W9-AGA-227

# FRANCES BURNEY

# *Evelina*

Bedford Cultural Editions

# FRANCES BURNEY
# *Evelina*

EDITED BY

## Kristina Straub
Carnegie Mellon University

BEDFORD/ST. MARTIN'S     BOSTON ◆ NEW YORK

For Bedford/St. Martin's
*President and Publisher:* Charles H. Christensen
*General Manager and Associate Publisher:* Joan E. Feinberg
*Managing Editor:* Elizabeth M. Schaaf
*Developmental Editor:* Katherine A. Retan
*Editorial Assistants:* Joanne Diaz and Adrian Harris
*Production Editor:* Maureen Murray
*Production Assistant:* Deborah Baker
*Copyeditor:* Barbara Sutton
*Cover Design:* Susan Pace
*Cover Art:* William Hogarth, *Canvassing for Votes,* engraving, sixth
state, February 1757.

Library of Congress Catalog Card Number: 96–86784

Copyright © 1997 by Bedford Books

Manufactured in the United States of America.
7   6
f   e


*For information, write:* Bedford/St. Martin's 75 Arlington Street, Boston,
MA 02116 (617–399–4000)


ISBN: 0–312–09729–8 (paperback)
ISBN: 0–312–12796–0 (hardcover)

Acknowledgments

# About the Series

The need to "historicize" literary texts — and even more to analyze the historical and cultural issues all texts embody — is now embraced by almost all teachers, scholars, critics, and theoreticians. But the question of how to teach such issues in the undergraduate classroom is still a difficult one. Teachers do not always have the historical information they need for a given text, and contextual documents and sources are not always readily available in the library — even if the teacher has the expertise (and students have the energy) to ferret them out. The Bedford Cultural Editions represent an effort to make available for the classroom the kinds of facts and documents that will enable teachers to use the latest historical approaches to textual analysis and cultural criticism. The best scholarly and theoretical work has for many years gone well beyond the "new critical" practices of formalist analysis and close reading, and we offer here a practical classroom model of the ways that many different kinds of issues can be engaged when texts are not thought of as islands unto themselves.

The impetus for the recent cultural and historical emphasis has come from many directions: the so-called new historicism of the late 1980s, the dominant historical versions of both feminism and Marxism, the cultural studies movement, and a sharply changed focus in older movements such as reader response, structuralism, deconstruction, and psychoanalytic theory. Emphases differ, of course, among schools and individuals, but what these movements and approaches have in common is a commitment to explore — and to have students in the classroom study interactively — texts in their full historical and cultural dimensions. The aim is to discover how older texts (and those from other traditions) differ from our own assumptions and expectations, and thus the focus in teaching falls on cultural and historical difference rather than on similarity or continuity.

The most striking feature of the Bedford Cultural Editions — and the one most likely to promote creative classroom discussion — is the inclusion of a generous selection of historical documents that contextualize the main text in a variety of ways. Each volume contains works (or passages from works) that are contemporary with the main text: legal and social documents, journalistic and autobiographical accounts, histories, sections from conduct books, travel books, poems, novels, and other historical sources. These materials have several uses. Often they provide information beyond what the main text offers. They provide, too, different perspectives on a particular theme, issue, or event central to the text, suggesting the range of opinions contemporary readers would have brought to their reading and allowing students to experience for themselves the details of cultural disagreement and debate. The documents are organized in thematic units — each with an introduction by the volume editor that historicizes a particular issue and suggests the ways in which individual selections work to contextualize the main text.

Each volume also contains a general introduction that provides students with information concerning the political, social, and intellectual context for the work as well as information concerning the material aspects of the text's creation, production, and distribution. There are also relevant illustrations, a chronology of important events, and, when helpful, an account of the reception history of the text. Finally, both the main work and its accompanying documents are carefully annotated in order to enable students to grasp the significance of historical references, literary allusions, and unfamiliar terms. Everywhere we have tried to keep the special needs of the modern student — especially the culturally conscious student of the turn of the millennium — in mind.

For each title, the volume editor has chosen the best teaching text of the main work and explained his or her choice. Old spellings and capitalizations have been preserved (except that the long "s" has been regularized to the modern "s") — the overwhelming preference of the two hundred teacher-scholars we surveyed in preparing the series.

Original habits of punctuation have also been kept, except for occasional places where the unusual usage would obscure the syntax for modern readers. Whenever possible, the supplementary texts and documents are reprinted from the first edition or the one most relevant to the issue at hand. We have thus meant to preserve — rather than counter — for modern students the sense of "strangeness" in older texts, expecting that the oddness will help students to see where older texts are *not* like modern ones, and expecting too that today's historically informed teachers will find their own creative ways to make something of such historical and cultural differences.

In developing this series, our goal has been to foreground the kinds of issues that typically engage teachers and students of literature and history now. We have not tried to move readers toward a particular ideological, political, or social position or to be exhaustive in our choice of contextual materials. Rather, our aim has been to be provocative — to enable teachers and students of literature to raise the most pressing political, economic, social, religious, intellectual, and artistic issues on a larger field than any single text can offer.

> J. Paul Hunter, University of Chicago
> William E. Cain, Wellesley College
> Series Editors

# About This Volume

*Evelina* is, as many students and teachers have found, a highly readable and teachable novel. It is also a highly topical novel, rich in references to the London of Frances Burney. Indeed, the concreteness of the novel's settings and events drew much delighted comment from contemporary readers who were familiar with High Holborn and Snowhill, who had walked through Vauxhall Gardens or "taken a turn" in fashionable St. James Park. They recognized their own urban experiences in Evelina's letters. Part of the purpose of this volume is to help readers over two hundred years later understand something about those experiences. Knowledge of London's topography is important to understanding and enjoying the novel but does not, in itself, offer a way into the richness enjoyed by readers who lived in or visited London in the 1770s. It is helpful but inadequate only to point to maps and pictures of the places Evelina visits; this volume therefore offers texts that will help readers construct their versions of the human experiences that are tied to those places.

Much of this experience is specific to middle-class English femininity in the late eighteenth century, and many of the materials included here speak to that experience. It is one of the main goals of this book, however, to show how femininity, as a form of experience and a set of meanings, cannot be isolated from apparently nongendered economic and political changes in English society and international position. England's growing dependence on a mercantile economy, its competition with other European nations for the conquest of Asia, the Americas, and the Caribbean, and its engagement in African slavery and colonial domination literally changed the face of London and resorts like Bath and Bristol Hotwells in the late eighteenth century. In the documents accompanying this edition, we can see, along with the growth of urban development, the proliferation of debates over the moral and social values those changes brought with them. Was England deteriorating into a decadent materialism in which traditional values would be lost? Or was England progressing toward military and economic ascendency over much of the known world? Representations of women as symbols of either decadence or progress are often central to these debates. As the documents suggest, women's historical experiences are shaped by economic and political factors that only *seem* to have little to do with the "feminine" world of leisure, courtship, and the domestic.

When Evelina goes shopping, her apparently trivial actions are part of larger patterns of consumption in a mercantile economy. When she retreats to the domestic haven of Lady Howard's country estate, she is followed by Captain Mirvan, a walking reminder of the military and economic conquests upon which British wealth (and the country estate as a locus of that wealth), increasingly depended in the late eighteenth century. The novel does not always make such connections explicit, but they are available to readers who know a bit about how eighteenth-century British trade and military expansion were changing the topography of London as well as the nature of the family and its domestic economies and practices. Evelina and Captain Mirvan might act and think as if they are from different species, but they are both part of the historical process of constructing "Englishness." Many of our current assumptions and debates about women, the family, and the role of the nation-state can be better understood in relation to this historical construction. This edition is offered as an aide to viewing Burney's novel — and women's literature in general — as central to understanding modern forms of social organization.

## ACKNOWLEDGMENTS

I owe thanks to many people and a few institutions for their help in compiling and editing this volume. A grant from Carnegie Mellon's Faculty Development Fund got me to the British Library, where I located most of the contextual materials. As always, I am grateful for the hard work and patience of the British Library staff and to my friends, Monty Davis and Nina Shandloff, for their fold-out couch and companionship in London.

My students at Carnegie Mellon have done their share. I thank the many undergraduate students who have good-naturedly borne with me as I worked to develop a cultural studies methodology that tried to be broadly accessible and not overly reductive. I owe the graduate students in our literary and cultural theory program at CMU more than I can adequately acknowledge. The instructors of our first-year curriculum should take credit for much of the methodology that informs this volume. Angela Todd provided useful information about Cox's Museum. Greg Bolton helped me understand the nature of London's pleasure gardens — and much more. Samantha Fenno enthusiastically joined in my obsession to know such facts as what a horse flime is; I am also grateful to her for cheering me on through what seemed, at times, an interminable process. Her sense of the project's worth fed my own and kept me going. In the final stages, she was able to help me fine-tune and trim my prose.

My colleagues at CMU, particularly my former colleague, Paul Smith, have thrown me the intellectual challenges that made me want to connect cultural theory with undergraduate education. Crystal Bartolovich's thrillingly lucid discussions of how to teach a material theory of language helped me bring Marxist theory into classes on literary history. My colleagues David Kaufer and Peggy Knapp have offered their support for my scholarship even when they needed me to be at faculty meetings instead of at the library.

The reference staff at Carnegie Mellon Library have been a scholar's delight. They have been unfailingly courteous, professional, and informed in response to my most frenzied queries. John Tofanelli, the English research librarian at CMU, is simply a wizard at retrieving the most inaccessible information. I owe him all of my knowledge about how to search for information in the computerized age.

The staff at Bedford Books have given me both material support and the freedom to explore my ideas. My editor, Kathy Retan, has provided wisdom and guidance at every stage of the process. She never steered me on a false course, and she stopped me from taking several wrong turns. Maureen Murray expertly guided the book through production, Margaret Hyre handled permissions, and Adrian Harris and Joanne Diaz assisted with numerous details. The readers of a very early and partial draft of the volume gave much excellent advice, most of which I have taken. Julia Epstein and James Thompson, in particular, were as generous as they were discerning in their critiques. Many of the features I now like best about the book came from their suggestions.

I thank my daughters, Bailey and Evie Clark, for their patience with hearing "Mommy has to work" so many times in their short lives. My partner, Danae Clark, has endured through this process, as she has in so many other ongoing, shared life narratives.

I end by thanking Paul Hunter, who set me this task, as he has so many others from which I've learned. Paul, I hope you never stop taking up years of my life with your "suggestions."

Kristina Straub
Carnegie Mellon University

# Contents

# Illustrations

Bedford Cultural Editions

# FRANCES BURNEY

## *Evelina*

Part One

---

*Evelina*
The Complete Text

# Introduction:
# Cultural and
# Historical Background

At first glance, the terms of Frances Burney's descriptive subtitle to *Evelina* seem clear and obvious, but after some consideration they evoke questions. When does the young lady enter the world? At birth? At her majority? What "world" does she enter, and why was she not "in" that world prior to the moment of her entry? Finally, what makes a lady "young" and what qualities, besides being female and human, go into the makeup of a "lady," young or old? Stepping back from these questions about specific terms, one might begin to wonder what is so significant about the young lady's "entrance." What would make it the subject of a novel that was a runaway bestseller at its first publication in 1778 and has never since been out of print?

The last question is perhaps best answered by the novel itself, which offers a highly readable version of what one might call a classic cultural narrative. By "cultural narrative" I mean a story that helps communities and individuals within communities organize and articulate their social and moral values. Cultural narratives are stories about human life that implicitly or explicitly teach people to make certain value judgments about kinds of people or behaviors. They are not fixed or stable forms or texts but can be told and retold in a variety of different ways and with different emphases on different values. For example, the fictional elements of a beautiful young girl who overcomes poverty and oppression through marriage to a rich and powerful man are components of a cultural narrative that informs a number of different stories. The Brothers Grimm version of the Cinderella story is just one of many versions of this narrative, and we can all think of movies we have seen or novels we have read that incorporate this cultural narrative while rewriting it with certain, significant differences.

*Evelina* incorporates a cultural narrative in that it shares elements with numerous other versions of Cinderella's story. A beautiful young woman leaves unglamorous domesticity for late-night dancing parties, city lights, and the excitement of mixed, unfamiliar company. She attracts the attention of a rich and powerful man, and the love story follows its course. Much of *Evelina*'s enduring appeal is surely tied to the historical tenacity of this cultural narrative. The appeal of a rags to riches story is one that has endured in Anglo-American traditions, and while American and British feminist critiques of women's economic dependence on men may have eroded our uncritical acceptance of Cinderella as an ideal of feminine success, the idea that romantic love is particularly important to women's sense of having "made it" has certainly not lost currency.

But *Evelina* is also very different from other variations on the Cinderella story. The various processes of producing and interpreting a cultural narrative are not merely idiosyncratic to specific writers and readers. Rather, these processes reflect different historical and cultural conditions. To take an example of how even a particular word might be given widely variant meanings in different social and historical contexts: when the sexually predatory Sir Clement Willoughby encounters Evelina walking by herself in London's Vauxhall Gardens, his rowdy friends, who do not know her, mistake her for an "actress." In Evelina's world, the word "actress" does not invoke the glamour of the movies or the artistry of "serious" theater. Many actresses supplemented their rather scanty salaries through high- or low-class prostitution, depending on their status and their skill and luck in attracting male "protectors." Some actresses became the mistresses of rich and powerful men. Others informally prostituted themselves for "gifts," while still others found the line between the stage and the brothel or the street distressingly permeable. In her use of the term "actress," Burney depended on this range of associations that would have been available to her eighteenth-century readers. Just as particular words can change their meanings in different situations, whole stories can shift meanings, as they are told and retold. For example, the tale that Evelina relates to her guardian, Mr. Villars, about her first experience at a ball, or ridotto, rewrites Cinderella's effortless conquest of the Prince as a story of personal confusion over the "right" way to behave.

The rich and various practices of storytelling and interpretation cannot be fully understood apart from historically specific cultural practices and assumptions that are themselves always changing. Stories, and the language that goes into making and understanding them, are a part of the larger — sometimes creative, sometimes destructive, but always complex — process we call cultural history. The definitions of words change, as we can see from the example of the word "actress," according to changing social relations and conditions. But it is important to remember that words are more than passive reflections of social reality. The words we use and the stories we tell shape social conditions and relations in addition to being shaped by them. The stories a community produces always serve an explanatory function, providing people within the community with ways of understanding both their lives and the social institutions and practices that shape those lives. *Evelina*, then, can be usefully understood by us as one of the stories by which late eighteenth-century society created its image of itself. Hence, my earlier questions about the meaning of the novel's subtitle are as much queries about cultural practices and conventions specific to English society in the mid- to late eighteenth century as they are questions about the novel itself.

*Evelina* and the materials accompanying it in this edition are not changeless artifacts that we can understand apart from their social contexts, but are a product of the lives lived by Frances Burney and others like her. A good way to begin understanding *Evelina*'s cultural narrative of a beautiful young woman entering public life for the first time is to start unpacking the cultural assumptions implicit in Burney's language. Just as "actress" takes its meaning from the particular social and historical context in which it is used, the terms "young lady" and "world" draw much of their significance from social relations and conditions specific to Burney's eighteenth-century, middle-class, English experience. What does it mean, in the context of those social relations and conditions, to be a "young lady" at the point of entry into "the world," and what are the characteristics of the world that Evelina enters?

## THE WORLD OF URBAN LEISURE AND TRADE

The subtitle of Burney's novel, "The History of a Young Lady's Entrance into the World," implies that the "world" Evelina enters is *not* Berry Hill, the retired country home of her guardian, Villars. The "world" that Evelina enters first is the city of London, for Villars does not seem to consider a visit to Lady Howard's country house as posing the danger to his ward that he sees in a visit to the city. Entering the "world" means going to town. Later in the novel Evelina enters the world of Bristol Hotwells, the resort town that includes the house of the wealthy and socially prominent Mrs. Beaumont. In both London and Bristol Hotwells, Evelina's experience is shaped by leisure activities. In London she goes to plays, the opera, public pleasure gardens, and other sites of amusement. In Bristol Hotwells the ladies walk, go for carriage rides, pay visits, and participate in balls. The work that people do to make a living is scarcely visible in Burney's novel. Except for Evelina's acquisition of new clothes in London and her time spent with the shopkeeping Branghtons, the young lady's "world" seems to have little to do with money-making or labor. The world that she enters is the world of leisure.

However, as most of us today are aware, a nation's economy is integrally connected with how its citizens spend their leisure time. Just as it would be a mistake to think of tourism as having nothing to do with the United States' balance of trade, it would be an error to think of Evelina's world of leisure and fashion as having nothing to do with the eighteenth-century English economy. Indeed, Burney and her contemporaries were just as aware as we are of the close connections between urban amusements and national economic conditions and relations. Evelina's experiences at Ranelagh, Vauxhall Gardens, the Pantheon, the theater, and the opera are richly meaningful in relation to changes that were taking place in both the British economy and the social relations that depended upon that economy. The fact that aristocrats such as Lord Orville have time for the fashionable London amusements to which Burney takes us in her novel is perhaps less remarkable than the fact that the shopkeeping, middle-class Branghtons do. Many, though not all, of the London amusements that help to define Evelina's "world" were enjoyed by people from a variety of class backgrounds. At a place such as Vauxhall Gardens, the traditionally leisured class of landed aristocrats mixed with both middle-class tradesmen and members of the working classes who were able to afford the price of entry. Evelina's nearly disastrous encounter with two prostitutes in the Gardens serves to underscore the mixed-class nature of the crowds at many of London's pleasure spots. While this mixing of different classes in public spaces was not entirely new to the eighteenth century (it had gone on intermittently in the London theaters, for example, for over a hundred years), it was becoming more pervasive and was more widely commented on by contemporaries as a characteristic of urban life.

Part of the reason for the relative heterogeneity of the crowds at London pleasure sites was economic. England was in a period of tremendous economic expansion, creating a higher standard of living for many, as well as the leisure time, to visit such sites as Vauxhall. English foreign trade nearly doubled between 1700 and 1780. This dramatic increase in import and export included trade with European markets but was also a product of England's colonial and mercantile ventures, including the traffic in African slaves in North America, North Africa, the West Indies, and India. At the same time, England was experiencing internal demographic and economic shifts. New systems of agricultural land use — for instance, the enclosure of "commons" that had been available for public use into private fields — reduced the possibilities for rural living in traditional settings of autonomous household production. Many people who would once have survived as independent farmers or as farmworkers or craftsmen attached to large, agriculturally supported households, migrated to such cities as Bristol and London to do work that involved them in larger networks of trade and commerce. The result was a larger and relatively more heterogeneous body of residents in urban centers, with sufficient leisure to partake of fashionable goods and pastimes.

Urban centers were becoming increasingly important to an economy that was rapidly expanding its trade, and thus the populations of cities such as London were growing at an unprecedented rate, leading to changes in occupations, living conditions, and places of residence within the city. While many of these changes were seen positively as part of England's growing wealth and developing culture, many were seen as carrying with them the urban blights of crime and poverty. It would be a terrible mistake, then, to assume that the picture of an urban, mixed-class population with leisure and the means to enjoy London and resort amusements was inclusive. What is not visible in this picture are the deadly realities of widespread poverty, illiteracy, sickness, alcohol abuse, and the general impoverishment of large numbers of working English people. While the standard of living for many improved, many others, such as numbers of displaced agricultural workers who sought their fortunes in the cities, ended up scratching out a bare subsistence or resorting to crime and prostitution to stay alive. Many did not stay alive. Children, in particular, frequently fell victim to poverty and its side effects: malnutrition, disease, and infanticide. English economic growth and urban expansion had a dark side that is hard to glimpse in Evelina's relatively privileged world of fashion and leisure. It is important to understand this darker side, however, if one is to comprehend how the novel engages in contemporary debates over the moral and ethical values implicit in this newly expanded world of leisure pursuits and consumer commodities. Here the concept of cultural narrative is again useful. What stories did Burney's culture tell itself about the "new" world of leisure and amusement, and what different assessments do these stories implicitly make of the economic and demographic trends that supported this world — an expanding urban population and the growth of the English economy?

Debates over the social and cultural effects of the economic and demographic changes overtaking England in the eighteenth century occurred on a variety of cultural fronts and in many forms. Concerns about the expanding urban population were expressed variously through a new interest in philanthropy, in caring for the urban poor and sick, and in a concurrent interest in defining and punishing the "criminal." Discussions about the use of bank notes, a newly important form of currency, and the use of national credit indicate both excitement at growing possibilities for English dominance in international trade and fears that the English economy was departing from a system in which land was the basis for wealth and power. Two opposing cultural narratives about the growing importance of commerce and its impact on urban life informed many of these debates as they appear in the materials provided in this text. While these two narratives are not entirely unique to eighteenth-century England, they have a particular importance to this historical time and place because of eighteenth-century England's dramatic growth in urban population and the concurrent proliferation of ways in which to spend one's leisure time in the city.

The first and more optimistic is the narrative of rational progress. This cultural narrative characterizes the leisure-time consumption of commodities and amusements as part of larger patterns of economic and political progress away from an older, feudal society based on land ownership and agricultural productivity and toward a new, "egalitarian" society based on the concept of a free market that is open to anyone with goods to buy or sell. In this narrative, material goods are exchanged in an atmosphere of rational understanding and productive commerce. The leisured consumption of goods and services by those who can afford them is represented as being of a piece with the economic health of the whole country. Indeed, in the following passage from Joseph Addison's 1711 *Spectator* portrait of the Royal Exchange, an important London center for international trade, the exchange of goods becomes a paradigm for the rational organization of the whole world.

> Nature seems to have taken a particular Care to disseminate her Blessings among the different Regions of the World, with an Eye to this mutual Intercourse and Traffick among Mankind, that the Natives of the several Parts of the Globe might have a kind of Dependance upon one another, and be united together by their common Interest. Almost every *Degree* produces something peculiar to it. The Food often grows in one Country, and the Sauce in another. The Fruits of *Portugal* are corrected by the Products of *Barbadoes*: The Infusion of a *China* Plant sweetened with the Pith of an *Indian* Cane: The *Philippick* Islands give a Flavour to our European Bowls. The single Dress of a Woman of Quality is often the Product of an hundred Climates. The Muff and the Fan come together from the different Ends of the Earth. The Scarf is sent from the Torrid Zone, and the Tippet from Beneath the Pole. The Brocade Petticoat rises out of the Mines of *Peru*, and the Diamond Necklace out of the Bowels of *Indostan*. (see Part Two, pp. 522–23)

One of the most striking aspects of Addison's view of the Royal Exchange is the way in which it obscures differences of nationality and class. The Dutchman, Jew, and Englishman are portrayed as equal participants in economic exchange, and the merchant's self-interest is seen as synonymous with the good of the whole society. The merchant, in this narrative of progress, is the representative of a new class whose identity is formed through the acquisition of wealth rather than the traditional bases of class identity: birth, ownership of land, or allegiance to a trade. He is also the cog that makes the machine of commerce run: "there are not more useful Members in a Commonwealth than Merchants. They knit Mankind together in a mutual Intercourse of good Offices, distribute the Gifts of Nature, find Work for the Poor, add Wealth to the Rich, and Magnificence to the Great" (see Part Two, p. 523). Class identity both is and isn't important in Addison's view. He is clearly celebrating the new kind of class identity invested in the merchant, but differences of class and nationality are overridden by the order of rational, free exchange. This cultural narrative of rational commercialism is an extremely important and enduring one, which we can recognize in recent celebrations of free-market capitalism's world dominance over communist systems of governance and economic exchange.

The second narrative, which we might refer to as that of luxury and decadence, paints a darker picture of Evelina's world. In this narrative, commercial exchange is morally and aesthetically disabling. Leisure and consumption signify moral and aesthetic chaos and the breakdown of traditional codes and institutions of social order. The cultural narrative of luxury is cynical about the possibilities for a social order in which differences of class and nationality are subordinate to a rational economic order. The Royal Exchange is, of course, very different from the London pleasure gardens of Vauxhall; such sites of pure leisure and recreation are harder to glorify as embodiments of commercial progress and rational understanding. Nonetheless, we can see claims for social decorum, even improvement, being made in texts such as *A Sketch of the Spring-Gardens* (see Part Two, Chapter 2). More typically, however, the London places of amusement that Evelina visits lend themselves to views informed by the cultural narrative of luxury. In Oliver Goldsmith's satiric portrait of an evening at Vauxhall (see Part Two, Chapter 2), class differences are portrayed as a problem for which economic exchange is hardly an adequate solution. Material exchange, in Goldsmith's view, is merely selfish consumption, not a basis for rational order. Goldsmith's satire points to the enduring nature of class distinctions within an allegedly class-blind economic system in which anyone with a minimum of money and leisure can buy the fashionable amusements of the town. Burney's portrayal of Madame Duval in *Evelina* has a similar satiric function. The former tavern girl can buy herself a Lyons silk gown, but she cannot transcend the class differences that cast her affluence as ridiculous.

Both cultural narratives — the narrative of rational progress and the narrative of luxury and decadence — inform the world that the young lady enters in *Evelina*. In fact, one might read many of the novel's scenes as dramatizing the struggle between these two narratives. The dispute over gambling between Lord Orville and his prospective brother-in-law, for instance, enacts the struggle between rational exchange and luxury by pitting Orville's concept of leisure as tied to the social good against his would-be relative's fashionable and thoughtless approach to leisure. Gambling is often targeted, in at-

tacks on luxury and decadence, as particularly symptomatic of reason's breakdown in the realm of public leisure. (It is worth pointing
out, however, that neither male antagonist in this dispute seems terribly concerned about the physical and mental abuse of elderly
women to which it leads.)

It is important, in any case, to remember that whatever the nature
of "the world," it is a young lady who enters it in Burney's novel.
Evelina's gender clearly makes a difference to her experience of the
world of leisure and fashion. While Lord Orville, for example, can be
in verbally profuse "spirits" at the performance of a slightly risqué
play, Evelina and Maria Mirvan are tongue-tied and "knew not
where even to look" (p. 124). The world Burney portrays poses difficulties for young ladies that it apparently does not pose for young
men, and one might argue that these difficulties are connected with
the problematic ways that "young ladies," and "femininity" figure
into both the cultural narrative of rational progress and that of luxury and decadence. However opposed they are in their characterization of leisure and fashion, both cultural narratives pose problems of
"fit" for the young lady.

Although Addison's view of the Royal Exchange includes diverse
nationalities and classes, one must look closely to find a woman.
Moving from Addison to the excerpts from the businesslike trade
manual, *The London Tradesman*, we find that women who entered
into business faced a rather bleak set of prospects in comparison to
their male counterparts. Here we see the relative economic disadvantage of the milliner and the sexual vulnerability of her female apprentices. While the economic impoverishment and hardship of women's
work are not directly addressed in *Evelina,* Burney's last novel, *The
Wanderer* (1814), takes this issue as a primary concern. Even in
*Evelina* the lack of vocational resources is an important subtext to
Villars's plans for the heroine and her dependence on them. Part of
women's disadvantage lies in their changing economic function in the
new order of trade and exchange. With the decline of the autonomous household as the commonest unit for producing goods,
women's part in manufacturing was, as Alice Clark's classic history
documents, severely curtailed. Leonore Davidoff and Catherine Hall
have more recently documented the decline of cottage industry,
which involved women's labor in the home, in the eighteenth-century
British economy. While working-class women continued to labor as
servants and participate in agricultural tasks and small trade, women
of the middle and upper ranks were increasingly excluded from the

production of goods. In sum, there was no function for women in the rapidly developing world of trade parallel to that of the male merchant celebrated by Addison. Not surprisingly, the woman who does appear in Addison's vision of international trade and economic progress is not a participant in the business of exchange but a symbol of it. She appears as a consumer decorated in the products of foreign exchange, and her decorated body symbolizes the wealth that men and nations reap from exchange. Addison elsewhere characterizes her as "a beautiful Romantick Animal, that may be adorned with Furs and Feathers, Pearls and Diamonds, Ores and Silks. The Lynx shall cast its Skin at her Feet to make her a Tippett; the Peacock, Parrot, and Swan, shall pay Contributions to her Muff; the Sea shall be searched for Shells, and the Rocks for Gems; and every Part of Nature furnish out its Share towards the Embellishment of a Creature that is the most consummate Work of it" (Addison and Steele, 2: 195).

Both the narrative of rational progress and the narrative of luxury situate women in roles outside of the productive parts available to men, and the latter often explicitly aligns women with the destructive effects of luxury. Specialists in women's education, such as Thomas Gisborne and James Fordyce, warn against young women becoming thoughtless consumers of fashion and leisure-time recreations (see Part Two, Chapter 1). We can also see the image of woman as mindless consumer writ large in Burney's character of Madame Duval, who values her clothes and her "curls" over her own dignity and comfort. While Duval is obviously a warning to women to avoid losing their integrity to the world of leisure and fashion, even the more positive image of Addison's "beautiful Romantick Animal" is difficult to take seriously as a role model for young women. What does the young lady do besides wear clothes? One of the difficulties that Evelina encounters in her entrance into this world is that of squaring her active intelligence and sense of humanity with the passivity of the ideal woman. At the same time, she must avoid alignment with the thoughtlessly consuming woman who fits all too well with the cultural narrative of luxury and decadence.

The world of leisure that the young lady enters is, in sum, highly contested territory. Is it a serene realm in which social equals enjoy the fruits of rational progress or a chaotic space of selfish consumption? Is fashion a shining emblem of social decorum or a symptom of moral decay? It is appropriate that the sites of fashion and leisure visited by Evelina often seem more like contentious boardrooms or disputatious playgrounds than places of unadulterated pleasure. In addition to their contested and contentious nature, fashion and leisure pose specific difficulties to the young lady of Burney's subtitle by giving her a no-win choice between nonparticipation and roles that threaten her very worth as a young lady. In a scene symptomatic of this double-bind, Maria Mirvan and Evelina find themselves unable to answer Lord Orville's questions about their reactions to fashionable London amusements without rendering themselves vulnerable to misinterpretation by Captain Mirvan. In the captain's hearing, Orville tells the company that he is

> "most desirous to hear the opinions of these young ladies, to whom all public places must, as yet, be new."
> We both, and with eagerness, declared that we had received as much, if not more pleasure, at the opera than any where: but we had better have been silent; for the Captain, quite displeased, said, "What signifies asking them girls? Do you think they know their own minds yet? Ask 'em after any thing that's called diversion, and you're sure they'll say it's vastly fine; — they are a set of parrots, and speak by rote, for they all say the same thing: but ask 'em how they like making puddings and pies, and I'll warrant you'll pose 'em." . . .
> This reproof effectually silenced us both for the rest of the evening.
> (p. 154)

The cultural narratives in which men like Mirvan believe place Evelina in an awkward, untenable relation to the leisured world that she enters. The young ladies' enjoyment of their leisure, however innocent and even intelligent and discerning, contributes to the negative stereotyping of young women.

However opposed they may be in their characterization of the leisure and amusements that we see in *Evelina,* the cultural narratives of both rational progress and luxury pose problems of "fit" for the young lady. What is the place of feminine innocence in an urban culture based on commercial exchange? Most answers to this question, such as Thomas Gisborne's or Joseph Addison's (see Part Two, Chapters 1 and 2), position women more as symbols than as participants. But Evelina must act. It is not enough to function as a passive symbol. And while femininity fits all too well into the narrative of luxury, as we can seen from Burney's characterization of Madame Duval, this placement hardly offers women a positive role to play in their entrance into the world.

## BEYOND THE WORLD OF LEISURE

While Evelina and Maria Mirvan's very real pleasure in the theater, the opera, and the sights of fashionable London suggests that girls do indeed just want to have fun, it is important to note that fun, in Evelina's world, often leads to verbal or even physical violence. Much as Captain Mirvan turns Orville's question about the young ladies' pleasure in town amusements into an occasion for verbal aggression against them, the aristocratic male "friends" of Lady Beaumont turn a puerile contest over who can drive the fastest into an occasion to torture elderly working-class women. Unable to settle a bet, these fashionable young men gleefully coerce two old women into racing against each other to settle the matter. This tendency in the novel for play to turn into violence can, and I think should, be read as Burney's commentary on how often "polite" society can turn uncomfortable or even lethal for those with less power, especially women. I would also suggest that this commentary should be read not as a "universal" or even feminist truth that can be detached from the novel's time and place, but rather as a direct response to the role that violence played in two increasingly important aspects of English national identity: the rapid expansion of urban centers, and the growth of English commitment to military conquest and dominance in international trade.

As we can see from the letters and journals of foreign visitors to London in the eighteenth century, the topography of the city was being reshaped by trade and trade interests. The old walled city was becoming a business center in which those in the commercial walk of life lived and worked. The former suburb of Westminster was concurrently emerging as the residence of the wealthy. The traditional English upper class, an aristocracy whose wealth remained largely in land and agricultural rents, made part of a growing urban population interested in "amusements." Merchants and tradesmen, whose money was made primarily from business, added to the numbers who could enjoy such places of leisure as the Spring Gardens at Vauxhall, Ranelagh, and the Pantheon. Urban public space was, then, both structured according to class differences, so that the Branghton's address of High Holborn was marked by its association with trade, and characterized by an increase in the mixing of classes that was relatively new in English culture. Class difference mattered, but it mattered in new ways. Cultural narratives upholding aristocratic superiority were still in circulation, and we can read them in Evelina's embarrassment over her cousins in trade and her nouveau riche grandmother. However, other narratives also circulated through London's public life, such as the travel journals of visitors to the country that note English egalitarian tendencies and the comparative cleanliness and decency of the English working classes (see Part Two, Chapter 3).

Another way in which urban change affects the young lady's leisure experience is rather more dramatic and markedly unpleasant. While urban wealth grew with the expansion of trade, bringing with it a proliferation of conveniences such as hackney coaches, indoor plumbing, sedan chairs, the penny post, and street lighting, so did urban poverty. The number of those who made a living through thievery — including pickpockets, housebreakers, and highwaymen — increased in and around London. So did the number of women who lived by prostitution. The emergence of public spaces in which different classes mixed on a regular basis created opportunities for these "trades" to prosper and eroded the protective distance between young ladies such as Evelina and the different forms of violence attending theft and prostitution. Trapped by Sir Clement Willoughby in the dark walks at Vauxhall, Evelina narrowly escapes the rape that her alleged status as an "actress" would legitimize in his moral view of the world. And while her brush with a highwayman is staged rather than real, it hints at a violence that moves just below the surface of London public amusements.

The cultural narratives of urban violence jar against those of urban pleasure and progress in the accounts of travelers to London in the eighteenth century. César de Saussure finds himself thrown against the wall by "chairmen" whose warning cry he did not, as a foreigner, understand. W. de Archenholtz joins Saussure in worrying about foot pads, pickpockets, and highwaymen, much as a modern-day visitor to New York City might worry about being mugged (for Saussure and Archenholtz see Part Two, Chapter 3). Also apparent from these accounts is a strong sense of English national identity: both its emergent egalitarian values and its propensity to do violence to those who represented rival interests in trade and imperial expansion. England's national stature as a naval and trading power was rising as the country extended its financial interests to parts of the globe newly opened to European conquest. Eighteenth-century international trade was not entirely the peaceful business implied in Addison's idealized view of the Royal Exchange. Rather, it depended quite literally on international aggression and defense. The enslavement and transportation of Africans to North America and the Caribbean constituted one form of sanctioned (though not uncontested) violence that was inextricably connected with economic expansion. Battles among European nations for mercantile supremacy constituted another form of violence that resulted in the loss of countless seamen's lives. Captain Mirvan might seem to interject an anomalous violence into the trivial and fashionable world of Evelina's leisured society, but the journals and letters of sea captains collected in this volume suggest that legitimized violence is a force upon which eighteenth-century English leisure and the market for amusement structurally depend (see Part Two, Chapter 3). English mercantile expansion underpins the decorum of rational economic exchange as envisioned by Addison. And in the eighteenth century, this expansion of trade is inextricably linked to violent conflict between nations and the concrete damage done to bodies and property in that conflict.

Both people and things French occupy a dangerous position in London public life, which is reflected in Saussure's advice to avoid looking like a Frenchman when walking a London public street. English Francophobia is not a phenomenon unique to Captain Mirvan. English fears of French visitors to London have a long and complex history. The events most relevant as a context for *Evelina* are the Seven Years War between France and England, which occurred at mid-century, and France's role in the American revolution. By the 1760s, England was entering a period of unprecedented advantage in naval trade and military domination, and France was among its rivals. One can easily gain a sense from Edward Boscawen's and James Anthony Gardner's journals of how trade and military dominance are linked upon the contested seas; the latter makes the former possible, while the former makes the latter desirable (see selections from these journals in Part Two, Chapter 3). Furthermore, the line between trade and military action is extremely thin at times; the two kinds of naval activity are inextricably related in the eighteenth century. Merchant ships often carried and used guns to fight off pirates and hostile foreign ships, and military ships were frequently used to convey merchant ships through contested waters. In fact, to be a military sea captain in the British navy was literally to be in business, since the greater part of the incentive for taking "hostile" vessels was the proceeds from confiscated property. Hence, the world of leisure and amusement, derived as it was from the accumulation of urban wealth through trade, literally depended on English military dominance on the seas. And, as Boscawen's, Gardner's, and Pasley's journals and letters demonstrate, this dominance was gained through considerable violence. Captain Mirvan's disregard for the physical comfort and safety of others comes as less of a shock when considered in the light of these accounts of the violent injury and death that were a part of both military conflict and the everyday work of seamanship at the time.

And while Burney's Captain Mirvan is clearly a domestic nightmare — a plague to any peaceful enjoyment of familial intimacy and a scourge to women, who looked to marriage for protection from violence — the letters of Edward Boscawen offer a very different view of the sea captain's relationship to domesticity. Whereas Mirvan embodies conflict between the goals and values of domesticity and those of English naval enterprise, Boscawen seems to have wedded the two as firmly together in his mind as he was wedded to his much-loved wife. Burney's brother James made a long and successful career at sea, so she was probably not ignorant of the quality of a sailor's experience. It is interesting to speculate about why she constructed Mirvan as so relentlessly antithetical to the ideal of a happy marriage. In any case, the violence that may seem puzzling in Mirvan seems more explicable in the broader context of the sea captain's historical experience, and can also be seen as part of the larger pattern of violence that bubbles up through the surface of fashionable life — a violence that is endemic to the maintenance of both public exchange and domestic serenity. Perhaps Boscawen saw no contradiction between the violence of his profession and the domestic peace that he bought through it, but one might read Burney's novel as suggesting that the disruption of domestic peace and quiet are implicit in the very economic and nationalistic activities that support it.

In Captain Mirvan's family, the balance between violence and domestic serenity is rather painfully and uncertainly maintained through the efforts of the Mirvan women. Lady Howard, for example, feigns ignorance of her son-in-law's most egregious pranks. Their agreement is unspoken but clear: she will turn her head away from the captain's violence, and he will, in return, allow her to maintain a dignified detachment from his aggressive "romps." Evelina continually comments on Mrs. Mirvan's efforts to sooth the captain's irritability and to control the damage that he does to those around and within his family. The domestic world of marriage and the family is no more insulated from the violence of the world "beyond" the family than is the world of leisure and fashionable amusements.

In both realms, the young lady comes up against verbal and physical aggression and the struggles between violent opponents such as Madame Duval and the captain. Evelina's entrance into the world involves learning how to act with wisdom and integrity when faced with such violence. No perfect heroine, she makes mistakes in dealing with those characters that offer violence. At the opera, she leaves the embarrassing and socially damaging protection of Duval (one kind of psychological and social "violence") only to find herself subject to the sexual predations of Sir Clement. She avoids receiving the brunt of Mirvan's violence but cannot prevent him from assaulting her grandmother. Burney does not, however, give us a heroine who is simply a passive victim of violence. Evelina can act heroically, as when confronted with Macartney's plans to commit criminal violence on himself and others. Even when Evelina cannot protect herself, Burney never absolves her of the responsibility to think intelligently about how to deal with the violence of the world she enters.

The subtitle "The History of a Young Lady's Entrance into the World" may conjure up a romantic image of Cinderella entering the ballroom and sweeping down a wide, curving staircase in her miraculous gown. Burney's novel certainly holds some of the sparkle of such an image in her portrayal of her lovely heroine's ultimately successful and happy entrance into the world, but it speaks even more strongly of the effort and difficulty of such an entrance. The cultural narrative of Cinderella is not the only context for understanding the young lady, and in writing her novel, Burney is responding to a variety of cultural narratives of female life that helped shape the meanings of both the "young lady" and her "entrance into the world."


## THE YOUNG LADY MAKES HER ENTRANCE

Burney's novel and the language she uses to tell her story are rich with meanings that are specific to how her community understood femininity and the lives and experiences of young women. *Evelina* is one thread in a vast cultural fabric of stories about femininity, and this edition offers you a few other snippets from this fabric in the materials that accompany the text of the novel. The stories circulating about femininity in eighteenth-century British culture did not necessarily agree with one another, and one can see how Thomas Gisborne's advice to young ladies differs from Burney's portrayal of

Evelina's experiences (see Part Two, Chapter 1). A better metaphor for how these different stories are related might be that of a conversation between people who hold differing views on a subject. Burney holds her own in this conversation; she does not merely repeat what James Fordyce and Thomas Gisborne say. Neither is she writing in a vacuum in which she is able to ignore other people's stories about the young lady and her entrance into the world. Rather, her story speaks to and about those of others.

The terms "young lady" and "entrance," then, take their meanings not only from Burney's novel but from their usage in narratives contemporary to it. Evelina thinks and acts in relation to two highly influential, commonly held cultural narratives about female life: the importance of a particular kind of youthful, feminine innocence and the inevitability of marriage as women's fate. Both of these narratives assume the necessity of women's economic dependence on men. Both narratives also assume that the period of time when a young lady enters the world is one of the most critical, exciting, and dangerous eras of her life.

When we first meet Evelina, she is on the verge of leaving the only home she has ever known, the rural Berry Hill, residence of her guardian and surrogate father, the Reverend Mr. Villars. The peculiarities of Evelina's family history have motivated Villars to keep her isolated in the country; his fear of exposing her to social ostracism, given the ambiguities of her mother's secret marriage, has kept her strictly within the limits of Villars's country circle of acquaintances, far from the "publicity" of town life. But Evelina's situation is similar to that of the daughters of country gentlemen, as described by the "expert" in female education, Thomas Gisborne: her interests and pastimes are, with the exception of occasional neighborhood visits, all confined within the space of the home and garden. Up to a point, both Villars and Gisborne see this confinement as desirable. Unlike modern parents who urge their daughters to play basketball, become involved in extracurricular activities at school, get part-time work, or participate in community activities and projects, these "fathers" see the line that separates domestic and public life as constituting a sharp, crucial distinction between what is safe and what is dangerous for their "daughters." They see the young lady's inevitable crossing of that line as she enters society as a period of great danger to her and anxiety to her parents.

Much of the concern over the young lady's entrance into the world has to do with the emphasis that late-eighteenth-century moralists and educators placed on innocence in young women, and their anxiety over the vulnerability of that innocence once exposed to a far-from-innocent world. To cross into public life, as Evelina is about to do at the opening of Burney's novel, is to endanger one's integrity as a young lady, at least in the eyes of men such as Villars, Gisborne, and James Fordyce, the fictional and real educators of young women. Villars fears for Evelina because she is innocent, and she is innocent because she has been exclusively "at home." At the same time, he values her innocence above all her other qualities. He has propagated a particularly attractive but fragile plant within a domestic greenhouse; the very isolation that has made her valuable also makes her vulnerable once she leaves the specialized conditions of the domestic.

The late-eighteenth-century ideal of the young lady, then, is built on a paradox: the exclusively domestic upbringing that gives the young lady value in the form of innocence also renders her vulnerable to losing that value by failing to prepare her for the experiences of public life. If we read between the lines of Burney, Fordyce, and Gisborne, it becomes apparent that one aspect of this innocence is sexual. Caroline Evelyn's secret marriage brings her sexual innocence into question, and though guiltless, she dies under the strain of that question. Evelina's terror at being trapped in a coach with Sir Clement is based on her unarticulated fear of rape. But sexual innocence is not isolatable from other forms of innocence. While too much knowledge of the world may lead to a general moral corruption that can, in turn, lead to the young lady's sexual undoing, too little knowledge of the world leaves the young lady ignorant of her danger and unable to defend herself from sexual seduction. Gisborne comments wryly on the effects of this paradox. If a young lady is not raised in innocence, she has lost her value before she even enters public life, but if she is raised in innocence, "that delicacy and that innocence are exposed under the greatest disadvantages to the sudden influence of highly fascinating allurements" (see Part Two, p. 458).

A healthy dose of skepticism should accompany our understanding of the narrative of feminine innocence and its circulation in Burney's culture: to say that innocence, defined as ignorance of public life, was an ideal for young ladies is not the same as to say that young women in Burney's day lived the secluded, domestic lives valued so highly by Fordyce and Gisborne. The ideal of the young lady whose innocence is nurtured in domestic privacy was certainly not closely related to the experience of working-class women, who worked outside the home from a young age and whose innocence often died young. But even the middle-class women whom Gisborne and Fordyce assumed to be their audience did not seem to have conformed to this ideal. Burney herself is a case in point. Her early diaries and letters, written when she was a young, unmarried woman living with her father and family in a London suburb, suggest that Burney herself, as a young lady, was seldom at home, except to receive a lively array of visitors, and only applied herself to the domestic tasks so valued by the educators of young women when under the surveillance of her stepmother's critical eye. Much other evidence, gleaned from the letters and journals of Burney's contemporaries, would suggest that middle-class women were not the purely domestic beings found in the pages of Gisborne.

Nonetheless, the cultural narrative of feminine innocence nurtured in domesticity held power over the lives and thoughts of real women, who did not necessarily conform to the ideal. Again, Burney herself is a case in point. She grew up in the household of a popular musician, Charles Burney, who was something of a celebrity in London. Through her father and other members of the gregarious Burney family, she had a more than lively social life among some of London's most famous artists, writers, and actors. She published *Evelina*, her first novel, anonymously, but once the news of her authorship got out, she was much sought after on the London literary scene. It is clear from her diary and letters that she thoroughly enjoyed the public attention and activity. Nonetheless, she wrote that she "would a thousand Times rather forfeit my character as a *Writer*, than risk ridicule or censure as a *Female*" (Burney 3: 212), and when "dear little Burney" appeared in a mild lampoon on contemporary writers, she was "for more than a week, unable to Eat, Drink, or sleep for vehemence of vexation" (Burney 3: 211). In short, the ideal of the young lady's innocence, defined as a lack of contamination by public experience, was important to female self-definition even if it did not entirely reflect the reality of women's lives. In Bristol Hotwells, Evelina is upset to find herself portrayed in a poem about the marriageable young women at the resort. However at odds the ideal of domestic innocence might have been with women's experience, it remained an idea very important to middle-class women such as Burney. At the same time, the ideal did not blind Burney and her contemporaries to its contradictory qualities.

The ideal of the young lady that emerges in the educational theories of Fordyce and Gisborne, and in the fictionalized philosophy of Villars, is represented as being rather difficult to sustain. The innocent young lady's worth is simultaneously her greatest vulnerability. The sphere from which the young lady enters into "the world" ideally allows entry only to carefully edited information. It is the sphere of private life, of domestic pursuits, of religious devotion and quiet, familial hours relieved from tedium by just the "right" sort of books and amusements. The goals of female education, as we see them reflected in Villars's letters, Fordyce's sermons, and Gisborne's advice, must be consonant with the preservation of the young lady's innocence as it is nurtured in this space. But young ladies do not, obviously, remain young. How does female educational theory reconcile its privileging of innocence with the need to prepare women for their roles in later life?

The answer to this question has a lot to do with what the young lady is being educated to do when she grows up. The range of occupations available to middle-class women such as Burney was extremely small; the excerpts given here from *The London Tradesman* (see Part Two, Chapter 2) cover a few of the possibilities in the world of commerce, and as we can see, these possibilities were among the worst-paid and least valued. Furthermore, many of them, such as the millinery trade, subjected women, as the *Tradesman* warns, to the dangers of casual seduction and eventual prostitution. Burney's *The Wanderer* dramatically states the tensions between the sexual vulnerability of this line of work and the moral sensibility of its upper-class heroine. The work of a paid companion or governess to children was among the few other choices. Young ladies were generally expected to marry a husband capable of supporting them and the children they were expected to produce and educate up to a certain age. The domestic realm that produces the innocent and virtuous young lady, then, is to be superseded by yet another domestic realm once she leaves the home of her early years.

What, then, are Fordyce, Gisborne, and Villars afraid of? What is the threat to a femininity that moves from the sphere of early innocence to that of maternal domestic virtue? To reach the safe haven of mature domestic life, the young lady must leave the sphere of youthful innocence in order to be met and married. She must come into contact with young men and the public realm in which they move, and she must make or be helped to make the right decision about whom to marry. The young lady's "entrance" is not, therefore, a simple step into a new phase of life, a transition that is quickly made and unimportant in and of itself. Rather, it signifies a dangerous passage with extremely high stakes attached to its successful completion. Villars hopes for Evelina's marriage to a man of quiet, domestic tastes. Gisborne admits the possibility that the young lady may not marry, but he assumes that she generally does. If she does not marry or her marriage is an unhappy one, he implies that it is probably her fault. While many late-eighteenth-century writers, including Burney, are sympathetic to the economic, social, and emotional difficulties of unmarried or unhappily married women, most assume that happy, companionate marriage is the only viable option for the respectable young lady once she has left her original shelter.

Hence, there are two terrible risks that the young lady must take in her entrance into the world. First, the passage itself is treacherous. Will the young lady find or be found by the appropriate young man? How will he be induced to marry her, especially if she does not bring with her the lure of money or prestige? He must fall in love with her, but in the process of being made available as the object of such love, the young lady may be besieged by less noble attentions than those that precede a marriage offer. What if her head, innocent and unprepared to distinguish honorable from dishonorable intentions, is turned by these attentions, and she loses her reputation? If she remains innocent but fails to attract an offer of marriage, she is condemned to a lifetime of economic dependence and social marginalization. If she loses her innocence along with her chance at marriage, she risks ostracism as well. The second risk occurs in the matter of whom she marries. What if she marries the wrong man, and instead of the domestic happiness that is supposed to shelter her feminine innocence in its mature phase she enters into a lifetime of mild to extreme abuse or, at best, boredom and loneliness? If she should try to alleviate the tedium of a bad marriage through public amusements and visits, she again risks losing the innocence that is so central to respectable femininity. While marriage did allow for more social mobility than was considered appropriate for unmarried young ladies, the wife who neglected her family and household duties for social pleasures was a stock figure of contempt in eighteenth-century literature, as was the widow (like Madame Duval) whose life became too public.

If in their youth middle-class Englishwomen encounter the paradox that the innocence which gives them value also makes them vulnerable, marriage, the goal of female life, constitutes a similar paradox: it is the site of both possible happiness and possible misery. As Burney comments in one of her journal entries, "it is such chance!" Elsewhere in her journals, she comments, after witnessing a wedding, "O [heavens]! how short a time does it take to put an eternal end to a Woman's liberty!" (Burney 1: 17). Her view of married life was far from idealistic, as she muses in her journal: " 'Tis preparing one to lead a long Journey, and to know the path is not altogether strew'd with Roses. . . . [The bride] may not find the Road it leads her to very short; be that as it may, she must trudge on, she can only return with her wishes, be she ever so wearied" (Burney 1: 65). Caught between the paradox of youth and the paradox of female maturity, the young lady at her entrance into the world is in a critical and interesting position, and it is not surprising that the happy resolution that Evelina shares with Cinderella should have appealed to readers who were anxious about this critical moment in middle-class women's lives. *Evelina*'s staging of the difficulties of achieving this resolution underscores the fact that the cultural narrative of Cinderella must be read in relation to other cultural narratives about young ladies. Burney's incorporation of the cultural narratives of innocence as the young lady's greatest source of value and vulnerability and female adolescence as that critical period when she wins or loses all place Evelina's Cinderella story in the context of mid-eighteenth-century English definitions of middle-class femininity.

*Evelina* offers more than a romantic placebo for the understandable fears of young ladies. It also offers critical distance on the young lady's entrance into society. Evelina's experience as a Cinderella at her first ball is far more anxious than romantic, and her story includes moments of real misery that counterbalance the romance of her rise to wealth and happiness. Evelina's observations concerning Mrs. Mirvan's marriage and the sad reality of Madame Duval's faded charms offer grim alternatives to the novel's "happily-ever-after" ending. Another way in which the novel establishes such critical distance is through humor. When Evelina attends her first ball, we view the world from her perspective, and it often appears to be an absurd place. Evelina may be awed by Lord Orville's handsome appearance and urbanity, but the "fashionable" refinement of a Lovel is downright silly in her eyes. Although Evelina's chortle at Mr. Lovel is ill-timed, her reflections on the social conventions attached to a young lady's entrance draw attention to the ridiculous nature of conventions that require her to be both knowing and innocent. A clear view of the gritty, sometimes even grim, aspects of feminine life and a good sense of humor are the young lady's best tools for avoiding the dangers inherent in the paradox of the young lady and the paradox or marriage — the danger of becoming the victim of an unscrupulous seducer or an unhappy marriage.

The young lady of Burney's England must strike a delicate balance between contradictory ways of thinking and living. She must be both knowledgeable and innocent in order to move successfully toward her goal of marriage, which itself holds out both the best and the worst of possibilities. The world of leisure that she enters is caught between narratives of orderly, rational progress on one hand and narratives of decay and violence on the other. At one point in Burney's novel, Villars cautions Evelina that "nothing is so delicate as the reputation of a woman: it is, at once, the most beautiful and most brittle of all human things" (p. 206). However resilient and resourceful she may be, Evelina's character is defined by cultural narratives that place her in a highly precarious position in the world of Burney's England. In turn, that world itself seems to hold what order it has through a tenuous balance between rational exchange and violence. It is probably no coincidence that Evelina and Lord Orville leave the world of urban leisure for the rural domesticity of Berry Hill at the novel's end. After reading *Evelina,* it is hard to imagine a public space that could truly accommodate the rational exchange of words and feelings that their marriage seems to represent. At the same time, the Mirvans' nightmare of a marriage reminds us that there are no guarantees of rational order or protection from violence in domestic life. The young lady's entrance into the world is a rather dark journey, however bright the ballroom lights.

## A WOMAN NOVELIST MAKES HER ENTRANCE

*Evelina* entered the world in 1778, when its author was twenty-six. Burney had already written an unpublished novel, *The History of Caroline Evelyn,* which she destroyed in 1767, and had for ten years kept a diary of her observations on the lively events of the Burney family social life — a life that included many of London's most famous artists, musicians, and writers. She was clearly addicted to writing as a pastime, preferring it to the more conventionally feminine needlework to which her stepmother urged her. With the publication of her first novel, she became a writer in the public eye, although she did not assume the public role of writer immediately. With the help of her brother Charles, a classical scholar and an author himself, Burney managed to publish *Evelina* anonymously. The novel was enthusiastically received by the influential periodical reviews of the time as the most exciting work of fiction to appear within what was, admittedly, a rather quiet period for new novels. *Evelina* was favorably compared to the earlier work of Samuel Richardson and Henry Fielding, and the identity of its author became a popular subject for speculation. The secret was short-lived, however, and Burney became, in her late twenties and early thirties, a celebrity in the world of literary London. We have asked questions and sketched some tentative answers about Evelina's "entrance," as a "young lady," into "the world." What remains to be done by way of introduction to the novel is to explore how these three terms work in relation to the novel's reception and Burney's career as a writer. What was the "world" of literature like in eighteenth-century London, and how would the eighteenth-century idea of the "young lady" have affected the "entrance" of a twenty-six-year-old woman writer into that "world"?

The English reading world of 1778 was quite small by today's standards. Readers were those who, for a variety of reasons, had the means and motivation to acquire the skill; men and women in the upper and middle classes were usually in this category, and literacy was increasing rapidly among women in merchant, trade, and professional families. While the lower order of workers was usually not literate, it was reasonably common for the upper servants of gentry and aristocrats to read. However limited "the reading public" was by today's standards, it is important to note that "the world" of literature seemed, in 1778, to have grown at an unprecedented rate during the first half of the eighteenth century, both in regard to readership and the amount of print literature available on the market. Publishing had become a lucrative business, and a few authors even found it possible to live on what they could make by selling their productions to publishers. Although the support of the rich and powerful was still an important part of making a reputation and livelihood as an author, writing for a living no longer depended as heavily as it had in the past on the economic and political patronage of the great. One could write plays for the London theaters and publish poetry, essays, and increasingly, novels. Many of the aspiring writers who took advantage of these new opportunities in the London literary marketplace were women.

Burney was by no means the first woman to publish successful prose fiction. Eliza Haywood's *Love in Excess* (1719), for example, was at the very top of the list of best-selling novels in the first half of the century. The eighteenth century is generally associated with the "birth" or "rise" of the novel, which gained prevalence in the literary marketplace during the first half of the century and continued to be published and sold in increasing numbers. By the 1770s, it is possible to discern in the popular periodical publications that reviewed works of fiction a certain problematic association between women and the novel. Reading was generally thought to be an inappropriate occupation for women, and the novel was seen as one of the most ideologically dangerous forms of reading material. In addition, women novelists were increasingly stereotyped, throughout the second half of the century, as "feminine" in ways that clearly carried the connotation of second rate. Men who wrote successful novels — for instance Tobias Smollett, Henry Fielding, and Samuel Richardson — did not entirely escape a "feminization" of their work that grew out of the association between women writers and readers and the genre, but their gender usually lent them a respectability that often eluded women. The fact that many women novelists *were* socially and economically marginal and needed to write for a living fed the popular stereotype of the woman novelist as a particularly pernicious hack writer. This is not to say that women writers never obtained praise and success. Rather, they inevitably encountered a world that thought of them *as* women writers — a world in which gender neutrality was nearly impossible. Burney's entrance into the world of literary London was marked by gendered assumptions about women and writing.

The reception of Burney's novel has been brilliantly explored by Julia Epstein, who argues convincingly that all of her fiction — *Evelina* (1778), *Cecilia* (1782), *Camilla* (1796), and *The Wanderer* (1814) — was reviewed with unremitting and sometimes quite maddeningly inaccurate references based on her gender. When Burney's secret authorship of *Evelina* came out, reviewers seem to have assumed that the novelist was the same age as her seventeen-year-old heroine. Throughout the eighteenth and nineteenth centuries, *Evelina* received consistent praise. This praise is often condescending, however, and almost always infantilizes both the novel and its author. Burney's contemporaries praise the novel for its "freshness," "youth," and "vivacity," but even when these critics and reviewers drop such infantilizing metaphors, gender still reigns as *the* category through which Burney's work is read. William Hazlitt's influential 1815 *Endinburgh Review* assessment sets out gender as the term through which Burney's writing has been read since its first publication:

> Women, in general, have a quicker perception of any oddity or singularity of character than men, and are more alive to every absurdity

which arises from a violation of the rules of society, or a deviation from established custom. This partly arises from the restraints on their own behaviour, which turn their attention constantly on the subject, and partly from other causes. The surface of their minds, like that of their bodies, seems a finer texture than ours; more soft, and susceptible of immediate impression. They have less muscular power, — less power of continued voluntary attention — of reason — passion and imagination. But they are more easily impressed with whatever appeals to their senses or habitual prejudices. The intuitive perception of their minds is less disturbed by any general reasonings on causes or consequences. They learn the idiom of character and manner, as they acquire that of language, by rote merely, without troubling themselves about the principles. Their observation is not the less accurate on that account, as far as it goes; for it has been well said, that "there is nothing so true as habit." (qtd. in Epstein 211)

Hazlitt's appreciative response to Burney in terms of her gender is representative, as Epstein notes, of the prevalent approach to her work through the late eighteenth and the nineteenth centuries. When Burney's novels are well received, as *Evelina* generally was, they are typed as "feminine": charming for their informant's-eye-view of a "young lady's" experience if rather limited in their "knowledge of the world." Even when Burney is granted some insight into the human condition, the reviewer manages to infantilize her, as in the 1782 *Gentleman's Magazine* review of *Cecilia*, which allows that the book shows "more knowledge of the world, or the *ton*, than could be expected from the years of the fair authoress" (485). (Burney was thirty-one.)

As irritating as this sort of condescension to Burney as a "young lady" might be, the gendering of her work carries with it the force of social reality — a social reality that Burney knew and dramatized in her writing. Burney's fiction is about, among other things, the constraints placed on female life and thought. That gender plays a highly useful role in thinking about Burney's fiction is evident from recent feminist reevaluations of her work, such as Patricia Spacks's, Epstein's, Margaret Doody's, and my own. The problem arises when femininity becomes the only category through which one reads the work. This problem is most apparent in the reception of Burney's last novel, *The Wanderer* (1814), considered by many recent critics, including myself, to be her best. *The Wanderer* drew the misogynist fire that *Evelina*'s alleged "youthfulness" had been spared. John Wilson Croker, in the 1814 *Quarterly Review*, describes Burney as "an old coquette who endeavours, by the wild tawdriness and laborious gaiety of her attire, to compensate for the loss of the natural charms of freshness, novelty, and youth" (126). *The Wanderer* itself is characterized as "Evelina grown old; the vivacity, the bloom, the elegance, 'the purple light of love' are vanished; the eyes are there, but dim; the cheek, but it is furrowed; the lips, but they are withered" (125–126).

Gender is the primary category through which the reception of Burney's novels has been filtered, and we might ask what impact this "feminization" of her novels had on Burney's career as a writer. Burney's extraordinary and rich life, which is discussed in fascinating detail by Doody and Epstein, certainly attests to how the complexity of human experience often exceeds such categorization. Nonetheless, her culture's idea of "the young lady" did have a profound effect on Burney's long career as a writer. After *Evelina*'s public acclaim, the question of what the young lady novelist would do next was on the minds of many who were connected to the world of literary London. Burney's inclination was not to write another novel, and her first literary production after *Evelina* was a play, the until recently unpublished *The Witlings*. Burney had received encouragement in this work from the playwright and man of letters Arthur Murphy. Though in her late twenties, and with some reason to think herself a skillful writer, Burney did not proceed with the business of getting the play performed and published, because she considered herself morally obliged to consult her father and Samuel Crisp, her informally adopted paternal advisor whom she referred to as "Daddy" Crisp. Charles Burney and Crisp did not dispute the quality of the work itself, which was not, in fact, much discussed. Rather, they objected to the career move that a public performance of *The Witlings* might entail.

Their objections seem to have arisen from a concern that the play, a satiric comedy, would offend the writer and intellectual Elizabeth Montagu, who was recognizable as the real-life model for one of its characters. Those who made up the literary and intellectual circle of "the Bluestockings," the name given the women intellectuals of Montagu's set, were the most prestigious and respectable models in Burney's society for women who wrote literature. Montagu had high-class standing, economic independence, and an impeccable moral reputation — facts that dissociated her from the more sexually vulnerable and socially and economically marginal figure of the woman who wrote for money. Burney, in her father's and Crisp's opinion, would have been alienated from Montagu and all that she represented had *The Witlings* been produced.

In addition, the London stage was arguably not the most respectable institution with which women could be associated. Actors of both genders were often considered morally and sexually suspect; Charles Burney's friend, the actor David Garrick, had only recently made it possible to think of the professional actor as highly respectable. Actresses in particular were marked as sexually disreputable, having been associated with high- and low-class prostitution since their entrance on the English stage in the late seventeenth century. The fact that so many of the women who had written for the stage had also acted on it must have created some slippage between "actress" and "woman playwright" in the minds of Burney's contemporaries. While the questionable morality of those associated with the theater was probably not enough in itself to make Charles Burney and Samuel Crisp discourage their "daughter" from writing for the stage, they may have felt that the satire on respectable female intellectuals in *The Witlings* would have increased the likelihood of Burney's association with the "wrong" kind of woman writer, while cutting her off from the "right" kind.

Burney acquiesced to her father's and Crisp's directions, but not without considerable anger and dismay. Later in her life, she wrote several more plays, one of which was performed, but this initial containment of her writing talent to the genre of the novel affected the course of her career as a writer. Characterized by her father and adopted paternal advisor as suited to the more "feminine" genre of the novel, Burney was pressured to stay within the limits of those forms of writing considered most appropriate for women: prose fiction and the writing of "private" forms such as diaries and letters, which she produced in prodigious quantities throughout her long life. The fact that she had started editing her journals and correspondence by the time she died in 1840 suggests that she did not regard these texts as entirely private. Burney's career as a writer might be characterized as one of acquiescence to external constraints coupled with as much resistance as she could muster, within those boundaries, against gendered limitations.

After the publication of Burney's diaries and letters in 1842 (see Part Two, Chapter 1, for selections from the diaries and letters), reviewers extended their views of the "young lady novelist" to the work of Burney the social observer and diarist. According to the 1842 *New Monthly Magazine,* Burney was the "gentlest, the softest, the most pure-minded, the most simple-thoughted, the most home-loving, the most retiring of her sex" (527). This characterization could be forgiven the reviewer, perhaps, given the fact that the published version of her diaries did not, at that time, include the account of Burney's search for her husband on the battlefields of the Napoleonic Wars or the agonizing journal she kept for her sister of the mastectomy she underwent without benefit of anesthesia in France at the age of fifty. Less forgivable is the tenacity of this image in the twentieth century. Until the late 1980s, Burney was predominantly seen as "the young lady novelist" who wrote *Evelina*. After that 1778 novel, the story told by twentieth-century literary criticism goes, the quality of the novels declined as "Miss Burney" aged into the less charming "Madame D'Arblay." Croker's "aging coquette" image endures in the twentieth-century reception of the later novels, especially *The Wanderer*, until the late 1980s, when feminist academic reassessments of the fiction begin to call attention to the violence, complexity, and critical edge of Burney's writing. As Epstein has noted, this reassessment has been made possible by social and political developments in the historical period in which we are now reading *Evelina*, much as Croker's misogynist dismissals were rendered creditable by his culture's attitudes toward gender and writing. As our cultural narratives about social difference and power relations change, our readings of texts change with them. While our reading of the novel is enriched by knowing more about how Burney's contemporaries understood the young lady's entrance into the world, that reading is inevitably grounded in our present thinking about culture. Working through past formulations of the young lady and her world leads us directly to our own place as thinkers, writers, and readers. As we interpret texts such as *Evelina*, we create our own cultural narratives about the world we live in and our place within it.

## WORKS CITED

Addison, Joseph, and Richard Steele. *The Tatler*. Ed. Donald Bond. 3 vols. Oxford: Clarendon, 1987.

Burney, Frances. *The Early Journals and Letters of Fanny Burney*. Ed. Lars E. Troide. 3 vols. Oxford: Clarendon, 1988.

Clark, Alice. *The Working Life of Women in the Seventeenth Century*. London: Cass, 1968.

Croker, John Wilson. "D'Arblay's Wanderer." *Quarterly Review* Apr. 1814: 123–130.

Davidoff, Leonore, and Catherine Hall. *Family Fortunes: Men and Women of the English Middle Class, 1780–1850.* Chicago: U of Chicago P, 1987.

Doody, Margaret Anne. *Frances Burney: The Life in the Works.* New Brunswick: Rutgers UP, 1988.

Epstein, Julia. *The Iron Pen: Frances Burney and the Politics of Women's Writing.* Madison: U of Wisconsin P, 1989.

"Impartial and Critical Review of New Publications." *Gentleman's Magazine* Oct. 1782: 485–92.

"Review of *Diary and Correspondences of Madame D'Arblay.*" *New Monthly Magazine and Humorist* Dec. 1842: 526–37.

Spacks, Patricia Ann Meyer. *The Female Imagination.* New York: Knopf, 1975.

———. *Imagining a Self: Autobiography and Novel in Eighteenth-Century England.* Cambridge: Harvard UP, 1976.

Straub, Kristina. *Divided Fictions: Fanny Burney and Feminine Strategy.* Lexington: UP of Kentucky, 1987.

# Chronology of
# Burney's Life and Times

## 1752

June 13: Frances Burney born in King's Lynn, third child of Esther Sleepe (?–1762) and Dr. Charles Burney (1726–1814). Two older siblings: Esther (1749–1832) and James (1750–1821); three younger: Susanna Elizabeth (1755–1800), Charles (1757–1817), and Charlotte Ann (1761–1838).

The London Hospital founded. New Style calendar begins.

## 1753

Passage of the Marriage Act, legislation that regularizes civil law on marriage, which was previously in a rather vague and unstable state. The bill specifies that marriages must be performed in a parish church after the publication of banns or with a special license from the archbishop.

*Opposite:* Detail of East London from *A Topographical Map of the County of Middlesex* by John Rocque, 1754. Holbourne Hill is clearly visible in the northwest quadrant, near Lincolns Inn Fields. Much of the area away from the banks of the Thames is still in agricultural use, although the area of Lambeth Marsh in the southwest is beginning to show the development of new roads. St. James Park and Vauxhall Spring Gardens are visible on the west side of town. Copyright Museum of London.

Passage of the "Jew Bill," legislation that extends naturalization, although not universally, to Jews in England. It is met with much popular agitation and violence against Jews and is repealed in 1754.

Samuel Richardson (1689–1761), *The History of Sir Charles Grandison.* Tobias Smollett (1721–1771), *The Adventures of Ferdinand Count Fathom.*

## 1755

Samuel Johnson (1709–1784), *Dictionary of the English Language.*

## 1756

Seven Years War with France declared, following five years of repeated military conflicts between France and England in North America and India. The French strike back at England by taking Minorca, an island crucially located in relation to Mediterranean trade routes. This military defeat is seen in England as a national disgrace.

Thomas Gray (1716–1771), *The Bard.* Edmund Burke (1729–1797), *A Philosophical Enquiry into the Origin of Our Ideas of the Sublime and Beautiful.*

## 1757

David Garrick's (1717–1779) *The Male Coquette* plays at Drury Lane. David Hume (1711–1776), *Natural History of Religion.* Smollett, *History of England.*

## 1758

General James Wolfe takes the French colony of Louisbourg in Canada. This victory establishes British dominance over France in North America.

Johnson begins *The Idler.*

## 1759

British Museum opens to public.

Johnson, *The Prince of Abissinia (Rasselas).* Laurence Sterne (1713–1768) begins the serial publication of *Tristram Shandy.*

## 1760

The Burneys move to London.

George II dies, is succeeded by George III. English capture Montreal and Guadaloupe.

Samuel Foote's (1720–1777) farce, *The Minor,* produced. Arthur Murphy's (1727–1805) *The Way to Keep Him* produced.

## 1761

Hume, *History of England*. Oliver Goldsmith (1730–1774), *Citizen of the World*.

## 1762

September 27: Burney's mother, Esther Sleepe Burney, dies.

Isaac Bickerstaffe's (1735?–1812?) musical, *Love in a Village*, produced. Jean-Jacques Rousseau (1712–1778), *Social Contract*.

## 1763

Samuel Crisp, who became Frances Burney's fatherly advisor, "Daddy" Crisp, becomes a close friend of the Burney family.

Peace of Paris is concluded, in which the French cede Canada and India to Britain. Riots in support of John Wilkes, M.P., whose *North Briton* had attacked the established government of Prime Minister Lord Bute.

George Colman's (1732–1794) *The Deuce Is in Him* is produced. Christopher Smart (1722–1771; a visitor to the Burney house), *Song to David*.

## 1764

Horace Walpole (1717–1797), *The Castle of Otranto*.

## 1765

Stamp Act is passed and is violently resisted in North America.

James Fordyce (1720–1796), *Sermons to Young Women*. Foote's *Commissary* produced. Sir William Blackstone (1723–1780) begins the serial publication of his *Commentaries on the Laws of England*.

## 1766

Goldsmith, *The Vicar of Wakefield*. Christopher Anstey (1724–1805), *A New Bath Guide*. Garrick and Colman collaborate on *The Clandestine Marriage*.

## 1767

June 13: Frances Burney destroys manuscript of a novel, *The History of Caroline Evelyn*.

October 2: Charles Burney marries Elizabeth Allen. This marriage brings together the six Burney children and three children of Allen's former marriage, Maria, Stephen, and Elizabeth. Two more children are born of this marriage, Richard Thomas (1768–1808) and Sarah Harriet (1772–1844). The two families do not maintain a single residence, however, for over two more years.

Charles Macklin's (1697?–1797) *The Trueborn Irishman* produced.

## 1768

Frances Burney begins keeping a diary.

Royal Academy of Arts founded in London with Sir Joshua Reynolds as the first president. Captain James Cook begins his exploratory expeditions in the South Pacific.

Sterne, *A Sentimental Journey*. *Encyclopaedia Britannica* begins publication. Goldsmith's *The Good-Natured Man* produced.

## 1769

James Watt invents steam engine.

## 1770

The combined Allen/Burney families move to house in Queen's Square, London. By 1772, it is clear from Burney's journals that the Burney children and their stepmother are not getting along as smoothly as was wished by Charles Burney.

Cook "discovers" Australia.

Goldsmith, *The Deserted Village*.

## 1771

First color fashion plate appears in *The Lady's Magazine*.

Charles Burney publishes his musical *Tours* of France and Italy. Smollett, *Humphry Clinker*. Henry Mackenzie (1745–1831), *The Man of Feeling*.

## 1772

Burney's brother James is made second lieutenant of the *Adventure*, under the command of Captain Cook, then undertaking his second expedition. Stepsister Maria Allen elopes with Martin Folkes Rishton.

Lord Mansfield, Lord Chief Justice, makes ruling in case of a slave brought to England from Jamaica that is interpreted to mean that slavery cannot exist on English soil.

Foote's *Nabob* produced.

## 1773

Charles Burney publishes his *Tour* of Germany.

Between 1770 and 1773, Burney enjoys family outings to Ranelagh, Marylebone Gardens, Vauxhall, the opera, and theater. She also spends many pleasurable evenings listening to the fine musicians who frequent her father's house.

Boston Tea Party.

Goldsmith's *She Stoops to Conquer* produced. Foote's *Piety in Pattens* produced.

## 1774

Burney family moves to house on St. Martin's Street, Leicester Square, that was once owned by Sir Isaac Newton.

Posthumous publication of Lord Chesterfield's (1694–1773) *Letter to His Son.*

## 1775

Unwanted marriage proposals made to Burney by Thomas Barlow.

Battles of Concord, Lexington, and Bunker Hill.

Richard Brinsley Sheridan's (1751–1816) *The Rivals* produced.

## 1776

Charles Burney begins publication of his *History of Music*, ending in 1789. Burney assists her father in producing this monumental work.

British parliament rejects universal male suffrage. American Declaration of Independence.

Adam Smith (1723–1790) publishes *The Wealth of Nations,* the classic work on political economy that offers the capitalist theory of free exchange. Edward Gibbon (1737–1794) publishes the first volume of his *Decline and Fall of the Roman Empire.* Thomas Paine (1737–1809), *Common Sense.* Foote's *Trip to Calais* produced.

## 1777

Elizabeth Allen (Burney's stepsister), sent to Paris to finish her education, elopes with an adventurer named Meeke. Charles Burney the younger is expelled from Caius College for stealing books from the college library.

October: Surrender of British army to American forces at Battle of Saratoga.

Sheridan's *School for Scandal* produced.

## 1778

January: Publication of *Evelina, or, The History of a Young Lady's Entrance into the World.*

After Burney's authorship is exposed, Charles Burney takes her with him to Streatham, the home of the literary patrons Henry and Hester Lynch Thrale. The latter and Burney become close friends for the next five years, and through Thrale she meets many of London's famous writers and artists, including Samuel Johnson and Richard Brinsley Sheridan.

Between 1778 and 1780, Burney spends lengthy visits in the resorts of Brighton and Bath with the Thrales.

June: France enters War of Independence on American side.

## 1779

Four more editions of *Evelina* published (one pirated). Frances Burney writes *The Witlings, a Comedy*. Samuel Crisp and Charles Burney discourage production, and Burney reluctantly complies. Burney is mildly satirized as a female author and friend of Samuel Johnson in George Huddlesford's *Warley: A Satire*.

Spain enters war against England; Siege of Gibraltar.

Sheridan's *The Critic* produced. Johnson publishes first installment of *The Lives of the Poets*.

## 1780

The Thrales and Samuel Johnson visit Burney and Samuel Crisp at the latter's home in Chessington.

Gorden riots in London over the proposed extension of civil rights to Roman Catholics. Burney, in Bath with the Thrales, sees burning and riots for "one whole dreadful night"; Mr. Thrale, suspected of being a "papist" for having supported a Bill for the Relief of Roman Catholics, is threatened, and the Thrale family flees to Brighton.

Holland enters war against England.

Hannah Cowley's (1743–1809) *The Belles' Strategem* produced.

## 1781

April:  Death of Henry Thrale.

October 19:  Surrender of the British army under Cornwallis to the Continental army at Yorktown.

## 1782

January 10:  Burney's sister Susanna marries Molesworth Phillips. Burney is concerned, as it turns out rightly, over her sister's health and happiness in this match.

June 12:  Publication of *Cecilia; or, Memoirs of an Heiress* (in five volumes).

December:  Burney meets Richard Owen Cambridge and his son, the Reverend George Owen Cambridge. Burney hopes for an offer of marriage from the latter, which never materializes.

## 1783

April 26: Samuel Crisp dies.

Burney meets Mary Delany, who eventually introduces her to the Royal Court.

September 3: Peace of Versailles formally concludes American War of Independence.

Cowley's *Bold Stroke for a Husband* produced. Hugh Blair (1718–1800), *Lectures on Rhetoric*.

## 1784

Spring: Susanna and Molesworth Phillips settle near Norbury Park, the estate of William and Frederica Locke. Burney meets the Lockes and begins a lifelong friendship.

July 23, 25: Hester Lynch Thrale marries the music teacher, Gabriel Piozzi, in two separate ceremonies, one Catholic and one Protestant. This marriage effectively ended Thrale's friendship with Burney.

December 13: Burney visits Samuel Johnson on his deathbed.

## 1785

Summer: Burney visits Mrs. Delany, who is grieving and in ill health after the death of her friend, the Duchess of Portland.

December: Burney first presented at Court.

William Cowper (1731–1800), *The Task*. Elizabeth Inchbald's (1753–1821) *I'll Tell You What* produced.

## 1786

February: Burney's sister Charlotte marries Clement Francis, a surgeon who had acted as secretary to William Hastings in India. Burney spends more time with the Lockes, as life at St. Martin's Street becomes increasingly lonely and difficult.

July 17: Burney becomes Second Keeper of the Robes to Queen Charlotte by royal invitation.

Robert Burns (1759–1796), *Poems*. William Beckford (1760–1844), *Vathek*. Inchbald's *Widow's Vow* produced. Cowley's *School for Greybeards* produced.

## 1787

Burney begins journals from Windsor and Kew for her sisters Susanna and Hetty.

Society for the Suppression of the Slave Trade founded by William Wilberforce and Thomas Clarkson. George III exhibits signs of apparent madness; from 1787 to 1789 Burney is privy to the scandal of the king's "madness" and the attempts to hide it for political reasons. Sierra Leone founded.

Inchbald's *Such Things Are* produced. Colman's (the younger) *Inkle and Yarico* produced.

## 1788

October: Burney begins blank-verse tragedy, *Edwy and Elgiva*. Burney's friend Mary Delany dies.

## 1789

Burney leaves for a three-month holiday in Dorset with the Royal Family.

July 14: Storming of the Bastille begins the French Revolution.

William Blake (1757–1827), *Songs of Innocence*.

## 1790

Burney becomes very ill as a result of her service at Court. From 1790 through 1791, she writes three more blank-verse tragedies — *Hubert De Vere, A Pastoral Tragedy, The Siege of Pevensey* — and the draft of a fourth, *Elberta*.

Burke, *Reflections on the Revolution in France*.

## 1791

July 7: Burney leaves the service of Queen Charlotte after a long illness and with a pension of £100 a year.

Paine publishes *The Rights of Man* as a rejoinder to Burke. Inchbald, *A Simple Story*.

## 1793

January 21: Execution of Louis XVI in France.

February 1: France declares war against Britain and Holland; war will continue between Britain and France until 1801.

Burney's courtship with Alexandre d'Arblay, exiled adjutant-general of the Marquis of Lafayette, begins. She meets Madame de Staël, daughter of the French minister of finance and the former hostess of one of Europe's most famous salons.

July 28: Burney marries d'Arblay in a Protestant ceremony.

July 30: Burney marries d'Arblay in a Catholic ceremony.

Burney publishes a pamphlet, *Brief Reflections Relative to the Emigrant French Clergy*, to call attention to the plight of expatriate French clergymen in England. William Godwin (1756–1836), *Enquiry Concerning Political Justice*.

## 1794

July 28: Execution of Robespierre ends "Reign of Terror" in France.

December 18: Burney's son, Alexander, is born.

Blake, *Songs of Experience*. Mary Wollstonecraft (1759–1797), *A Vindication of the Rights of Woman*. Godwin, *Caleb Williams*. Ann Radcliffe (1764–1823), *The Mysteries of Udolpho*.

## 1795

January: Burney, nursing her two-week-old infant, develops an abscess in her breast and is dangerously ill for some months.

March 21: Production of Burney's *Edwy and Elgiva* at Drury Lane theater for a one-night run.

June: Burney's sister Susanna leaves her home near Norbury Park and is forced to move to Ireland with her philandering and abusive husband.

Edward Jenner develops vaccination for smallpox using a dead form of the virus from cows. (Lady Mary Wortley Montagu had first brought idea of inoculation from Turkey to England in 1718.)

## 1796

Summer: Burney publishes *Camilla: or, A Picture of Youth* (in five volumes).

October 20: Burney's stepmother, Elizabeth Allen Burney, dies.

With the permission of William Locke, d'Arblay begins work on Camilla cottage at Norbury, the Locke's estate, doing much of the work with his own hands. This project was financed by advance proceeds from Burney's *Camilla*.

Matthew Gregory Lewis (1775–1818), *The Monk*.

## 1797

Burney has son, Alexander, inoculated for smallpox.

Thomas Gisborne (1758–1846), *An Enquiry into the Duties of the Female Sex*.

## 1798

September 2: James Burney, unhappy in his marriage, runs off with his half-sister, Sarah Harriet. They cohabit for five years, to the horror of the Burney family.

Burney writes *Love and Fashion*, a comedy. Burney's sister Charlotte, now a widow, marries Ralph Broome in what is to be an unhappy match.

William Wordsworth (1770–1850) and Samuel Taylor Coleridge (1772–1834), *Lyrical Ballads*.

## 1799

November 9: Napoleon Bonaparte becomes emperor of France.

## 1800

January 6: Death of Burney's beloved sister, Susanna. Burney, unable to cry, screams "for some vent to the mighty oppression upon [her] soul." Burney commemorates Susanna's death by keeping January 6 as a day of prayer and mourning for the rest of her life.

## 1801

Burney writes *A Busy Day; or, An Arrival from India* and *The Woman-Hater*, both comedies.

October 1: Peace of Amiens: war between France and England ends in a stalemate.

October 28: D'Arblay returns to France in hopes of recouping some of his lost rights and property.

## 1802

April 20: Burney and her son join d'Arblay in France.

## 1803

May 18: England declares war on France. Burney and her son are unable to return to England.

## 1807

Gas lighting is first used in London.

## 1808

Napoleon strengthens Continental Blockade, making communication between England and France more difficult.

## 1809

Hannah More (1745–1833), *Coelebs in Search of a Wife*.

## 1811

September: Burney undergoes a radical mastectomy for an apparent cancer.

Jane Austen (1775–1817), *Sense and Sensibility*.

## 1812

August 16: Burney and her son return to England, leaving d'Arblay to deal with his financial and military interests.

Napoleon leads disastrous invasion of Russia.

George Gordon, Lord Byron (1788–1824), first two cantos of "Childe Harold."

## 1813

October: Alexander d'Arblay enters Cambridge.

Napoleon regroups his troops in Prussia.

Austen, *Pride and Prejudice.*

## 1814

March: Publication of Burney's *The Wanderer; or, Female Difficulties* (in five volumes). This work was begun some time before 1800.

April 6: Napoleon abdicates after Wellington's decisive victory at Vittoria; Bourbons return to the throne of France.

April 12: Charles Burney dies.

May: D'Arblay receives a summons from the Duc de Luxembourg to enter the Garde du Corps de son Roi.

May: The d'Arblays learn that they will lose Camilla cottage. William Locke, dying in 1810, had left Norbury to his son. When the latter sells the estate, it is discovered that the d'Arblays have no deed to the land on which the cottage is built.

November: Burney returns to France, leaving her son, who has rejected his father's designs of a military career, at Cambridge.

Sir Walter Scott (1771–1832), *Waverley* (anonymously).

## 1815

March: D'Arblay joins royalist troops opposing Napoleon, who has returned from Elba to attempt to retake France after the demolition of his empire; Burney escapes to Belgium from a war-torn France.

June 18: Napoleon is defeated at Waterloo.

July: Burney witnesses the aftermath of war in Belgium, helps to tend wounded, and is horrified by the masses of dead and maimed. Embarks on a harrowing journey across war-torn France to find her husband.

July 24: Burney and d'Arblay, ill from the hardships of his military duties, are reunited at Trèves.

October 17: Burney returns to England with the wounded Lieutenant-General d'Arblay.

## 1817

Burney, trapped in a seaside cavern at Wildersmouth at high tide, narrowly escapes drowning.

November 17: Burney and Hester Thrale Piozzi meet at Bath and are reconciled.

December 28: Burney's brother Charles dies.

## 1818

May 3: D'Arblay dies after a painful illness.

Lord Byron, first five cantos of *Don Juan*. Mary Shelley (1797–1851), *Frankenstein; or The Modern Prometheus*.

## 1819

April 11: Burney's son, Alexander d'Arblay, is ordained a priest in Church of England.

Percy Bysshe Shelley (1792–1822) begins to write some of his most famous lyrics, including "Ode to the West Wind" and "To a Sky-lark."

## 1820

Alexander d'Arblay's general health begins to fail probably from some then-undiagnosed medical condition that caused weakness and depression.

January 29: George III dies, is succeeded by George IV.

## 1821

May 2: Hester Thrale Piozzi dies.

July 19: Burney's brother James is appointed rear-admiral in British navy.

November: James Burney dies.

## 1824

Alexander d'Arblay is made curate at Camden Town.

## 1829

Sir Robert Peel founds the Metropolitan Police in London.

*Opposite:* Detail from *A New Plan of the City and Liberty of Westminster, etc.* by Robert Sayer, Thomas Jefferys, and Carington Bowles, 1766. This map shows the proliferation of roads on the south bank of the Thames. Stairs down to the water for the benefit of visitors seeking their way across the river are clearly marked. The watermen of the Thames were still extremely important to London transportation, in part because they were effective in preventing the building of more bridges to connect the south and north banks of the Thames. By permission of the British Library.

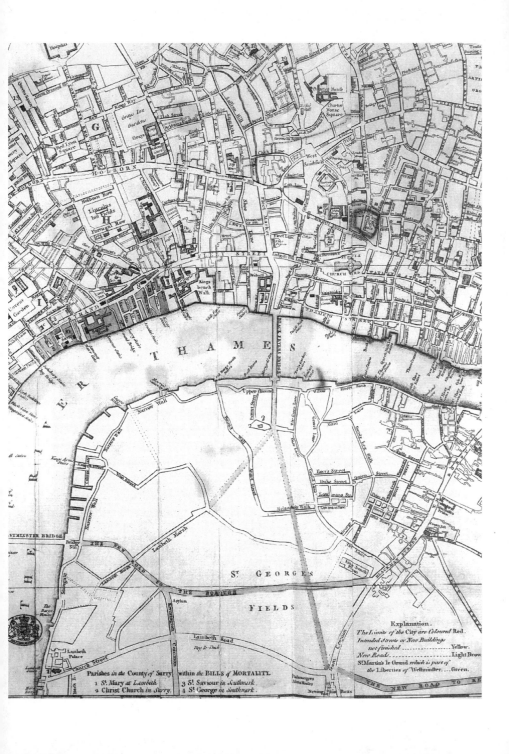

THAMES

St. GEORGES

FIELDS

Explanation.
The Limits of the City are Coloured Red.
Intended Streets or New Buildings
not finished .................... Yellow.
New Roads .................... Light Brown
St. Martin's le Grand which is part of
the Liberties of Westminster.....Green.

Parishes in the County of Surry within the BILLS of MORTALITY.
1 St. Mary at Lambeth        3 St. Saviour in Southwark.
2 Christ Church in Surry.   4 St. George in Southwark.

## 1831
Opening of New London Bridge.

## 1832
February:  Burney's sister Esther dies.

Publication of *Memoirs of Doctor Burney* (in three volumes).

## 1837
January 19.  Burney's son, Alexander, dies.

## 1838
September 12:  Burney's sister Charlotte dies.

## 1840
January 6:  Burney dies in London. She is buried in Bath, next to her husband and son.

# A Note on the Text

This volume reprints Edward A. and Lillian D. Bloom's edition of the text of *Evelina*, published in 1968 by Oxford University Press. I thank Oxford for permission to use this edition. The Blooms based their work on the first edition of *Evelina* (January 1778), incorporating both the corrections and alterations made by Burney after she had seen Thomas Lowndes's proof sheets, and a number of additions that were made to the narrative in the second edition (1779). They also corrected obvious misprints and modernized the long *s*. I have retained their practice of bracketing Burney's 1779 additions to the novel.

Students should be aware that the Oxford Edition preserves certain peculiarities in spelling and punctuation in order to be faithful to Burney's late-eighteenth-century style. I have added footnotes when the text refers to events, objects, and people that might be unfamiliar to modern readers, or when eighteenth-century usage differs from that of the present day.

Wherever possible, the documents in Part Two are from the original editions or the most authoritative scholarly editions. Unless otherwise indicated in the headnote for a document, the text is that of the original edition. I have modernized the long *s* in these selections but have otherwise left them as found in the copy text. Students should expect to encounter some archaic or variant spellings and punctuation conventions.

# EVELINA,

## OR, A

## YOUNG LADY'S

## ENTRANCE

### INTO THE

## WORLD.

### VOL. I.

## LONDON:

Printed for T. Lowndes, Nº 77, in
Fleet-Street.

M.DCC.LXXVIII.

Title page from Volume 1 of the first edition of *Evelina* (1778). The Bodleian Library, shelf mark Don.e.500. In subsequent editions the novel's subtitle was changed to *The History of a Young Lady's Entrance into the World*.

# Evelina,

## or,
## The History of a Young Lady's Entrance into the World

### TO —— ——[1]

Oh author of my being! — far more dear
To me than light, than nourishment, or rest,
Hygieia's[2] blessings, Rapture's burning tear,
Or the life blood that mantles[3] in my breast!

If in my heart the love of Virtue glows,
'Twas planted there by an unerring rule;
From thy example the pure flame arose,
Thy life, my precept — thy good works, my school.

Could my weak pow'rs thy num'rous virtues trace,
By filial love each fear should be repress'd;
The blush of Incapacity I'd chace,
And stand, recorder of thy worth, confess'd:

But since my niggard stars that gift refuse,
Concealment is the only boon I claim;[4]

---

[1] *To* —— ——*:* Burney's father, Charles, is the addressee. [All notes are the editor's unless identified otherwise.]
[2] *Hygieia:* The goddess of health.
[3] *mantles:* Bubbles up, as with desire or warm emotion.
[4] *Concealment is the only boon I claim:* With the help of her brother Charles, Burney published *Evelina* anonymously.

Obscure be still the unsuccessful Muse,
Who cannot raise, but would not sink, your fame.
Oh! of my life at once the source and joy!
If e'er thy eyes these feeble lines survey,
Let not their folly their intent destroy;
Accept the tribute — but forget the lay.[5]

[5] *lay:* Verse or song.

## TO THE AUTHORS OF THE MONTHLY
## AND CRITICAL REVIEWS[1]

GENTLEMEN,

The liberty which I take in addressing to You the trifling production of a few idle hours, will, doubtless, move your wonder, and,
probably, your contempt. I will not, however, with the futility of
apologies, intrude upon your time, but briefly acknowledge the motives of my temerity: lest, by a premature exercise of the patience
from which I hope to profit, I should abate of its benevolence, and be
myself accessary to my own condemnation.

Without name, without recommendation, and unknown alike to
success and disgrace, to whom can I so properly apply for patronage,
as to those who publicly profess themselves Inspectors of all literary
performances?

The extensive plan of your critical observations, — which, not
confined to works of utility or ingenuity, is equally open to those of
frivolous amusement, and yet worse than frivolous dullness, — encourages me to seek for your protection, since, — perhaps for my
sins! — it entitles me to your annotations. To resent, therefore, this
offering, however insignificant, would ill become the universality of
your undertaking, tho' not to despise it may, alas! be out of your
power.

The language of adulation, and the incense of flattery, though the
natural inheritance, and constant resource, from time immemorial, of

[1] *Authors of the Monthly and Critical Reviews: The Monthly Review* was founded
in 1749 by the bookseller Ralph Griffiths. Oliver Goldsmith (see the headnote to "On
London Shops" in Part Two, Chapter 2) contributed essays in literary criticism. *The
Critical Review* was established in 1756 by Archibald Hamilton, an Edinburgh printer,
in opposition to *The Monthly Review*. It was edited by Tobias Smollett (see headnote
to "On a Visit to Bath" in Part Two, Chapter 2) between 1756 and 1759 and tended
to support the Tory party and the Anglican Church.

the Dedicator, to me offer nothing but the wistful regret that I dare not invoke their aid. Sinister views would be imputed to all I could say; since, thus situated, to extol your judgment, would seem the effect of art, and to celebrate your impartiality, be attributed to suspecting it.

As Magistrates of the press, and Censors for the Public, — to which you are bound by the sacred ties of integrity to exert the most spirited impartiality, and to which your suffrages[2] should carry the marks of pure, dauntless, irrefragable truth, — to appeal for your MERCY, were to solicit your dishonour; and therefore, — though 'tis sweeter than frankincense, — more grateful to the senses than all the odorous perfumes of Arabia, — and though

> It droppeth like the gentle rain from heaven
> Upon the place beneath, ——.[3]

I court it not! to your Justice alone I am entitled, and by that I must abide. Your engagements are not to the supplicating author, but to the candid public, which will not fail to crave

> The penalty and forfeit of your bond.[4]

No hackneyed writer, inured to abuse, and callous to criticism, here braves your severity; — neither does a half-starved garretteer,[5]

> Compell'd by hunger, — and request of friends, — [6]

implore your lenity; your examination will be alike unbiassed by partiality and prejudice; — no refractory murmuring will follow your censure, no private interest be gratified by your praise.

Let not the anxious solicitude with which I recommend myself to your notice, expose me to your derision. Remember, Gentlemen, you were all young writers once, and the most experienced veteran of your corps, may, by recollecting his first publication, renovate his first terrors, and learn to allow for mine. For, though Courage is one

---

[2] *suffrages:* Votes; that is, reviews that endorse or criticize a particular writer or text.

[3] *It droppeth . . . beneath:* Slightly misquoted from Shakespeare's *The Merchant of Venice,* 4.1.181.

[4] *The penalty . . . bond:* Another misquote from *The Merchant of Venice,* 4.1.203.

[5] *garretteer:* Literally, one who lives, and by implication writes, in a garret or attic. The higher the floor in the house, the lower the rent. Hence, those who scraped a living by writing were stereotyped as living and working in garretts.

[6] *Compell'd . . . friends:* Misquote from Alexander Pope's *Epistle to Dr. Arbuthnot,* line 44.

of the noblest virtues of this nether sphere, and, though scarcely more requisite in the field of battle, to guard the fighting hero from disgrace, than in the private commerce of the world, to ward off that littleness of soul which leads, by steps imperceptible, to all the base train of the inferior passions, and by which the too timid mind is betrayed into a servility derogatory to the dignity of human nature; — yet is it a virtue of no necessity in a situation such as mine; a situation which removes, even from cowardice itself, the sting of ignominy; — for surely that Courage may easily be dispensed with, which would rather raise disgust than admiration? Indeed, it is the peculiar privilege of an author, to rob terror of contempt, and pusillanimity of reproach.

*Here let me rest,* — and snatch myself, while yet I am able, from the fascination of EGOTISM, — a monster who has more votaries than ever did homage to the most popular deity of antiquity; and whose singular quality is, that while he excites a blind and involuntary adoration in almost every individual, his influence is universally disallowed, his power universally contemned, and his worship, even by his followers, never mentioned but with abhorrence.

In addressing you jointly, I mean but to mark the generous sentiments by which liberal criticism, to the utter annihilation of envy, jealousy, and all selfish views, ought to be distinguished.

> I have the honour to be,
> GENTLEMEN,
> Your most obedient
> humble servant,

* * * * * * *

## PREFACE

*In the republic of letters, there is no member of such inferior rank, or who is so much disdained by his brethren of the quill, as the humble Novelist: nor is his fate less hard in the world at large, since, among the whole class of writers, perhaps not one can be named, of whom the votaries are more numerous, but less respectable.*

*Yet, while in the annals of those few of our predecessors, to whom this species of writing is indebted for being saved from contempt, and rescued from depravity, we can trace such names as Rousseau, John-*

son,[1] *Marivaux, Fielding, Richardson, and Smollet, no man need blush at starting from the same post, though many, nay, most men, may sigh at finding themselves distanced.*

*The following letters are presented to the public — for such, by novel writers, novel readers will be called, — with a very singular mixture of timidity and confidence, resulting from the peculiar situation of the editor;[2] who, though trembling for their success from a consciousness of their imperfections, yet fears not being involved in their disgrace, while happily wrapped up in a mantle of impenetrable obscurity.*

*To draw characters from nature, though not from life, and to mark the manners of the times, is the attempted plan of the following letters. For this purpose, a young female, educated in the most secluded retirement, makes, at the age of seventeen, her first appearance upon the great and busy stage of life; with a virtuous mind, a cultivated understanding, and a feeling heart, her ignorance of the forms, and inexperience in the manners, of the world, occasion all the little incidents which these volumes record, and which form the natural progression of the life of a young woman of obscure birth, but conspicuous beauty, for the first six months after her* Entrance into the World.

*Perhaps were it possible to effect the total extirpation of novels, our young ladies in general, and boarding-school damsels in particular, might profit from their annihilation: but since the distemper they have spread seems incurable, since their contagion bids defiance to the medicine of advice or reprehension, and since they are found to baffle all the mental art of physic, save what is prescribed by the slow regimen of Time, and bitter diet of Experience, surely all attempts to contribute to the number of those which may be read, if not with advantage, at least without injury, ought rather to be encouraged than contemned.*

*Let me, therefore, prepare for disappointment those who, in the perusal of these sheets, entertain the gentle expectation of being transported to the fantastic regions of Romance, where Fiction is*

---

[1] However superior the capacities in which these great writers deserve to be considered, they must pardon me that, for the dignity of my subject, I here rank the authors of Rasselas and Eloïse as Novelists. [Burney's note.]

[2] *editor:* It was a convention of eighteenth-century epistolary fiction (that is, novels in the form of letters) to present the author as an "editor" who discovers and collects the letters that compose the novel.

*coloured by all the gay tints of luxurious Imagination, where Reason
is an outcast, and where the sublimity of the* Marvellous *rejects all
aid from sober Probability. The heroine of these memoirs, young, artless, and inexperienced, is*

No faultless Monster, that the World ne'er saw,[3]

*but the offspring of Nature, and of Nature in her simplest attire.
In all the Arts, the value of copies can only be proportioned to the
scarceness of originals: among sculptors and painters a fine statue, or
a beautiful picture, of some great master, may deservedly employ the
imitative talents of younger and inferior artists, that their appropria-
tion to one spot, may not wholly prevent the more general expansion
of their excellence; but, among authors, the reverse is the case, since
the noblest productions of literature, are almost equally attainable
with the meanest. In books, therefore, imitation cannot be shunned
too sedulously; for the very perfection of a model which is frequently
seen, serves but more forcibly to mark the inferiority of a copy.*

*To avoid what is common, without adopting what is unnatural,
must limit the ambition of the vulgar herd of authors; however zealous, therefore, my veneration of the great writers I have mentioned,
however I may feel myself enlightened by the knowledge of Johnson,
charmed with the eloquence of Rousseau, softened by the pathetic
powers of Richardson, and exhilarated by the wit of Fielding, and
humour of Smollet; I yet presume not to attempt pursuing the same
ground which they have tracked; whence, though they may have
cleared the weeds, they have also culled the flowers, and though they
have rendered the path plain, they have left it barren.*

*The candour of my readers, I have not the impertinence to doubt,
and to their indulgence, I am sensible I have no claim: I have, therefore, only to entreat, that my own words may not pronounce my condemnation, and that what I have here ventured to say in regard to
imitation, may be understood, as it is meant, in a general sense, and
not be imputed to an opinion of my own originality, which I have not
the vanity, the folly, or the blindness, to entertain.*

*Whatever may be the fate of these letters, the editor is satisfied
they will meet with justice; and commits them to the press, though
hopeless of fame, yet not regardless of censure.*

---

[3] *No faultless Monster . . . saw:* A slight misquote from John Sheffield's *Essay on
Poetry*, a well-regarded example of literary criticism.

# Volume I

## LETTER I

### Lady Howard to the Rev. Mr. Villars

Howard Grove

Can there, my good Sir, be any thing more painful to a friendly mind, than a necessity of communicating disagreeable intelligence? Indeed, it is sometimes difficult to determine, whether the relator or the receiver of evil tidings is most to be pitied.

I have just had a letter from Madame Duval; she is totally at a loss in what manner to behave; she seems desirous to repair the wrongs she has done, yet wishes the world to believe her blameless. She would fain cast upon another the odium of those misfortunes for which she alone is answerable. Her letter is violent, sometimes abusive, and that of *you! — you*, to whom she is under obligations which are greater even than her faults, but to whose advice she wickedly imputes all the sufferings of her much-injured daughter, the late Lady Belmont. The chief purport of her writing I will acquaint you with; the letter itself is not worthy your notice.

She tells me that she has, for many years past, been in continual expectation of making a journey to England, which prevented her writing for information concerning this melancholy subject, by giving her hopes of making personal enquiries; but family occurrences have still detained her in France, which country she now sees no prospect of quitting. She has, therefore, lately used her utmost endeavours to obtain a faithful account of whatever related to her *ill-advised* daughter; the result of which giving her *some reason* to apprehend that, upon her death-bed, she bequeathed an infant orphan to the world, she most graciously says that if *you*, with whom *she understands* the child is placed, will procure authentic proofs of its relationship to her, you may send it to Paris, where she will properly provide for it.

This woman is, undoubtedly, at length, conscious of her most unnatural conduct: it is evident, from her writing, that she is still as vulgar and illiterate as when her first husband, Mr. Evelyn, had the weakness to marry her; nor does she at all apologise for addressing herself to me, though I was only once in her company.

This letter has excited in my daughter Mirvan, a strong desire to be informed of the motives which induced Madame Duval to abandon the unfortunate Lady Belmont, at a time when a mother's protection was so peculiarly necessary for her peace and her reputation. Notwithstanding I was personally acquainted with all the parties concerned in that affair, the subject always appeared of too delicate a nature to be spoken of with the principals; I cannot, therefore, satisfy Mrs. Mirvan otherwise than by applying to you.

By saying that you *may* send the child, Madame Duval aims at *conferring*, where she most *owes* obligation. I pretend not to give you advice; you, to whose generous protection this helpless orphan is indebted for every thing, are the best and only judge of what she ought to do; but I am much concerned for the trouble and uneasiness which this unworthy woman may occasion you.

My daughter and my grandchild join with me in desiring to be most kindly remembered to the amiable girl; and they bid me remind you, that the annual visit to Howard Grove, which we were formerly promised, has been discontinued for more than four years. I am, dear Sir,

> with great regard,
> Your most obedient servant and friend,
> M. Howard

## LETTER II

### Mr. Villars to Lady Howard

Berry Hill, Dorsetshire

Your Ladyship did but too well foresee the perplexity and uneasiness of which Madame Duval's letter has been productive. However, I ought rather to be thankful that I have so many years remained unmolested, than repine at my present embarrassment; since it proves, at least, that this wretched woman is at length awakened to remorse.

In regard to my answer, I must humbly request your Ladyship to write to this effect: "That I would not, upon any account, intentionally offend Madame Duval, but that I have weighty, nay unanswerable reasons for detaining her grand-daughter at present in England; the principal of which is, that it was the earnest desire of one to whose will she owes implicit duty. Madame Duval may be assured that she meets with the utmost attention and tenderness; that her education, however short of my wishes, almost exceeds my abilities;

and that I flatter myself, when the time arrives that she shall pay her duty to her grandmother, Madame Duval will find no reason to be dissatisfied with what has been done for her."

Your Ladyship will not, I am sure, be surprised at this answer. Madame Duval is by no means a proper companion or guardian for a young woman: she is at once uneducated and unprincipled; ungentle in her temper, and unamiable in her manners. I have long known that she has persuaded herself to harbour an aversion for me — Unhappy woman! I can only regard her as an object of pity!

I dare not hesitate at a request from Mrs. Mirvan, yet, in complying with it, I shall, for her own sake, be as concise as I possibly can; since the cruel transactions which preceded the birth of my ward, can afford no entertainment to a mind so humane as her's.

Your Ladyship may probably have heard, that I had the honour to accompany Mr. Evelyn, the grandfather of my young charge, when upon his travels, in capacity of tutor. His unhappy marriage, immediately upon his return to England, with Madame Duval, then a waiting-girl at a tavern, contrary to the advice and entreaties of all his friends, among whom I was myself the most urgent to dissuade him, induced him to abandon his native land, and fix his abode in France. Thither he was followed by shame and repentance; feelings which his heart was not framed to support: for, notwithstanding he had been too weak to resist the allurements of beauty, which nature, though a niggard to her of every other boon, had with a lavish hand bestowed on his wife; yet he was a young man of excellent character, and, till thus unaccountably infatuated, of unblemished conduct. He survived this ill-judged marriage but two years. Upon his death-bed, with an unsteady hand, he wrote me the following note:

"My friend! forget your resentment, in favour of your humanity; — a father, trembling for the welfare of his child, bequeaths her to your care. — O Villars! hear! pity! and relieve me!"

Had my circumstances permitted [me], I should have answered these words by an immediate journey to Paris; but I was obliged to act by the agency of a friend, who was upon the spot, and present at the opening of the will.

Mr. Evelyn left to me a legacy of a thousand pounds, and the sole guardianship of his daughter's person till her eighteenth year, conjuring me, in the most affecting terms, to take the charge of her education till she was able to act with propriety for herself; but in regard to fortune, he left her wholly dependent on her mother, to whose tenderness he earnestly recommended her.

Thus, though he would not, to a woman low-bred and illiberal as Mrs. Evelyn, trust the mind and morals of his daughter, he nevertheless thought proper to secure to her that respect and duty which, from her own child, were certainly her due; but, unhappily, it never occurred to him that the mother, on her part, could fail in affection or justice.

Miss Evelyn, Madam, from the second to the eighteenth year of her life, was brought up under my care, and, except when at school, under my roof. I need not speak to your Ladyship of the virtues of that excellent young creature. She loved me as her father; nor was Mrs. Villars less valued by her; while to me she became so dear, that her loss was little less afflicting to me than that which I have since sustained of Mrs. Villars herself.

At that period of her life we parted; her mother, then married to Monsieur Duval, sent for her to Paris. How often have I since regretted that I did not accompany her thither! protected and supported by me, the misery and disgrace which awaited her, might, perhaps, have been avoided. But — to be brief, Madame Duval, at the instigation of her husband, earnestly, or rather tyrannically, endeavoured to effect an union between Miss Evelyn and one of his nephews. And, when she found her power inadequate to her attempt, enraged at her non-compliance, she treated her with the grossest unkindness, and threatened her with poverty and ruin.

Miss Evelyn, to whom wrath and violence had hitherto been strangers, soon grew weary of this usage; and rashly, and without a witness, consented to a private marriage with Sir John Belmont, a very profligate young man, who had but too successfully found means to insinuate himself into her favour. He promised to conduct her to England — he did. —— O, Madam, you know the rest! — Disappointed of the fortune he expected, by the inexorable rancour of the Duvals, he infamously burnt the certificate of their marriage, and denied that they had ever been united!

She flew to me for protection. With what mixed transports of joy and anguish did I again see her! By my advice she endeavoured to procure proofs of her marriage; — but in vain: her credulity had been no match for his art.

Every body believed her innocent, from the guiltless tenor of her unspotted youth, and from the known libertinism[1] of her barbarous betrayer. Yet her sufferings were too acute for her tender frame, and

---

[1] *libertinism:* A set of beliefs, commonly attributed to aristocratic young males in the late seventeenth and eighteenth centuries, that included a much-criticized glorification of male sexual freedom.

the same moment that gave birth to her infant, put an end at once to the sorrows and the life of its mother.

The rage of Madame Duval at her elopement, abated not while this injured victim of cruelty yet drew breath. She probably intended, in time, to have pardoned her, but time was not allowed. When she was informed of her death, I have been told, that the agonies of grief and remorse, with which she was seized, occasioned her a severe fit of illness. But, from the time of her recovery to the date of her letter to your Ladyship, I had never heard that she manifested any desire to be made acquainted with the circumstances which attended the death of Lady Belmont, and the birth of her helpless child.

That child, Madam, shall never, while life is lent me, know the loss she has sustained. I have cherished, succoured, and supported her, from her earlicst infancy to her sixteenth year; and so amply has she repaid my care and affection, that my fondest wish is now bounded in the desire of bestowing her on one who may be sensible of her worth, and then sinking to eternal rest in her arms.

Thus it has happened that the education of the father, daughter, and grand-daughter, has devolved on me. What infinite misery have the two first caused me! Should the fate of the dear survivor be equally adverse, how wretched will be the end of my cares — the end of my days!

Even had Madame Duval merited the charge she claims, I fear my fortitude would have been unequal to such a parting; but, being such as she is, not only my affection, but my humanity recoils, at the barbarous idea of deserting the sacred trust reposed in me. Indeed, I could but ill support her former yearly visits to the respectable mansion at Howard Grove; pardon me, dear Madam, and do not think me insensible of the honour which your Ladyship's condescension confers upon us both; but so deep is the impression which the misfortunes of her mother have made on my heart, that she does not, even for a moment, quit my sight, without exciting apprehensions and terrors which almost overpower me. Such, Madam, is my tenderness, and such my weakness! But she is the only tie I have upon earth, and I trust to your Ladyship's goodness not to judge of my feelings with severity.

I beg leave to present my humble respects to Mrs. and Miss Mirvan; and have the honour to be,

> Madam,
> Your Ladyship's most obedient
> and most humble servant,
> ARTHUR VILLARS

## LETTER III
### [Written some months after the last.]

### Lady Howard to the Rev. Mr. Villars

Howard Grove, March 8.

Dear and Rev. Sir,

Your last letter gave me infinite pleasure: after so long and tedious an illness, how grateful to yourself and to your friends must be your returning health! You have the hearty wishes of every individual of this place for its continuance and increase.

Will you not think I take advantage of your acknowledged recovery, if I once more venture to mention your pupil and Howard Grove together? Yet you must remember the patience with which we submitted to your desire of not parting with her during the bad state of your health, though it was with much reluctance we forbore to solicit her company. My grand-daughter, in particular, has scarce been able to repress her eagerness to again meet the friend of her infancy; and for my own part, it is very strongly my wish to manifest the regard which I had for the unfortunate Lady Belmont, by proving serviceable to her child; which seems to me the best respect that can be paid to her memory. Permit me, therefore, to lay before you a plan which Mrs. Mirvan and I have formed, in consequence of your restoration to health.

I would not frighten you; — but do you think you could bear to part with your young companion for two or three months? Mrs. Mirvan proposes to spend the ensuing spring in London, whither, for the first time, my grandchild will accompany her: Now, my good friend, it is very earnestly their wish to enlarge and enliven their party by the addition of your amiable ward, who would share, equally with her own daughter, the care and attention of Mrs. Mirvan. Do not start at this proposal; it is time that she should see something of the world. When young people are too rigidly sequestered from it, their lively and romantic imaginations paint it to them as a paradise of which they have been beguiled; but when they are shown it properly, and in due time, they see it such as it really is, equally shared by pain and pleasure, hope and disappointment.

You have nothing to apprehend from her meeting with Sir John Belmont, as that abandoned man is now abroad, and not expected home this year.

Well, my good Sir, what say you to our scheme? I hope it will meet with your approbation; but if it should not, be assured I can never be displeased at any decision made by one who is so much respected and esteemed as yourself by,

Dear Sir,
Your most faithful humble servant,
M. HOWARD

## LETTER IV

### Mr. Villars to Lady Howard

Berry Hill, March 12.

I am grieved, Madam, to appear obstinate, and I blush to incur the imputation of selfishness. In detaining my young charge thus long with myself in the country, I consulted not solely my own inclination. Destined, in all probability, to possess a very moderate fortune, I wished to contract her views to something within it. The mind is but too naturally prone to pleasure, but too easily yielded to dissipation: it has been my study to guard her against their delusions, by preparing her to expect, — and to despise them. But the time draws on for experience and observation to take place of instruction: if I have, in some measure, rendered her capable of using the one with discretion, and making the other with improvement, I shall rejoice myself with the assurance of having largely contributed to her welfare. She is now of an age that happiness is eager to attend, — let her then enjoy it! I commit her to the protection of your Ladyship, and only hope she may be found worthy half the goodness I am satisfied she will meet with at your hospitable mansion.

Thus far, Madam, I chearfully submit to your desire. In confiding my ward to the care of Lady Howard, I can feel no uneasiness from her absence, but what will arise from the loss of her company, since I shall be as well convinced of her safety, as if she were under my own roof; — but, can your Ladyship be serious in proposing to introduce her to the gaieties of a London life? Permit me to ask, for what end, or what purpose? A youthful mind is seldom totally free from ambition; to curb that, is the first step to contentment, since to diminish expectation, is to increase enjoyment. I apprehend nothing more than too much raising her hopes and her views, which the natural vivacity of her disposition would render but too easy to effect. The town-acquaintance of Mrs. Mirvan are all in the circle of high life; this art-less young creature, with too much beauty to escape notice, has too much sensibility[1] to be indifferent to it; but she has too little wealth to be sought with propriety by men of the fashionable world.

Consider, Madam, the peculiar cruelty of her situation; only child of a wealthy baronet,[2] whose person she has never seen, whose character she has reason to abhor, and whose name she is forbidden to claim; entitled as she is to lawfully inherit his fortune and estate, is there any probability that he will *properly* own her? And while he continues to persevere in disavowing his marriage with Miss Evelyn, she shall never, at the expence of her mother's honour, receive a part of her right, as the donation of his bounty.

And as to Mr. Evelyn's estate, I have no doubt but that Madame Duval and her relations will dispose of it among themselves.

It seems, therefore, as if this deserted child, though legally heiress to two large fortunes, must owe all her rational expectations to adoption and friendship. Yet her income will be such as may make her happy, if she is disposed to be so in private life; though it will by no means allow her to enjoy the luxury of a London fine lady.

Let Miss Mirvan, then, Madam, shine in all the splendor of high life, but suffer my child still to enjoy the pleasures of humble retirement, with a mind to which greater views are unknown.

I hope this reasoning will be honoured with your approbation; and I have yet another motive that has some weight with me; I would not willingly give offence to any human being, and surely Madame Duval might accuse me of injustice, if, while I refuse to let her grand-daughter wait upon her, I consent to her joining a party of pleasure to London.

In sending her to Howard Grove, not one of these scruples arise; and therefore Mrs. Clinton, a most worthy woman, formerly her nurse, and now my housekeeper, shall attend her thither next week.

Though I have always called her by the name of Anville, and reported in this neighbourhood that her father, my intimate friend, left her to my guardianship, yet I have thought it necessary to let her be herself acquainted with the melancholy circumstances attending her birth; for, though I am very desirous of guarding her from curiosity and impertinence, by concealing her name, family, and story, yet I would not leave it in the power of chance, to shock her gentle nature with a tale of so much sorrow.

---

[1] *sensibility:* A capacity for feeling; sensitivity.
[2] *baronet:* The lowest hereditary title of honor held by a commoner, ranking just below a baron.

You must not, Madam, expect too much from my pupil. She is quite a little rustic, and knows nothing of the world; and tho' her education has been the best I could bestow in this retired place, to which Dorchester,[3] the nearest town, is seven miles distant, yet I shall not be surprised if you should discover in her a thousand deficiencies of which I have never dreamt. She must be very much altered since she was last at Howard Grove, — but I will say nothing of her; I leave her to your Ladyship's own observations, of which I beg a faithful relation; and am,

> Dear Madam, with great respect,
> Your obedient and most humble servant,
> ARTHUR VILLARS

[3] *Dorchester:* The principal town of Dorsetshire, a rural county in southwest England.


## LETTER V

## Mr. Villars to Lady Howard

March 18.

Dear Madam,

This letter will be delivered to you by my child, — the child of my adoption, — my affection! Unblest with one natural friend, she merits a thousand. I send her to you, innocent as an angel, and artless as purity itself: and I send you with her the heart of your friend, the only hope he has on earth, the subject of his tenderest thoughts, and the object of his latest cares. She is one, Madam, for whom alone I have lately wished to live; and she is one whom to serve I would with transport die! Restore her but to me all innocence as you receive her, and the fondest hope of my heart will be amply gratified!

> A. VILLARS


## LETTER VI

## Lady Howard to the Rev. Mr. Villars

Howard Grove.

Dear and Rev. Sir,

The solemn manner in which you have committed your child to my care, has in some measure dampt the pleasure which I receive from the trust, as it makes me fear that you suffer from your compliance, in which case I shall very sincerely blame myself for the earnestness with which I have requested this favour; but remember, my good Sir, she is within a few days summons, and be assured I will not detain her a moment longer than you wish.

You desire my opinion of her.

She is a little angel! I cannot wonder that you sought to monopolize her. Neither ought you, at finding it impossible.

Her face and person answer my most refined ideas of complete beauty: and this, though a subject of praise less important to you, or to me, than any other, is yet so striking, it is not possible to pass it unnoticed. Had I not known from whom she received her education, I should, at first sight of so perfect a face, have been in pain for her understanding; since it has been long and justly remarked, that folly has ever sought alliance with beauty.

She has the same gentleness in her manners, the same natural grace in her motions, that I formerly so much admired in her mother. Her character seems truly ingenuous and simple; and, at the same time that nature has blessed her with an excellent understanding, and great quickness of parts, she has a certain air of inexperience and innocency that is extremely interesting.

You have no reason to regret the retirement in which she has lived; since that politeness which is acquired by an acquaintance with high life, is in her so well supplied by a natural desire of obliging, joined to a deportment infinitely engaging.

I observe with great satisfaction a growing affection between this amiable girl and my grand-daughter, whose heart is as free from selfishness or conceit, as that of her young friend is from all guile. Their attachment may be mutually useful, since much is to be expected from emulation, where nothing is to be feared from envy. I would have them love each other as sisters, and reciprocally supply the place of that tender and happy relationship to which neither of them have a natural claim.

Be satisfied, my good Sir, that your child shall meet with the same attention as our own. We all join in most hearty wishes for your health and happiness, and in returning our sincere thanks for the favour you have conferred on us.

> I am, Dear Sir,
> Your most faithful servant,
> M. HOWARD

## LETTER VII

Lady Howard to the Rev. Mr. Villars

Howard Grove, March 26.

Be not alarmed, my worthy friend, at my so speedily troubling you again; I seldom use the ceremony of waiting for answers, or writing with any regularity, and I have at present immediate occasion for begging your patience.

Mrs. Mirvan has just received a letter from her long-absent husband, containing the welcome news of his hoping to reach London by the beginning of next week. My daughter and the Captain have been separated almost seven years, and it would therefore be needless to say what joy, surprise, and consequently confusion, his, at present, unexpected return has caused at Howard Grove. Mrs. Mirvan, you cannot doubt, will go instantly to town to meet him; her daughter is under a thousand obligations to attend her; I grieve that her mother cannot.

And now, my good Sir, I almost blush to proceed; — but, tell me, may I ask — will you permit — that your child may accompany them? Do not think us unreasonable, but consider the many inducements which conspire to make London the happiest place at present she can be in. The joyful occasion of the journey; the gaiety of the whole party; opposed to the dull life she must lead if left here, with a solitary old woman for her sole companion, while she so well knows the chearfulness and felicity enjoyed by the rest of the family, — are circumstances that seem to merit your consideration. Mrs. Mirvan desires me to assure you, that one week is all she asks, as she is certain that the Captain, who hates London, will be eager to revisit Howard Grove: and Maria is so very earnest in wishing to have the company of her friend, that, if you are inexorable, she will be deprived of half the pleasure she otherwise hopes to receive.

However, I will not, my good Sir, deceive you into an opinion that they intend to live in a retired manner, as that cannot be fairly expected. But you have no reason to be uneasy concerning Madame Duval; she has no correspondent in England, and only gains intelligence by common report. She must be a stranger to the name your child bears; and, even should she hear of this excursion, so short a time as a week, or less, spent in town upon so particular an occasion, though previous to their meeting, cannot be construed into disrespect to herself.

Mrs. Mirvan desires me to assure you, that if you will oblige her, her *two* children shall equally share her time and her attention. She has sent a commission to a friend in town to take a house for her, and while she waits for an answer concerning it, I shall for one from you to our petition. However, your child is writing herself, and that, I doubt not, will more avail than all we can possibly urge.

My daughter desires her best compliments to you, *if*, she says, you will grant her request, but *not else*.

Adieu, my dear Sir, — we all hope every thing from your goodness.

M. HOWARD

## LETTER VIII

### Evelina to the Rev. Mr. Villars

Howard Grove, March 26.

This house seems to be the house of joy; every face wears a smile, and a laugh is at every body's service. It is quite amusing to walk about, and see the general confusion; a room leading to the garden is fitting up for Captain Mirvan's study. Lady Howard does not sit a moment in a place; Miss Mirvan is making caps;[1] every body so busy! — such flying from room to room! — so many orders given, and retracted, and given again! — nothing but hurry and perturbation.

Well but, my dear Sir, I am desired to make a request to you. I hope you will not think me an incroacher; Lady Howard insists upon my writing! — yet I hardly know how to go on; a petition implies a want, — and have you left me one? No, indeed.

I am half ashamed of myself for beginning this letter. But these dear ladies are so pressing — I cannot, for my life, resist wishing for the pleasures they offer me, — provided you do not disapprove them.

They are to make a very short stay in town. The captain will meet them in a day or two. Mrs. Mirvan and her sweet daughter both go; — what a happy party! Yet I am not *very* eager to accompany them: at least, I shall be very well contented to remain where I am, if you desire that I should.

---

[1] *caps:* A cap was a light fabric covering for the head, sometimes decorated with lace, which was fashionable for women's wear indoors and under bonnets for much of the eighteenth century.

Assured, my dearest Sir, of your goodness, your bounty, and your indulgent kindness, ought I to form a wish that has not your sanction? Decide for me, therefore, without the least apprehension that I shall be uneasy, or discontented. While I am yet in suspense, perhaps I may *hope,* but I am most certain, that when you have once determined, I shall not repine.

They tell me that London is now in full splendour. Two Playhouses are open, — the Opera-House, — Ranelagh, — the Pantheon.[2] — You see I have learned all their names. However, pray don't suppose that I make any point of going, for I shall hardly sigh to see them depart without me; though I shall probably never meet with such another opportunity. And, indeed, their domestic happiness will be so great, — it is natural to wish to partake of it.

I believe I am bewitched! I made a resolution when I began, that I would not be urgent; but my pen — or rather my thoughts, will not suffer me to keep it — for I acknowledge, I must acknowledge, I cannot help wishing for your permission.

I almost repent already that I have made this confession; pray forget that you have read it, if this journey is displeasing to you. But I will not write any longer; for the more I think of this affair, the less indifferent to it I find myself.

Adieu, my most honoured, most reverenced, most beloved father! for by what other name can I call you? I have no happiness or sorrow, no hope or fear, but what your kindness bestows, or your displeasure may cause. You will not, I am sure, send a refusal, without reasons unanswerable, and therefore I shall chearfully acquiesce. Yet I hope — I hope you will be able to permit me to go!

I am,
With the utmost affection,
gratitude and duty,
Your
EVELINA———

I cannot to *you* sign *Anville,* and what other name may I claim?

---

[2] *Two Playhouses . . . Pantheon:* The two playhouses — probably Drury Lane and Covent Garden — were open every month but July, August, and September, traditionally times when fashionable people exited the town for their rural estates. The Opera-House could be either the Haymarket Opera-House, built in 1705, or the opera house for Italian operas. Ranelagh was a fashionable garden that included "Chinese" buildings and a "rotunda," or circular room in which tea or coffee could be taken for the price of admission. The Pantheon, a huge, opulent hall, provided in the wintertime a splendid indoor alternative to the outdoor pleasure gardens of London, Ranelagh, and Vauxhall. Concerts and masquerade balls made up the entertainment, and refreshments were included for the price of admission.

## LETTER IX

### Mr. Villars to Evelina

Berry-Hill, March 28.
To resist the urgency of entreaty, is a power which I have not yet acquired: I aim not at an authority which deprives you of liberty, yet I would fain guide myself by a prudence which should save me the pangs of repentance. Your impatience to fly to a place which your imagination has painted to you in colours so attractive, surprises me not; I have only to hope that the liveliness of your fancy may not deceive you: to refuse, would be to raise it still higher. To see my Evelina happy, is to see myself without a wish: go then, my child, and may that Heaven which alone can, direct, preserve, and strengthen you! To That, my love, will I daily offer prayers for your felicity; O may it guard, watch over you! defend you from danger, save you from distress, and keep vice as distant from your person as from your heart! And to Me, may it grant the ultimate blessing of closing these aged eyes in the arms of one so dear — so deservedly beloved!

ARTHUR VILLARS

## LETTER X

### Evelina to the Rev. Mr. Villars

Queen-Ann-Street, London, Saturday, April 2.
This moment arrived. Just going to Drury-Lane theatre. The celebrated Mr. Garrick[1] performs Ranger. I am quite in extacy. So is Miss Mirvan. How fortunate, that he should happen to play! We would not let Mrs. Mirvan rest till she consented to go; her chief objection was to our dress, for we have had no time to *Londonize*[2] ourselves; but we teized her into compliance, and so we are to sit in

---

[1] *Garrick:* David Garrick, arguably the most prominent British actor of the century, was a close friend of Burney's father, Charles, and a frequent and popular guest in the Burney household. Garrick is noted for introducing a revolutionary "natural" style of acting to the English stage; he was also instrumental in the elevation of acting from a socially marginal occupation to a relatively respectable profession. Besides acting, he wrote plays and managed the Drury Lane Theatre for a quarter of a century. He made his last appearances in 1776, in the principal male role of Ranger in Benjamin Hoadly's *The Suspicious Husband.*

[2] *Londonize:* To furnish themselves with the most current London fashions in dress.

some obscure place, that she may not be seen. As to me, I should be alike unknown in the most conspicuous or most private part of the house.

I can write no more now. I have hardly time to breathe — only just this, the houses and streets are not quite so superb as I expected. However, I have seen nothing yet, so I ought not to judge.

Well, adieu, my dearest Sir, for the present; I could not forbear writing a few words instantly on my arrival; though I suppose my letter of thanks for your consent is still on the road.

Saturday Night.

O my dear Sir, in what raptures am I returned! Well may Mr. Garrick be so celebrated, so universally admired — I had not any idea of so great a performer.

Such ease! such vivacity in his manner! such grace in his motions! such fire and meaning in his eyes! — I could hardly believe he had studied a written part, for every word seemed spoke from the impulse of the moment.

His action — at once so graceful and so free! — his voice — so clear, so melodious, yet so wonderfully various in its tones — such animation! — every look *speaks!*

I would have given the world to have had the whole play acted over again. And when he danced — O how I envied Clarinda.[3] I almost wished to have jumped on the stage and joined them.

I am afraid you will think me mad, so I won't say any more; yet I really believe Mr. Garrick would make you mad too, if you could see him. I intend to ask Mrs. Mirvan to go to the play every night while we stay in town. She is extremely kind to me, and Maria, her charming daughter, is the sweetest girl in the world.

I shall write to you every evening all that passes in the day, and that in the same manner as, if I could see, I should tell you.

Sunday.

This morning we went to Portland chapel,[4] and afterwards we walked in the Mall in St. James's Park, which by no means answered my expectations: it is a long straight walk, of dirty gravel,

---

[3] *O how I envied Clarinda:* Burney has confused the female roles in *The Suspicious Husband*; Ranger dances with Mrs. Strickland at the end of the play.

[4] *Portland chapel:* St. Paul's Cathedral, located on Great Portland Street.

very uneasy to the feet; and at each end, instead of an open prospect, nothing is to be seen but houses built of brick. When Mrs. Mirvan pointed out the *Palace*[5] to me — I think I was never much more surprised.

However, the walk was very agreeable to us; every body looked gay, and seemed pleased, and the ladies were so much dressed, that Miss Mirvan and I could do nothing but look at them. Mrs. Mirvan met several of her friends. No wonder, for I never saw so many people assembled together before. I looked about for some of *my* acquaintance, but in vain, for I saw not one person that I knew, which is very odd, for all the world seemed there.

Mrs. Mirvan says we are not to walk in the Park again next Sunday, even if we should be in town, because there is better company in Kensington Gardens.[6] But really if you had seen how much every body was dressed, you would not think that possible.

Monday.

We are to go this evening to a private ball, given by Mrs. Stanley, a very fashionable lady of Mrs. Mirvan's acquaintance.

We have been *a shopping,* as Mrs. Mirvan calls it, all this morning, to buy silks, caps, gauzes, and so forth.

The shops are really very entertaining, especially the mercers;[7] there seem to be six or seven men belonging to each shop, and every one took care, by bowing and smirking, to be noticed; we were conducted from one to another, and carried from room to room, with so much ceremony, that at first I was almost afraid to follow.

I thought I should never have chosen a silk, for they produced so many, I knew not which to fix upon, and they recommended them all so strongly, that I fancy they thought I only wanted persuasion to buy every thing they shewed me. And, indeed, they took so much trouble, that I was almost ashamed I could not.

---

[5] *the Mall . . . the Palace:* The Mall in St. James Park was a fashionable place to walk, to see and be seen. The Palace was then known as the Queen's House, having become Queen Charlotte's in 1775 by order of George III. It was built in 1705 by John Sheffield, duke of Buckingham, and known as Buckingham House.

[6] *Kensington Gardens:* Another very fashionable promenade at the time, this park dates back to the reign of Queen Anne early in the century and was and still remains a huge expanse of well-tended lawns, gardens, and groves, about three and a half miles across in 1778.

[7] *mercers:* Dealers in fine fabrics such as silks and velvets.

At the milliners,[8] the ladies we met were so much dressed, that I should rather have imagined they were making visits than purchases. But what most diverted me was, that we were more frequently served by men than by women; and such men! so finical, so affected! they seemed to understand every part of a woman's dress better than we do ourselves; and they recommended caps and ribbands with an air of so much importance, that I wished to ask them how long they had left off wearing them!

The dispatch with which they work in these great shops is amazing, for they have promised me a compleat suit of linen against the evening.

I have just had my hair dressed.[9] You can't think how oddly my head feels; full of powder and black pins, and a great *cushion* on the top of it. I believe you would hardly know me, for my face looks quite different to what it did before my hair was dressed. When I shall be able to make use of a comb for myself I cannot tell, for my hair is so much entangled, *frizled* they call it, that I fear it will be very difficult.

I am half afraid of this ball to-night, for, you know, I have never danced but at school; however, Miss Mirvan says there is nothing in it. Yet I wish it was over.

Adieu, my dear Sir; pray excuse the wretched stuff I write, perhaps I may improve by being in this town, and then my letters will be less unworthy your reading. Mean time I am,

> Your dutiful and affectionate,
> though unpolished,
> EVELINA

Poor Miss Mirvan cannot wear one of the caps she made, because they dress her hair too large for them.

---

[8] *milliners:* Sellers of fashionable accessories to female dress, such as bonnets and gloves. It was often noted that this traditionally female-dominated trade was being taken up more and more frequently by men, further narrowing the possibilities for professions open to women in the last quarter of the eighteenth century.

[9] *I have just had my hair dressed.* Fashionable hairstyles for English women in the 1770s were highly elaborate and usually only undertaken by professional hairdressers or experienced personal servants. The hair was back-combed from end to root, or "frizzled," to create height and mass. Often the natural hair was supplemented with false hair pieces and cushions or even wire frames over which the natural hair was combed. The whole creation could rise several feet over a woman's forehead. Once frizzled and pulled up into place, the hair was covered with pomatum, a hairdressing ointment, and powdered white, pink, or blue. Ribbons, bows, knots, small figures and ornaments, and jewels were sometimes added as decorations.

## LETTER XI

### Evelina in Continuation

Queen-Ann-Street, April 5, Tuesday morning.

I have a vast deal to say, and shall give all this morning to my pen. As to my plan of writing every evening the adventures of the day, I find it impracticable; for the diversions here are so very late, that if I begin my letters after them, I could not go to bed at all.

We past a most extraordinary evening. A *private* ball this was called, so I expected to have seen about four or five couple; but, Lord! my dear Sir, I believe I saw half the world! Two very large rooms were full of company; in one, were cards for the elderly ladies, and in the other, were the dancers. My mamma Mirvan, for she always calls me her child, said she would sit with Maria and me till we were provided with partners, and then join the card-players.

The gentlemen, as they passed and repassed, looked as if they thought we were quite at their disposal, and only waiting for the honour of their commands; and they sauntered about, in a careless indolent manner, as if with a view to keep us in suspense. I don't speak of this in regard to Miss Mirvan and myself only, but to the ladies in general; and I thought it so provoking, that I determined, in my own mind, that, far from humouring such airs, I would rather not dance at all, than with any one who should seem to think me ready to accept the first partner who would condescend to take me.

Not long after, a young man, who had for some time looked at us with a kind of negligent impertinence, advanced, on tiptoe, towards me; he had a set smile on his face, and his dress was so foppish,[1] that I really believe he even wished to be stared at; and yet he was very ugly.

Bowing almost to the ground, with a sort of swing, and waving his hand with the greatest conceit, after a short and silly pause, he said, "Madam — may I presume?" — and stopt, offering to take my hand. I drew it back, but could scarce forbear laughing. "Allow me, Madam," (continued he, affectedly breaking off every half moment)

---

[1] *foppish:* "Fop" was a term applied to a fashionable male, usually of the middle or upper classes, who affected an air of outlandish frivolity in dress and speech. The fop was a character type in Restoration and eighteenth-century drama, but social commentary of the time often complained of real-life fops who were more interested in their clothing, hairstyles, and fashionable amusements than in more substantive, "manly" pursuits.

"the honour and happiness — if I am not so unhappy as to address you too late — to have the happiness and honour —— "

Again he would have taken my hand, but, bowing my head, I begged to be excused, and turned to Miss Mirvan to conceal my laughter. He then desired to know if I had already engaged myself to some more fortunate man? I said No, and that I believed I should not dance at all. He would keep himself, he told me, disengaged, in hopes I should relent; and then, uttering some ridiculous speeches of sorrow and disappointment, though his face still wore the same invariable smile, he retreated.

It so happened, as we have since recollected, that during this little dialogue, Mrs. Mirvan was conversing with the lady of the house. And very soon after another gentleman, who seemed about six-and-twenty years old, gayly, but not foppishly, dressed, and indeed extremely handsome, with an air of mixed politeness and gallantry, desired to know if I was engaged, or would honour him with my hand. So he was pleased to say, though I am sure I know not what honour he could receive from me; but these sort of expressions, I find, are used as words of course, without any distinction of persons, or study of propriety.

Well, I bowed, and I am sure I coloured; for indeed I was frightened at the thoughts of dancing before so many people, all strangers, and, which was worse, *with* a stranger; however, that was unavoidable, for though I looked round the room several times, I could not see one person that I knew. And so, he took my hand, and led me to join in the dance.

The minuets[2] were over before we arrived, for we were kept late by the milliner's making us wait for our things.

He seemed very desirous of entering into conversation with me; but I was seized with such a panic, that I could hardly speak a word, and nothing but the shame of so soon changing my mind, prevented my returning to my seat, and declining to dance at all.

He appeared to be surprised at my terror, which I believe was but too apparent: however, he asked no questions, though I fear he must think it very odd; for I did not choose to tell him it was owing to my never before dancing but with a school-girl.

---

[2] *minuets:* The minuet was a rather formal dance of French derivation for two partners. These were apparently danced as an exhibition before the assembled group of dancers. They were occasions for personal display, often exhibited by those willing to show off their skill and grace.

His conversation was sensible and spirited; his air and address were open and noble; his manners gentle, attentive, and infinitely engaging; his person is all elegance, and his countenance the most animated and expressive I have ever seen.

In a short time we were joined by Miss Mirvan, who stood next couple to us. But how was I startled, when she whispered me that my partner was a nobleman! This gave me a new alarm; how will he be provoked, thought I, when he finds what a simple rustic he has honoured with his choice! one whose ignorance of the world makes her perpetually fear doing something wrong!

That he should be so much my superior every way, quite disconcerted me; and you will suppose my spirits were not much raised, when I heard a lady, in passing us, say, "This is the most difficult dance I ever saw."

"O dear, then," cried Maria to her partner, "with your leave, I'll sit down till the next."

"So will I too, then," cried I, "for I am sure I can hardly stand."

"But you must speak to your partner first," answered she; for he had turned aside to talk with some gentlemen. However, I had not sufficient courage to address him, and so away we all three tript, and seated ourselves at another end of the room.

But, unfortunately for me, Miss Mirvan soon after suffered herself to be prevailed upon to attempt the dance; and just as she rose to go, she cried, "My dear, yonder is your partner, Lord Orville, walking about the room in search of you."

"Don't leave me, then, dear girl!" cried I; but she was obliged to go. And then I was more uneasy than ever; I would have given the world to have seen Mrs. Mirvan, and begged of her to make my apologies; for what, thought I, can I possibly say for myself in excuse for running away? he must either conclude me a fool, or half mad, for any one brought up in the great world, and accustomed to its ways, can have no idea of such sort of fears as mine.

I was in the utmost confusion, when I observed that he was every where seeking me, with apparent perplexity and surprise; but when, at last, I saw him move towards the place where I sat, I was ready to sink with shame and distress. I found it absolutely impossible to keep my seat, because I could not think of a word to say for myself, and so I rose, and walked hastily towards the card-room, resolving to stay with Mrs. Mirvan the rest of the evening, and not to dance at all. But before I could find her, Lord Orville saw and approached me.

He begged to know if I was not well? You may easily imagine how much I was confused. I made no answer, but hung my head, like a fool, and looked on my fan.

He then, with an air the most respectfully serious, asked if he had been so unhappy as to offend me?

"No, indeed!" cried I: and then, in hopes of changing the discourse, and preventing his further inquiries, I desired to know if he had seen the young lady who had been conversing with me?

No; — but would I honour him with my commands to see for her?

"O by no means!"

Was there any other person with whom I wished to speak?

I said *no*, before I knew I had answered at all.

Should he have the pleasure of bringing me any refreshment?

I bowed, almost involuntarily. And away he flew.

I was quite ashamed of being so troublesome, and so much *above* myself as these seeming airs made me appear; but indeed I was too much confused to think or act with any consistency.

If he had not been swift as lightning, I don't know whether I should not have stolen away again; but he returned in a moment. When I had drunk a glass of lemonade, he hoped, he said, that I would again honour him with my hand, as a new dance was just begun. I had not the presence of mind to say a single word, and so I let him once more lead me to the place I had left.

Shocked to find how silly, how childish a part I had acted, my former fears of dancing before such a company, and with such a partner, returned more forcibly than ever. I suppose he perceived my uneasiness, for he intreated me to sit down again, if dancing was disagreeable to me. But I was quite satisfied with the folly I had already shewn, and therefore declined his offer, tho' I was really scarce able to stand.

Under such conscious disadvantages, you may easily imagine, my dear Sir, how ill I acquitted myself. But, though I both expected and deserved to find him very much mortified and displeased at his ill fortune in the choice he had made, yet, to my very great relief, he appeared to be even contented, and very much assisted and encouraged me. These people in high life have too much presence of mind, I believe, to *seem* disconcerted, or out of humour, however they may feel: for had I been the person of the most consequence in the room, I could not have met with more attention and respect.

When the dance was over, seeing me still very much flurried, he led me to a seat, saying that he would not suffer me to fatigue myself from politeness.

And then, if my capacity, or even if my spirits had been better, in how animated a conversation might I have been engaged! It was then that I saw the rank of Lord Orville was his least recommendation, his understanding and his manners being far more distinguished. His remarks upon the company in general were so apt, so just, so lively, I am almost surprised myself that they did not re-animate me; but indeed I was too well convinced of the ridiculous part I had myself played before so nice an observer, to be able to enjoy his pleasantry: so self-compassion gave me feeling for others. Yet I had not the courage to attempt either to defend them, or to rally in my turn, but listened to him in silent embarrassment.

When he found this, he changed the subject, and talked of public places, and public performers; but he soon discovered that I was totally ignorant of them.

He then, very ingeniously, turned the discourse to the amusements and occupations of the country.

It now struck me, that he was resolved to try whether or not I was capable of talking upon *any* subject. This put so great a constraint upon my thoughts, that I was unable to go further than a monosyllable, and not even so far, when I could possibly avoid it.

We were sitting in this manner, he conversing with all gaiety, I looking down with all foolishness, when that fop who had first asked me to dance, with a most ridiculous solemnity, approached, and after a profound bow or two, said, "I humbly beg pardon, Madam, — and of you too, my Lord, — for breaking in upon such agreeable conversation — which must, doubtless, be much more delectable — than what I have the honour to offer — but — "

I interrupted him — I blush for my folly, — with laughing; yet I could not help it, for, added to the man's stately foppishness, (and he actually took snuff[3] between every three words) when I looked round at Lord Orville, I saw such extreme surprise in his face, — the cause of which appeared so absurd, that I could not for my life preserve my gravity.

I had not laughed before from the time I had left Miss Mirvan, and I had much better have cried then; Lord Orville actually stared at me; the beau, I know not his name, looked quite enraged. "Refrain —

---

[3] *snuff*: A tobacco product in powdery form that is inserted into the nostrils or inside a cheek. Snuff boxes were often highly ornate objects, and taking snuff was associated with those who affected to be highly fashionable.

Madam," (said he, with an important air,) "a few moments refrain! —
I have but a sentence to trouble you with. — May I know to what accident I must attribute not having the honour of your hand?"

"Accident, Sir!" repeated I, much astonished.

"Yes, accident, Madam — for surely, — I must take the liberty to
observe — pardon me, Madam, — it ought to be no common one —
that should tempt a lady — so young a one too, — to be guilty of ill
manners."

A confused idea now for the first time entered my head, of something I had heard of the rules of assemblies; but I was never at one
before, — I have only danced at school, — and so giddy and heedless
I was, that I had not once considered the impropriety of refusing one
partner, and afterwards accepting another. I was thunderstruck at the
recollection: but, while these thoughts were rushing into my head,
Lord Orville, with some warmth, said, "This lady, Sir, is incapable of
meriting such an accusation!"

The creature — for I am very angry with him, — made a low bow,
and with a grin the most malicious I ever saw, "My Lord," said he,
"far be it from me to *accuse* the lady, for having the discernment to
distinguish and prefer — the superior attractions of your Lordship."

Again he bowed, and walked off.

Was ever any thing so provoking? I was ready to die with shame.
"What a coxcomb!" exclaimed Lord Orville; while I, without know-
ing what I did, rose hastily, and moving off, "I can't imagine," cried
I, "where Mrs. Mirvan has hid herself!"

"Give me leave to see," answered he. I bowed and sat down again,
not daring to meet his eyes; for what must he think of me, between
my blunder and the supposed preference?

He returned in a moment, and told me that Mrs. Mirvan was at
cards, but would be glad to see me; and I went immediately. There
was but one chair vacant, so, to my great relief, Lord Orville
presently left us. I then told Mrs. Mirvan my disasters, and she good-
naturedly blamed herself for not having better instructed me, but said
she had taken it for granted that I must know such common customs.
However, the man may, I think, be satisfied with his pretty speech,
and carry his resentment no farther.

In a short time, Lord Orville returned. I consented, with the best
grace I could, to go down another dance, for I had had time to recollect myself, and therefore resolved to use some exertion, and, if possible, appear less a fool than I hitherto had; for it occurred to me
that, insignificant as I was, compared to a man of his rank and figure,

yet, since he had been so unfortunate as to make choice of me for a partner, why I should endeavour to make the best of it.

The dance, however, was short, and he spoke very little; so I had no opportunity of putting my resolution in practice. He was satisfied, I suppose, with his former successless efforts to draw me out: or, rather, I fancied, he has been inquiring *who I was*. This again disconcerted me, and the spirits I had determined to exert, again failed me. Tired, ashamed, and mortified, I begged to sit down till we returned home, which we did soon after. Lord Orville did me the honour to hand me to the coach, talking all the way of the honour *I* had done *him!* O these fashionable people!

Well, my dear Sir, was it not a strange evening? I could not help being thus particular, because, to me, every thing is so new. But it is now time to conclude. I am, with all love and duty,

Your

EVELINA

## LETTER XII

### Evelina in Continuation

Tuesday, April 5.

There is to be no end to the troubles of last night. I have, this moment, between persuasion and laughter, gathered from Maria the most curious dialogue that ever I heard. You will, at first, be startled at my vanity; but, my dear Sir, have patience!

It must have passed while I was sitting with Mrs. Mirvan in the card-room. Maria was taking some refreshment, and saw Lord Orville advancing for the same purpose himself; but he did not know her, though she immediately recollected him. Presently after, a very gay-looking man, stepping hastily up to him, cried, "Why, my Lord, what have you done with your lovely partner!"

"*Nothing!*" answered Lord Orville, with a smile and a shrug.

"By Jove," cried the man, "she is the most beautiful creature I ever saw in my life!"

Lord Orville, as he well might, laughed, but answered, "Yes, a pretty modest-looking girl."

"O my Lord!" cried the madman, "she is an angel!"

"A *silent* one," returned he.

"Why ay, my Lord, how stands she as to that? She looks all intelligence and expression."

"A poor weak girl!" answered Lord Orville, shaking his head.

"By Jove," cried the other, "I am glad to hear it!"

At that moment, the same odious creature who had been my former torment, joined them. Addressing Lord Orville with great respect, he said, "I beg pardon, my Lord, — if I was — as I fear might be the case — rather too severe in my censure of the lady who is honoured with your protection — but, my Lord, ill-breeding is apt to provoke a man."

"Ill-breeding!" cried my unknown champion, "impossible! that elegant face can never be so vile a mask!"

"O Sir, as to that," answered he, "you must allow *me* to judge; for though I pay all deference to your opinion — in other things, — yet I hope you will grant — and I appeal to your Lordship also — that I am not totally despicable as a judge of good or ill manners."

"I was so wholly ignorant," said Lord Orville gravely, "of the provocation you might have had, that I could not but be surprised at your singular resentment."

"It was far from my intention," answered he, "to offend your Lordship; but really, for a person who is nobody, to give herself such airs, — I own I could not command my passions. For, my Lord, though I have made diligent enquiry — I cannot learn who she is."

"By what I can make out," cried my defender, "she must be a country parson's daughter."

"He! he! he! very good, 'pon honour!" cried the fop, — "well, so I could have sworn by her manners."

And then, delighted at his own wit, he laughed, and went away, as I suppose, to repeat it.

"But what the deuce is all this?" demanded the other.

"Why a very foolish affair," answered Lord Orville; "your Helen first refused this coxcomb, and then — danced with me. This is all I can gather of it."

"O Orville," returned he, "you are a happy man! — But, *ill-bred?* — I can never believe it! And she looks too sensible to be *ignorant.*"

"Whether ignorant, or mischievous, I will not pretend to determine, but certain it is, she attended to all I could say to her, though I have really fatigued myself with fruitless endeavours to entertain her, with the most immoveable gravity; but no sooner did Lovel begin his complaint, than she was seized with a fit of laughing first affronting the poor beau, and then enjoying his mortification."

"Ha! ha! ha! why there's some *genius* in that, my Lord, though perhaps rather — *rustick.*"

Here Maria was called to dance, and so heard no more.

Now tell me, my dear Sir, did you ever know any thing more provoking? *"A poor weak girl!" "ignorant or mischievous!"* What mortifying words! I'm resolved, however, that I will never again be tempted to go to an assembly. I wish I had been in Dorsetshire.

Well, after this, you will not be surprised that Lord Orville contented himself with an enquiry after our healths this morning, by his servant, without troubling himself to call;[1] as Miss Mirvan had told me he would: but perhaps it may be only a country custom.

I would not live here for the world. I don't care how soon we leave town. London soon grows tiresome. I wish the Captain would come. Mrs. Mirvan talks of the opera for this evening; however, I am very indifferent about it.

Wednesday morning.

Well, my dear Sir, I have been pleased, against my will, I could almost say, for I must own I went out in very ill-humour, which I think you can't wonder at: but the music and the singing were charming; they soothed me into a pleasure the most grateful, the best suited to my present disposition in the world. I hope to persuade Mrs. Mirvan to go again on Saturday. I wish the opera was every night. It is, of all entertainments, the sweetest, and most delightful. Some of the songs seemed to melt my very soul. It was what they call a *serious* opera, as the *comic* first singer was ill.

To-night we go to Ranelagh. If any of those three gentlemen who conversed so freely about me should be there —— but I won't think of it.

Thursday morning.

Well, my dear Sir, we went to Ranelagh. It is a charming place, and the brilliancy of the lights, on my first entrance, made me almost think I was in some inchanted castle, or fairy palace, for all looked like magic to me.

The very first person I saw was Lord Orville. I felt so confused! — but he did not see me. After tea, Mrs. Mirvan being tired, Maria and I walked round the room alone. Then again we saw him, standing by the orchestra. We, too, stopt to hear a singer. He bowed to me; I

---

[1] *without troubling himself to call:* A good deal of time during the fashionable season in London was spent in the polite custom of paying and returning social calls. It was customary for a gentleman to inquire after the health of a dance partner the morning after a ball. Sending a servant was a rather perfunctory way of fulfilling this obligation.

courtsied, and I am sure I coloured. We soon walked on, not liking our situation; however, he did not follow us, and when we past by the orchestra again, he was gone. Afterwards, in the course of the evening, we met him several times, but he was always with some party, and never spoke to us, tho' whenever he chanced to meet my eyes, he condescended to bow.

I cannot but be hurt at the opinion he entertains of me. It is true, my own behaviour incurred it — yet he is himself the most agreeable, and, seemingly, the most amiable man in the world, and therefore it is, that I am grieved to be thought ill of by him: for of whose esteem ought we to be ambitious, if not of those who most merit our own? — But it is too late to reflect upon this now. Well, I can't help it; — However, I think I have done with assemblies!

This morning was destined for *seeing sights*, auctions, curious shops,[2] and so forth; but my head ached, and I was not in a humour to be amused, and so I made them go without me, though very un-willingly. They are all kindness.

And now I am sorry I did not accompany them, for I know not what to do with myself. I had resolved not to go to the play tonight; but I believe I shall. In short, I hardly care whether I do or not.

* * * * * * * *

I thought I had done wrong! Mrs. Mirvan and Maria have been half the town over, and so entertained! — while I, like a fool, stayed at home to do nothing. And, at an auction in Pall-Mall, who should they meet but Lord Orville! He sat next to Mrs. Mirvan, and they talked a great deal together: but she gave me no account of the conversation.

I may never have such another opportunity of seeing London; I am quite sorry that I was not of the party; but I deserve this mortifica-tion, for having indulged my ill-humour.

Thursday night.

We are just returned from the play, which was King Lear, and has made me very sad. We did not see any body we knew.

Well, adieu, it is too late to write more.

---

[2] *auctions, curious shops:* Going to Christie's to watch or participate in bidding on elegant household goods was a popular amusement; "curious shops" probably refers to the growing eighteenth-century English appetite for exotic and "curious" decorative objects witnessed by, among other phenomena, the invention of the museum and the curiosity cabinet.

Friday.

Captain Mirvan is arrived. I have not spirits to give an account of his introduction, for he has really shocked me. I do not like him. He seems to be surly, vulgar, and disagreeable.

Almost the same moment that Maria was presented to him, he began some rude jests upon the bad shape of her nose, and called her a tall, ill-formed thing. She bore it with the utmost good-humour; but that kind and sweet-tempered woman, Mrs. Mirvan, deserved a better lot. I am amazed she would marry him.

For my own part, I have been so shy, that I have hardly spoken to him, or he to me. I cannot imagine why the family was so rejoiced at his return. If he had spent his whole life abroad, I should have supposed they might rather have been thankful than sorrowful. However, I hope they do not think so ill of him as I do. At least, I am sure they have too much prudence to make it known.

Saturday night.

We have been to the opera, and I am still more pleased than I was on Tuesday. I could have thought myself in paradise, but for the continual talking of the company around me. We sat in the pit,[3] where every body was dressed in so high a style, that, if I had been less delighted with the performance, my eyes would have found me sufficient entertainment from looking at the ladies.

I was very glad I did not sit next the Captain, for he could not bear the music, or singers, and was extremely gross in his observations on both. When the opera was over, we went into a place called the coffee-room,[4] where ladies as well as gentlemen assemble. There are all sorts of refreshments, and the company walk about, and *chat*, with the same ease and freedom as in a private room.

On Monday we go to a ridotto,[5] and on Wednesday we return to Howard Grove. The Captain says he won't stay here to be *smoked with filth* any longer; but, having been seven years *smoked with a burning sun*, he will retire to the country, and sink into a *fair-weather chap*.

Adieu, my dear Sir.

[3] *We sat in the pit:* The pit, or lower level of the opera house, had become a highly fashionable place to sit and required elaborate formal dress.

[4] *coffee-room:* A fashionable gathering place at the opera.

[5] *ridotto:* A fashionable London social gathering during the eighteenth century that featured music and dancing.

## LETTER XIII

### Evelina in Continuation

Tuesday, April 12.

My dear Sir,

We came home from the ridotto so late, or rather, so early, that it was not possible for me to write. Indeed we did not *go,* you will be frightened to hear it, — till past eleven o'clock: but nobody does. A terrible reverse of the order of nature! We sleep with the sun, and wake with the moon.

The room was very magnificent, the lights and decorations [were] brilliant, and the company gay and splendid. But I should have told you, that I made very many objections to being of the party, according to the resolution I had formed. However, Maria laughed me out of my scruples, and so, once again — I went to an assembly.

Miss Mirvan danced a minuet, but I had not the courage to follow her example. In our walks I saw Lord Orville. He was quite alone, but did not observe us. Yet, as he seemed of no party, I thought it was not impossible that he might join us; and tho' I did not wish much to dance at all, — yet, as I was more acquainted with him than with any other person in the room, I must own I could not help thinking it would be infinitely more desireable to dance again with him, than with an entire stranger. To be sure, after all that had passed, it was very ridiculous to suppose it even probable, that Lord Orville would again honour me with his choice; yet I am compelled to confess my absurdity, by way of explaining what follows.

Miss Mirvan was soon engaged; and, presently after, a very fashionable, gay-looking man, who seemed about 30 years of age, addressed himself to me, and begged to have the honour of dancing with me. Now Maria's partner was a gentleman of Mrs. Mirvan's acquaintance; for she had told us it was highly improper for young women to dance with strangers, at any public assembly. Indeed it was by no means my wish so to do; yet I did not like to confine myself from dancing at all; neither did I dare refuse this gentleman, as I had done Mr. Lovel, and then, if any acquaintance should offer, accept him: and so, all these reasons combining, induced me to tell him — yet I blush to write it to you! — that I was *already engaged;* by which I meant to keep myself at liberty to dance or not, as matters should fall out.

I suppose my consciousness betrayed my artifice, for he looked at me as if incredulous; and, instead of being satisfied with my answer, and leaving me, according to my expectation, he walked at my side, and, with the greatest ease imaginable, began a conversation, in that free style which only belongs to old and intimate acquaintance. But, what was most provoking, he asked me a thousand questions concerning *the partner to whom I was engaged*. And, at last, he said, "Is it really possible that a man whom you have honoured with your acceptance, can fail to be at hand to profit from your goodness?"

I felt extremely foolish, and begged Mrs. Mirvan to lead to a seat, which she very obligingly did. The Captain sat next her, and, to my great surprise, this gentleman thought proper to follow, and seat himself next to me.

"What an insensible!" continued he, "why, Madam, you are missing the most delightful dance in the world! The man must be either mad, or a fool. — Which do you incline to think him yourself?"

"Neither, Sir," answered I in some confusion.

He begged my pardon for the freedom of his supposition, saying, "I really was off my guard, from astonishment that any man can be so much and so unaccountably his own enemy. But where, Madam, can he possibly be? — has he left the room? — or has not he been in it?"

"Indeed, Sir," said I peevishly, "I know nothing of him."

"I don't wonder that you are disconcerted, Madam, it is really very provoking. The best part of the evening will be absolutely lost. He deserves not that you should wait for him."

"I do not, Sir," said I, "and I beg you not to —— "

"Mortifying, indeed, Madam," interrupted he, "a lady to wait for a gentleman! — O fie! — careless fellow! — what can detain him? — Will you give me leave to seek him?"

"If you please, Sir," answered I, quite terrified lest Mrs. Mirvan should attend to him, for she looked very much surprised at seeing me enter into conversation with a stranger.

"With all my heart," cried he; "pray what coat has he on?"

"Indeed I never looked at it."

"Out upon him!" cried he; "What! did he address you in a coat not worth looking at? — What a shabby dog!"

How ridiculous! I really could not help laughing, which, I fear, encouraged him, for he went on.

"Charming creature! — and can you really bear ill usage with so much sweetness? — Can you, *like patience on a monument*,[1] smile in the midst of disappointment? — For my part, though I am not the offended person, my indignation is so great, that I long to kick the fellow round the room! — unless, indeed, — (hesitating and looking earnestly at me,) unless, indeed — it is a partner of your own *creating?*"

I was dreadfully abashed, and could not make any answer.

"But no!" cried he, (again, and with warmth,) "it cannot be that you are so cruel! Softness itself is painted in your eyes: — You could not, surely, have the barbarity so wantonly to trifle with my misery?"

I turned away from this nonsense, with real disgust. Mrs. Mirvan saw my confusion, but was perplexed what to think of it, and I could not explain to her the cause, lest the Captain should hear me. I therefore proposed to walk, she consented, and we all rose; but, would you believe it? this man had the assurance to rise too, and walk close by my side, as if of my party!

"Now," cried he, "I hope we shall see this ingrate. — Is that he?" — pointing to an old man, who was lame, "or that?" And in this manner he asked me of whoever was old or ugly in the room. I made no sort of answer; and when he found that I was resolutely silent, and walked on, as much as I could, without observing him, he suddenly stamped his foot, and cried out, in a passion, "Fool! idiot! booby!"

I turned hastily toward him: "O Madam," continued he, "forgive my vehemence, but I am distracted to think there should exist a wretch who can slight a blessing for which I would forfeit my life! — O! that I could but meet him! — I would soon — — But I grow angry: pardon me, Madam, my passions are violent, and your injuries affect me!"

I began to apprehend he was a madman, and stared at him with the utmost astonishment. "I see you are moved, Madam," said he, "generous creature! — but don't be alarmed, I am cool again, I am indeed, — upon my soul I am, — I entreat you, most lovely of mortals! I entreat you to be easy."

"Indeed, Sir," said I very seriously, "I must insist upon your leaving me; you are quite a stranger to me, and I am both unused, and averse to your language and your manners."

[1] *patience on a monument:* A quotation from Shakespeare's *Twelfth Night,* 2.4.117.

This seemed to have some effect on him. He made me a low bow, begged my pardon, and vowed he would not for the world offend me.

"Then, Sir, you must leave me," cried I.

"I am gone, Madam, I am gone!" with a most tragical air; and he marched away, a quick pace, out of sight in a moment; but before I had time to congratulate myself, he was again at my elbow.

"And could you really let me go, and not be sorry? — Can you see me suffer torments inexpressible, and yet retain all your favour for that miscreant who flies you? — Ungrateful puppy! — I could bastinado[2] him!"

"For Heaven's sake, my dear," cried Mrs. Mirvan, "who is he talking of?"

"Indeed — I do not know, Madam," said I, "but I wish he would leave me."

"What's all that there?" cried the Captain.

The man made a low bow, and said, "Only, Sir, a slight objection which this young lady makes to dancing with me, and which I am endeavouring to obviate. I shall think myself greatly honoured, if you will intercede for me."

"That lady, Sir," said the Captain coldly, "is her own mistress." And he walked sullenly on.

"You, Madam," said the man, (who looked delighted, to Mrs. Mirvan) "you, I hope, will have the goodness to speak for me."

"Sir," answered she gravely, "I have not the pleasure of being acquainted with you."

"I hope when you have, Ma'am," cried he, (undaunted,) "you will honour me with your approbation; but, while I am yet unknown to you, it would be truly generous in you to countenance me; and I flatter myself, Madam, that you will not have cause to repent it."

Mrs. Mirvan, with an embarrassed air, replied, "I do not at all mean, Sir, to doubt your being a gentleman, — but — "

"But *what*, Madam? — that doubt removed, why a *but?*"

"Well, Sir," said Mrs. Mirvan, (with a good-humoured smile,) "I will even treat you with your own plainness, and try what effect that will have on you: I must therefore tell you, once for all, —— "

"O pardon me, Madam!" interrupted he eagerly, "you must not proceed with those words, *once for all*; no, if *I* have been too *plain,* and though a *man,* deserve a rebuke, remember, dear ladies, that if you *copy,* you ought, in justice, to *excuse* me."

---

[2] *bastinado:* To beat with a stick or a cudgel.

We both stared at the man's strange behaviour.

"Be nobler than your sex," continued he, turning to me, "honour me with one dance, and give up the ingrate who has merited so ill your patience."

Mrs. Mirvan looked with astonishment at us both. "Who does he speak of, my dear? — you never mentioned —— "

"O Madam!" exclaimed he, "he was not worth mentioning — it is pity he was ever thought of; but let us forget his existence. One dance is all I solicit; permit me, madam, the honour of this young lady's hand; it will be a favour I shall ever most gratefully acknowledge."

"Sir," answered she, "favours and strangers have with me no connection."

"If you have hitherto," said he, "confined your benevolence to your intimate friends, suffer me to be the first for whom your charity is enlarged."

"Well, Sir, I know not what to say to you, — but — "

He stopt her *but* with so many urgent entreaties, that she at last told me, I must either go down one dance, or avoid his importunities by returning home. I hesitated which alternative to chuse; but this impetuous man at length prevailed, and I was obliged to consent to dance with him.

And thus was my deviation from truth punished; and thus did this man's determined boldness conquer.

During the dance, before we were too much engaged in it for conversation, he was extremely provoking about *my partner,* and tried every means in his power to make me own that I had deceived him; which, though I would not so far humble myself, was, indeed, but too obvious.

Lord Orville, I fancy, did not dance at all; he seemed to have a large acquaintance, and joined several different parties: but you will easily suppose I was not much pleased to see him, in a few minutes after I was gone, walk towards the place I had just left, and bow to, and join Mrs. Mirvan!

How unlucky I thought myself, that I had not longer withstood this stranger's importunities! The moment we had gone down the dance, I was hastening away from him, but he stopt me, and said that I could by no means return to my party, without giving offence, before we had *done our duty of walking up the dance.*[3] As I

---

[3] *walking up the dance:* To form a part of the two lines of dancers that usually characterized English country dancing. Individual couples would dance "down" between these lines, while the other dancers "walked up" the lines.

know nothing at all of these rules and customs, I was obliged to submit to his directions; but I fancy I looked rather uneasy, for he took notice of my inattention, saying, in his free way, "Whence that anxiety? — Why are those lovely eyes perpetually averted?"

"I wish you would say no more to me, Sir," (cried I peevishly) "you have already destroyed all my happiness for this evening."

"Good Heaven! what is it I have done? — How have I merited this scorn?"

"You have tormented me to death; you have forced me from my friends, and intruded yourself upon me, against my will, for a partner."

"Surely, my dear madam, we ought to be better friends, since there seems to be something of sympathy in the frankness of our dispositions — And yet, were you not an angel — how do you think I could brook such contempt?"

"If I have offended you, cried I, you have but to leave me — and O how I wish you would!"

"My dear creature," (cried he, half laughing) "why where could you be educated?"

"Where I most sincerely wish I now was!"

"How conscious you must be, all beautiful that you are, that those charming airs serve only to heighten the bloom of your complexion!"

"Your freedom, Sir, where you are more acquainted, may perhaps be less disagreeable; but to *me* —— "

"You do me justice," (cried he, interrupting me) "yes, I do indeed improve upon acquaintance; you will hereafter be quite charmed with me."

"Hereafter, Sir, I hope I shall never — "

"O hush! — hush! — have you forgot the situation in which I found you? — Have you forgot, that when deserted, I pursued you, — when betrayed, I adored you? — but for me —— "

"But for you, Sir, I might, perhaps, have been happy."

"What, then, am I to conclude that, *but for me,* your *partner* would have appeared? — poor fellow! — and did my presence awe him?"

"I wish *his* presence, Sir, could awe *you!*"

"His presence! — perhaps then you see him?"

"Perhaps, Sir, I do," cried I, quite wearied of his raillery.

"Where? — where? — for Heaven's sake shew me the wretch!"

"Wretch, Sir?"

"O, a very savage! — a sneaking, shame-faced, despicable puppy!"
I know not what bewitched me, — but my pride was hurt, and my
spirits were tired, and — in short — I had the folly, looking at Lord
Orville, to repeat, "*Despicable,* you think?"

His eyes instantly followed mine; "why, is *that* the gentleman?"

I made no answer; I could not affirm, and I would not deny; for I
hoped to be relieved from his teizing, by his mistake.

The very moment we had done what he called our duty, I eagerly
desired to return to Mrs. Mirvan.

"To your *partner,* I presume, Madam?" said he, very gravely.

This quite confounded me; I dreaded lest this mischievous man, ignorant of his rank, should address himself to Lord Orville, and say
something which might expose my artifice. Fool! to involve myself in
such difficulties! I now feared what I had before wished, and therefore, to *avoid* Lord Orville, I was obliged myself to *propose* going
down another dance, though I was ready to sink with shame while I
spoke.

"But your *partner,* Ma'am?" (said he, affecting a very solemn air)
"perhaps he may resent my detaining you: if you will give me leave to
ask his consent — "

"Not for the universe."

"Who is he, Madam?"

I wished myself a hundred miles off. He repeated his question,
"What is his name?"

"Nothing — nobody — I don't know. — "

He assumed a most important solemnity; "How! — not know? —
Give me leave, my dear madam, to recommend this caution to you;
never dance in public with a stranger, — with one whose name you
are unacquainted with, — who may be a mere adventurer, — a man
of no character, — consider to what impertinence you may expose
yourself."

Was ever any thing so ridiculous? I could not help laughing, in
spite of my vexation.

At this instant, Mrs. Mirvan, followed by Lord Orville, walked up
to us. You will easily believe it was not difficult for me to recover my
gravity; but what was my consternation, when this strange man, destined to be the scourge of my artifice, exclaimed, "Ha! my Lord
Orville! — I protest I did not know your Lordship. What can I say for
my usurpation? — Yet, faith, my Lord, such a prize was not to be
neglected."

My shame and confusion were unspeakable. Who could have supposed or foreseen that this man knew Lord Orville! But falsehood is not more unjustifiable than unsafe.

Lord Orville — well he might, — looked all amazement.

"The philosophic coldness of your Lordship," continued this odious creature, "every man is not endowed with. I have used my utmost endeavours to entertain this lady, though I fear without success; and your Lordship would be not a little flattered, if acquainted with the difficulty which attended my procuring the honour of only one dance." Then, turning to me, who was sinking with shame, while Lord Orville stood motionless, and Mrs. Mirvan astonished, — he suddenly seized my hand, saying, "Think, my Lord, what must be my reluctance to resign this fair hand to your Lordship!"

In the same instant, Lord Orville took it of him; I coloured violently, and made an effort to recover it. "You do me too much honour, Sir," cried he, (with an air of gallantry, pressing it to his lips ere he let it go) "however, I shall be happy to profit by it, if this lady," (turning to Mrs. Mirvan) "will permit me to seek for her party."

To compel him thus to dance, I could not endure, and eagerly called out, "By no means, — not for the world! — I must beg —— "

"Will you honour *me*, Madam, with your commands," cried my tormentor; "may *I* seek the lady's party?"

"No, Sir," answered I, turning from him.

"What *shall* be done, my dear?" said Mrs. Mirvan.

"Nothing, Ma'am; — any thing, I mean. —— "

"But do you dance, or not? you see his Lordship waits."

"I hope not, — I beg that — I would not for the world — I am sure I ought to — to — "

I could not speak; but that confident man, determined to discover whether or not I had deceived him, said to Lord Orville, who stood suspended, "My Lord, this affair, which, at present, seems perplexed, I will briefly explain; — this lady proposed to me another dance, — nothing could have made me more happy — I only wished for your Lordship's permission, which, if now granted, will, I am persuaded, set every thing right."

I glowed with indignation. "No, Sir — It is your absence, and that alone, can set every thing right."

"For Heaven's sake, my dear," (cried Mrs. Mirvan, who could no longer contain her surprise,) "what does all this mean? — were you pre-engaged? — had Lord Orville —— "

"No, Madam, cried I, — only — only I did not know that gentleman, — and so, — and so I thought — I intended — I — "

Overpowered by all that had passed, I had not strength to make
my mortifying explanation; — my spirits quite failed me, and I burst
into tears.

They all seemed shocked and amazed.

"What is the matter, my dearest love?" cried Mrs. Mirvan, with
the kindest concern.

"What have I done?" exclaimed my evil genius, and ran officiously
for a glass of water.

However, a hint was sufficient for Lord Orville, who compre-
hended all I would have explained. He immediately led me to a seat,
and said, in a low voice, "Be not distressed, I beseech you; I shall ever
think my name honoured by your making use of it."

This politeness relieved me. A general murmur had alarmed Miss
Mirvan, who flew instantly to me; while Lord Orville, the moment
Mrs. Mirvan had taken the water, led my tormentor away.

"For Heaven's sake, dear Madam," cried I, "let me go home, —
indeed I cannot stay here any longer."

"Let us all go," cried my kind Maria.

"But the Captain — what will he say? — I had better go home in a
chair."[4]

Mrs. Mirvan consented, and I rose to depart. Lord Orville and
that man both came to me. The first, with an attention I had but ill
merited from him, led me to a chair, while the other followed, pester-
ing me with apologies. I wished to have made mine to Lord Orville,
but was too much ashamed.

It was about one o'clock. Mrs. Mirvan's servants saw me home.

And now, — what again shall ever tempt me to an assembly? I
dread to hear what you will think of me, my most dear and honoured
Sir: you will need your utmost partiality to receive me without displeasure.

This morning Lord Orville has sent to enquire after our healths:
and Sir Clement Willoughby, for that, I find, is the name of my perse-
cutor, has called: but I would not go down stairs till he was gone.

And now, my dear Sir, I can somewhat account for the strange,
provoking, and ridiculous conduct of this Sir Clement last night; for

---

[4] *chair:* Sedan chairs, carried by two chairmen, were common means of conveyance
for the fashionable Londoner.

Miss Mirvan says, he is the very man with whom she heard Lord Orville conversing at Mrs. Stanley's, when I was spoken of in so mortifying a manner. He was pleased to say he was glad to hear I was a fool, and therefore, I suppose, he concluded he might talk as much nonsense as he pleased to me: however, I am very indifferent as to his opinion; — but for Lord Orville, — if then he thought me an idiot, now, I am sure, he must believe me both bold and presuming. Make use of his name! — what impertinence! — he can never know how it happened — he can only imagine it was from an excess of vanity: — well, however, I shall leave this bad city to-morrow, and never again will I enter it!

The Captain intends to take us to-night to the Fantocini.[5] I cannot bear that Captain; I can give you no idea how gross he is. I heartily rejoice that he was not present at the disagreeable conclusion of yesterday's adventure, for I am sure he would have contributed to my confusion; which might perhaps have diverted him, as he seldom or never smiles but at some other person's expence.

And here I conclude my London letters, — and without any regret, for I am too inexperienced and ignorant to conduct myself with propriety in this town, where every thing is new to me, and many things are unaccountable and perplexing.

Adieu, my dear Sir; Heaven restore me safely to you! I wish I was to go immediately to Berry Hill; yet the wish is ungrateful to Mrs. Mirvan, and therefore I will repress it. I shall write an account of the Fantocini from Howard Grove. We have not been to half the public places that are now open, though I dare say you will think we have been to all. But they are almost as innumerable as the persons who fill them.

[5] *Fantocini:* Derived from the Italian name for puppets and meaning a marionette show.

## LETTER XIV

### Evelina in Continuation

Queen-Ann-street, April 13.

How much will you be surprised, my dearest Sir, at receiving another letter from London of your Evelina's writing! But, believe me, it was not my fault, neither is it my happiness, that I am still here: our journey has been postponed by an accident equally unexpected and disagreeable.

We went last night to see the Fantocini, where we had infinite entertainment from the performance of a little comedy, in French and Italian, by puppets, so admirably managed, that they both astonished and diverted us all, except the Captain, who has a fixed and most prejudiced hatred of whatever is not English.

When it was over, while we waited for the coach, a tall elderly woman brushed quickly past us, calling out, "My God! what shall I do?"

"Why what *would* you do," cried the Captain.

"*Ma foi, Monsieur,*" answered she, "I have lost my company, and in this place I don't know nobody."

There was something foreign in her accent, though it was difficult to discover whether she was an English or a French woman. She was very well dressed, and seemed so entirely at a loss what to do, that Mrs. Mirvan proposed to the Captain to assist her.

"Assist her!" cried he, "ay, with all my heart; — let a link-boy[1] call her a coach."

There was not one to be had, and it rained very fast.

"*Mon Dieu,*" exclaimed the stranger, "what shall become of me? *Je suis au désespoir!*"

"Dear Sir," cried Miss Mirvan, "pray let us take the poor lady into our coach. She is quite alone, and a foreigner — ."

"She's never the better for that," answered he: "she may be a woman of the town,[2] for any thing you know."

"She does not appear such," said Mrs. Mirvan, "and indeed she seems so much distressed, that we shall but follow the golden rule, if we carry her to her lodgings."

"You are mighty fond of new acquaintance," returned he, "but first let us know if she be going our way."

Upon enquiry, we found that she lived in Oxford Road, and, after some disputing, the Captain, surlily, and with a very bad grace, consented to admit her into his coach; though he soon convinced us, that he was determined she should not be too much obliged to him, for he seemed absolutely bent upon quarrelling with her: for which strange inhospitality, I can assign no other reason, than that she appeared to be a foreigner.

---

[1] *link-boy:* A boy hired to light pedestrians' way with a torch.
[2] *woman of the town:* A prostitute.

The conversation began, by her telling us, that she had been in England only two days; that the gentlemen belonging to her were Parisians, and had left her, to see for a hackney-coach, as her own carriage was abroad; and that she had waited for them till she was quite frightened, and concluded that they had lost themselves.

"And pray," said the Captain, "why did you go to a public place without an Englishman?"

"*Ma foi,* Sir," answered she, "because none of my acquaintance is in town."

"Why then," said he, "I'll tell you what; your best way is to go out of it yourself."

"*Pardie, Monsieur,*" returned she, "and so I shall; for, I promise you, I think the English a parcel of brutes; and I'll go back to France as fast as I can, for I would not live among none of you."

"Who wants you?" cried the Captain; "do you suppose, Madam French, we have not enough of other nations to pick our pockets already? I'll warrant you, there's no need of you for to put in your oar."

"Pick your pockets, Sir! I wish nobody wanted to pick your pockets no more than I do; and I'll promise you, you'd be safe enough. But there's no nation under the sun can beat the English for ill-politeness: for my part, I hate the very sight of them, and so I shall only just visit a person of quality or two, of my particular acquaintance, and then I shall go back again to France."

"Ay, do," cried he, "and then go to the devil together, for that's the fittest voyage for the French and the quality."[3]

"We'll take care, however," cried the stranger, with great vehemence, "not to admit none of your vulgar, unmannered English among us."

"O never fear," (returned he coolly) "we shan't dispute the point with you; you and the quality may have the devil all to yourselves."

Desirous of changing the subject of a conversation which now became very alarming, Miss Mirvan called out, "Lord, how slow the man drives!"

"Never mind, Moll," said her father, "I'll warrant you he'll drive fast enough to-morrow, when you're going to Howard Grove."

"To Howard Grove!" exclaimed the stranger; "why, *mon Dieu,* do you know Lady Howard?"

---

[3] *quality:* Generally, those with pretensions to positions of power and fashion in upper-class society. The captain is using the term sneeringly to refer to those who affect French fashions.

"Why, what if we do?" answered he, "that's nothing to you; she's none of *your* quality, I'll promise you."

"Who told you that?" cried she, "you don't know nothing about the matter; besides, you're the ill-bredest person ever I see; and as to your knowing Lady Howard, I don't believe no such a thing; unless, indeed, you are her steward."[4]

The Captain, swearing terribly, said, with great fury, "*you* would much sooner be taken for her wash-woman."

"Her wash-woman, indeed! — Ha, ha, ha! — why you han't no eyes; did you ever see a wash-woman in such a gown as this? — besides, I'm no such mean person, for I'm as good as Lady Howard, and as rich too; and besides, I'm now come to England to visit her."

"You may spare yourself that there trouble," said the Captain, "she has paupers enough about her already."

"Paupers, Mr.! — no more a pauper than yourself, nor so much neither; — but you're a low, dirty fellow, and I shan't stoop to take no more notice of you."

"Dirty fellow!" (exclaimed the Captain, seizing both her wrists) "hark you, Mrs. Frog, you'd best hold your tongue, for I must make bold to tell you, if you don't, that I shall make no ceremony of tripping you out of the window; and there you may lie in the mud till some of your Monsieurs come to help you out of it."

Their encreasing passion quite terrified us; and Mrs. Mirvan was beginning to remonstrate with the Captain, when we were all silenced by what follows.

"Let me go, villain that you are, let me go, or I'll promise you I'll get you put to prison for this usage; I'm no common person, I assure you, and, *ma foie*, I'll go to Justice Fielding[5] about you; for I'm a person of fashion, and I'll make you know it, or my name i' n't Duval."

I heard no more: amazed, frightened, and unspeakably shocked, an involuntary exclamation of *Gracious Heaven!* escaped me, and, more dead than alive, I sunk into Mrs. Mirvan's arms. But let me draw a veil over a scene too cruel for a heart so compassionately tender as yours; it is sufficient that you know this supposed foreigner proved to be Madame Duval, — the grandmother of your Evelina!

---

[4] *steward:* An upper-level servant or hireling, in charge of a gentleman's estate.

[5] *Justice Fielding:* John Fielding, half-brother to the novelist and magistrate Henry Fielding, served as a well-known and highly respected magistrate in Westminster from 1761 to 1780.

O, Sir, to discover so near a relation in a woman who had thus introduced herself! — what would become of me, were it not for you, my protector, my friend, and my refuge?

My extreme concern, and Mrs. Mirvan's surprise, immediately betrayed me. But I will not shock you with the manner of her acknowledging me, or the bitterness, the *grossness* — I cannot otherwise express myself, — with which she spoke of those unhappy past transactions you have so pathetically related to me. All the misery of a much-injured parent, dear, though never seen, regretted, though never known, crowded so forcibly upon my memory, that they rendered this interview — one only excepted — the most afflicting I can ever know.

When we stopt at her lodgings, she desired me to accompany her into the house, and said she could easily procure a room for me to sleep in. Alarmed and trembling, I turned to Mrs. Mirvan. "My daughter, Madam," said that sweet woman, "cannot so abruptly part with her young friend; you must allow a little time to wean them from each other."

"Pardon me, Ma'am," answered Madame Duval, (who, from the time of her being known somewhat softened her manners) "Miss can't possibly be so nearly connected to this child as I am."

"No matter for that," cried the Captain, (who espoused my cause to satisfy his own pique, though an awkward apology had passed between them) "she was sent to us, and so, d'ye see, we don't chuse for to part with her."

I promised to wait upon her at what time she pleased the next day, and, after a short debate, she desired me to breakfast with her, and we proceeded to Queen-Ann-Street.

What an unfortunate adventure! I could not close my eyes the whole night. A thousand times I wished I had never left Berry Hill; however, my return thither shall be accelerated to the utmost of my power; and, once more in that abode of tranquil happiness, I will suffer no temptation to allure me elsewhere.

Mrs. Mirvan was so kind as to accompany me to Madame Duval's house this morning. The Captain, too, offered his service, which I declined, from a fear she should suppose I meant to insult her.

She frowned most terribly upon Mrs. Mirvan, but she received me with as much tenderness as I believe she is capable of feeling. Indeed, our meeting seems really to have affected her; for when, overcome by the variety of emotions which the sight of her occasioned, I almost fainted in her arms, she burst into tears, and said, "Let me not lose

my poor daughter a second time!" This unexpected humanity softened me extremely; but she very soon excited my warmest indignation, by the ungrateful mention she made of the best of men, my dear,
and most generous benefactor. However, grief and anger mutually
gave way to terror, upon her avowing the intention of her visiting
England was to make me return with her to France. This, she said,
was a plan she had formed from the instant she had heard of my
birth, which, she protested, did not reach her ears till I must have
been twelve years of age; but Monsieur Duval, who, she declared,
was the worst husband in the world, would not permit her to do any
thing she wished: he had been dead but three months, which had
been employed in arranging certain affairs, that were no sooner settled, than she set off for England. She was already out of mourning,[6]
for she said nobody here could tell how long she had been a widow.

She must have been married very early in life; what her age is, I do
not know, but she really looks to be less than fifty. She dresses very
gaily, paints very high,[7] and the traces of former beauty are still very
visible in her face.

I know not, when, or how, this visit would have ended, had not
the Captain called for Mrs. Mirvan, and absolutely insisted upon my
attending her. He is become, very suddenly, so warmly my friend,
that I quite dread his officiousness. Mrs. Mirvan, however, whose
principal study seems to be healing those wounds which her husband
inflicts, appeased Madame Duval's wrath, by a very polite invitation
to drink tea and spend the evening here. Not without great difficulty
was the Captain prevailed upon to defer his journey some time
longer; but what could be done? it would have been indecent for me
to have quitted town the very instant I discovered that Madame
Duval was in it; and to have stayed here solely under her protection —
Mrs. Mirvan, thank Heaven, was too kind for such a thought. That she
should follow us to Howard Grove, I almost equally dreaded; it is,
therefore, determined that we remain in London for some days, or a
week: though the Captain has declared that the *old French hag*, as he is
pleased to call her, shall fare never the better for it.

---

[6] *mourning:* It was customary for the upper and middle classes to wear specially
made, dark clothes, often of silk, for a considerable period of time after the death of a
close family member.

[7] *paints very high:* Rouge and white lead powder, among other cosmetics, were
commonly used to enhance both male and female appearance, but the older woman
who used a lot of rouge was a negative stereotype indicating a ridiculous, sexually
predatory female.

My only hope, is to get safe to Berry Hill; where, counselled and sheltered by you, I shall have nothing more to fear. Adieu, my ever dear and most honoured Sir! I shall have no happiness till I am again with you!

## LETTER XV

### Mr. Villars to Evelina

Berry Hill, April 16.

In the belief and hope that my Evelina would ere now have bid adieu to London, I had intended to have deferred writing, till I heard of her return to Howard Grove; but the letter I have this moment received, with intelligence of Madame Duval's arrival in England, demands an immediate answer.

Her journey hither equally grieves and alarms me: how much did I pity my child, when I read of a discovery at once so unexpected and unwished! I have long dreaded this meeting and its consequence; to claim you, seems naturally to follow acknowledging you: I am well acquainted with her disposition, and have for many years foreseen the contest which now threatens us.

Cruel as are the circumstances of this affair, you must not, my love, suffer it to depress your spirits; remember, that while life is lent me, I will devote it to your service; and, for future time, I will make such provision as shall seem to me most conducive to your future happiness. Secure of my protection, and relying on my tenderness, let no apprehensions of Madame Duval disturb your peace; conduct yourself towards her with all the respect and deference due to so near a relation, remembering always, that the failure of duty on her part, can by no means justify any neglect on yours: indeed, the more forcibly you are struck with improprieties and misconduct in another, the greater should be your observance and diligence to avoid even the shadow of similar errors. Be careful, therefore, that no remissness of attention, no indifference of obliging, make known to her the independence I assure you of; but when she fixes the time for her leaving England, trust to me the task of refusing your attending her: disagreeable to myself I own it will be, yet to you, it would be improper, if not impossible.

In regard to her opinion of me, I am more sorry than surprised at her determined blindness; the palliation, which she feels the want of, for her own conduct, leads her to seek for failings in all who were concerned in those unhappy transactions which she has so much reason to lament. And this, as it is the cause, so we must, in some measure, consider it as the excuse of her inveteracy.

How grateful to me are your wishes to return to Berry Hill! your lengthened stay in London, and the dissipation in which I find you are involved, fill me with uneasiness: I mean not, however, that I would have you sequester yourself from the party to which you belong, since Mrs. Mirvan might thence infer a reproof which your youth and her kindness would render inexcusable. I will not, therefore, enlarge upon this subject, but content myself with telling you, that I shall heartily rejoice when I hear of your safe arrival at Howard Grove, for which place I hope you will be preparing at the time you receive this letter.

I cannot too much thank you, my best Evelina, for the minuteness of your communications; continue to me this indulgence, for I should be miserable if in ignorance of your proceedings.

How new to you is the scene of life in which you are now engaged, — balls — plays — operas — ridottos — Ah, my child! at your return hither, how will you bear the change? My heart trembles for your future tranquility. — Yet I will hope every thing from the unsullied whiteness of your soul, and the native liveliness of your disposition.

I am sure I need not say, how much more I was pleased with the mistakes of your inexperience at the private ball, than with the attempted adoption of more fashionable manners at the ridotto. But your confusion and mortifications were such as to entirely silence all reproofs on my part.

I hope you will see no more of Sir Clement Willoughby, whose conversation and boldness are extremely disgustful to me. I was gratified by the good-nature of Lord Orville, upon your making use of his name, but I hope you will never again put it to such a trial.

Heaven bless thee, my dear child, and grant that neither misfortune nor vice may ever rob thee of that gaiety of heart which, resulting from innocence, while it constitutes your own, contributes also to the felicity of all who know you!

ARTHUR VILLARS

## LETTER XVI

### Evelina to the Rev. Mr. Villars

Queen-Ann-street, Thursday morning, April 14.

Before our dinner was over yesterday, Madame Duval came to tea: though it will lessen your surprise, to hear that it was near five o'clock, for we never dine till the day is almost over.[1] She was asked into another room, while the table was cleared, and then was invited to partake of the desert.

She was attended by a French gentleman, whom she introduced by the name of Monsieur Du Bois:[2] Mrs. Mirvan received them both with her usual politeness; but the Captain looked very much displeased, and, after a short silence, very sternly said to Madame Duval, "Pray who asked you to bring that there spark with you?"

"O," cried she, "I never go no-where without him."

Another short silence ensued, which was terminated by the Captain's turning roughly to the foreigner, and saying, "Do you know, Monsieur, that you're the first Frenchman I ever let come into my house?"

Monsieur Du Bois made a profound bow. He speaks no English, and understands it so imperfectly, that he might, possibly, imagine he had received a compliment.

Mrs. Mirvan endeavoured to divert the Captain's ill-humour, by starting new subjects; but he left to her all the trouble of supporting them, and leant back in his chair in gloomy silence, except when any opportunity offered of uttering some sarcasm upon the French. Finding her efforts to render the evening agreeable were fruitless, Mrs. Mirvan proposed a party to Ranelagh. Madame Duval joyfully consented to it, and the Captain, tho' he railed against the dissipation of the women, did not oppose it, and therefore Maria and I ran up stairs to dress ourselves.

Before we were ready, word was brought us, that Sir Clement Willoughby was in the drawing-room. He introduced himself under the pretence of enquiring after all our healths, and entered the room

---

[1] *we never dine till the day is almost over:* Tea, often a substantial meal in eighteenth-century London, was commonly served in the early evening, while dinner, the heavy meal of the day, was served at midday. Evelina's late, town hours move this schedule back by several hours, so that dinner might occur at the usual hour for tea.

[2] *Du Bois:* The maiden name of Burney's French grandmother.

with the easy air of an old acquaintance; though Mrs. Mirvan con-
fesses that he seemed embarrassed, when he found how coldly he was
received, not only by the Captain, but by herself.

I was extremely disconcerted at the thoughts of seeing this man
again, and did not go down stairs till I was called to tea. He was then
deeply engaged in a discourse upon French manners with Madame
Duval and the Captain, and the subject seemed so entirely to engross
him, that he did not, at first, observe my entrance into the room.
Their conversation was supported with great vehemence; the Captain
roughly maintaining the superiority of the English in every particular,
and Madame Duval warmly refusing to allow of it in any; while Sir
Clement exerted all his powers of argument and of ridicule to second
and strengthen whatever was advanced by the Captain: for he had
the sagacity to discover, that he could take no method so effectual for
making the master of the house his friend, as to make Madame Duval
his enemy: and indeed, in a very short time, he had reason to congratulate himself upon his successful discernment.

As soon as he saw me, he made a most respectful bow, and hoped
I had not suffered from the fatigue of the ridotto: I made no other answer than a slight inclination of the head, for I was very much
ashamed of that whole affair. He then returned to the disputants,
where he managed the argument so skilfully, at once provoking
Madame Duval, and delighting the Captain, that I could not forbear
admiring his address, though I condemned his subtlety. Mrs. Mirvan,
dreading such violent antagonists, attempted frequently to change the
subject; and she might have succeeded, but for the interposition of Sir
Clement, who would not suffer it to be given up, and supported it
with such humour and satire, that he seems to have won the Captain's heart; though their united forces so enraged and overpowered
Madame Duval, that she really trembled with passion.

I was very glad when Mrs. Mirvan said it was time to be gone. Sir
Clement arose to take leave; but the Captain very cordially invited
him to join our party: he *had* an engagement, he said, but would give
it up to have that pleasure.

Some little confusion ensued in regard to our manner of setting
off: Mrs. Mirvan offered Madame Duval a place in her coach, and
proposed that we four females should go all together: however, this
she rejected, declaring she would by no means go so far without a
gentleman, and wondering so polite a lady could make *so English* a
proposal. Sir Clement Willoughby said his chariot was waiting at the

door, and begged to know if it could be of any use. It was, at last, decided, that a hackney-coach[3] should be called for Monsieur Du Bois
and Madame Duval, in which the Captain, and, at his request, Sir
Clement, went also; Mrs. and Miss Mirvan and I had a peaceful and
comfortable ride by ourselves.

I don't doubt but they quarrelled all the way; for when we met at
Ranelagh, every one seemed out of humour: and, though we joined
parties, poor Madame Duval was avoided as much as possible by all
but me, and I did not dare quit her for an instant; indeed I believe she
was resolved I should not, for she leant upon my arm almost all the
evening.

The room was so very much crowded, that, but for the uncommon
assiduity of Sir Clement Willoughby, we should not have been able to
procure a box (which is the name given to the arched recesses which
are appropriated for tea-parties) till half the company had retired. As
we were taking possession of our places, some ladies of Mrs. Mirvan's acquaintance stopped to speak to her, and persuaded her to
*take a round* with them.[4] When she returned to us, what was my surprise, to see that Lord Orville had joined her party! The ladies walked
on; Mrs. Mirvan seated herself, and made a slight, though respectful,
invitation to Lord Orville to drink his tea with us, which, to my no
small consternation, he accepted.

I felt a confusion unspeakable at again seeing him, from the recollection of the ridotto adventure: nor did my situation lessen it, for I
was seated between Madame Duval and Sir Clement, who seemed as
little as myself to desire Lord Orville's presence. Indeed, the continual
wrangling and ill-breeding of Captain Mirvan and Madame Duval,
made me blush that I belonged to them. And poor Mrs. Mirvan and
her amiable daughter had still less reason to be satisfied.

A general silence ensued after he was seated: his appearance, from
different motives, gave a universal restraint to every body. What his
own reasons were for honouring us with his company, I cannot imag-

---

[3] *hackney-coach:* One of the innovations of travel in eighteenth-century London
was the hackney-coach, a closed carriage drawn by two horses and available for private hire. This conveyance made it possible for anyone with the fairly moderate rental
fee to travel in some style, without the expense of maintaining a coach. Sir Clement
keeps his own chariot, a closed carriage with seating for only two people. A private
coach, such as that kept by Lord Orville, was a roomier vehicle with seating for up to
six people and drawn by four horses.
[4] *take a round with them:* To stroll around, with the intent to see and be seen by
others of one's acquaintance.

ine, unless, indeed, he had a curiosity to know whether I should invent any new impertinence concerning him.

The first speech was made by Madame Duval, who said, "It's quite a shocking thing to see ladies come to so genteel a place as Ranelagh with hats on; it has a monstrous vulgar look: I can't think what they wear them for. There's no such a thing to be seen in Paris."

"Indeed," cried Sir Clement, "I must own myself no advocate for hats; I am sorry the ladies ever invented or adopted so tantalizing a fashion; for, where there is beauty, they only serve to shade it, and where there is none, to excite a most unavailing curiosity. I fancy they were originally worn by some young and whimsical coquet."

"More likely," answered the Captain, "they were invented by some wrinkled old hag, who'd a mind for to keep the young fellows in chace, let them be never so weary."

"I don't know what you may do in England," cried Madame Duval, "but I know in Paris no woman need n't be at such a trouble as that, to be taken very genteel notice of."

"Why, will you pretend for to say," returned the Captain, "that they don't distinguish the old from the young there as well as here?"

"They don't make no distinguishments at all," said she; "they're vastly too polite."

"More fools they!" said the Captain, sneeringly.

"Would to Heaven," cried Sir Clement, "that, for our own sakes, we Englishmen too were blest with so accommodating a blindness!"

"Why the devil do you make such a prayer as that?" demanded the Captain: "them are the first foolish words I've heard you speak; but I suppose you're not much used to that sort of work. Did you ever make a prayer before, since you were a sniveler?"

"Ay, now," cried Madame Duval, "that's another of the unpolitenesses of you English, to go to talking of such things as that: now in Paris, nobody never says nothing about religion, no more than about politics."

"Why then," answered he, "it's a sign they take no more care of their souls, than of their country, and so both one and t'other go to old Nick."[5]

"Well, if they do," said she, "who's the worse, so long as they don't say nothing about it? it's the tiresomest thing in the world to be always talking of them sort of things, and nobody that's ever been abroad troubles their heads about them."

---

[5] old Nick: The devil.

"Pray then," cried the Captain, "since you know so much of the matter, be so good as to tell us what they *do* trouble their heads about? — hay, Sir Clement! ha'n't we a right to know that much?"

"A very comprehensive question," said Sir Clement, "and I expect much instruction from the lady's answer."

"Come, Madam," continued the Captain, "never flinch; speak at once; don't stop for thinking."

"I assure you I am not going," answered she; "for as to what they *do* do, why they've enough to do, I promise you, what with one thing or another."

"But *what, what* do they do, these famous Monsieurs?" demanded the Captain; "can't you tell us? do they game?[6] — or drink? — or fiddle? — or are they jockies? — or do they spend all their time in flummering[7] old women?"

"As to that, Sir, — but indeed I sha'n't trouble myself to answer such a parcel of low questions, so don't ask me no more about it." And then, to my great vexation, turning to Lord Orville, she said, "Pray, Sir, was you ever in Paris?"

He only bowed.

"And pray, Sir, how did you like it?"

This *comprehensive* question, as Sir Clement would have called it, though it made him smile, also made him hesitate; however, his answer was expressive of his approbation.

"I thought you would like it, Sir, because you look so like a gentleman. As to the Captain, and as to that other gentleman, why they may very well not like what they don't know: for I suppose, Sir, you was never abroad?"

"Only three years, Ma'am," answered Sir Clement, drily.

"Well, that's very surprising! I should never have thought it: however, I dare say you only kept company with the English."

"Why pray, who *should* he keep company with?" cried the Captain: "what, I suppose you'd have him ashamed of his own nation, like some other people, not a thousand miles off, on purpose to make his own nation ashamed of him."

"I'm sure it wou'd be a very good thing if you'd go abroad yourself."

"How will you make out that, hay, Madam? come, please to tell me, where would be the good of that?"

---

[6] *game:* Gamble.
[7] *flummering:* Deceiving, making fools of.

"Where! why a great deal. They'd make quite another person of you."

"What, I suppose you'd have me learn to cut capers? — and dress like a monkey? — and palaver in French gibberish? — hay, would you? — And powder, and daub, and make myself up, like some other folks?"

"I would have you learn to be more politer, Sir, and not to talk to ladies in such a rude, old-fashion way as this. You, Sir, as have been in Paris" (again addressing herself to Lord Orville) "can tell this English gentleman how he'd be despised, if he was to talk in such an ungenteel manner as this, before any foreigners. Why there is n't a hair-dresser, nor a shoe-maker, nor nobody, that would n't blush to be in your company."

"Why look ye, Madam," answered the Captain, "as to your hair-pinchers and shoe-blacks, you may puff off[8] their manners, and welcome; and I am heartily glad you like 'em so well; but as to me, since you must needs make so free of your advice, I must e'en tell you, I never kept company with any such gentry."

"Come, ladies and gentlemen," said Mrs. Mirvan, "as many of you as have done tea, I invite to walk with me." Maria and I started up instantly; Lord Orville followed; and I question whether we were not half round the room ere the angry disputants knew that we had left the box.

As the husband of Mrs. Mirvan had borne so large a share in this disagreeable altercation, Lord Orville forbore to make any comments upon it; so that the subject was immediately dropt, and the conversation became calmly sociable, and politely chearful, and, to every body but me, must have been highly agreeable: — but, as to myself, I was so eagerly desirous of making some apology to Lord Orville for the impertinence of which he must have thought me guilty at the ridotto, and yet so utterly unable to assume sufficient courage to speak to him concerning an affair in which I had so terribly exposed myself, that I hardly ventured to say a word all the time we were walking. Besides, the knowledge of his contemptuous opinion, haunted and dispirited me, and made me fear he might possibly misconstrue whatever I should say. So that, far from enjoying a conversation that might, at any other time, have delighted me, I continued silent, uncomfortable, and ashamed. O Sir, shall I ever again involve myself in so foolish an

---

[8] *puff off:* Boast of.

embarrassment? I am sure that if I do, I shall deserve yet greater mortification.

We were not joined by the rest of the party till we had taken three or four turns round the room, and then, they were so quarrelsome, that Mrs. Mirvan complained of being fatigued, and proposed going home. No one dissented. Lord Orville joined another party, having first made an offer of his services, which the gentlemen declined, and we proceeded to an outward room, where we waited for the carriages. It was settled that we should return to town in the same manner we came to Ranelagh, and, accordingly, Monsieur Du Bois handed Madame Duval into a hackney-coach, and was just preparing to follow her, when she screamed, and jumpt hastily out, declaring she was wet through all her clothes. Indeed, upon examination, the coach was found to be in a dismal condition; for the weather proved very bad, and the rain had, though I know not how, made its way into the carriage.

Mrs. and Miss Mirvan, and myself, were already disposed of as before; but no sooner did the Captain hear this account, than, without any ceremony, he was so civil as to immediately take possession of the vacant seat in his own coach, leaving Madame Duval and Monsieur Du Bois to take care of themselves. As to Sir Clement Willoughby, his own chariot was in waiting.

I instantly begged permission to offer Madame Duval my own place, and made a motion to get out; but Mrs. Mirvan stopped me, saying that I should then be obliged to return to town with only the foreigner, or Sir Clement.

"O never mind the old Beldame," cried the Captain, "she's weather-proof, I'll answer for her; and besides, as we are all, I hope, *English*, why she'll meet with no worse than she expects from us."

"I do not mean to defend her," said Mrs. Mirvan; "but indeed, as she belongs to our party, we cannot, with any decency, leave the place, till she is, by some means, accommodated."

"Lord, my dear," cried the Captain, whom the distress of Madame Duval had put into very good humour, "why she'll break her heart, if she meets with any civility from a filthy Englishman."

Mrs. Mirvan, however, prevailed, and we all got out of the coach, to wait till Madame Duval could meet with some better carriage. We found her, attended by Monsieur Du Bois, standing amongst the servants, and very busy in wiping her negligee,[9] and endeavouring to

---

[9] *negligee:* A loose gown, fashionable in the eighteenth century.

save it from being stained by the wet, as she said it was a new Lyon's silk. Sir Clement Willoughby offered her the use of his chariot, but she had been too much piqued by his raillery to accept it. We waited some time, but in vain, for no hackney-coach could be procured. The Captain, at last, was persuaded to accompany Sir Clement himself, and we four females were handed into Mrs. Mirvan's carriage, though not before Madame Duval had insisted upon our making room for Monsieur Du Bois, to which the Captain only consented in preference to being incommoded by him in Sir Clement's chariot.

Our party drove off first. We were silent and unsociable; for the difficulties attending this arrangement had made every one languid and fatigued. Unsociable, I must own, we continued; but very short was the duration of our silence, as we had not proceeded thirty yards, ere every voice was heard at once, — for the coach broke down! I suppose we concluded of course, that we were all half killed, by the violent shrieks that seemed to come from every mouth. The chariot was stopped, the servants came to our assistance, and we were all taken out of the carriage, without having been at all hurt. The night was dark and wet; but I had scarce touched the ground, when I was lifted suddenly from it, by Sir Clement Willoughby, who begged permission to assist me, though he did not wait it have it granted, but carried me in his arms back to Ranelagh.

He enquired very earnestly if I was not hurt by the accident? I assured him I was perfectly safe, and free from injury, and desired he would leave me, and return to the rest of the party, for I was very uneasy to know whether they had been equally fortunate. He told me he was happy in being honoured with my commands, and would joyfully execute them; but insisted upon first conducting me to a warm room, as I had not wholly escaped being wet. He did not regard my objections, but made me follow him to an apartment, where we found an excellent fire, and some company waiting for carriages. I readily accepted a seat, and then begged he would go.

And go, indeed, he did; but he returned in a moment, telling me that the rain was more violent than ever, and that he had sent his servants to offer their assistance, and acquaint *the Mirvans* of my situation. I was very mad that he would not go himself; but as my acquaintance with him was so very slight, I did not think proper to urge him contrary to his inclination.

Well, he drew a chair close to mine, and, after again enquiring how I did, said, in a low voice, "You will pardon me, Miss Anville, if the eagerness I feel to vindicate myself, induces me to snatch this opportunity of making sincere acknowledgments for the impertinence with which I tormented you at the last ridotto. I can assure you, Madam, I have been a true and sorrowful penitent ever since; but — shall I tell you honestly what encouraged me to —— ."

He stopt; but I said nothing, for I thought instantly of the conversation Miss Mirvan had overheard, and supposed he was going to tell me himself what part Lord Orville had borne in it; and really I did not wish to hear it repeated. Indeed, the rest of his speech convinces me that such was his intention; with what view, I know not, except to make a merit of his defending me.

"And yet," he continued, "my excuse may only expose my own credulity, and want of judgment and penetration. I will, therefore, merely beseech your pardon, and hope that some future time —— "

Just then, the door was opened by Sir Clement's servant, and I had the pleasure of seeing the Captain, Mrs. and Miss Mirvan, enter the room.

"O ho," cried the former, "you have got a good warm birth here; but we shall beat up your quarters.[10] Here, Lucy, Moll, come to the fire, and dry your trumpery. But, hey-day, — why where's old Madam French?"

"Good God," cried I, "is not Madame Duval then with you?"

"With me! No, — thank God."

I was very uneasy to know what might have become of her, and, if they would have suffered me, I should have gone out in search of her myself; but all the servants were dispatched to find her, and the Captain said we might be very sure her *French beau* would take care of her.

We waited some time without any tidings, and were soon the only party in the room. My uneasiness encreased so much, that Sir Clement now made a voluntary offer of seeking her. However, the same moment that he opened the door with this design, she presented herself at it, attended by Monsieur Du Bois.

"I was this instant, Madam," said he, "coming to see for you."

"You are mighty good, truly," cried she, "to come when all the mischief's over."

She then entered, — in such a condition! — entirely covered with mud, and in so great a rage, it was with difficulty she could speak. We all expressed our concern, and offered our assistance, — except

---

[10] *beat up your quarters:* To unceremoniously join Evelina in her place by the fire. An example of the Captain's nautical jargon.

the Captain; who no sooner beheld her, than he burst into a loud laugh.

We endeavoured, by our enquiries and condolements, to prevent her attending to him; and she was, for some time, so wholly engrossed by her anger and her distress, that we succeeded without much trouble. We begged her to inform us how this accident had happened. "How!" repeated she, — why "it was all along of your all going away, — and there poor Monsieur Du Bois — but it was n't his fault, — for he's as bad off as me."

All eyes were then turned to Monsieur Du Bois, whose clothes were in the same miserable plight with those of Madame Duval, and who, wet, shivering, and disconsolate, had crept to the fire.

The Captain laughed yet more heartily; while Mrs. Mirvan, ashamed of his rudeness, repeated her enquiries to Madame Duval; who answered, "Why, as we were a-coming along, all in the rain, Monsieur Du Bois was so obliging, though I'm sure it was an unlucky obligingness for me, as to lift me up in his arms, to carry me over a place that was ancle-deep in mud; but instead of my being ever the better for it, just as we were in the worst part, — I'm sure I wish we had been fifty miles off, — for, somehow or other, his foot slipt, — at least, I suppose so, — though I can't think how it happened, for I'm no such great weight, — but, however that was, down we both came together, all in the mud; and the more we tried to get up, the more deeper we got covered with the nastiness, — and my new Lyon's negligee, too, quite spoilt! — however, it's well we got up at all, for we might have laid there till now, for aught you all cared; for nobody never came near us."

This recital put the Captain into an extacy; he went from the lady to the gentleman, and from the gentleman to the lady, to enjoy alternately the sight of their distress. He really shouted with pleasure; and, shaking Monsieur Du Bois strenuously by the hand, wished him joy of having *touched English ground;* and then he held a candle to Madame Duval, that he might have a more complete view of her disaster, declaring repeatedly, that he had never been better pleased in his life.

The rage of poor Madame Duval was unspeakable; she dashed the candle out of his hand, stamped upon the floor, and, at last, spat in his face.

This action seemed immediately to calm them both, as the joy of the Captain was converted into resentment, and the wrath of Madame Duval into fear; for he put his hands upon her shoulders, and gave her so violent a shake, that she screamed out for help; assuring her, at the same time, that if she had been one ounce less old, or less ugly, she should have had it all returned on her own face.

Monsieur Du Bois, who had seated himself very quietly at the fire, approached them, and expostulated very warmly with the Captain; but he was neither understood nor regarded, and Madame Duval was not released, till she quite sobbed with passion.

When they were parted, I entreated her to permit the woman who has the charge of the ladies cloaks to assist in drying her clothes; she consented, and we did what was possible to save her from catching cold. We were obliged to wait in this disagreeable situation near an hour, ere a hackney-coach could be found; and then we were disposed in the same manner as before our accident.

I am going this morning to see poor Madame Duval, and to enquire after her health, which I think must have suffered by her last night's misfortunes; though, indeed, she seems to be naturally strong and hearty.

Adieu, my dear Sir, till to-morrow.


## LETTER XVII

### Evelina in Continuation

Friday Morning, April 15.
Sir Clement Willoughby called here yesterday at noon, and Captain Mirvan invited him to dinner. For my part, I spent the day in a manner the most uncomfortable imaginable.

I found Madame Duval at breakfast in bed, though Monsieur Du Bois was in the chamber; which so much astonished me, that I was, involuntarily, retiring, without considering how odd an appearance my retreat would have, when Madame Duval called me back, and laughed very heartily at my ignorance of foreign customs.

The conversation, however, very soon took a more serious turn; for she began, with great bitterness, to inveigh against the *barbarous brutality of that fellow the Captain*, and the horrible ill-breeding of the English in general, declaring she should make her escape with all expedition from so *beastly a nation*. [But nothing can be more strangely absurd, than to hear politeness recommended in language so repugnant to it as that of Madame Duval.]

She lamented, very mournfully, the fate of her Lyon's silk, and protested she had rather have parted with all the rest of her wardrobe, because it was the first gown she had bought to wear upon leaving off her weeds.[1] She has a very bad cold, and Monsieur Du Bois is so hoarse, he can hardly speak.

She insisted upon my staying with her all day, as she intended, she said, to introduce me to some of my own relations. I would very fain have excused myself, but she did not allow me any choice.

Till the arrival of these relations, one continued series of questions on her side, and of answers on mine, filled up all the time we passed together. Her curiosity was insatiable; she enquired into every action of my life, and every particular that had fallen under my observation, in the lives of all I knew. Again, she was so cruel as to avow the most inveterate rancour against the sole benefactor her deserted child and grand-child have met with; and such was the indignation her ingratitude raised, that I would actually have quitted her presence and house, had she not, in a manner the most peremptory, absolutely forbid me. But what, good Heaven! can induce her to such shocking injustice? O my friend and father! I have no command of myself when this subject is started.

She talked very much of taking me to Paris, and said I greatly wanted the polish of a French education. She lamented that I had been brought up in the country, which, she observed, had given me a very *bumpkinish air*. However, she bid me not despair, for she had known many girls, much worse than me, who had become very fine ladies after a few years residence abroad; and she particularly instanced a Miss Polly Moore, daughter of a chandler's-shop[2] woman, who, by an accident not worth relating, happened to be sent to Paris, where, from an awkward, ill-bred girl, she so much improved, that she has since been taken for a woman of quality.

The relations to whom she was pleased to introduce me, consisted of a Mr. Branghton, who is her nephew, and three of his children, the eldest of which is a son, and the two younger are daughters.

Mr. Branghton appears about forty years of age. He does not seem to want a common understanding, though he is very contracted and prejudiced: he has spent his whole time in the city,[3] and I believe feels a great contempt for all who reside elsewhere.

---

[1] *weeds:* Mourning dress for a widow.
[2] *chandler's-shop:* A shop where candles are made and sold.
[3] *he has spent his whole time in the city:* "City" here refers to the old, walled city of London that was, at the time of *Evelina*'s writing, the commercial center of the city. Branghton's association with the city underscores his mercantile, practical, unfashionable interests.

His son seems weaker in his understanding, and more gay in his temper; but his gaiety is that of a foolish, over-grown school-boy, whose mirth consists in noise and disturbance. He disdains his father for his close attention to business, and love of money, though he seems himself to have no talents, spirit, or generosity, to make him superior to either. His chief delight appears to be tormenting and ridiculing his sisters, who, in return, most heartily despise him.

Miss Branghton, the eldest daughter, is by no means ugly, but looks proud, ill-tempered, and conceited. She hates the city, though without knowing why; for it is easy to discover she has lived no where else.

Miss Polly Branghton is rather pretty, very foolish, very ignorant, very giddy, and, I believe, very good-natured.

The first half hour was allotted to *making themselves comfortable,* for they complained of having had a very dirty walk, as they came on foot from Snow Hill, where Mr. Branghton keeps a silver-smith's shop;[4] and the young ladies had not only their coats to brush, and shoes to dry, but to adjust their head-dress, which their bonnets had totally discomposed.

The manner in which Madame Duval was pleased to introduce me to this family, extremely shocked me. "Here, my dears," said she, "here's a relation you little thought of; but you must know my poor daughter Caroline had this child after she run away from me, — though I never knew nothing of it, not I, for a long while after; for they took care to keep it a secret from me; though the poor child has never a friend in the world besides."

"Miss seems very tender-hearted, aunt," said Miss Polly, "and to be sure she's not to blame for her mama's undutifulness, for she could n't help it."

"Lord no," answered she, "and I never took no notice of it to her; for indeed, as to that, my own poor daughter was n't so much to blame as you may think, for she'd never have gone astray, if it had not been for that meddling old parson I told you of."

"If aunt pleases," said young Mr. Branghton, "we'll talk o' somewhat else, for Miss looks very uneasy-like."

The next subject that was chosen, was the age of the three young Branghtons and myself. The son is twenty; the daughters, upon hear-

---

[4] *Snow Hill . . . silver-smith's shop:* The address, a winding, narrow street in London, and vocation identify the Branghtons as moderately well-off shopkeepers, a far cry, in class terms, from the noble Orville or even the baronet, Sir Clement Willoughby.

ing that I was seventeen, said that was just the age of Miss Polly; but their brother, after a long dispute, proved that she was two years older, to the great anger of both sisters, who agreed that he was very ill-natured and spiteful.

When this point was settled, the question was put, Which was tallest? — We were desired to measure, as the Branghtons were all of different opinions. They, none of them, however, disputed my being the tallest in the company, but, in regard to one another, they were extremely quarrelsome: the brother insisted upon their measuring *fair*, and not with *heads* and *heels;*[5] but they would by no means consent to lose these privileges of our sex, and therefore the young man was *cast*, as shortest; though he appealed to all present upon the injustice of the decree.

This ceremony over, the young ladies began, very freely, to examine my dress, and to interrogate me concerning it. "This apron's your own work, I suppose, Miss? but these sprigs[6] a'n't in fashion now. Pray, if it is not impertinent, what might you give a yard for this lutestring?[7] — Do you make your own caps, Miss? — " and many other questions equally interesting and well-bred.

They then asked me *how I liked London?* and whether I should not think the country a very *dull place*, when I returned thither? "Miss must try if she can't get a good husband," said Mr. Branghton, "and then she may stay and live here."

The next topic was public places, or rather the theatres, for they knew of no other; and the merits and defects of all the actors and actresses were discussed: the young man here took the lead, and seemed to be very conversant on the subject. But, during this time, what was my concern, and, suffer me to add, my indignation, when I found, by some words I occasionally heard, that Madame Duval was entertaining Mr. Branghton with all the most secret and cruel particulars of my situation! The eldest daughter was soon drawn to them by the recital; the youngest and the son still kept their places, intending, I believe, to divert me, though the conversation was all their own.

In a few minutes, Miss Branghton, coming suddenly up to her sister, exclaimed, "Lord, Polly, only think! Miss never saw her papa!"

"Lord, how odd!" cried the other; "why then, Miss, I suppose you would n't know him?"

---

[5] *heads and heels:* Fashionable female footwear and hairdressing gave women a considerable height advantage over most men. See footnote 9 to Volume I, Letter X.

[6] *sprigs:* A design stamped or embroidered on fabric.

[7] *lutestring:* A silk fabric.

This was quite too much for me; I rose hastily, and ran out of the room: but I soon regretted I had so little command of myself, for the two sisters both followed, and insisted upon comforting me, notwithstanding my earnest entreaties to be left alone.

As soon as I returned to the company, Madame Duval said, "Why, my dear, what was the matter with you? why did you run away so?"

This question almost made me run again, for I knew not how to answer it. But is it not very extraordinary, that she can put me in situations so shocking, and then wonder to find me sensible of any concern?

Mr. Branghton junior now enquired of me, whether I had seen the Tower, or St. Paul's church? and, upon my answering in the negative, they proposed making a party to shew them to me. Among other questions, they also asked if I had ever seen *such a thing as an Opera?* I told them I had. "Well," said Mr. Branghton, "I never saw one in my life, so long as I've lived in London, and I never desire to see one, if I live here as much longer."

"Lord, Papa," cried Miss Polly, "why not? you might as well for once, for the curiosity of the thing: besides, Miss Pomfret saw one, and she says it was very pretty."

"Miss will think us very vulgar," said Miss Branghton, "to live in London, and never have been to an Opera; but it's no fault of mine, I assure you, Miss, only Papa don't like to go."

The result was, that a party was proposed, and agreed to, for some early opportunity. I did not dare oppose them; but I said that my time, while I remained in town, was at the disposal of Mrs. Mirvan. However, I am sure I will not attend them, if I can possibly avoid so doing.

When we parted, Madame Duval desired to see me the next day; and the Branghtons told me, that the first time I went towards Snow Hill, they should be very glad if I would call upon them.

I wish we may not meet again till that time arrives.

I am sure I shall not be very ambitious of being known to any more of my relations, if they have any resemblance to those whose acquaintance I have been introduced to already.


## LETTER XVIII

### Evelina in Continuation

I had just finished my letter to you this morning, when a violent rapping at the door made me run down stairs; and who should I see in the drawing-room, but — Lord Orville!

He was quite alone, for the family had not assembled to breakfast. He enquired, first of mine, then of the health of Mrs. and Miss Mirvan, with a degree of concern that rather surprised me, till he said that he had just been informed of the accident we had met with at Ranelagh. He expressed his sorrow upon the occasion with the utmost politeness, and lamented that he had not been so fortunate as to hear of it in time to offer his services. "But, I think," he added, "Sir Clement Willoughby had the honour of assisting you?"

"He was with Captain Mirvan, my Lord."

"I had heard of his being of your party."

I hope that flighty man has not been telling Lord Orville he only assisted *me?* however, he did not pursue the subject, but said, "This accident, though extremely unfortunate, will not, I hope, be the means of frightening you from gracing Ranelagh with your presence in future?"

"Our time, my Lord, for London, is almost expired already."

"Indeed! do you leave town so very soon?"

"O yes, my Lord, our stay has already exceeded our intentions."

"Are you, then, so particularly partial to the country?"

"We merely came to town, my Lord, to meet Captain Mirvan."

"And does Miss Anville feel no concern at the idea of the many mourners her absence will occasion?"

"O, my Lord, — I'm sure you don't think — " I stopt there, for, indeed, I hardly knew what I was going to say. My foolish embarrassment, I suppose, was the cause of what followed; — for he came to me, and took my hand, saying, "I *do* think, that whoever has once seen Miss Anville, must receive an impression never to be forgotten."

This compliment, — from Lord Orville, — so surprised me, that I could not speak; but felt myself change colour, and stood, for some moments, silent and looking down: however, the instant I recollected my situation, I withdrew my hand, and told him that I would see if Mrs. Mirvan was not dressed. He did not oppose me, so away I went.

I met them all on the stairs, and returned with them to breakfast.

I have since been extremely angry with myself for neglecting so excellent an opportunity of apologizing for my behaviour at the Ridotto: but, to own the truth, that affair never once occurred to me during the short *tête-à-tête* which we had together. But, if ever we should happen to be so situated again, I will certainly mention it; for I am inexpressibly concerned at the thought of his harbouring an opinion that I am bold or impertinent, and I could almost kill myself for having given him the shadow of a reason for so shocking an idea.

But was it not very odd, that he should make me such a compliment? I expected it not from him; — but gallantry, I believe, is common to all men, whatever other qualities they may have in particular.

Our breakfast was the most agreeable meal, if it may be called a *meal,* that we have had since we came to town. Indeed, but for Madame Duval I should like London extremely.

The conversation of Lord Orville is really delightful. His manners are so elegant, so gentle, so unassuming, that they at once engage esteem, and diffuse complacence. Far from being indolently satisfied with his own accomplishments, as I have already observed many men here are, tho' without any pretensions to his merit, he is most assiduously attentive to please and to serve all who are in his company; and, though his success is invariable, he never manifests the smallest degree of consciousness.

I could wish that *you,* my dearest Sir, knew Lord Orville, because I am sure you would love him; and I have felt that wish for no other person I have seen since I came to London. I sometimes imagine, that, when his youth is flown, his vivacity abated, and his life is devoted to retirement, he will, perhaps, resemble him whom I most love and honour. His present sweetness, politeness, and diffidence, seem to promise in future the same benevolence, dignity, and goodness. But I must not expatiate upon this subject.

When Lord Orville was gone, — and he made but a very short visit, — I was preparing, most reluctantly, to wait upon Madame Duval; but Mrs. Mirvan proposed to the Captain, that she should be invited to dinner in Queen-Ann-Street, and he readily consented, for he said he wished to ask after her Lyon's negligee.

The invitation is accepted, and we expect her every moment. But to me, it is very strange, that a woman, who is the uncontrolled mistress of her time, fortune, and actions, should chuse to expose herself voluntarily to the rudeness of a man who is openly determined to make her his sport. But she has very few acquaintance, and, I fancy, scarce knows how to employ herself.

How great is my obligation to Mrs. Mirvan, for bestowing her time in a manner so disagreeable to herself, merely to promote my happiness! every dispute in which her undeserving husband engages, is productive of pain, and uneasiness to herself; of this I am so sensible, that I even besought her not to send to Madame Duval, but she declared she could not bear to have me pass all my time, while in town, with her only. Indeed she is so infinitely kind to me, that one would think she was your daughter.

## LETTER XIX

### Evelina in Continuation

Saturday Morning, April 16.

Madame Duval was accompanied by Monsieur Du Bois. I am surprised that she should chuse to introduce him where he is so unwelcome; and, indeed, it is strange that they should be so constantly together; though I believe I should not have taken notice of it, but that Captain Mirvan is perpetually rallying me upon my *grandmama's beau.*

They were both received by Mrs. Mirvan with her usual good breeding; but the Captain, most provokingly, attacked her immediately, saying, "Now, Madam, you that have lived abroad, please to tell me this here; Which did you like best, the *warm room* at Ranelagh, or the *cold bath* you went into afterwards? though, I assure you, you look so well that I should advise you to take another dip."

"*Ma foi,* Sir," cried she, "nobody asked for your advice, so you may as well keep it to yourself: besides, it's no such great joke to be splashed, and to catch cold, and spoil all one's things, whatever you may think of it."

"*Splashed,* qhoth-a! — why I thought you were soused all over. — Come, come, don't mince the matter, never spoil a good story; you know you had n't a dry thread about you — 'Fore George, I shall never think on't without hallowing! such a poor, forlorn, draggle-tailed — *gentlewoman!* and poor Monsieur French, here, like a drowned rat, by your side! — "

"Well, the worse pickle we was in, so much the worser in you not to help us, for you knowed where we was fast enough, because, while I laid in the mud, I'm pretty sure I heard you snigger; so it's like enough you jostled us down yourself, for Monsieur Du Bois says, that he is sure he had a great jolt given him, or he should n't have fell."

The Captain laughed so immoderately, that he really gave me also a suspicion that he was not entirely innocent of the charge: however, he disclaimed it very peremptorily.

"Why then," continued she, "if you did n't do that, why did n't you come to help us?"

"Who, I? — what, do you suppose I had forgot I was an *Englishman,* a filthy, beastly *Englishman?*"

"Very well, Sir, very well; but I was a fool to expect any better, for it's all of a piece with the rest; you know you wanted to fling me out of the coach-window, the very first time ever I see you: but I'll never go to Ranelagh with you no more, that I'm resolved; for I dare say, if the horses had runn'd over me, as I laid in that nastiness, you'd never have stirred a step to save me."

"Lord, no, to be sure, Ma'am, not for the world! I know your opinion of our nation too well, to affront you by supposing a *Frenchman* would want *my* assistance to protect you. Did you think that Monsieur here, and I, had changed characters, and that he should pop you into the mud, and I help you out of it? Ha, ha, ha!"

"O, very well, Sir, laugh on, it's like your manners; however, if poor Monsieur Du Bois had n't met with that unlucky accident himself, I should n't have wanted nobody's help."

"O, I promise you, Madam, you'd never have had mine; I knew my distance better; and as to your being a little ducked, or so, why, to be sure, Monsieur and you settled that between yourselves; so it was no business of mine."

"What, then, I suppose, you want to make me believe as Monsieur Du Bois served me that trick o' purpose?"

"O' purpose! ay, certainly, who ever doubted that? Do you think a *Frenchman* ever made a blunder? If he had been some clumsy-footed *English* fellow, indeed, it might have been accidental: but what the devil signifies all your hopping and capering with your dancing-masters, if you can't balance yourselves upright?"

In the midst of this dialogue, Sir Clement Willoughby made his appearance. He affects to enter the house with the freedom of an old acquaintance, and this very *easiness*, which, to me, is astonishing, is what most particularly recommends him to the Captain. Indeed, he seems very successfully to study all the humours of that gentleman.

After having heartily welcomed him, "You are just come in time, my boy," said he, "to settle a little matter of a dispute between this here gentlewoman and I; do you know, she has been trying to persuade me, that she did not above half like the ducking Monsieur gave her t'other night?"

"I should have hoped," (said Sir Clement, with the utmost gravity) "that the friendship subsisting between that lady and gentleman, would have guarded them against any actions professedly disagreeable to each other; but, probably, they might not have discussed the matter previously; in which case, the gentleman, I must own, seems to have been guilty of inattention, since, in my humble opinion, it was his business first to have enquired whether the lady preferred soft, or hard ground, before he dropt her."

"O very fine, Gentlemen, very fine," cried Madame Duval, "you may try to set us together by the ears as much as you will; but I'm not such an ignorant person as to be made a fool of so easily; so you need n't talk no more about it, for I sees into your designs."

Monsieur Du Bois, who was just able to discover the subject upon which the conversation turned, made his defence, in French, with great solemnity: he hoped, he said, that the company would at least acknowledge, he did not come from a nation of brutes, and consequently, that to wilfully offend any lady, was, to him, utterly impossible; but that, on the contrary, in endeavouring, as was his duty, to save and guard her, he had himself suffered, in a manner which he would forbear to relate, but which, he greatly apprehended, he should feel the ill effects of for many months; and then, with a countenance exceedingly lengthened, he added, that he hoped it would not be attributed to him as national prejudice, when he owned that he must, to the best of his memory, aver, that his unfortunate fall was owing to a sudden, but violent push, which, he was shocked to say, some malevolent person, with a design to his injury, must certainly have given him; but whether with a view to mortify him, by making him let the lady fall, or whether merely to spoil his cloaths, he could not pretend to determine.

This disputation was, at last, concluded by Mrs. Mirvan's proposing that we should all go to Cox's Museum.[1] Nobody objected, and carriages were immediately ordered.

In our way down stairs, Madame Duval, in a very passionate manner, said, "*Ma foi*, if I would n't give fifty guineas, only to know who gave us that shove!"

This Museum is very astonishing, and very superb; yet, it afforded me but little pleasure, for it is a mere show, though a wonderful one.

Sir Clement Willoughby, in our walk round the room, asked me what my opinion was of this brilliant *spectacle?*

---

[1] *Cox's Museum:* Eighteenth-century England experienced a marked expansion in popular interest in displayed collections of natural and mechanical oddities. Some of the more "scientific" collections, such as that of Sir Hans Sloane, which became the basis for the British Museum, were intended to instruct the public. Others, like Don Saltero's collection of novelties (see footnote 3 to Volume II, Letter XIII), were designed purely for entertainment. Cox's Museum specialized in mechanical creations, such as the singing birds in the pineapple described by Evelina. The first of such automata were designed by Vaucanson in France and displayed in England in the 1740s.

"It is very fine, and very ingenious," answered I, "and yet — I don't know how it is, — but I seem to miss something."

"Excellently answered!" cried he, "you have exactly defined my own feelings, tho' in a manner I should never have arrived at. But I was certain your taste was too well formed, to be pleased at the expence of your understanding."

"*Pardie,*" cried Madame Duval, "I hope you two is difficult enough! I'm sure if you don't like this, you like nothing; for it's the grandest, prettiest, finest sight that ever I see, in England."

"What," (cried the Captain, with a sneer) "I suppose this may be in your French taste? It's like enough, for it's all *kickshaw*[2] work. But, pr'ythee, friend," (turning to the person who explained the devices) "will you tell me the *use* of all this? for I'm not enough of a conjurer to find it out."

"Use, indeed!" (repeated Madame Duval disdainfully) "Lord, if every thing's to be useful! — "

"Why, Sir, as to that, Sir," said our conductor, "the ingenuity of the mechanism, — the beauty of the workmanship, — the — undoubtedly, Sir, any person of taste may easily discern the utility of such extraordinary performances."

"Why then, Sir," answered the Captain, "your person of taste must be either a coxcomb, or a Frenchman; though, for the matter of that, 'tis the same thing."

Just then, our attention was attracted by a pine-apple, which, suddenly opening, discovered a nest of birds, who immediately began to sing. "Well," cried Madame Duval, "this is prettier than all the rest! I declare, in all my travels, I never see nothing eleganter."

"Hark ye, friend," said the Captain, "hast never another pine apple?"

"Sir? — "

"Because, if thou hast, pr'ythee give it us without the birds; for, d'ye see, I'm no Frenchman, and should relish something more substantial."

This entertainment concluded with a concert of mechanical music: I cannot explain how it was produced, but the effect was pleasing. Madame Duval was in extacies; and the Captain flung himself into so many ridiculous distortions, by way of mimicking her, that he engaged the attention of all the company; and, in the midst of the per-

---

[2] *kickshaw work:* Something delicately made but trivial, a useless item.

formance of the Coronation Anthem,[3] while Madame Duval was affecting to beat time, and uttering many expressions of delight, he called suddenly for salts,[4] which a lady, apprehending some distress, politely handed to him, and which, instantly applying to the nostrils of poor Madame Duval, she involuntarily snuffed up such a quantity, that the pain and surprise made her scream aloud. When she recovered, she reproached him, with her usual vehemence; but he protested he had taken that measure out of pure friendship, as he concluded, from her raptures, that she was going into hysterics. This excuse by no means appeased her, and they had a violent quarrel; but the only effect her anger had on the Captain, was to encrease his diversion. Indeed, he laughs and talks so terribly loud in public, that he frequently makes us ashamed of belonging to him.

Madame Duval, notwithstanding her wrath, made no scruple of returning to dine in Queen-Ann-Street. Mrs. Mirvan had secured places for the play at Drury Lane Theatre, and, though ever uneasy in her company, she very politely invited Madame Duval to be of our party; however, she had a bad cold, and chose to nurse it. I was sorry for her indisposition, but I knew not how to be sorry she did not accompany us, for she is — I must not say what, but very unlike other people.

[3] *Coronation Anthem:* George Frederick Handel was commissioned to compose several of the anthems sung at the coronation of George II. *Zadok the Priest*, the most famous of these, was also performed at the coronation of George III in 1760 and became known as the Coronation Anthem.
[4] *salts:* Smelling salts; ammonia was sometimes sniffed to counter a fainting spell.

## LETTER XX

### Evelina in Continuation

Our places were in the front row of a side-box. Sir Clement Willoughby, who knew our intention, was at the door of the Theatre, and handed us from the carriage.

We had not been seated five minutes, ere Lord Orville, who we saw in the stage-box,[1] came to us; and he honoured us with his company all the evening. Miss Mirvan and I both rejoiced that Madame Duval

[1] *side-box . . . stage-box:* Box seats were, as is often the case today, the most expensive in the theater. The side-boxes were at the side of the theater, just to the front of the stage. The stage-boxes were over the front of the stage, just outside the curtain.

was absent, as we hoped for the enjoyment of some conversation, uninterrupted by her quarrels with the Captain: but I soon found that her presence would have made very little alteration, for so far was I from daring to speak, that I knew not where even to look.

The play was Love for Love,[2] and tho' it is fraught with wit and entertainment, I hope I shall never see it represented again; for it is so extremely indelicate, — to use the softest word I can, — that Miss Mirvan and I were perpetually out of countenance, and could neither make any observations ourselves, nor venture to listen to those of others. This was the more provoking, as Lord Orville was in excellent spirits, and exceedingly entertaining.

When the Play was over, I flattered myself I should be able to look about me with less restraint, as we intended to stay the Farce;[3] but the curtain had hardly dropped when the box-door opened, and in came Mr. Lovel, the man by whose foppery and impertinence I was so much teazed at the ball where I first saw Lord Orville.

I turned away my head, and began talking to Miss Mirvan, for I was desirous to avoid speaking to him; — but in vain, for as soon as he had made his compliments to Lord Orville and Sir Clement Willoughby, who returned them very coldly, he bent his head forward, and said to me, "I hope, Ma'am, you have enjoyed your health since I had the honour — I beg ten thousand pardons, but I protest I was going to say the honour of *dancing* with you — however, I mean the honour of *seeing* you dance?"

He spoke with a self-complacency that convinced me he had studied this address, by way of making reprisals for my conduct at the ball: I therefore bowed slightly, but made no answer.

---

[2] *Love for Love:* A comedy by William Congreve, first produced in 1695, which was still popular with the London theaters. In the first quarter of the eighteenth century critics and writers such as Joseph Addison and Richard Steele made a number of efforts to "reform" the sexually frank comedy of the Restoration English theater. The results of these efforts were uneven, and the new "sentimental" comedy was performed alongside late seventeenth-century favorites such as *Love for Love* throughout the century. As the difference between Lord Orville's and the ladies' responses to the play suggests, the "reform" in eighteenth-century comedy had much to do with changing attitudes towards gender and sexuality. It's not the degree of sexual explicitness in and of itself that determines a play's acceptability, so much as the degree of sexual license granted to women, in particular. Maria and Evelina, as "nice girls," are embarrassed by the humor that Lord Orville can comfortably enjoy.

[3] *to stay the Farce:* An evening at the theater included a short play, often a broad comedy, in addition to the longer theatrical presentation.

After a short silence, he again called my attention, by saying, in an easy, negligent way, "I think, Ma'am, you was never in town before?" "No, Sir."

"So I did presume. Doubtless, Ma'am, every thing must be infinitely novel to you. Our customs, our manners, and *les etiquettes de nous autres*,[4] can have very little resemblance to those you have been used to. I imagine, Ma'am, your retirement is at no very small distance from the capital?"

I was so much disconcerted at this sneering speech, that I said not a word; though I have since thought my vexation both stimulated and delighted him.

"The air we breathe here, however, Ma'am," (continued he, very conceitedly) "though foreign to that you have been accustomed to, has not, I hope, been at variance with your health?"

"Mr. Lovel," said Lord Orville, "could not your *eye* have spared that question?"

"O, my Lord," answered he, "if *health* were the only cause of a lady's bloom, my eye, I grant, had been infallible from the first glance; but — "

"Come, come," cried Mrs. Mirvan, "I must beg no insinuations of that sort; Miss Anville's colour, as you have successfully tried, may, you see, be heightened; — but I assure you, it would be past your skill to lessen it."

"Pon honour, Madam," returned he, "you wrong me; I presumed not to infer that *rouge* was the only succedaneum[5] for health; but, really, I have known so many different causes for a lady's colour, such as flushing, — anger, — *mauvaise honte*,[6] — and so forth, that I never dare decide to which it may be owing."

"As to such causes as them there," cried the Captain, "they must belong to those that they keep company with."

"Very true, Captain," said Sir Clement; "the natural complexion has nothing to do with occasional sallies of the passions, or any accidental causes."

"No, truly," returned the Captain, "for now here's me, why I look like any other man just now; and yet, if you were to put me in a passion, 'fore George, you'd soon see me have as fine a high colour as any painted Jezabel in all this place, be she never so bedaubed."

---

[4] *les etiquettes de nous autres:* "The etiquette of us others" (i.e., Londoners).
[5] *succedaneum:* An artificial replacement.
[6] *mauvaise honte:* A painful and socially backward shyness.

"But," said Lord Orville, "the difference of natural and of artificial colour, seems to me very easily discerned; that of Nature, is mottled, and varying; that of art, *set,* and *too* smooth; it wants that animation, that glow, that *indescribable something* which, even now that I see it, wholly surpasses all my powers of expression."

"Your Lordship," said Sir Clement, "is universally acknowledged to be a *connoisseur* in beauty."

"And you, Sir Clement," returned he, "an *enthusiast.*"

"I am proud to own it," cried Sir Clement; "in such a cause, and before such objects, enthusiasm is simply the consequence of not being blind."

"Pr'ythee a truce with all this palavering," cried the Captain, "the women are vain enough already; no need for to puff 'em up more."

"We must all submit to the commanding officer," said Sir Clement, "therefore let us call another subject. Pray, Ladies, how have you been entertained with the play?"

"Want of entertainment," said Mrs. Mirvan, "is its least fault; but I own there are objections to it, which I should be glad to see removed."

"I could have ventured to answer for the Ladies," said Lord Orville, "since I am sure this is not a play that can be honoured with their approbation."

"What, I suppose it is not sentimental enough!" cried the Captain, "or else it's too good for them; for I'll maintain it's one of the best comedies in the language, and has more wit in one scene, than there is in all the new plays put together."

"For my part," said Mr. Lovel, "I confess I seldom listen to the players: one has so much to do, in looking about, and finding out one's acquaintance, that, really, one has no time to mind the stage. Pray, — (most affectedly fixing his eyes upon a diamond-ring on his little finger) pray — what was the play to-night?"

"Why, what the D — l," cried the Captain, "do you come to the play, without knowing what it is?"

"O yes, Sir, yes, very frequently; I have no time to read playbills; one merely comes to meet one's friends, and shew that one's alive."

"Ha, ha, ha! — and so," cried the Captain, "it costs you five shillings a night, just to shew that you're alive! Well, faith, my friends should all think me dead and under ground, before I'd be at that expence for 'em. Howsomever, this here you may take from me; — they'll find you out fast enough, if you've any thing to give 'em. And so you've been here all this time, and don't know what the play was?"

"Why, really, Sir, a play requires so much attention, — it is scarce possible to keep awake, if one listens; — for, indeed, by the time it is evening, one has been so fatigued, with dining, — or wine, — or the house,[7] — or studying, — that it is — it is perfectly an impossibility. But, now I think of it, I believe I have a bill in my pocket; O, ay, here it is — Love for Love, ay, — true, — ha, ha, — how could I be so stupid!"

"O, easily enough as to that, I warrant you," said the Captain; "but, by my soul, this is one of the best jokes I ever heard! Come to a play, and not know what it is! — Why, I suppose you would n't have found it out, if they had *fob'd* you off with a scraping of fiddlers, or an opera? — Ha! ha! ha! — why now, I should have thought you might have taken some notice of one Mr. *Tattle* that is in this play!"

This sarcasm, which caused a general smile, made him colour: but, turning to the Captain with a look of conceit, which implied that he had a retort ready, he said, "Pray, Sir, give me leave to ask, — what do *you* think of *one* Mr. *Ben*, who is also in this play?"

The Captain, regarding him with the utmost contempt, answered in a loud voice, "Think of him! — why I think he's a *man!*" And then, staring full in his face, he struck his cane on the ground, with a violence that made him start. He did not, however, chuse to take any notice of this; but, having bit his nails some time, in manifest confusion, he turned very quick to me, and, in a sneering tone of voice, said, "For my part, I was most struck with the *country* young lady, Miss Prue;[8] pray what do *you* think of her, Ma'am?"

"Indeed, Sir," cried I, very much provoked, "I think — that is, I do not think any thing about her."

"Well, really, Ma'am, you prodigiously surprise me! — *mais, apparement ce n'est qu'un façon à parler?*[9] — though I should beg your pardon, for probably you do not understand French?"

I made no answer, for I thought his rudeness intolerable; but Sir Clement, with great warmth, said, "I am surprised that you can

---

[7] *house:* The House of Commons.

[8] *Mr. Tattle . . . Mr. Ben . . . Miss Prue:* All characters in *Love for Love*. Tattle is a scandal-monger and gossip; Mr. Ben, an ignorant seaman; and Miss Prue, a country girl who combines ignorance of town manners with an unseemly sexual aggressiveness.

[9] *mais . . . parler:* "But apparently this is just a manner of speaking."

suppose such an object as Miss Prue would engage the attention of Miss Anville even for a moment."

"O Sir," returned this fop, "'tis the first character in the piece! — so well drawn, — so much the thing! — such true country-breeding, — such rural ignorance! — ha! ha! ha! — 'tis most admirably hit off, 'pon honour!"

I could almost have cried, that such impertinence should be levelled at me; and yet, chagrined as I was, I could never behold Lord Orville and this man at the same time, and feel any regret for the cause I had given of displeasure.

"The only character in the play," said Lord Orville, "worthy of being mentioned to these ladies, is Angelica."

"Angelica," cried Sir Clement, "is a noble girl; she tries her lover severely, but she rewards him generously."

"Yet, in a trial so long," said Mrs. Mirvan, "there seems rather too much consciousness of her power."

"Since my opinion has the sanction of Mrs. Mirvan's," added Lord Orville, "I will venture to say, that Angelica bestows her hand rather with the air of a benefactress, than with the tenderness of a mistress. Generosity without delicacy, like wit without judgment, generally give as much pain as pleasure. The uncertainty in which she keeps Valentine,[10] and her manner of trifling with his temper, give no very favourable idea of her own."

"Well, my Lord," said Mr. Lovel, "it must, however, be owned, that uncertainty is not the *ton*[11] among our ladies at present; nay, indeed, I think they say, though, faith," taking a pinch of snuff, "I hope it is not true — but they say, that *we* now are most shy and backward."

The curtain then drew up, and our conversation ceased. Mr. Lovel finding we chose to attend to the players, left the box. How strange it is, Sir, that this man, not contented with the large share of foppery and nonsense which he has from nature, should think proper to affect yet more! for what he said of Tattle and of Miss Prue, convinced me that he really had listened to the play, though he was so ridiculous and foolish as to pretend ignorance.

But how malicious and impertinent in this creature to talk to me in such a manner! I am sure I hope I shall never see him again. I should have despised him heartily as a fop, had he never spoken to me at all;

---

[10] *Angelica . . . Valentine:* The romantic leads in *Love for Love.*
[11] *ton:* Fashion.

but now, that he thinks proper to resent his supposed ill-usage, I am really quite afraid of him.

The entertainment was, The Deuce is in him,[12] which Lord Orville observed to be the most finished and elegant *petite piece* that was ever written in English.

In our way home, Mrs. Mirvan put me into some consternation, by saying it was evident, from the resentment which this Mr. Lovel harbours of my conduct, that he would think it a provocation sufficiently important for a duel, if his courage equalled his wrath.

I am terrified at the very idea. Good Heaven! that a man so weak and frivolous should be so revengeful! However, if bravery would have excited him to affront Lord Orville, how much reason have I to rejoice, that cowardice makes him contented with venting his spleen upon me! But we shall leave town soon, and, I hope, see him no more.

It was some consolation to me, to hear, from Miss Mirvan, that, while he was speaking to me so cavalierly, Lord Orville regarded him with great indignation.

But, really, I think there ought to be a book, of the laws and customs *à-la-mode*, presented to all young people, upon their first introduction into public company.

To-night we go to the opera, where I expect very great pleasure. We shall have the same party as at the play; for Lord Orville said he should be there, and would look for us.

[12] *the entertainment:* See footnote 3. *The Deuce Is in Him* was a frequently acted farce by George Colman. It was first performed at Drury Lane Theatre in 1763 and was repeated at least forty times prior to 1776.


## LETTER XXI

### Evelina in Continuation

I have a volume to write, of the adventures of yesterday.

In the afternoon, — at Berry Hill, I should have said the *evening*, for it was almost six o'clock, — while Miss Mirvan and I were dressing for the opera, and in high spirits, from the expectation of great entertainment and pleasure, we heard a carriage stop at the door, and concluded that Sir Clement Willoughby, with his usual assiduity, was come to attend us to the Haymarket; but, in a few moments, what was our surprise, to see our chamber-door flung open, and the two

Miss Branghtons enter the room! They advanced to me with great familiarity, saying, "How do you do, cousin? — so we've caught you at the glass! — well, I'm determined I'll tell my brother of that!"

Miss Mirvan, who had never before seen them, and could not, at first, imagine who they were, looked so much astonished, that I was ready to laugh myself, till the eldest said, "We're come to take you to the opera, Miss; papa and my brother are below, and we are to call for your grand-mama as we go along."

"I am very sorry," answered I, "that you should have taken so much trouble, as I am engaged already."

"Engaged! Lord, Miss, never mind that," cried the youngest, "this young lady will make your excuses, I dare say; it's only doing as one would be done by, you know."

"Indeed, Ma'am," said Miss Mirvan, "I shall myself be very sorry to be deprived of Miss Anville's company this evening."

"Well, Miss, that is not so very good-natured in you," said Miss Branghton, "considering we only come to give our cousin pleasure; it's no good to us; it's all upon her account; for we came, I don't know how much round about to take her up."

"I am extremely obliged to you," said I, "and very sorry you have lost so much time; but I cannot possibly help it, for I engaged myself without knowing you would call."

"Lord, what signifies that?" said Miss Polly, "you're no old maid, and so you need n't be so very formal: besides, I dare say those you are engaged to, a'n't half so near related to you as we are."

"I must beg you not to press me any further, for I assure you it is not in my power to attend you."

"Why we came all out of the city on purpose: besides, your grand-mama expects you; — and, pray, what are we to say to her?"

"Tell her, if you please, that I am much concerned, — but that I am pre-engaged."

"And who to?" demanded the abrupt Miss Branghton.

"To Mrs. Mirvan, — and a large party."

"And, pray, what are you all going to do, that it would be such a mighty matter for you to come along with us?"

"We are going to — to the opera."

"O dear, if that be all, why can't we go all together?"

I was extremely disconcerted at this forward and ignorant behaviour, and yet their rudeness very much lessened my concern at refusing them. Indeed, their dress was such as would have rendered their scheme of accompanying our party impracticable, even if I had de-

sired it; and this, as they did not themselves find out, I was obliged, in
terms the least mortifying I could think of, to tell them.

They were very much chagrined, and asked where I should sit?

"In the pit," answered I.

"In the pit!" repeated Miss Branghton, "well, really, I must own I
should never have supposed that my gown was not good enough for
the pit:[1] but come, Polly, let's go; if Miss does not think us fine
enough for her, why to be sure she may chuse."

Surprised at this ignorance, I would have explained to them that
the pit at the opera required the same dress as the boxes; but they
were so much affronted, they would not hear me, and, in great displeasure, left the room, saying they would not have troubled me, only
they thought I should not be so proud with my own relations, and
that they had at least as good a right to my company as strangers.

I endeavoured to apologize, and would have sent a long message
to Madame Duval; but they hastened away without listening to me;
and I could not follow them down stairs, because I was not dressed.
The last words I heard them say, were, "Well, her grand-mama will
be in a fine passion, that's one good thing."

Though I was extremely mad at this visit, yet I so heartily rejoiced
at their going, that I would not suffer myself to think gravely about it.

Soon after, Sir Clement actually came, and we all went down
stairs. Mrs. Mirvan ordered tea; and we were engaged in a very lively
conversation, when the servant announced Madame Duval, who instantly followed him into the room.

Her face was the colour of scarlet, and her eyes sparkled with fury.
She came up to me with a hasty step, saying, "So, Miss, you refuses to
come to me, do you? And pray who are you, to dare to disobey me?"

I was quite frightened; — I made no answer; — I even attempted to
rise, and could not, but sat still, mute and motionless.

Every body, but Miss Mirvan, seemed in the utmost astonishment;
and the Captain, rising and approaching Madame Duval, with a
voice of authority, said, "Why how now, Mrs. Turkey Cock, what's
put you into this here fluster?"

"It's nothing to you," answered she, "so you may as well hold your
tongue, for I sha'n't be called to no account to you, I assure you."

"There you're out, Madam Fury," returned he, "for you must
know I never suffer any body to be in a passion in my house, but
myself."

---

[1] *the pit:* See footnote 4 to Volume I, Letter XII.

"But you *shall*," cried she, in a great rage, "for I'll be in as great a passion as ever I please, without asking your leave, so don't give yourself no more airs about it. And as for you, Miss," again advancing to me, "I order you to follow me this moment, or else I'll make you repent it all your life." And, with these words, she flung out of the room.

I was in such extreme terror, at being addressed and threatened in a manner to which I am so wholly unused, that I almost thought I should have fainted.

"Don't be alarmed, my love," cried Mrs. Mirvan, "but stay where you are, and I will follow Madame Duval, and try to bring her to reason."

Miss Mirvan took my hand, and most kindly endeavoured to raise my spirits: Sir Clement, too, approached me, with an air so interested in my distress, that I could not but feel myself obliged to him; and, taking my other hand, said, "For Heaven's sake, my dear Madam, compose yourself; surely the violence of such a wretch ought merely to move your contempt: she can have no right, I imagine, to lay her commands upon you, and I only wish that you would allow *me* leave to speak to her."

"O no! not for the world! — indeed, I believe, — I am afraid — I had better follow her."

"Follow her! Good God, my dear Miss Anville, would you trust yourself with a mad woman? for what else can you call a creature whose passions are so insolent? No, no; send her word at once to leave the house, and tell her you desire that she will never see you again."

"O Sir! you don't know who you talk of! — it would ill become me to send Madame Duval such a message."

"But *why*," cried he, (looking very inquisitive,) "*why* should you scruple to treat her as she deserves?"

I then found that his aim was to discover the nature of her connection with me; but I felt so much ashamed of my near relationship to her, that I could not persuade myself to answer him, and only entreated that he would leave her to Mrs. Mirvan, who just then entered.

Before she could speak to me, the Captain called out, "Well, Goody, what have you done with Madame French? is she cooled a little? 'cause, if she be n't, I've just thought of a most excellent device to bring her to."

"My dear Evelina," said Mrs. Mirvan, "I have been vainly endeavouring to appease her; I pleaded your engagement, and promised your future attendance: but I am sorry to say, my love, that I fear her rage will end in a total breach (which I think you had better avoid) if she is any further opposed."

"Then I will go to her, Madam," cried I, "and, indeed, it is now no matter, for I should not be able to recover my spirits sufficiently to enjoy much pleasure *any* where this evening."

Sir Clement began a very warm expostulation, and entreaty, that I would not go; but I begged him to desist, and told him, very honestly, that, if my compliance were not indispensably necessary, I should require no persuasion to stay. He then took my hand, to lead me down stairs; but the Captain desired him to be quiet, saying he would 'squire me himself, "because," he added, (exultingly rubbing his hands,) "I have a wipe ready for the old lady, which may serve her to *chew*[2] as she goes along."

We found her in the parlour. "O, you're come at last, Miss, are you? — fine airs you give yourself; indeed! — *ma foi*, if you had n't come, you might have stayed, I assure you, and have been a beggar for your pains."

"Heyday, Madam," cried the Captain, (prancing forward, with a look of great glee,) "what, a'n't you got out of that there passion yet? why then, I'll tell you what to do to cool yourself; call upon your old friend, Monsieur Slippery, who was with you at Ranelagh, and give my service to him, and tell him, if he sets any store by your health, that I desire he'll give you such another souse as he did before: he'll know what I mean, and I'll warrant you he'll do't for my sake."

"Let him, if he dares!" cried Madame Duval; "but I sha'n't stay to answer you no more; you are a vulgar fellow, — and so, child, let us leave him to himself."

"Hark ye, Madam," cried the Captain, "you'd best not call names, because, d'ye see, if you do, I shall make bold to show you the door."

She changed colour, and, saying, "*Pardie,* I can shew it myself," hurried out of the room, and I followed her into a hackney-coach. But, before we drove off, the Captain, looking out of the parlour window, called out, "D'ye hear, Madam, — don't forget my message to Monsieur."

----

[2] *a wipe . . . to chew:* A trick to play on her.

You will believe, our ride was not the most agreeable in the world; indeed, it would be difficult to say which was least pleased, Madame Duval or me, though the reasons of our discontent were so different: however, Madame Duval soon got the start of me; for we had hardly turned out of Queen-Ann-street, when a man, running full speed, stopt the coach. He came up to the window, and I saw he was the Captain's servant. He had a broad grin on his face, and panted for breath. Madame Duval demanded his business; "Madam," answered he, "my master desires his compliments to you, and — and — and he says he wishes it well over with you. He! he! he! — "

Madame Duval instantly darted forward, and gave him a violent blow on the face; "Take that back for your answer, sirrah," cried she, "and learn to grin at your betters another time. Coach-man, drive on!"

The servant was in a violent passion, and swore terribly; but we were soon out of hearing.

The rage of Madame Duval was greater than ever, and she inveighed against the Captain with such fury, that I was even apprehensive she would have returned to his house, purposely to reproach him, which she repeatedly threatened to do; nor would she, I believe, have hesitated a moment, but that, notwithstanding her violence, he has really made her afraid of him.

When we came to her lodgings, we found all the Branghtons in the passage, impatiently waiting for us, with the door open.

"Only see, here's Miss!" cried the brother.

"Well, I declare I thought as much!" said the younger sister.

"Why, Miss," said Mr. Branghton, "I think you might as well have come with your cousins at once; it's throwing money in the dirt, to pay two coaches for one fare."

"Lord, father," cried the son, "make no words about that; for I'll pay for the coach that Miss had."

"O, I know very well," answered Mr. Branghton, "that you're always more ready to spend than to earn."

I then interfered, and begged that I might myself be allowed to pay the fare, as the expence was incurred upon my account; they all said no, and proposed that the same coach should carry us on to the opera.

While this passed, the Miss Branghtons were examining my dress, which, indeed, was very improper for my company; and, as I was extremely unwilling to be so conspicuous amongst them, I requested Madame Duval to borrow a hat or bonnet for me of the people of the house. But she never wears either herself, and thinks them very *English* and barbarous; therefore she insisted that I should go full dressed, as I had prepared myself for the pit, though I made many objections.

We were then all crowded into the same carriage; but when we arrived at the opera-house, I contrived to pay the coachman. They made a great many speeches; but Mr. Branghton's reflection had determined me not to be indebted to him.

If I had not been too much chagrined to laugh, I should have been extremely diverted at their ignorance of whatever belongs to an opera. In the first place, they could not tell at what door we ought to enter, and we wandered about for some time, without knowing which way to turn: they did not chuse to apply to me, though I was the only person of the party who had ever before been at an opera; because they were unwilling to suppose that their *country cousin,* as they were pleased to call me, should be better acquainted with any London public place than themselves. I was very indifferent and careless upon this subject, but not a little uneasy at finding that my dress, so different from that of the company to which I belonged, attracted general notice and observation.

In a short time, however, we arrived at one of the door-keeper's *bars.* Mr. Branghton demanded for what part of the house they took money? They answered the pit, and regarded us all with great earnestness. The son then advancing, said, "Sir, if you please, I beg that I may treat Miss."

"We'll settle that another time," answered Mr. Branghton, and put down a guinea.

Two tickets of admission were given to him.

Mr. Branghton, in his turn, now stared at the door-keeper, and demanded what he meant by giving him only two tickets for a guinea?

"Only two, Sir!" said the man, "why don't you know that the tickets are half a guinea each?"

"Half a guinea each!" repeated Mr. Branghton, "why I never heard of such a thing in my life! And pray, Sir, how many will they admit?"

"Just as usual, Sir, one person each."

"But one person for half a guinea! — why I only want to sit in the pit, friend."

"Had not the Ladies better sit in the gallery, Sir; for they'll hardly chuse to go into the pit with their hats on?"

"O, as to that," cried Miss Branghton, "if our hats are too high, we'll take them off when we get in. I sha'n't mind it, for I did my hair on purpose."

Another party then approaching, the door-keeper could no longer attend to Mr. Branghton, who, taking up the guinea, told him it should be long enough before he'd see it again, and walked away.

The young ladies, in some confusion, expressed their surprise, that their *papa* should not know the Opera prices, which, for their parts, they had read in the papers a thousand times.

"The price of stocks," said he, "is enough for me to see after; and I took it for granted it was the same thing here as at the playhouse."

"I knew well enough what the price was," said the son, "but I would not speak, because I thought perhaps they'd take less, as we're such a large party."

The sisters both laughed very contemptuously at this idea, and asked him if he ever heard of *people's abating*³ any thing at a public place?

"I don't know whether I have or no," answered he, "but I'm sure if they would, you'd like it so much the worse."

"Very true, Tom," cried Mr. Branghton; "tell a woman that any thing is reasonable, and she'll be sure to hate it."

"Well," said Miss Polly, "I hope that Aunt and Miss will be of our side, for Papa always takes part with Tom."

"Come, come," cried Madame Duval, "if you stand talking here, we sha'n't get no place at all."

Mr. Branghton then enquired the way to the gallery, and, when we came to the door-keeper, demanded what was to pay.

"The usual price, Sir," said the man.

"Then give me change," cried Mr. Branghton, again putting down his guinea.

"For how many, Sir?"

"Why — let's see, — for six."

"For six, Sir? why you've given me but a guinea."

"But a guinea! why how much would you have? I suppose it i'n't half a guinea apiece here too?"

"No, Sir, only five shillings."

Mr. Branghton again took up his unfortunate guinea, and protested he would submit to no such imposition. I then proposed that we should return home, but Madame Duval would not consent, and we were conducted, by a woman who sells books of the Opera, to another gallery-door, where, after some disputing, Mr. Branghton at last paid, and we all went up stairs.

---

³ *people's abating:* Reducing the price.

Madame Duval complained very much of the trouble of going so high, but Mr. Branghton desired her not to hold the place too cheap, "for, whatever you may think," cried he, "I assure you I paid pit price; so don't suppose I come here to save my money."

"Well, to be sure," said Miss Branghton, "there's no judging of a place by the outside, else, I must needs say, there's nothing very extraordinary in the stair-case."

But, when we entered the gallery, their amazement and disappointment became general. For a few instants, they looked at one another without speaking, and then they all broke silence at once.

"Lord, Papa," exclaimed Miss Polly, "why you have brought us to the one-shilling gallery!"

"I'll be glad to give you two shillings, though," answered he, "to pay. I was never so fooled out of my money before, since the hour of my birth. Either the door-keeper's a knave, or this is the greatest imposition that ever was put upon the public."

"*Ma foi*," cried Madame Duval, "I never sat in such a mean place in all my life; — why it's as high! — we sha'n't see nothing."

"I thought, at the time," said Mr. Branghton, "that three shillings was an exorbitant price for a place in the gallery, but as we'd been asked so much more at the other doors, why I paid it without many words; but then, to be sure, thinks I, it can never be like any other gallery, — we shall see some *crinkum-crankum*[4] or other for our money; — but I find it's as arrant a take-in as ever I met with."

"Why it's as like the twelvepenny gallery at Drury-lane," cried the son, "as two peas are one to another. I never knew father so bit[5] before."

"Lord," said Miss Branghton, "I thought it would have been quite a fine place, — all over I don't know what, — and done quite in taste."

In this manner they continued to express their dissatisfaction till the curtain drew up; after which, their observations were very curious. They made no allowance for the customs, or even for the language of another country, but formed all their remarks upon comparisons with the English theatre.

Notwithstanding all my vexation at having been forced into a party so very disagreeable, and that, too, from one so much — so very much the contrary — yet, would they have suffered me to listen,

---

[4] *crinkum-crankum:* Anything full of twists and turns, as in a winding way.
[5] *so bit:* Taken in.

I should have forgotten every thing unpleasant, and felt nothing but delight, in hearing the sweet voice of Signor Millico,[6] the first singer; but they tormented me with continual talking.

"What a jabbering they make!" cried Mr. Branghton; "there's no knowing a word they say. Pray what's the reason they can't as well sing in English? — but I suppose the fine folks would not like it, if they could understand it."

"How unnatural their action is!" said the son; "why now who ever saw an Englishman put himself in such out-of-the-way postures?"

"For my part," said Miss Polly, "I think it's very pretty, only I don't know what it means."

"Lord, what does that signify?" cried her sister; "mayn't one like a thing without being so very particular? — You may see that Miss likes it, and I don't suppose she knows more of the matter than we do."

A gentleman, soon after, was so obliging as to make room in the front row for Miss Branghton and me. We had no sooner seated ourselves, than Miss Branghton exclaimed, "Good gracious! only see! — why, Polly, all the people in the pit are without hats, dressed like any thing!"

"Lord, so they are," cried Miss Polly, "well, I never saw the like! — it's worth coming to the Opera if one saw nothing else."

I was then able to distinguish the happy party I had left; and I saw that Lord Orville had seated himself next to Mrs. Mirvan. Sir Clement had his eyes perpetually cast towards the five shilling gallery, where I suppose he concluded that we were seated; however, before the Opera was over, I have reason to believe that he had discovered me, high and distant as I was from him. Probably he distinguished me by my head-dress.

At the end of the first act, as the green curtain dropped, to prepare for the dance, they imagined that the Opera was done, and Mr. Branghton expressed great indignation that he had been *tricked* out of his money with so little trouble. "Now if any Englishman was to do such an impudent thing as this," said he, "why he'd be pelted;[7] —

---

[6] *Signor Millico:* An opera singer at the height of his London career in the early 1770s. He was a friend of the musical Burney family.

[7] *be pelted:* It was not uncommon for London theater audiences to show their displeasure with a performance by throwing rotten fruit, and worse, at the offending actor.

but here, one of these outlandish gentry may do just what he pleases, and come on, and squeak out a song or two, and then pocket your money without further ceremony."

However, so determined he was to be dissatisfied, that, before the conclusion of the third act, he found still more fault with the Opera for being too long, and wondered whether they thought their singing good enough to serve us for supper.

During the symphony of a song of Signor Millico's, in the second act, young Mr. Branghton said, "It's my belief that that fellow's going to sing another song! — why there's nothing but singing! — I wonder when they'll speak."

This song, which was slow and pathetic, caught all my attention, and I lean'd my head forward to avoid hearing their observations, that I might listen without interruption; but, upon turning round, when the song was over, I found that I was the object of general diversion to the whole party; for the Miss Branghtons were tittering, and the two gentlemen making signs and faces at me, implying their contempt of my affectation.

This discovery determined me to appear as inattentive as themselves; but I was very much provoked at being thus prevented enjoying the only pleasure, which, in such a party, was within my power.

"So, Miss," said Mr. Branghton, "you're quite in the fashion, I see; — so you like Operas? well, I'm not so polite; I can't like nonsense, let it be never so much the taste."

"But pray, Miss," said the son, "what makes that fellow look so doleful while he's singing?"

"Probably because the character he performs is in distress."

"Why then I think he might as well let alone singing 'till he's in better cue: it's out of all nature for a man to be piping when he's in distress. For my part, I never sing but when I'm merry; yet I love a song as well as most people."

When the curtain dropt, they all rejoiced.

"How do *you* like it? — and how do *you* like it?" passed from one to another with looks of the utmost contempt. "As for me," said Mr. Branghton, "they've caught me once, but if ever they do again, I'll give 'em leave to sing me to Bedlam[8] for my pains: for such a heap of stuff never did I hear; there is n't one ounce of sense in the whole Opera, nothing but one continued squeaking and squalling from beginning to end."

---

[8] *Bedlam:* Bethleham Hospital, an institution in London for the insane.

"If I had been in the pit," said Madame Duval, "I should have liked it vastly, for music is my passion; but sitting in such a place as this, is quite unbearable."

Miss Branghton, looking at me, declared, that she was not *genteel* enough to admire it.

Miss Polly confessed, that, if they would but sing *English,* she should like it *very well.*

The brother wished he could raise a riot in the house, because then he might get his money again.

And, finally, they all agreed, that it was *monstrous dear.*

During the last dance, I perceived, standing near the gallery-door, Sir Clement Willoughby. I was extremely vexed, and would have given the world to have avoided being seen by him: my chief objection was, from the apprehension that he wou'd hear Miss Branghton call me *cousin.* — I fear you will think this London journey has made me grow very proud, but indeed this family is so low-bred and vulgar, that I should be equally ashamed of such a connexion in the country, or any where. And really I had already been so much chagrined that Sir Clement had been a witness of Madame Duval's power over me, that I could not bear to be exposed to any further mortification.

As the seats cleared, by parties going away, Sir Clement approached nearer to us; the Miss Branghtons observed with surprise, what a fine gentleman was come into the gallery, and they gave me great reason to expect, that they would endeavour to attract his notice, by familiarity with me, whenever he should join us; and so, I formed a sort of plan, to prevent any conversation. I am afraid you will think it wrong; and so I do myself now, — but, at the time, I only considered how I might avoid immediate humiliation.

As soon as he was within two seats of us, he spoke to me, "I am very happy, Miss Anville, to have found you, for the Ladies below have each an humble attendant, and therefore I am come to offer my services here."

"Why then," cried I, (not without hesitating) "if you please, — I will join them."

"Will you allow me the honour of conducting you?" cried he eagerly; and, instantly taking my hand, he would have marched away with me: but I turned to Madame Duval, and said, "As our party is so large, Madam, if you will give me leave, I will go down to Mrs. Mirvan, that I may not crowd you in the coach."

And then, without waiting for an answer, I suffered Sir Clement to hand me out of the gallery.

Madame Duval, I doubt not, will be very angry, and so I am with myself, now, and therefore I cannot be surprised: but Mr. Branghton, I am sure, will easily comfort himself, in having escaped the additional coach expence of carrying me to Queen-Ann-street: as to his daughters, they had no time to speak, but I saw they were in utter amazement.

My intention was to join Mrs. Mirvan, and accompany her home. Sir Clement was in high spirits and good-humour; and, all the way we went, I was fool enough to rejoice in secret at the success of my plan; nor was it till I got down stairs, and amidst the servants, that any difficulty occurred to me of meeting with my friends.

I then asked Sir Clement how I should contrive to acquaint Mrs. Mirvan that I had left Madame Duval?

"I fear it will be almost impossible to find her," answered he; "but you can have no objection to permitting me to see you safe home."

He then desired his servant, who was waiting, to order his chariot to draw up.

This quite startled me; I turned to him hastily, and said that I could not think of going away without Mrs. Mirvan.

"But how can we meet with her?" cried he; "you will not chuse to go into the pit yourself; I cannot send a servant there; and it is impossible for me to go and leave you alone."

The truth of this was indisputable, and totally silenced me. Yet, as soon as I could recollect myself, I determined not to go in his chariot, and told him I believed I had best return to my party up stairs.

He would not hear of this; and earnestly entreated me not to withdraw the trust I had reposed in him.

While he was speaking, I saw Lord Orville, with several ladies and gentlemen, coming from the pit passage: unfortunately, he saw me too, and, leaving his company, advanced instantly towards me, and, with an air and voice of surprise, said, "Good God, do I see Miss Anville!"

I now most severely felt the folly of my plan, and the aukwardness of my situation; however, I hastened to tell him, though in a hesitating manner, that I was waiting for Mrs. Mirvan: but what was my disappointment, when he acquainted me that she was already gone home!

I was inexpressibly distressed; to suffer Lord Orville to think me satisfied with the single protection of Sir Clement Willoughby, I could not bear; yet I was more than ever averse to returning to a party which I dreaded his seeing: I stood some moments in suspense, and could not help exclaiming, "Good Heaven, what can I do!"

"Why, my dear Madam," cried Sir Clement, "should you be thus uneasy? — you will reach Queen-Ann-street almost as soon as Mrs. Mirvan, and I am sure you cannot doubt being as safe."

I made no answer, and Lord Orville then said, "My coach is here; and my servants are ready to take any commands Miss Anville will honour me with for them. I shall myself go home in a chair, and therefore — "

How grateful did I feel for a proposal so considerate, and made with so much delicacy! I should gladly have accepted it, had I been permitted, but Sir Clement would not let him even finish his speech; he interrupted him with evident displeasure, and said, "My Lord, my own chariot is now at the door."

And just then the servant came, and told him the carriage was ready. He begged to have the honour of conducting me to it, and would have taken my hand, but I drew it back, saying, "I can't — I can't indeed! pray go by yourself — and as to me, let me have a chair."

"Impossible!" (cried he with vehemence) "I cannot think of trusting you with strange chairmen, — I cannot answer it to Mrs. Mirvan, — come, dear Madam, we shall be home in five minutes."

Again I stood suspended. With what joy would I then have compromised with my pride, to have been once more with Madame Duval and the Branghtons, provided I had not met with Lord Orville! However, I flatter myself that he not only saw, but pitied my embarrassment, for he said, in a tone of voice unusually softened, "To offer my services in the presence of Sir Clement Willoughby would be superfluous; but I hope I need not assure Miss Anville, how happy it would make me to be of the least use to her."

I courtsied my thanks. Sir Clement with great earnestness pressed me to go; and while I was thus uneasily deliberating what to do, the dance, I suppose, finished, for the people crowded down stairs. Had Lord Orville then repeated his offer, I would have accepted it, notwithstanding Sir Clement's repugnance; but I fancy he thought it would be impertinent. In a very few minutes I heard Madame Duval's voice, as she descended from the gallery; "Well," cried I, hastily, "if I must go — " I stopt, but Sir Clement immediately handed me into his chariot, called out "Queen-Ann-street," and then jumped in himself. Lord Orville, with a bow and a half smile, wished me good night.

My concern was so great, at being seen and left by Lord Orville in so strange a situation, that I should have been best pleased to have remained wholly silent during our ride home: but Sir Clement took care to prevent that.

He began by making many complaints of my unwillingness to trust myself with him, and begged to know what could be the reason. This question so much embarrassed me, that I could not tell what to answer, but only said, that I was sorry to have taken up so much of his time.

"O Miss Anville," (cried he, taking my hand) "if you knew with what transport I would dedicate to you not only the present but all the future time allotted to me, you would not injure me by making such an apology."

I could not think of a word to say to this, nor to a great many other equally fine speeches with which he ran on, though I would fain have withdrawn my hand, and made almost continual attempts; but in vain, for he actually grasped it between both his, without any regard to my resistance.

Soon after, he said that he believed the coachman was going the wrong way, and he called to his servant, and gave him directions. Then again addressing himself to me, "How often, how assiduously have I sought an opportunity of speaking to you, without the presence of that brute Captain Mirvan! Fortune has now kindly favoured me with one, and permit me," (again seizing my hand) "permit me to use it, in telling you that I adore you!"

I was quite thunderstruck at this abrupt and unexpected declaration. For some moments I was silent, but, when I recovered from my surprise, I said, "Indeed, Sir, if you were determined to make me repent leaving my own party so foolishly, you have very well succeeded."

"My dearest life," cried he, "is it possible you can be so cruel? Can your nature and your countenance be so totally opposite? Can the sweet bloom upon those charming cheeks, which appears as much the result of good-humour as of beauty — "

"O, Sir," cried I, interrupting him, "this is very fine; but I had hoped we had had enough of this sort of conversation at the Ridotto, and I did not expect you would so soon resume it."

"What I then said, my sweet reproacher, was the effect of a mistaken, a prophane idea, that your understanding held no competition with your beauty; but now, now that I find you equally incomparable in both, all words, all powers of speech, are too feeble to express the admiration I feel of your excellencies."

"Indeed," cried I, "if you did not talk in one language, and think in another, you would never suppose that I could give credit to praise so very much above my desert."

This speech, which I made very gravely, occasioned still stronger protestations, which he continued to pour forth, and I continued to disclaim, till I began to wonder that we were not in Queen-Ann-Street, and begged he would desire the coachman to drive faster.

"And does this little moment," cried he, "which is the first of happiness I have ever known, does it already appear so very long to you?"

"I am afraid the man has mistaken the way," answered I, "or else we should ere now have been at our journey's end. I must beg you will speak to him."

"And you can think me so much my own enemy? — if my good genius has inspired the man with a desire of prolonging my happiness, can you expect that I should counter-act its indulgence?"

I now began to apprehend that he had himself ordered the man to go a wrong way, and I was so much alarmed at the idea, that, the very instant it occurred to me, I let down the glass, and made a sudden effort to open the chariot-door myself, with a view of jumping into the street; but he caught hold of me, exclaiming, "For Heaven's sake, what is the matter?"

"I — I don't know," cried I, (quite out of breath) "but I am sure the man goes wrong, and, if you will not speak to him, I am determined I will get out myself."

"You amaze me," answered he, (still holding me) "I cannot imagine what you apprehend. Surely you can have no doubts of my honour?"

He drew me towards him as he spoke. I was frightened dreadfully, and could hardly say, "No, Sir, no, — none at all, — only Mrs. Mirvan, — I think she will be uneasy."

"Whence this alarm, my dearest angel? — What can you fear? — my life is at your devotion, and can you, then, doubt my protection?"

And so saying, he passionately kissed my hand.

Never, in my whole life, have I been so terrified. I broke forcibly from him, and, putting my head out of the window, called aloud to the man to stop. Where we then were I know not, but I saw not a human being, or I should have called for help.

Sir Clement, with great earnestness, endeavoured to appease and compose me; "If you do not intend to murder me," cried I, "for mercy's, for pity's sake, let me get out!"

"Compose your spirits, my dearest life," cried he, "and I will do every thing you would have me." And then he called to the man himself, and bid him make haste to Queen-Ann-Street. "This stupid fellow," continued he, "has certainly mistaken my orders; but I hope you are now fully satisfied."

I made no answer, but kept my head at the window, watching which way he drove, but without any comfort to myself, as I was quite unacquainted with either the right or the wrong.

Sir Clement now poured forth abundant protestations of honour, and assurances of respect, entreating my pardon for having offended me, and beseeching my good opinion; but I was quite silent, having too much apprehension to make reproaches, and too much anger to speak without.

In this manner we went through several streets, till at last, to my great terror, he suddenly ordered the man to stop, and said, "Miss Anville, we are now within twenty yards of your house; but I cannot bear to part with you, till you generously forgive me for the offence you have taken, and promise not to make it known to the Mirvans."

I hesitated between fear and indignation.

"Your reluctance to speak, redoubles my contrition for having displeased you, since it shews the reliance I might have on a promise which you will not give without consideration."

"I am very, very much distressed," cried I, "you ask a promise which you must be sensible I ought not to grant, and yet dare not refuse."

"Drive on!" cried he to the coachman; — "Miss Anville, I will not compel you; I will exact no promise, but trust wholly to your generosity."

This rather softened me; which advantage he no sooner perceived, than he determined to avail himself of, for he flung himself on his knees, and pleaded with so much submission, that I was really obliged to forgive him, because his humiliation made me quite ashamed: and, after that, he would not let me rest till I gave him my word that I would not complain of him to Mrs. Mirvan.

My own folly and pride, which had put me in his power, were pleas which I could not but attend to in his favour. However, I shall take very particular care never to be again alone with him.

When, at last, we arrived at our house, I was so overjoyed, that I should certainly have pardoned him then, if I had not before. As he handed me up stairs, he scolded his servant aloud, and very angrily, for having gone so much out of the way. Miss Mirvan ran out to meet me, — and who should I see behind her, but — Lord Orville!

All my joy now vanished, and gave place to shame and confusion; for I could not endure that he should know how long a time Sir Clement and I had been together, since I was not at liberty to assign any reason for it.

They all expressed great satisfaction at seeing me, and said they had been extremely uneasy and surprised that I was so long coming home, as they had heard from Lord Orville that I was not with Madame Duval. Sir Clement, in an affected passion, said that his booby of a servant had misunderstood his orders, and was driving us to the upper end of Piccadilly. For my part, I only coloured, for though I would not forfeit my word, I yet disdained to confirm a tale in which I had myself no belief.

Lord Orville, with great politeness, congratulated me that the troubles of the evening had so happily ended, and said, that he had found it impossible to return home, before he enquired after my safety.

In a very short time he took leave, and Sir Clement followed him. As soon as they were gone, Mrs. Mirvan, though with great softness, blamed me for having quitted Madame Duval. I assured her, and with truth, that for the future I would be more prudent.

The adventures of the evening so much disconcerted me, that I could not sleep all night. I am under the most cruel apprehensions, lest Lord Orville should suppose my being on the gallery-stairs with Sir Clement was a concerted scheme, and even that our continuing so long together in his chariot, was with my approbation, since I did not say a word on the subject, nor express any dissatisfaction at the coachman's pretended blunder.

Yet, his coming hither to wait our arrival, though it seems to imply some doubt, shews also some anxiety. Indeed Miss Mirvan says, that he appeared *extremely* anxious, nay uneasy and impatient for my return. If I did not fear to flatter myself, I should think it not impossible but that he had a suspicion of Sir Clement's design, and was therefore concerned for my safety.

What a long letter is this! however, I shall not write many more from London, for the Captain said this morning, that he would leave town on Tuesday next. Madame Duval will dine here to-day, and then she is to be told his intention.

I am very much amazed that she accepted Mrs. Mirvan's invitation, as she was in such wrath yesterday. I fear that to-day I shall myself be the principal object of her displeasure; but I must submit patiently, for I cannot defend myself.

Adieu, my dearest Sir. Should this letter be productive of any uneasiness to you, more than ever shall I repent the heedless imprudence which it recites.


## LETTER XXII

### Evelina in Continuation

Monday Morning, April 18.

Mrs. Mirvan has just communicated to me an anecdote concerning Lord Orville, which has much surprised, half pleased, and half pained me.

While they were sitting together during the Opera, he told her that he had been greatly concerned at the impertinence which the young lady under her protection had suffered from Mr. Lovel; but that he had the pleasure of assuring her, she had no future disturbance to apprehend from him.

Mrs. Mirvan, with great eagerness, begged he would explain himself, and said she hoped he had not thought so insignificant an affair worthy his serious attention.

"There is nothing," answered he, "which requires more immediate notice than impertinence, for it ever encroaches when it is tolerated." He then added, that he believed he ought to apologize for the liberty he had taken of interfering, but that, as he regarded himself in the light of a *party concerned,* from having had the honour of dancing with Miss Anville, he could not possibly reconcile to himself a patient neutrality.

He then proceeded to tell her, that he had waited upon Mr. Lovel the morning after the play; that the visit had proved an amicable one, but the particulars were neither entertaining nor necessary; he only assured her, Miss Anville might be perfectly easy, since Mr. Lovel had engaged his honour never more to mention, or even to hint at what had passed at Mrs. Stanley's assembly.

Mrs. Mirvan expressed her satisfaction at this conclusion, and thanked him for his polite attention to her young friend.

"It would be needless," said he, "to request that this affair may never transpire, since Mrs. Mirvan cannot but see the necessity of keeping it inviolably secret; but I thought it incumbent upon me, as the young lady is under your protection, to assure both you and her of Mr. Lovel's future respect."

Had I know of this visit previous to Lord Orville's making it, what dreadful uneasiness would it have cost me! Yet that he should so much interest himself in securing me from offence, gives me, I must own, an internal pleasure greater than I can express, for I feared he had too contemptuous an opinion of me, to take any trouble upon my account. Though, after all, this interference might rather be to satisfy his own delicacy, than from thinking well of me.

But how cool, how quiet is true courage! Who, from seeing Lord Orville at the play, would have imagined his resentment would have hazarded his life? yet his displeasure was evident, though his real bravery and his politeness equally guarded him from entering into any discussion in our presence.

Madame Duval, as I expected, was most terribly angry yesterday; she scolded me for I believe two hours, on account of having left her, and protested she had been so much surprised at my going, without giving her time to answer, that she hardly knew whether she was awake or asleep. But she assured me, that if ever I did so again, she would never more take me into public. And she expressed an equal degree of displeasure against Sir Clement, because he had not even spoken to her, and because he was always of the Captain's side in an argument. The Captain, as bound in honour, warmly defended him, and then followed a dispute in the usual style.

After dinner, Mrs. Mirvan introduced the subject of our leaving London. Madame Duval said she should stay a month or two longer. The Captain told her she was welcome, but that he and his family should go into the country on Tuesday morning.

A most disagreeable scene followed; Madame Duval insisted upon keeping me with her; but Mrs. Mirvan said, that as I was actually engaged on a visit to Lady Howard, who had only consented to my leaving her for a few days, she could not think of returning without me.

Perhaps if the Captain had not interfered, the good-breeding and mildness of Mrs. Mirvan might have had some effect upon Madame Duval; but he passes no opportunity of provoking her, and therefore made so many gross and rude speeches, all of which she retorted, that, in conclusion, she vowed she would sooner go to law, in right of her relationship, than that I should be taken away from her.

I heard this account from Mrs. Mirvan, who was so kindly considerate as to give me a pretence for quitting the room, as soon as this dispute begun, lest Madame Duval should refer to me, and insist on my obedience.

The final result of the conversation was, that, to soften matters for the present, Madame Duval should make one in the party for Howard Grove, whither we are positively to go next Wednesday. [And though we are none of us satisfied with this plan, we know not how to form a better.]

Mrs. Mirvan is now writing to Lady Howard, to excuse bringing this unexpected guest, and to prevent the disagreeable surprise, which must, otherwise, attend her reception. This dear lady seems eternally studying my happiness and advantage.

To-night we go to the Pantheon, which is the last diversion we shall partake of in London, for to-morrow ——

\* \* \* \*

This moment, my dearest Sir, I have received your kind letter.

If you thought us too dissipated the first week, I almost fear to know what you will think of us this second; — however, the Pantheon this evening will probably be the last public place which I shall ever see.

The assurance of your support and protection in regard to Madame Duval, though what I never doubted, excites my utmost gratitude: how, indeed, cherished under your roof, the happy object of your constant indulgence, how could I have borne to become the slave of her tyrannical humours? — pardon me that I speak so hardly of her, but, whenever the idea of passing my days with her occurs to me, the comparison which naturally follows, takes from me all that forbearance, which, I believe, I owe her.

You are already displeased with Sir Clement: to be sure, then, his behavior after the opera will not make his peace with you. Indeed, the more I reflect upon it, the more angry I am. I was entirely in his power, and it was cruel in him to cause me so much terror.

O my dearest Sir, were I but worthy the prayers and the wishes you offer for me, the utmost ambition of my heart would be fully satisfied! but I greatly fear you will find me, now that I am out of the reach of your assisting prudence, more weak and imperfect than you could have expected.

I have not now time to write another word, for I must immediately hasten to dress for the evening.

## LETTER XXIII

### Evelina in Continuation

Queen-Ann-Street, Tuesday, April 19.
There is something to me half melancholy in writing an account of our last adventures in London; however, as this day is merely appropriated to packing, and preparations for our journey, and as I shall shortly have no more adventures to write, I think I may as well complete my town journal at once. And, when you have it all together, I hope, my dear Sir, you will send me your observations and thoughts upon it to Howard Grove.

About eight o'clock we went to the Pantheon. I was extremely struck with the beauty of the building, which greatly surpassed whatever I could have expected or imagined. Yet, it has more the appearance of a chapel, than of a place of diversion; and, though I was quite charmed with the magnificence of the room, I felt that I could not be as gay and thoughtless there as at Ranelagh, for there is something in it which rather inspires awe and solemnity, than mirth and pleasure. However, perhaps it may only have this effect upon such a novice as myself.

I should have said, that our party consisted only of Captain, Mrs. and Miss Mirvan, as Madame Duval spent the day in the city: — which I own I could not lament.

There was a great deal of company; but the first person we saw was Sir Clement Willoughby. He addressed us with his usual ease, and joined us for the whole evening. I felt myself very uneasy in his presence; for I could not look at him, nor hear him speak, without recollecting the chariot adventure; but, to my great amazement, I observed that he looked at *me* without the least apparent discomposure, tho' certainly he ought not to think of his behavior without blushing. I really wish I had not forgiven him, and then he could not have ventured to speak to me any more.

There was an exceeding good concert, but too much talking to hear it well. Indeed I am quite astonished to find how little music is attended to in silence; for though every body seems to admire, hardly any body listens.

We did not see Lord Orville, till we went into the tea-room, which is large, low, and under ground, and serves merely as a foil to the apartments above; he then sat next to us; he seemed to belong to a large party, chiefly of ladies; but, among the gentlemen attending them, I perceived Mr. Lovel.

I was extremely irresolute whether or not I ought to make any acknowledgments to Lord Orville for his generous conduct in securing me from the future impertinence of that man; and I thought, that as he had seemed to allow Mrs. Mirvan to acquaint me, though no one else, of the measures which he had taken, he might perhaps suppose me ungrateful if silent: however, I might have spared myself the trouble of deliberating, as I never once had the shadow of an opportunity of speaking unheard by Sir Clement. On the contrary, he was so exceedingly officious and forward, that I could not say a word to any body, but instantly he bent his head forward, with an air of profound attention, as if I had addressed myself wholly to him: and yet, I never once looked at him, and would not have spoken to him on any account.

Indeed, Mrs. Mirvan herself, though unacquainted with the behaviour of Sir Clement after the opera, says it is not right for a young woman to be seen so frequently in public with the same gentleman; and, if our stay in town was to be lengthened, she would endeavour to represent to the Captain the impropriety of allowing his constant attendance; for Sir Clement, with all his *easiness*, could not be so eternally of our parties, if the Captain was less fond of his company.

At the same table with Lord Orville, sat a gentleman, — I call him so only because he *was* at the same table, — who, almost from the moment I was seated, fixed his eyes stedfastly on my face, and never once removed them to any other object during tea-time, notwithstanding my dislike of his staring must, I am sure, have been very evident. I was quite surprised, that a man whose boldness was so offensive, could have gained admission into a party of which Lord Orville made one; for I naturally concluded him to be some low-bred, and uneducated man; and I thought my idea was indubitably confirmed, when I heard him say to Sir Clement Willoughby, in an *audible whisper,* — which is a mode of speech very distressing and disagreeable to by-standers, — "For Heaven's sake, Willoughby, who is that lovely creature?"

But what was my amazement, when, listening attentively for the answer, though my head was turned another way, I heard Sir Clement say, "I am sorry I cannot inform your Lordship, but I am ignorant myself."

*Lordship!* — how extraordinary! that a *nobleman,* accustomed, in all probability, to the first rank of company in the kingdom, from his earliest infancy, can possibly be deficient in *good manners,* however faulty in morals and principles! Even Sir Clement Willoughby appeared modest in comparison with this person.

During tea, a conversation was commenced upon the times, fashions, and public places, in which the company of both tables joined. It began by Sir Clement's enquiring of Miss Mirvan and of me if the Pantheon had answered our expectations.

We both readily agreed that it had greatly exceeded them.

"Ay, to be sure," said the Captain, "why you don't suppose they'd confess they did n't like it, do you? Whatever's the fashion, they must like of course; — or else I'd be bound for it they'd own, that there never was such a dull place as this here invented."

"And has, then, this building," said Lord Orville, "no merit that may serve to lessen your censure? Will not your eye, Sir, speak something in its favour?"

"Eye," cried the Lord, (I don't know his name,) "and is there any eye here, that can find any pleasure in looking at dead walls or statues, when such heavenly living objects as I now see demand all their admiration?"

"O, certainly," said Lord Orville, "the lifeless symmetry of architecture, however beautiful the design and proportion, no man would be so mad as to put in competition with the animated charms of nature: but when, as to-night, the eye may be regaled at the same time, and in one view, with all the excellence of art, and all the perfection of nature, I cannot think that either suffer by being seen together."

"I grant, my Lord," said Sir Clement, "that the cool eye of unimpassioned philosophy may view both with equal attention, and equal safety; but, where the heart is not so well guarded, it is apt to interfere, and render, even to the eye, all objects but one insipid and uninteresting."

"Aye, aye," cried the Captain, "you may talk what you will of your eye here, and your eye there, and, for the matter of that, to be sure you have two, — but we all know they both squint one way."

"Far be it from me," said Lord Orville, "to dispute the *magnetic* power of beauty, which irresistibly draws and attracts whatever has soul and sympathy: and I am happy to acknowledge, that though we have now no *gods* to occupy a mansion professedly built for them, yet we have secured their *better halves,* for we have *goddesses* to whom we all most willingly bow down." And then, with a very droll air, he made a profound reverence to the ladies.

"They'd need be goddesses with a vengeance," said the Captain, "for they're mortal dear to look at. Howsomever, I should be glad to know what you can see in e'er a face among them that's worth half a guinea[1] for a sight."

"Half a guinea!" exclaimed that same Lord, "I would give half I am worth, for a sight of only *one*, provided I make my own choice. And, prithee, how can money be better employed than in the service of fine women?"

"If the ladies of his own party can pardon the Captain's speech," said Sir Clement, "I think he has a fair claim to the forgiveness of all."

"Then you depend very much, as I doubt not but you may," said Lord Orville, "upon the general sweetness of the sex; — but, as to the ladies of the Captain's party, they may easily pardon, for they cannot be hurt."

"But they must have a devilish good conceit of themselves, though," said the Captain, "to believe all that. Howsomever, whether or no, I should be glad to be told, by some of you who seem to be knowing in them things, what kind of diversion can be found in such a place as this here, for one who has had, long ago, his full of face-hunting?"

Every body laughed, but nobody spoke.

"Why look you there, now," continued the Captain, "you're all at a dead stand! — not a man among you can answer that there question. Why, then, I must make bold to conclude, that you all come here for no manner of purpose but to stare at one another's pretty faces; — though, for the matter of that, half of 'em are plaguy ugly, — and, as to t'other half, — I believe it's none of God's manufactory."

"What the ladies may come hither for, Sir," said Mr. Lovel, (stroking his ruffles, and looking down,) "it would ill become *us* to determine; but as to we men, doubtless we can have no other view, than to admire them."

"If I be n't mistaken," cried the Captain, (looking earnestly in his face,) "you are that same person we saw at Love for Love t'other night; — be n't you?"

Mr. Lovel bowed.

"Why then, Gentlemen," continued he, with a loud laugh, "I must tell you a most excellent good joke; — when all was over, as sure as you're alive, he asked what the play was! Ha, ha, ha!"

---

[1] *half a guinea:* The cost of a ticket to the Pantheon during concert evenings.

"Sir," said Mr. Lovel, colouring, "if you were as much used to a town life as I am, — which, I presume, is not precisely the case, — I fancy you would not find so much diversion from a circumstance so common."

"Common! what, is it common?" repeated the Captain; "why then, 'fore George, such chaps are more fit to be sent to school, and well disciplined with a cat o' nine tails, than to poke their heads into a play-house. Why, a play is the only thing left, now-a-days, that has a grain of sense in it; for as to all the rest of your public places, d'ye see, if they were all put together, I would n't give *that* for 'em!" snapping his fingers. "And now we're talking of them sort of things, there's your operas, — I should like to know, now, what any of you can find to say for them."

Lord Orville, who was most able to have answered, seemed by no means to think the Captain worthy an argument, upon a subject concerning which he had neither knowledge nor feeling: but, turning to us, he said, "The ladies are silent, and we seem to have engrossed the conversation to ourselves, in which we are much more our own enemies than theirs. But," addressing himself to Miss Mirvan and me, "I am most desirous to hear the opinions of these young ladies, to whom all public places must, as yet, be new."

We both, and with eagerness, declared that we had received as much, if not more pleasure, at the opera than any where: but we had better have been silent; for the Captain, quite displeased, said, "What signifies asking them girls? Do you think they know their own minds yet? Ask 'em after any thing that's called diversion, and you're sure they'll say it's vastly fine; — they are a set of parrots, and speak by rote, for they all say the same thing: but ask 'em how they like making puddings and pies, and I'll warrant you'll pose 'em. As to them operas, I desire I may hear no more of their liking such nonsense; and for you, Moll," to his daughter, "I charge you, as you value my favour, that you'll never again be so impertinent as to have a taste of your own before my face. There are fools enough in the world, without your adding to their number. I'll have no daughter of mine affect them sort of megrims.[2] It is a shame they a'n't put down; and if I'd my will, there's not a magistrate in this town, but should be knocked of the head for suffering them. If you've a mind to praise any thing, why you may praise a play, and welcome, for I like it myself."

---

[2] *megrims:* Literally, a headache, associated with the "vapours," an eighteenth-century version of depression. The term could also mean a whimsical affectation.

This reproof effectually silenced us both for the rest of the evening. Nay, indeed, for some minutes it seemed to silence every body else; till Mr. Lovel, not willing to lose an opportunity of returning the Captain's sarcasm, said, "Why, really, Sir, it is but natural, to be most pleased with what is most familiar, and, I think, of all our diversions, there is not one so much in common between us and the country, as a play. Not a village but has its barns and comedians; and as for the stage-business, why it may be pretty equally done any where; and even in regard to *us*, and the *canaille*,[3] confined as we all are within the semi-circle of a theatre, there is no place where the distinction is less obvious."

While the Captain seemed considering for Mr. Lovel's meaning, Lord Orville, probably with a view to prevent his finding it, changed the subject to Cox's Museum, and asked what he thought of it?

"Think! — " said he, "why I think as how it i'n't worth thinking about. I like no such *jem cracks*. It is only fit, in my mind, for monkeys, — though, for aught I know, they too might turn up their noses at it."

"May we ask your Lordship's own opinion?" said Mrs. Mirvan.

"The mechanism," answered he, "is wonderfully ingenious: I am sorry it is turned to no better account; but its purport is so frivolous, so very remote from all aim at instruction or utility, that the sight of so fine a shew, only leaves a regret on the mind, that so much work, and so much ingenuity, should not be better bestowed."

"The truth is," said the Captain, "that in all this huge town, so full as it is of folks of all sorts, there i'n't so much as one public place, besides the play-house, where a man, that's to say a man who *is* a man, ought not to be ashamed to shew his face. T'other day, they got me to a ridotto; but I believe it will be long enough before they get me to another. I knew no more what to do with myself, than if my ship's company had been metamorphosed into Frenchmen. Then, again, there's your famous Ranelagh, that you make such a fuss about, — why what a dull place is that! — it's the worst of all."

"Ranelagh dull!" — "Ranelagh dull!" was echoed from mouth to mouth, and all the ladies, as if of one accord, regarded the Captain with looks of the most ironical contempt.

"As to Ranelagh," said Mr. Lovel, "most indubitably, though the price is plebeian, it is by no means adapted to the plebeian taste. It requires a certain acquaintance with high life; and — and — and some-

---

[3] *canaille:* The populace, contemptuously named, as in mob, pack, or herd.

thing of — of — something *d'un vrai goût,* to be really sensible of its merit. Those whose — whose connections, and so forth, are not among *les gens comme il faut,* can feel nothing but *ennui* at such a place as Ranelagh."

"Ranelagh!" cried Lord ——, "O, 'tis the divinest place under heaven, — or, indeed, — for aught I know —— "

"O you creature!" cried a pretty, but affected young lady, patting him with her fan, "you sha'n't talk so; I know what you are going to say; but, positively, I won't sit by you, if you're so wicked."

"And how can one sit by you, and be good?" said he, "when only to look at you is enough to make one wicked — or wish to be so?"

"Fie, my Lord!" returned she, "you are really insufferable. I don't think I shall speak to you again these seven years."

"What a metamorphosis," cried Lord Orville, "should you make a patriarch of his Lordship!"[4]

"Seven years!" said he: "dear Madam, be contented with telling me you will not speak to me *after* seven years, and I will endeavour to submit."

"O, very well, my Lord," answered she, "pray date the end of our speaking to each other as early as you please, I'll promise to agree to your time."

"You know, dear Madam," said he, sipping his tea, "you know I only live in your sight."

"O yes, my Lord, I have long known that. But I begin to fear we shall be too late for Ranelagh this evening."

"O no, Madam," said Mr. Lovel, looking at his watch, "it is but just past ten."

"No more!" cried she, "O then we shall do very well."

All the ladies then started up, and declared they had no time to lose.

"Why what the D — l," cried the Captain, (leaning forward with both his arms on the table,) "are you going to Ranelagh at this time of night?"

The ladies looked at one another, and smiled.

"To Ranelagh?" cried Lord ——, "Yes, and I hope you are going too; for we cannot possibly excuse these ladies."

---

[4] *seven years . . . a patriarch of his Lordship:* See Genesis, book 29: Jacob, the son of Isaac, saw and fell in love with Rachel, daughter of Laban. He offered to serve Laban for seven years in return for her hand in marriage. At the end of seven years, Laban brought Jacob Rachel's older sister Leah instead, and Jacob was forced to serve Laban another seven years to gain Rachel as a second wife.

"I go to Ranelagh? — if I do, I'll be —— "

Every body now stood up, and the stranger Lord, coming round to me, said, "*You* go, I hope?"

"No, my Lord, I believe not."

"O you cannot, must not be so barbarous." And he took my hand, and ran on saying such fine speeches and compliments, that I might almost have supposed myself a goddess, and him a pagan, paying me adoration. As soon as I possibly could, I drew back my hand; but he frequently, in the course of conversation, contrived to take it again, though it was extremely disagreeable to me; and the more so, as I saw that Lord Orville had his eyes fixed upon us, with a gravity of attention that made me uneasy.

And, surely, my dear Sir, it was a great liberty in this Lord, notwithstanding his rank, to treat me so freely. As to Sir Clement, he seemed in misery.

They all endeavoured to prevail with the Captain to join the Ranelagh party; and this Lord told me, in a low voice, that *it was tearing his heart out* to go without me.

During this conversation, Mr. Lovel came forward, and assuming a look of surprise, made me a bow, and enquired how I did, protesting, upon his honour, that he had not seen me before, or would sooner have paid his respects to me.

Though his politeness was evidently constrained, yet I was very glad to be thus assured of having nothing more to fear from him.

The Captain, far from listening to their persuasions of accompanying them to Ranelagh, was quite in a passion at the proposal, and vowed he would sooner go to the *Black-hole in Calcutta*.[5]

"But," said Lord —— , "if the *ladies* will take their tea at Ranelagh, you may depend upon our seeing them safe home, for we shall all be proud of the honour of attending them."

"May be so," said the Captain; "but I'll tell you what, if one of these places be n't enough for them to-night, why to-morrow they shall go to ne'er a one."

We instantly declared ourselves very ready to go home.

"It is not for yourselves that we petition," said Lord —— , "but for *us;* if you have any charity, you will not be so cruel as to deny us; we only beg you to prolong our happiness for a few minutes, — the

---

[5] *Black-hole in Calcutta:* Fort William, an English colonialist outpost in Calcutta, was taken by Suraj-ud Dowlah, the Nabob of Bengal in 1756. One hundred forty-six prisoners were held in a grossly small room with inadequate ventilation. Only twenty-three survived one night's imprisonment.

favour is but a small one for you to grant, though so great a one for us to receive."

"To tell you a piece of my mind," said the Captain, surlily, "I think you might as well not give the girls so much of this palaver: they'll take it all for gospel. As to Moll, why she's well enough, but nothing extraordinary, though, perhaps, you may persuade her that her pug-nose is all the fashion: and as to the other, why she's good white and red, to be sure; but what of that? — I'll warrant she'll moulder away as fast as her neighbours."

"Is there," cried Lord —— , "another man in this place, who, see-ing such objects, could make such a speech?"

"As to that there," returned the Captain, "I don't know whether there be or no, and, to make free, I don't care; for I sha'n't go for to model myself by any of these fair-weather chaps, who dare not so much as say their souls are their own, — and, for aught I know, no more they ben't. I'm almost as much ashamed of my countrymen, as if I was a Frenchman, and I believe in my heart there i'n't a pin to chuse between them; and, before long, we shall hear the very sailors talking that lingo, and see never a swabber without a bag and a sword."[6]

"He, he, he! — well, 'pon honour," cried Mr. Lovel, "you gentle-men of the ocean have a most severe way of judging."

"Severe! 'fore George, that is impossible; for, to cut the matter short, the men, as they call themselves, are no better than monkeys; and as to the women, why they are mere dolls. So, now you've got my opinion of this subject; and so I wish you good night."

The ladies, who were very impatient to be gone, made their court-sies, and tripped away, followed by all the gentlemen of their party, except the Lord I have before mentioned, and Lord Orville, who stayed to make enquiries of Mrs. Mirvan concerning our leaving town; and then saying, with his usual politeness, something civil to each of us, with a very grave air, he quitted us.

Lord —— remained some minutes longer, which he spent in mak-ing a profusion of compliments to me, by which he prevented my hearing distinctly what Lord Orville said, to my great vexation, espe-

---

[6] *swabber without a bag and a sword:* "Swabber" could refer to either a seaman (one who swabs the decks) or, negatively, to one who has the manners of an ordinary seaman. A bag was a small pouch, usually of silk, that held a man's hair at the nape of the neck in one fashionable manner of hair-dressing. Swords were usually worn only by gentlemen, or those who affected to be gentlemen.

cially as he looked — I thought so, at least, — as if displeased at his particularity of behaviour to me.

In going to an outward room,[7] to wait for the carriage, I walked, and could not possibly avoid it, between this nobleman and Sir Clement Willoughby; and, when the servant said the coach stopped the way, though the latter offered me his hand, which I should much have preferred, this same Lord, without any ceremony, took mine himself; and Sir Clement, with a look extremely provoked, conducted Mrs. Mirvan.

In all ranks and all stations of life, how strangely do characters and manners differ! Lord Orville, with a politeness which knows no intermission, and makes no distinction, is as unassuming and modest, as if he had never mixed with the great, and was totally ignorant of every qualification he possesses; this other Lord, though lavish of compliments and fine speeches, seems to me an entire stranger to real good-breeding; whoever strikes his fancy, engrosses his whole attention. He is forward and bold, has an air of haughtiness towards men, and a look of libertinism towards women, and his conscious quality seems to have given him a freedom in his way of speaking to either sex, that is very little short of rudeness.

When we returned home, we were all low-spirited; the evening's entertainment had displeased the Captain, and his displeasure, I believe, disconcerted us all.

And here I thought to have concluded my letter; but, to my great surprise, just now we had a visit from Lord Orville. He called, he said, to pay his respects to us before we left town, and made many enquiries concerning our return; and, when Mrs. Mirvan told him we were going into the country without any view of again quitting it, he expressed his concern in such terms — so polite, so flattering, so serious — , that I could hardly forbear being sorry myself. Were I to go immediately to Berry Hill, I am sure I should feel nothing but joy; — but, now we are joined by this Captain, and by Madame Duval, I must own I expect very little pleasure at Howard Grove.

Before Lord Orville went, Sir Clement Willoughby called. He was more grave than I had ever seen him, and made several attempts to speak to me in a low voice, and to assure me that his regret upon the occasion of our journey, was entirely upon my account. But I was not in spirits, and could not bear to be teazed by him. However, he has so

---

[7] *outward room:* A lobby or a foyer; a room designated for waiting or the business of entering or leaving a public building.

well paid his court to Captain Mirvan, that he gave him a very hearty invitation to the Grove. At this, he brightened, — and, just then, Lord Orville took leave!

No doubt but he was disgusted at this ill-timed, ill-bred partiality: for surely it was very wrong to make an invitation before Lord Orville, in which he was not included! I was so much chagrined, that, as soon as he went, I left the room; and I shall not go down stairs till Sir Clement is gone.

Lord Orville cannot but observe his assiduous endeavours to ingratiate himself into my favour; and does not this extravagant civility of Captain Mirvan, give him reason to suppose, that it meets with our general approbation? I cannot think upon this subject, without inexpressible uneasiness; — and yet, I can think of nothing else.

Adieu, my dearest Sir. Pray write to me immediately. How many long letters has this one short fortnight produced! More than I may, probably, ever write again: I fear I shall have tired you with reading them; but you will now have time to rest, for I shall find but little to say in future.

And now, most honoured Sir, with all the follies and imperfections which I have thus faithfully recounted, can you, and with unabated kindness, suffer me to sign myself

Your dutiful,
and most affectionate
Evelina?

## LETTER XXIV

### Mr. Villars to Evelina

Berry Hill, April 22.

How much do I rejoice that I can again address my letters to Howard Grove! My Evelina would have grieved, had she known the anxiety of my mind, during her residence in the great world. My apprehensions have been inexpressibly alarming; and your journal, at once exciting and relieving my fears, has almost wholly occupied me, since the time of your dating it from London.

Sir Clement Willoughby must be an artful, designing man; I am extremely irritated at his conduct. The passion he pretends for you has neither sincerity nor honour; the manner and the opportunities he has chosen to declare it, are bordering upon insult.

His unworthy behaviour after the opera, convinces me, that, had not your vehemence frightened him, Queen-Ann-street would have been the last place whither he would have ordered his chariot. O my child, how thankful am I for your escape! I need not now, I am sure, enlarge upon your indiscretion and want of thought, in so hastily trusting yourself with a man so little known to you, and whose gaiety and flightiness should have put you on your guard.

The nobleman you met at the Pantheon, bold and forward as you describe him to be, gives me no apprehension; a man who appears so openly licentious, and who makes his attack with so little regard to decorum, is one who, to a mind such as my Evelina's, can never be seen but with the disgust which his manners ought to excite.

But Sir Clement, though he seeks occasions to give real offence, contrives to avoid all appearance of intentional evil. He is far more dangerous, because more artful; but I am happy to observe, that he seems to have made no impression upon your heart, and therefore a very little care and prudence may secure you from those designs which I fear he has formed.

Lord Orville appears to be of a better order of beings. His spirited conduct to the meanly impertinent Lovel, and his anxiety for you after the opera, prove him to be a man of sense and of feeling. Doubtless he thought there was much reason to tremble for your safety, while exposed to the power of Sir Clement; and he acted with a regard to real honour, that will always incline me to think well of him, in so immediately acquainting the Mirvan family with your situation. Many men of this age, from a false and pretended delicacy to a friend, would have quietly pursued their own affairs, and thought it more honourable to leave an unsuspecting young creature to the mercy of a libertine, than to risk his displeasure by taking measures for her security.

Your evident concern at leaving London, is very natural; and yet it afflicts me. I ever dreaded your being too much pleased with a life of dissipation, which youth and vivacity render but too alluring; and I almost regret the consent for your journey, which I had not the resolution to withhold.

Alas, my child, the artlessness of your nature, and the simplicity of your education, alike unfit you for the thorny paths of the great and busy world. The supposed obscurity of your birth and situation, makes you liable to a thousand disagreeable adventures. Not only my views, but my hopes for your future life, have ever centered in the country. Shall I own to you, that, however I may differ from Captain

Mirvan in other respects, yet my opinion of the town, its manners, inhabitants, and diversions, is much upon a level with his own? Indeed it is the general harbour of fraud and of folly, of duplicity and of impertinence; and I wish few things more fervently, than that you may have taken a lasting leave of it.

Remember, however, that I only speak in regard to a public and dissipated life; in private families, we may doubtless find as much goodness, honesty, and virtue, in London as in the country.

If contented with a retired station, I still hope I shall live to see my Evelina the ornament of her neighbourhood, and the pride and delight of her family: giving and receiving joy from such society as may best deserve her affection, and employing herself in such useful and innocent occupations as may secure and merit the tenderest love of her friends, and the worthiest satisfaction of her own heart.

Such are my hopes, and such have been my expectations. Disappoint them not, my beloved child, but chear me with a few lines, that may assure me, this one short fortnight spent in town, has not undone the work of seventeen years spent in the country.

ARTHUR VILLARS

## LETTER XXV

### Evelina to the Rev. Mr. Villars

Howard Grove, April 25.

No, my dear Sir, no; *the work of seventeen years* remains such as it was, ever unworthy your time and your labour, but not more so now, — at least I hope not, — than before that fortnight which has so much alarmed you.

And yet, I must confess, that I am not half so happy here at present, as I was ere I went to town: but the change is in the place, not in me. Captain Mirvan and Madame Duval have ruined Howard Grove. The harmony that reigned here, is disturbed, our schemes are broken, our way of life is altered, and our comfort is destroyed. But do not suppose *London* to be the source of these evils; for, had our excursion been any where else, so disagreeable an addition to our household, must have caused the same change at our return.

I was sure you would be displeased with Sir Clement Willoughby, and therefore I am by no means surprised at what you say of him: but for Lord Orville — I must own I had greatly feared, that my weak and imperfect account would not have procured him the good opinion which he so well deserves, and which I am delighted to find you seem to have of him. O Sir, could I have done justice to the merit of which I believe him possessed, — could I have painted him to *you* such as he appeared to *me*, — then, indeed, you would have had some idea of the claim which he has to your approbation!

After the last letter which I wrote in town, nothing more passed previous to our journey hither, except a very violent quarrel between Captain Mirvan and Madame Duval. As the Captain intended to travel on horseback, he had settled that we four females should make use of his coach. Madame Duval did not come to Queen-Ann-street, till the carriage had waited some time at the door, and then, attended by Monsieur Du Bois, she made her appearance.

The Captain, impatient to be gone, would not suffer them to enter the house, but insisted that we should immediately get into the coach. We obeyed; but were no sooner seated, than Madame Duval said, "Come, Monsieur Du Bois, these girls can make very good room for you; sit closer, children."

Mrs. Mirvan looked quite confounded, and M. Du Bois, after making some apologies about crowding us, actually got into the coach, on the side with Miss Mirvan and me. But no sooner was he seated, than the Captain, who had observed this transaction very quietly, walked up to the coach-door, saying, "What, neither with your leave, nor by your leave?"

M. Du Bois seemed rather shocked, and began to make abundance of excuses; but the Captain neither understood nor regarded him, and, very roughly, said, "Look'ee, Monsieur, this here may be a French fashion, for aught I know; — but Give and Take is fair in all nations; and so now, d'ye see, I'll make bold to shew you an English one."

And then, seizing his wrist, he made him jump out of the coach.

M. Du Bois instantly put his hand upon his sword, and threatened to resent this indignity. The Captain, holding up his stick, bid him draw at his peril. Mrs. Mirvan, greatly alarmed, got out of the coach, and, standing between them, entreated her husband to re-enter the house.

"None of your clack!" cried he, angrily, "what the D — l, do you suppose I can't manage a Frenchman?"

Mean time, Madame Duval called out to M. Du Bois, "*Eh, laissez-le, mon ami, ne le corrigez pas; c'est un vilain bête qui n'en vaut pas la peine.*"[1]

---

[1] *Eh . . . peine:* "Oh, leave him alone, my friend, don't bother to chastise him; he's a stupid rascal who's not worth your trouble."

"*Monsieur le Capitaine,*" cried M. Du Bois, "*voulez-vous bien me demander pardon?*"[2]

"O ho, you demand pardon; do you?" said the Captain, "I thought as much; I thought you'd come to; — so you have lost your relish for an English salutation, have you?" strutting up to him with looks of defiance.

A crowd was now gathering, and Mrs. Mirvan again besought her husband to go into the house.

"Why what a plague is the woman afraid of? — did you ever know a Frenchman that could not take an affront? — I warrant Monsieur knows what he is about; — don't you, Monsieur?"

M. Du Bois, not understanding him, only said, "*plait-il, Monsieur?*"[3]

"No, nor *dish* me, neither," answered the Captain; "but be that as it may, what signifies our parleying here? If you've any thing to propose, speak at once; if not, why let us go on our journey without more ado."

"*Parbleu, je n'entends rien, moi!*"[4] cried M. Du Bois, shrugging his shoulders, and looking very dismal.

Mrs. Mirvan then advanced to him, and said, in French, that she was sure the Captain had not any intention to affront him, and begged he would desist from a dispute which could only be productive of mutual misunderstanding, as neither of them knew the language of the other.

This sensible remonstrance had the desired effect, and M. Du Bois, making a bow to every one, except the Captain, very wisely gave up the point, and took leave.

We then hoped to proceed quietly on our journey; but the turbulent Captain would not yet permit us: he approached Madame Duval with an exulting air, and said, "Why how's this, Madam? what, has your champion deserted you? why I though you told me that you old gentlewomen had it all your own way, among them French sparks?"

"As to that, Sir," answered she, "it's not of no consequence what you thought; for a person who can behave in such a low way, may think what he pleases for me, for I sha'n't mind."

"Why, then, Mistress, since you must needs make so free," cried he, "please to tell me the reason why you took the liberty for to ask

[2] *Monsieur . . . pardon:* "Mister Captain, . . . would you like to beg my pardon?"
[3] *plait-il, Monsieur:* "If you please, Sir?"
[4] *je n'entends rien, moi:* "I don't understand anything."

any of your followers into my coach, without my leave? Answer me to that."

"Why then, pray, Sir," returned she, "tell me the reason why you took the liberty to treat the gentleman in such a impolite way, as to take and pull him neck and heels out? I'm sure he had n't done nothing to affront you, nor nobody else; and I don't know what great hurt he would have done you, by just sitting still in the coach; he would not have eat it."

"What, do you think, then, that my horses have nothing to do, but to carry about your sniveling Frenchmen? If you do, Madame, I must make bold to tell you, you are out, for I'll see 'em hanged first."

"More brute you, then! for they've never carried nobody half so good."

"Why, look'ee, Madam, if you must needs provoke me, I'll tell you a piece of my mind; you must know, I can see as far into a millstone[5] as another man; and so, if you thought for to fob me off with one of your smirking French puppies for a son-in-law, why you'll find yourself in a hobble,[6] — that's all."

"Sir, you're a —— but I won't say what; — but, I protest, I had n't no such a thought, no more had n't Monsieur Du Bois."

"My dear," said Mrs. Mirvan, "we shall be very late."

"Well, well," answered he, "get away then; off with you, as fast as you can, it's high time. As to Molly, she's fine lady enough in all conscience; I want none of your French chaps to make her worse."

And so saying, he mounted his horse, and we drove off. And I could not but think with regret of the different feelings we experienced upon leaving London, to what had belonged to our entering it!

During the journey, Madame Duval was so very violent against the Captain, that she obliged Mrs. Mirvan to tell her, that, when in her presence, she must beg her to chuse some other subject of discourse.

We had a most affectionate reception from Lady Howard, whose kindness and hospitality cannot fail of making every body happy, who is disposed so to be.

Adieu, my dearest Sir. I hope, though I have hitherto neglected to mention it, that you have always remembered me to whoever has made any enquiry concerning me.

---

[5] *see as far into a millstone:* Understand as much as anyone.
[6] *in a hobble:* In an awkward situation from which it is hard to escape; the term can imply a legal threat, as it was slang for being arrested.

## LETTER XXVI

### Evelina to the Rev. Mr. Villars

Howard Grove, April 27.

O my dear Sir, I now write in the greatest uneasiness! Madame Duval has made a proposal which terrifies me to death, and which was as unexpected, as it is shocking.

She had been employed for some hours this afternoon in reading letters from London, and, just about tea-time, she sent for me into her room, and said, with a look of great satisfaction, "Come here, child, I've got some very good news to tell you: something that will surprise you, I'll give you my word, for you ha'n't no notion of it."

I begged her to explain herself; and then, in terms which I cannot repeat, she said she had been considering what a shame it was, to see me such a poor country, shame-faced thing, when I ought to be a fine lady; and that she had long, and upon several occasions, blushed for me, though she must own the fault was none of mine: for nothing better could be expected from a girl who had been so immured. However, she assured me she had, at length, hit upon a plan, which would make quite another creature of me.

I waited, without much impatience, to hear what this preface led to; but I was soon awakened to more lively sensations, when she acquainted me, that her intention was to prove my birthright, and to claim, by law, the inheritance of my real family!

It would be impossible for me to express my extreme consternation, when she thus unfolded her scheme. My surprise and terror were equally great. I could say nothing; I heard her with a silence which I had not the power to break.

She then expatiated very warmly upon the advantages I should reap from her plan; talked in a high style of my future grandeur; assured me how heartily I should despise almost every body and every thing I had hitherto seen; predicted my marrying into some family of the first rank in the kingdom; and, finally, said I should spend a few months in Paris, where my education and manners might receive their last polish.

She enlarged also upon the delight she should have, in common with myself, from mortifying the pride of certain people, and shewing them, that she was not to be slighted with impunity.

In the midst of this discourse, I was relieved by a summons to tea. Madame Duval was in great spirits; but my emotion was too painful for concealment, and every body enquired into the cause. I would fain have waved the subject, but Madame Duval was determined to make it public. She told them, that she had it in her head to *make something* of me, and that they should soon call me by another name than that of Anville, and yet that she was not going to have the child married, neither.

I could not endure to hear her proceed, and was going to leave the room; which, when Lady Howard perceived, she begged Madame Duval would defer her intelligence to some other opportunity; but she was so eager to communicate her scheme, that she could bear no delay, and therefore they suffered me to go, without opposition. Indeed, whenever my situation or affairs are mentioned by Madame Duval, she speaks of them with such bluntness and severity, that I cannot be enjoined a task more cruel than to hear her.

I was afterwards acquainted with some particulars of the conversation by Miss Mirvan, who told me that Madame Duval informed them of her plan with the utmost complacency, and seemed to think herself very fortunate in having suggested it; but soon after, she accidentally betrayed, that she had been instigated to the scheme by her relations the Branghtons, whose letters, which she received to-day, first mentioned the proposal. She declared that she would have nothing to do with any *round-about ways,* but go openly and instantly to law, in order to prove my birth, real name, and title to the estate of my ancestors.

How impertinent and officious, in these Branghtons, to interfere thus in my concerns! You can hardly imagine what a disturbance this plan has made in the family. The Captain, without enquiring into any particulars of the affair, has peremptorily declared himself against it, merely because it has been proposed by Madame Duval, and they have battled the point together with great violence. Mrs. Mirvan says she will not even *think,* till she hears your opinion. But Lady Howard, to my great surprise, openly avows her approbation of Madame Duval's intention: however, she will write her reasons and sentiments upon the subject to you herself.

As to Miss Mirvan, she is my second self, and neither hopes nor fears but as I do. And as to *me,* — I know not what to say, nor even what to wish; I have often thought my fate peculiarly cruel, to have but one parent, and from that one to be banished for ever; — while, on the other side, I have but too well known and felt the propriety of the separation. And yet, you may much better imagine than I can express, the internal anguish which sometimes oppresses my heart, when I reflect upon the strange indifferency, that must occasion a father never to make the least enquiry after the health, the welfare, or even the life of his child!

O Sir, to *me,* the loss is nothing! — greatly, sweetly, and most benevolently have you guarded me from feeling it; — but for *him,* I grieve indeed! — I must be divested, not merely of all filial piety, but of all humanity, could I ever think upon this subject, and not be wounded to the soul.

Again I must repeat, I know not what to *wish:* think for me, therefore, my dearest Sir, and suffer my doubting mind, that knows not which way to direct its hopes, to be guided by your wisdom and unerring counsel.

EVELINA

## LETTER XXVII

### Lady Howard to the Rev. Mr. Villars

Howard Grove.

Dear Sir,

I cannot give a greater proof of the high opinion I have of your candour, than by the liberty I am now going to take, of presuming to offer you advice, upon a subject concerning which you have so just a claim to act for yourself: but I know you have too unaffected a love of justice, to be partially tenacious of your own judgment.

Madame Duval has been proposing a scheme which has put us all in commotion, and against which, at first, in common with the rest of my family, I exclaimed; but upon more mature consideration, I own my objections have almost wholly vanished.

This scheme is no other than to commence a law-suit with Sir John Belmont, to prove the validity of his marriage with Miss Evelyn; the necessary consequence of which proof, will be securing his fortune and estate to his daughter.

And why, my dear Sir, should not this be? I know that, upon first hearing, this plan conveys ideas that must shock you; but I know, too, that your mind is superior to being governed by prejudices, or to opposing any important cause on account of a few disagreeable attendant circumstances.

Your lovely charge, now first entering into life, has merit which ought not to be buried in obscurity. She seems born for an ornament to the world. Nature has been bountiful to her of whatever she had to bestow; and the peculiar attention you have given to her education, has formed her mind to a degree of excellence, that, in one so young, I have scarce ever seen equalled. Fortune, alone, has hitherto been sparing of her gifts; and she, too, now opens the way which leads to all that is left to wish for her.

What your reasons may have been, my good Sir, for so carefully concealing the birth, name, and pretensions of this amiable girl, and forbearing to make any claim upon Sir John Belmont, I am totally a stranger to; but, without knowing, I respect them, from the high opinion I have of your character and judgment: but I hope they are not insuperable; for I cannot but think, that it was never designed, for one who seems meant to grace the world, to have her life devoted to retirement.

Surely Sir John Belmont, wretch as he has shewn himself, could never see his accomplished daughter, and not be proud to own her, and eager to secure her the inheritance of his fortune. The admiration she met with in town, though merely the effect of her external attractions, was such, that Mrs. Mirvan assures me, she would have had the most splendid offers, had there not seemed to be some mystery in regard to her birth, which, she was well informed, was assiduously, though vainly, endeavoured to be discovered.

Can it be right, my dear Sir, that this promising young creature should be deprived of the fortune, and rank of life, to which she is lawfully entitled, and which you have prepared her to support and to use so nobly? To despise riches, may, indeed, be philosophic, but to dispense them worthily, must surely be more beneficial to mankind.

Perhaps a few years, or indeed, a much shorter time, may make this scheme impracticable: Sir John, though yet young, leads a life too dissipated for long duration; and, when too late, we may regret that something was not sooner done; for it will be next to impossible, after he is gone, to settle or prove any thing with his heirs and executors.

Pardon the earnestness with which I write my sense of this affair; but your charming ward has made me so warmly her friend, that I cannot be indifferent upon a subject of such importance to her future life.

Adieu, my dear Sir; — send me speedily an answer to this remonstrance, and believe me to be, &c.

M. HOWARD

## LETTER XXVIII

## Mr. Villars to Lady Howard

Berry Hill, May 2.

Your letter, Madam, has opened a source of anxiety to which I look forward with dread, and which to see closed, I scarcely dare expect. I am unwilling to oppose my opinion to that of your Ladyship, nor, indeed, can I, but by arguments which, I believe, will rather rank me as a hermit, ignorant of the world, and fit only for my cell, than as a proper guardian, in an age such as this, for an accomplished young woman. Yet, thus called upon, it behoves me to explain, and endeavour to vindicate, the reasons by which I have been hitherto guided.

The mother of this dear child, — who was led to destruction by her own imprudence, the hardness of heart of Madame Duval, and the villainy of Sir John Belmont, — was once, what her daughter is now, the best beloved of my heart; and her memory, so long as my own holds, I shall love, mourn, and honour! On the fatal day that her gentle soul left its mansion, and not many hours ere she ceased to breathe, I solemnly plighted my faith, *That her child, if it lived, should know no father, but myself, or her acknowledged husband.*

You cannot, Madam, suppose that I found much difficulty in adhering to this promise, and forbearing to make any *claim* upon Sir John Belmont. Could I feel an affection the most paternal for this poor sufferer, and not abominate her destroyer? Could I wish to deliver to *him,* who had so basely betrayed the mother, the helpless and innocent offspring, who, born in so much sorrow, seemed entitled to all the compassionate tenderness of pity?

For many years, the *name* alone of that man, accidentally spoken in my hearing, almost divested me of my christianity, and scarce could I forbear to execrate him. Yet I sought not, neither did I desire, to deprive him of his child, had he, with any appearance of contrition, or, indeed, of humanity, endeavoured to become less unworthy such a blessing; — but he is a stranger to all parental feelings, and has, with a savage insensibility, forborne to enquire even into the existence of this sweet orphan, though the situation of his injured wife was but too well known to him.

You wish to be acquainted with my intentions. — I must acknowledge, they were such as I now perceive would not be honoured with your Ladyship's approbation: for though I have sometimes thought of presenting Evelina to her father, and demanding the justice which is her due, yet, at other times, I have both disdained and feared the application; disdained, lest it should be refused, and feared, lest it should be accepted!

Lady Belmont, who was firmly persuaded of her approaching dissolution, frequently and earnestly besought me, that if her infant was a female, I would not abandon her to the direction of a man so wholly unfit to take the charge of her education; but, should she be importunately demanded, that I would retire with her abroad, and carefully conceal her from Sir John, till some apparent change in his sentiments and conduct should announce him less improper for such a treat. And often would she say, "Should the poor babe have any feelings correspondent with its mother's, it will have no want, while under your protection." Alas! she had no sooner quitted it herself, than she was plunged into a gulph of misery, that swallowed up her peace, reputation, and life.

During the childhood of Evelina, I suggested a thousand plans for the security of her birth-right; — but I as oftentimes rejected them. I was in a perpetual conflict, between the desire that she should have justice done her, and the apprehension that, while I improved her fortune, I should endanger her mind. However, as her character began to be formed, and her disposition to be displayed, my perplexity abated; the road before me seemed less thorny and intricate, and I thought I could perceive the right path from the wrong: for, when I observed the artless openness, the ingenuous simplicity of her nature; when I saw that her guileless and innocent soul fancied all the world to be pure and disinterested as herself, and that her heart was open to every impression with which love, pity, or art might assail it; — then did I flatter myself, that to follow my own inclination, and to secure her welfare, was the same thing; since, to expose her to the snares and dangers inevitably encircling a house of which the master is dissipated and unprincipled, without the guidance of a mother, or any prudent and sensible female, seemed to me no less than suffering her to stumble into some dreadful pit, when the sun was in its meridian. My plan, therefore, was not merely to educate and to cherish her as my own, but to adopt her the heiress of my small fortune, and to bestow her upon some worthy man, with whom she might spend her days in tranquillity, chearfulness, and good-humour, untainted by vice, folly, or ambition.

So much for the time past. Such have been the motives by which I have been governed; and I hope they will be allowed not merely to account for, but also to justify, the conduct which has resulted from them. It now remains to speak of the time to come.

And here, indeed, I am sensible of difficulties which I almost despair of surmounting according to my wishes. I pay the highest deference to your Ladyship's opinion, which it is extremely painful to me not to concur with; yet, I am so well acquainted with your goodness, that I presume to hope it would not be absolutely impossible for me to offer such arguments as might lead you to think with me, that this young creature's chance of happiness seems less doubtful in retirement, than it would be in the gay and dissipated world: but why should I perplex your Ladyship with reasoning that can turn to so little account? for, alas! what arguments, what persuasions can I make use of, with any prospect of success, to such a woman as Madame Duval? Her character, and the violence of her disposition, intimidate me from making the attempt: she is too ignorant for instruction, too obstinate for entreaty, and too weak for reason.

I will not, therefore, enter into a contest from which I have nothing to expect but altercation and impertinence. As soon would I discuss the effect of sound with the deaf, or the nature of colours with the blind, as aim at illuminating with conviction a mind so warped by prejudice, so much the slave of unruly and illiberal passions. Unused as she is to controul, persuasion would but harden, and opposition incense her. I yield, therefore, to the necessity which compels my reluctant acquiescence, and shall now turn all my thoughts upon considering of such methods for the conducting this enterprize, as may be most conducive to the happiness of my child, and least liable to wound her sensibility.

The law-suit, therefore, I wholly and absolutely disapprove.

Will you, my dear Madam, forgive the freedom of an old man, if I own myself greatly surprised, that you could, even for a moment, listen to a plan so violent, so public, so totally repugnant to all female delicacy? I am satisfied your Ladyship has not weighed this project. There was a time, indeed, when, to assert the innocence of Lady Belmont, and to blazon to the world the *wrongs,* not *guilt,* by which she suffered, I proposed, nay attempted, a similar plan: but then, all assistance and encouragement was denied. How cruel to the remembrance I bear of her woes, is this tardy resentment of Madame Duval! She was deaf to the voice of Nature, though she has hearkened to that of Ambition.

Never can I consent to have this dear and timid girl brought forward to the notice of the world by such a method; a method, which will subject her to all the impertinence of curiosity, the sneers of conjecture, and the stings of ridicule. And for what? — the attainment of wealth, which she does not want, and the gratification of vanity, which she does not feel. — A child to appear against a father! — no, Madam, old and infirm as I am, I would even yet sooner convey her myself to some remote part of the world, though I were sure of dying in the expedition.

Far different had been the motives which would have stimulated her unhappy mother to such a proceeding; all her felicity in this world was irretrievably lost; her life was become a burthen to her, and her fair fame, which she had early been taught to prize above all other things, had received a mortal wound: therefore, to clear her own honour, and to secure from blemish the birth of her child, was all the good which Fortune had reserved herself the *power* of bestowing. But even this last consolation was with-held from her!

Let milder measures be adopted; and — since it must be so, — let application be made to Sir John Belmont; but as to a law-suit, I hope, upon this subject, never more to hear it mentioned.

With Madame Duval, all pleas of delicacy would be ineffectual; her scheme must be opposed by arguments better suited to her understanding. I will not, therefore, talk of its impropriety, but endeavour to prove its inutility. Have the goodness, then, to tell her, that her own intentions would be frustrated by her plan, since, should the law-suit be commenced, and even should the cause be gained, Sir John Belmont would still have it in his power, and, if irritated, no doubt in his inclination, to cut off her granddaughter with a shilling.

She cannot do better, herself, than to remain quiet and inactive in the affair: the long and mutual animosity between her and Sir John, will make her interference merely productive of debates and ill-will. Neither would I have Evelina appear till summoned. And as to myself, I must wholly decline *acting,* though I will, with unwearied zeal, devote all my thoughts to giving counsel; but, in truth, I have neither inclination nor spirits adequate to engaging personally with this man.

My opinion is, that he would pay more respect to a letter from your Ladyship upon this subject, than from any other person. I therefore advise and hope, that you will yourself take the trouble of writing to him, in order to open the affair. When he shall be inclined to see Evelina, I have for him a posthumous letter, which his much-injured lady left to be presented to him, if ever such a meeting should take place.

The views of the Branghtons, in suggesting this scheme, are obviously interested; they hope, by securing to Evelina the fortune of her father, to induce Madame Duval to settle her own upon themselves. In this, however, they would probably be mistaken, for little minds have ever a propensity to bestow their wealth upon those who are already in affluence, and, therefore, the less her grand-child requires her assistance, the more gladly she will give it.

I have but one thing more to add, from which, however, I can by no means recede: my word so solemnly given to Lady Belmont, that her child should never be owned but with herself, must be inviolably adhered to.

I am, dear Madam, with great respect,
                    Your Ladyship's most obedient servant,
                    ARTHUR VILLARS


## LETTER XXIX

### Mr. Villars to Evelina

                                    Berry Hill, May 2.
How sincerely do I sympathise in the uneasiness and concern which my beloved Evelina has so much reason to feel! The cruel scheme in agitation is equally repugnant to my judgment and my inclination, — yet to oppose it, seems impracticable. To follow the dictates of my own heart, I should instantly recall you to myself, and never more consent to your being separated from me; but the manners and opinion of the world demand a different conduct. Hope, however, for the best, and be satisfied you shall meet with no indignity; if you are not received into your own family as you ought to be, and with the distinction that is your due, you shall leave it for ever; and, once again restored to my protection, secure your own tranquillity, and make, as you have hitherto done, all the happiness of my life!


## LETTER XXX

### Evelina to the Rev. Mr. Villars

                                    Howard Grove, May 6.
The die is thrown, and I attend the event in trembling! Lady Howard has written to Paris, and sent her letter to town, to be for-

warded in the ambassador's packet, and in less than a fortnight, therefore, she expects an answer. O Sir, with what anxious impatience shall
I wait its arrival! upon it seems to depend the fate of my future life. My
solicitude is so great, and my suspence so painful, that I cannot rest a
moment in peace, or turn my thoughts into any other channel.

Deeply interested as I now am in the event, most sincerely do I regret that the plan was ever proposed: methinks it *cannot* end to my
satisfaction; for either I must be torn from the arms of my *more* than
father, — or I must have the misery of being finally convinced, that I
am cruelly rejected by him who has the natural claim to that dear
title; a title, which to write, mention, or think of, fills my whole soul
with filial tenderness.

The subject is discussed here eternally. Captain Mirvan and
Madame Duval, as usual, quarrel whenever it is started: but I am so
wholly engrossed by my own reflections, that I cannot even listen to
them. My imagination changes the scene perpetually: at one moment,
I am embraced by a kind and relenting parent, who takes me to that
heart from which I have hitherto been banished, and supplicates,
through me, peace and forgiveness from the ashes of my mother! —
at another, he regards me with detestation, considers me as the living
image of an injured saint, and repulses me with horror! — But I will
not afflict you with the melancholy phantasms of my brain. I will endeavour to compose my mind to a more tranquil state, and forbear to
write again, till I have, in some measure, succeeded.

May Heaven bless you, my dearest Sir! and long, long may it continue you on earth, to bless

Your grateful
EVELINA!

## LETTER XXXI

### Lady Howard to Sir John Belmont, Bart.

Howard Grove, May 5.

Sir,

You will, doubtless, be surprised at receiving a letter from one
who had for so short a period the honour of your acquaintance, and
that at so great a distance of time; but the motive which has induced
me to take this liberty, is of so delicate a nature, that were I to commence making apologies for my officiousness, I fear my letter would
be too long for your patience.

You have, probably, already conjectured the subject upon which I mean to treat. My regard for Mr. Evelyn and his amiable daughter, was well known to you: nor can I ever cease to be interested in whatever belongs to their memory or family.

I must own myself somewhat distressed in what manner to introduce the purport of my writing; yet, as I think that, in affairs of this kind, frankness is the first requisite to a good understanding between the parties concerned, I will neither torment you nor myself with punctilious ceremonies, but proceed instantly and openly to the business which occasions my giving you this trouble.

I presume, Sir, it would be superfluous to tell you, that your child resides still in Dorsetshire, and is still under the protection of the Reverend Mr. Villars, in whose house she was born: for, though no enquiries concerning her have reached his ears, or mine, I can never suppose it possible you have forborne to make them. It only remains, therefore, to tell you, that your daughter is now grown up; that she has been educated with the utmost care, and the utmost success; and that she is now a most deserving, accomplished, and amiable young woman.

Whatever may be your view for her future destination in life, it seems time to declare it. She is greatly admired, and, I doubt not, will be very much sought after: it is proper, therefore, that her future expectations, and your pleasure concerning her, should be made known.

Believe me, Sir, she merits your utmost attention and regard. You could not see and know her, and remain unmoved by those sensations of affection which belong to so near and tender a relationship. She is the lovely resemblance of her lovely mother; — pardon me, Sir, that I mention that unfortunate lady, but I think it behoves me, upon this occasion, to shew the esteem I felt for her; allow me, therefore, to say, and be not offended at my freedom, that the memory of that excellent lady has but too long remained under the aspersions of calumny; surely it is time to vindicate her fame! — and how can that be done in a manner more eligible, more grateful to her friends, or more honourable to yourself, than by openly receiving as your child, *the daughter of the late Lady Belmont?*

The venerable man who has had the care of her education, deserves your warmest acknowledgments, for the unremitting pains he has taken, and attention he has shewn, in the discharge of his trust. Indeed she has been peculiarly fortunate in meeting with such a friend and guardian: a more worthy man, or one whose character seems nearer to perfection, does not exist.

Permit me to assure you, Sir, she will amply repay whatever regard and favour you may hereafter shew her, by the comfort and happiness you cannot fail to find in her affection and duty. To be owned *properly* by you, is the first wish of her heart; and I am sure, that to merit your approbation will be the first study of her life.

I fear that you will think this address impertinent; but I must rest upon the goodness of my intention to plead my excuse.

I am, Sir,

Your most obedient humble servant,

M. HOWARD

END OF THE FIRST VOLUME

# Volume II

## LETTER I

### Evelina to the Rev. Mr. Villars

Howard Grove, May 10.

Our house has been enlivened to-day, by the arrival of a London visitor; and the necessity I have been under of concealing the uneasiness of my mind, has made me exert myself so effectually, that I even think it is really diminished; or, at least, my thoughts are not so totally, so very anxiously occupied by one only subject, as they lately were.

I was strolling this morning with Miss Mirvan, down a lane about a mile from the grove, when we heard the trampling of horses; and, fearing the narrowness of the passage, we were turning hastily back, but stopped upon hearing a voice call out "Pray, Ladies, don't be frightened, for I will walk my horse." We turned again, and then saw Sir Clement Willoughby. He dismounted, and approaching us, with the reins in his hand, presently recollected us. "Good Heaven," cried he, with his usual quickness, "do I see Miss Anville? — and you, too, Miss Mirvan?"

He immediately ordered his servant to take charge of his horse, and then, advancing to us, took a hand of each, which he pressed to his lips, and said a thousand fine things concerning his good fortune, our improved looks, and the charms of the country, when inhabited by *such* rural deities. "The town, Ladies, has languished since your absence, — or, at least, I have so much languished myself, as to be absolutely insensible to all it had to offer. One refreshing breeze, such as I now enjoy, awakens me to new vigour, life, and spirit. But I never before had the good luck to see the country in such perfection."

"Has not almost every body left town, Sir?" said Miss Mirvan.

"I am ashamed to answer you, Madam — but indeed it is as full as ever, and will continue so, till after the birth-day.[1] However, you Ladies were so little seen, that there are but few who know what it has lost. For my own part, I felt it too sensibly, to be able to endure the place any longer."

"Is there any body remaining there, that we were acquainted with?" cried I.

"O yes, Ma'am." And then he named two or three persons we had seen when with him; but he did not mention Lord Orville, and I would not ask him, lest he should think me curious. Perhaps, if he stays here some time, he may speak of him by accident.

He was proceeding in this complimentary style, when we were met by the Captain; who no sooner perceived Sir Clement, than he hastened up to him, gave him a hearty shake of the hand, a cordial slap on the back, and some other equally gentle tokens of satisfaction, assuring him of his great joy at his visit, and declaring he was as glad to see him as if he had been a messenger who brought news that a French ship was sunk. Sir Clement, on the other side, expressed himself with equal warmth, and protested he had been so eager to pay his respects to Captain Mirvan, that he had left London in its full lustre, and a thousand engagements unanswered, merely to give himself that pleasure.

"We shall have rare sport," said the Captain, "for do you know the old French-woman is among us? 'Fore George, I have scarce made any use of her yet, by reason I have had nobody with me that could enjoy a joke; howsomever, it shall go hard but we'll have some diversion now."

Sir Clement very much approved of the proposal; and we then went into the house, where he had a very grave reception from Mrs.

---

[1] *it is as full . . . till after the birth-day:* June 4, George III's birthday, was the end of the fashionable London "season." It was customary for those who had a country estate (or an invitation to visit one) to leave London for the hotter summer months.

Mirvan, who is by no means pleased with his visit, and a look of much discontent from Madame Duval, who said to me, in a low voice, "I'd as soon have seen Old Nick as that man, for he's the most impertinentest person in the world, and is n't never of my side."

The Captain is now actually occupied in contriving some scheme which, he says, is *to play the old Dowager off;* and so eager and delighted is he at the idea, that he can scarcely constrain his raptures sufficiently to conceal his design, even from herself. I wish, however, since I do not dare put Madame Duval upon her guard, that he had the delicacy not to acquaint me with his intention.

## LETTER II

### Evelina in Continuation

May 13th.

The Captain's operations are begun, — and, I hope, ended; for indeed poor Madame Duval has already but too much reason to regret Sir Clement's visit to Howard Grove.

Yesterday morning, during breakfast, as the Captain was reading the news-paper, Sir Clement suddenly begged to look at it, saying he wanted to know if there was any account of a transaction, at which he had been present the evening before his journey hither, concerning a poor Frenchman, who had got into a scrape which might cost him his life.

The Captain demanded particulars; and then Sir Clement told a long story, of being with a party of country friends, at the Tower,[1] and hearing a man call out for mercy in French; and that, when he enquired into the occasion of his distress, he was informed, that he had been taken up upon suspicion of treasonable practices against the government. "The poor fellow," continued he, "no sooner found that I spoke French, than he besought me to hear him, protesting that he had no evil designs; that he had been but a short time in England, and only waited the return of a Lady from the country, to quit it for ever."

---

[1] *the Tower:* Originally built by William the Conquerer, the Tower of London stands on the banks of the Thames within the old walled city of London. It was traditionally used as a prison for deposed or soon to be deposed kings and queens and other eminent persons, including captive foreign rulers.

Madame Duval changed colour, and listened with the utmost attention.

"Now, though I by no means approve of so many foreigners continually flocking into our country," added he, addressing himself to the Captain, "yet I could not help pitying the poor wretch, because he did not know enough of English to make his defence: however, I found it impossible to assist him, for the mob would not suffer me to interfere. In truth, I am afraid he was but roughly handled."

"Why, did they duck him?"[2] said the Captain.

"Something of that sort," answered he.

"So much the better! so much the better!" cried the Captain, "an impudent French puppy! — I'll bet you what you will he was a rascal. I only wish all his countrymen were served the same."

"I wish you had been in his place, with all my soul!" cried Madame Duval, warmly; — "but pray, Sir did n't nobody know who this poor gentleman was?"

"Why I did hear his name spoke," answered Sir Clement, "but I cannot recollect it."

"It was n't, — it was n't — Du Bois?" stammered out Madame Duval.

"The very name!" answered he, "yes, Du Bois, I remember it now."

Madame Duval's cup fell from her hand, as she repeated "Du Bois! Monsieur Du Bois, did you say?"

"Du Bois! why that's *my* friend," cried the Captain, "that's *Monsieur Slippery*, i'n't it? — Why he's plaguy fond of sousing work; howsomever, I'll be sworn they gave him his fill of it."

"And I'll be sworn," cried Madame Duval, "that you're a — but I don't believe nothing about it, so you need n't be so overjoyed, for I dare say it was no more Monsieur Du Bois than I am."

"I thought at the time," said Sir Clement, very gravely, "that I had seen the gentleman before, and now I recollect, I think it was in company with you, Madam."

"With *me,* Sir!" cried Madame Duval.

---

[2]*duck him:* In an age when no real standing police force existed, unofficial policing of criminal — or perceived criminal — behavior frequently took the form of ducking by the hands of a London crowd. The alleged culprit was tied up, sometimes wrapped in a blanket, and dragged through a pond. Often she or he was held under water for periods of time with long sticks. The result could be death by choking on water and mud.

"Say you so!" said the Captain, "why then, it must be he, as sure as you're alive! — Well but, my good friend, what will they do with poor Monsieur?"

"It is difficult to say," answered Sir Clement, very thoughtfully, "but, I should suppose, that if he has not good friends to appear for him, he will be in a very unpleasant situation; for these are serious sort of affairs."

"Why, do you think they'll hang him?" demanded the Captain.

Sir Clement shook his head, but made no answer.

Madame Duval could no longer contain her agitation; she started from her chair, repeating, with a voice half choaked, "Hang him! — they can't, — they sha'n't, — let them at their peril! — however, it's all false, and I won't believe a word of it; — but I'll go to town this very moment, and see M. Du Bois myself; — I won't wait for nothing."

Mrs. Mirvan begged her not to be alarmed; but she flew out of the room, and up stairs into her own apartment. Lady Howard blamed both the gentlemen for having been so abrupt, and followed her. I would have accompanied her, but the Captain stopped me; and, having first laughed very heartily, said he was going to read his commission to his ship's company.

"Now, do you see," said he, "as to Lady Howard, I sha'n't pretend for to enlist her into my service, and so I shall e'en leave her to make it out as well as she can; but as to all you, I expect obedience and submission to orders; I am now upon a hazardous expedition, having undertaken to convoy a crazy vessel to the shore of Mortification; so, d'ye see, if any of you have any thing to propose, that will forward the enterprize, — why speak and welcome; but if any of you, that are of my chosen crew, capitulate, or enter into any treaty with the enemy, — I shall look upon you as mutinying, and turn you adrift."

Having finished this harangue, which was interlarded with many expressions, and sea-phrases, that I cannot recollect, he gave Sir Clement a wink of intelligence, and left us to ourselves.

Indeed, notwithstanding the attempts I so frequently make of writing some of the Captain's conversation, I can only give you a faint idea of his language; for almost every other word he utters, is accompanied by an oath, which, I am sure, would be as unpleasant for you to read, as for me to write. And, besides, he makes use of a thousand sea-terms, which are to me quite unintelligible.

Poor Madame Duval sent to enquire at all probable places, whether she could be conveyed to town in any stage-coach; but the Captain's servant brought her for answer, that no London stage would pass near Howard Grove till to-day. She then sent to order a chaise; but was soon assured, that no horses could be procured. She was so much inflamed by these disappointments, that she threatened to set out for town on foot, and it was with difficulty that Lady Howard dissuaded her from this mad scheme.

The whole morning was filled up with these enquiries. But, when we were all assembled to dinner, she endeavoured to appear perfectly unconcerned, and repeatedly protested that she gave not any credit to the report, as far as it regarded M. Du Bois, being very certain that he was not the person in question.

The Captain used the most provoking efforts to convince her that she deceived herself; while Sir Clement, with more art, though not less malice, affected to be of her opinion; but, at the same time that he pretended to relieve her uneasiness, by saying that he doubted not having mistaken the name, he took care to enlarge upon the danger to which the *unknown gentleman* was exposed, and expressed great concern at his perilous situation.

Dinner was hardly removed, when a letter was delivered to Madame Duval. The moment she had read it, she hastily demanded from whom it came? "A country boy brought it," answered the servant, "but he would not wait."

"Run after him this instant!" cried she, "and be sure you bring him back. *Mon Dieu! quelle aventure! que ferai-je?*"[3]

"What's the matter? what's the matter?" said the Captain.

"Why nothing, — nothing's the matter. *O mon Dieu!*"

And she rose, and walked about the room.

"Why, what — has Monsieur sent to you?" continued the Captain: "is that there letter from him?"

"No, — it i'n't; — besides, if it is, it's nothing to you."

"O then, I'm sure it is! Pray now, Madame, don't be so close; come, tell us all about it, — what does he say? how did he relish the horse-pond? — which did he find best, sousing *single* or *double?* — 'Fore George, 'twas plaguy unlucky you was not with him!"

"It's no such a thing, Sir," cried she, very angrily, "and if you're so very fond of a horse-pond, I wish you'd put yourself into one, and not be always a thinking about other people's being served so."

---

[3] *Mon Dieu . . . ferai-je:* "My God! What a mess! What am I to do?"

The man then came in, to acquaint her they could not overtake the boy. She scolded violently, and was in such perturbation, that Lady Howard interfered, and begged to know the cause of her uneasiness, and whether she could assist her?

Madame Duval cast her eyes upon the Captain and Sir Clement, and said she should be glad to speak to her Ladyship, without so many witnesses.

"Well, then, Miss Anville," said the Captain, turning to me, "do you and Molly go into another room, and stay there till Mrs. Duval has opened her mind to us."

"So you may think, Sir," cried she, "but who's fool then? no, no, you need n't trouble yourself to make a ninny of me, neither, for I'm not so easily taken in, I'll assure you."

Lady Howard then invited her into the dressing-room,[4] and I was desired to attend her.

As soon as we had shut the door, "O my Lady," exclaimed Madame Duval, "here's the most cruellest thing in the world has happened! — But that Captain is such a beast, I can't say nothing before him, — but it's all true! poor M. Du Bois is tooked up!"

Lady Howard begged her to be comforted, saying that, as M. Du Bois was certainly innocent, there could be no doubt of his ability to clear himself.

"To be sure, my Lady," answered she, "I know he is innocent; and to be sure they'll never be so wicked as to hang him for nothing?"

"Certainly not;" replied Lady Howard, "you have no reason to be uneasy. This is not a country where punishment is inflicted without proof."

"Very true, my Lady; but the worst thing is this: I cannot bear that that fellow, the Captain, should know about it; for if he does, I sha'n't never hear the last of it; — no more won't poor M. Du Bois."

"Well, well," said Lady Howard, "shew me the letter, and I will endeavour to advise you."

The letter was then produced. It was signed by the clerk of a country justice; who acquainted her, that a prisoner, then upon trial for suspicion of treasonable practices against the government, was just upon the point of being committed to jail, but having declared that he was known to her, this clerk had been prevailed upon to write, in

---

[4] *dressing-room:* A lady's sitting room, for informal visits.

order to enquire if she really could speak to the character and family of a Frenchman who called himself Pierre Du Bois.

When I heard the letter, I was quite amazed at its success. So improbable did it seem, that a foreigner should be taken before a *country* justice of peace, for a crime of so dangerous a nature, that I cannot imagine how Madame Duval could be alarmed, even for a moment. But, with all her violence of temper, I see that she is easily frightened, and, in fact, more cowardly than many who have not half her spirit; and so little does she reflect upon circumstances, or probability, that she is continually the dupe of her own — I ought not to say *ignorance,* but yet, I can think of no other word.

I believe that Lady Howard, from the beginning of the transaction, suspected some contrivance of the Captain, and this letter, I am sure, must confirm her suspicion: however, though she is not at all pleased with his frolick, yet she would not hazard the consequence of discovering his designs: her looks, her manner, and her character, made me draw this conclusion from her apparent perplexity; for not a word did she say, that implied any doubt of the authenticity of the letter. Indeed there seems to be a sort of tacit agreement between her and the Captain, that she should not appear to be acquainted with his schemes; by which means she at once avoids quarrels, and supports her dignity.

While she was considering what to propose, Madame Duval begged to have the use of her Ladyship's chariot, that she might go immediately to the assistance of her friend. Lady Howard politely assured her, that it would be extremely at her service; and then Madame Duval besought her not to own to the Captain what had happened, protesting that she could not endure he should know poor M. Du Bois had met with so unfortunate an accident. Lady Howard could not help smiling, though she readily promised not to *inform* the Captain of the affair. As to me, she desired my attendance; which I was by no means rejoiced at, as I was certain she was going upon a fruitless errand.

I was then commissioned to order the chariot.

At the foot of the stairs I met the Captain, who was most impatiently waiting the result of the conference. In an instant we were joined by Sir Clement. A thousand enquiries were then made concerning Madame Duval's opinion of the letter, and her intentions upon it: and when I would have left them, Sir Clement, pretending equal eagerness with the Captain, caught my hand, and repeatedly detained me, to ask some frivolous question, to the answer of which he must be totally indifferent. At length, however, I broke from them; they retired into the parlour, and I executed my commission.

The carriage was soon ready, and Madame Duval, having begged Lady Howard to say she was not well, stole softly down stairs, desiring me to follow her. The chariot was ordered at the garden-door; and when we were seated, she told the man, according to the clerk's directions, to drive to Mr. Justice[5] Tyrell's, asking, at the same time, how many miles off he lived?

I expected he would have answered that he knew of no such person; but, to my great surprize, he said, "Why 'Squire Tyrell lives about nine miles beyond the park."

"Drive fast, then," cried she, "and you sha'n't be no worse for it."

During our ride, which was extremely tedious, she tormented herself with a thousand fears for M. Du Bois' safety; and piqued herself very much upon having escaped unseen by the Captain, not only that she avoided his triumph, but because she knew him to be so much M. Du Bois' enemy, that she was sure he would prejudice the Justice against him, and endeavour to take away his life. For my part, I was quite ashamed of being engaged in so ridiculous an affair, and could only think of the absurd appearance we should make upon our arrival at Mr. Tyrell's.

When we had been out near two hours, and expected every moment to stop at the place of our destination, I observed that Lady Howard's servant, who attended us on horseback, rode on forward till he was out of sight, and soon after returning, came up to the chariot-window, and delivering a note to Madame Duval, said he had met a boy, who was just coming with it to Howard Grove, from the Clerk of Mr. Tyrell.

While she was reading it, he rode round to the other window, and, making a sign for secrecy, put into my hand a slip of paper, on which was written, "Whatever happens, be not alarmed, — for *you* are safe, — though you endanger all mankind!"

I readily imagined that Sir Clement must be the author of this note, which prepared me to expect some disagreeable adventure: but I had no time to ponder upon it, for Madame Duval had no sooner read her own letter, than, in an angry tone of voice, she exclaimed, "Why now what a thing is this! here we're come all this way for nothing!"

---

[5] *Justice:* The title could apply to a justice of the peace as well as to a higher court justice.

She then gave me the note, which informed her, that she need not trouble herself to go to Mr. Tyrell's, as the prisoner had had the address[6] to escape. I congratulated her upon this fortunate incident; but she was so much concerned at having rode so far in vain, that she seemed less pleased then provoked. However, she ordered the man to make what haste he could home, as she hoped, at least, to return before the Captain should suspect what had passed.

The carriage turned about, and we journeyed so quietly for near an hour, that I began to flatter myself we should be suffered to proceed to Howard Grove without further molestation, when, suddenly, the footman called out, "John, are we going right?"

"Why I a'n't sure," said the coachman, "but I'm afraid we turned wrong."

"What do you mean by that, Sirrah?" said Madame Duval, "why if you lose your way, we shall be all in the dark."

"I think we should turn to the left," said the footman.

"To the left!" answered the other, "No, no, I'm partly sure we should turn to the right."

"You had better make some enquiry," said I.

"*Ma foi,*" cried Madame Duval, "we're in a fine hole, here! — they neither of them know no more than the post. However, I'll tell my Lady, as sure as you're born, so you'd better find the way."

"Let's try this lane," said the footman.

"No," said the coachman, "that's the road to Canterbury; we had best go straight on."

"Why that's the direct London road," returned the footman, "and will lead us twenty miles about."

"*Pardie,*" cried Madame Duval, "why they won't go one way nor t'other! and, now we're come all this jaunt for nothing, I suppose we sha'n't get home to-night!"

"Let's go back to the public-house," said the footman, "and ask for a guide."

"No, no," said the other, "if we stay here a few minutes, somebody or other will pass by; and the horses are almost knocked up already."

"Well, I protest," cried Madame Duval, "I'd give a guinea to see them sots both horse-whipped! As sure as I'm alive, they're drunk! Ten to one but they'll overturn us next!"

[6] *address:* Cleverness.

After much debating, they, at length, agreed to go on, till we came to some inn, or met with a passenger who could direct us. We soon arrived at a small farm-house, and the footman alighted, and went into it.

In a few minutes he returned, and told us we might proceed, for that he had procured a direction; "But," added he, "it seems there are some thieves hereabouts; and so the best way will be for you to leave your watches and purses with the farmer, who I know very well, and who is an honest man, and a tenant of my Lady's."

"Thieves!" cried Madame Duval, looking aghast, "the Lord help us! — I've no doubt but we shall be all murdered!"

The farmer came to us, and we gave him all we were worth, and the servants followed our example. We then proceeded, and Madame Duval's anger so entirely subsided, that, in the mildest manner imaginable, she intreated them to make haste, and promised to tell their Lady how diligent and obliging they had been. She perpetually stopped them, to ask if they apprehended any danger; and was, at length, so much overpowered by her fears, that she made the footman fasten his horse to the back of the carriage, and then come and seat himself within it. My endeavours to encourage her were fruitless; she sat in the middle, held the man by the arm, and protested that if he did but save her life, she would make his fortune. Her uneasiness gave me much concern, and it was with the utmost difficulty I forbore to acquaint her that she was imposed upon; but the mutual fear of the Captain's resentment to me, and of her own to him, neither of which would have any moderation, deterred me. As to the footman, he was evidently in torture from restraining his laughter, and I observed that he was frequently obliged to make most horrid grimaces, from pretended fear, in order to conceal his risibility.

Very soon after, "The robbers are coming!" cried the coachman.

The footman opened the door, and jumped out of the chariot.

Madame Duval gave a loud scream.

I could no longer preserve my silence. "For Heaven's sake, my dear Madam," said I, "don't be alarmed, — you are in no danger — you are quite safe, — there is nothing but — "

Here the chariot was stopped, by two men in masks, who, at each side, put in their hands, as if for our purses. Madame Duval sunk to the bottom of the chariot, and implored their mercy. I shrieked involuntarily, although prepared for the attack: one of them held me fast, while the other tore poor Madame Duval out of the carriage, in spite of her cries, threats, and resistance.

I was really frightened, and trembled exceedingly. "My angel!" cried the man who held me, "you cannot surely be alarmed, — do you not know me? — I shall hold myself in eternal abhorrence, if I have really terrified you."

"Indeed, Sir Clement, you have," cried I, — "but, for Heaven's sake, where is Madame Duval? — why is she forced away?"

"She is perfectly safe; the Captain has her in charge: but suffer me now, my adored Miss Anville, to take the only opportunity that is allowed me, to speak upon another, a much dearer, much sweeter subject."

And then he hastily came into the chariot, and seated himself next to me. I would fain have disengaged myself from him, but he would not let me; "Deny me not, most charming of women," cried he, "deny me not this only moment that is lent me, to pour forth my soul into your gentle ears, — to tell you how much I suffer from your absence, — how much I dread your displeasure, — and how cruelly I am affected by your coldness!"

"O Sir, this is no time for such language, — pray leave me, pray go to the relief of Madame Duval, — I cannot bear that she should be treated with such indignity."

"And will you, — can you command my absence? — When may I speak to you, if not now? — does the Captain suffer me to breathe a moment out of his sight? — and are not a thousand impertinent people for ever at your elbow?"

"Indeed, Sir Clement, you must change your style, or I will not hear you. The *impertinent people* you mean, are among my best friends, and you would not, if you really wished me well, speak of them so disrespectfully."

"Wish you well! — O Miss Anville, point but out to me how, in what manner, I may convince you of the fervour of my passion, — tell me but what services you will accept from me, — and you shall find my life, my fortune, my whole soul at your devotion."

"I want *nothing*, Sir, that you can offer; — I beg you not to talk to me so — so strangely. Pray leave me, and pray assure yourself, you cannot take any method so successless to shew any regard for me, as entering into schemes so frightful to Madame Duval, and so disagreeable to myself."

"The scheme was the Captain's; I even opposed it: though, I own, I could not refuse myself the so-long-wished-for happiness, of speaking to you once more, without so many of — your *friends* to watch me. And I had flattered myself that the note I charged the footman to give you would have prevented the alarm you have received."

"Well, Sir, you have now, I hope, said enough; and, if you will not go yourself to see for Madame Duval, at least suffer *me* to enquire what is become of her."

"And when may I speak to you again?"

"No matter when, — I don't know, — perhaps — "

"Perhaps what, my angel?"

"Perhaps *never*, Sir, — if you torment me thus."

"Never! O Miss Anville, how cruel, how piercing to my soul is that icy word! — Indeed, I cannot endure such displeasure."

"Then, Sir, you must not provoke it. Pray leave me directly."

"I will, Madam: but let me, at least, make a merit of my obedience, — allow me to hope, that you will, in future, be less averse to trusting yourself for a few moments alone with me."

I was surprised at the freedom of this request; but, while I hesitated how to answer it, the other mask came up to the chariot-door, and, in a voice almost stifled with laughter, said, "I've done for her! — the old buck[7] is safe; — but we must sheer off directly, or we shall be all aground."

Sir Clement instantly left me, mounted his horse, and rode off. The Captain, having given some directions to the servants, followed him.

I was both uneasy and impatient to know the fate of Madame Duval, and immediately got out of the chariot to seek her. I desired the footman to shew me which way she was gone; he pointed with his finger, by way of answer, and I saw that he dared not trust his voice to make any other. I walked on, a very quick pace, and soon, to my great consternation, perceived the poor lady, seated upright in a ditch. I flew to her, with unfeigned concern at her situation. She was sobbing, nay, almost roaring, and in the utmost agony of rage and terror. As soon as she saw me she redoubled her cries, but her voice was so broken, I could not understand a word she said. I was so much shocked, that it was with difficulty I forbore exclaiming against the cruelty of the Captain, for thus wantonly ill-treating her; and I could not forgive myself for having passively suffered the deception. I

---

[7] *buck*: This term, usually meaning the male of a species or a young and gay man, seems oddly applied to Duval. The nautical context in which it occurs suggests that Mirvan is drawing on another of the word's meanings, denoting a wash-tub, or some kind of vessel. One could imagine a sea captain referring to a ship he is "convoying" as a buck or tub.

used my utmost endeavors to comfort her, assuring her of our present safety, and begging her to rise, and return to the chariot.

Almost bursting with passion, she pointed to her feet, and with frightful violence, she actually beat the ground with her hands.

I then saw, that her feet were tied together with a strong rope, which was fastened to the upper branch of a tree, even with an hedge which ran along the ditch where she sat. I endeavoured to untie'the knot, but soon found it was infinitely beyond my strength. I was, therefore, obliged to apply to the footman; but being very unwilling to add to his mirth, by the sight of Madame Duval's situation, I desired him to lend me a knife; I returned with it, and cut the rope. Her feet were soon disentangled, and then, though with great difficulty, I assisted her to rise. But what was my astonishment, when, the moment she was up, she hit me a violent slap on the face! I retreated from her with precipitation and dread, and she then loaded me with reproaches, which, though almost unintelligible, convinced me that she imagined I had voluntarily deserted her; but she seemed not to have the slightest suspicion that she had not been attacked by real robbers.

I was so much surprised and confounded at the blow, that, for some time, I suffered her to rave, without making any answer; but her extreme agitation, and real suffering, soon dispelled my anger, which all turned into compassion. I then told her, that I had been forcibly detained from following her, and assured her of my real sorrow at her ill usage.

She began to be somewhat appeased; and I again entreated her to return to the carriage, or give me leave to order that it should draw up to the place where we stood. She made no answer, till I told her, that the longer we remained still, the greater would be the danger of our ride home. Struck with this hint, she suddenly, and with hasty steps, moved forward.

Her dress was in such disorder, that I was quite sorry to have her figure exposed to the servants, who all of them, in imitation of their master, hold her in derision: however, the disgrace was unavoidable.

The ditch, happily, was almost quite dry, or she must have suffered still more seriously; yet, so forlorn, so miserable a figure, I never before saw. Her head-dress had fallen off; her linen was torn; her negligee had not a pin left in it; her petticoats she was obliged to hold on; and her shoes were perpetually slipping off. She was covered with dirt, weeds, and filth, and her face was really horrible, for the pomatum and powder from her head, and the dust from the road, were quite *pasted* on her skin by her tears, which, with her *rouge*, made so frightful a mixture, that she hardly looked human.

The servants were ready to die with laughter, the moment they saw her; but not all my remonstrances could prevail upon her to get into the carriage, till she had most vehemently reproached them both, for not rescuing her. The footman, fixing his eyes on the ground, as if fearful of again trusting himself to look at her, protested that the robbers had vowed they would shoot him, if he moved an inch, and that one of them had stayed to watch the chariot, while the other carried her off; adding, that the reason of their behaving so barbarously, was to revenge our having secured our purses. Notwithstanding her anger, she gave immediate credit to what he said, and really imagined that her want of money had irritated the pretended robbers to treat her with such cruelty. I determined, therefore, to be carefully upon my guard, not to betray the imposition, which could now answer no other purpose, than occasioning an irreparable breach between her and the Captain.

Just as we were seated in the chariot, she discovered the loss which her head had sustained, and called out, "My God! what is becomed of my hair? — why the villain has stole all my curls!"

She then ordered the man to run and see if he could find any of them in the ditch. He went, and presently returning, produced a great quantity of hair, in such a nasty condition, that I was amazed she would take it; and the man, as he delivered it to her, found it impossible to keep his countenance; which she no sooner observed, than all her stormy passions were again raised. She flung the battered curls in his face, saying, "Sirrah, what do you grin for? I wish you'd been served so yourself, and you would n't have found it no such joke: you are the impudentest fellow ever I see, and if I find you dare grin at me any more, I shall make no ceremony of boxing your ears."

Satisfied with the threat, the man hastily retired, and we drove on.

Her anger now subsiding into grief, she began most sorrowfully to lament her case. "I believe," she cried, "never nobody was so unlucky as I am! and so here, because I ha'n't had misfortunes enough already, that puppy has made me lose my curls! — Why, I can't see nobody without them: — only look at me, — I was never so bad off in my life before. *Pardie*, if I'd know'd as much, I'd have brought two or three sets with me: but I'd never a thought of such a thing as this."

Finding her now somewhat pacified, I ventured to ask an account of her adventure, which I will endeavour to write in her own words.

"Why, child, all this misfortune comes of that puppy's making us leave our money behind us; for as soon as the robber see I did not put nothing in his hands, he lugged me out of the chariot by main force, and I verily thought he'd have murdered me. He was as strong as a lion; I was no more in his hands than a child. But I believe never nobody was so abused before, for he dragged me down the road, pulling and hawling me all the way, as if I'd no more feeling than a horse. I'm sure I wish I could see that man cut up and quartered alive! however, he'll come to the gallows, that's one good thing. So, as soon as we'd got out of sight of the chariot, — though he need n't have been afraid, for if he'd beat me to a mummy,[8] those cowardly fellows would n't have said nothing to it. — So, when I was got there, what does he do, but, all of a sudden, he takes me by both the shoulders, and he gives me such a shake! — *Mon Dieu!* I shall never forgot it, if I live to be an hundred. I'm sure I dare say I'm out of joint all over. And, though I made as much noise as ever I could, he took no more notice of it than nothing at all, but there he stood, shaking me in that manner, as if he was doing it for a wager. I'm determined, if it costs me all my fortune, I'll see that villain hanged. He shall be found out, if there's e'er a justice in England. So when he had shooked me till he was tired, and I felt all over like a jelly, without saying never a word, he takes and pops me into the ditch! I'm sure I thought he'd have murdered me, as much as I ever thought any thing in my life, for he kept bumping me about, as if he thought nothing too bad for me. However, I'm resolved I'll never leave my purse behind me again, the longest day I have to live. So when he could n't stand over me no longer, he holds out his hands again for my money; but he was as cunning as could be, for he would n't speak a word, because I should n't swear to his voice; however, that sha'n't save him, for I'll swear to him any day in the year, if I can but catch him. So, when I told him I had no money, he fell to jerking me again, just as if he had but that moment begun! And, after that, he got me close by a tree, and out of his pocket he pulls a great cord! — It's a wonder I did not swoon away, for as sure as you're alive, he was going to hang me to that tree. I screamed like any thing mad, and told him if he would but spare my life, I'd never prosecute him, nor tell nobody what he'd done to me: so he stood some time, quite in a brown study, a thinking what he should do. And so, after that, he forced me to sit down in the ditch, and he tied my feet together, just as you see them, and then,

[8] *beat me to a mummy:* Into a bloody pulp.

as if he had not done enough, he twitched off my cap, and, without saying nothing, got on his horse, and left me in that condition, thinking, I suppose, that I might lie there and perish."

Though this narrative almost compelled me to laugh, yet I was really irritated with the Captain, for carrying his love of tormenting, — *sport*, he calls it, — to such barbarous and unjustifiable extremes. I consoled and soothed her as well as I was able, and told her that, since M. Du Bois had escaped, I hoped, when she recovered from her fright, all would end well.

"Fright, child!" repeated she, "why, that's not half; — I promise you, I wish it was; but here I'm bruised from top to toe, and it's well if ever I have the right use of my limbs again. However, I'm glad the villain got nothing but his trouble for his pains. But here the worst is to come, for I can't go out, because I've got no curls, and so he'll be escaped, before I can get to the Justice to stop him. I'm resolved I'll tell Lady Howard how her man served me, for if he had n't made me fling 'em away, I dare say I could have pinned them up well enough for the country."

"Perhaps Lady Howard may be able to lend you a cap that will wear without them."

"Lady Howard, indeed! why, do you think I'd wear one of her dowdies?[9] No, I'll promise you, I sha'n't put on no such disguisement. It's the unluckiest thing in the world that I did not make the man pick up the curls again; but he put me in such a passion, I could not think of nothing. I know I can't get none at Howard Grove for love nor money, for of all the stupid places ever I see, that Howard Grove is the worst! there's never no getting nothing one wants."

This sort of conversation lasted till we arrived at our journey's end; and then, a new distress occurred; Madame Duval was eager to speak to Lady Howard and Mrs. Mirvan, and to relate her misfortunes, but she could not endure that Sir Clement or the Captain should see her in such disorder, for she said they were so ill-natured, that instead of pitying her, they would only make a jest of her disasters. She therefore sent me first into the house, to wait for an opportunity of their being out of the way, that she might steal up stairs unobserved. In this I succeeded, as the gentlemen thought it most prudent not to seem watching for her; though they both contrived to divert themselves with peeping at her as she passed.

---

[9] *dowdies:* A woman's cap, often a nightcap.

She went immediately to bed, where she had her supper. Lady Howard and Mrs. Mirvan both of them very kindly sat with her, and listened to her tale with compassionate attention; while Miss Mirvan and I retired to our own room, where I was very glad to end the troubles of the day in a comfortable conversation.

The Captain's raptures, during supper, at the success of his plan, were boundless. I spoke, afterwards, to Mrs. Mirvan, with the openness which her kindness encourages, and begged her to remonstrate with him upon the cruelty of tormenting Madame Duval so causelessly. She promised to take the first opportunity of starting the subject, but said he was, at present, so much elated that he would not listen to her with any patience. However, should he make any new efforts to molest her, I can by no means consent to be passive. Had I imagined he would have been so violent, I would have risked his anger in her defence much sooner.

She has kept her bed all day, and declares she is almost bruised to death.

Adieu, dear Sir. What a long letter have I written! I could almost fancy I sent it you from London!

## LETTER III

### Evelina in Continuation

Howard Grove, May 15th.

This insatiable Captain, if left to himself, would not, I believe, rest, till he had tormented Madame Duval into a fever. He seems to have no delight but in terrifying or provoking her, and all his thoughts apparently turn upon inventing such methods as may do it most effectually.

She had her breakfast again in bed yesterday morning; but, during ours, the Captain, with a very significant look at Sir Clement, gave us to understand, that he thought she had now rested long enough to bear the hardships of a fresh campaign.

His meaning was obvious, and, therefore, I resolved to endeavour immediately to put a stop to his intended exploits. When breakfast was over, I followed Mrs. Mirvan out of the parlour, and begged her to lose no time in pleading the cause of Madame Duval with the Captain. "My love," answered she, "I have already expostulated with him; but all I can say is fruitless, while his favourite Sir Clement contrives to urge him on."

"Then I will go and speak to Sir Clement," said I, "for I know he will desist, if I request him."

"Have a care, my dear," said she, smiling, "it is sometimes dangerous to make requests to men, who are too desirous of receiving them."

"Well then, my dear Madam, will you give me leave to speak myself to the Captain?"

"Willingly; nay, I will accompany you to him."

I thanked her, and we went to seek him. He was walking in the garden with Sir Clement. Mrs. Mirvan most obligingly made an opening for my purpose, by saying, "Mr. Mirvan, I have brought a petitioner with me."

"Why, what's the matter now?" cried he.

I was fearful of making him angry, and stammered very much, when I told him, I hoped he had no new plan for alarming Madame Duval.

"*New* plan!" cried he, "why, you don't suppose the *old* one would do again, do you? Not but what it was a very good one, only I doubt she would n't bite."

"Indeed, Sir," said I, "she has already suffered too much, and I hope you will pardon me, if I take the liberty of telling you, that I think it my duty to do all in my power to prevent her being again so much terrified."

A sullen gloominess instantly clouded his face, and, turning short from me, he said, I might do as I pleased, but that I should much sooner repent than repair my officiousness.

I was too much disconcerted at this rebuff, to attempt making any answer, and, finding that Sir Clement warmly espoused my cause, I walked away, and left them to discuss the point together.

Mrs. Mirvan, who never speaks to the Captain when he is out of humour, was glad to follow me, and, with her usual sweetness, made a thousand apologies for her husband's ill-manners.

When I left her, I went to Madame Duval, who was just risen, and employed in examining the cloaths she had on the day of her ill usage.

"Here's a sight!" cried she. "Come here, child, — only look — *Pardie*, so long as I've lived, I never see so much before! Why, all my things are spoilt, and, what's worse, my sacque[1] was as good as new. Here's the second negligee I've had used in this manner! — I am sure I

---

[1] *sacque:* A style of gown; French in origin but also worn in England in the eighteenth century.

was a fool to put it on, in such a lonesome place as this; however, if I
stay here these ten years, I'll never put on another good gown, that
I'm resolved."

"Will you let the maid try if she can iron it out, or clean it,
Ma'am?"

"No, she'll only make bad worse. — But look here, now, here's a
cloak! *Mon Dieu!* why, it looks like a dish-clout! Of all the unlucki-
nesses that ever I met, this is the worst! for, do you know, I bought it
but the day before I left Paris? — Besides, into the bargain, my cap's
quite gone; where the villain twitched it, I don't know, but I never see
no more of it, from that time to this. Now you must know this was
the becomingest cap I had in the world, for I've never another with
pink ribbon in it; and, to tell you the truth, if I had n't thought to
have seen M. Du Bois, I'd no more have put it on than I'd have
flown; for as to what one wears in such a stupid place as this, it signifies no more than nothing at all."

She then told me, that she had been thinking all night of a contrivance to hinder the Captain's finding out her loss of curls; which
was, having a large gauze handkerchief pinned on her head as a
hood, and saying she had the tooth-ach.

"To tell you the truth," added she, "I believe that Captain is one
of the worst men in the world; he's always making a joke of me; and
as to his being a gentleman, he has no more manners than a bear, for
he's always upon the grin when one's in distress; and, I declare, I'd
rather be done any thing to than laugh'd at, for, to my mind, it's one
or other the disagreeablest thing in the world."

Mrs. Mirvan, I found, had been endeavouring to dissuade her
from the design she had formed, of having recourse to the law, in
order to find out the supposed robbers; for she dreads a discovery of
the Captain, during Madame Duval's stay at Howard Grove, as it
could not fail being productive of infinite commotion. She has, therefore, taken great pains to shew the inutility of applying to justice, unless she were more able to describe the offenders against whom she
would appear, and has assured her, that as she neither heard their
voices, nor saw their faces, she cannot possibly swear to their persons, or obtain any redress.

Madame Duval, in telling me this, extremely lamented her hard
fate, that she was thus prevented from revenging her injuries; which,
however, she vowed she would not be persuaded to *pocket tamely,*
"because," added she, "if such villains as these are let to have their
own way, and nobody takes no notice of their impudence, they'll

make no more ado than nothing at all of tying people in ditches, and such things as that: however, I shall consult with M. Du Bois, as soon as I can ferret out where he's hid himself. I'm sure I've a right to his advice, for it's all along of his gaping about at the Tower that I've met with these misfortunes."

"M. Du Bois," said I, "will, I am sure, be very sorry when he hears what has happened."

"And what good will that do now? — that won't unspoil all my cloaths; I can tell him, I a'n't much obliged to him, though it's no fault of his; — yet it i'n't the less provokinger for that. I'm sure, if he had been there, to have seen me served in that manner, and put neck and heels into a ditch, he'd no more have thought it was me, than the Pope of Rome. I'll promise you, whatever you may think of it, I sha'n't have no rest, night nor day, till I find out that rogue."

"I have no doubt, Madam, but you will soon discover him."

"*Pardie,* if I do, I'll hang him, as sure as fate! — but what's the oddest, is that he should take such a 'special spite against *me,* above all the rest! it was as much for nothing, as could be, for I don't know what I had done, so particular bad, to be used in that manner: I'm sure, I had n't given him no offence, as I know of, for I never see his face all the time; and as to screaming a little, I think it's very hard if one must n't do such a thing as that, when one's put in fear of one's life."

During this conversation, she endeavoured to adjust her head dress, but could not at all please herself. Indeed, had I not been present, I should have thought it impossible for a woman at her time of life to be so very difficult in regard to dress. What she may have in view, I cannot imagine, but the labour of the toilette seems the chief business of her life.

When I left her, in my way down stairs, I met with Sir Clement, who, with great earnestness, said he must not be denied the honour of a moment's conversation with me; and then, without waiting for an answer, he led me to the garden, at the door of which, however, I absolutely insisted upon stopping.

He seemed very serious, and said, in a grave tone of voice, "At length, Miss Anville, I flatter myself that I have hit upon an expedient that will oblige you, and therefore, though it is death to myself, I will put it in practice."

I begged him to explain himself.

"I saw your desire of saving Madame Duval, and scarce could I refrain giving the brutal Captain my real opinion of his savage conduct;

but I am unwilling to quarrel with him, lest I should be denied entrance into a house which you inhabit: I have been endeavouring to prevail with him to give up his absurd new scheme, but I find him impenetrable; — I have therefore determined to make a pretence for suddenly leaving this place, dear as it is to me, and containing all I most admire and adore; — and I will stay in town till the violence of this boobyish humour is abated."

He stopped; but I was silent, for I knew not what I ought to say. He took my hand, which he pressed to his lips, saying, "And must I, then, Miss Anville, must I quit you — sacrifice voluntarily my greatest felicity, — and yet not be honoured with one word, one look of approbation?" —

I withdrew my hand, and said, with a half laugh, "You know so well, Sir Clement, the value of the favours you confer, that it would be superfluous for me to point it out."

"Charming, charming girl! how does your wit, your understanding rise upon me daily! and must I, can I part with you? — will no other method — "

"O Sir, do you so soon repent the good office you had planned for Madame Duval?"

"For Madame Duval! — cruel creature, and will you not even suffer me to place to your account the sacrifice I am about to make?"

"You must place it, Sir, to what account you please; but I am too much in haste now to stay here any longer."

And then I would have left him, but he held me, and, rather impatiently, said, "If, then, I cannot be so happy as to oblige *you*, Miss Anville, you must not be surprised, should I seek to oblige myself. If my scheme is not honoured with your approbation, for which alone it was formed, why should I, to my own infinite dissatisfaction, pursue it?"

We were then, for a few minutes, both silent; I was really unwilling he should give up a plan which would so effectually break into the Captain's designs, and, at the same time, save me the pain of disobliging him; and I should instantly and thankfully have accepted his offered civility, had not Mrs. Mirvan's caution made me fearful. However, when he pressed me to speak, I said, in an ironical voice, "I had thought, Sir, that the very strong sense you have yourself of the favour you propose to me, would sufficiently have repaid you, but, as I was mistaken, I must thank you myself. And now," making a low court'sy, "I hope, Sir, you are satisfied."

"Loveliest of thy sex — " he began, but I forced myself from him, and ran up stairs.

Soon after, Miss Mirvan told me that Sir Clement had just received a letter, which obliged him instantly to leave the Grove, and that he had actually ordered a chaise. I then acquainted her with the real state of the affair. Indeed, I conceal nothing from her, she is so gentle and sweet-tempered, that it gives me great pleasure to place an entire confidence in her.

At dinner, I must own, we all missed him; for though the flightiness of his behaviour to me, when we are by ourselves, is very distressing, yet, in large companies, and general conversation, he is extremely entertaining and agreeable. As to the Captain, he has been so much chagrined at his departure, that he has scarce spoken a word since he went: but Madame Duval, who made her first public appearance since her accident, was quite in raptures that she escaped seeing him.

The money which we left at the farm-house, has been returned to us. What pains the Captain must have taken to arrange and manage the adventures which he chose we should meet with! Yet he must certainly be discovered, for Madame Duval is already very much perplexed, at having received a letter this morning from M. Du Bois, in which he makes no mention of his imprisonment. However, she has so little suspicion, that she imputes his silence upon the subject, to his fears that the letter might be intercepted.

Not one opportunity could I meet with, while Sir Clement was here, to enquire after his friend Lord Orville: but I think it was strange he should never mention him unasked. Indeed, I rather wonder that Mrs. Mirvan herself did not introduce the subject, for she always seemed particularly attentive to him.

And now, once more, all my thoughts involuntarily turn upon the letter I so soon expect from Paris. This visit of Sir Clement has, however, somewhat diverted my fears, and therefore I am very glad he made it at this time. Adieu, my dear Sir.

## LETTER IV

### Sir John Belmont to Lady Howard

Paris, May 11.

Madam,

I have this moment the honour of your Ladyship's letter, and I will not wait another, before I return an answer.

It seldom happens that a man, though extolled as a saint, is really without blemish; or that another, though reviled as a devil, is really without humanity. Perhaps the time is not very distant, when I may have the honour to convince your Ladyship of this truth, in regard to Mr. Villars and myself.

As to the young Lady, whom Mr. Villars so obligingly proposes presenting to me, I wish her all the happiness to which, by your Ladyship's account, she seems entitled; and, if she has a third part of the merit of *her* to whom you compare her, I doubt not but Mr. Villars will be more successful in every other application he may make for her advantage, than he can ever be in any with which he may be pleased to favour me.

> I have the honour to be,
> Madam,
> your Ladyship's most humble
> and most obedient servant
> JOHN BELMONT

## LETTER V

### Evelina to the Rev. Mr. Villars

Howard-Grove, May 18.

Well, my dear Sir, all is now over! the letter so anxiously expected, is at length arrived, and my doom is fixed. The various feelings which oppress me, I have not language to describe; nor need I — you know my heart, you have yourself formed it, — and its sensations upon this occasion, you may but too readily imagine.

Outcast as I am, and rejected for ever by him to whom I of right belong, — shall I now implore *your* continued protection?—no, no, — I will not offend your generous heart (which, open to distress, has no wish but to relieve it) with an application that would seem to imply a doubt. I am more secure than ever of your kindness, since you now know upon that is my sole dependance.

I endeavour to bear this stroke with composure, and in such a manner as if I had already received your counsel and consolation. Yet, at times, my emotions are almost too much for me. O Sir, what a letter for a parent to write! must I not myself be deaf to the voice of Nature, if I could endure to be thus absolutely abandoned, without regret? I dare not, even to you, nor would I, could I help it, to myself, acknowledge all that I think; for, indeed, I have, sometimes, sentiments upon this rejection, which my strongest sense of duty can scarcely correct. Yet, suffer me to ask, — might not this answer have been softened? — was it not enough to disclaim me for ever, without treating me with contempt, and wounding me with derision?

But, while I am thus thinking of myself, I forget how much more *he* is the object of sorrow, than I am! Alas, what amends can he make himself, for the anguish he is hoarding up for time to come! My heart bleeds for him, whenever this reflection occurs to me.

What is said of *you*, my protector, my friend, my benefactor! — I dare not trust myself to comment upon. Gracious Heaven! what a return for goodness so unparalleled!

I would fain endeavour to divert my thoughts from this subject, but even that is not in my power; for, afflicting as this letter is to me, I find that it will not be allowed to conclude the affair, though it does all my expectations: for Madame Duval has determined not to let it rest here. She heard the letter in great wrath, and protested she would not be so easily answered; she regretted her facility, in having been prevailed upon to yield the direction of this affair to those who knew not how to manage it, and vowed she would herself undertake and conduct it in future.

It is in vain that I have pleaded against her resolution, and besought her to forbear an attack, where she has nothing to expect but resentment; especially as there seems to be a hint, that Lady Howard will one day be more openly dealt with: she will not hear me; she is furiously bent upon a project which is terrible to think of, — for she means to go herself to Paris, take me with her, and there, *face to face,* demand justice!

How to appease or to persuade her, I know not; but for the universe would I not be dragged, in such a manner, to an interview so awful, with a parent I have never yet beheld!

Lady Howard and Mrs. Mirvan are both of them infinitely shocked at the present situation of affairs, and they seem to be even more kind to me than ever; and my dear Maria, who is the friend of my heart, uses her utmost efforts to console me, and, when she fails in her design, with still greater kindness, she sympathises in my sorrow.

I very much rejoice, however, that Sir Clement Willoughby had left us before this letter arrived. I am sure the general confusion of the house would, otherwise, have betrayed to him the whole of a tale which I now, more than ever, wish to have buried in oblivion.

Lady Howard thinks I ought not to disoblige Madame Duval, yet she acknowledges the impropriety of my accompanying her abroad upon such an enterprize. Indeed I would rather die, than force myself into his presence. But so vehement is Madame Duval, that she would instantly have compelled me to attend her to town, in her way to Paris, had not Lady Howard so far exerted herself, as to declare she could by no means consent to my quitting her house, till she gave me up to you, by whose permission I had entered it.

She was extremely angry at this denial; and the Captain, by his sneers and raillery, so much encreased her rage, that she has positively declared, should your next letter dispute her authority to guide me by her own pleasure, she will, without hesitation, make a journey to Berry Hill, and *teach you to know who she is.*

Should she put this threat in execution, nothing could give me greater uneasiness, for her violence and volubility would almost distract you.

Unable as I am to act for myself, or to judge what conduct I ought to pursue, how grateful do I feel myself, that I have such a guide and director to counsel and instruct me as yourself!

Adieu, my dearest Sir! Heaven, I trust, will never let me live to be repulsed and derided by *you*, to whom I may now sign myself

Wholly your
EVELINA

## LETTER VI

### Mr. Villars to Evelina

Berry Hill, May 25.

Let not my Evelina be depressed by a stroke of fortune for which she is not responsible. No breach of duty on your part, has incurred the unkindness which has been shewn you, nor have you, by any act of imprudence, provoked either censure or reproach. Let me entreat you, therefore, my dearest child, to support yourself with that courage which your innocency ought to inspire; and let all the affliction you allow yourself, be for him only, who, not having that support, must one day be but too severely sensible how much he wants it.

The hint thrown out concerning myself, is wholly unintelligible to me: my heart, I dare own, fully acquits me of vice, but *without blemish,* I have never ventured to pronounce myself. However, it seems his intention to be hereafter more explicit, and *then,* — should any thing appear, that has on *my* part, contributed to those misfortunes we lament, let me, at least, say, that the most partial of my friends cannot be so much astonished as I shall myself be, at such a discovery.

The mention, also, of any *future applications* I may make, is equally beyond my comprehension. But I will not dwell upon a subject which almost compels from me reflections that cannot but be wounding to a heart so formed for filial tenderness as my Evelina's. There is an air of mystery throughout the letter, the explanation of which I will await in silence.

The scheme of Madame Duval is such as might be reasonably expected from a woman so little inured to disappointment, and so totally incapable of considering the delicacy of your situation. Your averseness to her plan gives me pleasure, for it exactly corresponds with my own. Why will she not make the journey she projects by herself? She would not have even the wish of an opposition to encounter. And then, once more, might my child and myself be left to the quiet enjoyment of that peaceful happiness, which she alone has interrupted. As to her coming hither, I could, indeed, dispense with such a visit; but, if she will not be satisfied with my refusal by letter, I must submit to the task of giving it her in person.

My impatience for your return is encreased by your account of Sir Clement Willoughby's visit to Howard Grove. I am but little surprised at the perseverance of his assiduities to interest you in his favour; but I am very much hurt that you should be exposed to addresses, which, by their privacy, have an air that shocks me. You cannot, my love, be too circumspect; the slightest carelessness on your part, will be taken advantage of, by a man of his disposition. It is not sufficient for you to be reserved; his conduct even calls for your resentment: and should he again, as will doubtless be his endeavour, contrive to solicit your favour in private, let your disdain and displeasure be so marked, as to constrain a change in his behaviour. Though, indeed, should his visit be repeated while you remain at the Grove, Lady Howard must pardon me if I shorten your's.

Adieu, my child. You will always make my respects to the hospitable family to which we are so much obliged.

## LETTER VII

### Mr. Villars to Lady Howard

Berry Hill, May 27.

Dear Madam,

I believe your Ladyship will not be surprised at hearing I have had a visit from Madame Duval, as I doubt not her having made known her intention before she left Howard Grove. I would gladly have excused myself this meeting, could I have avoided it decently; but, after so long a journey, it was not possible to refuse her admittance.

She told me, that she came to Berry Hill, in consequence of a letter I had sent to her grand-daughter, in which I had forbid her going to Paris. Very roughly, she then called me to account for the authority which I assumed; and, had I been disposed to have argued with her, she would very angrily have disputed the right by which I used it. But I declined all debating. I therefore listened very quietly, till she had so much fatigued herself with talking, that she was glad, in her turn, to be silent. And then, I begged to know the purport of her visit.

She answered, that she came to make me relinquish the power I had usurped over her grand-daughter, and assured me she would not quit the place till she succeeded.

But I will not trouble your Ladyship with the particulars of this disagreeable conversation; nor should I, but on account of the result, have chosen so unpleasant a subject for your perusal. However, I will be as concise as I possibly can, that the better occupations of your Ladyship's time may be the less impeded.

When she found me inexorable in refusing Evelina's attending her to Paris, she peremptorily insisted, that she should, at least, live with her in London, till Sir John Belmont's return. I remonstrated against this scheme with all the energy in my power; but the contest was vain; she lost her patience, and I my time. She declared that if I was resolute in opposing her, she would instantly make a will, in which she would leave all her fortune to strangers, though, otherwise, she intended her grand-daughter for her sole heiress.

To me, I own, this threat seemed of little consequence; I have long accustomed myself to think, that, with a competency, of which she is sure, my child might be as happy as in the possession of millions: but the incertitude of her future fate, deters me from following implicitly the dictates of my present judgment. The connections she may hereafter form, the style of life for which she may be destined, and the future family to which she may belong, are considerations which give but too much weight to the menaces of Madame Duval. In short, Madam, after a discourse infinitely tedious, I was obliged, though very reluctantly, to compromise with this ungovernable woman, by consenting that Evelina should pass one month with her.

I never made a concession with so bad a grace, or so much regret. The violence and vulgarity of this woman, her total ignorance of propriety, the family to which she is related, and the company she is likely to keep, are objections so forcible to her having the charge of this dear child, that nothing less than my diffidence of the right I have of depriving her of so large a fortune, would have induced me to listen to her proposal. Indeed we parted, at last, equally discontented, she, at what I had refused, I, at what I had granted.

It now only remains for me to return your Ladyship my humble acknowledgements for the kindness which you have so liberally shewn to my ward, and to beg you would have the goodness to part with her, when Madame Duval thinks proper to claim the promise which she has extorted from me. I am,

Dear Madam, &c.<br>Arthur Villars


## LETTER VIII

### Mr. Villars to Evelina

Berry Hill, May 28.

With a reluctance which occasions me inexpressible uneasiness, I have been almost compelled to consent that my Evelina should quit the protection of the hospitable and respectable Lady Howard, and accompany Madame Duval to a city to which I had hoped she had bid an eternal adieu. But alas, my dear child, we are the slaves of custom, the dupes of prejudice, and dare not stem the torrent of an opposing world, even though our judgments condemn our compliance! however, since the die is cast, we must endeavour to make the best of it.

You will have occasion, in the course of the month you are to pass with Madame Duval, for all the circumspection and prudence you can call to your aid: she will not, I know, propose any thing to you which she thinks wrong herself; but you must learn not only to *judge* but to *act* for yourself: if any schemes are started, any engagements made, which your understanding represents to you as improper, exert yourself resolutely in avoiding them, and do not, by a too passive facility, risk the censure of the world, or your own future regret.

You cannot too assiduously attend to Madame Duval herself; but I would wish you to mix as little as possible with her associates, who are not likely to be among those whose acquaintance would reflect credit upon you. Remember, my dear Evelina, nothing is so delicate as the reputation of a woman: it is, at once, the most beautiful and most brittle of all human things.

Adieu, my beloved child; I shall be but ill at ease till this month is elapsed.

A. V.

## LETTER IX

### Evelina to the Rev. Mr. Villars

London, June 6.

Once more, my dearest Sir, I write to you from this great city. Yesterday morning, with the truest concern, I quitted the dear inhabitants of Howard Grove, and most impatiently shall I count the days till I see them again. Lady Howard and Mrs. Mirvan took leave of me with the most flattering kindness; but indeed I knew not how to part with Maria, whose own apparent sorrow redoubled mine. She made me promise to send her a letter every post. And I shall write to her with the same freedom, and almost the same confidence, you allow me to make use of to yourself.

The Captain was very civil to me, but he wrangled with poor Madame Duval to the last moment; and, taking me aside, just before we got into the chaise, he said, "Hark'ee, Miss Anville, I've a favour for to ask of you, which is this; that you will write us word how the old gentlewoman finds herself, when she sees it was all a trick; and what the French lubber says to it, and all about it."

I answered that I would obey him, though I was very little pleased with the commission, which, to me, was highly improper: but he will either treat me as an *informer,* or make me a party in his frolic.

As soon as we drove away, Madame Duval, with much satisfaction, exclaimed *"Dieu merci,* we've got off at last! I'm sure I never desire to see that place again. It's a wonder I've got away alive; for I believe I've had the worst luck ever was known, from the point I set my foot upon the threshold. I know I wish I'd never a gone. Besides,

into the bargain, it's the most dullest place in all Christendom: there's
never no diversions, nor nothing at all."

Then she bewailed M. Du Bois, concerning whose adventures she
continued to make various conjectures during the rest of our journey.

When I asked her what part of London she should reside in, she told
me that Mr. Branghton was to meet us at an inn, and would conduct us
to a lodging. Accordingly, we proceeded to a house in Bishopsgate
Street, and were led by a waiter into a room where we found Mr.
Branghton.

He received us very civilly, but seemed rather surprised at seeing
me, saying "Why I did n't think of your bringing Miss; however she's
very welcome."

"I'll tell you how it was," said Madame Duval; "you must know
I've a mind to take the girl to Paris, that she may see something of the
world, and improve herself a little; besides, I've another reason, that
you and I will talk more about; but do you know, that meddling old
parson as I told you of, would not let her go: however, I'm resolved
I'll be even with him, for I shall take her on with me, without saying
never a word more to nobody."

I started at this intimation, which very much surprised me. But I
am very glad she has discovered her intention, as I shall be carefully
upon my guard not to venture from town with her.

Mr. Branghton then hoped we had passed our time agreeably in
the country.

"O Lord, Cousin," cried she, "I've been the miserablest creature in
the world! I'm sure all the horses in London sha'n't drag me into the
country again of one while: why how do you think I've been served? —
only guess."

"Indeed, Cousin, I can't pretend to do that."

"Why then I'll tell you. Do you know, I've been robbed? — that is,
the villain would have robbed me if he could, only I'd secured all my
money."

"Why then, Cousin, I think your loss can't have been very great."

"O Lord, you don't know what you're saying; you're talking in the
unthinkingest manner in the world: why it was all along of not having no money, that I met with that misfortune."

"How's that, Cousin? I don't see what great misfortune you can
have met with, if you'd secured all your money."

"That's because you don't know nothing of the matter; for there
the villain came to the chaise, and because we had n't got nothing to
give him, though he'd no more right to our money than the man in

the moon, yet, do you know, he fell into the greatest passion ever you see, and abused me in such a manner, and put me in a ditch, and got a rope, o' purpose to hang me, — and I'm sure, if that was n't misfortunate enough, why I don't know what is."

"This is a hard case, indeed, Cousin. Buy why don't you go to Justice Fielding?"

"O, as to that, I'm a going to him directly; but only I want first to see poor M. Du Bois, for the oddest thing of all is, that he has wrote to me, and never said nothing of where he is, nor what's become of him, nor nothing else."

"M. Du Bois! why he's at my house at this very time."

"M. Du Bois at your house! well, I declare this is the surprisingest part of all! however, I assure you, I think he might have comed for me, as well as you, considering what I have gone through on his account; for, to tell you the truth, it was all along of him that I met with that accident; so I don't take it very kind of him, I promise you."

"Well but, Cousin, tell me some of the particulars of this affair."

"As to the particulars, I'm sure they'd make your hair stand an end to hear them; however, the beginning of it all was thro' the fault of M. Du Bois: but, I'll assure you, he may take care of himself in future, since he don't so much as come to see if I'm dead or alive; — but there I went for him to a justice of peace, and rode all out of the way, and did every thing in the world, and was used worser than a dog, and all for the sake of serving of him, and now, you see, he don't so much — well, I was a fool for my pains, — however, he may get somebody else to be treated so another time, for if he's taken up every day in the week, I'll never go after him no more."

This occasioned an explanation, in the course of which, Madame Duval, to her utter amazement, heard that M. Du Bois had never left London during her absence! nor did Mr. Branghton believe that he had ever been to the Tower, or met with any kind of accident.

Almost instantly, the whole truth of the transaction seemd to *rush upon her mind,* and her wrath was inconceivably violent. She asked me a thousand questions in a breath, but, fortunately, was too vehement to attend to my embarrassment, which must, otherwise, have betrayed my knowledge of the deceit. Revenge was her first wish, and she vowed she would go the next morning to Justice Fielding, and enquire what punishment she might lawfully inflict upon the Captain for his assault.

I believe we were an hour in Bishopsgate-street, ere poor Madame Duval could allow any thing to be mentioned but her own story; at length, however, Mr. Branghton told her, that M. Du Bois, and all his own family, were waiting for her at his house. A hackney-coach was then called, and we proceeded to Snow-hill.[1]

Mr. Branghton's house is small and inconvenient, though his shop, which takes in all the ground floor, is large and commodious. I believe I told you before that he is a silver-smith.

We were conducted up two pair of stairs, for the dining-room, Mr. Branghton told us, was *let*. His two daughters, their brother, M. Du Bois, and a young man, were at tea. They had waited some time for Madame Duval, but I found they had not any expectation that I should accompany her; and the young ladies, I believe, were rather more surprised than pleased when I made my appearance; for they seemed hurt that I should see their apartment. Indeed I would willingly have saved them that pain, had it been in my power.

The first person who saw me was M. Du Bois: "*Ah, mon Dieu!*" exclaimed he, "*voilà Mademoiselle!*"

"Goodness," cried young Branghton, "if there is n't Miss!"

"Lord, so there is," said Miss Polly; "well, I'm sure I should never have dreamed of Miss's coming."

"Nor I neither, I'm sure," cried Miss Branghton, "or else I would not have been in this room to see her; I'm quite ashamed about it, — only not thinking of seeing any body but my aunt — however, Tom, it's all your fault, for you know very well I wanted to borrow Mr. Smith's room, only you were so *grumpy*, you would not let me."

"Lord, what signifies?" said the brother, "I dare be sworn Miss has been up two pair of stairs before now; — Ha'n't you, Miss?"

I begged that I might not give them the least disturbance, and assured them that I had not any choice in regard to what room we sat in.

"Well," said Miss Polly, "when you come next, Miss, we'll have Mr. Smith's room; and it's a very pretty one, and only up one pair of stairs, and nicely furnished, and every thing."

"To say the truth," said Miss Branghton, "I thought that my cousin would not, upon any account, have come to town in the summer-time; for it's not at all the *fashion,* — so, to be sure, thinks I, she'll stay till September, when the play-houses open."

This was my reception, which I believe you will not call a very *cordial* one. Madame Duval, who, after having severely reprimanded M. Du Bois for his negligence, was just entering upon the story of her misfortunes, now wholly engaged the company.

---

[1] *Snow-hill:* See footnote 4 to Volume I, Letter XVII.

M. Du Bois listened to her with a look of the utmost horror, repeatedly lifting up his eyes and hands, and exclaiming, "*O ciel! quel
barbare!*"[2] The young ladies gave her the most earnest attention; but
their brother, and the young man, kept a broad grin upon their faces
during the whole recital. She was, however, too much engaged to observe them: but, when she mentioned having been tied in a ditch,
young Branghton, no longer able to constrain himself, burst into a
loud laugh, declaring that he had never heard any thing so *funny* in
his life! His laugh was heartily re-echoed by his friend; the Miss
Branghtons could not resist the example; and poor Madame Duval,
to her extreme amazement, was absolutely overpowered and stopped
by the violence of their mirth.

For some minutes the room seemed quite in an uproar; the rage of
Madame Duval, the astonishment of M. Du Bois, and the angry interrogatories of Mr. Branghton, on one side; the convulsive tittering
of the sisters, and the loud laughs of the young men, on the other,
occasioned such noise, passion, and confusion, that had any one
stopped an instant on the stairs, he must have concluded himself in
Bedlam. At length, however, the father brought them to order; and
half laughing, half frightened, they made Madame Duval some very
awkward apologies. But she would not be prevailed upon to continue
her narrative, till they had protested they were laughing at the Captain, and not at her. Appeased by this, she resumed her story; which,
by the help of stuffing handkerchiefs into their mouths, the young
people heard with tolerable decency.

Every body agreed, that the ill usage the Captain had given her
was *actionable*, and Mr. Branghton said he was sure she might recover
what damages she pleased, since she had been put in fear of her life.

She then, with great delight, declared, that she would lose no time
in satisfying her revenge, and vowed she would not be contented with
less than half his fortune: "For though," said she, "I don't put no
value upon the money, because, *Dieu merci*, I ha'n't no want of it, yet
I don't wish for nothing so much as to punish that fellow; for, I'm
sure, whatever's the cause of it, he owes me a great *grudge*, and I
know no more what it's for than you do, but he's always been doing
me one spite or other, ever since I knew him."

Soon after tea, Miss Branghton took an opportunity to tell me, in
a whisper, that the young man I saw was a lover of her sister's, that

[2] *O . . . barbare:* "Oh heavens! what barbarity!"

his name was Brown, and that he was a haberdasher,[3] with many
other particulars of his circumstances and family; and then she declared her utter aversion to the thoughts of such a match; but added,
that her sister had no manner of spirit or ambition, though, for her
part, she would ten times rather die an old maid, than marry any person but a gentleman. "And, for that matter," added she, "I believe
Polly herself don't care much for him, only she's in such a hurry, because, I suppose, she's a mind to be married before me; however,
she's very welcome, for, I'm sure, I don't care a pin's point whether I
ever marry at all; — it's all one to me."

Some time after this, Miss Polly contrived to tell *her* story. She assured me, with much tittering, that her sister was in a great fright, lest
she should be married first, "So I make her believe that I will," continued she, "for I love dearly to plague her a little; though, I declare, I
don't intend to have Mr. Brown in reality; I'm sure I don't like him
half well enough, — do you, Miss?"

"It is not possible for me to judge of his merits," said I, "as I am
entirely a stranger to him."

"But, what do you think of him, Miss?"

"Why, really, I — I don't know — "

"But do you think him handsome? Some people reckon him to
have a good pretty person, — but, I'm sure, for my part, I think he's
monstrous ugly: — don't *you*, Miss?"

"I am no judge, — but I think his person is very — very well — ."

"*Very well!* — Why, pray, Miss," in a tone of vexation, "what
fault can you find with it?"

"O, none at all!"

"I'm sure you must be very ill-natured if you could. Now there's
Biddy says she thinks nothing of him, — but I know it's all out of
spite. You must know, Miss, it makes her as mad as can be, that I
should have a lover before her, but she's so proud, that nobody will
court her, and I often tell her she'll die an old maid. But, the thing is,
she has taken it into her head, to have a liking for Mr. Smith, as
lodges on the first floor; but, Lord, he'll never have her, for he's
quite a fine gentleman; and besides, Mr. Brown heard him say, one
day, that he'd never marry as long as he lived, for he'd no opinion of
matrimony."

---

[3] *haberdasher:* A dealer in small articles pertaining to dress, such as ribbons,
thread, and so forth.

"And did you tell your sister this?"

"O, to be sure, I told her directly; but she did not mind me; however, if she will be a fool, she must."

This extreme want of affection, and good-nature, increased the distaste I already felt for these unamiable sisters; and a confidence so entirely unsolicited and unnecessary, manifested equally their folly and their want of decency.

I was very glad when the time for our departing arrived. Mr. Branghton said our lodgings were in Holborn,[4] that we might be near his house, and neighbourly. He accompanied us to them himself.

Our rooms are large, and not inconvenient; our landlord is an hosier. I am sure I have a thousand reasons to rejoice that I am so little known; for my present situation is, in every respect, very unenviable, and I would not, for the world, be seen by any acquaintance of Mrs. Mirvan.

This morning Madame Duval, attended by all the Branghtons, actually went to a Justice in the neighbourhood, to report the Captain's ill usage of her. I had great difficulty in excusing myself from being of the party, which would have given me very serious concern. Indeed, I was extremely anxious, though at home, till I heard the result of the application; for I dread to think of the uneasiness which such an affair would occasion the amiable Mrs. Mirvan. But, fortunately, Madame Duval has received very little encouragement to proceed in her design, for she has been informed that, as she neither heard the voice, nor saw the face of the person suspected, she will find it difficult to cast him upon *conjecture*,[5] and will have but little probability of gaining her cause, unless she can procure witnesses of the transaction. Mr. Branghton, therefore, who has considered all the circumstances of the affair, is of opinion, that the law-suit will not only be expensive, but tedious and hazardous, and has advised against it. Madame Duval, though very unwillingly, has acquiesced in his decision; but vows that if ever she is so affronted again, she will be revenged, even if she ruins herself, I am extremely glad that this ridiculous adventure seems now likely to end without more serious consequences.

Adieu, my dearest Sir. My direction[6] is at Mr. Dawkins's, a hosier in High Holborn.

---

[4] *Holborn:* Like the Branghtons' address, this location in London was unfashionably associated with business.

[5] *to cast him upon conjecture:* To arrest him upon suspicion of criminal behavior.

[6] *direction:* Address.

## LETTER X

### Evelina to Miss Mirvan

June 7th.

I have no words, my sweet friend, to express the thankfulness I feel for the unbounded kindness which you, your dear mother, and the much-honoured Lady Howard, have shewn me; and still less can I find language to tell you with what reluctance I parted from such dear and generous friends, whose goodness reflects, at once, so much honour on their own hearts, and on her to whom it has been so liberally bestowed. But I will not repeat what I have already written to the kind Mrs. Mirvan; I will remember your admonitions, and confine to my own breast that gratitude with which you have filled it, and teach my pen to dwell upon subjects less painful to my generous correspondent.

O Maria, London now seems no longer the same place where I lately enjoyed so much happiness; every thing is new and strange to me; even the town itself has not the same aspect: — my situation so altered! my home so different! — my companions so changed! — But you well know my averseness to this journey.

Indeed, to me, London now seems a desart; that gay and busy appearance it so lately wore, is now succeeded by a look of gloom, fatigue, and lassitude; the air seems stagnant, the heat is intense, the dust intolerable, and the inhabitants illiterate and under-bred. At least, such is the face of things in the part of the town where I at present reside.

Tell me, my dear Maria, do you never re-trace in your memory the time we past here when together? to mine, it recurs for ever! And yet, I think I rather recollect a dream, or some visionary fancy, than a reality. — That I should ever have been known to Lord Orville, — that I should have spoken to — have danced with him, — seems now a romantic illusion: and that elegant politeness, that flattering attention, that high-bred delicacy, which so much distinguished him above all other men, and which struck us with such admiration, I now re-trace the remembrance of, rather as belonging to an object of ideal perfection, formed by my own imagination, than to a being of the same race and nature as those with whom I at present converse.

I have no news for you, my dear Miss Mirvan, for all that I could venture to say of Madame Duval, I have already written to your sweet mother; and as to adventures, I have none to record. Situated as I now am, I heartily hope I shall not meet with any; my wish is to remain quiet and unnoticed.

Adieu! excuse the gravity of this letter, and believe me,

> Your most sincerely
> affectionate and obliged
> EVELINA ANVILLE


## LETTER XI

### Evelina to the Rev. Mr. Villars

Holborn, June 9th.

Yesterday morning, we received an invitation to dine and spend the day at Mr. Branghton's; and M. Du Bois, who was also invited, called to conduct us to Snow-hill.

Young Branghton received us at the door, and the first words he spoke were, "Do you know, Sisters a'n't dressed yet?"

Then hurrying us into the house, he said to me, "Come, Miss, you shall go up stairs and catch 'em, — I dare say they're at the glass."

He would have taken my hand, but I declined his civility, and begged to follow Madame Duval. Mr. Branghton then appeared, and led the way himself. We went, as before, up two pair of stairs; but the moment the father opened the door, the daughters both gave a loud scream. We all stopped, and then Miss Branghton called out, "Lord, Papa, what do you bring the company up here for? why, Polly and I a'n't half dressed."

"More shame for you," answered he, "here's your aunt, and cousin, and M. Du Bois, all waiting, and ne'er a room to take them to."

"Who'd have thought of their coming so soon?" cried she: "I'm sure for my part I thought Miss was used to nothing but quality hours."

"Why, I sha'n't be ready this half-hour yet," said Miss Polly; "can't they stay in the shop till we're dressed?"

Mr. Branghton was very angry, and scolded them violently; however, we were obliged to descend, and stools were procured for us in the shop, where we found the brother, who was highly delighted, he said, that his sisters had been *catched;* and he thought proper to entertain me with a long account of their tediousness, and the many quarrels they all had together.

When, at length, these ladies were equipped to their satisfaction, they made their appearance; but before any conversation was suffered to pass between them and us, they had a long and most disagreeable dialogue with their father, to whose reprimands, though so justly incurred, they replied with the utmost pertness and rudeness, while their brother, all the time, laughed aloud.

The moment they perceived this, they were so much provoked, that, instead of making any apologies to Madame Duval, they next began a quarrel with him. "Tom, what do you laugh for? I wonder what business you have to be always a laughing when Papa scolds us."

"Then what business have you to be such a while getting on your cloathes? You're never ready, you know well enough."

"Lord, Sir, I wonder what that's to you! I wish you'd mind your own affairs, and not trouble yourself about ours. How should a boy like you know any thing?"

"A boy, indeed! not such a boy, neither; I'll warrant you'll be glad to be as young, when you come to be old maids."

This sort of dialogue we were amused with till dinner was ready, when we again mounted up two pair of stairs.

In our way, Miss Polly told me that her sister had asked Mr. Smith for his room to dine in, but he had refused to lend it; "because," she said, "one day it happened to be a little greased: however, we shall have it to drink tea in, and then, perhaps, you may see him, and I assure you he's quite like one of the quality, and dresses as fine, and goes to balls and dances, and every thing quite in taste; — and besides, Miss, he keeps a foot-boy of his own, too."

The dinner was ill-served, ill-cooked, and ill-managed. The maid who waited had so often to go down stairs for something that was forgotten, that the Branghtons were perpetually obliged to rise from table themselves, to get plates, knives and forks, bread, or beer. Had they been without *pretensions,* all this would have seemed of no consequence; but they aimed at appearing to advantage, and even fancied they succeeded. However, the most disagreeable part of our fare was, that the whole family continually disputed whose turn it was to rise, and whose to be allowed to sit still.

When this meal was over, Madame Duval, Mr. Branghton, and, in broken English, M. Du Bois, entered into an argument concerning the French nation; and Miss Polly, then addressing herself to me, said, "Don't you think, Miss, it's very dull sitting up stairs here? we'd better go down *to shop,* and then we shall see the people go by."

"Lord, Poll," said the brother, "you're always wanting to be staring and gaping; and I'm sure you need n't be so fond of shewing yourself, for you're ugly enough to frighten a horse."

"Ugly, indeed! I wonder which is best, you or me. But, I tell you what, Tom, you've no need to give yourself such airs, for if you do, I'll tell Miss of you know what — ."

"Who cares if you do? You may tell her what you will; I don't mind — "

"Indeed," cried I, "I do not desire to hear any secrets."

"O, but I'm resolved I'll tell you, because Tom's so very spiteful. You must know, Miss, t'other night — "

"Poll," cried the brother, "if you tell of that, Miss shall know all about your meeting young Brown, — you know when! — So I'll be quits with you, one way or another."

Miss Polly coloured, and again proposed our going down stairs till Mr. Smith's room was ready for our reception.

"Aye, so we will," said Miss Branghton; "I'll assure you, Cousin, we have some very genteel people pass by our shop sometimes. Polly and I always go and sit there, when we've cleaned ourselves."

"Yes, Miss," cried the brother, "they do nothing else all day long, when father don't scold them. But the best fun is, when they've got all their dirty things on, and all their hair about their ears, sometimes I send young Brown up stairs to them; and then, there's such a fuss! — there they hide themselves, and run away, and squeal and squall like any thing mad: and so then I puts the two cats into the room, and I gives 'em a good whipping, and so that sets them a squalling too; so there's such a noise, and such an uproar! — Lord, you can't think, Miss, what fun it is!"

This occasioned a fresh quarrel with the sisters; at the end of which, it was, at length, decided that we should go to the shop.

In our way down stairs, Miss Branghton said aloud, "I wonder when Mr. Smith's room will be ready."

"So do I," answered Polly; "I'm sure we should not do any harm to it now."

This hint had not the desired effect; for we were suffered to proceed very quietly.

As we entered the shop, I observed a young man, in deep mourning, leaning against the wall, with his arms folded, and his eyes fixed on the ground, apparently in profound and melancholy meditation: but the moment he perceived us, he started, and, making a passing bow, very abruptly retired. As I found he was permitted to go quite unnoticed, I could not forbear enquiring who he was.

"Lord!" answered Miss Branghton, "he's nothing but a poor Scotch poet."

"For my part," said Miss Polly, "I believe he's just starved, for I don't find he has any thing to live upon."

"Live upon!" cried the brother, "why he's a poet, you know, so he may live upon learning."

"Aye, and good enough for him too," said Miss Branghton, "for he's as proud as he's poor."

"Like enough," replied the brother, "but, for all that, you won't find he will live without meat and drink: no, no, catch a Scotchman at that if you can! why, they only come here for what they can get."

"I'm sure," said Miss Branghton, "I wonder Papa 'll be such a fool as to let him stay in the house, for I dare say he'll never pay for his lodging."

"Why, no more he would, if he could get another Lodger: you know the bill's been put up this fortnight. Miss, if you should hear of a person that wants a room, I assure you it is a very good one, for all it's up three pair of stairs."

I answered, that as I had no acquaintance in London, I had not any chance of assisting them: but both my compassion and my curiosity were excited for this poor young man; and I asked them some further particulars concerning him.

They then acquainted me, that they had only known him three months. When he first lodged with them, he agreed to board also; but had lately told them, he would eat by himself, though they all believed he had hardly ever tasted a morsel of meat since he left their table. They said, that he had always appeared very low-spirited, but, for the last month, he had been *duller* than ever, and, all of a sudden, had put himself into mourning, though they knew not for whom, nor for what, but they supposed it was only for convenience, as no person had ever been to see or enquire for him since his residence amongst them: and they were sure he was very poor, as he had not paid for his lodgings the last three weeks: and finally, they concluded he was a poet, or else half-crazy, because they had, at different times, found scraps of poetry in his room.

They then produced some unfinished verses, written on small pieces of paper, unconnected, and of a most melancholy cast. Among them was the fragment of an ode, which, at my request, they lent me to copy; and, as you may perhaps like to see it, I will write it now.

> O LIFE! thou lingering dream of grief, of pain,
> And every ill that nature can sustain,
>    Strange, mutable, and wild!
> Now flattering with Hope most fair,
> Depressing now with fell Despair,
>    The nurse of Guilt, the slave of Pride,
>       That, like a wayward child,
>       Who, to himself a foe,
> Sees joy alone in what's denied,
>    In what is granted, woe!
>
> O thou poor, feeble, fleeting pow'r,
> By Vice seduc'd, by Folly woo'd,
> By Mis'ry, Shame, Remorse, pursu'd!
> And as thy toilsome steps proceed,
> Seeming to Youth the fairest flow'r
> Proving to Age the rankest weed,
>    A guilded, but a bitter pill,
>    Of varied, great, and complicated ill!

These lines are harsh, but they indicate an internal wretchedness which, I own, affects me. Surely this young man must be involved in misfortunes of no common nature: but I cannot imagine what can induce him to remain with this unfeeling family, where he is, most unworthily, despised for being poor, and, most illiberally, detested for being a Scotchman. He may, indeed, have motives which he cannot surmount, for submitting to such a situation. Whatever they are, I most heartily pity him, and cannot but wish it were in my power to afford him some relief.

During this conversation, Mr. Smith's foot-boy came to Miss Branghton, and informed her, that his master said she might have the room now when she liked it, for that he was presently going out.

This very genteel message, though it perfectly satisfied the Miss Branghtons, by no means added to my desire of being introduced to this gentleman: and upon their rising, with intention to accept his offer, I begged they would excuse my attending them, and said I would sit with Madame Duval till the tea was ready.

I therefore once more went up two pair of stairs, with young Branghton, who insisted upon accompanying me; and there we remained, till Mr. Smith's foot-boy summoned us to tea, when I followed Madame Duval into the dining-room.

The Miss Branghtons were seated at one window, and Mr. Smith was lolling indolently out of the other. They all approached us at our entrance, and Mr. Smith, probably to shew he was master of the apartment, most officiously handed me to a great chair, at the upper end of the room, without taking any notice of Madame Duval, till I rose, and offered her my own seat.

Leaving the rest of the company to entertain themselves, he, very abruptly, began to address himself to me, in a style of gallantry equally new and disagreeable to me. It is true, no man can possibly pay me greater compliments, or make more fine speeches, than Sir Clement Willoughby, yet his language, though too flowery, is always that of a gentleman, and his address and manners are so very superior to those of the inhabitants of this house, that to make any comparison between him and Mr. Smith would be extremely unjust. This latter seems very desirous of appearing a man of gaiety and spirit; but his vivacity is so low-bred, and his whole behaviour so forward and disagreeable, that I should prefer the company of *dullness* itself, even as that goddess is described by Pope,[1] to that of this *sprightly* young man.

He made many apologies, that he had not lent his room for our dinner, which, he said, he should certainly have done, had he seen me first; and he assured me, that when I came again, he should be very glad to oblige me.

I told him, and with sincerity, that every part of the house was equally indifferent to me.

"Why, Ma'am, the truth is, Miss Biddy and Polly take no care of any thing, else, I'm sure, they should be always welcome to my room; for I'm never so happy as in obliging the ladies, — that's my character, Ma'am; — but, really, the last time they had it, every thing was made so greasy and so nasty, that, upon my word, to a man who wishes to have things a little genteel, it was quite cruel. Now, as to you, Ma'am, it's quite another thing; for I should not mind if every thing I had was spoilt, for the sake of having the pleasure to oblige you; and, I assure you, Ma'am, it makes me quite happy, that I have a room good enough to receive you."

This elegant speech was followed by many others, so much in the same style, that to write them would be superfluous; and, as he did not allow me a moment to speak to any other person, the rest of the

---

[1] *dullness* . . . *Pope:* Alexander Pope personified dullness as a goddess in several versions of *The Dunciad,* his mock-epic satire on London literary and political culture.

evening was consumed in a painful attention to this irksome young man, who seemed to intend appearing before me to the utmost advantage.

Adieu, my dear Sir. I fear you will be sick of reading about this family; yet I must write of them, or not of any, since I mix with no other. Happy shall I be, when I quit them all, and again return to Berry Hill!

## LETTER XII

### Evelina in Continuation

June 10th.

This morning, Mr. Smith called, *on purpose*, he said, to offer me a ticket for the next Hampstead assembly.[1] I thanked him, but desired to be excused in accepting it; he would not, however, be denied, nor answered, and, in a manner both vehement and free, pressed and urged his offer till I was wearied to death: but, when he found me resolute, he seemed thunderstruck with amazement, and thought proper to desire I would tell him my reasons.

Obvious as they must, surely, have been to any other person, they were such as I knew not how to repeat to him; and, when he found I hesitated, he said, "Indeed, Ma'am, you are too modest; I assure you the ticket is quite at your service, and I shall be very happy to dance with you; so pray don't be so coy."

"Indeed, Sir," I returned, "you are mistaken; I never supposed you would offer a ticket, without wishing it should be accepted; but it would answer no purpose to mention the reasons which make me decline it, since they cannot possible by removed."

This speech seemed very much to mortify him, which I could not be concerned at, as I did not chuse to be treated by him with so much freedom. When he was, at last, convinced that his application to me was ineffectual, he addressed himself to Madame Duval, and begged she would interfere in his favour, offering, at the same time, to procure another ticket for herself.

---

[1] *Hampstead assembly:* A spa and resort near London, Hampstead afforded visitors taverns, bowling greens, shops, concerts, and dances, in addition to its supposedly curative waters. The "assembly" referred to was a public entertainment, unlike the private ridotto attended by Evelina in the company of the Mirvans.

"*Ma foi,* Sir," answered she, angrily, "you might as well have had the complaisance² to ask me before, for, I assure you, I don't approve of no such rudeness: however, you may keep your tickets to yourself, fo we don't want none of 'em."

This rebuke almost overset him; he made many apologies, and said that he should certainly have first applied to her, but that he had no notion the *young* lady would have refused him, and, on the contrary, had concluded that she would have assisted him to persuade Madame Duval herself.

This excuse appeased her; and he pleaded his cause so successfully, that, to my great chagrin, he gained it; and Madame Duval promised that she would go herself, and take me to the Hampstead assembly whenever he pleased.

Mr. Smith then, approaching me with an air of triumph, said "Well, Ma'am, now, I think, you can't possibly keep to your denial."

I made no answer, and he soon took leave, though not till he had so wonderfully gained the favour of Madame Duval, that she declared, when he was gone, he was the prettiest young man she had seen since she came to England.

As soon as I could find an opportunity, I ventured, in the most humble manner, to entreat Madame Duval would not insist upon my attending her to this ball; and represented to her, as well as I was able, the impropriety of my accepting any present from a young man so entirely unknown to me: but she laughed at my scruples, called me a foolish, ignorant country girl, and said she should make it her business to teach me something of the world.

This ball is to be next week. I am sure it is not more improper for, than unpleasant to me, and I will use every possible endeavour to avoid it. Perhaps I may apply to Miss Branghton for advice, as I believe she will be willing to assist me, from disliking, equally with myself, that I should dance with Mr. Smith.

June 11th.

O, my dear Sir! I have been shocked to death, — and yet, at the same time, delighted beyond expression, in the hope that I have happily been the instrument of saving a human creature from destruction!

---

² *complaisance:* Good manners.

This morning, Madame Duval said she would invite the Branghton family to return our visit to-morrow; and, not chusing to rise herself, — for she generally spends the morning in bed, — she desired me to wait upon them with her message. M. Du Bois, who just then called, insisted upon attending me.

Mr. Branghton was in the shop, and told us that his son and daughters were out; but desired me to step up stairs, as he very soon expected them home. This I did, leaving M. Du Bois below. I went into the room where we had dined the day before, and, by a wonderful chance, I happened to seat myself, that I had a view of the stairs, and yet could not be seen from them.

In about ten minutes time, I saw, passing by the door, with a look perturbed and affrighted, the same young man I mentioned in my last letter. Not heeding, as I suppose, how he went, in turning the corner of the stairs, which are narrow and winding, his foot slipped, and he fell, but, almost instantly rising, I plainly perceived the end of a pistol, which started from his pocket, by hitting against the stairs.

I was inexpressibly shocked. All that I had heard of his misery occuring to my memory, made me conclude, that he was, at that very moment, meditating suicide! Struck with the dreadful idea, all my strength seemed to fail me; — I sat motionless; — I lost all power of action, — and grew almost stiff with horror.

He moved on slowly, — yet I soon lost sight of him. I then trembled so violently, that my chair actually shook under me; — till, recollecting that it was yet possible to prevent the fatal deed, all my faculties seemed to return, with the hope of saving him.

My first thought was to fly to Mr. Branghton, but I feared that an instant of time lost, might for ever be rued; and therefore, guided by the impulse of my apprehensions, as well I was able, I followed him up stairs, stepping very softly, and obliged to support myself by the banisters.

When I came within a few stairs of the landing-place, I stopped, for I could then see into his room, as he had not yet shut the door.

He had put the pistol upon a table, and had his hand in his pocket, whence, in a few moments, he took out another: He then emptied something on the table from a small leather bag; after which, taking up both the pistols, one in each hand, he dropt hastily upon his knees, and called out "O God! — forgive me!"

In a moment, strength and courage seemed lent me as by inspiration: I started, and rushing precipitately into the room, just caught his arm, and then, overcome by my own fears, I fell down at his side, breathless and senseless. My recovery, however, was, I believe, almost instantaneous; and then the sight of this unhappy man, regarding me with a look of unutterable astonishment, mixed with concern, presently restored to me my recollection. I arose, though with difficulty; he did the same; the pistols, as I soon saw, were both on the floor.

Unwilling to leave them, and, indeed, too weak to move, I leant one hand on the table, and then stood perfectly still: while he, his eyes cast wildly towards me, seemed too infinitely amazed to be capable of either speech or action.

I believe we were some minutes in this extraordinary situation; but, as my strength returned, I felt myself both ashamed and awkward, and making a slight courtesie, I moved towards the door. Pale, and motionless, he suffered me to pass, without changing his posture, or uttering a syllable; and, indeed,

He looked a bloodless image of despair![3]

When I reached the door, I turned round; I looked fearfully at the pistols, and, impelled by an emotion I could not repress, I hastily stepped back, with an intention of carrying them away: but their wretched owner, perceiving my design, and recovering from his astonishment, darting suddenly down, seized them both himself.

Wild with fright, and scarce knowing what I did, I caught, almost involuntarily, hold of both his arms, and exclaimed, "O Sir! have mercy on yourself!"

The guilty pistols fell from his hands, which, disengaging from me, he fervently clasped, and cried, "Sweet Heaven! is this thy angel?"

Encouraged by such gentleness, I again attempted to take the pistols, but, with a look half frantic, he again prevented me, saying, "What would you do?"

"Awaken you," I cried, with a courage I now wonder at, "to worthier thoughts, and rescue you from perdition."

I then seized the pistols; he said not a word, — he made no effort to stop me; — I glided quick by him, and tottered down stairs, ere he had recovered from the extremest amazement.

The moment I reached again the room I had so fearfully left, I threw away the pistols, and flinging myself on the first chair, gave free vent to the feelings I had most painfully stifled, in a violent burst of tears, which, indeed, proved a happy relief to me.

---

[3] Pope's Iliad. [Burney's note.] "With chatt'ring teeth he stands, and stiff'ning hair, / And looks a bloodless image of despair!"

In this situation I remained some time; but when, at length, I lifted up my head, the first object I saw, was the poor man who had occasioned my terror, standing, as if petrified, at the door, and gazing at me with eyes of wild wonder.

I started from the chair, but trembled so excessively, that I almost instantly sunk again into it. He then, though without advancing, and in a faltering voice, said, "Whoever or whatever you are, relieve me, I pray you, from the suspence under which my soul labours — and tell me if indeed I do not dream!"

To this address, so singular and so solemn, I had not then the presence of mind to frame any answer: but, as I presently perceived that his eyes turned from me to the pistols, and that he seemed to intend regaining them, I exerted all my strength, and saying "O for Heaven's sake forbear!" I rose and took them myself.

"Do my senses deceive me!" cried he, "do *I* live — ? and do *you* — ?"

As he spoke, he advanced towards me, and I, still guarding the pistols, retreated, saying "No, no — you must not — must not have them!" —

"Why — for what purpose, tell me! — do you withhold them?" —

"To give you time to *think*, — to save you from eternal misery, — and, I hope, to reserve you for mercy and forgiveness."

"Wonderful!" cried he, with uplifted hands and eyes, "most wonderful!"

For some time, he seemed wrapped in deep thought, till a sudden noise of tongues below, announcing the approach of the Branghtons, made him start from his reverie: he sprung hastily forward, — dropt on one knee, — caught hold of my gown, which he pressed to his lips, and then, quick as lightening, he rose, and flew up stairs to his own room.

There was something in the whole of this extraordinary and shocking adventure, really too affecting to be borne; and so entirely had I spent my spirits and exhausted my courage, that, before the Branghtons reached me, I had sunk on the ground, without sense or motion.

I believe I must have been a very horrid sight to them, on their entrance into the room; for, to all appearance, I seemed to have suffered a violent death, either by my own rashness, or the cruelty of some murderer; as the pistols were fallen close by my side.

How soon I recovered, I know not, but, probably, I was more indebted to the loudness of their cries, than to their assistance; for they all concluded that I was dead, and, for some time, did not make any effort to revive me.

Scarcely could I recollect *where,* or, indeed, *what* I was, ere they poured upon me such a torrent of questions and enquiries, that I was almost stunned with their vociferation. However, as soon and as well as I was able, I endeavoured to satisfy their curiosity, by re-counting what had happened as clearly as was in my power. They all looked aghast at the recital, but, not being well enough to enter into any discussions, I begged to have a chair called, and to return instantly home.

Before I left them, I recommended, with great earnestness, a vigilant observance of their unhappy lodger, and that they would take especial care to keep from him, if possible, all means of self-destruction.

M. Du Bois, who seemed extremely concerned at my indisposition, walked by the side of the chair, and saw me safe to my own apartment.

The rashness and the misery of this ill-fated young man, engross all my thoughts. If, indeed, he is bent upon destroying himself, all efforts to save him will be fruitless. How much do I wish it were in my power to discover the nature of the malady which thus maddens him, and to offer or to procure alleviation to his sufferings! I am sure, my dearest Sir, you will be much concerned for this poor man, and, were you here, I doubt not but you would find some method of awakening him from the error which blinds him, and of pouring the balm of peace and comfort into his afflicted soul!

## LETTER XIII

### Evelina in Continuation

Holborn, June 13th.

Yesterday all the Branghtons dined here.

Our conversation was almost wholly concerning the adventure of the day before. Mr. Branghton said, that his first thought was instantly to turn his lodger out of doors, "Lest," continued he, "his killing himself in my house, should bring me into any trouble; but then, I was afraid I should never get the money he owes me, whereas, if he dies in my house, I have a right to all he leaves behind him, if he goes off in my debt. Indeed, I would put him in prison,[1] — but what should I get by that? he could not earn any thing there to pay me. So I considered about it some time, and then I determined to ask him, point-blank, for my money out of hand. And so I did, but he told me he'd pay me next week: however, I gave him to understand, that, though I was no Scotchman, yet I did not like to be over-reached any more than he; so then, he gave me a ring, which, to my certain knowledge, must be worth ten guineas, and told me he would not part with it for his life, and a good deal more such sort of stuff, but that I might keep it till he could pay me."

"It is ten to one, Father," said young Branghton, "if he came fairly by it."

"Very likely not," answered he, "but that will make no great difference; for I shall be able to prove my right to it all one."

What principles! I could hardly stay in the room.

"I'm determined," said the son, "I'll take some opportunity to affront him soon, now I know how poor he is, because of the airs he gave himself to me when he first came."

"And pray how was that, child?" said Madame Duval.

"Why you never knew such a fuss in your life as he made, because, one day at dinner, I only happened to say, that I supposed he had never got such a good meal in his life, before he came to England: there he fell in such a passion as you can't think; but, for my part, I took no notice of it, for to be sure, thinks I, he must needs be a gentleman, or he'd never go to be so angry about it. However, he won't put his tricks upon me again, in a hurry."

"Well," said Miss Polly, "he's grown quite another creature to what he was, and he does n't run away from us, nor hide himself, nor any thing; and he's as civil as can be, and he's always in the shop, and he saunters about the stairs, and he looks at every body who comes in."

"Why you may see what he's after plain enough," said Mr. Branghton; "he wants to see Miss again."

"Ha, ha, ha! Lord, how I should laugh," said the son, "if he should have fell in love with Miss!"

"I'm sure," said Miss Branghton, "Miss is welcome; but, for my part, I should be quite ashamed of such a beggarly conquest."

---

[1] *I would put him in prison:* It was possible to have otherwise inoffensive people arrested for bad debt and imprisoned in such brutal conditions as those common to Newgate Prison.

Such was the conversation till tea-time, when the appearance of Mr. Smith gave a new turn to the discourse.

Miss Branghton desired me to remark with what a *smart air* he entered the room, and asked me if he had not very much a *quality look?*

"Come," cried he, advancing to us, "you ladies must not sit together; wherever I go, I always make it a rule to part the ladies."

And then, handing Miss Branghton to the next chair, he seated himself between us.

"Well, now, ladies, I think we sit very well. What say you? for my part, I think it was a very good motion."

"If my Cousin likes it," said Miss Branghton, "I'm sure I've no objection."

"O," cried he, "I always study what the ladies like, — that's my first thought. And, indeed, it is but natural that you should like best to sit by the gentlemen, for what can you find to say to one another?"

"Say!" cried young Branghton, "O, never you think of that, they'll find enough to say, I'll be sworn. You know the women are never tired of talking."

"Come, come, Tom," said Mr. Smith, "don't be severe upon the ladies; when I'm by, you know I always take their part."

Soon after, when Miss Branghton offered me some cake, this man of gallantry said, "Well, if I was that lady, I'd never take any thing from a woman."

"Why not, Sir?"

"Because I should be afraid of being poisoned for being so handsome."

"Who is severe upon the ladies *now?*" said I.

"Why, really, Ma'am, it was a slip of the tongue; I did not intend to say such a thing; but one can't always be on one's guard."

Soon after, the conversation turning upon public places, young Branghton asked if I had ever been to *George*'s at Hampstead?[2]

"Indeed I never heard the place mentioned."

"Did n't you, Miss?" cried he, eagerly, "why then you've a deal of fun to come, I'll promise you; and, I tell you what, I'll treat you there some Sunday soon. So now, Bid and Poll, be sure you don't tell Miss about the chairs, and all that, for I've a mind to surprise her; and if I pay, I think I've a right to have it my own way."

---

[2] *George's at Hampstead:* Probably New Georgia, a cottage and gardens laid out by Robert Caston in 1737 and opened to the public for tea. The main attraction of the place, aside from the garden and surrounding wilderness itself, was a variety of mechanical contraptions.

"George's at Hampstead!" repeated Mr. Smith, contemptuously, "how came you to think the young Lady would like to go to such a low place as that? But, pray Ma'am, have you ever been to Don Saltero's at Chelsea?"[3]

"No, Sir."

"No! — nay, then, I must insist on having the pleasure of conducting you there before long. I assure you, Ma'am, many genteel people go, or else, I give you my word, *I* should not recommend it."

"Pray, Cousin," said Mr. Branghton, "have you been to Sadler's Wells,[4] yet ?"

"No, Sir."

"No! why then you've seen nothing!"

"Pray, Miss," said the Son, "how do you like the Tower of London?"[5]

"I have never been to it, Sir."

"Goodness!" exclaimed he, "not seen the Tower! — why may be you ha'n't been o' top of the Monument,[6] neither?"

"No, indeed, I have not."

"Why then you might as well not have come to London, for aught I see, for you've been no where."

"Pray, Miss," said Polly, "have you been all over Paul's Church,[7] yet?"

---

[3] *Don Saltero's at Chelsea:* Salter's was originally a coffeehouse, combined with a barbershop. Sir Hans Sloane, the famous collector and one of the founders of the British Museum, gave some unwanted specimens from his collection of curiosities to Salter, and the resulting museum became the dominant attraction of the place. The 1729 catalog accompanying Don Saltero's collection included "the Queen of Sheba's Fan and Cordial Bottle, Robinson Crusoe's and his Man Friday's shirt, the Four Evangelists cut on a cherry stone, a curious Ball of Fishbones found near Plymouth, and Pontius Pilate's Wife's Chambermaid's Sister's Sister's Hat" (quoted from Edward Miller, *That Noble Cabinet*, 1974).

[4] *Sadler's Wells:* This pleasure spot was begun in the Restoration as a garden with such "lower-class" entertainment as tightrope dancing, tumbling, and music-hall concerts. A theater was built there in 1765. It was considered, up until the nineteenth century, a rowdy and somewhat disreputable place.

[5] *Tower of London:* An "attraction" to London visitors then as now. See footnote 1 to Volume II, Letter II.

[6] *top of the Monument:* Sir Christopher Wren's design, the two-hundred-plus foot Doric column was erected to commemorate the Great Fire that destroyed much of the old walled city of London in 1666. It is hollow on the inside, and visitors can climb more than three hundred steps to the top.

[7] *Paul's Church:* Another of Sir Christopher Wren's constructions, St. Paul's, like the Monument, is a London architectural attraction.

"No, Ma'am."

"Well, but, Ma'am," said Mr. Smith, "how do you like Vauxhall and Marybone?"[8]

"I never saw either, Sir."

"No! — God bless me! — you really surprise me, — why Vauxhall is the first pleasure in life! — I know nothing like it. — Well, Ma'am, you must have been with strange people, indeed, not to have taken you to Vauxhall. Why you have seen nothing of London yet. — However, we must try if *we* can't make you amends."

In the course of this *catechism,* many other places were mentioned, of which I have forgotten the names; but the looks of surprise and contempt that my repeated negatives incurred, were very diverting.

"Come," said Mr. Smith, after tea, "as this Lady has been with such a queer set of people, let's shew her the difference; suppose we go somewhere to-night? — I love to do things with spirit! — Come, Ladies, where shall we go? For my part, I should like Foote's,[9] — but the Ladies must chuse; I never speak myself."

"Well, Mr. Smith is always in such spirits!" said Miss Branghton.

"Why yes, Ma'am, yes, thank G — , pretty good spirits; — I have not yet the cares of the world upon me, — I am not *married,* — ha, ha, ha, — you'll excuse me, Ladies, — but I can't help laughing! — "

---

[8] *Vauxhall and Marybone:* Vauxhall Gardens opened to the public in 1661 and became unique among London pleasure gardens in its appeal to visitors of various classes. The attractions consisted of formal gardens, buildings such as alcoves and a theater, paintings, and refreshments. Marylebone Gardens, prior to 1738, consisted of formal gardens, detached from the old Marylebone Manor House in 1650, and a bowling green. The Rose tavern, which was located at the main entrance to the gardens, was infamous as a gambling house. From the beginning of Daniel Gough's proprietorship in 1738 until its closing in 1776, Marylebone was known for its musical entertainments, balls, and fireworks displays.

[9] *Foote's:* Samuel Foote (1720–1777) was a well-known actor and writer of comedies. In 1760, he opened the Little Theatre in the Haymarket to provide summer entertainment when the primary London theaters were closed. Much of Foote's success as an actor and writer depended on his satirical "take-offs" of famous London personages, particularly other actors. Always considered somewhat marginal by more "respectable" theater professionals such as David Garrick, and a thorn in the side of the rich and powerful whom he "took off," Foote never achieved complete financial security, and the end of his acting career in the 1770s was darkened by his being charged with sodomy, a hangable offense. Foote was acquitted but seems never to have regained his zest for performing, despite the encouragement of loyal audiences.

No objection being made, to my great relief, we all proceeded to the little theatre in the Haymarket, where I was extremely entertained by the performance of the Minor and the Commissary.[10]

They all returned hither to supper.

[10] *the Minor and the Commissary:* The titles of two separate plays by Foote, here conflated into one title. They might well have been performed together at the Little Theatre for a single evening's entertainment, which could last for five or six hours.

## LETTER XIV

### Evelina in Continuation

June 15th.

Yesterday morning, Madame Duval again sent me to Mr. Branghton's, attended by M. Du Bois, to make some party for the evening; because she had had the vapours[1] the preceding day, from staying at home.

As I entered the shop, I perceived the unfortunate North Briton, seated in a corner, with a book in his hand. He cast his melancholy eyes up, as we came in, and, I believe, immediately recollected my face, for he started and changed colour. I delivered Madame Duval's message to Mr. Branghton; who told me I should find Polly up stairs, but that the others were gone out.

Up stairs, therefore, I went; and seated on a window, with Mr. Brown at her side, sat Miss Polly. I felt a little awkward at disturbing them, and much more so, at their behaviour afterwards: for, as soon as the common enquiries were over, Mr. Brown grew so fond, and so foolish, that I was extremely disgusted. Polly, all the time, only rebuked him with "La, now, Mr. Brown, do be quiet, can't you? — you should not behave so before company. — Why now what will Miss think of me?" — while her looks plainly shewed not merely the pleasure, but the pride which she took in his caresses.

I did not, by any means, think it necessary to punish myself by witnessing their tenderness, and, therefore, telling them I would see if Miss Branghton were returned home, I soon left them, and again descended into the shop.

"So, Miss, you've come again," said Mr. Branghton, "what, I suppose, you've a mind to sit a little in the shop, and see how the world goes, hay, Miss?"

[1] *vapours:* Depression, melancholy.

I made no answer; and M. Du Bois instantly brought me a chair.

The unhappy stranger, who had risen at my entrance, again seated himself; and, though his head leant towards his book, I could not help observing, that his eyes were most intently and earnestly turned towards me.

M. Du Bois, as well as his broken English would allow him, endeavoured to entertain us, till the return of Miss Branghton and her brother.

"Lord, how tired I am!" cried the former, "I have not a foot to stand upon." And then, without any ceremony, she flung herself into the chair from which I had risen to receive her.

"You tired!" said the brother, "why then what must I be, that have walked twice as far?" And with equal politeness, he paid the same compliment to M. Du Bois which his sister had done to me.

Two chairs and three stools compleated the furniture of the shop, and Mr. Branghton, who chose to keep his own seat himself, desired M. Du Bois to take another; and then, seeing that I was without any, called out to the stranger, "Come, Mr. Macartney, lend us your stool."

Shocked at their rudeness, I declined the offer, and approaching Miss Branghton, said, "If you will be so good as to make room for me on your chair, there will be no occasion to disturb that gentleman."

"Lord, what signifies that?" cried the brother, "he has had his share of sitting, I'll be sworn."

"And if he has not," said the sister, "he has a chair up stairs; and the shop is our own, I hope."

This grossness so much disgusted me, that I took the stool, and carrying it back to Mr. Macartney myself, I returned him thanks, as civilly as I could, for his politeness, but said that I had rather stand.

He looked at me as if unaccustomed to such attention, bowed very respectfully, but neither spoke, nor yet made use of it.

I soon found that I was an object of derision to all present, except M. Du Bois, and, therefore, I begged Mr. Branghton would give me an answer for Madame Duval, as I was in haste to return.

"Well, then, Tom, — Biddy, — where have you a mind to go to-night? your Aunt and Miss want to be abroad and amongst them."

"Why then, Papa," said Miss Branghton, "we'll go to Don Saltero's. Mr. Smith likes that place, so may be he'll go along with us."

"No, no," said the son, "I'm for White-Conduit House;[2] so let's go there."

"White-Conduit House, indeed!" cried his sister, "no, Tom, that I won't."

"Why then let it alone; nobody wants your company; — we shall do as well without you, I'll be sworn, and better too."

"I'll tell you what, Tom, if you don't hold your tongue, I'll make you repent it, — that I assure you."

Just then, Mr. Smith came into the shop, which he seemed to intend passing through; but when he saw me, he stopped and began a most courteous enquiry after my health, protesting that, had he known I was there, he should have come down sooner. "But, bless me, Ma'am," added he, "what is the reason you stand?" and then he flew to bring me the seat from which I had just parted.

"Mr. Smith, you are come in very good time," said Mr. Branghton, "to end a dispute between my son and daughter, about where they shall all go to-night."

"O fie, Tom, — dispute with a lady!" cried Mr. Smith, "Now, as for me, I'm for where you will, provided this young Lady is of the party, — one place is the same as another to me, so that it be but agreeable to the ladies, — I would go any where with you, Ma'am," (to me) "unless, indeed, it were to *church;* — ha, ha, ha, — you'll excuse me, Ma'am, but, really, I never could conquer my fear of a parson; — ha, ha, ha, — really, ladies, I beg your pardon, for being so rude, but I can't help laughing for my life!"

"I was just saying, Mr. Smith," said Miss Branghton, "that I should like to go to Don Saltero's; — now pray where should *you* like to go?"

"Why really, Miss Biddy, you know I always let the ladies decide; I never fix any thing myself; but I should suppose it would be rather hot at the coffee-house, — however, pray, Ladies, settle it among yourselves, — I'm agreeable to whatever you chuse."

It was easy for me to discover, that this man, with all his parade of *conformity,* objects to every thing that is not proposed by himself: but he is so much admired, by this family, for his *gentility,* that he thinks himself a complete fine gentleman!

"Come," said Mr. Branghton, "the best way will be to put it to the vote, and then every body will speak their minds. Biddy, call Poll down stairs. We'll start fair."

---

[2] *White-Conduit House:* A coffeehouse that was particularly popular for Saturday-afternoon outings. It contained bowling greens, a cricket field, and a garden pool by which visitors could sit and consume refreshments.

"Lord, Papa," said Miss Branghton, "why can't you as well send Tom? — you're always sending me of the errands."

A dispute then ensued, but Miss Branghton was obliged to yield.

When Mr. Brown and Miss Polly made their appearance, the latter uttered many complaints of having been called, saying she did not want to come, and was very well where she was.

"Now, Ladies, your votes," cried Mr. Smith, "and so, Ma'am," (to me) "we'll begin with you. What place shall you like best?" and then, in a whisper, he added, "I assure you, I shall say the same as you do, whether I like it or not."

I said, that as I was ignorant what choice was in my power, I must beg to hear their decisions first. This was reluctantly assented to; and then miss Branghton voted for Saltero's Coffeehouse; her sister, for a party to *Mother Red Cap's*;[3] the brother, for White-Conduit House; Mr. Brown, for Bagnigge Wells;[4] Mr. Branghton for Sadler's Wells; and Mr. Smith for Vauxhall.

"Well, now, Ma'am," said Mr. Smith, "we have all spoken, and so you must give the casting vote. Come, what will you fix upon?"

"Sir," answered I, "I was to speak *last*."

"Well, so you will," said Miss Branghton, "for we've all spoke first."

"Pardon me," returned I, "the voting has not yet been quite general."

And I looked towards Mr. Macartney, to whom I wished extremely to shew that I was not of the same brutal nature with those by whom he was treated so grossly.

"Why pray," said Mr. Branghton, "who have we left out? would you have the cats and dogs vote?"

"No, Sir," cried I, with some spirit, "I would have *that gentleman* vote, — if, indeed, he is not superior to joining our party."

They all looked at me, as if they doubted whether or not they had heard me right: but, in a few moments, their surprise gave way to a rude burst of laughter.

Very much displeased, I told M. Du Bois that if he was not ready to go, I would have a coach called for myself.

O yes, he said, he was always ready to attend me.

Mr. Smith then advancing, attempted to take my hand, and begged me not to leave them till I had settled the evening's plan.

[3] *Mother Red Cap's:* A popular public house.
[4] *Bagnigge Wells:* Another pleasure garden, originally popular for its mineral springs. It included a teahouse and drew its largest crowds on Sundays from among shopkeepers and other tradesmen.

"I have nothing, Sir," said I, "to do with it, as it is my intention to stay at home; and therefore Mr. Branghton will be so good as to send Madame Duval word what place is fixed upon, when it is convenient to him."

And then, making a slight courtesie, I left them.

How much does my disgust of these people encrease my pity for poor Mr. Macartney! I will not see them when I can avoid so doing; but I am determined to take every opportunity in my power, to shew civility to this unhappy man, whose misfortunes, with this family, only render him an object of scorn. I was, however, very well pleased with M. Du Bois, who, far from joining in their mirth, expressed himself extremely shocked at their ill-breeding.

We had not walked ten yards, ere we were followed by Mr. Smith, who came to make excuses, and to assure me they were *only joking,* and hoped I took nothing ill, for, if I did, he would make a quarrel of it himself with the Branghtons, rather than I should receive any offence.

I begged him not to take any trouble about so immaterial an affair, and assured him I should not myself. He was so officious, that he would not be prevailed upon to return home, till he had walked with us to Mr. Dawkins's.

Madame Duval was very much displeased that I brought her so little satisfaction. White-Conduit House was, at last, fixed upon; and, notwithstanding my great dislike of such parties and such places, I was obliged to accompany them.

Very disagreeable, and much according to my expectations, the evening proved. There were many people all smart and gaudy, and so pert and low-bred, that I could hardly endure being amongst them; but the party to which, unfortunately, I belonged, seemed all *at home.*

## LETTER XV

### Evelina in Continuation

Holborn, June 17th.

Yesterday Mr. Smith carried his point, of making a party for Vauxhall, consisting of Madame Duval, M. Du Bois, all the Branghtons, Mr. Brown, himself, — and me! — for I find all endeavours vain to escape any thing which these people desire I should not.

There were twenty disputes previous to our setting out; first, as to the *time* of our going: Mr. Branghton, his son, and young Brown, were for six o'clock; and all the Ladies and Mr. Smith were for eight; — the latter, however, conquered.

Then, as to the *way* we should go; some were for a boat, others for a coach,[1] and Mr. Branghton himself was for walking: but the boat, at length, was decided upon. Indeed this was the only part of the expedition that was agreeable to me, for the Thames was delightfully pleasant.

The Garden is very pretty, but too formal; I should have been better pleased, had it consisted less of strait walks, where

Grove nods at grove, each alley has its brother.[2]

The trees, the numerous lights, and the company in the circle around the orchestra make a most brilliant and gay appearance; and, had I been with a party less disagreeable to me, I should have thought it a place formed for animation and pleasure. There was a concert, in the course of which, a hautbois concerto was so charmingly played, that I could have thought myself upon enchanted ground, had I had spirits more gentle to associate with. The hautboy in the open air is heavenly.

Mr. Smith endeavoured to attach himself to me, with such officious assiduity, and impertinent freedom, that he quite sickened me. Indeed, M. Du Bois was the only man of the party to whom, voluntarily, I ever addressed myself. He is civil and respectful, and I have found nobody else so since I left Howard Grove. His English is very bad, but I prefer it to speaking French myself, which I dare not venture to do. I converse with him frequently, both to disengage myself from others, and to oblige Madame Duval, who is always pleased when he is attended to.

As we were walking about the orchestra, I heard a bell ring, and, in a moment, Mr. Smith, flying up to me, caught my hand, and, with a motion too quick to be resisted, ran away with me many yards before I had breath to ask his meaning, tho' I struggled as well as I could to get from him. At last, however, I insisted upon stopping;

---

[1] *some were for a boat, others for a coach:* One could walk or ride to the gardens via Westminster Bridge or cross the Thames by boat.

[2] *Grove nods at grove, each alley has its brother:* A slight misquotation of Alexander Pope's *Moral Essays*, Epistle IV, line 117.

"Stopping, Ma'am!" cried he, "why, we must run on, or we shall lose the cascade!"[3]

And then again, he hurried me away, mixing with a crowd of people, all running with so much velocity, that I could not imagine what had raised such an alarm. We were soon followed by the rest of the party; and my surprise and ignorance proved a source of diversion to them all, that was not exhausted the whole evening. Young Branghton, in particular, laughed till he could hardly stand.

The scene of the cascade I thought extremely pretty, and the general effect striking and lively.

But this was not the only surprise which was to divert them at my expence; for they led me about the garden, purposely to enjoy my first sight of various other deceptions.

About ten o'clock, Mr. Smith having chosen a *box* in a very conspicuous place, we all went to supper. Much fault was found with every thing that was ordered, though not a morsel of any thing was left; and the dearness of the provisions, with conjectures upon what profit was made by them, supplied discourse during the whole meal.

When wine and cyder were brought, Mr. Smith said, "Now let's enjoy ourselves; now is the time, or never. Well, Ma'am, and how do you like Vauxhall?"

"Like it!" cried young Branghton, "why, how can she help liking it? she has never seen such a place before, that I'll answer for."

"For my part," said Miss Branghton, "I like it because it is not vulgar."

"This must have been a fine treat for you, Miss," said Mr. Branghton; "why, I suppose you was never so happy in all your life before?"

I endeavoured to express my satisfaction with some pleasure, yet I believe they were much amazed at my coldness.

"Miss ought to stay in town till the last night," said young Branghton, "and then, it's my belief, she'd say something to it! Why, Lord, it's the best night of any; there's always a riot,[4] — and there the

---

[3] *the cascade:* At nine o'clock visitors were summoned by a bell to the north side of the gardens to view "the Cascade," an artificial landscape complete with a waterfall and mill. See Oliver Goldsmith's account of an evening at Vauxhall in "On a Visit to Vauxhall Gardens" in Part Two, Chapter 2.

[4] *riot:* It was a commonly decried practice during the peak of the gardens' popularity in the 1770s for young "bucks" and "beaux" to become rowdy and damage property on the last night of the season.

folks run about, — and then there's such squealing and squalling! — and there all the lamps are broke, — and the women run skimper scamper; — I declare I would not take five guineas to miss the last night!"

I was very glad when they all grew tired of sitting, and called for the waiter to pay the bill. The Miss Branghtons said they would walk on, while the gentlemen settled the account, and asked me to accompany them; which, however, I declined.

"You girls may do as you please," said Madame Duval, "but as to me, I promise you, I sha'n't go no where without the gentlemen."

"No more, I suppose, will my *Cousin*," said Miss Branghton, looking reproachfully towards Mr. Smith.

This reflection, which I feared would flatter his vanity, made me, most unfortunately, request Madame Duval's permission to attend them. She granted it, and away we went, having promised to meet in the room.

To the room, therefore, I would immediately have gone; but the sisters agreed that they would first have a *little pleasure*, and they tittered, and talked so loud, that they attracted universal notice.

"Lord, Polly," said the eldest, "suppose we were to take a turn in the dark walks!"[5]

"Ay, do," answered she, "and then we'll hide ourselves, and then Mr. Brown will think we are lost."

I remonstrated very warmly against this plan, telling them that it would endanger our missing the rest of the party all the evening.

"O dear," cried Miss Branghton, "I thought how uneasy Miss would be, without a beau!"

This impertinence I did not think worth answering; and, quite by compulsion, I followed them down a long alley, in which there was hardly any light.

By the time we came near the end, a large party of gentlemen, apparently very riotous, and who were hallowing, leaning on one another, and laughing immoderately, seemed to rush suddenly from behind some trees, and, meeting us face to face, put their arms at their sides, and formed a kind of circle, that first stopped our proceeding, and then our retreating, for we were presently entirely inclosed. The Miss Branghtons screamed aloud, and I was frightened exceedingly: our screams were answered with bursts of laughter, and, for some

---

[5] *dark walks:* Enclosed by overarching trees, the walks were closed off in 1763 because of complaints about people using them as a cover for illicit sex.

minutes, we were kept prisoners, till, at last, one of them, rudely, seizing hold of me, said I was a pretty little creature.

Terrified to death, I struggled with such vehemence to disengage myself from him, that I succeeded, in spite of his efforts to detain me; and immediately, and with a swiftness which fear only could have given me, I flew rather than ran up the walk, hoping to secure my safety by returning to the lights and company we had so foolishly left: but, before I could possibly accomplish my purpose, I was met by another party of men, one of whom placed himself so directly in my way, calling out, "Whither so fast, my love?" — that I could only have proceeded, by running into his arms.

In a moment, both my hands, by different persons, were caught hold of; and one of them, in a most familiar manner, desired to accompany me in a race, when I ran next; while the rest of the party stood still and laughed.

I was almost distracted with terror, and so breathless with running, that I could not speak, till another advancing, said, I was as handsome as an angel, and desired to be of the party. I then just articulated, "For Heaven's sake, Gentlemen, let me pass!"

Another, then, rushing suddenly forward, exclaimed, "Heaven and earth! what voice is that? — "

"The voice of the prettiest little actress I have seen this age," answered one of my persecutors.

"No, — no, — no, — " I *panted* out, "I am no actress,[6] — pray let me go, — pray let me pass — ."

"By all that's sacred," cried the same voice, which I then knew for Sir Clement Willoughby's, 'tis herself!"

"Sir Clement Willoughby!" cried I. "O Sir, assist — assist me — or I shall die with terror! — "

"Gentlemen," cried he, disengaging them all from me in an instant, "pray leave this lady to me."

Loud laughs proceeded from every mouth, and two or three said, "*Willoughby has all the luck!*" But one of them, in a passionate manner, vowed he would not give me up, for that he had the first right to me, and would support it.

"You are mistaken," said Sir Clement, "this lady is — I will explain myself to you another time; but, I assure you, you are all mistaken."

---

[6] *actress:* While many English actresses achieved social respectability in the 1770s, young and relatively unknown women who worked on the stage were often assumed to be engaged in or at least open to casual prostitution as a supplementary source of income.

And then, taking my willing hand, he led me off, amidst the loud acclamations, laughter, and gross merriment of his impertinent companions.

As soon as we had escaped from them, Sir Clement, with a voice of surprise, exclaimed, "My dearest creature, what wonder, what strange revolution, has brought you to such a spot as this?"

Ashamed of my situation, and extremely mortified to be thus recognized by him, I was for some time silent, and when he repeated his question, only stammered out, "I have, — I hardly know how, — lost myself from my party. — "

He caught my hand, and eagerly pressing it, in a passionate voice, said, "O that I had sooner met with thee!"

Surprised at a freedom so unexpected, I angrily broke from him, saying, "Is this the protection you give me, Sir Clement?"

And then I saw, what the perturbation of my mind had prevented my sooner noticing, that he had led me, though I know not how, into another of the dark alleys, instead of the place whither I meant to go.

"Good God!" I cried, "where am I? — What way are you going? — "

"Where," answered he, "we shall be least observed."

Astonished at this speech, I stopped short, and declared I would go no further.

"And why not, my angel?" again endeavouring to take my hand.

My heart beat with resentment; I pushed him away from me with all my strength, and demanded how he dared treat me with such insolence?

"Insolence!" repeated he.

"Yes, Sir Clement, *insolence;* from you, who know me, I had a claim for protection, — not to such treatment as this."

"By Heaven," cried he with warmth, "you distract me, — why, tell me, — why do I see you here? — Is this a place for Miss Anville? — these dark walks! — no party! — no companion! — by all that's good, I can scarce believe my senses!"

Extremely offended at this speech, I turned angrily from him, and, not deigning to make any answer, walked on towards that part of the garden whence I perceived the lights and company.

He followed me; but we were both some time silent.

"So you will not explain to me your situation?" said he, at length.

"No, Sir," answered I, disdainfully.

"Nor yet — suffer me to make my own interpretation? — "

I could not bear this strange manner of speaking; it made my very soul shudder, — and I burst into tears.

He flew to me, and actually flung himself at my feet, as if regardless who might see him, saying, "O Miss Anville — loveliest of women — forgive my — my — I beseech you forgive me; — if I have offended, — if I have hurt you — I could kill myself at the thought! — "

"No matter, Sir, no matter," cried I, "if I can but find my friends, — I will never speak to — never see you again!"

"Good God! — good Heaven! — my dearest life, what is it I have done? — what is it I have said? — "

"You best know, Sir, *what* and *why;* — but don't hold me here, — let *me* be gone, and do *you!*"

"Not till you forgive me! — I cannot part with you in anger."

"For shame, for shame, Sir!" cried I indignantly, "do you suppose I am to be thus compelled? — do you take advantage of the absence of my friends, to affront me?"

"No, Madam," cried he, rising, "I would sooner forfeit my life than act so mean a part. But you have flung me into amazement unspeakable, and you will not condescend to listen to my request of giving me some explanation."

"The manner, Sir," said I, "in which you spoke that request, made, and will make me scorn to answer it."

"Scorn! — I will own to you, I expected not such displeasure from Miss Anville."

"Perhaps, Sir, if you had, you would less voluntarily have merited it."

"My dearest life, surely it must be known to you, that the man does not breathe, who adores you so passionately, so fervently, so tenderly as I do! — why then will you delight in perplexing me? — in keeping me in suspense — in torturing me with doubt? — "

"I, Sir, delight in perplexing you! — You are much mistaken. — Your suspence, your doubts, your perplexities, — are of your own creating; and, believe me, Sir, they may *offend,* but they can never *delight* me: — but, as you have yourself raised, you must yourself satisfy them."

"Good God! — that such haughtiness and such sweetness can inhabit the same mansion!"

I made no answer, but quickening my pace, I walked on silently and sullenly; till this most impetuous of men, snatching my hand, which he grasped with violence, besought me to forgive him, with such earnestness of supplication, that, merely to escape his importunities, I was forced to speak, and, in some measure, to grant the pardon he requested: though it was accorded with a very ill grace; but, indeed, I knew not how to resist the humility of his entreaties: yet never shall I recollect the occasion he gave me of displeasure, without feeling it renewed.

We now soon arrived in the midst of the general crowd, and my own safety being then insured, I grew extremely uneasy for the Miss Branghtons, whose danger, however imprudently incurred by their own folly, I too well knew how to tremble for. To this consideration all my pride of heart yielded, and I determined to seek my party with the utmost speed; though not without a sigh did I recollect the fruitless attempt I had made, after the opera, of concealing from this man my unfortunate connections, which I was now obliged to make known.

I hastened, therefore, to the room, with a view of sending young Branghton to the aid of his sisters. In a very short time, I perceived Madame Duval, and the rest, looking at one of the paintings. I must own to you, honestly, my dear Sir, that an involuntary repugnance seized me, at presenting such a set to Sir Clement, — he, who had been used to see me in parties so different! — My pace slackened as I approached them, — but they presently perceived me.

"*Ah, Mademoiselle!*" cried M. Du Bois, "*Que je suis charmé de vous voir!*"[7]

"Pray, Miss," cried Mr. Brown, "where's Miss Polly?"

"Why, Miss, you've been a long while gone," said Mr. Branghton; "we thought you'd been lost. But what have you done with your cousins?"

I hesitated, — for Sir Clement regarded me with a look of wonder.

"*Pardie,*" cried Madame Duval, "I sha'n't let you leave me again in a hurry. Why, here we've been in such a fright! — and, all the while, I suppose you've been thinking nothing about the matter."

"Well," said young Branghton, "as long as Miss is come back, I don't mind, for as to Bid and Poll, they can take care of themselves. But the best joke is, Mr. Smith is gone all about a looking for you."

These speeches were made almost all in a breath: but when, at last, they waited for an answer, I told them, that in walking up one of the long alleys, we had been frightened and separated.

"The long alleys!" repeated Mr. Branghton, "and, pray, what had you to do in the long alleys? why, to be sure, you must all of you have had a mind to be affronted!"

---

[7] *Que . . . voir:* "How I am charmed to see you!"

This speech was not more impertinent to me, than surprising to Sir Clement, who regarded all the party with evident astonishment. However, I told young Branghton that no time ought to be lost, for that his sisters might require his immediate protection.

"But how will they get it?" cried this brutal brother; "if they've a mind to behave in such a manner as that, they ought to protect themselves; and so they may for me."

"Well," said the simple Mr. Brown, "whether you go or no, I think I may as well see after Miss Polly."

The father, then, interfering, insisted that his son should accompany him; and away they went.

It was now that Madame Duval first perceived Sir Clement; to whom turning with a look of great displeasure, she angrily said, "*Ma foi*, so you are comed here, of all the people in the world! — I wonder, child, you would let such a — such a *person* as that keep company with you."

"I am very sorry, Madam," said Sir Clement, in a tone of surprise, "if I have been so unfortunate as to offend you; but I believe you will not regret the honour I now have of attending Miss Anville, when you hear that I have been so happy as to do her some service."

Just as Madame Duval, with her usual *Ma foi*, was beginning to reply, the attention of Sir Clement was wholly drawn from her, by the appearance of Mr. Smith, who coming suddenly behind me, and freely putting his hands on my shoulders, cried, "Oh ho, my little runaway, have I found you at last? I have been scampering all over the gardens for you; for I was determined to find you, if you were above ground. — But how could you be so cruel as to leave us?"

I turned round to him, and looked with a degree of contempt that I hoped would have quieted him; but he had not the sense to understand me; and, attempting to take my hand, he added, "Such a demure looking lady as you are, who'd have thought of your leading one such a dance? — Come, now, don't be so coy, — only think what a trouble I have had in running after you!"

"The trouble, Sir," said I, "was of your own choice, — not mine." And I walked round to the other side of Madame Duval.

Perhaps I was too proud, — but I could not endure that Sir Clement, whose eyes followed him with looks of the most surprised curiosity, should witness his unwelcome familiarity.

Upon my removal, he came up to me, and, in a low voice, said, "You are not, then, with the Mirvans?"

"No, Sir."

"And pray — may I ask, — have you left them long?"

"No, Sir."

"How unfortunate I am! — but yesterday I sent to acquaint the Captain I should reach the Grove by to-morrow noon! However, I shall get away as fast as possible. Shall you be long in town?"

"I believe not, Sir."

"And then, when you leave it, — which way — will you allow me to ask, which way you shall travel?"

"Indeed, — I don't know."

"Not know! — But do you return to the Mirvans any more?"

"I — I can't tell, Sir."

And then, I addressed myself to Madame Duval, with such a pretended earnestness, that he was obliged to be silent.

As he cannot but observe the great change in my situation, which he knows not how to account for, there is something in all these questions, and this unrestrained curiosity, that I did not expect from a man, who when he pleases can be so well-bred, as Sir Clement Willoughby. He seems disposed to think that the alteration in my companions authorizes an alteration in his manners. It is true, he has always treated me with uncommon freedom, but never before with so disrespectful an abruptness. This observation, which he has given me cause to make, of his *changing with the tide,* has sunk him more in my opinion, than any other part of his conduct.

Yet I could almost have laughed, when I looked at Mr. Smith, who no sooner saw me addressed by Sir Clement, than, retreating aloof from the company, he seemed to lose at once all his happy self-sufficiency and conceit; looking now at the baronet, now at himself, surveying, with sorrowful eyes, his dress, struck with his air, his gestures, his easy gaiety; he gazed at him with envious admiration, and seemed himself, with conscious inferiority, to shrink into nothing.

Soon after, Mr. Brown, running up to us, called out, "La, what, i'n't Miss Polly come yet?"

"Come!" said Mr. Branghton, "why, I thought you went to fetch her yourself, did n't you?"

"Yes, but I could n't find her; — yet I dare say I've been over half the garden."

"Half! but why did not you go over it all?"

"Why, so I will: but only I thought I'd just come and see if she was here first?"

"But where's Tom?"

"Why, I don't know; for he would not stay with me, all as ever I could say; for we met some young gentlemen of his acquaintance, and so he bid me go and look by myself, for he said, says he, I can divert myself better another way, says he."

This account being given, away again went this silly young man; and Mr. Branghton, extremely incensed, said he would go and see after them himself.

"So now," cried Madame Duval, "he's gone too! why, at this rate we shall have to wait for one or other of them all night!"

Observing that Sir Clement seemed disposed to renew his enquiries, I turned towards one of the paintings,[8] and, pretending to be very much occupied in looking at it, asked M. Du Bois some questions concerning the figures.

"O, *Mon Dieu!*" cried Madame Duval, "don't ask him; your best way is to ask Mr. Smith, for he's been here the oftenest. Come, Mr. Smith, I dare say you can tell us all about them."

"Why, yes, Ma'am," said Mr. Smith, who, brightening up at this application, advanced towards us, with an air of assumed importance (which, however, sat very uneasily upon him) and begged to know what he should explain first; "For I have attended," said he, "to all these paintings, and know every thing in them perfectly well; for I am rather fond of pictures, Ma'am; and, really, I must say, I think a pretty picture is a — a very — is really a very — is something very pretty. — "

"So do I too," said Madame Duval, "but pray now, Sir, tell us who that is meant for," pointing to a figure of Neptune.

"That! — why that, Ma'am, is, — Lord bless me, I can't think how I come to be so stupid, but really I have forgot his name, — and yet, I know it as well as my own, too, — however, he's a *general,* Ma'am, they are all generals."

I saw Sir Clement bite his lips; and, indeed, so did I mine.

"Well," said Madame Duval, "it's the oddest dress for a general ever I see!"

"He seems so capital a figure," said Sir Clement to Mr. Smith, "that I imagine he must be *generalissimo* of the whole army."

"Yes, Sir, yes," answered Mr. Smith, respectfully bowing, and highly delighted at being thus referred to, "you are perfectly right, —

---

[8] *one of the paintings:* Another of Vauxhall's attractions was the Picture Room, where one could view the work of current artists.

but I cannot for my life think of his name; — perhaps, Sir, you may remember it?"

"No, really," replied Sir Clement, "my acquaintance among the generals is not so extensive."

The ironical tone of voice in which Sir Clement spoke, entirely disconcerted Mr. Smith; who, again retiring to an humble distance, seemed sensibly mortified at the failure of his attempt to recover his consequence.

Soon after, Mr. Branghton returned, with his youngest daughter, whom he had rescued from a party of insolent young men; but he had not yet been able to find the eldest. Miss Polly was really frightened, and declared she would never go into the dark walks again. Her father, leaving her with us, went in quest of her sister.

While she was relating her adventures, to which nobody listened more attentively than Sir Clement, we saw Mr. Brown enter the room. "O la!" cried Miss Polly, "let me hide myself, and don't tell him I'm come."

She then placed herself behind Madame Duval, in such a manner that she could not be seen.

"So Miss Polly is not come yet!" said the simple swain;[9] "well, I can't think where she can be! I've been a looking, and looking, and looking all about, and I can't find her, all I can do."

"Well but, Mr. Brown," said Mr. Smith, "sha'n't you go and look for the lady again?"

"Yes, Sir," said he, sitting down, "but I must rest me a little bit first. You can't think how tired I am."

"O fie, Mr. Brown, fie," cried Mr. Smith, winking at us, "tired of looking for a lady! Go, go, for shame!"

"So I will, Sir, presently; but you'd be tired too, if you'd walked so far: besides, I think she's gone out of the garden, or else I must have seen something or other of her."

A *he, he, he!* of the tittering Polly, now betrayed her, and so ended this ingenious little artifice.

At last appeared Mr. Branghton and Miss Biddy, who, with a face of mixed anger and confusion, addressing herself to me, said, "So Miss, so you ran away from me! Well, see if I don't do as much by you, some day or other! But I thought how it would be, you'd no mind to leave the *gentlemen,* though you'd run away from *me.*"

---

[9] *swain:* A gallant or lover, usually associated with the rural lower classes.

I was so much surprised at this attack, that I could not answer her for very amazement; and she proceeded to tell us how ill she had been used, and that two young men had been making her walk up and down the dark walks by absolute force, and as fast as ever they could tear her along; and many other particulars, which I will not tire you with relating. In conclusion, looking at Mr. Smith, she said, "But, to be sure, thought I, at least all the company will be looking for me; so I little expected to find you all here, talking as comfortably as ever you can. However, I know I may thank my cousin for it!"

"If you mean *me*, Madam," said I, very much shocked, "I am quite ignorant in what manner I can have been accessary to your distress."

"Why, by running away so. If you'd stayed with us, I'll answer for it, Mr. Smith and M. Du Bois would have come to look for us; but I suppose they could not leave your ladyship."

The folly and unreasonableness of this speech would admit of no answer. But what a scene was this for Sir Clement! his surprise was evident; and, I must acknowledge, my confusion was equally great.

We had now to wait for young Branghton, who did not appear for some time; and, during this interval, it was with difficulty that I avoided Sir Clement, who was on the rack of curiosity, and dying to speak to me.

When, at last, the hopeful youth returned, a long and frightful quarrel ensued between him and his father, in which his sisters occasionally joined, concerning his neglect; and he defended himself only by a brutal mirth, which he indulged at their expence.

Every one, now, seemed inclined to depart, — when, as usual, a dispute arose, upon the *way* of our going, whether in a coach or a boat. After much debating, it was determined that we should make two parties, one by the water and the other by land; for Madame Duval declared she would not, upon any account, go into a boat at night.

Sir Clement then said, that if she had no carriage in waiting, he should be happy to see her and me safe home, as his was in readiness.

Fury started into her eyes, and passion inflamed every feature, as she answered, "*Pardie*, no, — you may take care of yourself, if you please; but as to me, I promise you I sha'n't trust myself with no such person."

He pretended not to comprehend her meaning, yet, to wave a discussion, acquiesced in her refusal. The coach-party fixed upon consisted of Madame Duval, M. Du Bois, Miss Branghton, and myself.

I now began to rejoice, in private, that, at least, our lodgings would be neither seen nor known by Sir Clement. We soon met with an hackney-coach, into which he handed me, and then took leave.

Madame Duval, having already given the coachman her direction, he mounted the box, and we were just driving off, when Sir Clement exclaimed, "By Heaven, this is the very coach I had in waiting for myself!"

"This coach, your honour!" said the man, "no, that it i'n't."

Sir Clement, however, swore that it was, and, presently, the man, begging his pardon, said he had really forgotten that he was engaged.

I have no doubt but that this scheme occurred to him at the moment, and that he made some sign to the coachman, which induced him to support it: for there is not the least probability that the accident really happened, as it is most likely his own chariot was in waiting.

The man then opened the coach-door, and Sir Clement advancing to it, said, "I don't believe there is another carriage to be had, or I would not incommode you; but, as it may be disagreeable to you to wait here any longer, I beg you will not get out, for you shall be set down before I am carried home, if you will be so good as to make a little room."

And so saying, in he jumpt, and seated himself between M. Du Bois and me, while our astonishment at the whole transaction was too great for speech. He then ordered the coachman to drive on, according to the directions he had already received.

For the first ten minutes, no one uttered a word; and then, Madame Duval, no longer able to contain herself, exclaimed, "*Ma foi,* if this is n't one of the impudentest things ever I see!"

Sir Clement, regardless of this rebuke, attended only to me; however, I answered nothing he said, when I could possibly avoid so doing. Miss Branghton made several attempts to attract his notice, but in vain, for he would not take the trouble of paying her any regard.

Madame Duval, during the rest of the ride, addressed herself to M. Du Bois in French, and in that language exclaimed with great vehemence against boldness and assurance.

I was extremely glad when I thought our journey must be nearly at an end, for my situation was very uneasy to me, as Sir Clement perpetually endeavoured to take my hand. I looked out of the coach-window, to see if we were near home; Sir Clement, stooping over me did the same, and then, in a voice of infinite wonder, called out,

"Where the d — l is the man driving to? — why we are in Broad St. Giles's!"

"O, he's very right," cried Madame Duval, "so never trouble your head about that, for I sha'n't go by directions of yours, I promise you."

When, at last, we stopped, at *an Hosier's* in *High Holborn,* — Sir Clement said nothing, but his *eyes,* I saw, were very busily employed in viewing the place, and the situation of the house. The coach he insisted upon settling himself, as he said it belonged to him; and then he took leave. M. Du Bois walked home with Miss Branghton, and Madame Duval and I retired to our apartments.

How disagreeable an evening's adventure! not one of the party seemed satisfied, except Sir Clement, who was in high spirits: but Madame Duval, was enraged at meeting with him; Mr. Branghton, angry with his children; the frolic of the Miss Branghtons had exceeded their plan, and ended in their own distress; their brother was provoked that there had been no riot; Mr. Brown was tired; and Mr. Smith mortified. As to myself, I must acknowledge, nothing could be more disagreeable to me, than being seen by Sir Clement Willoughby with a party at once so vulgar in themselves, and so familiar to me.

And you, too, my dear Sir, will, I know, be sorry that I have met him; however, there is no apprehension of his visiting here, as Madame Duval is far too angry to admit him.


## LETTER XVI

### Evelina in Continuation

Holborn, June 18th.

Madame Duval rose very late this morning, and, at one o'clock, we had but just breakfasted, when Miss Branghton, her brother, Mr. Smith, and Monsieur Du Bois, called to enquire after our healths.

This civility in young Branghton, I much suspect, was merely the result of his father's commands; but his sister and Mr. Smith, I soon found, had motives of their own. Scarce had they spoken to Madame Duval, when, advancing eagerly to me, "Pray, Ma'am," said Mr. Smith, "who was that gentleman?"

"Pray, Cousin," cried Miss Branghton, "was not he the same gentleman you ran away with that night at the opera?"

"Goodness! that he was," said young Branghton; "and, I declare, as soon as ever I saw him, I thought I knew his face."

"I'm sure I'll defy you to forget him," answered his sister, "if once you had seen him: he is the finest gentleman I ever saw in my life; don't you think so, Mr. Smith?"

"Why, you won't give the Lady time to speak," said Mr. Smith. — "Pray, Ma'am, what is the gentleman's name?"

"Willoughby, Sir."

"Willoughby! I think I have heard the name. Pray, Ma'am, is he married?"

"Lord, no, that he is not," cried Miss Branghton; "he looks too smart, by a great deal, for a married man. Pray, Cousin, how did you get acquainted with him?"

"Pray, Miss," said young Branghton, in the same breath, "what's his business?"

"Indeed I don't know," answered I.

"Something very genteel, I dare say," added Miss Branghton, "because he dresses so fine."

"It ought to be something that brings in a good income," said Mr. Smith, "for I'm sure he did not get that suit of cloaths he had on, under thirty or forty pounds; for I know the price of cloaths pretty well: — pray, Ma'am, can you tell me what he has a year?"

"Don't talk no more about him," cried Madame Duval, "for I don't like to hear his name; I believe he's one of the worst persons in the world; for, though I never did him no manner of harm, nor so much as hurt a hair of his head, I know he was an accomplice with that fellow, Captain Mirvan, to take away my life."

Every body, but myself, now crowding around her for an explanation, a violent rapping at the street-door was unheard; and, without any previous notice, in the midst of her narration, Sir Clement Willoughby entered the room. They all started, and, with looks of guilty confusion, as if they feared his resentment for having listened to Madame Duval, they scrambled for chairs, and, in a moment, were all formally seated.

Sir Clement, after a general bow, singling out Madame Duval, said, with his usual easiness, "I have done myself the honour of waiting on you, Madam, to enquire if you have any commands to Howard Grove, whither I am going to-morrow morning."

Then, seeing the storm that gathered in her eyes, before he allowed her time to answer, he addressed himself to me; — "And if you, Madam, have any with which you will honour me, I shall be happy to execute them."

"None at all, Sir."

"None! — not to Miss Mirvan! — no message! no letter! — "

"I wrote to Miss Mirvan yesterday by the post."

"My application should have been earlier, had I sooner known your address."

"*Ma foi*," cried Madame Duval, recovering from her surprise, "I believe never nobody saw the like of this!"

"Of what! Madam!" cried the undaunted Sir Clement, turning quick towards her, "I hope no one has offended you!"

"You don't hope no such a thing!" cried she, half choaked with passion, and rising from her chair. This motion was followed by the rest, and, in a moment, every body stood up.

Still Sir Clement was not abashed; affecting to make a bow of *acknowledgment* to the company in general, he said, "Pray — I beg — Ladies, — Gentlemen, — pray don't let me disturb you, — pray keep your seats."

"Pray, Sir," said Miss Branghton, moving a chair towards him, "won't you sit down yourself?"

"You are extremely good, Ma'am: — rather than make any disturbance — "

And so saying, this strange man seated himself, as did, in an instant, every body else, even Madame Duval herself, who, overpowered by his boldness, seemed too full for utterance.

He then, and with as much composure as if he had been an expected guest, began to discourse on the weather, — its uncertainty, — the heat of the public places in summer, — the emptiness of the town, — and other such common topics.

Nobody, however, answered him; Mr. Smith seemed afraid, young Branghton ashamed, M. Du Bois amazed, Madame Duval enraged, and myself determined not to interfere. All that he could obtain, was the notice of Miss Branghton, whose nods, smiles, and attention, had some appearance of entering into conversation with him.

At length, growing tired, I suppose, of engaging every body's eyes, and nobody's tongue, addressing himself to Madame Duval and to me, he said, "I regard myself as peculiarly unfortunate, Ladies, in having fixed upon a time for my visit to Howard Grove, when you are absent from it."

"So I suppose, Sir, so I suppose," cried Madame Duval, hastily rising, and the next moment as hastily seating herself, "you'll be a wanting of somebody to make your game of, and so you may think to get *me* there again; — but, I promise you, Sir, you won't find it so easy a matter to make me a fool: and besides that," raising her voice, "I've found you out, I assure you; so if ever you go to play your tricks upon me again, I'll make no more ado, but go directly to a justice of peace; so, Sir, if you can't think of nothing but making people ride about the country, at all hours of the night, just for your diversion, why you'll find I know some justices, as well as Justice Tyrrel."

Sir Clement was evidently embarrassed at this attack; yet he affected a look of surprise, and protested he did not understand her meaning.

"Well," cried she, "if I don't wonder where people can get such impudence! if you'll say that, you'll say any thing; however, if you swear till you're black in the face, I sha'n't believe you; for nobody sha'n't persuade me out of my senses, that I'll promise you."

"Doubtless not, Madam," answered he with some hesitation, "and I hope you do not suspect I ever had such an intention; my respect for you — "

"O Sir, you're vastly polite, all of a sudden! but I know what it's all for; — it's only for what you can get! — you could treat me like nobody at Howard Grove — but now you see I've a house of my own, you've a mind to wheedle yourself into it; but I sees your design, so you need n't trouble yourself to take no more trouble about that, for you shall never get nothing at my house,—not so much as a dish of tea: — so now, Sir, you see I can play you trick for trick."

There was something so extremely gross in this speech, that it even disconcerted Sir Clement, who was too much confounded to make any answer.

It was curious to observe the effect which his embarrassment, added to the freedom with which Madame Duval addressed him, had upon the rest of the company: every one, who, before, seemed at a loss how, or if at all, to occupy a chair, now filled it with the most easy composure: and Mr. Smith, whose countenance had exhibited the most striking picture of mortified envy, now began to recover his usual expression of satisfied conceit. Young Branghton, too, who had been apparently awed by the presence of so fine a gentleman, was again himself, rude and familiar; while his mouth was wide distended into a broad grin, at hearing *his aunt give the beau such a trimming.*

Madame Duval, encouraged by this success, looked around her with an air of triumph, and continued her harangue: "And so, Sir, I suppose you thought to have had it all your own way, and to have come here as often as you pleased, and to have got me to Howard Grove again, on purpose to have served me as you did before; but you shall see I'm as cunning as you, so you may go and find somebody else to use in that manner, and to put your mask on, and to make a fool of; for as to me, if you go to tell me your stories about the Tower again, for a month together, I'll never believe 'em no more; and I'll promise you, Sir, if you think I like such jokes, you'll find I'm no such person."

"I assure you, Ma'am, — upon my honour — I really don't comprehend — I fancy there is some misunderstanding — "

"What, I suppose you'll tell me next you don't know nothing of the matter?"

"Not a word, upon my honour."

O Sir Clement! thought I, is it thus you prize your honour!

"*Pardie*," cried Madame Duval, "this is the most provokingest part of all! why you might as well tell me I don't know my own name."

"Here is certainly some mistake; for I assure you, Ma'am — "

"Don't assure me nothing," cried Madame Duval, raising her voice, "I know what I'm saying, and so do you too; for did not you tell me all that about the Tower, and about M. Du Bois? — why M. Du Bois was n't never there, nor nigh it, and so it was all your own invention."

"May there not be two persons of the same name? the mistake was but natural, — "

"Don't tell me of no mistake, for it was all on purpose; besides, did not you come, all in a mask, to the chariot-door, and help to get me put in that ditch? — I'll promise you, I've had the greatest mind in the world to take the law of you, and if ever you do as much again, so I will, I assure you!"

Here Miss Branghton tittered; Mr. Smith smiled contemptuously, and young Branghton thrust his handkerchief into his mouth to stop his laughter.

The situation of Sir Clement, who saw all that passed, became now very awkward, even to himself, and he stammered very much in saying, "Surely, Madam — surely you — you cannot do me the — the injustice to think — that I had any share in the — the — the misfortune which — "

"*Ma foi*, Sir," cried Madame Duval, with increasing passion, "you'd best not stand talking to me at that rate; I know it *was* you, — and if you stay there, provoking me in such a manner, I'll send for a constable this minute."

Young Branghton, at these words, in spite of all his efforts, burst into a loud laugh; nor could either his sister, or Mr. Smith, though with more moderation, forbear joining in his mirth.

Sir Clement darted his eyes towards them, with looks of the most angry contempt, and then told Madame Duval, that he would not now detain her, to make his vindication, but would wait on her some time when she was alone.

"O *pardie,* Sir," cried she, "I don't desire none of your company; and if you was n't the most impudentest person in the world, you would not dare look me in the face."

The ha, ha, ha's, and he, he, he's, grew more and more uncontroulable, as if the restraint from which they had burst, had added to their violence. Sir Clement could no longer endure being the object who excited them, and, having no answer ready for Madame Duval, he hastily stalked towards Mr. Smith and young Branghton, and sternly demanded what they laughed at?

Struck by the air of importance which he assumed, and alarmed at the angry tone of his voice, their merriment ceased, as instantaneously as if it had been directed by clock-work, and they stared foolishly, now at him, now at each other, without making any answer but a simple *"Nothing, Sir!"*

"O *pour le coup,*" cried Madame Duval, "this is too much! pray, Sir, what business have you to come here, a ordering people that comes to see me? I suppose, next, nobody must laugh but yourself!"

"With me, Madam," said Sir Clement, bowing, "a *lady* may do any thing, and, consequently, there is no liberty in which I shall not be happy to indulge *you:* — but it has never been my custom to give the same license to *gentlemen.*"

Then, advancing to me, who had sat very quietly, on a window, during this scene, he said, "Miss Anville, I may at least acquaint our friends at Howard Grove, that I had the honour of leaving you in good health." And then, lowering his voice, he added, "For Heaven's sake, my dearest creature, who are these people? and how came you so strangely situated?"

"I beg my respects to all the family, Sir," answered I, aloud, "and I hope you will find them well."

He looked at me reproachfully, but kissed my hand; and then, bowing to Madame Duval and Miss Branghton, passed hastily by the men, and made his exit.

I fancy he will not be very eager to repeat his visits, for I should imagine he has rarely, if ever, been before in a situation so awkward and disagreeable.

Madame Duval has been all spirits and exultation ever since he went, and only wishes Captain Mirvan would call, that she might *do the same by him.* Mr. Smith, upon hearing that he was a baronet, and seeing him drive off in a very beautiful chariot, declared that he would not have laughed upon any account, had he known his rank, and regretted extremely having missed such an opportunity of making so *genteel* an *acquaintance.* Young Branghton vowed that, if he had known as much, he would have *asked for his custom:*[1] and his sister has sung his praises ever since, protesting she thought, *all along,* he was a man of *quality* by his *look.*

[1] *asked for his custom:* Solicited Sir Clement to buy goods from him.

## LETTER XVII

### Evelina in Continuation

The last three evenings have passed tolerably quiet, for the Vauxhall adventures had given Madame Duval a surfeit of public places: home, however, soon growing tiresome, she determined to-night, she said, to relieve her *ennui,* by some amusement; and it was therefore settled that we should call upon the Branghtons, at their house, and thence proceed to Marybone Gardens.

But, before we reached Snow-Hill, we were caught in a shower of rain: we hurried into the shop, where the first object I saw was Mr. Macartney, with a book in his hand, seated in the same corner where I saw him last; but his looks were still more wretched than before, his face yet thinner, and his eyes sunk almost hollow into his head. He lifted them up as we entered, and I even thought that they emitted a gleam of joy: involuntarily, I made to him my first courtesie; he rose and bowed, with a precipitation that manifested surprise and confusion.

In a few minutes, we were joined by all the family, except Mr. Smith, who, fortunately, was engaged.

Had all the future prosperity of our lives depended upon the good or bad weather of this evening, it could not have been treated as a subject of greater importance. "Sure never any thing was so unlucky!" — "Lord, how provoking!" — "It might rain for ever, if it would hold up now!" — These, and such expressions, with many anxious observations upon the kennels,[1] filled up all the conversation till the shower was over.

[1] *kennels:* An open drain running down the center of the road which formed the primary means of waste and water drainage in London.

And then a very warm debate arose, whether we should pursue our plan, or defer it to some finer evening; [the] Miss Branghtons were for the former; their father was sure it would rain again; Madame Duval, though she detested returning home, yet dreaded the dampness of the gardens.

M. Du Bois then proposed going to the top of the house, to examine whether the clouds looked threatening or peaceable; Miss Branghton, starting at this proposal, said they might go to Mr. Macartney's room, if they would, but not to her's.

This was enough for the brother; who, with a loud laugh, declared he would have some *fun*, and immediately led the way, calling to us all to follow. His sisters both ran after him, but no one else moved.

In a few minutes, young Branghton, coming half way down stairs, called out, "Lord, why don't you all come? why here's Poll's things all about the room!"

Mr. Branghton then went, and Madame Duval, who cannot bear to be excluded from whatever is going forward, was handed up stairs by M. Du Bois.

I hesitated a few moments whether or not to join them; but, soon perceiving that Mr. Macartney had dropped his book, and that I engrossed his whole attention, I prepared, from mere embarrassment, to follow them.

As I went, I heard him move from his chair, and walk slowly after me. Believing that he wished to speak to me, and earnestly desiring myself to know if, by your means, I could possibly be of any service to him, I first slackened my pace, and then turned back. But, though I thus met him half-way, he seemed to want courage or resolution to address me; for, when he saw me returning, with a look extremely disordered, he retreated hastily from me.

Not knowing what I ought to do, I went to the street-door, where I stood some time, hoping he would be able to recover himself: but, on the contrary, his agitation increased every moment; he walked up and down the room, in a quick, but unsteady pace, seeming equally distressed and irresolute: and, at length, with a deep sigh, he flung himself into a chair.

I was so much affected by the appearance of such extreme anguish, that I could remain no longer in the room; I therefore glided by him, and went up stairs; but, ere I had gone five steps, he precipitately followed me, and, in a broken voice, called out, "Madam! — for Heaven's sake — "

He stopped, but I instantly descended, restraining, as well as I was able, the fullness of my own concern. I waited some time, in painful expectation, for his speaking: all that I had heard of his poverty, occurring to me, I was upon the point of presenting him my purse, but the fear of mistaking or offending him, deterred me. Finding, however, that he continued silent, I ventured to say, "Did you — Sir, wish to speak to me?"

"I did!" cried he, with quickness, "but now — I cannot!"

"Perhaps, Sir, another time, perhaps if you recollect yourself — "

"Another time!" repeated he mournfully, "alas! I look not forward but to misery and despair!"

"O Sir," cried I, extremely shocked, "you must not talk thus! — if you forsake *yourself*, how can you expect — "

I stopped. "Tell me, tell me," cried he, with eagerness, "who you are? — whence you come? — and by what strange means you seem to be arbitress and ruler of the destiny of such a wretch as I am?"

"Would to Heaven," cried I, "I could serve you!"

"You can!"

"And how? pray tell me how?"

"To tell you — is death to me! yet I *will* tell you, — I have a *right* to your assistance, — you have deprived me of the only resource to which I could apply, — and therefore — "

"Pray, pray, speak;" cried I, putting my hand into my pocket, "they will be down stairs in a moment!"

"I will, Madam. — Can you — will you — I think you will! — may I then — " he stopped and paused, "say, will you —— " then suddenly turning from me, "Great Heaven! I cannot speak!" and he went back to the shop.

I now put my purse in my hand, and following him, said, "If indeed, Sir, I can assist you, why should you deny me so great a satisfaction? Will you permit me to — "

I dared not go on; but with a countenance very much softened, he approached me, and said, "Your voice, Madam, is the voice of compassion! — such a voice as these ears have long been strangers to!"

Just then, young Branghton called out vehemently to me, to come up stairs; I seized the opportunity of hastening away: and therefore saying, "Heaven, Sir, protect and comfort you! — " I let fall my purse upon the ground, not daring to present it to him, and ran up stairs with the utmost swiftness.

Too well do I know you, my ever honoured Sir, to fear your displeasure for this action: I must, however, assure you I shall need no fresh supply during my stay in town, as I am at little expence, and hope soon to return to Howard Grove.

Soon, did I say! when not a fortnight is yet expired, of the long and tedious month I must linger out here!

I had many witticisms to endure from the Branghtons, upon account of my staying so long with the *Scotch mope,* as they call him; but I attended to them very little, for my whole heart was filled with pity and concern. I was very glad to find the Marybone scheme was deferred, another shower of rain having put a stop to the dissention upon this subject; the rest of the evening was employed in most violent quarrelling between Miss Polly and her brother, on account of the discovery made by the latter, of the state of her apartment.

We came home early; and I have stolen from Madame Duval and M. Du Bois, who is here for ever, to write to my best friend.

I am most sincerely rejoiced that this opportunity has offered for my contributing what little relief was in my power, to this unhappy man; and I hope it will be sufficient to enable him to pay his debts to this pitiless family.

## LETTER XVIII

### Mr. Villars to Evelina

Berry Hill.

Displeasure? my Evelina! — you have but done your duty; you have but shewn that humanity without which I should blush to own my child. It is mine, however, to see that your generosity be not repressed by your suffering from indulging it; I remit to you, therefore, not merely a token of my approbation, but an acknowledgement of my desire to participate in your charity.

O my child, were my fortune equal to my confidence in thy benevolence, with what transport should I, through thy means, devote it to the relief of indigent virtue! yet let us not repine at the limitation of our power, for, while our bounty is proportioned to our ability, the difference of the greater or less donation, can weigh but little in the scale of justice.

In reading your account of the misguided man, whose misery has so largely excited your compassion, I am led to apprehend, that his unhappy situation is less the effect of misfortune, than of misconduct.

If he is reduced to that state of poverty represented by the Branghtons, he should endeavour by activity and industry to retrieve his affairs; and not pass his time in idle reading in the very shop of his creditor.

The pistol scene made me shudder: the courage with which you pursued this desperate man, at once delighted and terrified me. Be ever thus, my dearest Evelina, dauntless in the cause of distress! let no weak fears, no timid doubts, deter you from the exertion of your duty, according to the fullest sense of it that Nature has implanted in your mind. Though gentleness and modesty are the peculiar attributes of your sex, yet fortitude and firmness, when occasion demands them, are virtues as noble and as becoming in women as in men: the right line of conduct is the same for both sexes, though the manner in which it is pursued, may somewhat vary, and be accommodated to the strength or weakness of the different travellers.

There is, however, something so mysterious in all you have yet seen or heard of this wretched man, that I am unwilling to stamp a bad impression of his character, upon so slight and partial a knowledge of it. Where any thing is doubtful, the ties of society, and the laws of humanity, claim a favourable interpretation; but remember, my dear child, that those of discretion have an equal claim to your regard.

As to Sir Clement Willoughby, I know not how to express my indignation at his conduct. Insolence so insufferable, and the implication of suspicions so shocking, irritate me to a degree of wrath, which I hardly thought my almost worn-out passions were capable of again experiencing. You must converse with him no more; he imagines, from the pliability of your temper, that he may offend you with impunity; but his behaviour justifies, nay, calls for, your avowed resentment: do not, therefore, hesitate in forbidding him your sight.

The Branghtons, Mr. Smith, and young Brown, however ill-bred and disagreeable, are objects too contemptible for serious displeasure: yet I grieve much that my Evelina should be exposed to their rudeness and impertinence.

The very day that this tedious month expires, I shall send Mrs. Clinton to town, who will accompany you to Howard Grove. Your stay there will, I hope, be short, for I feel daily an increasing impatience to fold my beloved child to my bosom!

ARTHUR VILLARS

## LETTER XIX

### Evelina to the Rev. Mr. Villars

Holborn, June 27th.
I have just received, my dearest Sir, your kind present, and still kinder letter. Surely never had orphan so little to regret as your grateful Evelina! Though motherless, though worse than fatherless, bereft from infancy of the two first and greatest blessings of life, never has she had cause to deplore their loss; never has she felt the omission of a parent's tenderness, care, or indulgence; never, but from sorrow for *them,* had reason to grieve at the separation! Most thankfully do I receive the token of your approbation, and most studiously will I endeavour so to dispose of it, as may merit your generous confidence in my conduct.

Your doubts concerning Mr. Macartney give me some uneasiness. Indeed, Sir, he has not the appearance of a man whose sorrows are the effect of guilt. But I hope, ere I leave town, to be better acquainted with his situation, and enabled, with more certainty of his worth, to recommend him to your favour.

I am very willing to relinquish all acquaintance with Sir Clement Willoughby, as far as it may depend upon myself so to do; but indeed, I know not how I should be able to absolutely *forbid him my sight.*

Miss Mirvan, in her last letter, informs me that he is now at Howard Grove, where he continues in high favour with the Captain, and is the life and spirit of the house. My time, since I wrote last, has passed very quietly; Madame Duval having been kept at home by a bad cold, and the Branghtons by bad weather. The young man, indeed, has called two or three times, and his behaviour, though equally absurd, is more unaccountable than ever: he speaks very little, takes hardly any notice of Madame Duval, and never looks at me, without a broad grin. Sometimes he approaches me, as if with intention to communicate intelligence of importance, and then, suddenly stopping short, laughs rudely in my face.

O how happy shall I be, when the worthy Mrs. Clinton arrives!

June 29th.
Yesterday morning, Mr. Smith called, to acquaint us that the Hampstead assembly was to be held that evening; and then he pre-

sented Madame Duval with one ticket, and brought another to me. I thanked him for his intended civility, but told him I was surprised he had so soon forgot my having already declined going to the ball.

"Lord, Ma'am," cried he, "how should I suppose you was in earnest? come, come, don't be cross; here's your Grandmama ready to take care of you, so you can have no fair objection, for she'll see that I don't run away with you. Besides, Ma'am, I got the tickets on purpose."

"If you were determined, Sir," said I, "in making me this offer, to allow me no choice of refusal or acceptance, I must think myself less obliged to your intention, than I was willing to do."

"Dear Ma'am," cried he, "you're so smart, there is no speaking to you; — indeed, you are monstrous smart, Ma'am! but come, your Grandmama shall ask you, and then I know you'll not be so cruel."

Madame Duval was very ready to interfere; she desired me to make no further opposition, said she should go herself, and insisted upon my accompanying her. It was in vain that I remonstrated; I only incurred her anger, and Mr. Smith, having given both the tickets to Madame Duval, with an air of triumph, said he should call early in the evening, and took leave.

I was much chagrined at being thus compelled to owe even the shadow of an obligation to so forward a young man; but I determined that nothing should prevail upon me to dance with him, however my refusal might give offence.

In the afternoon, when he returned, it was evident that he purposed to both charm and astonish me by his appearance; he was dressed in a very showy manner, but without any taste, and the inelegant smartness of his air and deportment, his visible struggle, against education, to put on the fine gentleman, added to his frequent conscious glances at a dress to which he was but little accustomed, very effectually destroyed his aim of *figuring*, and rendered all his efforts useless.

During tea, entered Miss Branghton and her brother. I was sorry to observe the consternation of the former, when she perceived Mr. Smith. I had intended applying to her for advice upon this occasion, but been always deterred by her disagreeable abruptness. Having cast her eyes several times from Mr. Smith to me, with manifest displeasure, she seated herself sullenly in the window, scarce answering Madame Duval's enquiries, and, when I spoke to her, turning absolutely away from me.

Mr. Smith, delighted at this mark of his importance, sat indolently quiet on his chair, endeavouring by his looks rather to display, than to conceal, his inward satisfaction.

"Good gracious!" cried young Branghton, "why, you're all as fine as five-pence! Why, where are you going?"

"To the Hampstead ball," answered Mr. Smith.

"To a ball!" cried he. "Why, what, is Aunt going to a ball? Ha, ha, ha!"

"Yes, to be sure," cried Madame Duval; "I don't know nothing need hinder me."

"And pray, Aunt, will you dance too?"

"Perhaps I may; but I suppose, Sir, that's none of your business, whether I do or not."

"Lord! well, I should like to go! I should like to see Aunt dance, of all things! But the joke is, I don't believe she'll get ever a partner."

"You're the most rudest boy ever I see," cried Madame Duval, an-grily: "but, I promise you, I'll tell your father what you say, for I've no notion of such rudeness."

"Why, Lord, Aunt, what are you so angry for? there's no speaking a word, but you fly into a passion: you're as bad as Biddy or Poll for that, for you're always a scolding."

"I desire, Tom," cried Miss Branghton, "you'd speak for yourself, and not make so free with my name."

"There, now, she's up! there's nothing but quarrelling with the women: it's my belief they like it better than victuals and drink."

"Fie, Tom," cried Mr. Smith, "you never remember your manners before the ladies: I'm sure you never heard *me* speak so rude to them."

"Why, Lord, *you* are a beau; but that's nothing to me. So, if you've a mind, you may be so polite as to dance with Aunt yourself." Then, with a loud laugh, he declared it would be *good fun* to see them.

"Let it be never so good, or never so bad," cried Madame Duval, "you won't see nothing of it, I promise you; so pray don't let me hear no more of such vulgar pieces of fun; for, I assure you, I don't like it. And as to my dancing with Mr. Smith, you may see wonderfuller things than that any day in the week."

"Why, as to that, Ma'am," said Mr. Smith, looking much sur-prised, "I always thought you intended to play at cards, and so I thought to dance with the young lady."

I gladly seized this opportunity to make my declaration, that I should not dance at all.

"Not dance at all!" repeated Miss Branghton; "yes, that's a likely matter truly, when people go to balls."

"I wish she mayn't," said the brother; "'cause then Mr. Smith will have nobody but Aunt for a partner. Lord, how mad he'll be!"

"O, as to that," said Mr. Smith, "I don't at all fear prevailing with the young lady, if once I get her to the room."

"Indeed, Sir," cried I, much offended by his conceit, "you are mistaken; and therefore I beg leave to undeceive you, as you may be assured my resolution will not alter."

"Then pray, Miss, if it is not impertinent," cried Miss Branghton, sneeringly, "what do you go for?"

"Merely and solely," answered I, "to comply with the request of Madame Duval."

"Miss," cried young Branghton, "Bid only wishes it was she, for she has cast a sheep's-eye at Mr. Smith this long while."

"Tom," cried the sister, rising, "I've the greatest mind in the world to box your ears! How dare you say such a thing of me?"

"No, hang it, Tom, no, that's wrong," said Mr. Smith, simpering, "it is indeed, to tell the lady's secrets. — But never mind him, Miss Biddy, for I won't believe him."

"Why, I know Bid would give her ears to go," returned the brother; "but only Mr. Smith likes Miss best, — so does every body else."

While the sister gave him a very angry answer, Mr. Smith said to me, in a low voice, "Why now, Ma'am, how can you be so cruel as to be so much handsomer than your cousins? Nobody can look at them when you are by."

"Miss," cried young Branghton, "whatever he says to you, don't mind him, for he means no good; I'll give you my word for it, he'll never marry you, for he has told me again and again, he'll never marry as long as he lives; besides, if he'd any mind to be married, there's Bid would have had him long ago, and thanked him too."

"Come, come, Tom, don't tell secrets; you'll make the ladies afraid of me: but, I assure you," lowering his voice, "if I *did* marry, it should be your cousin."

*Should* be! — did you ever, my dear Sir, hear such unauthorised freedom? I looked at him with a contempt I did not wish to repress, and walked to the other end of the room.

Very soon after, Mr. Smith sent for a hackney-coach. When I would have taken leave of Miss Branghton, she turned angrily from me, without making any answer. She supposes, perhaps, that I have rather sought, than endeavored to avoid, the notice and civilities of this conceited young man.

The ball was at the *long room* at Hampstead.

This room seems very well named, for I believe it would be difficult to find any other epithet which might, with propriety, distinguish it, as it is without ornament, elegance, or any sort of singularity, and merely to be marked by its length.

I was saved from the importunities of Mr. Smith, the beginning of the evening, by Madame Duval's declaring her intention to dance the two first dances with him herself. Mr. Smith's chagrin was very evident, but as she paid no regard to it, he was necessitated to lead her out.

I was, however, by no means pleased, when she said she was determined to dance a minuet. Indeed I was quite astonished, not having had the least idea she would have consented to, much less proposed, such an exhibition of her person. She had some trouble to make her intentions known, as Mr. Smith was rather averse to speaking to the Master of the ceremonies.

During this minuet, how much did I rejoice in being surrounded only with strangers! She danced in a style so uncommon; her age, her showy dress, and an unusual quantity of *rouge,* drew upon her the eyes, and, I fear, the derision of the whole company. Who she danced with, I know not; but Mr. Smith was so ill-bred as to laugh at her very openly, and to speak of her with as much ridicule as was in his power. But I would neither look at, nor listen to him; nor would I suffer him to proceed with a speech which he began, expressive of his vexation at being forced to dance with her. I told him, very gravely, that complaints upon such a subject might, with less impropriety, be made to every person in the room, than to me.

When she returned to us, she distressed me very much, by asking what I thought of her minuet. I spoke as civilly as I could, but the coldness of my compliment evidently disappointed her. She then called upon Mr. Smith to secure a good place among the country-dancers,[1] and away they went, though not before he had taken the

---

[1] *country-dancers:* Originally the term "country dance" was applied to dances indigenous to the English countryside. In this sense, it is meant to describe generically all dances of English origin, either rural or urban, in which an indefinite number of couples stand up to dance together, forming two long lines.

liberty to say to me in a low voice, "I protest to you, Ma'am, I shall be quite out of countenance, if any of my acquaintance should see me dancing with the old lady!"

For a few moments I very much rejoiced at being relieved from this troublesome man; but scarce had I time to congratulate myself, ere I was accosted by another, who *begged the favour of hopping a dance* with me.

I told him that I should not dance at all; but he thought proper to importune me, very freely, not to be so cruel; and I was obliged to assume no little haughtiness ere I could satisfy him I was serious.

After this, I was addressed, much in the same manner, by several other young men, of whom the appearance and language were equally inelegant and low-bred: so that I soon found my situation was both disagreeable and improper; since, as I was quite alone, I fear I must seem rather to invite, than to forbid, the offers and notice I received. And yet, so great was my apprehension of this interpretation, that I am sure, my dear Sir, you would have laughed had you seen how proudly grave I appeared.

I knew not whether to be glad or sorry, when Madame Duval and Mr. Smith returned. The latter instantly renewed his tiresome entreaties, and Madame Duval said she would go to the card-table: and, as soon as she was accommodated, she desired us to join the dancers.

I will not trouble you with the arguments that followed. Mr. Smith teazed me till I was weary of resistance; and I should at last have been obliged to submit, had I not fortunately recollected the affair of Mr. Lovel, and told my persecuter, that it was impossible I should dance with him, even if I wished it, as I had refused several persons in his absence.

He was not contented with being extremely chagrined, but took the liberty, openly and warmly, to expostulate with me upon not having said I was engaged.

The total disregard with which, involuntarily, I heard him, made him soon change the subject. In truth, I had no power to attend to him, for all my thoughts were occupied in re-tracing the transactions of the two former balls at which I had been present. The party — the conversation — the company — O how great the contrast!

In a short time, however, he contrived to draw my attention to himself, by his extreme impertinence; for he chose to express what he called his *admiration* for me, in terms so open and familiar, that he forced me to express my displeasure with equal plainness.

But how was I surprised, when I found he had the temerity —
what else can I call it? — to impute my resentment to doubts of his
honour; for he said, "My dear Ma'am, you must be a little patient; I
assure you I have no bad designs, I have not upon my word; but,
really, there is no resolving upon such a thing as matrimony all at
once; what with the loss of one's liberty, and what with the ridicule
of all one's acquaintance, — I assure you, Ma'am, you are the first
lady who ever made me even demur upon this subject; for, after all,
my dear Ma'am, marriage is the devil!"

"Your opinion, Sir," answered I, "of either the married or the
single life, can be of no manner of consequence to me, and therefore I
would by no means trouble you to discuss their different merits."

"Why, really, Ma'am, as to your being a little out of sorts, I must
own I can't wonder at it, for, to be sure, marriage is all in all with the
ladies; but with us gentleman it's quite another thing! Now only put
yourself in my place, — suppose you had such a large acquaintance of
gentleman as I have, — and that you had always been used to appear
a little — a little smart among them, — why now, how should you
like to let yourself down all at once into a married man?"

I could not tell what to answer; so much conceit, and so much ignorance, both astonished and silenced me.

"I assure you, Ma'am," added he, "there is not only Miss Biddy, —
though I should have scorned to mention her, if her brother had not
blab'd, for I'm quite particular in keeping ladies' secrets, — but there
are a great many other ladies that have been proposed to me, — but I
never thought twice of any of them, — that is, not in a *serious* way,
— so you may very well be proud," offering to take my hand, "for I
assure you, there is nobody so likely to catch me at last as yourself."

"Sir," cried I, drawing myself back as haughtily as I could, "you
are totally mistaken, if you imagine you have given me any pride I felt
not before, by this conversation; on the contrary, you must allow me
to tell you, I find it too humiliating to bear with it any longer."

I then placed myself behind the chair of Madame Duval; who,
when she heard of the partners I had refused, pitied my ignorance of
the world, but no longer insisted upon my dancing.

Indeed, the extreme vanity of this man makes me exert a spirit
which I did not, till now, know that I possessed: but I cannot endure
that he should think me at his disposal.

The rest of the evening passed very quietly, as Mr. Smith did not
attempt again to speak to me; except, indeed, after we had left the
room, and while Madame Duval was seating herself in the coach, he

said in a voice *pique,* "Next time I take the trouble to get any tickets for a young lady, I'll make a bargain beforehand that she sha'n't turn me over to her grandmother."

We came home very safe; and thus ended this so long projected, and most disagreeable affair.

## LETTER XX

### Evelina in Continuation

I have just received a most affecting letter from Mr. Macartney. I will inclose it, my dear Sir, for your perusal. More than ever have I cause to rejoice that I was able to assist him.

### "Mr. Macartney to Miss Anville"

"Madam,

"Impressed with the deepest, the most heart-felt sense of the exalted humanity with which you have rescued from destruction an unhappy stranger, allow me, with the humblest gratitude, to offer you my fervent acknowledgments, and to implore your pardon for the terror I have caused you.

"You bid me, Madam, live: I have now, indeed, a motive for life, since I should not willingly quit the world, while I withhold from the needy and distressed any share of that charity which a disposition so noble would, otherwise, bestow upon them.

"The benevolence with which you have interested yourself in my concerns, induces me to suppose you would wish to be acquainted with the cause of that desperation from which you snatched me, and the particulars of that misery of which you have, so wonderfully, been a witness. Yet, as this explanation will require that I should divulge secrets of a nature the most delicate, I must entreat you to regard them as sacred, even though I forbear to mention the names of the parties concerned.

"I was brought up in Scotland, though my mother, who had the sole care of me, was an Englishwoman, and had not one relation in that country. She devoted to me her whole time. The retirement in which we lived, and the distance from our natural friends, she often told me were the effect of an unconquerable melancholy with which she was seized, upon the sudden loss of my father, some time before I was born.

"At Aberdeen, where I finished my education, I formed a friendship with a young man of fortune, which I considered as the chief happiness of my life; — but, when he quitted his studies, I considered it as my chief misfortune, for he immediately prepared, by direction of his friends, to make the tour of Europe. For my part, designed for the church, and with no prospect even of maintenance but from my own industry, I scarce dared permit even a wish of accompanying him. It is true, he would joyfully have borne my expences; but my affection was as free from meanness as his own, and I made a determination the most solemn never to lessen its dignity, by submitting to pecuniary obligations.

"We corresponded with great regularity, and the most unbounded confidence, for the space of two years, when he arrived at Lyons in his way home. He wrote me, thence, the most pressing invitation to meet him at Paris, where he intended to remain for some time. My desire to comply with his request, and shorten our absence, was so earnest, that my mother, too indulgent to controul me, lent me what assistance was in her power, and, in an ill-fated moment I set out for that capital.

"My meeting with this dear friend was the happiest event of my life: he introduced me to all his acquaintance; and so quickly did time seem to pass at that delightful period, that the six weeks I had allotted for my stay were gone, ere I was sensible I had missed so many days. But I must now own, that the company of my friend was not the sole subject of my felicity: I became acquainted with a young lady, daughter of an Englishman of distinction, with whom I formed an attachment which I have a thousand times vowed, a thousand times sincerely thought would be lasting as my life. She had but just quitted a convent, in which she had been placed when a child, and though English by birth, she could scarcely speak her native language. Her person and disposition were equally engaging; but chiefly I adored her for the greatness of the expectations which, for my sake, she was willing to resign.

"When the time for my residence in Paris expired, I was almost distracted at the idea of quitting it; yet I had not the courage to make our attachment known to her father, who might reasonably form for her such views as would make him reject, with a contempt which I could not bear to think of, such an offer as mine. Yet I had free access to the house, where she seemed to be left almost wholly to the guidance of an old servant, who was my fast friend.

"But, to be brief, the sudden and unexpected return of her father, one fatal afternoon, proved the beginning of the misery which has ever since devoured me. I doubt not but he had listened to our conversation, for he darted into the room with the rage of a madman. Heavens! what a scene followed! — what abusive language did the shame of a clandestine affair, and the consciousness of acting ill, induce me to brook! At length, however, his fury exceeded my patience, — he called me a beggarly, cowardly Scotchman. Fired at the words, I drew my sword; he, with equal alertness, drew his; for he was not an old man, but on the contrary, strong and able as myself. In vain his daughter pleaded;—in vain did I, repentant of my anger, retreat; — his reproaches continued; myself, my country, were loaded with infamy, — till, no longer constraining my rage, — we fought, — and he fell!

"At that moment I could almost have destroyed myself! The young lady fainted with terror; the old servant, drawn to us by the noise of the scuffle, entreated me to escape, and promised to bring intelligence of what should pass to my apartment. The disturbance which I heard raised in the house obliged me to comply, and, in a state of mind inconceivably wretched, I tore myself away.

"My friend, who I found at home, soon discovered the whole affair. It was near midnight ere the woman came. She told me that her master was living, and her young mistress restored to her senses. The absolute necessity for my leaving Paris, while any danger remained, was forcibly urged by my friend: the servant promised to acquaint him of whatever passed, and he, to transmit to me her information. Thus circumstanced, with the assistance of this dear friend, I effected my departure from Paris, and, not long after, I returned to Scotland. I would fain have stopped by the way, that I might have been nearer the scene of all my concerns, but the low state of my finances denied me that satisfaction.

"The miserable situation of my mind was soon discovered by my mother; nor would she rest till I communicated the cause. She heard my whole story with an agitation which astonished me; — the *name* of the parties concerned, seemed to strike her with horror; — but when I said, We *fought, and he fell;* — "My son," cried she, "you have then murdered your father!" and she sunk breathless at my feet. Comments, Madam, upon such a scene as this, would to you be superfluous, and to me agonizing: I cannot, for both our sakes, be too concise. When she recovered, she confessed all the particulars of a tale which she had hoped never to have revealed. — Alas! the loss she had sustained of my father was not by death! — bound to her by no ties but those of honour, he had voluntarily deserted her! — Her settling in Scotland was not the effect of choice, — she was banished thither by a family but too justly incensed; — pardon, Madam, that I cannot be more explicit!

"My senses, in the greatness of my misery, actually forsook me, and for more than a week I was wholly delirious. My unfortunate mother was yet more to be pitied, for she pined with unmitigated sorrow, eternally reproaching herself for the danger to which her too strict silence had exposed me. When I recovered my reason, my impatience to hear from Paris almost deprived me of it again; and though the length of time I waited for letters might justly be attributed to contrary winds, I could not bear the delay, and was twenty times upon the point of returning thither at all hazards. At length, however, several letters arrived at once, and from the most insupportable of my afflictions I was then relieved, for they acquainted me that the horrors of parricide were not in reserve for me. They informed me also, that as soon as the wound was healed, a journey would be made to England, where my unhappy *sister* was to be received by an aunt with whom she was to live.

"This intelligence somewhat quieted the violence of my sorrows. I instantly formed a plan of meeting them in London, and, by revealing the whole dreadful story, convincing this irritated parent that he had nothing more to apprehend from his daughter's unfortunate choice. My mother consented, and gave me a letter to prove the truth of my assertions. As I could but ill afford to make this journey, I travelled in the cheapest way that was possible. I took an obscure lodging, I need not, Madam, tell you where, — and boarded with the people of the house.

"Here I languished, week after week, vainly hoping for the arrival of my *family;* but my impetuosity had blinded me to the imprudence of which I was guilty in quitting Scotland so hastily. My wounded father, after his recovery, relapsed; and when I had waited in the most comfortless situation for six weeks, my friend wrote me word, that the journey was yet deferred for some time longer.

"My finances were then nearly exhausted, and I was obliged, though most unwillingly, to beg further assistance from my mother, that I might return to Scotland. Oh! Madam! — my answer was not from herself, — it was written by a lady who had long been her companion, and acquainted me that she had been taken suddenly ill of a fever, — and was no more!

"The compassionate nature of which you have given such noble proofs, assures me I need not, if I could, paint to you the anguish of a mind overwhelmed with such accumulated sorrows.

"Inclosed was a letter to a near relation, which she had, during her illness, with much difficulty, written, and in which, with the strongest maternal tenderness, she described my deplorable situation, and entreated his interest to procure me some preferment. Yet so sunk was I by misfortune, that a fortnight elapsed ere I had the courage or spirit to attempt delivering this letter. I was then compelled to it by want. To make my appearance with some decency, I was necessitated, myself, to the melancholy task of changing my coloured cloaths for a suit of mourning; — and then I proceeded to seek my relation.

"I was informed that he was not in town.

"In this desperate situation, the pride of my heart, which hitherto had not bowed to adversity, gave way, and I determined to entreat the assistance of my friend, whose offered services I had a thousand times rejected. Yet, Madam, so hard is it to root from the mind its favourite principles, or prejudices, call them which you please, that I lingered another week ere I had the resolution to send away a letter which I regarded as the death of my independence.

"At length, reduced to my last shilling, dunned insolently by the people of the house, and almost famished, I sealed this fatal letter, and, with a heavy heart, determined to take it to the post-office. But Mr. Branghton and his son suffered me not to pass through their shop with impunity; they insulted me grossly, and threatened me with imprisonment, if I did not immediately satisfy their demands. Stung to the soul, I bid them have but a day's patience, and flung from them, in a state of mind too terrible for description.

"My letter, which I now found would be received too late to save me from disgrace, I tore into a thousand pieces, and scarce could I refrain from putting an instantaneous, an unlicensed period to my existence.

"In this disorder of my senses, I formed the horrible plan of turning foot-pad,[1] for which purpose I returned to my lodging, and collected whatever of my apparel I could part with, which I immediately sold, and with the profits purchased a brace of pistols, powder and shot. I hope, however, you will believe me, when I most solemnly assure you, my sole intention was to *frighten* the passengers I should as-

---

[1] *foot-pad:* A thief who accosted other pedestrians, often at gunpoint, to take their money.

sault, with these dangerous weapons, which I had not loaded, but from a resolution, — a dreadful one, I own, — to save *myself* from an ignominious death if seized. And, indeed, I thought that if I could but procure money sufficient to pay Mr. Branghton, and make a journey to Scotland, I should soon be able, by the public papers, to discover whom I had injured, and to make private retribution.

"But, Madam, new to every species of villainy, my perturbation was so great that I could with difficulty support myself: yet the Branghtons observed it not as I passed through the shop.

"Here I stop: what followed is better known to yourself. But no time can ever efface from my memory that moment, when in the very action of preparing for my own destruction, or the lawless seizure of the property of others, you rushed into the room, and arrested my arm! — It was, indeed, an awful moment! — the hand of Providence seemed to intervene between me and eternity; I beheld you as an angel! — I thought you dropt from the clouds; — the earth, indeed, had never before presented to my view a form so celestial! — What wonder, then, that a spectacle so astonishing should, to a man disordered as I was, appear too beautiful to be human?

"And now, Madam, that I have performed this painful task, the more grateful one remains of rewarding, as far as is in my power, your generous goodness, by assuring you it shall not be thrown away. You have awakened me to a sense of the false pride by which I have been actuated, — a pride which, while it scorned assistance from a friend, scrupled not to compel it from a stranger, though at the hazard of reducing that stranger to a situation as destitute as my own. Yet, Oh! how violent was the struggle which tore my conflicting soul, ere I could persuade myself to profit by the benevolence which you were so evidently disposed to exert in my favour!

"By means of a ring, the gift of my much-regretted mother, I have for the present satisfied Mr. Branghton; and by means of your compassion, I hope to support myself, either till I hear from my friend, to whom, at length, I have written, or till the relation of my mother returns to town.

"To talk to you, Madam, of paying my debt, would be vain; I never can! the service you have done me exceeds all power of return; you have restored me to my senses, you have taught me to curb those passions which bereft me of them, and, since I cannot avoid calamity, to bear it as a man! An interposition so wonderfully circumstanced can never be recollected without benefit. Yet allow me to say, the pecuniary part of my obligation must be settled by my first ability.

"I am, Madam, with the most profound respect, and heart-felt gratitude,

"Your obedient,

"and devoted humble servant,

"J. MACARTNEY"

## LETTER XXI

### Evelina in Continuation

Holborn, July 1, 5 o'clock in the morn.

O sir, what an adventure have I to write! — all night it has occupied my thoughts, and I am now risen thus early, to write it to you.

Yesterday it was settled that we should spend the evening in Marybone-gardens, where M. Torre,[1] a celebrated foreigner, was to exhibit some fireworks. The party consisted of Madame Duval, all the Branghtons, M. Du Bois, Mr. Smith, and Mr. Brown.

We were almost the first persons who entered the Gardens, Mr. Branghton having declared he would have *all he could get for his money*, which, at best, was only fooled away, at such silly and idle places.

We walked in parties, and very much detached from one another; Mr. Brown and Miss Polly led the way by themselves; Miss Branghton and Mr. Smith followed, and the latter seemed determined to be revenged for my behaviour at the ball, by transferring all his former attention for me, to Miss Branghton, who received it with an air of exultation: and very frequently they each of them, though from different motives, looked back, to discover whether I observed their good intelligence. Madame Duval walked with M. Du Bois; and Mr. Branghton by himself; but his son would willingly have attached himself wholly to me, saying frequently, "Come, Miss, let's you and I have a little fun together; you see they have all left us, so now let us leave them." But I begged to be excused, and went to the other side of Madame Duval.

This Garden, as it is called, is neither striking for magnificence nor for beauty; and we were all so dull and languid, that I was extremely glad when we were summoned to the orchestra, upon the opening of

---

[1] *M. Torre:* A print-seller who also specialized in spectacular fireworks displays at Marylebone Gardens between 1772 and 1774.

a concert; in the course of which, I had the pleasure of hearing a concerto on the violin by Mr. Barthelemon,[2] who, to me, seems a player of exquisite fancy, feeling, and variety.

When notice was given us, that the fireworks were preparing, we hurried along to secure good places for the site: but, very soon, we were so encircled and incommoded by the crowd, that Mr. Smith proposed the *ladies* should make interest for a form to stand upon; this was soon effected, and the men then left us, to accommodate themselves better, saying they would return the moment the exhibition was over.

The firework was really beautiful, and told, with wonderful ingenuity, the story of Orpheus and Eurydice:[3] but, at the moment of the fatal look, which separated them for ever, there was such an explosion of fire, and so horrible a noise, that we all, as of one accord, jumpt hastily from the form, and ran away some paces, fearing that we were in danger of mischief, from the innumerable sparks of fire which glittered in the air.

For a moment or two, I neither knew nor considered whither I had run; but my recollection was soon awakened by a stranger's addressing me with, "Come along with me, my dear, and I'll take care of you."

I started, and then, to my great terror, perceived that I had outrun all my companions, and saw not one human being I knew! with all the speed in my power, and forgetful of my first fright, I hastened back to the place I had left; — but found the form occupied by a new set of people.

In vain, from side to side, I looked for some face I knew; I found myself in the midst of a crowd, yet without party, friend, or acquaintance. I walked, in disordered haste, from place to place, without knowing which way to turn, or whither I went. Every other moment, I was spoken to, by some bold and unfeeling man, to whom my dis-

---

[2] *Mr. Barthelemon:* François Hippolite Barthelemon was a French/Irish violinist and the composer of several operas. He was the first violinist at Marylebone Gardens in 1770 and later became conductor of the orchestra at Vauxhall.

[3] *Orpheus and Eurydice:* Orpheus was a poet in Greek mythology whose music was legendary in its power over animals, humans, and gods. He was passionately in love with his wife, Eurydice, and when she died Orpheus charmed Pluto and Persephone, the rulers of Hades, to allow him to enter the underworld of the dead and bring her back. The rulers of the underworld imposed one condition: Orpheus was not to look back at his wife until he had emerged from Hades. Just as he was about to step from the underworld, he forgot this condition and looked back at his wife, who vanished from his sight, never to reappear.

tress, which, I think, must be very apparent, only furnished a pretence for impertinent witticisms, or free gallantry.

At last, a young officer, marching fiercely up to me, said, "You are a sweet pretty creature, and I enlist you in my service;" and then, with great violence, he seized my hand. I screamed aloud with fear, and forcibly snatching it away, I ran hastily up to two ladies, and cried, "For Heaven's sake, dear ladies, afford me some protection!"

They heard me with a loud laugh, but very readily said, "Ay, let her walk between us;" and each of them took hold of an arm.

Then, in a drawling, ironical tone of voice, they asked *what had frightened my little Ladyship?* I told them my adventure very simply, and entreated they would have the goodness to assist me in finding my friends.

O yes, to be sure, they said, I should not want for friends, whilst I was with them. Mine, I said, would be very grateful for any civilities with which they might favour me. But imagine, my dear Sir, how I must be confounded, when I observed, that every other word I spoke produced a loud laugh! However, I will not dwell upon a conversation, which soon, to my inexpressible horror, convinced me I had sought protection from insult, of those who were themselves most likely to offer it! You, my dearest Sir, I well know, will both feel for, and pity my terror, which I have no words to describe.

Had I been at liberty, I should have instantly run away from them, when I made the shocking discovery; but, as they held me fast, that was utterly impossible: and such was my dread of their resentment or abuse, that I did not dare make any open attempt to escape.

They asked me a thousand questions, accompanied by as many hallows,[4] of who I was, what I was, and whence I came. My answers were very incoherent, — but what, good Heaven! were my emotions, when, a few moments afterwards, I perceived advancing our way, — Lord Orville!

Never shall I forget what I felt at that instant: had I, indeed, been sunk to the guilty state, which such companions might lead him to suspect, I could scarce have had feelings more cruelly depressing.

However, to my infinite joy, he passed us without distinguishing me; though I saw that, in a careless manner, his eyes surveyed the party.

As soon as he was gone, one of these unhappy women said, "Do you know that young fellow?"

---

[4] *hallows:* Cries made to incite action or attract attention.

Not thinking it possible she should mean Lord Orville by such a term, I readily answered, "No, Madam."

"Why then," answered she, "you have a monstrous good stare, for a little country Miss."

I now found I had mistaken her, but was glad to avoid an explanation.

A few minutes after, what was my delight, to hear the voice of Mr. Brown, who called out, "Lord, i'n't that Miss what's her name?"

"Thank God," cried I, suddenly springing from them both, "thank God, I have found my party!"

Mr. Brown was, however, alone, and, without knowing what I did, I took hold of his arm.

"Lord, Miss," cried he, "we've had such a hunt you can't think! some of them thought you was gone home; but I says, says I, I don't think, says I, that she'll like to go home all alone, says I."

"So that gentleman belongs to you, Miss, does he?" said one of the women.

"Yes, madam," answered I, "and I now thank you for your civility; but, as I am safe, will not give you any further trouble."

I courtsied slightly, and would have walked away; but, most unfortunately, Madame Duval and the two Miss Branghtons just then joined us.

They all began to make a thousand enquiries, to which I briefly answered, that I had been obliged to these two ladies for walking with me, and would tell them more another time: for, though I felt great *comparative* courage, I was yet too much intimidated by their presence, to dare be explicit.

Nevertheless, I ventured, once more, to wish them good night, and proposed seeking Mr. Branghton. These unhappy women listened to all that was said with a kind of callous curiosity, and seemed determined not to take any hint. But my vexation was terribly augmented, when, after having whispered something to each other, they very cavalierly declared, that they intended joining our party! and then, one of them, very boldly, took hold of my arm, while the other, going round, seized that of Mr. Brown; and thus, almost forcibly, we were moved on between them, and followed by Madame Duval and the Miss Branghtons.

It would be very difficult to say which was greatest, my fright, or Mr. Brown's consternation; who ventured not to make the least resistance, though his uneasiness made him tremble almost as much as myself. I would instantly have withdrawn my arm; but it was held so tight, I could not move it; and poor Mr. Brown was circumstanced in the same manner on the other side; for I heard him say, "Lord, Ma'am, there's no need to squeeze one's arm so!"

And this was our situation, — for we had not taken three steps, when, — O Sir, — we again met Lord Orville! — but not again did he pass quietly by us, — unhappily I caught his eye; — both mine, immediately, were bent to the ground; but he approached me, and we all stopped.

I then looked up. He bowed. Good God, with what expressive eyes did he regard me! Never were surprise and concern so strongly marked — yes, my dear Sir, he looked *greatly* concerned; and that, the remembrance of that, is the only consolation I feel, for an evening the most painful of my life.

What he first said, I know not; for, indeed, I seemed to have neither ears nor understanding; but I recollect that I only courtsied in silence. He paused for an instant, as if — I believe so, — as if unwilling to pass on; but then, finding the whole party detained, he again bowed, and took leave.

Indeed, my dear Sir, I thought I should have fainted, so great was my emotion from shame, vexation, and a thousand other feelings, for which I have no expressions. I absolutely tore myself from the woman's arm, and then, disengaging myself from that of Mr. Brown, I went to Madame Duval, and besought that she would not suffer me to be again parted from her.

I fancy — that Lord Orville saw what passed; for scarcely was I at liberty, ere he returned. Methought, my dear Sir, the pleasure, the surprise of that moment, recompensed me for all the chagrin I had before felt: for do you not think, that this return, manifests, from a character so quiet, so reserved as Lord Orville's, something like solicitude in my concerns? — such, at least, was the interpretation I involuntarily made upon again seeing him.

With a politeness to which I have been some time very little used, he apologised for returning, and then enquired after the health of Mrs. Mirvan, and the rest of the Howard Grove family. The flattering conjecture which I have just acknowledged, had so wonderfully restored my spirits, that I believe I never answered him so readily, and with so little constraint. Very short, however, was the duration of this conversation: for we were soon most disagreeably interrupted.

The Miss Branghtons, though they saw almost immediately the characters of the women to whom I had so unfortunately applied, were, nevertheless, so weak and foolish, as merely to *titter* at their behaviour. As to Madame Duval, she was really for some time so strangely imposed upon, that she thought they were two real fine ladies. Indeed it is wonderful to see how easily and how frequently she is deceived: our disturbance, however, arose from young Brown, who was now between the two women, by whom his arms were absolutely pinioned to his sides: for a few minutes, his complaints had been only murmured; but he now called out aloud, "Goodness, Ladies, you hurt me like any thing! why I can't walk at all, if you keep pinching my arms so!"

This speech raised a loud laugh in the women, and redoubled the tittering of the Miss Branghtons. For my own part, I was most cruelly confused; while the countenance of Lord Orville manifested a sort of indignant astonishment; and, from that moment, he spoke to me no more, till he took leave.

Madame Duval, who now began to suspect her company, proposed our taking the first box we saw empty, bespeaking a supper, and waiting till Mr. Branghton should find us.

Miss Polly mentioned one she had remarked, to which we all turned; Madame Duval instantly seated herself; and the two bold women, forcing the frightened Mr. Brown to go between them, followed her example.

Lord Orville, with an air of gravity that wounded my very soul, then wished me good night. I said not a word; but my face, if it had any connection with my heart, must have looked melancholy indeed: and so, I have reason to believe, it did; for he added, with much more softness, though not less dignity, "Will Miss Anville allow me to ask her address, and to pay my respects to her before I leave town?"

O how I changed colour at this unexpected request! — yet what was the mortification I suffered, in answering, "My Lord, I am — in Holborn."

He then bowed and left us.

What, what can he think of this adventure! how strangely, how cruelly have all appearances turned against me! Had I been blessed with any presence of mind, I should instantly have explained to him the accident which occasioned my being in such terrible company; — but I have none!

As to the rest of the evening, I cannot relate the particulars of what passed; for, to you, I only write of what I think, and I can think of nothing but this unfortunate, this disgraceful meeting. These two poor women continued to torment us all, but especially poor Mr. Brown, who seemed to afford them uncommon diversion, till we were discovered by Mr. Branghton, who very soon found means to release us from their persecutions, by frightening them away. We stayed but a short time after they left us, which was all employed in explanations.

Whatever may be the construction which Lord Orville may put upon this affair, to me it cannot fail of being unfavourable; to be seen — gracious Heaven! — to be seen in company with two women of such character! — How vainly, how proudly have I wished to avoid meeting him when only with the Branghtons and Madame Duval, — but now, how joyful should I be had he seen me to no greater disadvantage! — Holborn, too! what a direction! — he who had always — but I will not torment you, my dearest Sir, with any more of my mortifying conjectures and apprehensions: perhaps he may call, — and then I shall have an opportunity of explaining to him all the most shocking part of the adventure. And yet, as I did not tell him at whose house I lived, he may not be able to discover me; I merely said *in Holborn,* and he, who I suppose saw my embarrassment, forbore to ask any other direction.

Well, I must take my chance!

Yet let me, in justice to Lord Orville, and in justice to the high opinion I have always entertained of his honour and delicacy, — let me observe the difference of his behaviour, when nearly in the same situation to that of Sir Clement Willoughby. He had at least equal cause to depreciate me in his opinion, and to mortify and sink me in my own: but far different was his conduct; — perplexed, indeed, he looked, and much surprised, — but it was benevolently, not with insolence. I am even inclined to think, that he could not see a young creature whom he had so lately known in a higher sphere, appear so suddenly, so strangely, so disgracefully altered in her situation, without some pity and concern. But, whatever might be his doubts and suspicions, far from suffering them to influence his behaviour, he spoke, he looked, with the same politeness and attention with which he had always honoured me when countenanced by Mrs. Mirvan.

Once again, let me drop this subject.

In every mortification, every disturbance, how grateful to my heart, how sweet to my recollection, is the certainty of your never-failing tenderness, sympathy, and protection! Oh Sir, could I, upon this subject, could I write as I feel, — how animated would be the language of

Your devoted
EVELINA!

## LETTER XXII

### Evelina to the Rev. Mr. Villars

Holborn, July 1.

Listless, uneasy, and without either spirit or courage to employ myself, from the time I had finished my last letter, I indolently seated myself at the window, where, while I waited Madame Duval's summons to breakfast, I perceived, among the carriages which passed by, a coronet coach,[1] and, in a few minutes, from the window of it, Lord Orville! I instantly retreated, but not, I believe, unseen; for the coach immediately drove up to our door.

Indeed, my dear Sir, I must own I was greatly agitated; the idea of receiving Lord Orville by myself, — the knowledge that his visit was entirely to *me*, — the wish of explaining the unfortunate adventure of yesterday, — and the mortification of my present circumstances, — all these thoughts, occurring to me nearly at the same time, occasioned me more anxiety, confusion, and perplexity, than I can possibly express.

I believe he meant to send up his name; but the maid, unused to such a ceremony, forgot it by the way, and only told me, that a great Lord was below, and desired to see me: and, the next moment, he appeared himself.

If formerly, when in the circle of high life, and accustomed to its manners, I so much admired and distinguished the grace, the elegance of Lord Orville, think, Sir, how they must strike me now, — now, when, far removed from that splendid circle, I live with those to whom even civility is unknown, and decorum a stranger!

I am sure I received him very awkwardly; depressed by a situation so disagreeable, could I do otherwise? When his first enquiries were made, "I think myself very fortunate," he said, "in meeting with Miss Anville at home, and still more so, in finding her disengaged."

I only courtsied. He then talked of Mrs. Mirvan; asked how long I had been in town, and other such general questions, which, happily, gave me time to recover from my embarrassment. After which, he said, "If Miss Anville will allow me the honour of sitting by her a few minutes" (for we were both standing) "I will venture to tell her the motive which, next to enquiring after her health, has prompted me to wait on her thus early."

---

[1] *coronet coach:* A private coach ornamented by the figure of a crown, indicating that the owner belongs to the nobility.

We were then both seated, and, after a short pause, he said, "How to apologize for so great a liberty as I am upon the point of taking, I know not; — shall I, therefore, rely wholly upon your goodness, and not apologize at all?"

I only bowed.

"I should be extremely sorry to appear impertinent, — yet hardly know how to avoid it."

"Impertinent! O my Lord," cried I, eagerly, "that, I am sure, is impossible!"

"You are very good," answered he, "and encourage me to be ingenuous — "

Again he stopped; but my expectation was too great for speech: at last, without looking at me, in a low voice and hesitating manner, he said, "Were those ladies with whom I saw you last night, ever in your company before?"

"No, my Lord," cried I, rising, and colouring violently, "nor will they ever be again."

He rose too, and, with an air of the most condescending concern, said, "Pardon, Madam, the abruptness of a question which I knew not how to introduce as I ought, and for which I have no excuse to offer, but my respect for Mrs. Mirvan, joined to the sincerest wishes for your happiness: yet I fear I have gone too far!"

"I am very sensible of the honour of your Lordship's attention," said I, "but —— "

"Permit me to assure you," cried he, finding I hesitated, "that officiousness is not my characteristic, and that I would by no means have risked your displeasure, had I not been fully satisfied you were too generous to be offended, without a real cause of offence."

"Offended!" cried I, "no, my Lord, I am only grieved, — grieved, indeed! to find myself in a situation so unfortunate, as to be obliged to make explanations which cannot but mortify and shock me."

"It is I alone," cried he, with some eagerness, "who am shocked, as it is I who deserve to be mortified; I seek no explanation, for I have no doubt; but, in mistaking me, Miss Anville injures herself: allow me, therefore, frankly and openly to tell you the intention of my visit."

I bowed, and we both returned to our seats.

"I will own myself to have been greatly surprised," continued he, "when I met you yesterday evening, in company with two persons who I was sensible merited not the honour of your notice; nor was it easy for me to conjecture the cause of your being so situated; yet, believe me, my incertitude did not for a moment do you injury; I was satisfied that their characters must be unknown to you, and I thought with concern of the shock you would sustain, when you discovered their unworthiness. I should not, however, upon so short an acquaintance, have usurped the privilege of intimacy, in giving my unasked sentiments upon so delicate a subject, had I not known that credulity is the sister of innocence, and therefore feared you might be deceived. A something, which I could not resist, urged me to the freedom I have taken to caution you; but I shall not easily forgive myself, if I have been so unfortunate as to give you pain."

The pride which his first question had excited, now subsided into delight and gratitude, and I instantly related to him, as well as I could, the accident which had occasioned my joining the unhappy women with whom he had met me. He listened with an attention so flattering, seemed so much interested during the recital, and, when I had done, thanked me, in terms so polite, for what he was pleased to call my condescension, that I was almost ashamed either to look at, or hear him.

Soon after, the maid came to tell me, that Madame Duval desired to have breakfast made in her own room.

"I fear," cried Lord Orville, instantly rising, "that I have intruded upon your time, — yet who, so situated, could do otherwise?" Then, taking my hand, "Will Miss Anville allow me thus to seal my peace?" He pressed it to his lips, and took leave.

Generous, noble Lord Orville! how disinterested his conduct! how delicate his whole behaviour! willing to advise, yet afraid to wound me! — Can I ever, in future, regret the adventure I met with at Marybone, since it has been productive of a visit so flattering? Had my mortifications been still more humiliating, my terrors still more alarming, such a mark of esteem — may I not call it so? — from Lord Orville, would have made me ample amends.

And indeed, my dear Sir, I require some consolation in my present very disagreeable situation; for, since he went, two incidents have happened, that, had not my spirits been particularly elated, would greatly have disconcerted me.

During breakfast, Madame Duval, very abruptly, asked if I should like to be married? and added, that Mr. Branghton had been proposing a match for me with his son. Surprised, and, I must own, provoked, I assured her that, in thinking of me, Mr. Branghton would very vainly lose his time.

"Why," cried she, "I have had grander views for you, myself, if once I could get you to Paris, and make you be owned; but, if I can't

do that, and you can do not better, why, as you are both my relations, I think to leave my fortune between you, and then, if you
marry, you never need want for nothing."

I begged her not to pursue the subject, as, I assured her, Mr.
Branghton was totally disagreeable to me: but she continued her admonitions and reflections, with her usual disregard of whatever I
could answer. She charged me, very peremptorily, neither wholly to
discourage, nor yet to accept Mr. Branghton's offer, till she saw what
could be done for me: the young man, she added, had often intended
to speak to me himself, but, not well knowing how to introduce the
subject, he had desired her to pave the way for him.

I scrupled not, warmly and freely to declare my aversion to this
proposal; but it was to no effect, as she concluded, just as she had
begun, by saying, that I should not *have him, if I could do better.*

Nothing, however, shall persuade me to listen to any other person
concerning this odious affair.

My second cause of uneasiness arises, very unexpectedly, from M.
Du Bois, who, to my infinite surprise, upon Madame Duval's quitting
the room after dinner, put into my hand a note, and immediately left
the house.

This note contains an open declaration of an attachment to me,
which, he says, he should never have presumed to have acknowledged, had he not been informed that Madame Duval destined my
hand to young Branghton, —— a match which he cannot endure to
think of. He beseeches me, earnestly, to pardon his temerity, professes the most inviolable respect, and commits his fate to time, patience, and pity.

This conduct in M. Du Bois gives me real concern, as I was disposed to think very well of him. It will not, however, be difficult to
discourage him, and therefore I shall not acquaint Madame Duval of
his letter, as I have reason to believe it would greatly displease her.

LETTER XXIII

Evelina in Continuation

July 3.

O sir, how much uneasiness must I suffer, to counterbalance one
short morning of happiness!

Yesterday, the Branghtons proposed a party to Kensington-
gardens, and, as usual, Madame Duval insisted upon my attendance.

We went in a hackney-coach to Piccadilly, and then had a walk through Hyde Park, which, in any other company, would have been delightful. I was much pleased with Kensington-gardens, and think them infinitely preferable to those of Vauxhall.

Young Branghton was extremely troublesome; he insisted upon walking by my side, and talked with me almost by compulsion: however, my reserve and coldness prevented his entering upon the hateful subject which Madame Duval had prepared me to apprehend. Once, indeed, when I was, accidentally, a few yards before the rest, he said, "I suppose, Miss, aunt has told you about you know what? — ha'n't she, Miss?" — But I turned from him without making any answer. Neither Mr. Smith nor Mr. Brown were of the party; and poor M. Du Bois, when he found that I avoided him, looked so melancholy, that I was really sorry for him.

While we were strolling round the garden, I perceived, walking with a party of ladies at some distance, Lord Orville! I instantly retreated behind Miss Branghton, and kept out of sight till we had passed him: for I dreaded being seen by him again, in a public walk, with a party of which I was ashamed.

Happily I succeeded in my design, and saw no more of him; for a sudden and violent shower of rain made us all hasten out of the gardens. We ran till we came to a small green-shop,[1] where we begged shelter. Here we found ourselves in company with two footmen, whom the rain had driven into the shop. Their livery,[2] I thought, I had before seen; and upon looking from the window, I perceived the same upon a coachman belonging to a carriage, which I immediately recollected to be Lord Orville's.

Fearing to be known, I whispered Miss Branghton not to speak my name. Had I considered but a moment, I should have been sensible of the inutility of such a caution, since not one of the party call me by any other appellation than that of *Cousin*, or of *Miss*; but I am perpetually involved in some distress or dilemma from my own heedlessness.

This request excited very strongly her curiosity; and she attacked me with such eagerness and bluntness of enquiry, that I could not avoid telling her the reason of my making it, and, consequently, that I was known to Lord Orville: an acknowledgment which proved the most unfortunate in the world; for she would not rest till she had drawn from me the circumstances attending my first making the

---

[1] *green-shop:* A vegetable shop.
[2] *livery:* The uniforms worn by servants of the affluent classes. The colors and style would be distinctive to their respective employers.

acquaintance. Then, calling to her sister, she said, "Lord, Polly, only think! Miss has danced with a Lord!"

"Well," cried Polly, "that's a thing I should never have thought of! And pray, Miss, what did he say to you?"

This question was much sooner asked than answered; and they both became so very inquisitive and earnest, that they soon drew the attention of Madame Duval and the rest of the party, to whom, in a very short time, they repeated all they had gathered from me.

"Goodness, then," cried young Branghton, "if I was Miss, if I would not make free with his Lordship's coach to take me to town."

"Why ay," said the father, "there would be some sense in that; that would be making some use of a Lord's acquaintance, for it would save us coach-hire."

"Lord, Miss," cried Polly, "I wish you would, for I should like of all things to ride in a coronet coach!"

"I promise you," said Madame Duval, "I'm glad you've thought of it, for I don't see no objection; — so let's have the coachman called."

"Not for the world," cried I, very much alarmed, "indeed it is utterly impossible."

"Why so?" demanded Mr. Branghton; "pray where's the good of your knowing a Lord, if you're never the better for him?"

"*Ma foi,* child," said Madame Duval, "you don't know no more of the world than if you was a baby. Pray, Sir," (to one of the footmen,) "tell that coachman to draw up, for I wants to speak to him."

The man stared, but did not move. "Pray, pray, Madam," said I, "pray, Mr. Branghton, have the goodness to give up this plan; I know but very little of his Lordship, and cannot, upon any account, take so great a liberty."

"Don't say nothing about it," said Madame Duval, "for I shall have it my own way: so if *you* won't call the coachman, Sir, I'll promise you I'll call him myself."

The footman, very impertinently, laughed and turned upon his heel. Madame Duval, extremely irritated, ran out in the rain, and beckoned the coachman, who instantly obeyed her summons. Shocked beyond all expression, I flew after her, and entreated her with the utmost earnestness, to let us return in a hackney-coach: — but oh! — she is impenetrable to persuasion! She told the man she wanted him to carry her directly to town,[3] and that she would answer

---

[3] *carry her directly to town:* Kensington was a village outside London proper in 1778.

for him to Lord Orville. The man, with a sneer, thanked her, but said he should answer for himself; and was driving off, when another footman came up to him, with information that his Lord was gone into Kensington palace,[4] and would not want him for an hour or two.

"Why then, friend," said Mr. Branghton, (for we were followed by all the party) "where will be the great harm of your taking us to town?"

"Besides," said the son, "I'll promise you a pot of beer for my own share."

These speeches had no other answer from the coachman than a loud laugh, which was echoed by the insolent footmen. I rejoiced at their resistance, though I was certain, that if their Lord had witnessed their impertinence, they would have been instantly dismissed his service.

"*Pardie,*" cried Madame Duval, "if I don't think all the footmen are the most impudentest fellows in the kingdom! But I'll promise you I'll have your master told of your airs, so you'll get no good by 'em."

"Why pray," said the coachman, rather alarmed, "did my Lord give you leave to use the coach?"

"It's no matter for that," answered she; "I'm sure if he's a gentleman he'd let us have it sooner than we should be wet to the skin: but I'll promise you he shall know how saucy you've been, for this young lady knows him very well."

"Ay, that she does," said Miss Polly; "and she's danced with him too."

Oh how I repented my foolish mismanagement! The men bit their lips, and looked at one another in some confusion. This was perceived by our party, who, taking advantage of it, protested they would write Lord Orville word of their ill behaviour without delay. This quite startled them, and one of the footmen offered to run to the palace and ask his Lord's permission for our having the carriage.

This proposal really made me tremble; and the Branghtons all hung back upon it: but Madame Duval is never to be dissuaded from a scheme she has once formed. "Do so," cried she, "and give this child's compliments to your master, and tell him, as we ha'n't no coach here, we should be glad to go just as far as Holborn in his."

---

[4] *Kensington palace:* A palace used by British royalty up to the time of George III. It contained a large collection of fine paintings.

"No, no, no!" cried I; "don't go, — I know nothing of his Lord-ship, — I send no message, — I have nothing to say to him!"

The men, very much perplexed, could with difficulty restrain themselves from resuming their impertinent mirth. Madame Duval scolded me very angrily, and then desired them to go directly. "Pray, then," said the coachman, "what name is to be given to my Lord?"

"Anville," answered Madame Duval, "tell him Miss Anville wants the coach; the young lady he danced with once."

I was really in an agony; but the winds could not have been more deaf to me, than those to whom I pleaded! and therefore the foot-man, urged by the repeated threats of Madame Duval, and perhaps recollecting the name himself, actually went to the palace with this strange message!

He returned in a few minutes, and bowing to me with the greatest respect, said, "My Lord desires his compliments, and his carriage will be always at Miss Anville's service."

I was so much affected by this politeness, and chagrined at the whole affair, that I could scarce refrain from tears. Madame Duval and the Miss Branghtons eagerly jumped into the coach, and desired me to follow. I would rather have submitted to the severest punish-ment; — but all resistance was vain.

During the whole ride, I said not a word; however, the rest of the party were so talkative, that my silence was very immaterial. We stopped at our lodgings; but when Madame Duval and I alighted, the Branghtons asked if they could not be carried on to Snow-Hill? The servants, now all civility, made no objection. Remonstrances from me, would, I too well knew, be fruitless; and therefore, with a heavy heart, I retired to my room, and left them to their own direction.

Seldom have I passed a night in greater uneasiness: — so lately to have cleared myself in the good opinion of Lord Orville, — so soon to forfeit it! — to give him reason to suppose I presumed to boast of his acquaintance, — to publish his having danced with me! — to take with him a liberty I should have blushed to have taken with the most intimate of my friends! — to treat with such impertinent freedom one who has honoured *me* with such distinguished respect! — indeed, Sir, I could have met with no accident that would so cruelly have tor-mented me!

If such were, then, my feelings, imagine, — for I cannot describe, what I suffered during the scene I am now going to write.

This morning, while I was alone in the dining-room, young Branghton called. He entered with a most important air, and strutting up to me, said, "Miss, *Lord Orville* sends his compliments to you."

"Lord Orville!" — repeated I, much amazed.

"Yes, Miss, Lord Orville; — for *I* know his Lordship now, as well as you. — And a very civil gentleman he is, for all he's a Lord."

"For Heaven's sake," cried I, "explain yourself."

"Why you must know, Miss, after we left you, we met with a little misfortune; but I don't mind it now, for it's all turned out for the best: but, just as we were a going up Snow-Hill, plump we comes against a cart, with such a jogg it almost pulled the coach-wheel off; however, that i'n't the worst, for as I went to open the door in a hurry, a thinking the coach would be broke down, as ill-luck would have it, I never minded that the glass was up, and so I poked my head fairly through it. Only see, Miss, how I've cut my forehead!"

A much worse accident to himself, would not, I believe, at that moment, have given me any concern for him: however, he proceeded with his account, for I was too much confounded to interrupt him.

"Goodness, Miss, we were in such a stew, us, and the servants, and all, as you can't think; for besides the glass being broke, the coachman said how the coach would n't be safe to go back to Kensington. So we did n't know what to do; however, the footmen said they'd go and tell his Lordship what had happened. So then father grew quite uneasy, like, for fear of his Lordship's taking offence, and prejudicing us in our business: so he said I should go this morning and ask his pardon, 'cause of having broke the glass. So then I asked the footman the direction, and they told me he lived in Berkeley-square; so this morning I went, — and I soon found out the house."

"You did!" cried I, quite out of breath with apprehension.

"Yes, Miss, and a very fine house it is. Did you ever see it?"

"No."

"No! — why then, Miss, I know more of his Lordship than you do, for all you knew him first. So, when I came to the door, I was in a peck of troubles, a thinking what I should say to him; however, the servants had no mind I should see him, for they told me he was busy, but I might leave my message. So I was just coming away, when I bethought myself to say I come from you."

"From *me!* — "

"Yes, Miss, — for you know why should I have such a long walk as that for nothing? So I says to the porter, says I, tell his Lordship, says I, one wants to speak to him as comes from one Miss Anville, says I."

"Good God," cried I, "and by what authority did you take such a liberty?"

"Goodness, Miss, don't be in such a hurry, for you'll be as glad as me when you hear how well it all turned out. So then they made way for me, and said his Lordship would see me directly; and there I was led through such a heap of servants, and so many rooms, that my heart quite misgave me; for I thought, thinks I, he'll be so proud he'll hardly let me speak; but he's no more proud than I am, and he was as civil as if I'd been a lord myself. So then I said, I hoped he would n't take it amiss about the glass, for it was quite an accident; but he bid me not mention it, for it did n't signify. And then he said he hoped you got safe home, and was n't frightened; and so I said yes, and I gave your duty to him."

"My duty to him!" exclaimed I, — "and who gave you leave? — who desired you?"

"O, I did it of my own head, just to make him think I came from you. But I should have told you before how the footman said he was going out of town to-morrow evening, and that his sister was soon to be married, and that he was a ordering a heap of things for that; so it come into my head, as he was so affable, that I'd ask him for his custom. So I says, says I, my Lord, says I, if your Lordship i'n't engaged particularly, my father is a silversmith, and he'd be very proud to serve you, says I; and Miss Anville, as danced with you, is his cousin, and she's my cousin too, and she'd be very much obligated to you, I'm sure."

"You'll drive me wild," (cried I, starting from my seat) "you have done me an irreparable injury; — but I will hear no more!" — and then I ran into my own room.

I was half frantic, I really raved; the good opinion of Lord Orville seemed now irretrievably lost: a faint hope, which in the morning I had vainly encouraged, that I might see him again, and explain the transaction, wholly vanished, now I found he was so soon to leave town: and I could not but conclude that, for the rest of my life, he would regard me as an object of utter contempt.

The very idea was a dagger to my heart! — I could not support it, and — but I blush to proceed — I fear your disapprobation, yet I should not be conscious of having merited it, but that the repugnance I feel to relate to you what I have done, makes me suspect I must have erred. Will you forgive me, if I own that I have *first* written an account of this transaction to Miss Mirvan? — and that I even thought of *concealing* it from you? — Short-lived, however, was the ungrateful idea, and sooner will I risk the justice of your displeasure, than unworthily betray your generous confidence.

You are now probably prepared for what follows — which is a letter, — a hasty letter, that, in the height of my agitation, I wrote to Lord Orville.

### "To Lord Orville

"My Lord,

"I am so infinitely ashamed of the application made yesterday for your Lordship's carriage in my name, and so greatly shocked at hearing how much it was injured, that I cannot forbear writing a few lines, to clear myself from the imputation of an impertinence which I blush to be suspected of, and to acquaint you, that the request for your carriage was made against my consent, and the visit with which you were importuned this morning, without my knowledge.

"I am inexpressibly concerned at having been the instrument, however innocently, of so much trouble to your Lordship; but I beg you to believe, that reading these lines is the only part of it which I have given voluntarily.

"I am, my Lord,
"Your Lordship's most humble servant,
"EVELINA ANVILLE"

I applied to the maid of the house to get this note conveyed to Berkeley-square; but scarce had I parted with it, ere I regretted having written at all, and I was flying down stairs to recover it, when the voice of Sir Clement Willoughby stopped me. As Madame Duval had ordered we should be denied to him, I was obliged to return up stairs; and after he was gone, my application was too late, as the maid had given it to a porter.

My time did not pass very serenely while he was gone; however, he brought me no answer, but that Lord Orville was not at home. Whether or not he will take the trouble to send any; — or whether he will condescend to call; — or whether the affair will rest as it is, I know not; — but, in being ignorant, am most cruelly anxious.


### LETTER XXIV

#### Evelina in Continuation

July 4.

You may now, my dear Sir, send Mrs. Clinton for your Evelina with as much speed as she can conveniently make the journey, for no further opposition will be made to her leaving this town: happy had it perhaps been for her had she never entered it!

This morning Madame Duval desired me to go to Snow-hill, with an invitation to the Branghtons and Mr. Smith, to spend the evening with her: and she desired M. Du Bois, who breakfasted with us, to accompany me. I was very unwilling to obey her, as I neither wished to walk with M. Du Bois, nor yet to meet young Branghton. And, indeed, another, a yet more powerful reason, added to my reluctance, — for I thought it possible that Lord Orville might send some answer, or perhaps might call, during my absence; however, I did not dare dispute her commands.

Poor M. Du Bois spoke not a word during our walk, which was, I believe, equally unpleasant to us both. We found all the family assembled in the shop. Mr. Smith, the moment he perceived me, addressed himself to Miss Branghton, whom he entertained with all the gallantry in his power. I rejoice to find that my conduct at the Hampstead ball has had so good an effect. But young Branghton was extremely troublesome, he repeatedly laughed in my face, and looked so impertinently significant, that I was obliged to give up my reserve to M. Du Bois, and enter into conversation with him, merely to avoid such boldness.

"Miss," said Mr. Branghton, "I'm sorry to hear from my son that you was n't pleased with what we did about that Lord Orville; but I should like to know what it was you found fault with, for we did all for the best."

"Goodness!" cried the son, "why if you'd seen Miss, you'd have been surprised, — she went out of the room quite in a huff, like."

"It is too late, now," said I, "to reason upon this subject; but, for the future, I must take the liberty to request, that my name may never be made use of without my knowledge. May I tell Madame Duval that you will do her the favour to accept her invitation?"

"As to me, Ma'am," said Mr. Smith, "I am much obliged to the old lady, but I've no mind to be taken in by her again; you'll excuse me, Ma'am."

All the rest promised to come, and I then took leave: but as I left the shop, I heard Mr. Branghton say, "Take courage, Tom, she's only coy." And, before I had walked ten yards, the youth followed.

I was so much offended that I would not look at him, but began to converse with M. Du Bois, who was now more lively than I had ever before seen him; for, most unfortunately, he misinterpreted the reason of my attention to him.

The first intelligence I received when I came home, was that two gentlemen had called, and left cards. I eagerly enquired for them, and read the names of Lord Orville and Sir Clement Willoughby. I by no means regretted that I missed seeing the latter, but perhaps I may all my life regret that I missed the former, for probably he has now left town, — and I may see him no more!

"My goodness!" cried young Branghton, rudely looking over me, "only think of that Lord's coming all this way! It's my belief he'd got some order ready for father, and so he'd a mind to call and ask you if I'd told him the truth."

"Pray, Betty," cried I, "how long has he been gone?"

"Not two minutes, Ma'am."

"Why then I'll lay you any wager," said young Branghton, "he saw you and I a-walking up Holborn Hill!"

"God forbid!" cried I, impatiently; and too much chagrined to bear with any more of his remarks, I ran up stairs: but I heard him say to M. Du Bois, "Miss is so *uppish* this morning, that I think I had better not speak to her again."

I wish M. Du Bois had taken the same resolution; but he chose to follow me into the dining-room, which we found empty.

"*Vous ne l'aimez donc pas, ce garçon, Mademoiselle!*"[1] cried he.

"Me!" cried I, "no, I detest him!" for I was quite sick at heart.

"*Ah, tu me rends la vie!*"[2] cried he, and flinging himself at my feet, he had just caught my hand, as the door was opened by Madame Duval.

Hastily, and with marks of guilty confusion in his face, he arose; but the rage of that lady quite amazed me! advancing to the retreating M. Du Bois, she began, in French, an attack which her extreme wrath and wonderful volubility almost rendered unintelligible; yet I understood but too much, since her reproaches convinced me she had herself proposed being the object of his affection.

He defended himself in a weak and evasive manner, and upon her commanding him from her sight, very readily withdrew: and then, with yet greater violence, she upbraided me with having *seduced* his heart, called me an ungrateful, designing girl, and protested she would neither take me to Paris, nor any more interest herself in my concerns, unless I would instantly agree to marry young Branghton.

Frightened as I had been at her vehemence, this proposal restored all my courage; and I frankly told her that in this point I never could obey her. More irritated than ever, she ordered me to quit the room.

Such is the present situation of affairs. I shall excuse myself from seeing the Branghtons this afternoon: indeed, I never wish to see them again. I am sorry, however innocently, that I have displeased Madame Duval, yet I shall be very glad to quit this town, for I believe it does not, now, contain one person I ever wish to again meet. Had I

---

[1] *Vous . . . Mademoiselle:* "You do not, then, love this boy, Miss!"
[2] *Ah . . . vie:* "Ah, you give me back my life!"

but seen Lord Orville, I should regret nothing: I could then have more fully explained what I so hastily wrote; yet it will always be a pleasure to me to recollect that he called, since I flatter myself it was in consequence of his being satisfied with my letter.

Adieu, my dear Sir; the time now approaches when I hope once more to receive your blessing, and to owe all my joy, all my happiness to your kindness.

## LETTER XXV

### Mr. Villars to Evelina

Berry Hill, July 7.

Welcome, thrice welcome, my darling Evelina, to the arms of the truest, the fondest of your friends! Mrs. Clinton, who shall hasten to you with these lines, will conduct you directly hither, for I can consent no longer to be parted from the child of my bosom! — the comfort of my age! — the sweet solace of all my infirmities! Your worthy friends at Howard Grove must pardon me that I rob them of the visit you purposed to make them before your return to Berry Hill, for I find my fortitude unequal to a longer separation.

I have much to say to you, many comments to make upon your late letters, some parts of which give me no little uneasiness; but I will reserve my remarks for our future conversations. Hasten, then, to the spot of thy nativity, the abode of thy youth, where never yet care or sorrow had power to annoy thee; — O that they might ever be banished this peaceful dwelling!

Adieu, my dearest Evelina! I pray but that thy satisfaction at our approaching meeting, may bear any comparison with mine!

ARTHUR VILLARS

## LETTER XXVI

### Evelina to Miss Mirvan

Berry Hill, July 14.

My sweet Maria will be much surprised, and, I am willing to flatter myself, concerned, when, instead of her friend, she receives this letter; — this cold, this inanimate letter, which will but ill express the feelings of the heart which indites it.

When I wrote to you last Friday, I was in hourly expectation of seeing Mrs. Clinton, with whom I intended to have set out for Howard Grove; Mrs. Clinton came, but my plan was necessarily altered, for she brought me a letter, — the sweetest that ever was penned, from the best and kindest friend that ever orphan was blest with, requiring my immediate attendance at Berry Hill.

I obeyed, — and pardon me if I own I obeyed without reluctance; after so long a separation, should I not else have been the most ungrateful of mortals? — And yet, — oh Maria! though I *wished* to leave London, the gratification of my wish afforded me no happiness! and though I felt an impatience inexpressible to return hither, no words, no language can explain the heaviness of heart with which I made the journey. I believe you would hardly have known me; — indeed, I hardly know myself. Perhaps had I first seen *you,* in your kind and sympathizing bosom I might have ventured to have reposed every secret of my soul; and then — but let me pursue my journal.

Mrs. Clinton delivered Madame Duval a letter from Mr. Villars, which requested her leave for my return, and, indeed, it was very readily accorded: yet, when she found, by my willingness to quit town, that M. Du Bois was really indifferent to me, she somewhat softened in my favour, and declared that, but for punishing his folly in thinking of such a child, she would not have consented to my being again buried in the country.

All the Branghtons called to take leave of me: but I will not write a word more about them; indeed I cannot with any patience think of that family, to whose forwardness and impertinence is owing all the uneasiness I at this moment suffer!

So great was the depression of my spirits upon the road, that it was with difficulty I could persuade the worthy Mrs. Clinton I was not ill: but alas, the situation of my mind was such as would have rendered any mere bodily pain, by comparison, even enviable!

And yet, when we arrived at Berry Hill, — when the chaise[1] stopped at this place, — how did my heart throb with joy! And when, through the window, I beheld the dearest, the most venerable of men, with uplifted hands, returning, as I doubt not, thanks for my safe arrival, — good God! I thought it would have burst my bosom! — I

---

[1] *chaise:* An enclosed carriage for hire, usually for up to three passengers.

opened the chaise-door myself, I flew, — for my feet did not seem to touch the ground, — into the parlour; he had risen to meet me, but the moment I appeared, he sunk into his chair, uttering with a deep sigh, though his face *beamed* with delight, "My God, I thank thee!"

I sprung forward, and with a pleasure that bordered upon agony, I embraced his knees, I kissed his hands, I wept over them, but could not speak: while he, now raising his eyes in thankfulness towards heaven, now bowing down his reverend head, and folding me in his arms, could scarce articulate the blessings with which his kind and benevolent heart overflowed.

O Miss Mirvan, to be so beloved by the best of men, — should I not be happy? — Should I have one wish save that of meriting his goodness? — Yet think me not ungrateful; indeed I am not, although the internal sadness of my mind unfits me, at present, for enjoying as I ought the bounties of providence.

I cannot journalise;[2] cannot arrange my ideas into order.

How little has situation to do with happiness! I had flattered myself that, when restored to Berry Hill, I should be restored to tranquillity: far otherwise have I found it, for never yet had tranquillity and Evelina so little intercourse.

I blush for what I have written. Can you, Maria, forgive my gravity? but I restrain it so much and so painfully in the presence of Mr. Villars, that I know not how to deny myself the consolation of indulging it to you.

Adieu, my dear Miss Mirvan.

Yet one thing I must add; do not let the seriousness of this letter deceive you; do not impute to a wrong cause the melancholy I confess, by supposing that the heart of your friend mourns a too great susceptibility; no, indeed! believe me it never was, never can be, more assuredly her own than at this moment. So witness in all truth,

Your affectionate
EVELINA

You will make my excuses to the honoured Lady Howard, and to your dear mother.

---

[2] *journalise:* To write in a journal.

## LETTER XXVII

### Evelina in Continuation

Berry Hill, July 21.

You accuse me of mystery, and charge me with reserve: I cannot doubt but I must have merited the accusation; — yet, to clear myself, — you know not how painful will be the task. But I cannot resist your kind entreaties, — indeed, I do not wish to resist them, for your friendship and affection will soothe my chagrin. Had it arisen from any other cause, not a moment would I have deferred the communication you ask; — but, as it is, I would, were it possible, not only conceal it from all the world, but endeavor to disbelieve it myself. Yet, since I *must* tell you, why trifle with your impatience?

I know not how to come to the point; twenty times have I attempted it in vain; — but I will *force* myself to proceed.

Oh, Miss Mirvan, could you ever have believed, that one who seemed formed as a pattern for his fellow-creatures, as a model of perfection, — one whose elegance surpassed all description, — whose sweetness of manners disgraced all comparison, — Oh, Miss Mirvan, could you ever have believed that *Lord Orville* would have treated me with indignity?

Never, never again will I trust to appearances, — never confide in my own weak judgment, — never believe that person to be good, who seems to be amiable! What cruel maxims are we taught by a knowledge of the world! — But while my own reflections absorb me, I forget you are still in suspence.

I had just finished the last letter which I wrote to you from London, when the maid of the house brought me a note. It was given to her, she said, by a footman, who told her he would call the next day for an answer.

This note, — but let it speak for itself.

### "To Miss Anville

"With transport, most charming of thy sex, did I read the letter with which you yesterday morning favoured me. I am sorry the affair of the carriage should have given you any concern, but I am highly flattered by the anxiety you express so kindly. Believe me, my lovely girl, I am truly sensible of the honour of your good opinion, and feel myself deeply penetrated with love and gratitude. The correspondence you have so sweetly commenced[1] I shall be proud of continuing, and I hope the strong sense I have of the favour you do me, will prevent your withdrawing it. Assure yourself that I desire nothing more ardently, than to pour forth my thanks at your feet, and to offer those vows which are so justly the tribute of your charms and accomplishments. In your next, I entreat you to acquaint me how long you shall remain in town. The servant whom I shall commission to call for an answer, has orders to ride post with it to me.[2] My impatience for his arrival will be very great, though inferior to that with which I burn, to tell you, in person, how much I am, my sweet girl,

"Your grateful admirer,
"Orville"

What a letter! how has my proud heart swelled every line I have copied! What I wrote to him you know; tell me then, my dear friend, do you think it merited such an answer? — and that I have deservedly incurred the liberty he has taken? I meant nothing but a simple apology, which I thought as much due to my own character, as to his; yet, by the construction he seems to have put upon it, should you not have imagined it contained the avowal of sentiments which might, indeed, have provoked his contempt?

The moment the letter was delivered to me, I retired to my own room to read it, and so eager was my first perusal, that, — I am ashamed to own it gave me no sensation but of delight. Unsuspicious of any impropriety from Lord Orville, I perceived not immediately the impertinence it implied, — I only marked the expressions of his own regard; and I was so much surprised, that I was unable, for some time, to compose myself, or read it again, — I could only walk up and down the room, repeating to myself, "Good God, is it possible! — am I, then, loved by Lord Orville?"

But this dream was soon over, and I awoke to far different feelings; upon a second reading, I thought every word changed, — it did not seem the same letter, — I could not find one sentence that I could look at without blushing: my astonishment was extreme, and it was succeeded by the utmost indignation.

---

[1] *correspondence you have so sweetly commenced:* It was considered a serious breach of good conduct for an unbetrothed young woman to correspond with a man, as it gave the couple opportunities for private, possibly illicit communication.

[2] *to ride post with it to me:* In other words, the letter-writer will use his servant to convey Evelina's answer rather than use the public mail — another indication of his desire to establish an illicit correspondence with her.

If, as I am very ready to acknowledge, I erred in writing to Lord Orville, was it for *him* to punish the error? If he was offended, could he not have been silent? If he thought my letter ill-judged, should he not have pitied my ignorance? have considered my youth, and allowed for my inexperience?

Oh Maria, how have I been deceived in this man! Words have no power to tell the high opinion I had of him; to that was owing the unfortunate solicitude which prompted my writing, — a solicitude I must for ever repent!

Yet perhaps I have rather reason to rejoice than to grieve, since this affair has shewn me his real disposition, and removed that partiality, which, covering his every imperfection, left only his virtues and good qualities exposed to view. Had the deception continued much longer, had my mind received any additional prejudice in his favour, who knows whither my mistaken ideas might have led me? Indeed I fear I was in greater danger than I apprehended, or can now think of without trembling, — for oh, if this weak heart of mine had been penetrated with too deep an impression of his merit, — my peace and happiness had been lost for ever!

I would fain encourage more chearful thoughts, fain drive from my mind the melancholy that has taken possession of it, — but I cannot succeed; for, added to the humiliating feelings which so powerfully oppress me, I have yet another cause of concern; — alas, my dear Maria, I have broken the tranquillity of the best of men!

I have never had the courage to shew him this cruel letter: I could not bear so greatly to depreciate in his opinion, one whom I had, with infinite anxiety, raised in it myself. Indeed, my first determination was to confine my chagrin totally to my own bosom; but your friendly enquiries have drawn it from me; and now I wish I had made no concealment from the beginning, since I know not how to account for a gravity which not all my endeavours can entirely hide or repress.

My greatest apprehension is, lest he should imagine that my residence in London has given me a distaste to the country. Every body I see takes notice of my being altered, and looking pale and ill. I should be very indifferent to all such observations, did I not perceive that they draw upon me the eyes of Mr. Villars, which glisten with affectionate concern.

This morning, in speaking of my London expedition, he mentioned Lord Orville. I felt so much disturbed, that I would instantly have changed the subject; but he would not allow me, and, very unexpectedly, he began his panegyric, extolling, in strong terms, his manly and honourable behaviour in regard to the Marybone adventure. My cheeks glowed with indignation every word he spoke; — so lately as I had myself fancied him the noblest of his sex, now that I was so well convinced of my mistake, I could not bear to hear his undeserved praises uttered by one so really good, so unsuspecting, so pure of heart!

What he thought of my silence and uneasiness I fear to know, but I hope he will mention the subject no more. I will not, however, with ungrateful indolence, give way to a sadness which I find infectious to him who merits the most chearful exertion of my spirits. I am thankful that he has forborne to probe my wound, and I will endeavour to heal it by the consciousness that I have not deserved the indignity I have received. Yet I cannot but lament to find myself in a world so deceitful, where we must suspect what we see, distrust what we hear, and doubt even what we feel!

## LETTER XXVIII

### Evelina in Continuation

Berry Hill, July 29.
I must own myself somewhat distressed how to answer your raillery: yet believe me, my dear Maria, your suggestions are those of *fancy*, not of *truth*. I am unconscious of the weakness you suspect; yet, to dispel your doubts, I will animate myself more than ever to conquer my chagrin, and to recover my spirits.

You wonder, you say, since my *heart* takes no part in this affair, why it should make me so unhappy? And can you, acquainted as you are with the high opinion I entertained of Lord Orville, can you wonder that so great a disappointment in his character should affect me? indeed, had so strange a letter been sent to me from *any* body, it could not have failed shocking me; how much more sensibly, then, must I feel such an affront, when received from the man in the world I had imagined least capable of giving it?

You are glad I made no reply; assure yourself, my dear friend, had this letter been the most respectful that could be written, the clandestine air given to it, by his proposal of sending his servant for my answer, instead of having it directed to his house, would effectually have prevented my writing. Indeed, I have an aversion the most sincere to all mysteries, all private actions; however foolishly and blame-ably, in regard to this letter, I have deviated from the open path which, from my earliest infancy, I was taught to tread.

He talks of my having *commenced a correspondence* with him; and could Lord Orville indeed believe I had such a design? believe me so forward, so bold, so strangely ridiculous? I know not if his man called or not, but I rejoice that I quitted London before he came, and without leaving any message for him. What, indeed, could I have said? it would have been a condescension very unmerited, to have taken any, the least notice of such a letter.

Never shall I cease to wonder how he could write it. Oh, Maria, what, what could induce him so causelessly to wound and affront one who would sooner have died than wilfully offended *him?* — How mortifying a freedom of style! how cruel an implication conveyed by his *thanks,* and expressions of gratitude! Is it not astonishing, that any man can *appear* so modest, who is so vain?

Every hour I regret the secrecy I have observed with my beloved Mr. Villars; I know not what bewitched me, but I felt, at first, a repugnance to publishing this affair that I could not surmount, — and now, I am ashamed of confessing that I have any thing to confess! Yet I deserve to be punished for the false delicacy which occasioned my silence; since, if Lord Orville himself was contented to forfeit his character, was it for me, almost at the expence of my own, to support it?

Yet I believe I should be very easy, now the first shock is over, and now that I see the whole affair with the resentment it merits, did not all my good friends in this neighbourhood, who think me extremely altered, teaze me about my gravity, and torment Mr. Villars with observations upon my dejection, and falling away.[1] The subject is no sooner started, than a deep gloom overspreads his venerable countenance, and he looks at me with a tenderness so melancholy, that I know not how to endure the consciousness of exciting it.

Mrs. Selwyn, a lady of large fortune, who lives about three miles from Berry Hill, and who has always honoured me with very distinguishing marks of regard, is going, in a short time, to Bristol,[2] and has proposed to Mr. Villars to take me with her, for the recovery of

---

[1] *falling away:* Losing weight.

[2] *Bristol:* Bristol Hotwell or Hotwells was a resort that grew in popularity originally because of the supposedly curative powers of its hot springs. As with Bath, Bristol Hotwells's more successful competitor as a resort, many came more for music, dancing, and socializing than for the waters, but Bristol Hotwells retained something of its reputation as a spa restorative to the health.

my health. He seemed very much distressed whether to consent or refuse; but I, without any hesitation, warmly opposed the scheme, protesting my health could no where be better than in this pure air. He had the goodness to thank me for this readiness to stay with him: but he is all goodness! Oh that it were in my power to be, indeed, what in the kindness of his heart he has called me, the comfort of his age, and solace of his infirmities!

Never do I wish to be again separated from him. If here I am grave, elsewhere I should be unhappy. In his presence, with a very little exertion, all the chearfulness of my disposition seems ready to return; the benevolence of his countenance reanimates, the harmony of his temper composes, the purity of his character edifies me! I owe to him every thing; and, far from finding my debt of gratitude a weight, the first pride, first pleasure of my life is the recollection of the obligations conferred upon me by a goodness so unequalled.

Once, indeed, I thought there existed another, — who, when *time had winterd o'er his locks,* would have shone forth among his fellow-creatures, with the same brightness of worth which dignifies my honoured Mr. Villars; a brightness, how superior in value to that which results from mere quickness of parts, wit, or imagination! a brightness, which, not contented with merely diffusing smiles, and gaining admiration from the sallies of the spirits, reflects a real and a glorious lustre upon all mankind! Oh how great was my error! how ill did I judge! how cruelly have I been deceived!

I will not go to Bristol, though Mrs. Selwyn is very urgent with me; — but I desire not to see any more of the world; the few months I have already passed in it, have sufficed to give me a disgust even to its name.

I hope, too, I shall see Lord Orville no more; accustomed, from my first knowledge of him, to regard him as a *being superior to his race,* his presence, perhaps, might banish my resentment, and I might forget his ill conduct, — for oh, Maria! — I should not know how to see *Lord Orville* — and to think of displeasure!

As a sister I loved him, — I could have entrusted him with every thought of my heart, had he deigned to wish my confidence; so steady did I think his honour, so *feminine* his delicacy, and so amiable his nature! I have a thousand times imagined that the whole study of his life, and whole purport of his reflections, tended solely to the good and happiness of others: — but I will talk, — write, — think of him no more!

Adieu, my dear friend!

## LETTER XXIX

### Evelina in Continuation

Berry Hill, August 10.
You complain of my silence, my dear Miss Mirvan, — but what have I to write? Narrative does not offer, nor does a lively imagination supply the deficiency. I have, however, at present, sufficient matter for a letter, in relating a conversation I had yesterday with Mr. Villars.

Our breakfast had been the most chearful we have had since my return hither; and, when it was over, he did not, as usual, retire to his study, but continued to converse with me while I worked. We might, probably, have passed all the morning thus sociably, but for the entrance of a farmer, who came to solicit advice concerning some domestic affairs. They withdrew together into the study.

The moment I was alone, my spirits failed me; the exertion with which I had supported them, had fatigued my mind: I flung away my work, and, leaning my arms on the table, gave way to a train of disagreeable reflections, which, bursting from the restraint that had smothered them, filled me with unusual sadness.

This was my situation, when, looking towards the door, which was open, I perceived Mr. Villars, who was earnestly regarding me. "Is Farmer Smith gone, Sir?" cried I, hastily rising, and snatching up my work.

"Don't let me disturb you," said he, gravely; "I will go again to my study."

"Will you, Sir? — I was in hopes you were coming to sit here."

"In hopes! — and why, Evelina, should you hope it?"

This question was so unexpected, that I knew not how to answer it; but, as I saw he was moving away, I followed, and begged him to return. "No, my dear, no," said he, with a forced smile, "I only interrupt your meditations."

Again I knew not what to say; and while I hesitated, he retired. My heart was with him, but I had not the courage to follow. The idea of an explanation, brought on in so serious a manner, frightened me. I recollected the suspicions *you* had drawn from my uneasiness, and I feared that he might make a similar interpretation.

Solitary and thoughtful, I passed the rest of the morning in my own room. At dinner I again attempted to be chearful; but Mr. Villars himself was grave, and I had not sufficient spirits to support a conversation merely by my own efforts. As soon as dinner was over, he took a book, and I walked to the window. I believe I remained near an hour in this situation. All my thoughts were directed to considering how I might dispel the doubts which I apprehended Mr. Villars had formed, without acknowledging a circumstance which I had suffered so much pain merely to conceal. But, while I was thus planning for the future, I forgot the present; and so intent was I upon the subject which occupied me, that the strange appearance of my unusual inactivity and extreme thoughtfulness, never occurred to me. But when, at last, I recollected myself, and turned round, I saw that Mr. Villars, who had parted with his book, was wholly engrossed in attending to me. I started from my reverie, and, hardly knowing what I said, asked if he had been reading?

He paused a moment, and then said, "Yes, my child; — a book that both afflicts and perplexes me!"

He means *me,* thought I; and therefore I made no answer.

"What if we read it together?" continued he, "will you assist me to clear its obscurity?"

I knew not what to say, but I sighed, involuntarily, from the bottom of my heart. He rose, and, approaching me, said, with emotion, "My child, I can no longer be a silent witness of thy sorrow, — is not *thy* sorrow *my* sorrow? — and ought I to be a stranger to the cause, when I so deeply sympathise in the effect?"

"Cause, Sir!" cried I, greatly alarmed, "what cause? — I don't know, — I can't tell — I — "

"Fear not," said he, kindly, "to unbosom thyself to me, my dearest Evelina; open to me thy whole heart, — it can have no feelings for which I will not make allowance. Tell me, therefore, what it is that thus afflicts us both, and who knows but I may suggest some means of relief?"

"You are too, too good," cried I, greatly embarrassed; "but indeed I know not what you mean."

"I see," said he, "it is painful to you to speak: suppose, then, I endeavour to save you by guessing?"

"Impossible! impossible!" cried I, eagerly, "no one living could ever guess, ever suppose — " I stopped abruptly; for I then recollected I was acknowledging something *was* to be guessed: however, he noticed not my mistake.

"At least let me try," answered he, mildly; "perhaps I may be a better diviner than you imagine: if I guess every thing that is probable, surely I must approach near the real reason. Be honest, then, my love, and speak without reserve, — does not the country, after so much gaiety, so much variety, does it not appear insipid and tiresome?"

"No, indeed! I love it more than ever, and more than ever do I wish I had never, never quitted it!"

"Oh my child! that I had not permitted the journey! My judgment always opposed it, but my resolution was not proof against persuasion."

"I blush, indeed," cried I, "to recollect my earnestness; — but I have been my own punisher!"

"It is too late, now," answered he, "to reflect upon this subject; let us endeavour to avoid repentance for the time to come, and we shall not have erred without reaping some instruction." Then seating himself, and making me sit by him, he continued: "I must now guess again; perhaps you regret the loss of those friends you knew in town, — perhaps you miss their society, and fear you may see them no more? — perhaps Lord Orville —— "

I could not keep my seat, but rising hastily, said, "Dear Sir, ask me nothing more! — for I have nothing to own, — nothing to say; — my gravity has been merely accidental, and I can give no reason for it at all. Shall I fetch you another book? — or will you have this again?"

For some minutes he was totally silent, and I pretended to employ myself in looking for a book: at last, with a deep sigh, "I see," said he, "I see but too plainly, that though Evelina is returned, — I have lost my child!"

"No, Sir, no," cried I, inexpressibly shocked, "she is more yours than ever! Without you, the world would be a desart to her, and life a burthen; — forgive her, then, and, — if you can, — condescend to be, once more, the confident of all her thoughts."

"How highly I value, how greatly I wish for her confidence," returned he, "she cannot but know; — yet to extort, to tear it from her, — my justice, my affection, both revolt at the idea. I am sorry that I was so earnest with you; — leave me, my dear, leave me and compose yourself; — we will meet again at tea."

"Do you then refuse to hear me?"

"No, but I abhor to compel you. I have long seen that your mind has been ill at ease, and mine has largely partaken of your concern: I forbore to question you, for I hoped that time, and absence from whatever excited your uneasiness, might best operate in silence: but alas! your affliction seems only to augment, — your health declines, — your look alters. — Oh Evelina, my aged heart bleeds to see the change! — bleeds to behold the darling it had cherished, the prop it

had reared for its support, when bowed down by years and infirmities, sinking itself under the pressure of internal grief! — struggling to
hide, what it should seek to participate! — But go, my dear, go to
your own room, — we both want composure, and we will talk of this
matter some other time."

"Oh Sir," cried I, penetrated to the soul, "bid me not leave you! —
think me not so lost to feeling, to gratitude — "

"Not a word of that," interrupted he; "it pains me you should
think upon that subject; pains me you should ever remember that you
have not a natural, an hereditary right to every thing within my
power. I meant not to affect you thus, — I hoped to have soothed
you! — but my anxiety betrayed me to an urgency that has distressed
you. Comfort yourself, my love, and doubt not but that time will
stand your friend, and all will end well."

I burst into tears: with difficulty had I so long restrained them; for
my heart, while it glowed with tenderness and gratitude, was oppressed with a sense of its own unworthiness. "You are all, all goodness!" cried I, in a voice scarce audible, "little as I deserve, — unable
as I am to repay, such kindness, — yet my whole soul feels, — thanks
you for it!"

"My dearest child," cried he, "I cannot bear to see thy tears; — for
*my* sake dry them, — such a sight is too much for me: think of that,
Evelina, and take comfort, I charge thee!"

"Say then," cried I, kneeling at his feet, "say then that you forgive
me! that you pardon my reserve, — that you will again suffer me to
tell you my most secret thoughts, and rely upon my promise never
more to forfeit your confidence! — my father! my protector! — my
ever-honoured — ever-loved — my best and only friend! — say you
forgive your Evelina, and she will study better to deserve your goodness!"

He raised, he embraced me; he called me his sole joy, his only
earthly hope, and the child of his bosom! He folded me to his heart,
and, while I wept from the fullness of mine, with words of sweetest
kindness and consolation, he soothed and tranquillised me.

Dear to my remembrance will ever be that moment, when, banish-
ing the reserve I had so foolishly planned and so painfully supported,
I was restored to the confidence of the best of men!

When, at length, we were again quietly and composedly seated by
each other, and Mr. Villars waited for the explanation I had begged
him to hear, I found myself extremely embarrassed how to introduce

the subject which must lead to it. He saw my distress, and, with a kind of benevolent pleasantry, asked me if I would let him *guess* any more? I assented in silence.

"Shall I, then, go back to where I left off?"

"If — if you please; — I believe so, — " said I, stammering.

"Well then, my love, I think I was speaking of the regret it was natural you should feel upon quitting those from whom you had received civility and kindness, with so little certainty of ever seeing them again, or being able to return their good offices? These are circumstances that afford but melancholy reflections to young minds; and the affectionate disposition of my Evelina, open to all social feelings, must be hurt more than usual by such considerations. — You are silent, my dear? — Shall I name those whom I think most worthy the regret I speak of? We shall then see if our opinions coincide."

Still I said nothing, and he continued.

"In your London journal, nobody appears in a more amiable, a more respectable light, than Lord Orville, and perhaps —— "

"I knew what you would say," cried I, hastily, "and I have long feared where your suspicions would fall; but indeed, Sir, you are mistaken: I hate Lord Orville, — he is the last man in the world in whose favour I should be prejudiced."

I stopped; for Mr. Villars looked at me with such infinite surprise, that my own warmth made me blush. "You *hate* Lord Orville!" repeated he.

I could make no answer, but took from my pocket-book the letter, and giving it to him, "See, Sir," said I, "how differently the same man can *talk*, and *write!*"

He read it three times ere he spoke; and then said, "I am so much astonished, that I know not what I read. When had you this letter?"

I told him. Again he read it; and, after considering its contents some time, said, "I can form but one conjecture concerning this most extraordinary performance: he must certainly have been intoxicated when he wrote it."

"Lord Orville intoxicated!" repeated I; "once I thought him a stranger to all intemperance, — but it is very possible, for I can believe any thing now."

"That a man who had behaved with so strict a regard to delicacy," continued Mr. Villars, "and who, as far as occasion had allowed, manifested sentiments the most honourable, should thus insolently, thus wantonly insult a modest young woman, in his perfect senses, I cannot think possible. But, my dear, you should have inclosed this letter in an empty cover,[1] and have returned it to him again: such a resentment would at once have become *your* character, and have given him an opportunity, in some measure, of clearing his own. He could not well have read this letter the next morning, without being sensible of the impropriety of having written it."

Oh Maria! why had not I this thought? I might then have received some apology; the mortification would then have been *his,* not *mine.* It is true, he could not have reinstated himself so highly in my opinion as I had once ignorantly placed him, since the conviction of such intemperance would have levelled him with the rest of his imperfect race; yet, my humbled pride might have been consoled by his acknowledgments.

But why should I allow myself to be humbled by a man who can suffer his reason to be thus abjectly debased, when I am exalted by one who knows no vice, and scarcely a failing, — but by hearsay? To think of his kindness, and reflect upon his praises, might animate and comfort me even in the midst of affliction. "Your indignation," said he, "is the result of virtue; you fancied Lord Orville was without fault — he had the appearance of infinite worthiness, and you supposed his character accorded with his appearance: guileless yourself, how could you prepare against the duplicity of another? Your disappointment has but been proportioned to your expectations, and you have chiefly owed its severity to the innocence which hid its approach."

I will bid these words dwell in my memory, and they shall cheer, comfort, and enliven me! This conversation, though extremely affecting to me at the time it passed, has relieved my mind from much anxiety. Concealment, my dear Maria, is the foe of tranquillity: however I may err in future, I will never be disingenuous in acknowledging my errors. To you, and to Mr. Villars, I vow an unremitting confidence.

And yet, though I am more at ease, I am far from well: I have been some time writing this letter; but I hope I shall send you, soon, a more chearful one.

Adieu, my sweet friend. I entreat you not to acquaint even your dear mother with this affair; Lord Orville is a favourite with her, and why should I publish that he deserves not that honour?

---

[1] *cover:* Private letters were often enclosed in a blank, folded sheet of paper that was then sealed shut with wax.

## LETTER XXX

### Evelina in Continuation

Bristol Hotwell, August 28.

You will be again surprised, my dear Maria, at seeing whence I date my letter: but I have been very ill, and Mr. Villars was so much alarmed, that he not only insisted upon my accompanying Mrs. Selwyn hither, but earnestly desired she would hasten her intended journey.

We travelled very slowly, and I did not find myself so much fatigued as I expected. We are situated upon a most delightful spot; the prospect is beautiful, the air pure, and the weather very favourable to invalids. I am already better, and I doubt not but I shall soon be well; as well, in regard to mere health, as I wish to be.

I cannot express the reluctance with which I parted from my revered Mr. Villars: it was not like that parting which, last April, preceded my journey to Howard Grove, when, all expectation and hope, tho' I wept, I rejoiced, and though I sincerely grieved to leave him, I yet wished to be gone: the sorrow I now felt was unmixed with any livelier sensation; expectation was vanished, and hope I had none! All that I held most dear upon earth, I quitted, and that upon an errand to the success of which I was totally indifferent, the re-establishment of my health. Had it been to have seen my sweet Maria, or her dear mother, I should not have repined.

Mrs. Selwyn is very kind and attentive to me. She is extremely clever; her understanding, indeed, may be called *masculine;* but, unfortunately, her manners deserve the same epithet; for, in studying to acquire the knowledge of the other sex, she has lost all the softness of her own. In regard to myself, however, as I have neither courage nor inclination to argue with her, I have never been personally hurt at her want of gentleness; a virtue which, nevertheless, seems so essential a part of the female character, that I find myself more awkward, and less at ease, with a woman who wants it, than I do with a man. She is not a favourite with Mr. Villars, who has often been disgusted at her unmerciful propensity to satire: but his anxiety that I should try the effect of the Bristol waters, overcame his dislike of committing me to her care. Mrs. Clinton is also here; so that I shall be as well attended as his utmost partiality could desire.

I will continue to write to you, my dear Miss Mirvan, with as much constancy as if I had no other correspondent; tho', during my absence from Berry Hill, my letters may, perhaps, be shortened on account of the minuteness of the journal which I must write to my beloved Mr. Villars: but you, who know his expectations, and how many ties bind me to fulfil them, will, I am sure, rather excuse any omission to yourself, than any negligence to him.

#### END OF THE SECOND VOLUME

# Volume III

### LETTER I

### Evelina to the Rev. Mr. Villars

Bristol Hotwell, Sept. 12.

The first fortnight that I passed here, was so quiet, so serene, that it gave me reason to expect a settled calm during my stay; but if I may now judge of the time to come, by the present state of my mind, the calm will be succeeded by a storm, of which I dread the violence!

This morning, in my way to the pump-room,[1] with Mrs. Selwyn, we were both very much incommoded by three gentlemen, who were sauntering by the side of the Avon,[2] laughing and talking very loud, and lounging so disagreeably that we knew not how to pass them. They all three fixed their eyes very boldly upon me, alternately looking under my hat, and whispering one another. Mrs. Selwyn assumed an air of uncommon sternness, and said, "You will please, Gentlemen, either to proceed yourselves, or to suffer us."

"Oh! Ma'am," cried one of them, "we will suffer *you,* with the greatest pleasure in life."

"You will suffer us *both,*" answered she, "or I am much mistaken; you had better, therefore, make way quietly, for I should be sorry to give my servant the trouble of teaching you better manners."

---

[1] *pump-room:* A room at a spa where supposedly medicinal waters are dispensed for drinking purposes. People gathered at the pump-room at resort towns such as Bristol Hotwells and Bath to socialize, to see and be seen, and to "take the waters."
[2] *Avon:* The river that runs through Bath.

Her commanding air struck them, yet they all chose to laugh, and one of them wished the fellow would begin his lesson, that he might have the pleasure of rolling him into the Avon; while another, advancing to me with a freedom that made me start, said, "By my soul I did not know you! — but I am sure I cannot be mistaken; — had not I the honour of seeing you, once, at the Pantheon?"

I then recollected the nobleman who, at that place, had so much embarrassed me. I courtsied without speaking. They all bowed, and making, though in a very easy manner, an apology to Mrs. Selwyn, they suffered us to pass on, but chose to accompany us.

"And where," continued this Lord, "can you so long have hid yourself? do you know I have been in search of you this age? I could neither find you out, nor hear of you: not a creature could inform me what was become of you. I cannot imagine where you could be immured. I went to two or three public places every night, in hopes of meeting you. Pray did you leave town?"

"Yes, my Lord."

"So early in the season! — what could possibly induce you to go before the birth-day?"

"I had nothing, my Lord, to do with the birth-day."

"By my soul, all the women who *had,* may rejoice you were away. Have you been here any time?"

"Not above a fortnight, my Lord."

"A fortnight! — how unlucky that I did not meet you sooner! but I have had a run of ill luck ever since I came. How long shall you stay?"

"Indeed, my Lord, I don't know."

"Six weeks, I hope; for I shall wish the place at the devil when you go."

"Do you, then, flatter yourself, my Lord," said Mrs. Selwyn, who had hitherto listened in silent contempt, "that you shall see such a beautiful spot as this, when you visit the dominions of the devil?"

"Ha, ha, ha! Faith, my Lord," said one of his companions, who still walked with us, though the other had taken leave; "the Lady is rather hard upon you."

"Not at all," answered Mrs. Selwyn; "for as I cannot doubt but his Lordship's rank and interest will secure him a place there, it would be reflecting on his understanding, to suppose he should not wish to enlarge and beautify his dwelling."

Much as I was disgusted with this Lord, I must own Mrs. Selwyn's severity rather surprised me: but you, who have so often observed it, will not wonder she took so fair an opportunity of indulging her humour.

"As to *places*," returned he, totally unmoved, "I am so indifferent to them, that the devil take me if I care which way I go! *objects*, indeed, I am not so easy about; and therefore I expect that those angels with whose beauty I am so much enraptured in this world, will have the goodness to afford me some little consolation in the other."

"What, my Lord!" cried Mrs. Selwyn, "would you wish to degrade the habitation of your friend, by admitting into it the insipid company of the upper regions?"

"What do you do with yourself this evening?" said his Lordship, turning to me.

"I shall be home, my Lord."

"O, à-propos — where are you?"

"Young ladies, my Lord," said Mrs. Selwyn, "are *no where*."

"Prithee," whispered his Lordship, "is that queer woman your mother?"

Good Heavens, Sir, what words for such a question!

"No, my Lord."

"Your maiden aunt, then?"

"No."

"Whoever she is, I wish she would mind her own affairs: I don't know what the devil a woman lives for after thirty: she is only in other folks way. Shall you be at the assembly?"

"I believe not, my Lord."

"No! — why then how in the world can you contrive to pass your time?"

"In a manner that your Lordship will think very extraordinary," cried Mrs. Selwyn; "for the young Lady *reads*."

"Ha, ha, ha! Egad, my Lord," cried the facetious companion, "you are got into bad hands."

"You had better, Madam," answered he, "attack Jack Coverley, here, for you will make nothing of me."

"Of *you*, my Lord!" cried she; "Heaven forbid I should ever entertain so idle an expectation! I only talk, like a silly woman, for the sake of talking; but I have by no means so low an opinion of your Lordship, as to suppose you vulnerable to censure."

"Do pray, Ma'am," cried he, "turn to Jack Coverley; he's the very man for you; — he'd be a wit himself if he was n't too modest."

"Prithee, my Lord, be quiet," returned the other; "if the Lady is contented to bestow all her favours upon *you*, why should you make such a point of my going snacks?"[3]

"Don't be apprehensive, Gentlemen," said Mrs. Selwyn, drily, "I am not romantic, — I have not the least design of doing good to either of you."

"Have not you been ill since I saw you?" said his Lordship, again addressing himself to me.

"Yes, my Lord."

"I thought so; you are paler than you was, and I suppose that's the reason I did not recollect you sooner."

"Has not your Lordship too much gallantry," cried Mrs. Selwyn, "to discover a young lady's illness by her looks?"

"The devil a word can I speak for that woman," said he, in a low voice; "do, prithee, Jack, take her in hand."

"Excuse, me, my Lord!" answered Mr. Coverley.

"When shall I see you again?" continued his Lordship; "do you go to the pump-room every morning?"

"No, my Lord."

"Do you ride out?"

"No, my Lord."

Just then we arrived at the pump-room, and an end was put to our conversation, if it is not an abuse of words to give such a term to a string of rude questions and free compliments.

He had not opportunity to say much more to me, as Mrs. Selwyn joined a large party, and I walked home between two ladies. He had, however, the curiosity to see us to the door.

Mrs. Selwyn was very eager to know how I had made acquaintance with this nobleman, whose manners so evidently announced the character of a confirmed libertine: I could give her very little satisfaction, as I was ignorant even of his name. But, in the afternoon, Mr. Ridgeway, the apothecary,[4] gave us very ample information.

As his person was easily described, for he is remarkably tall, Mr. Ridgeway told us he was Lord Merton, a nobleman but lately come to his title, though he had already dissipated more than half his fortune: a professed admirer of beauty, but a man of most licentious

---

[3] *going snacks:* To share with.
[4] *apothecary:* As today, one who dispenses medicines. In the eighteenth century the apothecary also fulfilled many of the health-maintenance functions of a general practitioner.

character: that among men, his companions consisted chiefly of gamblers and jockies, and among women, he was rarely admitted.

"Well, Miss Anville," said Mrs. Selwyn, "I am glad I was not more civil to him. You may depend upon *me* for keeping him at a distance."

"O, Madam," said Mr. Ridgeway, "he may now be admitted any where, for he is going to *reform.*"

"Has he, under that notion, persuaded any fool to marry him?"

"Not yet, Madam, but a marriage is expected to take place shortly: it has been some time in agitation, but the friends of the Lady have obliged her to wait till she is of age: however, her brother, who has chiefly opposed the match, now that she is near being at her own disposal, is tolerably quiet. She is very pretty, and will have a large fortune. We expect her at the Wells every day."

"What is her name?" said Mrs. Selwyn.

"Larpent," answered he, "Lady Louisa Larpent, sister of Lord Orville."

"Lord Orville!" repeated I, all amazement.

"Yes, Ma'am; his Lordship is coming with her. I have had certain information. They are to be at the honourable Mrs. Beaumont's. She is a relation of my Lord's, and has a very fine house upon Clifton Hill."

*His Lordship is coming with her!* — Good God, what an emotion did those words give me! How strange, my dear Sir, that, just at this time, he should visit Bristol! It will be impossible for me to avoid seeing him, as Mrs. Selwyn is very well acquainted with Mrs. Beaumont. Indeed, I have had an escape in not being under the same roof with him, for Mrs. Beaumont invited us to her house immediately upon our arrival; but the inconveniency of being so distant from the pump-room made Mrs. Selwyn decline her civility.

Oh that the first meeting was over! — or that I could quit Bristol without seeing him! — inexpressibly do I dread an interview: should the same impertinent freedom be expressed by his looks, which dictated his cruel letter, I shall not know how to endure either him or myself. Had I but returned it, I should be easier, because my sentiments of it would then be known to him; but now, he can only gather them from my behaviour, and I tremble lest he should mistake my indignation for confusion! — lest he should misconstrue my reserve into embarrassment! — for how, my dearest Sir, how shall I be able totally to divest myself of the respect with which I have been used to think of him? — the pleasure with which I have been used to see him?

Surely he, as well as I, must think of the letter at the moment of our meeting, and he will, probably, mean to gather my thoughts of it from my looks; — oh that they could but convey to him my real detestation of impertinence and vanity! then would he see how much he had mistaken my disposition when he imagined them my due.

There was a time, when the very idea that such a man as Lord Merton would ever be connected with Lord Orville, would have both surprised and shocked me, and even yet I am pleased to hear of his repugnance to the marriage.

But how strange, that a man of so abandoned a character should be the choice of a sister of Lord Orville! and how strange that, almost at the moment of the union, he should be so importunate in gallantry to another woman! What a world is this we live in! how corrupt, how degenerate! well might I be contented to see no more of it! If I find that the *eyes* of Lord Orville agree with his *pen*, — I shall then think, that of all mankind, the only virtuous individual resides at Berry Hill!

## LETTER II

### Evelina in Continuation

Bristol Hotwell, Sept 16.

Oh, Sir, Lord Orville is still himself! still, what from the moment I beheld, I believed him to be, all that is amiable in man! and your happy Evelina, restored at once to spirits and tranquillity, is no longer sunk in her own opinion, nor discontented with the world; — no longer, with dejected eyes, sees the prospect of passing her future days in sadness, doubt, and suspicion! — with revived courage she now looks forward, and expects to meet with goodness, even among mankind; — though still she feels, as strongly as ever, the folly of hoping, in any *second* instance, to meet with *perfection*.

Your conjecture was certainly right; Lord Orville, when he wrote that letter, could not be in his senses. Oh that intemperance should have power to degrade so low, a man so noble!

This morning I accompanied Mrs. Selwyn to Clifton Hill, where, beautifully situated, is the house of Mrs. Beaumont. Most uncomfortable were my feelings during our walk, which was very slow, for the agitation of my mind made me more than usually sensible how weak I still continue. As we entered the house, I summoned all my resolution to my aid, determined rather to die than give Lord Orville reason to attribute my weakness to a wrong cause. I was happily relieved from my perturbation, when I saw Mrs. Beaumont was alone. We sat with her for, I believe, an hour without interruption, and then we saw a phaeton[1] drive up to the gate, and a lady and gentleman alight from it.

They entered the parlour with the ease of people who were at home. The gentleman, I soon saw, was Lord Merton; he came shuffling into the room with his boots on, and his whip in his hand; and, having made something like a bow to Mrs. Beaumont, he turned towards me. His surprise was very evident, but he took no manner of notice of me. He waited, I believe, to discover, first, what chance had brought me to that house, where he did not look much rejoiced at meeting me. He seated himself very quietly at the window, without speaking to any body.

Mean time, the lady, who seemed very young, hobbling[2] rather then walking into the room, made a passing courtsie to Mrs. Beaumont, saying, "How are you, Ma'am?" and then, without noticing any body else, with an air of languor, she flung herself upon a sofa, protesting, in a most affected voice, and speaking so softly she could hardly be heard, that she was fatigued to death. "Really, Ma'am, the roads are so monstrous dusty, — you can't imagine how troublesome the dust is to one's eyes! — and the sun, too, is monstrous disagreeable! — I dare say I shall be so tanned I sha'n't be fit to be seen[3] this age. Indeed, my Lord, I won't go out with you any more, for you don't care where you take one."

"Upon my honour," said Lord Merton, "I took you the pleasantest ride in England; the fault was in the sun, not me."

"Your Lordship is in the right," said Mrs. Selwyn, "to transfer the fault to the *sun,* because it has so many excellencies to counterbalance partial inconveniences, that a *little* blame will not injure *that* in our estimation."

Lord Merton looked by no means delighted at this attack; which I believe she would not so readily have made, but to revenge his neglect of us.

"Did you meet your brother, Lady Louisa?" said Mrs. Beaumont.

"No, Ma'am. Is he rode out this morning?"

---

[1] *phaeton:* A light, open, four-wheeled carriage, usually seating two and drawn by a pair of horses. The name derives from Phaeton of Greek mythology, whose driving of his father Phoebus's chariot — the sun — proved unlucky and disastrous.

[2] *hobbling:* To walk unsteadily, weaving from side to side.

[3] *so tanned I sha'n't be fit to be seen:* A very pale complexion was not only fashionable and a mark of beauty but a sign of upper-class standing.

I then found, what I had before suspected, that this Lady was Lord Orville's sister: how strange, that such near relations should be so different to each other! There is, indeed, some resemblance in their features, but in their manners, not the least.

"Yes," answered Mrs. Beaumont, "and I believe he wished to see you."

"My Lord drove so monstrous fast," said Lady Louisa, "that perhaps we passed him. He frighted me out of my senses; I declare my head is quite giddy. Do you know, Ma'am, we have done nothing but quarrel all the morning? — You can't think how I've scolded; — have not I, my Lord?" and she smiled expressively at Lord Merton.

"You have been, as you always are," said he, twisting his whip with his fingers, "all sweetness."

"O fie, my Lord," cried she, "I know you don't think so; I know you think me very ill-natured; — don't you, my Lord?"

"No, upon my honour; — how can your Ladyship ask such a question? Pray how goes time? my watch stands."

"It is almost three," answered Mrs. Beaumont.

"Lord, Ma'am, you frighten me!" cried Lady Louisa; and then turning to Lord Merton, "why now, you wicked creature, you, did not you tell me it was but one?"

Mrs. Selwyn then rose to take leave; but Mrs. Beaumont asked if she would look at the shrubbery. "I should like it much," answered she, "but that I fear to fatigue Miss Anville."

Lady Louisa then, raising her head from her hand, on which it had leant, turned round to look at me, and, having fully satisfied her curiosity, without any regard to the confusion it gave me, turned about, and, again leaning on her hand, took no further notice of me.

I declared myself very able to walk, and begged that I might accompany them. "What say you, Lady Louisa," cried Mrs. Beaumont, "to a strole in the garden?"

"Me, Ma'am! — I declare I can't stir a step; the heat is so excessive, it would kill me. I'm half dead with it already; besides, I shall have no time to dress. Will any body be here to-day, Ma'am?"

"I believe not, unless Lord Merton will favour us with his company."

"With great pleasure, Madam."

"Well, I declare you don't deserve to be asked," cried Lady Louisa, "you wicked creature, you! — I *must* tell you one thing, Ma'am, — you can't think how abominable he was! do you know we met Mr. Lovel in his new phaeton, and my Lord was so cruel as to drive against it?[4] — we really flew. I declare I could not breathe. Upon my word, my Lord, I'll never trust myself with you again, — I won't indeed!"

We then went into the garden, leaving them to discuss the point at their leisure.

Do you remember a *pretty but affected young lady* I mentioned to have seen, in Lord Orville's party, at the Pantheon? How little did I then imagine her to be his sister! yet Lady Louisa Larpent is the very person. I can now account for the piqued manner of her speaking to Lord Merton that evening, and I can now account for the air of displeasure with which Lord Orville marked the undue attention of his future brother-in-law to me.

We had not walked long, ere, at a distance, I perceived Lord Orville, who seemed just dismounted from his horse, enter the garden. All my perturbation returned at the sight of him! — yet I endeavoured to repress every feeling but resentment. As he approached us, he bowed to the whole party; but I turned away my head, to avoid taking any share in his civility. Addressing himself immediately to Mrs. Beaumont, he was beginning to enquire after his sister, but upon seeing my face, he suddenly exclaimed "Miss Anville! — " and then he advanced, and made his compliments to me, — not with an air of vanity or impertinence, nor yet with a look of consciousness or shame, — but with a smile that indicated pleasure, and eyes that sparkled with delight! on *my* side was all the consciousness, for by him, I really believe, the letter was, at that moment, entirely forgotten.

With what politeness did he address me! with what sweetness did he look at me! the very tone of his voice seemed flattering! he congratulated himself upon his good fortune in meeting with me, — hoped I should spend some time at Bristol, and enquired, even with anxiety enquired, if my health was the cause of my journey, in which case his satisfaction would be converted into apprehension.

Yet, struck as I was with his manner, and charmed to find him such as he was wont to be, imagine not, my dear Sir, that I forgot the resentment I owe him, or the cause he has given me of displeasure; no, my behaviour was such as, I hope, had you seen, you would not have disapproved: I was grave and distant, I scarce looked at him when he spoke, or answered him when he was silent.

As he must certainly observe this alteration in my conduct, I think it could not fail making him both recollect and repent the provoca-

---

[4] *drive against it:* To race against it.

tion he had so causelessly given me: for surely he was not so wholly lost to reason, as to be now ignorant he had ever offended me.

The moment that, without absolute rudeness, I was able, I turned entirely from him, and asked Mrs. Selwyn if we should not be late home. How Lord Orville looked I know not, for I avoided meeting his eyes, but he did not speak another word as we proceeded to the garden-gate. Indeed I believe my abruptness surprised him, for he did not seem to expect I had so much spirit. And, to own the truth, convinced as I was of the propriety, nay, necessity of shewing my displeasure, I yet almost hated myself for receiving his politeness so ungraciously.

When we were taking leave, my eyes accidentally meeting his, I could not but observe that his gravity equalled my own, for it had entirely taken place of the smiles and good-humor with which he had met me.

"I am afraid this young Lady," said Mrs. Beaumont, "is too weak for another long walk till she is again rested."

"If the Ladies will trust to my driving," said Lord Orville, "and are not afraid of a phaeton, mine shall be ready in a moment."

"You are very good, my Lord," said Mrs. Selwyn, "but my will is yet unsigned, and I don't chuse to venture in a phaeton with a young man while that is the case."

"O," cried Mrs. Beaumont, "you need not be afraid of my Lord Orville, for he is remarkably careful."

"Well, Miss Anville," answered she, "what say you?"

"Indeed," cried I, "I had much rather walk. — " But then, looking at Lord Orville, I perceived in his face a surprise so serious at my abrupt refusal, that I could not forbear adding, "for I should be sorry to occasion so much trouble."

Lord Orville brightening at these words, came forward, and pressed his offer in a manner not to be denied; — so the phaeton was ordered! And indeed, my dear Sir, — I know not how it was, — but, from that moment, my coldness and reserve insensibly wore away! You must not be angry; — it was my intention, nay, my endeavour, to support them with firmness; but, when I formed the plan, I thought only of the letter, — not of Lord Orville; — and how is it possible for resentment to subsist without provocation? yet, believe me, my dearest Sir, had he sustained the part he began to act when he wrote the ever-to-be-regretted letter, your Evelina would not have forfeited her title to your esteem, by contentedly submitting to be treated with indignity.

We continued in the garden till the phaeton was ready. When we parted from Mrs. Beaumont, she repeated her invitation to Mrs. Selwyn to accept an apartment in her house, but the same reasons made it be again declined.

Lord Orville drove very slow, and so cautiously, that, notwithstanding the height of the phaeton, fear would have been ridiculous. I supported no part in the conversation, but Mrs. Selwyn extremely well supplied the place of two. Lord Orville himself did not speak much, but the excellent sense and refined good-breeding which accompany every word he utters, give a *zest* to whatever he says.

"I suppose, my Lord," said Mrs. Selwyn, "when we stopped at our lodgings, you would have been extremely confused had we met any gentlemen who have the honour of knowing you."

"If I had," answered he, gallantly, "it would have been from mere compassion at their envy."

"No, my Lord," answered she, "it would have been from mere shame, that, in an age so daring, you alone should be such a coward as to forbear to frighten women."

"O," cried he, laughing, "when a man is in a fright for himself, the ladies cannot but be in security; for you have not had half the apprehension for the safety of your persons, that I have for that of my heart." He then alighted, handed us out, took leave, and again mounting the phaeton, was out of sight in a minute.

"Certainly," said Mrs. Selwyn, when he was gone, "there must have been some mistake in the birth of that young man; he was, undoubtedly, designed for the last age; for, if you observed, he is really polite."

And now, my dear Sir, do not you think, according to the present situation of affairs, I may give up my resentment, without imprudence or impropriety? I hope you will not blame me. Indeed, had you, like me, seen his respectful behaviour, you would have been convinced of the impracticability of supporting any further indignation.

## LETTER III

### Evelina in Continuation

Bristol Hotwells, Sept. 19th.

Yesterday morning, Mrs. Selwyn received a card from Mrs. Beaumont, to ask her to dinner to-day; and another, to the same purpose, came to me. The invitation was accepted, and we are but just arrived from Clifton-Hill.

We found Mrs. Beaumont alone in the parlour. I will write you that lady's character, as I heard it from our satirical friend Mrs. Selwyn, and in her own words. "She is an absolute *Court Calendar bigot;*[1] for, chancing herself to be born of a noble and ancient family, she thinks proper to be of opinion, that *birth* and *virtue* are one and the same thing. She has some good qualities, but they rather originate from pride than principle, as she piques herself upon being too high born to be capable of an unworthy action, and thinks it incumbent upon her to support the dignity of her ancestry. Fortunately for the world in general, she has taken it into her head, that condescension is the most distinguishing virtue of high life; so that the same pride of family which renders others imperious, is with her the motive of affability. But her civility is too formal to be comfortable, and too mechanical to be flattering. That she does *me* the honour of so much notice, is merely owing to an accident which, I am sure, is very painful to her remembrance; for it so happened that I once did her some service, in regard to an apartment, at Southampton; and I have since been informed, that, at the time she accepted my assistance, she thought I was a woman of quality: and I make no doubt but she was miserable when she discovered me to be a mere country gentlewoman:[2] however, her nice notions of decorum have made her load me with favours ever since. But I am not much flattered by her civilities, as I am convinced I owe them neither to attachment nor gratitude, but solely to a desire of cancelling an obligation which she cannot brook being under, to one whose name is no where to be found in the Court Calendar."

You well know, my dear Sir, the delight this lady takes in giving way to her satirical humour.

Mrs. Beaumont received us very graciously, though she somewhat distressed me by the questions she asked concerning my family, — such as, whether I was related to the Anvilles in the North? — Whether some of my name did not live in Lincolnshire? and many other enquiries, which much embarrassed me.

The conversation, next, turned upon the intended marriage in her family. She treated the subject with reserve, but it was evident she disapproved Lady Louisa's choice. She spoke in terms of the highest

---

[1] *Court Calendar bigot:* One who pays inordinate attention to a yearly almanac of royal families and those who are part of their courts.

[2] *a mere country gentlewoman:* Mrs. Selwyn, while from a respectable and probably land-owning family, is not related to nobility.

esteem of Lord Orville, calling him, in Marmontel's words, *Un jeune homme comme il y en a peu.*[3]

I did not think this conversation very agreeably interrupted by the entrance of Mr. Lovel. Indeed I am heartily sorry he is now at the Hot-wells. He made his compliments with the most obsequious respect to Mrs. Beaumont, but took no sort of notice of any other person.

In a few minutes Lady Louisa Larpent made her appearance. The same manners prevailed; for courtsying, with, "I hope you are well, Ma'am," to Mrs. Beaumont, she passed straight forward to her seat on the sofa, where, leaning her head on her hand, she cast her languishing eyes round the room, with a vacant stare, as if determined, though she looked, not to see who was in it.

Mr. Lovel, presently approaching her, with reverence the most profound, hoped her Ladyship was not indisposed.

"Mr. Lovel," cried she, raising her head, "I declare I did not see you: Have you been here long?"

"By my *watch*, Madam," said he, "only five minutes, — but by your Ladyship's absence, as many hours."

"O! now I think of it," cried she, "I am very angry with you, — so go along, do, for I sha'n't speak to you all day."

"Heaven forbid your La'ship's displeasure should last so long! in such cruel circumstances, a day would seem an age. But in what have I been so unfortunate as to offend?"

"O, you half-killed me, the other morning, with terror! I have not yet recovered from my fright. How could you be so cruel as to drive your phaeton against my Lord Merton's?"

" 'Pon honour, Ma'am, your La'ship does me wrong; it was all owing to the horses, — there was no curbing them. I protest I suffered more than your Ladyship from the terror of alarming you."

Just then entered Lord Merton; stalking up to Mrs. Beaumont, to whom alone he bowed; he hoped he had not made her wait; and then advancing to Lady Louisa, said, in a careless manner, "How is your Ladyship this morning?"

"Not well at all," answered she; "I have been dying with the head-ach ever since I got up."

---

[3] *Un jeune homme comme il y en a peu:* "A young man like whom there are few." Jean François Marmontel (1723–1799) wrote *Contes Moraux*, of which one tale is called *La Femme comme il y en a peu.*

"Indeed!" cried he, with a countenance wholly unmoved, "I am very unhappy to hear it. But should not your Ladyship have some advice?"[4]

"I am quite sick of advice," answered she; "Mr. Ridgeway has but just left me, — but he has done me no good. Nobody here knows what is the matter with me, yet they all see how indifferent I am."

"You Ladyship's constitution," said Mr. Lovel, "is infinitely delicate.

"Indeed, it is," cried she, in a low voice, "I am nerve[5] all over!"

"I am glad, however," said Lord Merton, "that you did not take the air this morning, for Coverley has been driving against me as if he was mad: he has got two of the finest spirited horses I ever saw."

"Pray, my Lord," cried she, "why did not you bring Mr. Coverley with you? he's a droll creature; I like him monstrously."

"Why, he promised to be here as soon as me. I suppose he'll come before dinner's over."

In the midst of this trifling conversation, Lord Orville made his appearance. O how different was his address! how superior did he look and move, to all about him! Having paid his respects to Mrs. Beaumont, and then to Mrs. Selwyn, he came up to me, and said, "I hope Miss Anville has not suffered from the fatigue of Monday morning!" Then, turning to Lady Louisa, who seemed rather surprised at his speaking to me, he added, "Give me leave, sister, to introduce Miss Anville to you."

Lady Louisa, half-rising, said, very coldly, that she should be glad of the honour of knowing me; and then, very abruptly turning to Lord Merton and Mr. Lovel, continued, in a half-whisper, her conversation.

For my part, I had risen and courtsied, and now, feeling very foolish, I seated myself again; first I had blushed at the unexpected politeness of Lord Orville, and immediately afterwards, at the contemptuous failure of it in his sister. How can that young lady see her brother so universally admired for his manners and deportment, and yet be so unamiably opposite to him in hers!

Lord Orville, I am sure, was hurt and displeased: he bit his lips, and turning from her, addressed himself wholly to me, till we were summoned to dinner. Do you think I was not grateful for his attention? yes, indeed, and every angry idea I had entertained, was totally obliterated.

---

[4] *advice:* Medical advice from a physician or apothecary.
[5] *I am nerve:* Prone to fits of nervousness.

As we were seating ourselves at the table, Mr. Coverley came into the room: he made a thousand apologies in a breath for being so late, but said he had been retarded by a little accident, for that he had overturned his phaeton, and broke it all to pieces. Lady Louisa screamed at this intelligence, and looking at Lord Merton, declared she would never go into a phaeton again.

"O," cried he, "never mind Jack Coverley, for he does not know how to drive."

"My Lord," cried Mr. Coverley, "I'll drive against *you* for a thousand pounds."

"Done!" returned the other, "Name your day, and we'll each choose a judge."

"The sooner the better," cried Mr. Coverley; "to-morrow, if the carriage can be repaired."

"These enterprises," said Mrs. Selwyn, "are very proper for men of rank, since 'tis a million to one but both parties will be incapacitated for any better employment."

"For Heaven's sake," cried Lady Louisa, changing colour, "don't talk so shockingly! Pray, my Lord, pray Mr. Coverley, don't alarm me in this manner."

"Compose yourself, Lady Louisa," said Mrs. Beaumont, "the gentlemen will think better of the scheme; they are neither of them in earnest."

"The very mention of such a scheme," said Lady Louisa, taking out her salts, "makes me tremble all over! Indeed, my Lord, you have frightened me to death! I sha'n't eat a morsel of dinner."

"Permit me," said Lord Orville, "to propose some other subject for the present, and we will discuss this matter another time."

"Pray, Brother, excuse me; my Lord must give me his word to drop this project, — for, I declare, it has made me sick as death."

"To compromise the matter," said Lord Orville, "suppose, if both parties are unwilling to give up the bet, that, to make the ladies easy, we change its object to something less dangerous?"

This proposal was so strongly seconded by all the party, that both Lord Merton and Mr. Coverley were obliged to comply with it: and it was then agreed that the affair should be finally settled in the afternoon.

"I shall now be entirely out of conceit[6] with phaetons again," said Mrs. Selwyn, "though Lord Orville had almost reconciled me to them."

[6] *out of conceit:* Out of humor with.

"My Lord Orville!" cried the witty Mr. Coverley, "why, my Lord Orville is as careful, — egad, as careful as an old woman! Why, I'd drive a one-horse cart against my Lord's phaeton for a hundred guineas!"

This sally occasioned much laughter; for Mr. Coverley, I find, is regarded as a man of infinite humour.

"Perhaps, Sir," said Mrs. Selwyn, "you have not discovered the *reason* my Lord Orville is so careful?"

"Why, no, Ma'am; I must own, I never heard any particular reason for it."

"Why then, Sir, I'll tell it you; and I believe you will confess it to be *very* particular; his Lordship's friends are not yet tired of him."

Lord Orville laughed and bowed. Mr. Coverley, a little confused, turned to Lord Merton, and said, "No foul play, my Lord! I remember your Lordship recommended me to the notice of this lady the other morning, and, egad, I believe you have been doing me the same office to-day."

"Give you joy, Jack!" cried Lord Merton, with a loud laugh.

After this, the conversation turned wholly upon eating, a subject which was discussed with the utmost delight; and, had I not known they were men of rank and fashion, I should have imagined that Lord Merton, Mr. Lovel, and Mr. Coverley, had all been professed cooks; for they displayed so much knowledge of sauces and made dishes, and of the various methods of dressing the same things, that I am persuaded they must have given much time, and much study, to make themselves such adepts in this *art*. It would be very difficult to determine, whether they were most to be distinguished as *gluttons*, or *epicures;* for they were, at once, dainty and voracious, understood the right and the wrong of every dish, and alike emptied the one and the other. I should have been quite sick of their remarks, had I not been entertained by seeing that Lord Orville, who, I am sure, was equally disgusted, not only read my sentiments, but, by his countenance, communicated to me his own.

When dinner was over, Mrs. Beaumont recommended the gentlemen to the care of Lord Orville, and then attended the ladies to the drawing-room.[7]

---

[7] *attended the ladies to the drawing-room:* It was customary for the ladies to withdraw from the dinner table before the men in order to leave the latter to drink and smoke.

The conversation, till tea-time, was extremely insipid; Mrs. Selwyn reserved herself for the gentlemen, Mrs. Beaumont was grave, and Lady Louisa languid.

But, at tea, every body revived; we were joined by the gentlemen, and gaiety took place of dullness.

Since I, as Mr. Lovel says, am *Nobody*,[8] I seated myself quietly on a window, and not very near to any body: Lord Merton, Mr. Coverley, and Mr. Lovel, severally passed me without notice, and surrounded the chair of Lady Louisa Larpent. I must own, I was rather piqued at the behaviour of Mr. Lovel, as he had formerly known me. It is true, I most sincerely despise his foppery, yet I should be grieved to meet with *contempt* from any body. But I was by no means sorry to find that Lord Merton was determined not to know me before Lady Louisa, as his neglect relieved me from much embarrassment. As to Mr. Coverley, his attention or disregard were equally indifferent to me. Yet, all together, I felt extremely uncomfortable in finding myself considered in a light very inferior to the rest of the company.

But, when Lord Orville appeared, the scene changed: he came up stairs last, and seeing me sit alone, not only spoke to me directly, but drew a chair next mine, and honoured me with his entire attention.

He enquired very particularly after my health, and hoped I had already found benefit from the Bristol air. "How little did I imagine," added he, "when I had last the pleasure of seeing you in town, that ill health would, in so short a time, have brought you hither! I am ashamed of myself for the satisfaction I feel at seeing you, — yet how can I help it!"

He then enquired after the Mirvan family, and spoke of Mrs. Mirvan in terms of most just praise. "She is gentle and amiable," said he, "a true feminine character."

"Yes, indeed," answered I, "and her sweet daughter, to say every thing of her at once, is just the daughter such a mother deserves."

"I am glad of it," said he, "for both their sakes, as such near relations must always reflect credit or disgrace on each other."

After this, he began to speak of the beauties of Clifton; but, in a few moments, was interrupted by a call from the company, to discuss the affair of the wager. Lord Merton and Mr. Coverley, though they had been discoursing upon the subject some time, could not fix upon any thing that satisfied them both.

---

[8] Vol. I, p. 81. [Burney's note.] In her early diaries, Burney had playfully identified herself as "Nobody."

When they asked the assistance of Lord Orville, he proposed that every body present should vote something, and that the two gentlemen should draw lots which, from the several votes, should decide the bet.

"We must then begin with the ladies," said Lord Orville; and applied to Mrs. Selwyn.

"With all my heart," answered she, with her usual readiness; "and, since the gentlemen are not allowed to risk their *necks,* suppose we decide the bet by their *heads?*"

"By our heads?" cried Mr. Coverley; "Egad, I don't understand you."

"I will then explain myself more fully. As I doubt not but you are both excellent classics,[9] suppose, for the good of your own memories, and the entertainment and surprise of the company, the thousand pounds should fall to the share of him who can repeat by heart the longest ode of Horace?"

Nobody could help laughing, the two gentlemen applied to excepted; who seemed, each of them, rather at a loss in what manner to receive this unexpected proposal. At length Mr. Lovel, bowing low, said, "Will your Lordship please to begin?"

"Devil take me if I do!" answered he, turning on his heel, and stalking to the window.

"Come, Gentlemen," said Mrs. Selwyn, "why do you hesitate? I am sure you cannot be afraid of a weak *woman?* Besides, if you should chance to be out, Mr. Lovel, I dare say, will have the goodness to assist you."

The laugh, now, turned against Mr. Lovel, whose change of countenance manifested no great pleasure at the transition.

"Me, Madam!" said he, colouring, "no, really I must beg to be excused."

"Why so, Sir?"

"Why so, Ma'am? — Why, really, — as to that, — 'pon honour, Ma'am, you are rather — a little severe; — for how is it possible for a man who is in the House, to study the classics? I assure you, Ma'am," (with an affected shrug) "I find quite business enough for *my* poor head, in studying politics."

"But, did you study politics at school, and at the university?"

---

[9] *classics:* Those learned in classical Greek and Roman literature, usually read in the original language by gentlemen educated at universities.

"At the university!" repeated he with an embarrassed look; "why, as to that, Ma'am, — no, I can't say I did; but then, what with riding, — and — and — and so forth, — really, one has not much time, even at the university, for mere reading."

"But, to be sure, Sir, you *have* read the classics?"

"O dear, yes, Ma'am! — very often, — but not very — not very lately."

"Which of the odes do you recommend to these gentlemen to begin with?"

"Which of the odes! — Really, Ma'am, as to that, I have no very particular choice, — for, to own the truth, that Horace was never a very great favourite with me."

"In truth I believe you!" said Mrs. Selwyn, very drily.

Lord Merton, again advancing into the circle, with a nod and a laugh, said, "Give you joy, Lovel!"

Lord Orville next applied to Mrs. Beaumont for her vote.

"It would very agreeably remind me of past times," said she, "when *bowing* was in fashion, if the bet was to depend upon the best-made bow."

"Egad, my Lord!" cried Mr. Coverley, "there I should beat you hollow, for your Lordship never bows at all."

"And, pray Sir, do *you?*" said Mrs. Selwyn.

"Do *I*, Ma'am?" cried he, "Why, only see!"

"I protest," cried she, "I should have taken *that* for a *shrug,* if you had not told me 'twas a bow."

"My Lord," cried Mr. Coverley, "let's practise;" and then, most ridiculously, they pranced about the room, making bows.

"We must now," said Lord Orville, turning to me, "call upon Miss Anville."

"O no, my Lord," cried I, "indeed I have nothing to propose." He would not, however, be refused, but urged me so much to say *something,* that at last, not to make him wait any longer, I ventured to propose an extempore couplet upon some given subject.

Mr. Coverley instantly made me a bow, or, according to Mrs. Selwyn, a *shrug,* crying, "Thank you, Ma'am; egad, that's my *forte!* — Why, my Lord, the Fates seem against you."

Lady Louisa was then applied to; and every body seemed eager to hear her opinion. "I don't know what to say, I declare," cried she, affectedly; "can't you pass me?"

"By no means!" said Lord Merton.

"It is possible your Ladyship can make so cruel a request?" said Mr. Lovel.

"Egad," cried Mr. Coverley, "if your Ladyship does not help us in this dilemma, we shall be forced to return to our phaetons."

"Oh," cried Lady Louisa, screaming, "you frightful creature, you, how can you be so abominable!"

I believe this trifling lasted near half an hour; when, at length, every body being tired, it was given up, and she said she would consider against another time.

Lord Orville now called upon Mr. Lovel, who, after about ten minutes deliberation, proposed, with a most important face, to determine the wager by who should draw the longest straw!

I had much difficulty to refrain laughing at this unmeaning scheme; but saw, to my great surprise, not the least change of countenance in any other person: and, since we came home, Mrs. Selwyn has informed me, that to *draw straws* is a fashion of betting by no means uncommon! Good God! my dear Sir, does it not seem as if money were of no value or service, since those who possess squander it away in a manner so infinitely absurd!

It now only remained for Lord Orville to speak; and the attention of the company shewed the expectations he had raised; yet, I believe, they by no means prevented his proposal from being heard with amazement; for it was no other, than that the money should be his due, who, according to the opinion of two judges, should bring the worthiest object with whom to share it!

They all stared, without speaking. Indeed, I believe every one, for a moment at least, experienced something like shame, from having either proposed or countenanced an extravagance so useless and frivolous. For my part, I was so much struck and affected by a rebuke so noble to these spendthrifts, that I felt my eyes filled with tears.

The short silence, and momentary reflection into which the company was surprised, Mr. Coverley was the first to dispel, by saying, "Egad, my Lord, your Lordship has a most remarkable odd way of taking things."

"Faith," said the incorrigible Lord Merton, "if this scheme takes, I shall fix upon my Swiss[10] to share with me; for I don't know a worthier fellow breathing."

---

[10] *Swiss:* A manservant from Switzerland.

After a few more of these attempts at wit, the two gentlemen agreed that they would settle the affair the next morning.

The conversation then took a different turn, but I did not give it sufficient attention to write any account of it. Not long after, Lord Orville resuming his seat next mine, said, "Why is Miss Anville so thoughtful?"

"I am sorry, my Lord," said I, "to consider myself one among those who have so justly incurred your censure."

"My censure! — you amaze me!"

"Indeed, my Lord, you have made me quite ashamed of myself, for having given my vote so foolishly, when an opportunity offered, had I but, like your Lordship, had the sense to use it, of shewing some humanity."

"You treat this too seriously," said he, smiling; "and I hardly know if you do not now mean a rebuke to *me*."

"To you, my Lord!"

"Nay, which deserves it most, the one who adapts the conversation to the company, or the one who chooses to be above it?"

"O, my Lord, who else would do you so little justice?"

"I flatter myself," answered he, "that, in fact, your opinion and mine, in this point, were the same, though you condescended to comply with the humour of the company. It is for me, therefore, to apologize for so unseasonable a gravity, which, but for a particular interest which I now take in the affairs of Lord Merton, I should not have been so officious to display."

Such a compliment as this could not fail to reconcile me to myself; and with revived spirits, I entered into a conversation, which he supported with me till Mrs. Selwyn's carriage was announced, and we returned home.

During our ride, Mrs. Selwyn very much surprised me, by asking if I thought my health would now permit me to give up my morning walks to the pump-room, for the purpose of spending a week at Clifton? "for this poor Mrs. Beaumont," added she, "is so eager to have a discharge in full of her debt to me, that, out of mere compassion, I am induced to listen to her. Besides, she has always a house full of people, and though they are chiefly fools and coxcombs, yet there is some pleasure in cutting them up."

I begged I might not, by any means, prevent her following her inclination, as my health was now very well established. And so, my dear Sir, to-morrow we are to be, actually, the guests of Mrs. Beaumont.

I am not much delighted at this scheme; for, flattered as I am by the attention of Lord Orville, it is not very comfortable to be neglected by every body else. Besides, as I am sure I owe the particularity of his civility to a generous feeling for my situation, I cannot expect him to support it so long as a week.

How often do I wish, since I am absent from you, that I was under the protection of Mrs. Mirvan! It is true, Mrs. Selwyn is very obliging, and, in every respect, treats me as an equal; but she is contented with behaving well herself, and does not, with a distinguishing politeness, raise and support me with others. Yet I mean not to blame her, for I know she is sincerely my friend; but the fact is, she is herself so much occupied in conversation, when in company, that she has neither leisure nor thought to attend to the silent.

Well, I must take my chance! But I knew not, till now, how requisite are birth and fortune to the attainment of respect and civility.

## LETTER IV

### Evelina in Continuation

Clifton, Sept. 20th.

Here I am, my dear Sir, under the same roof, and inmate of the same house, as Lord Orville! Indeed, if this were not the case, my situation would be very disagreeable, as you will easily believe, when I tell you the light in which I am generally considered.

"My dear," said Mrs. Selwyn, "did you ever before meet with that egregious fop, Lovel?"

I very readily satisfied her as to my acquaintance with him.

"O then," said she, "I am the less surprised at his ill-nature, since he has already injured you."

I begged her to explain herself; and then she told me, that while Lord Orville was speaking to me, Lady Louisa said to Mr. Lovel, "Do you know who that is?"

"Why, Ma'am, no, 'pon honour," answered he, "I can't absolutely say I do; I only know she is a kind of a toad-eater.[1] She made her first appearance in that capacity last Spring, when she attended Miss Mirvan, a young lady of Kent."

---

[1] *toad-eater:* Term for a dependent, usually a woman, who serves as a companion to her social superiors in exchange for support.

How cruel is it, my dear Sir, to be thus exposed to the impertinent suggestions of a man who is determined to do me ill offices! Lady Louisa may well despise a *toad-eater;* but, thank Heaven, her brother has not heard, or does not credit, the mortifying appellation. Mrs. Selwyn said, she would advise me to *pay my court* to this Mr. Lovel; "for," said she, "though he is malicious, he is fashionable, and may do you some harm in the great world." But I should disdain myself as much as I do him, were I capable of such duplicity, as to flatter a man whom I scorn and despise.

We were received by Mrs. Beaumont with great civility, and by Lord Orville with something more. As to Lady Louisa, she scarcely perceived that we were in the room.

There has been company here all day; part of which I have spent most happily; for after tea, when the ladies played at cards, Lord Orville, who does not, and I who cannot, play, were consequently at our own disposal; and then his Lordship entered into a conversation with me, which lasted till supper-time.

Almost insensibly, I find the constraint, the reserve, I have been wont to feel in his presence, wear away; the politeness, the sweetness, with which he speaks to me, restore all my natural chearfulness, and make me almost as easy as he is himself; and the more so, as, if I may judge by his looks, I am rather raised, than sunk, of late in his opinion.

I asked him, how the bet was, at last, to be decided? He told me, that, to his great satisfaction, the parties had been prevailed upon to lower the sum from one thousand to one hundred pounds; and that they had determined it should be settled by a race between two old women,[2] one chose by each side, and both of them to be proved more than eighty, though, in other respects, strong and healthy as possible.

When I expressed my surprise at this extraordinary method of spending so much money, "I am charmed," said he, "at the novelty of meeting with one so unhackneyed in the world, as not to be yet influenced by custom to forget the use of reason: for certain it is, that the prevalence of fashion makes the greatest absurdities pass uncensured, and the mind naturally accommodates itself even to the most ridiculous improprieties, if they occur frequently."

"I should have hoped," said I, "that the humane proposal made yesterday by your Lordship, would have had more effect."

---

[2] *a race between two old women:* Pedestrianism, either long-distance walking or footraces, was of some popular interest in eighteenth-century England. It was not uncommon to arrange matches between opponents, such as old people, who were chosen more for their oddity as athletes than for their abilities.

"O," cried he, laughing, "I was so far from expecting any success, that I shall think myself very fortunate if I escape the wit of Mr. Coverley in a lampoon! yet I spoke openly, because I do not wish to conceal that I am no friend to gaming."

After this, he took up the New Bath Guide,[3] and read it with me till supper-time. In our way down stairs, Lady Louisa said, "I thought, Brother, you were engaged this evening?"

"Yes, Sister," answered he, "and I *have* been engaged." And he bowed to me with an air of gallantry that rather confused me.

September 23d.

Almost insensibly have three days glided on since I wrote last, and so serenely, that, but for your absence, I could not have formed a wish. My residence here is much happier than I had dared expect. The attention with which Lord Orville honours me is as uniform as it is flattering, and seems to result from a benevolence of heart that proves him as much a stranger to caprice as to pride; for, as his particular civilities arose from a generous resentment at seeing me neglected, so will they, I trust, continue as long as I shall, in any degree, deserve them. I am now not merely easy, but even gay in his presence: such is the effect of true politeness, that it banishes all restraint and embarrassment. When we walk out, he condescends to be my companion, and keeps by my side all the way we go. When we read, he marks the passages most worthy to be noticed, draws out my sentiments, and favours me with his own. At table, where he always sits next to me, he obliges me by a thousand nameless attentions, while the distinguishing good-breeding with which he treats me, prevents my repining at the visibly-felt superiority of the rest of the company. A thousand occasional meetings could not have brought us to that degree of social freedom, which four days spent under the same roof have, insensibly, been productive of: and, as my only friend in this house, Mrs. Selwyn, is too much engrossed in perpetual conversation to attend much to me, Lord Orville seems to regard me as a helpless stranger, and, as such, to think me entitled to his good offices and protection. Indeed, my dear Sir, I have reason to hope, that the depreciating opinion he formerly entertained of me is succeeded by one infinitely more partial. — It may be that I flatter myself, but yet his looks, his attentions, his desire of drawing me into conversation, and

---

[3] *New Bath Guide:* See the headnote to Christopher Anstey, "From *The New Bath Guide*" in Part Two, Chapter 2.

his solicitude to oblige me, all conspire to make me hope I do not. In short, my dearest Sir, these last four happy days would repay me for months of sorrow and pain!

## LETTER V

### Evelina in Continuation

Clifton, Sept. 24th.

This morning I came down stairs very early, and, supposing that the family would not assemble for some time, I strolled out, purposing to take a long walk, in the manner I was wont to do at Berry Hill, before breakfast. But I had scarce shut the garden-gate, ere I was met by a gentleman, who, immediately bowing to me, I recollected to be the unhappy Mr. Macartney. Very much surprised, I courtsied, and stopped till he came up to me. He was still in mourning, but looked better than when I saw him last, though he had the same air of melancholy which so much struck me at first sight of him.

Addressing me with the utmost respect, "I am happy, Madam," said he, "to have met with you so soon. I came to Bristol but yesterday, and have had no small difficulty in tracing you to Clifton."

"Did you know, then, of my being here?"

"I did, Madam; the sole motive of my journey was to see you. I have been to Berry Hill, and there I had my intelligence, and, at the same time, the unwelcome information of your ill health."

"Good God! Sir, — and can you possibly have taken so much trouble?"

"Trouble! Oh, Madam, could there be any, to return you, the moment I had the power, my personal acknowledgments for your goodness?"

I then enquired after Madame Duval, and the Snow-Hill family. He told me they were all well, and that Madame Duval proposed soon returning to Paris. When I congratulated him upon looking better, "It is *yourself*, Madam," said he, "you should congratulate, for to your humanity alone it may now be owing that I exist at all." He then told me, that his affairs were now in a less desperate situation, and that he hoped, by the assistance of time and reason, to accommodate his mind to a more chearful submission to his fate. "The interest you so generously took in my affliction," added he, "assures me you will not be displeased to hear of my better fortune: I was therefore eager to acquaint you with it." He then told me, that his friend, the

moment he had received his letter, quitted Paris, and flew to give him
his personal assistance and consolation. With a heavy heart, he acknowledged, he accepted it; "but yet," he added, "I *have* accepted it,
and therefore, as bound equally by duty and honour, my first step
was to hasten to the benefactress of my distress, and to return" (presenting me something in a paper) "the only part of my obligations
that *can* be returned; for the rest, I have nothing but my gratitude to
offer, and must always be contented to consider myself her debtor."

I congratulated him most sincerely upon his dawning prosperity, but
begged he would not deprive me of the pleasure of being his friend, and
declined receiving the money, till his affairs were more settled.

While this point was in agitation, I heard Lord Orville's voice, enquiring of the gardener if he had seen me? I immediately opened the
garden-gate, and his Lordship, advancing to me with quickness, said,
"Good God, Miss Anville, have you been out alone? Breakfast has
been ready some time, and I have been round the garden in search of
you."

"Your Lordship has been very good," said I; "but I hope you have
not waited."

"Not waited!" repeated he, smiling, "Do you think we could sit
down quietly to breakfast, with the idea that you had run away from
us? But come," (offering to hand me) "if we do not return, they will
suppose *I* am run away too; and they very naturally may, as they
know the attraction of the magnet that draws me."

"I will come, my Lord," said I, rather embarrassed, "in two minutes." Then, turning to Mr. Macartney, with yet more embarrassment, I wished him good morning.

He advanced towards the garden, with the paper still in his hand.

"No, no," cried I, "some other time."

"May I then, Madam, have the honour of seeing you again?"

I did not dare take the liberty of inviting any body to the house of
Mrs. Beaumont, nor yet had I the presence of mind to make an excuse; and therefore, not knowing how to refuse him, I said, "Perhaps
you may be this way again to-morrow morning, — and I believe I
shall walk out before breakfast."

He bowed, and went away; while I, turning again to Lord Orville,
saw his countenance so much altered, that I was frightened at what I
had so hastily said. He did not again offer me his hand, but walked,
silent and slow, by my side. Good Heaven! thought I, what may he
not suppose from this adventure? May he not, by my desire of meeting Mr. Macartney to-morrow, imagine it was by design I walked out
to meet him to-day? Tormented by this apprehension, I determined to

avail myself of the freedom which his behaviour since I came hither has encouraged; and, since he would not ask any questions, begin an explanation myself. I therefore slackened my pace, to gain time, and then said, "Was not your Lordship surprised to see me speaking with a stranger?"

"A stranger!" repeated he; "is it possible that gentleman can be a stranger to you?"

"No, my Lord," — said I, stammering, "not to *me*, — but only it might look — he might seem — "

"No, believe me," said he, with a forced smile, "I could never believe Miss Anville would take an appointment with a stranger."

"An appointment, my Lord!" repeated I, colouring violently.

"Pardon me, Madam," answered he, "but I thought I had heard one."

I was so much confounded, that I could not speak; yet, finding he walked quietly on, I could not endure he should make his own interpretation of my silence; and therefore, as soon as I recovered from my surprise, I said, "Indeed, my Lord, you are much mistaken, — Mr. Macartney had particular business with me, — and I could not, — I knew not how to refuse seeing him, — but indeed, my Lord, — I had not, — he had not, — " I stammered so terribly that I could not go on.

"I am very sorry," said he, gravely, "that I have been so unfortunate as to distress you; but I should not have followed you, had I not imagined you were merely walked out for the air."

"And so I was!" cried I, eagerly, "indeed, my Lord, I was! My meeting with Mr. Macartney was quite accidental; and if your Lordship thinks there is any impropriety in my seeing him tomorrow, I am ready to give up that intention."

"If *I* think!" said he, in a tone of surprise, "surely Miss Anville must best judge for herself! surely she cannot leave the arbitration of a point so delicate, to one who is ignorant of all the circumstances which attend it?"

"If," said I, "it was worth your Lordship's time to hear them, — you should *not* be ignorant of the circumstances which attend it."

"The sweetness of Miss Anville's disposition," said he, in a softened voice, "I have long admired, and the offer of a communication which does me so much honour, is too grateful to me not to be eagerly caught at."

Just then, Mrs. Selwyn opened the parlour-window, and our conversation ended. I was rallied upon my passion for solitary walking, but no questions were asked me.

When breakfast was over, I hoped to have had some opportunity of speaking with Lord Orville; but Lord Merton and Mr. Coverley came in, and insisted upon his opinion of the spot they had fixed upon for the old women's race. The ladies declared they would be of the party, and, accordingly, we all went.

The race is to be run in Mrs. Beaumont's garden; the two gentlemen are as anxious as if their joint lives depended upon it. They have, at length, fixed upon objects, but have found great difficulty in persuading them to practise running, in order to try their strength. This grand affair is to be decided next Thursday.

When we returned to the house, the entrance of more company still prevented my having any conversation with Lord Orville. I was very much chagrined, as I knew he was engaged at the Hotwells in the afternoon. Seeing, therefore, no probability of speaking to him before the time of my meeting Mr. Macartney arrived, I determined that, rather than risk his ill opinion, I would leave Mr. Macartney to his own suggestions.

Yet, when I reflected upon his peculiar situation, his misfortunes, his sadness, and, more than all the rest, the idea I knew he entertained of what he calls his obligations to me, I could not resolve upon a breach of promise, which might be attributed to causes of all others the most offensive to one whom sorrow has made extremely suspicious of slights and contempt.

After the most uneasy consideration, I at length determined upon writing an excuse, which would, at once, save me from either meeting or affronting him. I therefore begged Mrs. Selwyn's leave to send her man to the Hotwells, which she instantly granted; and then I wrote the following note.


### "To Mr. Macartney

"Sir,

"As it will not be in my power to walk out to-morrow morning, I would by no means give you the trouble of coming to Clifton. I hope, however, to have the pleasure of seeing you before you quit Bristol. I am,

"Sir,
"Your obedient servant,
"EVELINA ANVILLE"

I desired the servant to enquire at the pump-room where Mr. Macartney lived, and returned to the parlour.

As soon as the company dispersed, the ladies retired to dress. I then, unexpectedly, found myself alone with Lord Orville; who, the moment I rose to follow Mrs. Selwyn, advanced to me, and said, "Will Miss Anville pardon my impatience, if I remind her of the promise she was so good as to make me this morning?"

I stopped, and would have returned to my seat, but, before I had time, the servants came to lay the cloth. He retreated, and went towards the window; and while I was considering in what manner to begin, I could not help asking myself what *right* I had to communicate the affairs of Mr. Macartney; and I doubted whether, to clear myself from one act of imprudence, I had not committed another.

Distressed by this reflection, I thought it best to quit the room, and give myself some time for consideration before I spoke; and therefore, only saying I must hasten to dress, I ran up stairs: rather abruptly, I own, and so, I fear, Lord Orville must think; yet what could I do? unused to the situations in which I find myself, and embarrassed by the slightest difficulties, I seldom, till too late, discover how I ought to act.

Just as we were all assembled to dinner, Mrs. Selwyn's man, coming into the parlour, presented to me a letter, and said, "I can't find out Mr. Macartney, Madam; but the post-office people will let you know if they hear of him."

I was extremely ashamed of this public message; and meeting the eyes of Lord Orville, which were earnestly fixed on me, my confusion redoubled, and I knew not which way to look. All dinner-time, he was silent as myself, and, the moment it was in my power, I left the table, and went to my own room. Mrs. Selwyn presently followed me, and her questions obliged me to own almost all the particulars of my acquaintance with Mr. Macartney, in order to excuse my writing to him. She said it was a most romantic affair, and spoke her sentiments with great severity, declaring that she had no doubt but he was an adventurer and an impostor.

And now, my dear Sir, I am totally at a loss what I ought to do: the more I reflect, the more sensible I am of the utter impropriety, nay, treachery, of revealing the story, and publishing the misfortunes and poverty of Mr. Macartney; who has an undoubted right to my secrecy and discretion, and whose letter charges me to regard his communication as sacred. — And yet, the appearance of mystery, —

perhaps something worse, which this affair must have to Lord Orville, — his seriousness, — and the promise I have made him, are inducements scarce to be resisted, for trusting him, with the openness he has reason to expect from me.

I am equally distressed, too, whether or not I should see Mr. Macartney to-morrow morning.

Oh Sir, could I now be enlightened by your counsel, from what anxiety and perplexity should I be relieved!

But no, — I ought not to betray Mr. Macartney, and I will not forfeit a confidence which would never have been reposed in me, but from a reliance upon my honour which I should blush to find myself unworthy of. Desirous as I am of the good opinion of Lord Orville, I will endeavour to act as if I was guided by your advice, and, making it my sole aim to *deserve* it, leave to time and to fate my success or disappointment.

Since I have formed this resolution, my mind is more at ease, but I will not finish my letter till the affair is decided.

Sept. 25th.

I rose very early this morning, and, after a thousand different plans, not being able to resolve upon giving poor Mr. Macartney leave to support I neglected him, I thought it incumbent upon me to keep my word, since he had not received my letter; I therefore determined to make my own apologies, not to stay with him two minutes, and to excuse myself from meeting him any more.

Yet, uncertain whether I was wrong or right, it was with fear and trembling that I opened the garden-gate, — judge, then, of my feelings, when the first object I saw was Lord Orville! — he, too, looked extremely disconcerted, and said, in a hesitating manner, "Pardon me, Madam, — I did not intend, — I did not imagine you would have been here so soon, — or, — or I would not have come." — And then, with a hasty bow, he passed me, and proceeded to the garden.

I was scarce able to stand, so greatly did I feel myself shocked; but, upon my saying, almost involuntarily, "Oh my Lord!" — he turned back, and, after a short pause, said, "Did you speak to *me*, Madam?"

I could not immediately answer; I seemed *choaked*, and was even forced to support myself by the garden-gate.

Lord Orville, soon recovering his dignity, said, "I know not how to apologise for being, just now, at this place; — and I cannot immediately, — if *ever,* — clear myself from the imputation of impertinent curiosity, to which I fear you will attribute it: however, I will, at present, only entreat your pardon, without detaining you any longer." Again he bowed, and left me.

For some moments, I remained fixed to the same spot, and in the same position, immoveably as if I had been transformed to stone. My first impulse was to call him back, and instantly tell him the whole affair; but I checked this desire, though I would have given the world to have indulged it; something like pride aided what I thought due to Mr. Macartney, and I determined not only to keep his secret, but to delay any sort of explanation, till Lord Orville should condescend to request it.

Slowly he walked, and before he entered the house, he looked back, but hastily withdrew his eyes, upon finding I observed him.

Indeed, my dear Sir, you cannot easily imagine a situation more uncomfortable than mine was at that time; to be suspected by Lord Orville of any clandestine actions, wounded my soul; I was too much discomposed to wait for Mr. Macartney, nor, in truth, could I endure to have the design of my staying so well known. Yet so extremely was I agitated, that I could hardly move, and, I have reason to believe, Lord Orville, from the parlour-window, saw me tottering along, for, before I had taken five steps, he came out, and hastening to meet me, said, "I fear you are not well; pray allow me," (offering his arm) "to assist you."

"No, my Lord," said I, with all the resolution I could assume; yet I was affected by an attention, at that time so little expected, and forced to turn away my head to conceal my emotion.

"You *must,*" said he, with earnestness, "indeed you must, — I am sure you are not well; — refuse me not the honour of assisting you," and, almost forcibly, he took my hand, and drawing it under his arm, obliged me to lean upon him. That I submitted, was partly the effect of surprise at an earnestness so uncommon in Lord Orville, and partly, that I did not, just then, dare trust my voice to make any objection.

When we came to the house, he led me into the parlour, and to a chair, and begged to know if I would not have a glass of water.

"No, my Lord, I thank you," said I, "I am perfectly recovered;" and, rising, I walked to the window, where, for some time, I pretended to be occupied in looking at the garden.

Determined as I was to act honourably by Mr. Macartney, I yet most anxiously wished to be restored to the good opinion of Lord

Orville; but his silence, and the thoughtfulness of his air, discouraged
me from speaking.

My situation soon grew disagreeable and embarrassing, and I resolved to return to my chamber till breakfast was ready. To remain
longer, I feared, might seem *asking* for his enquiries; and I was sure
it would ill become me to be more eager to speak, than he was to
hear.

Just as I reached the door, turning to me hastily, he said, "Are you
going, Miss Anville?"

"I am, my Lord," answered I, yet I stopped.

"Perhaps to return to — but I beg your pardon!" he spoke with a
degree of agitation that made me readily comprehend he meant to
*the garden,* and I instantly said, "To my own room, my Lord." And
again I would have gone; but, convinced by my answer that I understood him, I believe he was sorry for the insinuation; he approached
me with a very serious air, though, at the same time, he forced a
smile, and said, "I know not what evil genius pursues me this morning, but I seem destined to do or to say something I ought not: I
am so much ashamed of myself, that I can scarce solicit your forgiveness."

"My forgiveness! my Lord?" cried I, abashed, rather than elated
by his condescension, "surely you cannot — you are not serious?"

"Indeed never more so; yet, if I may be my own interpreter, Miss
Anville's countenance pronounces my pardon."

"I know not, my Lord, how any one can *pardon,* who has never
been offended."

"You are very good; yet I could expect no less from a sweetness of
disposition which baffles all comparison: will you not think I am an
encroacher, and that I take advantage of your goodness, should I
once more remind you of the promise you vouchsafed me yesterday?"

"No, indeed; on the contrary, I shall be very happy to acquit myself in your Lordship's opinion."

"Acquittal you need not," said he, leading me again to the window, "yet I own my curiosity is strongly excited."

When I was seated, I found myself much at a loss what to say; yet,
after a short silence, assuming all the courage in my power, "Will you
not, my Lord," said I, "think me trifling and capricious, should I own
I have repented the promise I made, and should I entreat your Lordship not to insist upon my strict performance of it? — I spoke so
hastily, that I did not, at the time, consider the impropriety of what I
said."

As he was entirely silent, and profoundly attentive, I continued to speak without interruption.

"If your Lordship, by an other means, knew the circumstances attending my acquaintance with Mr. Macartney, I am most sure you would yourself disapprove my relating them. He is a gentleman, and has been very unfortunate, — but I am not, — I think not, — at liberty to say more: yet I am sure, if he knew your Lordship wished to hear any particulars of his affairs, he would readily consent to my acknowledging them; — shall I, my Lord, ask his permission?"

"*His* affairs!" repeated Lord Orville; "by no means, I have not the least curiosity about them."

"I beg your Lordship's pardon, — but indeed I had understood the contrary."

"Is it possible, Madam, you could suppose the affairs of an utter stranger can excite my curiosity?"

The gravity and coldness with which he asked this question, very much abashed me; but Lord Orville is the most delicate of men, and, presently recollecting himself, he added, "I mean not to speak with indifference of any friend of yours, — far from it; any such will always command my good wishes: yet I own I am rather disappointed; and though I doubt not the justice of your reasons, to which I implicitly submit, you must not wonder, that, when upon the point of being honoured with your confidence, I should feel the greatest regret at finding it withdrawn."

Do you think, my dear Sir, I did not, at that moment, require all my resolution to guard me from frankly telling him whatever he wished to hear? yet I rejoice that I did not; for, added to the actual wrong I should have done, Lord Orville himself, when he had heard, would, I am sure, have blamed me. Fortunately, this thought occurred to me, and I said, "Your Lordship shall yourself be my judge; the promise I made, though voluntary, was rash and inconsiderate; yet, had it concerned myself, I would not have hesitated in fulfilling it; but the gentleman whose affairs I should be obliged to relate — "

"Pardon me," cried he, "for interrupting you; yet allow me to assure you, I have not the slightest desire to be acquainted with his affairs, further than what belongs to the motives which induced you, yesterday morning — " He stopped; but there was no occasion to say more.

"That, my Lord," cried I, "I will tell you honestly. Mr. Macartney had some particular business with me, — and I could not take the liberty to ask him hither."

"And why not? — Mrs. Beaumont, I am sure, — "

"I could not, my Lord, think of intruding upon Mrs. Beaumont's complaisance; and so, with the same hasty folly I promised your Lordship, I much *more* rashly, promised to meet him."

"And did you?"

"No, my Lord," said I, colouring, "I returned before he came."

Again, for some time, we were both silent; yet, unwilling to leave him to reflections which could not but be to my disadvantage, I summoned sufficient courage to say, "There is no young creature, my Lord, who so greatly wants, or so earnestly wishes for, the advice and assistance of her friends, as I do; I am new to the world, and unused to acting for myself, — my intentions are never wilfully blameable, yet I err perpetually! — I have, hitherto, been blest with the most affectionate of friends, and, indeed, the ablest of men, to guide and instruct me upon every occasion; — but he is too distant, now, to be applied to at the moment I want his aid; — and *here,* — there is not a human being whose counsel I can ask!"

"Would to Heaven," cried he, with a countenance from which all coldness and gravity were banished, and succeeded by the mildest benevolence, "that *I* were worthy, — and capable, — of supplying the place of such a friend to Miss Anville!"

"You do me but too much honour," said I; "yet I hope your Lordship's candour, — perhaps I ought to say indulgence, — will make some allowance, on account of my inexperience, for behaviour so inconsiderate: — May I, my Lord, hope that you will?"

"May *I,*" cried he, "hope that you will pardon the ill-grace with which I have submitted to my disappointment? and that you will permit me," (kissing my hand) "thus to seal my peace?"

"*Our* peace, my Lord," said I, with revived spirits.

"This, then," said he, again pressing it to his lips, "for *our* peace: and now, — are we not friends?"

Just then, the door opened, and I had only time to withdraw my hand, ere the ladies came in to breakfast.

I have been, all day, the happiest of human beings! — to be thus reconciled to Lord Orville, and yet to adhere to my resolution, — what could I wish for more? — he, too, has been very chearful, and more attentive, more obliging to me than ever. Yet Heaven forbid I should again be in a similar situation, for I cannot express how much uneasiness I have suffered from the fear of incurring his ill opinion.

But what will poor Mr. Macartney think of me? happy as I am, I much regret the necessity I have been under of disappointing him.

Adieu, my dearest Sir.

## LETTER VI

### Mr. Villars to Evelina

Berry Hill, Sept. 28.

Dead to the world, and equally insensible to its pleasures or its pains, I long since bid adieu to all joy, and defiance to all sorrow, but what should spring from my Evelina, — sole source, to me, of all earthly felicity. How strange, then, is it, that the letter in which she tells me she is the *happiest of human beings,* should give me the most mortal inquietude!

Alas, my child! — that innocence, the first, best gift of Heaven, should, of all others, be the blindest to its own danger, — the most exposed to treachery, — and the least able to defend itself, in a world where it is little known, less valued, and perpetually deceived!

Would to Heaven you were here! — then, by degrees, and with gentleness, I might enter upon a subject too delicate for distant discussion. Yet is it too interesting, and the situation too critical, to allow of delay. — Oh my Evelina, your situation is critical indeed! — your peace of mind is at stake, and every chance for your future happiness may depend upon the conduct of the present moment.

Hitherto I have forborne to speak with you upon the most important of all concerns, the state of your heart: — alas, I needed no information! I have been silent, indeed, but I have not been blind.

Long, and with the deepest regret, have I perceived the ascendancy which Lord Orville has gained upon your mind. — You will start at the mention of his name, — you will tremble every word you read; — I grieve to give pain to my gentle Evelina, but I dare not any longer spare her.

Your first meeting with Lord Orville was decisive. Lively, fearless, free from all other impressions, such a man as you describe him could not fail exciting your admiration, and the more dangerously, because he seemed as unconscious of his power as you of your weakness; and therefore you had no alarm, either from *his* vanity or *your own* prudence.

Young, animated, entirely off your guard, and thoughtless of consequences, *imagination* took the reins, and *reason,* slow-paced, though sure-footed, was unequal to a race with so eccentric and flighty a companion. How rapid was then my Evelina's progress through those regions of fancy and passion whither her new guide conducted her! — She saw Lord Orville at a ball, — and he was *the most amiable of men!* — She met him again at another — and *he had every virtue under Heaven!*

I mean not to depreciate the merit of Lord Orville, who, one mysterious instance alone excepted, seems to have deserved the idea you formed of his character; but it was not time, it was not the knowledge of his worth, obtained your regard; your new comrade had not patience to wait any trial; her glowing pencil, dipt in the vivid colours of her creative ideas, painted to you, at the moment of your first acquaintance, all the excellencies, all the good and rare qualities, which a great length of time, and intimacy, could alone have really discovered.

You flattered yourself, that your partiality was the effect of esteem, founded upon a general love of merit, and a principle of justice: and your heart, which fell the sacrifice of your error, was totally gone ere you suspected it was in danger.

A thousand times have I been upon the point of shewing you the perils of your situation; but the same inexperience which occasioned your mistake, I hoped, with the assistance of time and absence, would effect a cure: I was, indeed, most unwilling to destroy your illusion, while I dared hope it might itself contribute to the restoration of your tranquillity; since your ignorance of the danger and force of your attachment, might possibly prevent that despondency with which young people, in similar circumstances, are apt to persuade themselves that what is only difficult, is absolutely impossible.

But now, since you have again met, and are become more intimate than ever, all my hope from silence and seeming ignorance is at an end.

Awake, then, my dear, my deluded child, awake to the sense of your danger, and exert yourself to avoid the evils with which it threatens you, — evils which, to a mind like yours, are most to be dreaded, secret repining, and concealed, yet consuming regret! Make a noble effort for the recovery of your peace, which now, with sorrow I see it, depends wholly upon the presence of Lord Orville. This effort, may, indeed, be painful, but trust to my experience, when I assure you it is requisite.

You must quit him! — his sight is baneful to your repose, his society is death to your future tranquillity! Believe me, my beloved child, my heart aches for your suffering, while it dictates its necessity.

Could I flatter myself that Lord Orville would, indeed, be sensible of your worth, and act with a nobleness of mind which should prove it reciprocal, then would I leave my Evelina to the unmolested enjoyment of the chearful society and encreasing regard of a man she so greatly admires: but this is not an age in which we may trust to appearances, and imprudence is much sooner regretted than repaired. Your health, you tell me, is much mended, — can you then consent to leave Bristol? — not abruptly, that I do not desire, but in a few days from the time you receive this? I will write to Mrs. Selwyn, and tell her how much I wish your return; and Mrs. Clinton can take sufficient care of you.

I have meditated upon every possible expedient that might tend to your happiness, ere I fixed upon exacting from you a compliance which I am convinced will be most painful to you; but I can satisfy myself in none. This will at least be safe, and as to success, — we must leave it to time.

I am very glad to hear of Mr. Macartney's welfare.

Adieu, my dearest child; Heaven preserve and strengthen you!

A. V.

## LETTER VII

### Evelina to the Rev. Mr. Villars

Clifton, Sept. 28.

Sweetly, most sweetly, have two days more passed since I wrote; but I have been too much engaged to be exact in my journal.

To-day has been less tranquil. It was destined for the decision of the important bet, and has been productive of general confusion throughout the house. It was settled that the race should be run at five o'clock in the afternoon. Lord Merton breakfasted here, and stayed till noon. He wanted to engage the ladies to *bet on his side,* in the true spirit of gaming, without seeing the racers. But he could only prevail on Lady Louisa, as Mrs. Selwyn said she never laid a wager against her own wishes, and Mrs. Beaumont would not *take sides.* As for *me,* I was not applied to. It is impossible for negligence to be more pointed, than that of Lord Merton to me, in the presence of Lady Louisa.

But, just before dinner, I happened to be alone in the drawing-room, when his Lordship suddenly returned, and coming in with his usual familiarity, he was beginning, "You see, Lady Louisa, — " but, stopping short, "Pray where's every body gone?"

"Indeed I don't know, my Lord."

He then shut the door, and, with a great alteration in his face and manner, advanced eagerly towards me, and said, "How glad I am, my sweet girl, to meet you, at last, alone! By my soul, I began to think there was a plot against me, for I've never been able to have you a minute to myself." And, very freely, he seized my hand.

I was so much surprised at this address, after having been so long totally neglected, that I could make no other answer than staring at him with unfeigned astonishment.

"Why now," continued he, "if you was not the cruellest little angel in the world, you would have helped me to some expedient: for you see how I am watched here: Lady Louisa's eyes are never off me. She gives me a charming foretaste of the pleasures of a wife! however, it won't last long."

Disgusted to the greatest degree, I attempted to draw away my hand, but I believe I should not have succeeded, had not Mrs. Beaumont made her appearance. He turned from me with the greatest assurance, and said, "How are you, Ma'am? — how is Lady Louisa? — you see I can't live a moment out of the house."

Could you, my dearest Sir, have believed it possible for such effrontery to be in man?"

Before dinner, came Mr. Coverley, and before five o'clock, Mr. Lovel and some other company. The place marked out for the race, was a gravel-walk in Mrs. Beaumont's garden, and the length of the ground twenty yards. When we were summoned to the *course*, the two poor old women made their appearance. Though they seemed very healthy for their time of life, they yet looked so weak, so infirm, so feeble, that I could feel no sensation but that of pity at the sight. However, this was not the general sense of the company, for they no sooner came forward, than they were greeted with a laugh from every beholder, Lord Orville excepted, who looked very grave during the whole transaction. Doubtless he must be greatly discontented at the dissipated conduct and extravagance, of a man with whom he is, soon, to be so nearly connected.

For some time, the scene was truly ridiculous; the agitation of the parties concerned, and the bets that were laid upon the old women, were absurd beyond measure. *Who are you for?* and *whose side are you of?* was echoed from mouth to mouth by the whole company. Lord Merton and Mr. Coverley were both so excessively gay and noisy, that I soon found they had been too free in drinking to their success. They handed, with loud shouts, the old women to the race-ground, and encouraged them, by liberal promises, to exert themselves.

When the signal was given for them to set off, the poor creatures, feeble and frightened, ran against each other, and, neither of them able to support the shock, they both fell on the ground.

Lord Merton and Mr. Coverley flew to their assistance. Seats were brought for them, and they each drank a glass of wine. They complained of being much bruised, for, heavy and helpless, they had not been able to save themselves, but fell, with their whole weight upon the gravel. However, as they seemed equal sufferers, both parties were too eager to have the affair deferred.

Again, therefore, they set off, and hobbled along, nearly even with each other, for some time, yet frequently, and to the inexpressible diversion of the company, they stumbled and tottered; and the confused hallowing of "*Now Coverley!*" "*Now Merton!*" rung from side to side during the whole affair.

Not long after, a foot of one of the poor women slipt, and, with great force, she came again to the ground. Involuntarily, I sprung forward to assist her, but Lord Merton, to whom she did not belong, stopped me, calling out "No foul play! no foul play!"

Mr. Coverley, then, repeating the same words, went himself to help her, and insisted that the other should stop. A debate ensued; but the poor creature was too much hurt to move, and declared her utter inability to make another attempt. Mr. Coverley was quite brutal; he swore at her with unmanly rage, and seemed scarce able to refrain even from striking her.

Lord Merton then, in great rapture, said it was a *hollow thing;*[1] but Mr. Coverley contended that the fall was accidental, and time should be allowed for the woman to recover. However, all the company being against him, he was pronounced the loser.

We then went to the drawing-room, to tea. After which, the evening being delightful, we all walked in the garden. Lord Merton was quite riotous, and Lady Louisa in high spirits; but Mr. Coverley endeavoured in vain to conceal his chagrin.

As Lord Orville was thoughtful, and walked by himself, I expected that, as usual, *I* should pass unnoticed, and be left to my own meditations; but this was not the case, for Lord Merton, entirely off his guard, giddy equally from wine and success, was very troublesome to me; and, regardless of the presence of Lady Louisa, which, hitherto, has restrained him even from common civility, he attached himself to me, during the walk, with a freedom of gallantry that put me ex-

---

[1] *a hollow thing:*  An empty point; that is, Coverley has no case.

tremely out of countenance. He paid me the most high-flown compliments, and frequently and forcibly seized my hand, though I repeatedly, and with undissembled anger, drew it back. Lord Orville, I saw, watched us with earnestness, and Lady Louisa's smiles were converted into looks of disdain.

I could not bear to be thus situated, and complaining I was tired, I quickened my pace, with intention to return to the house; but Lord Merton, hastily following, caught my hand, and saying the *day was his own,* vowed he would not let me go.

"You *must,* my Lord," cried I, extremely flurried.

"You are the most charming girl in the world," said he, "and never looked better than at this moment."

"My Lord," cried Mrs. Selwyn, advancing to us, "you don't consider, that the better Miss Anville looks, the more striking is the contrast with your Lordship; therefore, for your own sake, I would advise you not to hold her."

"Egad, my Lord," cried Mr. Coverley, "I don't see what right you have to the best *old,* and the best *young* woman too, in the same day."

"*Best young woman!*" repeated Mr. Lovel; " 'pon honour, Jack, you have made a most unfortunate speech; however, if Lady Louisa can pardon you, — and her Ladyship is all goodness, — I am sure nobody else can, for you have committed an outrageous solecism in good manners."

"And pray, Sir," and Mrs. Selwyn, "under what denomination may your own speech pass?"

Mr. Lovel, turning another way, affected not to hear her: and Mr. Coverley, bowing to Lady Louisa, said, "Her Ladyship is well acquainted with my devotion, — but egad, I don't know how it is, — I had always an unlucky turn at an epigram, and never could resist a smart play upon words in my life."

"Pray, my Lord," cried I, "let go my hand! pray, Mrs. Selwyn, speak for me."

"My Lord," said Mrs. Selwyn, "in detaining Miss Anville any longer, you only lose time, for we are already as well convinced of your valour and your strength as if you were to hold her an age."

"My Lord," said Mrs. Beaumont, "I must beg leave to interfere; I know not if Lady Louisa can pardon you, but, as this young Lady is at my house, I do not chuse to have her made uneasy."

"*I* pardon him!" cried Lady Louisa, "I declare I am monstrous glad to get rid of him."

"Egad, my Lord," cried Mr. Coverley, "while you are grasping at a shadow, you'll lose a substance; you'd best make your peace while you can."

"Pray, Mr. Coverley, be quiet," said Lady Louisa, peevishly, "for I declare I won't speak to him. Brother," (taking hold of Lord Orville's arm) "will you walk in with me?"

"Would to Heaven," cried I, frightened to see how much Lord Merton was in liquor, "that I, too, had a brother! — and then I should not be exposed to such treatment!"

Lord Orville, instantly quitting Lady Louisa, said, "Will Miss Anville allow *me* the honour of taking that title?" and then, without waiting for any answer, he disengaged me from Lord Merton, and, handing me to Lady Louisa, "Let me," added he, "take equal care of *both* my sisters;" and then, desiring her to take hold of one arm, and begging me to make use of the other, we reached the house in a moment. Lord Merton, disordered as he was, attempted not to stop us.

As soon as we entered the house, I withdrew my arm, and courtsied my thanks, for my heart was too full for speech. Lady Louisa, evidently hurt at her brother's condescension, and piqued extremely by Lord Merton's behaviour, silently drew away her's, and biting her lips, with a look of infinite vexation, walked sullenly up the hall.

Lord Orville asked her if she would not go into the parlour?

"No," answered she, haughtily; "I leave you and your new sister together," and then she walked up stairs.

I was quite confounded at the pride and rudeness of this speech. Lord Orville himself seemed thunderstruck; I turned from him, and went into the parlour; he followed me, saying, "Must I, now, apologise to Miss Anville for the liberty of my interference? — or ought I to apologise that I did not, as I wished, interfere sooner?"

"O my Lord," cried I, with an emotion I could not repress, "it is from you alone I meet with any respect, — all others treat me with impertinence or contempt!"

I am sorry I had not more command of myself, as he had reason, just then, to suppose I particularly meant his sister, which, I am sure, must very much hurt him.

"Good Heaven," cried he, "that so much sweetness and merit can fail to excite the love and admiration so justly their due! I cannot, — I dare not express to you half the indignation I feel at this moment!"

"I am sorry, my Lord," said I, more calmly, "to have raised it; but yet, — in a situation that calls for protection, to meet only with mortifications, — indeed, I am but ill formed to bear them!"

"My *dear* Miss Anville," cried he, warmly, "allow *me* to be your friend; think of me as if I were indeed your brother, and let me entreat you to accept my best services, if there is any thing in which I can be so happy as to shew my regard, — my respect for you!"

Before I had time to speak, the rest of the party entered the parlour, and, as I did not wish to see any thing more of Lord Merton, at least before he had slept, I determined to leave it. Lord Orville, seeing my design, said, as I passed him, "Will you go?" "Had not I best, my Lord?" said I. "I am afraid," said he, smiling, "since I must now speak as your *brother*, I am afraid you *had*; — you see you may trust me, since I can advise against my own interest."

I then left the room, and have been writing ever since. And methinks I can never lament the rudeness of Lord Merton, as it has more than ever confirmed to me the esteem of Lord Orville.


## LETTER VIII

### Evelina in Continuation

Sept. 30.

Oh Sir, what a strange incident have I to recite! what a field of conjecture to open!

Yesterday evening, we all went to an assembly. Lord Orville presented tickets to the whole family, and did me the honour, to the no small surprise of all here, I believe, to dance with me. But every day abounds in fresh instances of his condescending politeness, and he now takes every opportunity of calling me his *friend*, and his *sister*.

Lord Merton offered a ticket to Lady Louisa; but she was so much incensed against him, that she refused it with the utmost disdain; neither could he prevail upon her to dance with him; she sat still the whole evening, and deigned not to look at, or speak to him. To me, her behaviour is almost the same, for she is cold, distant, and haughty, and her eyes express the greatest contempt. But for Lord Orville, how miserable would my residence here make me!

We were joined, in the ball-room, by Mr. Coverley, Mr. Lovel, and Lord Merton, who looked as if he was doing penance, and sat all the evening next to Lady Louisa, vainly endeavouring to appease her anger.

Lord Orville began the minuets; he danced with a young Lady who seemed to engage the general attention, as she had not been seen here before. She is pretty, and looks mild and good-humoured.

"Pray, Mr. Lovel," said Lady Louisa, "who is that?"

"Miss Belmont," answered he, "the young heiress; she came to the Wells yesterday."

Struck with the name, I involuntarily repeated it, but nobody heard me.

"What is her family?" said Mrs. Beaumont.

"Have you not heard of her, Ma'am?" cried he, "she is only daughter and heiress of Sir John Belmont."

Good Heaven, how did I start! the name struck my ear like a thunder-bolt. Mrs. Selwyn, who immediately looked at me, said, "Be calm, my dear, and we will learn the truth of all this."

Till then, I had never imagined her to be acquainted with my story; but she has since told me, that she knew my unhappy mother, and was well informed of the whole affair.

She asked Mr. Lovel a multitude of questions, and I gathered from his answers, that this young Lady was just come from abroad, with Sir John Belmont, who was now in London; that she was under the care of his sister, Mrs. Paterson; and that she would inherit a considerable estate.

I cannot express the strange feelings with which I was agitated during this recital. What, my dearest Sir, can it possibly mean? Did you ever hear of any after-marriage? — or must I suppose, that, while the lawful child is rejected, another is adopted? — I know not what to think! I am bewildered with a contrariety of ideas!

When we came home, Mrs. Selwyn passed more than an hour in my room, conversing upon this subject. She says that I ought instantly to go to town, find out my father, and have the affair cleared up. She assures me I have too strong a resemblance to my dear, though unknown mother, to allow of the least hesitation in my being owned, when once I am seen. For my part, I have no wish but to act by your direction.

I can give no account of the evening; so disturbed, so occupied am I by this subject, that I can think of no other. I have entreated Mrs. Selwyn to observe the strictest secrecy, and she has promised that she will. Indeed, she has too much sense to be idly communicative.

Lord Orville took notice of my being absent and silent, but I ventured not to entrust him with the cause. Fortunately, he was not of the party at the time Mr. Lovel made the discovery.

Mrs. Selwyn says that if you approve my going to town, she will herself accompany me. I had a thousand times rather ask the protection of Mrs. Mirvan, but, after this offer, that will not be possible.

Adieu, my dearest Sir. I am sure you will write immediately, and I shall be all impatience till your letter arrives.


## LETTER IX

### Evelina in Continuation

Oct. 1st.

Good God, my dear Sir, what a wonderful tale have I again to relate! even yet, I am not recovered from my extreme surprise.

Yesterday morning, as soon as I had finished my hasty letter, I was summoned to attend a walking party to the Hotwells. It consisted only of Mrs. Selwyn and Lord Orville. The latter walked by my side all the way, and his conversation dissipated my uneasiness, and insensibly restored my serenity.

At the pump-room, I saw Mr. Macartney; I courtsied to him twice ere he would speak to me. When he did, I began to apologise for having disappointed him; but I did not find it very easy to excuse myself, as Lord Orville's eyes, with an expression of anxiety that distressed me, turned from him to me, and me to him, every word I spoke. Convinced, however, that I had really trifled with Mr. Macartney, I scrupled not to beg his pardon. He was, then, not merely appeased, but even grateful.

He requested me to see him to-morrow: but I had not the folly to be again guilty of an indiscretion which had, already, caused me so much uneasiness; and therefore, I told him, frankly, that it was not in my power, at present, to see him, but by accident: and, to prevent his being offended, I hinted to him the reason I could not receive him as I wished to do.

When I had satisfied both him and myself upon this subject, I turned to Lord Orville, and saw, with concern, the gravity of his countenance. I would have spoken to him, but knew not how; I believe, however, he read my thoughts, for, in a little time, with a sort of serious smile, he said, "Does not Mr. Macartney complain of his disappointment?"

"Not much, my Lord."

"And how have you appeased him?" Finding I hesitated what to answer, "Am I not your brother," continued he, "and must I not enquire into your affairs?"

"Certainly, my Lord," said I, laughing, "I only wish it were better worth your Lordship's while."

"Let me, then, make immediate use of my privilege. When shall you see Mr. Macartney again?"

"Indeed, my Lord, I can't tell."

"But, — do you know that I shall not suffer *my sister* to make a private appointment?"

"Pray, my Lord," cried I, earnestly, "use that word no more! indeed you shock me extremely."

"That would I not do for the world," cried he; "yet you know not how warmly, how deeply I am interested, not only in all your concerns, but in all your actions."

This speech, — the most particular one Lord Orville had ever made to me, ended our conversation for that time, for I was too much struck by it to make any answer.

Soon after, Mr. Macartney, in a low voice, entreated me not to deny him the gratification of returning the money. While he was speaking, the young Lady I saw yesterday at the assembly, with a large party, entered the pump-room. Mr. Macartney turned as pale as death, his voice faltered, and he seemed not to know what he said. I was myself almost equally disturbed, by the croud of confused ideas that occurred to me. Good Heaven, thought I, why should he be thus agitated? — is it possible this can be the young Lady he loved? —

In a few minutes, we quitted the pump-room, and though I twice wished Mr. Macartney good morning, he was so absent he did not hear me.

We did not immediately return to Clifton, as Mrs. Selwyn had business at a pamphlet-shop.[1] While she was looking at some new poems, Lord Orville again asked me when I should see Mr. Macartney?

"Indeed, my Lord," cried I, "I know not, but I would give the universe for a few moments conversation with him!" I spoke this with a simple sincerity, and was not aware of the force of my own words.

"The universe!" repeated he, "Good God, Miss Anville, do you say this to *me?*"

---

[1] *pamphlet-shop:* In his introduction to *British Pamphleteers* (1948), George Orwell muses that "To ask 'What is a pamphlet?' is rather like asking 'What is a dog?' We all know a dog when we see one, or at least we think we do, but it is not easy to give a clear verbal definition, nor even to distinguish at sight between a dog and some kindred creature such as a wolf or jackal." Pamphlets were relatively short texts, between five hundred and ten thousand words, available unbound, and therefore cheap. They proliferated after the liberalization of British censorship laws in 1695 and usually dealt with topical political matters, which, as Horace Walpole noted, are "meat to our printers."

"I would say it," returned I, "to any body, my Lord."

"I beg your pardon," said he, in a voice that shewed him ill pleased, "I am answered!"

"My Lord," cried I, "you must not judge hardly of me. I spoke inadvertently; but if you knew the painful suspence I suffer at this moment, you would not be surprised at what I have said."

"And would a meeting with Mr. Macartney relieve you from that suspence?"

"Yes, my Lord, two words might be sufficient."

"Would to Heaven," cried he, after a short pause, "that I were worthy to know their import!"

"Worthy, my Lord! — O, if that were all, your Lordship could ask nothing I should not be ready to answer! If I were but at liberty to speak, I should be *proud* of your Lordship's enquiries; but indeed I am not, I have no right to communicate the affairs of Mr. Macartney, — your Lordship cannot suppose I have."

"I will own to you," answered he, "I know not *what* to suppose; yet there seems a frankness even in your mystery, — and such an air of openness in your countenance, that I am willing to hope, — " He stopped a moment, and then added, "This meeting, you say, is essential to your repose?"

"I did not say *that,* my Lord; but yet I have the most important reasons for wishing to speak to him."

He paused a few minutes, and then said, with warmth, "Yes, you *shall* speak to him! — I will myself assist you! — Miss Anville, I am sure, cannot form a wish against propriety, I will ask no questions, I will rely upon her own purity, and uninformed, blindfold as I am, I will serve her with all my power!" And then he went into the shop, leaving me so strangely affected by his generous behaviour, that I almost wished to follow him with my thanks.

When Mrs. Selwyn had transacted her affairs, we returned home.

The moment dinner was over, Lord Orville went out, and did not come back till just as we were summoned to supper. This is the longest time he has spent from the house since I have been at Clifton, and you cannot imagine, my dear Sir, how much I missed him. I scarce knew before how infinitely I am indebted to him alone for the happiness I have enjoyed since I have been at Mrs. Beaumont's.

As I generally go down stairs last, he came to me the moment the ladies had passed by, and said, "Shall you be at home to-morrow morning?"

"I believe so, my Lord."

"And will you, then, receive a visitor for me?"

"For you, my Lord!"

"Yes; — I have made acquaintance with Mr. Macartney, and he has promised to call upon me to-morrow about three o'clock."[2]

And then, taking my hand, he led me down stairs.

O Sir! — was there ever such another man as Lord Orville? — Yes, *one* other now resides at Berry Hill!

This morning there has been a great deal of company here, but at the time appointed by Lord Orville, doubtless with that consideration, the parlour is almost always empty, as every body is dressing.[3]

Mrs. Beaumont, however, was not gone up stairs, when Mr. Macartney sent in his name.

Lord Orville immediately said, "Beg the favour of him to walk in. You see, Madam, that I consider myself as at home."

"I hope so," answered Mrs. Beaumont, "or I should be very uneasy."

Mr. Macartney then entered. I believe we both felt very conscious to whom the visit was paid: but Lord Orville received him as his own guest, and not merely entertained him as such while Mrs. Beaumont remained in the room, but for some time after she went; a delicacy that saved me from the embarrassment I should have felt, had he immediately quitted us.

In a few minutes, however, he gave Mr. Macartney a book, — for I, too, by way of pretence for continuing in the room, pretended to be reading, — and begged he would be so good as to look it over, while he answered a note, which he would dispatch in a few minutes, and return to him.

When he was gone, we both parted with our books, and Mr. Macartney, again producing the paper with the money, besought me to accept it.

"Pray," said I, still declining it, "did you know the young lady who came into the pump-room yesterday morning?"

"Know her!" repeated he, changing colour, "Oh, but too well!"

"Indeed!"

"Why, Madam, do you ask?"

---

[2] *three o'clock:* This time would fall between the usual hours for breakfast and dinner, hence in the "morning." See footnote 1 to Volume 1, Letter XVI.

[3] *every body is dressing:* At a gathering such as the one at Mrs. Beaumont's it was customary to dress formally for dinner.

"I must beseech you to satisfy me further upon this subject; pray tell me who she is."

"Inviolably as I meant to keep my secret, I can refuse you, Madam, nothing; — that lady — is the daughter of Sir John Belmont! — of my father!"

"Gracious Heaven!" cried I, involuntarily laying my hand on his arm, "you are then — ", *my brother,* I would have said, but my voice failed me, and I burst into tears.

"Oh, Madam," cried he, "what can this mean? — What can thus distress you?"

I could not answer him, but held out my hand to him. He seemed greatly surprised, and talked in high terms of my condescension.

"Spare yourself," cried I, wiping my eyes, "spare yourself this mistake, — you have a *right* to all I can do for you; the similarity of our circumstances — "

We were then interrupted by the entrance of Mrs. Selwyn; and Mr. Macartney, finding no probability of our being left alone, was obliged to take leave, tho', I believe, very reluctantly, while in such suspence.

Mrs. Selwyn then, by dint of interrogatories, drew from me the state of this affair. She is so penetrating, that there is no possibility of evading to give her satisfaction.

Is not this a strange event? Good Heaven, how little did I think that the visits I so unwillingly paid at Mr. Branghton's would have introduced me to so near a relation! I will never again regret the time I spent in town this summer: a circumstance so fortunate will always make me think of it with pleasure.

*    *    *    *

I have just received your letter, — and it has almost broken my heart! — Oh, Sir! the illusion is over indeed! — How vainly have I flattered, how miserably deceived myself! Long since, doubtful of the situation of my heart, I dreaded a scrutiny, — but now, now that I have so long escaped, I began, indeed, to think my safety insured, to hope that my fears were causeless, and to believe that my good opinion and esteem of Lord Orville might be owned without suspicion, and felt without danger: — miserably deceived, indeed!

*His sight is baneful to my repose, — his society is death to my future tranquillity!* — Oh, Lord Orville! could I have believed that a friendship so grateful to my heart, so soothing to my distresses, — a friendship which, in every respect, did me so much honour, would only serve to embitter all my future moments! — What a strange, what an unhappy circumstance, that my gratitude, though so justly excited, should be so fatal to my peace!

Yes, Sir, I *will* quit him; — would to Heaven I could at this moment! without seeing him again, — without trusting to my now conscious emotion! — Oh, Lord Orville, how little do you know the evils I owe to you! how little suppose that, when most dignified by your attention, I was most to be pitied, — and when most exalted by your notice, you were most my enemy!

You, Sir, relied upon my ignorance; — I, alas, upon your experience; and, whenever I doubted the weakness of my heart, the idea that *you* did not suspect it, reassured me, — restored my courage, and confirmed my error! — Yet am I most sensible of the kindness of your silence.

Oh, Sir! why have I ever quitted you! why been exposed to dangers to which I am so unequal?

But I will leave this place, — leave Lord Orville, — leave him, perhaps, for ever! — no matter; your counsel, your goodness, may teach me how to recover the peace and the serenity of which my unguarded folly has beguiled me. To you alone do I trust, — in you alone confide for every future hope I may form.

The more I consider of parting with Lord Orville, the less fortitude do I feel to bear the separation; — the friendship he has shewn me, — his politeness, — his sweetness of manners, — his concern in my affairs, — his solicitude to oblige me, — all, all to be given up! —

No, I cannot tell him I am going, — I dare not trust myself to take leave of him, — I will run away without seeing him: — implicitly will I follow your advice, avoid his sight, and shun his society!

To-morrow morning I will set off for Berry Hill. Mrs. Selwyn and Mrs. Beaumont shall alone know my intention. And to-day, — I will spend in my own room. The readiness of my obedience is the only atonement I can offer, for the weakness which calls for its exertion.

Can you, will you, most honoured, most dear Sir! — sole prop by which the poor Evelina is supported, — can you, without reproach, without displeasure, receive the child you have so carefully reared, — from whose education better fruit might have been expected, and who, blushing for her unworthiness, fears to meet the eye by which she has been cherished? — Oh, yes, I am sure you will! Your Evelina's errors are those of the judgment, — and you, I well know, pardon all but those of the heart!

## LETTER X

### Evelina in Continuation

Clifton, October 1st.

I have only time, my dearest Sir, for three words, to overtake my last letter, and prevent your expecting me immediately; for, when I communicated my intention to Mrs. Selwyn, she would not hear of it, and declared it would be highly ridiculous for me to go before I received an answer to my intelligence concerning the journey from Paris. She has, therefore, insisted upon my waiting till your next letter arrives. I hope you will not be displeased at my compliance, though it is rather against my own judgment; but Mrs. Selwyn quite overpowered me with the force of her arguments. I will, however, see very little of Lord Orville; I will never come down stairs before breakfast; give up all my walks in the garden, — seat myself next to Mrs. Selwyn, and not merely avoid his conversation, but shun his presence. I will exert all the prudence and all the resolution in my power, to prevent this short delay from giving you any further uneasiness.

Adieu, my dearest Sir. I shall not now leave Clifton till I have your directions.


## LETTER XI

### Evelina in Continuation

October 2d.

Yesterday, from the time I received your kind, though heart-piercing letter, I kept my room, — for I was equally unable and unwilling to see Lord Orville: but this morning, finding I seemed destined to pass a few days longer here, I endeavoured to calm my spirits, and to appear as usual; though I determined to avoid him as much as should be in my power. Indeed, as I entered the parlour, when called to breakfast, my thoughts were so much occupied with your letter, that I felt as much confusion at his sight, as if he had himself been informed of its contents.

Mrs. Beaumont made me a slight compliment upon my recovery, for I had pleaded illness to excuse keeping my room: Lady Louisa spoke not a word: but Lord Orville, little imagining himself the cause of my indisposition, enquired concerning my health with the most distinguishing politeness. I hardly made any answer, and, for the first time since I have been here, contrived to sit at some distance from him.

I could not help observing that my reserve surprised him; yet he persisted in his civilities, and seemed to wish to remove it. But I paid him very little attention; and the moment breakfast was over, instead of taking a book, or walking in the garden, I retired to my own room.

Soon after, Mrs. Selwyn came to tell me that Lord Orville had been proposing I should take an airing, and persuading her to let him drive us both in his phaeton. She delivered the message with an archness that made me blush, and added, that an airing, in *my Lord Orville's carriage*, could not fail to revive my spirits. There is no possibility of escaping her discernment; she has frequently rallied me upon his Lordship's attention, — and, alas! — upon the pleasure with which I have received it! However, I absolutely refused the offer.

"Well," said she, laughing, "I cannot just now indulge you with any solicitation; for, to tell you the truth, I have business to transact at the Wells, and am glad to be excused myself. I would ask you to walk with *me*, — but, since *Lord Orville* is refused, *I* have not the presumption to hope for success."

"Indeed," cried I, "you are mistaken; I will attend *you* with pleasure."

"O rare coquetry!" cried she, "surely it must be inherent in our sex, or it could not have been imbibed at Berry Hill."

I had not spirits to answer her, and therefore put on my hat and cloak in silence.

"I presume," continued she, drily, "his Lordship may walk with us?"

"If so, Madam," cried I, "you will have a companion, and I will stay at home."

"My dear child," said she, "did you bring the certificate of your birth with you?"

"Dear Madam, no!"

"Why then, we shall never be known again at Berry Hill."

I felt too conscious to enjoy her pleasantry; but I believe she was determined to torment me; for she asked if she should inform Lord Orville that I desired him not to be of the party?

"By no means, Madam; — but, indeed, I had rather not walk myself."

"My dear," cried she, "I really do not know you this morning, — you have certainly been taking a lesson of Lady Louisa."

She then went down stairs; but presently returning, told me she had acquainted Lord Orville that I did not choose to go out in the phaeton, but preferred a walk, *tête-à-tête* with her, by way of *variety*. I said nothing, but was really vexed. She bid me go down stairs, and said she would follow immediately.

Lord Orville met me in the hall. "I fear," said he, "Miss Anville is not yet quite well?" and he would have taken my hand, but I turned from him, and courtsying slightly, went into the parlour.

Mrs. Beaumont and Lady Louisa were at work: Lord Merton was talking with the latter; for he has now made his peace, and been again received into favour.

I seated myself, as usual, by the window. Lord Orville, in a few minutes, came to me, and said, "Why is Miss Anville so grave?"

"Not grave, my Lord," said I, "only stupid,"[1] and I took up a book.

"You will go," said he, after a short pause, "to the assembly to night?"

"No, my Lord, certainly not."

"Neither, then, will I; for I should be sorry to sully the remembrance I have of the happiness I enjoyed at the last."

Mrs. Selwyn then coming in, general enquiries were made, to all but me, of who would go to the assembly. Lord Orville instantly declared he had letters to write at home; but every one else settled to go.

I then hastened Mrs. Selwyn away, tho' not before she had said to Lord Orville, "Pray has your Lordship obtained Miss Anville's leave to favour us with your company?"

"I have not, Madam," answered he, "had the vanity to ask it."

During our walk, Mrs. Selwyn tormented me unmercifully. She told me, that since I declined any addition to our party, I must, doubtless, be conscious of my own powers of entertainment; and begged me, therefore, to exert them freely. I repented a thousand times having consented to walk alone with her; for though I made the most painful efforts to appear in spirits, her raillery quite overpowered me.

The first place we went to was the pump-room. It was full of company; and the moment we entered, I heard a murmuring of, *"That's she!"* and, to my great confusion, I saw every eye turned towards me. I pulled my hat over my face, and, by the assistance of Mrs. Selwyn, endeavoured to screen myself from observation: nevertheless, I found

---

[1] *stupid:* Dull, lifeless.

I was so much the object of general attention, that I entreated her to hasten away. But, unfortunately, she had entered into conversation, very earnestly, with a gentleman of her acquaintance, and would not listen to me, but said, that if I was tired of waiting, I might walk on to the milliner's with the Miss Watkins, two young ladies I had seen at Mrs. Beaumont's, who were going thither.

I accepted the offer very readily, and away we went. But we had not gone three yards, ere we were followed by a party of young men, who took every possible opportunity of looking at us, and, as they walked behind, talked aloud, in a manner at once unintelligible and absurd. "Yes," cried one, " 'tis certainly she! — mark but her *blushing cheek!*"

"And then her *eye,* — her *downcast eye!*" cried another.

"True, oh most true," said a third, "*every beauty is her own!*"

"But then," said the first, "her *mind,* — now the difficulty is, to find out the truth of *that,* — for she will not say a word."

"She is *timid,*" answered another; "mark but her *timid air.*"

During this conversation, we all walked on, silent and quick; as we knew not to whom it was particularly addressed, we were all equally ashamed, and equally desirous to avoid such unaccountable observations.

Soon after, we were caught in a violent shower of rain. We hurried on, and the care of our cloaths occupying our hands, we were separated from one another. These gentlemen offered their services in the most pressing manner, begging us to make use of their arms; and two of them were so particularly troublesome to me, that, in my haste to avoid them, I unfortunately stumbled, and fell down. They both assisted in helping me up; and that very instant, while I was yet between them, upon raising my eyes, the first object they met was Sir Clement Willoughby!

He started; so, I am sure, did I. "Good God!" exclaimed he, with his usual quickness, "Miss Anville! — I hope to Heaven you are not hurt?"

"No," cried I, "not at all; but I am terribly dirtied." I then, without much difficulty, disengaged myself from my tormentors, who immediately gave way to Sir Clement, and entirely quitted us.

He teized me to make use of his arm; and, when I declined it, asked, very significantly, if I was much acquainted with those gentlemen who had just left me?

"No," answered I, "they are quite unknown to me."

"And yet," said he, "you allowed *them* the honour of assisting you. Oh, Miss Anville, to me alone will you ever be thus cruel?"

"Indeed, Sir Clement, their assistance was *forced* upon me, for I would have given the world to have avoided them."

"Good God!" cried he, "why did I not sooner know your situation? — But I only arrived here this morning, and I had not even learnt where you lodged."

"Did you know, then, that I was at Bristol?"

"Would to Heaven," cried he, "that I *could* remain in ignorance of your proceedings with the same contentment you do of mine! then should I not for ever journey upon the wings of hope, to meet my own despair! *You* cannot even judge of the cruelty of my fate, for the ease and serenity of your mind, incapacitates you from feeling for the agitation of mine."

The ease and serenity of *my* mind! alas, how little do I merit those words!

"But," added he, "had *accident* brought me hither, had I not known of your journey, the voice of fame would have proclaimed it to me instantly upon my arrival."

"The voice of fame!" repeated I.

"Yes, for your's was the first name I heard at the pump-room. But, had I *not* heard your name, such a description could have painted no one else."

"Indeed," said I, "I do not understand you." But, just then arriving at the milliner's, our conversation ended; for I ran up stairs to wipe the dirt off my gown. I should have been glad to have remained there till Mrs. Selwyn came, but the Miss Watkins called me into the shop, to look at caps and ribbons.

I found Sir Clement busily engaged in looking at lace ruffles. Instantly, however, approaching me, "How charmed I am," said he, "to see you look so well! I was told you were ill, — but I never saw you in better health, — never more infinitely lovely!"

I turned away, to examine the ribbons, and soon after Mrs. Selwyn made her appearance. I found that she was acquainted with Sir Clement, and her manner of speaking to him, convinced me that he was a favourite with her.

When their mutual compliments were over, she turned to me, and said, "Pray, Miss Anville, how long can you live without nourishment?"

"Indeed, Ma'am," said I, laughing, "I have never tried."

"Because so long, and no longer," answered she, "you may remain at Bristol."

"Why, what is the matter, Ma'am?"

"The matter! — why, all the ladies are at open war with you, — the whole pump-room is in confusion; and you, innocent as you pretend to look, are the cause. However, if you take my advice, you will be very careful how you eat and drink during your stay."

I begged her to explain herself: and she then told me, that a copy of verses had been dropt in the pump-room, and read there aloud: "The beauties of the wells," said she, "are all mentioned, but *you* are the Venus to whom the prize is given."

"Is it then possible," cried Sir Clement, "that you have not seen these verses?"

"I hardly know," answered I, "whether *any* body has."

"I assure you," said Mrs. Selwyn, "if you give *me* the invention of them, you do me an honour I by no means deserve."

"I wrote down in my tablets," said Sir Clement, "the stanzas which concern Miss Anville, this morning at the pump-room; and I will do myself the honour of copying them for her this evening."

"But why the part that concerned *Miss Anville?*" said Mrs. Selwyn; "Did you ever see her before this morning?"

"Oh yes," answered he, "I have had that happiness frequently at Captain Mirvan's. Too, too frequently!" added he, in a low voice, as Mrs. Selwyn turned to the milliner: and, as soon as she was occupied in examining some trimmings, he came to me, and, almost whether I would or not, entered into conversation with me.

"I have a thousand things," cried he, "to say to you. Pray where are you?"

"With Mrs. Selwyn, Sir."

"Indeed! — then, for once, Chance is my friend. And how long have you been here?"

"About three weeks."

"Good Heaven! what an anxious search have I had, to discover your abode, since you so suddenly left town! The termagant Madame Duval refused me all intelligence. Oh, Miss Anville, did you know what I have endured! the sleepless, restless state of suspence I have been tortured with, you could not, all cruel as you are, you could not have received me with such frigid indifference!"

"*Received* you, Sir!"

"Why, is not my visit to *you?* Do you think I should have made this journey, but for the happiness of again seeing you?"

"Indeed it is possible I might, — since so many others do."

"Cruel, cruel girl! you *know* that I adore you! — you *know* you are the mistress of my soul, and arbitress of my fate!"

Mrs. Selwyn then advancing to us, he assumed a more disengaged air, and asked if he should not have the pleasure of seeing her, in the evening, at the assembly?

"Oh yes," cried she, "we shall certainly be there; so you may bring the verses with you, if Miss Anville can wait for them so long."

"I hope, then," returned he, "that you will do me the honour to dance with me?"

I thanked him, but said I should not be at the assembly.

"Not be at the assembly!" cried Mrs. Selwyn, "Why, have *you*, too, letters to write?"

She looked at me with a significant archness that made me colour; and I hastily answered, "No, indeed, Ma'am!"

"You have not!" cried she, yet more drily, "then pray, my dear, do you stay at home to *help*, — or to *hinder* others?"

"To do neither, Ma'am," answered I, in much confusion; "so, if you please, I will *not* stay at home."

"You allow me, then," said Sir Clement, "to hope for the honour of your hand?"

I only bowed, — for the dread of Mrs. Selwyn's raillery made me not dare refuse him.

Soon after this, we walked home; Sir Clement accompanied us, and the conversation that passed between Mrs. Selwyn and him was supported in so lively a manner, that I should have been much entertained, had my mind been more at ease: but alas! I could think of nothing but the capricious, the unmeaning appearance which the alteration in my conduct must make in the eyes of Lord Orville! And, much as I wish to avoid him, greatly as I desire to save myself from having my weakness known to him, — yet I cannot endure to incur his ill opinion, — and, unacquainted as he is with the reasons by which I am actuated, how can he fail contemning a change, to him so unaccountable?

As we entered the garden, he was the first object we saw. He advanced to meet us, and I could not help observing, that at sight of each other both he and Sir Clement changed colour.

We went into the parlour, where we found the same party we had left. Mrs. Selwyn presented Sir Clement to Mrs. Beaumont; Lady Louisa and Lord Merton he seemed well acquainted with already.

The conversation was upon the general subjects, of the weather, the company at the Wells, and the news of the day. But Sir Clement, drawing his chair next to mine, took every opportunity of addressing himself to me in particular.

I could not but remark the striking difference of *his* attention, and that of Lord Orville: the latter has such gentleness of manners, such delicacy of conduct, and an air so respectful, that, when he flatters most, he never distresses, and when he most confers honour, appears to receive it! The former *obtrudes* his attention, and *forces* mine; it is so pointed, that it always confuses me, and so public, that it attracts general notice. Indeed I have sometimes thought that he would rather *wish,* than dislike to have his partiality for me known, as he takes great care to prevent my being spoken to by any body but himself.

When, at length, he went away, Lord Orville took his seat, and said with a half-smile, "Shall *I* call Sir Clement, — or will *you* call me an usurper, for taking this place? — You make me no answer? — Must I then suppose that Sir Clement — "

"It is little worth your Lordship's while," said I, "to suppose any thing upon so insignificant an occasion."

"Pardon me," cried he, — "to *me* nothing is insignificant in which you are concerned."

To this I made no answer, neither did he say any thing more, till the ladies retired to dress; and then, when I would have followed them, he stopped me, saying, "One moment, I entreat you!"

I turned back, and he went on. "I greatly fear that I have been so unfortunate as to offend you; yet so repugnant to my very soul is the idea, that I know not how to suppose it possible I can unwittingly have done the thing in the world that, designedly, I would most wish to avoid."

"No, indeed, my Lord, you have not!" said I.

"You sigh!" cried he, taking my hand, "would to Heaven I were the sharer of your uneasiness whencesoever it springs! with what earnestness would I not struggle to alleviate it! — Tell me, my dear Miss Anville, — my new-adopted sister, my sweet and most amiable friend! — tell me, I beseech you, if I can afford you any assistance?"

"None, none, my Lord!" cried I, withdrawing my hand, and moving towards the door.

"Is it then impossible I can serve you? — perhaps you wish to see Mr. Macartney again?"

"No, my Lord." And I held the door open.

"I am not, I own, sorry for that. Yet, oh, Miss Anville, there *is* a question, — there is a conjecture, — I know not how to mention, because I dread the result! — But I see you are in haste; — perhaps in the evening I may have the honour of a longer conversation. — Yet one thing will you have the goodness to allow me to ask? — Did you, this morning when you went to the Wells, — did you *know* who you should meet there?"

"Who, my Lord?"

"I beg your pardon a thousand times for a curiosity so unlicensed, — but I will say no more at present."

He bowed, expecting me to go, — and then, with quick steps, but a heavy heart, I came to my own room. His question, I am sure, meant Sir Clement Willoughby; and, had I not imposed upon myself the severe task of avoiding, flying Lord Orville with all my power, I would instantly have satisfied him of my ignorance of Sir Clement's journey. And yet more did I long to say something of the assembly, since I found he depended upon my spending the evening at home.

I did not go down stairs again till the family was assembled to dinner. My dress, I saw, struck Lord Orville with astonishment; and I was myself so much ashamed of appearing whimsical and unsteady, that I could not look up.

"I understood," said Mrs. Beaumont, "that Miss Anville did not go out this evening?"

"Her intention in the morning," said Mrs. Selwyn, "was to stay at home; but there is a fascinating power in an *assembly,* which, upon second thoughts, is not to be resisted."

"The assembly!" cried Lord Orville, "are you then going to the assembly?"

I made no answer; and we all took our places at table.

It was not without difficulty that I contrived to give up my usual seat; but I was determined to adhere to the promise in my yesterday's letter, though I saw that Lord Orville seemed quite confounded at my visible endeavours to avoid him.

After dinner, we all went into the drawing-room together, as there were no gentlemen to detain his Lordship; and then, before I could place myself out of his way, he said, "You are then really going to the assembly? — May I ask if you shall dance?"

"I believe not, — my Lord."

"If I did not fear," continued he, "that you would be tired of the same partner at two following assemblies, I would give up my letter-writing till to-morrow, and solicit the honour of your hand."

"If I *do* dance," said I, in great confusion, "I believe I am engaged."

"Engaged!" cried he, with earnestness, "May I ask to whom?"

"To — Sir Clement Willoughby, my Lord."

He said nothing, but looked very little pleased, and did not address himself to me any more all the afternoon. Oh, Sir! — thus situated, how comfortless were the feelings of your Evelina!

Early in the evening, with his accustomed assiduity, Sir Clement came to conduct us to the assembly. He soon contrived to seat himself next me, and, in a low voice, paid me so many compliments, that I knew not which way to look.

Lord Orville hardly spoke a word, and his countenance was grave and thoughtful; yet, whenever I raised my eyes, his, I perceived, were directed towards me, though instantly, upon meeting mine, he looked another way.

In a short time, Sir Clement, taking from his pocket a folded paper, said, almost in a whisper, "Here, loveliest of women, you will see a faint, a successless attempt to paint the object of all my adoration! yet, weak as are the lines for the purpose, I envy beyond expression the happy mortal who has dared make the effort."

"I will look at them," said I, "some other time." For, conscious that I was observed by Lord Orville, I could not bear he should see me take a written paper, so privately offered, from Sir Clement. But Sir Clement is an impracticable man, and I never yet succeeded in any attempt to frustrate whatever he had planned.

"No," said he, still in a whisper, "you must take it now, while Lady Louisa is away," (for she and Mrs. Selwyn were gone up stairs to finish their dress) "as she must by no means see them."

"Indeed," said I, "I have no intention to shew them."

"But the only way," answered he, "to avoid suspicion, is to take them in her absence. I would have read them aloud myself, but that they are not proper to be seen by any body in this house, yourself and Mrs. Selwyn excepted."

Then again he presented me the paper, which I now was obliged to take, as I found declining it was vain. But I was sorry that this action should be seen, and the whispering remarked, though the purport of the conversation was left to conjecture.

As I held it in my hand, Sir Clement teazed me to look at it immediately; and told me, that the reason he could not produce the lines publicly, was, that, among the ladies who were mentioned, and supposed to be rejected, was Lady Louisa Larpent. I am much concerned at this circumstance, as I cannot doubt but that it will render me more disagreeable to her than ever, if she should hear of it.

I will now copy the verses, which Sir Clement would not let me rest till I had read.

SEE last advance, with bashful grace,
    Downcast eye, and blushing cheek,
Timid air, and beauteous face,
    Anville, — whom the Graces seek.

Though ev'ry beauty is her own,
    And though her mind each virtue fills,
Anville, — to her power unknown,
    Artless, strikes, — unconscious, kills!

I am sure, my dear Sir, you will not wonder that a panegyric such as this, should, in reading, give me the greatest confusion; and, unfortunately, before I had finished it, the ladies returned.

"What have you there, my dear?" said Mrs. Selwyn.

"Nothing, Ma'am," said I, hastily folding, and putting it in my pocket.

"And has *nothing*," cried she, "the power of *rouge?*"

I made no answer; a deep sigh which escaped Lord Orville at that moment, reached my ears, and gave me sensations — which I dare not mention!

Lord Merton then handed Lady Louisa and Mrs. Beaumont to the latter's carriage. Mrs. Selwyn led the way to Sir Clement's, who handed me in after her.

During the ride, I did not once speak; but when I came to the assembly-room, Sir Clement took care that I should not preserve my silence. He asked me immediately to dance; I begged him to excuse me, and seek some other partner. But on the contrary, he told me he was very glad I would sit still, as he had a million of things to say to me.

He then began to tell me how much he had suffered from absence; how greatly he was alarmed when he heard I had left town, and how cruelly difficult he had found it to trace me; which, at last, he could only do by sacrificing another week to Captain Mirvan.

"And Howard Grove," continued he, "which, at my first visit, I thought the most delightful spot upon earth, now appeared to be the most dismal; the face of the country seemed altered: the walks which I had thought most pleasant, were now most stupid: Lady Howard, who had appeared a chearful and respectable old lady, now seemed in the common John Trot style[2] of other aged dames: Mrs. Mirvan, whom I had esteemed as an amiable piece of still-life,

---

[2] *John Trot style:* Countrified; a hick or bumpkin.

now became so insipid, that I could hardly keep awake in her company: the daughter too, whom I had regarded as a good-humoured, pretty sort of girl, now seemed too insignificant for notice: and as to the Captain, I had always thought him a booby, — but now, he appeared a savage!"

"Indeed, Sir Clement," cried I, angrily, "I will not hear you talk thus of my best friends."

"I beg your pardon," said he, "but the contrast of my two visits was too striking, not to be mentioned."

He then asked what I thought of the verses?

"Either," said I, "that they are written ironically, or by some madman."

Such a profusion of compliments ensued, that I was obliged to propose dancing, in my own defence. When we stood up, "I intended," said he, "to have discovered the author by his looks; but I find you so much the general loadstone of attention, that my suspicions change their object every moment. Surely you must yourself have some knowledge who he is?"

I told him, no. But, my dear Sir, I must own to you, I have no doubt but that Mr. Macartney must be the author; no one else would speak of me so partially; and, indeed, his poetical turn puts it, with me, beyond dispute.

He asked me a thousand questions concerning Lord Orville; how long he had been at Bristol? — what time I had spent at Clifton? — whether he rode out every morning? — whether I ever trusted myself in a phaeton? and a multitude of other enquiries, [all tending to discover if I was honoured with much of his Lordship's attention,] and all made with his usual freedom and impetuosity.

Fortunately, as I much wished to retire early, Lady Louisa makes a point of being among the first who quit the rooms, and therefore we got home in very tolerable time.

Lord Orville's reception of us was grave and cold: far from distinguishing me, as usual, by particular civilities, Lady Louisa herself could not have seen me enter the room with more frigid unconcern, nor have more scrupulously avoided honouring me with any notice. But chiefly I was struck to see, that he suffered Sir Clement, who stayed supper, to sit between us, without any effort to prevent him, though, till then, he had seemed to be even tenacious of a seat next mine.

This little circumstance affected me more than I can express: yet I endeavoured to *rejoice* at it, since neglect and indifference from him may be my best friends. — But, alas! — so suddenly, so abruptly to forfeit his attention! — to lose his friendship! — Oh Sir, these thoughts pierced my soul! — scarce could I keep my seat; for not all my efforts could restrain the tears from trickling down my cheeks: however, as Lord Orville saw them not, (for Sir Clement's head was constantly between us) I tried to collect my spirits, and succeeded so far as to keep my place with decency, till Sir Clement took leave: and then, not daring to trust my eyes to meet those of Lord Orville, I retired.

I have been writing ever since; for, certain that I could not sleep, I would not go to bed. Tell me, my dearest Sir, if you possibly can, tell me that you approve my change of conduct, — tell me that my altered behaviour to Lord Orville is right, — that my flying his society, and avoiding his civilities, are actions which *you* would have dictated. — Tell me this, and the sacrifices I have made will comfort me in the midst of my regret, — for never, never can I cease to regret that I have lost the friendship of Lord Orville! — Oh Sir, I have slighted, have rejected, — have thrown it away! — No matter, it was an honour I merited not to preserve, and I now see, — that my mind was unequal to sustaining it without danger.

Yet so strong is the desire you have implanted in me to act with uprightness and propriety, that, however the weakness of my heart may distress and afflict me, it will never, I humbly trust, render me wilfully culpable. The wish of doing well governs every other, as far as concerns my conduct, — for am I not *your* child? — the creature of your own forming? — Yet, oh Sir, friend, parent of my heart! — my feelings are all at war with my duties; and, while I most struggle to acquire self-approbation, my peace, my hopes, my happiness, — are lost!

'Tis you alone can compose a mind so cruelly agitated; you, I well know, can feel pity for the weakness to which you are a stranger; and, though you blame the affliction, soothe and comfort the afflicted.

## LETTER XII

### Mr. Villars to Evelina

Berry Hill, Oct. 3.

Your last communication, my dearest child, is indeed astonishing; that an acknowledged daughter and heiress of Sir John Belmont should be at Bristol, and still my Evelina bear the name of Anville, is to me inexplicable: yet the mystery of the letter to Lady Howard prepared me to expect something extraordinary upon Sir John Belmont's return to England.

Whoever this young lady may be, it is certain she now takes a place to which you have a right indisputable. An *after-marriage* I never heard of; yet, supposing such a one to have happened, Miss Evelyn was certainly the first wife, and therefore her daughter must, at least, be entitled to the name of Belmont.

Either there are circumstances in this affair at present utterly incomprehensible, or else some strange and most atrocious fraud has been practised; which of these two is the case, it now behoves us to enquire.

My reluctance to this step, gives way to my conviction of its propriety, since the reputation of your dear and much-injured mother must now either be fully cleared from blemish, or receive its final and indelible wound.

The public appearance of a daughter of Sir John Belmont will revive the remembrance of Miss Evelyn's story to all who have heard it, — who the *mother* was, will be universally demanded, — and if any other Lady Belmont shall be named, — the birth of my Evelina will receive a stigma, against which honour, truth, and innocence may appeal in vain! a stigma which will eternally blast the fair fame of her virtuous mother, and cast upon her blameless self the odium of a title, which not all her purity can rescue from established shame and dishonour.

No, my dear child, no; I will not quietly suffer the ashes of your mother to be treated with ignominy. Her spotless character shall be justified to the world, — her marriage shall be acknowledged, and her child shall bear the name to which she is lawfully entitled.

It is true, that Mrs. Mirvan would conduct this affair with more delicacy than Mrs. Selwyn; yet, perhaps, to save time is, of all considerations, the most important, since the longer this mystery is suffered to continue, the more difficult may be rendered its explanation. The sooner, therefore, you can set out for town, the less formidable will be your task.

Let not your timidity, my dear love, depress your spirits: I shall, indeed, tremble for you at a meeting so singular, and so affecting, yet there can be no doubt of the success of your application: I enclose a letter from your unhappy mother, written, and reserved purposely for this occasion: Mrs. Clinton, too, who attended her in her last illness, must accompany you to town. — But, without any other certificate of your birth, that which you carry in your countenance, as it could not be effected by artifice, so it cannot admit of a doubt.

And now, my Evelina, committed, at length, to the care of your real parent, receive the fervent prayers, wishes, and blessings, of him who so fondly adopted you!

May'st thou, oh child of my bosom! may'st thou, in this change of situation, experience no change of disposition! but receive with humility, and support with meekness, the elevation to which thou art rising! May thy manners, language, and deportment, all evince that modest equanimity, and chearful gratitude, which not merely deserve, but dignify prosperity! May'st thou, to the last moments of an unblemished life, retain thy genuine simplicity, thy singleness of heart, thy guileless sincerity! And may'st thou, stranger to ostentation, and superior to insolence, with true greatness of soul, shine forth conspicuous only in beneficence!

ARTHUR VILLARS

## LETTER XIII
### [Inclosed in the preceding Letter.]

#### Lady Belmont to Sir John Belmont

In the firm hope that the moment of anguish which approaches will prove the period of my sufferings, once more I address myself to Sir John Belmont, in behalf of the child, who, if it survives its mother, will hereafter be the bearer of this letter.

Yet in what terms, — oh most cruel of men! — can the lost Caroline address you, and not address you in vain? Oh deaf to the voice of compassion, — deaf to the sting of truth, — deaf to every tie of honour, — say, in what terms may the lost Caroline address you, and not address you in vain?

Shall I call you by the loved, the respected title of husband? — No, you disclaim it! — the father of my infant? — No, you doom it to infamy! — the lover who rescued me from a forced marriage? — No, you have yourself betrayed me! — the friend from whom I hoped succour and protection? — No, you have consigned me to misery and destruction!

Oh hardened against every plea of justice, remorse, or pity! how, and in what manner, may I hope to move thee? Is there one method I have left untried? remains there one resource unessayed? No; I have exhausted all the bitterness of reproach, and drained every sluice of compassion!

Hopeless, and almost desperate, twenty times have I flung away my pen; — but the feelings of a mother, a mother agonizing for the fate of her child, again animating my courage, as often I have resumed it.

Perhaps when I am no more, when the measure of my woes is compleated, and the still, silent, unreproaching dust has received my sad remains, — then, perhaps, when accusation is no longer to be feared, nor detection to be dreaded, the voice of equity, and the cry of nature may be heard.

Listen, oh Belmont, to their dictates! reprobate not your child, though you have reprobated its mother. The evils that are past, perhaps, when too late, you may wish to recall; the young creature you have persecuted, perhaps, when too late, you may regret that you have destroyed; — you may think with horror of the deceptions you have practised, and the pangs of remorse may follow me to the tomb: — oh Belmont, all my resentment softens into pity at the thought! what will become of thee, good heaven, when with the eye of penitence, thou reviewest thy past conduct!

Hear, then, the solemn, the last address with which the unhappy Caroline will importune thee.

If, when the time of thy contrition arrives, — for arrive it must! — when the sense of thy treachery shall rob thee of almost every other, if then thy tortured heart shall sigh to expiate thy guilt, — mark the conditions upon which I leave thee my forgiveness.

Thou know'st I am thy wife! — clear, then, to the world the reputation thou hast sullied, and receive as thy lawful successor the child who will present thee this my dying request.

The worthiest, the most benevolent, the best of men, to whose consoling kindness I owe the little tranquillity I have been able to preserve, has plighted me his faith that, upon no other conditions, he will part with his helpless charge.

Should'st thou, in the features of this deserted innocent, trace the resemblance of the wretched Caroline, — should its face bear the marks of its birth, and revive in thy memory the image of its mother, wilt thou not, Belmont, wilt thou not therefore renounce it? — Oh babe of my fondest affection! for whom already I experience all the tenderness of maternal pity! — look not like thy unfortunate mother, — lest the parent whom the hand of death may spare, shall be snatched from thee by the more cruel means of unnatural antipathy!

I can write no more. The small share of serenity I have painfully acquired, will not bear the shock of the dreadful ideas that crowd upon me.

Adieu, — for ever! —

Yet oh! — shall I not, in this last farewell, which thou wilt not read till every stormy passion is extinct, — and the kind grave has embosomed all my sorrows, — shall I not offer to the man once so dear to me, a ray of consolation to those afflictions he has in reserve? Suffer me, then, to tell thee, that my pity far exceeds my indignation, — that I will pray for thee in my last moments, — and that the recollection of the love I once bore thee, shall swallow up every other!

Once more, adieu!

CAROLINE BELMONT

## LETTER XIV

### Evelina to the Rev. Mr. Villars

Clifton, Oct. 3d.

This morning I saw from my window, that Lord Orville was walking in the garden; but I would not go down stairs till breakfast was ready: and then, he paid me his compliments almost as coldly as Lady Louisa paid her's.

I took my usual place, and Mrs. Beaumont, Lady Louisa, and Mrs. Selwyn, entered into their usual conversation. — Not so your Evelina: disregarded, silent, and melancholy, she sat like a cypher, whom to nobody belonging, by nobody was noticed.

Ill brooking such a situation, and unable to support the neglect of Lord Orville, the moment breakfast was over, I left the room; and was going up stairs, when, very unpleasantly, I was stopped by Sir Clement Willoughby, who, flying into the hall, prevented my proceeding.

He enquired very particularly after my health, and entreated me to return into the parlour. Unwillingly I consented, but thought any thing preferable to continuing alone with him; and he would neither leave me, nor suffer me to pass on. Yet, in returning, I felt not a little ashamed of appearing thus to take the visit of Sir Clement to myself. And, indeed, he took pains, by his manner of addressing me, to give it that air.

He stayed, I believe, two hours; nor would he, perhaps, even then have gone, had not Mrs. Beaumont broken up the party, by proposing an airing in her coach. Lady Louisa consented to accompany her: but Mrs. Selwyn, when applied to, said, "If my Lord, or Sir Clement, will join us, I shall be happy to make one; — but really, a trio of females will be nervous to the last degree."

Sir Clement readily agreed to attend them; indeed, he makes it his evident study to court the favour of Mrs. Beaumont. Lord Orville excused himself from going out; and I retired to my own room. What he did with himself I know not, for I would not go down stairs till dinner was ready: his coldness, though my own change of behaviour has occasioned it, so cruelly depresses my spirits, that I know not how to support myself in his presence.

At dinner, I found Sir Clement again of the party. Indeed he manages every thing his own way; for Mrs. Beaumont, though by no means easy to please, seems quite at his disposal.

The dinner, the afternoon, and the evening, were to me the most irksome imaginable: I was tormented by the assiduity of Sir Clement, who not only *took*, but *made* opportunities of speaking to me, — and I was hurt, — oh how inexpressibly hurt! — that Lord Orville not only forbore, as hitherto, *seeking*, he even *neglected* all occasions of talking with me!

I begin to think, my dear Sir, that the sudden alteration in my behaviour was ill-judged and improper; for, as I had received no offence, as the cause of the change was upon *my* account, not *his,* I should not have assumed, so abruptly, a reserve for which I dared assign no reason, — nor have shunned his presence so obviously, without considering the strange appearance of such a conduct.

Alas, my dearest Sir, that my reflections should always be too late to serve me! dearly, indeed, do I purchase experience! and much I fear I shall suffer yet more severely, from the heedless indiscretion of my temper, ere I attain that prudence and consideration, which, by foreseeing distant consequences, may rule and direct in present exigencies.

Oct. 4th.

Yesterday morning, every body rode out, except Mrs. Selwyn and myself: and we two sat for some time together in her room; but, as soon as I could, I quitted her, to saunter in the garden; for she diverts herself so unmercifully with rallying me, either upon my gravity, —

or concerning Lord Orville, — that I dread having any conversation with her.

Here I believe I spent an hour by myself; when, hearing the garden-gate open, I went into an arbour at the end of a long walk, where, ruminating, very unpleasantly, upon my future prospects, I remained quietly seated but a few minutes, ere I was interrupted by the appearance of Sir Clement Willoughby.

I started; and would have left the arbour, but he prevented me. Indeed I am almost certain he had heard in the house where I was, as it is not, otherwise, probable he would have strolled down the garden alone.

"Stop, stop," cried he, "loveliest and most beloved of women, stop and hear me!"

Then, making me keep my place, he sat down by me, and would have taken my hand; but I drew it back, and said I could not stay.

"Can you, then," cried he, "refuse me even the smallest gratification, though, but yesterday, I almost suffered martyrdom for the pleasure of seeing you?"

"Martyrdom! Sir Clement."

"Yes, beauteous Insensible! *martyrdom:* for did I not compel myself to be immured in a carriage, the tedious length of a whole morning, with the three most fatiguing women in England?"

"Upon my word the Ladies are extremely obliged to you."

"O," returned he, "they have, every one of them, so copious a share of their own personal esteem, that they have no right to repine at the failure of it in the world; and, indeed, they will themselves be the last to discover it."

"How little," cried I, "are those Ladies aware of such severity from *you!*"

"They are guarded," answered he, "so happily and so securely by their own conceit, that they are not aware of it from any body. Oh Miss Anville, to be torn away from *you,* in order to be shut up with *them,* — is there a human being, except your cruel self, could forbear to pity me?"

"I believe, Sir Clement, however hardly you may choose to judge of them, your situation, by the world in general, would rather have been envied, than pitied."

"The world in general," answered he, "has the same opinion of them that I have myself: Mrs. Beaumont is every where laughed at, Lady Louisa ridiculed, and Mrs. Selwyn hated."

"Good God, Sir Clement, what cruel strength of words do you use!"

"It is you, my angel, are to blame, since your perfections have rendered their faults so glaring. I protest to you, during our whole ride, I thought the carriage drawn by snails. The absurd pride of Mrs. Beaumont, and the respect she exacts, are at once insufferable and stupifying; had I never before been in her company, I should have concluded that this had been her first airing from the herald's-office,[1] — and wished her nothing worse than that it might also be the last. I assure you, that but for gaining the freedom of her house, I would fly her as I would plague, pestilence, and famine. Mrs. Selwyn, indeed, afforded some relief from this formality, but the unbounded licence of her tongue — "

"O Sir Clement, do *you* object to that?"

"Yes, my sweet reproacher, in a *woman*, I do; in a *woman* I think it intolerable. She has wit, I acknowledge, and more understanding than half her sex put together; but she keeps alive a perpetual expectation of satire, that spreads a general uneasiness among all who are in her presence; and she talks so much, that even the best things she says, weary the attention. As to the little Louisa, 'tis such a pretty piece of languor, that 'tis almost cruel to speak rationally about her, — else I should say, she is a mere compound of affectation, impertinence, and airs."

"I am quite amazed," said I, "that, with such opinions, you can behave to them all with so much attention and civility."

"Civility! my angel, — why I could worship, could adore them, only to procure myself a moment of your conversation! Have you not seen me pay my court to the gross Captain Mirvan, and the virago Madame Duval? Were it possible that a creature so horrid could be formed, as to partake of the worst qualities of all these characters, — a creature who should have the haughtiness of Mrs. Beaumont, the brutality of Captain Mirvan, the self-conceit of Mrs. Selwyn, the affectation of Lady Louisa, and the vulgarity of Madame Duval, — even to such a monster as that, I would pay homage, and pour forth adulation, only to obtain one word, one look from my adored Miss Anville!"

"Sir Clement," said I, "you are greatly mistaken if you suppose such duplicity of character recommends you to my good opinion. But I must take this opportunity of begging you never more to talk to me in this strain."

[1] *herald's-office:* The office of the Herald's College, or College of Arms, responsible for recording noble pedigrees and granting the rights to armorial bearings (more commonly called coats of arms).

"Oh Miss Anville, your reproofs, your coldness, pierce me to the soul! look upon me with less rigour, and make me what you please; — you shall govern and direct all my actions, — you shall new-form, new-model me: — I will not have even a wish but of your suggestion; — only deign to look upon me with pity, — if not with favour!"

"Suffer me, Sir," said I, very gravely, "to make use of this occasion to put a final conclusion to such expressions. I entreat you never again to address me in a language so flighty, and so unwelcome. You have already given me great uneasiness; and I must frankly assure you, that if you do not desire to banish me from wherever you are, you will adopt a very different style and conduct in future."

I then rose, and was going, but he flung himself at my feet to prevent me, exclaiming, in a most passionate manner, "Good God! Miss Anville, what do you say? — is it, can it be possible, that so unmoved, that with such petrifying indifference, you can tear from me even the remotest hope?"

"I know not, Sir," said I, endeavouring to disengage myself from him, "what hope you mean, but I am sure that I never intended to give you any."

"You distract me!" cried he, "I cannot endure such scorn; — I beseech you to have some moderation in your cruelty, lest you make me desperate: — say, then, that you pity me, — O fairest inexorable! loveliest tyrant! — say, tell me, at least, that you pity me!"

Just then, who should come in sight, as if intending to pass by the arbour, but Lord Orville! Good Heaven, how did I start! and he, the moment he saw me, turned pale, and was hastily retiring; — but I called out, "Lord Orville! — Sir Clement, release me, — let go my hand!"

Sir Clement, in some confusion, suddenly rose, but still grasped my hand. Lord Orville, who had turned back, was again walking away; but, still struggling to disengage myself, I called out, "Pray, pray, my Lord, don't go! — Sir Clement, I *insist* upon your releasing me!"

Lord Orville then, hastily approaching us, said, with great spirit, "Sir Clement, you cannot wish to detain Miss Anville by force!"

"Neither, my Lord," cried Sir Clement, proudly, "do I request the honour of your Lordship's interference."

However, he let go my hand, and I immediately ran into the house.

I was now frightened to death lest Sir Clement's mortified pride should provoke him to affront Lord Orville: I therefore ran hastily to Mrs. Selwyn, and entreated her, in a manner hardly to be understood, to walk towards the arbour. She asked no questions, for she is quick as lightening in taking a hint, but instantly hastened into the garden.

Imagine, my dear Sir, how wretched I must be till I saw her return! scarce could I restrain myself from running back; however, I checked my impatience, and waited, though in agonies, till she came.

And, now, my dear Sir, I have a conversation to write, the most interesting to me, that I ever heard. The comments and questions with which Mrs. Selwyn interrupted her account, I shall not mention; for they are such as you may very easily suppose.

Lord Orville and Sir Clement were both seated very quietly in the arbour: and Mrs. Selwyn, standing still, as soon as she was within a few yards of them, heard Sir Clement say, "Your question, my Lord, alarms me, and I can by no means answer it, unless you will allow me to propose another?"

"Undoubtedly, Sir."

"You ask me, my Lord, what are my intentions? — I should be very happy to be satisfied as to your Lordship's."

"I have never, Sir, professed *any*."

Here they were both, for a few moments, silent; and then Sir Clement said, "To what, my Lord, must I, then, impute your desire of knowing mine?"

"To an unaffected interest in Miss Anville's welfare."

"Such an interest," said Sir Clement, drily, "is, indeed, very generous; but, except in a father, — a brother, — or a lover — "

"Sir Clement," interrupted his Lordship, "I know your inference; and I acknowledge I have not the right of enquiry which any of those three titles bestow, and yet I confess the warmest wishes to serve her, and to see her happy. Will you, then, excuse me, if I take the liberty to repeat my question?"

"Yes, if your Lordship will excuse my repeating that I think it a rather extraordinary one."

"It may be so," said Lord Orville; "but this young lady seems to be peculiarly situated; she is very young, very inexperienced, yet appears to be left totally to her own direction. She does not, I believe, see the dangers to which she is exposed, and I will own to you, I feel a strong desire to point them out."

"I don't rightly understand your Lordship, — but I think you cannot mean to prejudice her against me?"

"Her sentiments of *you*, Sir, are as much unknown to me as your intentions towards *her*. Perhaps, were I acquainted with either, my officiousness might be at an end; but I presume not to ask upon what terms — "

Here he stopped; and Sir Clement said, "You know, my Lord, I am not given to despair; I am by no means such a puppy as to tell you I am upon *sure ground,* however, perseverance — "

"You are, then, determined to persevere?"

"I am, my Lord."

"Pardon me, then, Sir Clement, if I speak to you with freedom. This young lady, though she seems alone, and, in some measure, unprotected, is not entirely without friends; she has been extremely well educated, and accustomed to good company; she has a natural love of virtue, and a mind that might adorn *any* station, however exalted: is such a young lady, Sir Clement, a proper object to trifle with? — for your principles, excuse me, Sir, are well known."

"As to that, my Lord, let Miss Anville look to herself; she has an excellent understanding, and needs no counsellor."

"Her understanding is, indeed, excellent; but she is too young for suspicion, and has an artlessness of disposition that I never saw equalled."

"My Lord," cried Sir Clement, warmly, "your praises make me doubt your disinterestedness, and there exists not the man who I would so unwillingly have for a rival as yourself. But you must give me leave to say, you have greatly deceived me in regard to this affair."

"How so, Sir," cried Lord Orville, with equal warmth.

"You were pleased, my Lord," answered Sir Clement, "upon our first conversation concerning this young lady, to speak of her in terms by no means suited to your present encomiums; you said she was a *poor, weak, ignorant girl,* and I had great reason to believe you had a most contemptuous opinion of her."

"It is very true," said Lord Orville, "that I did not, at our first acquaintance, do justice to the merit of Miss Anville; but I knew not, then, how new she was to the world; at present, however, I am convinced, that whatever might appear strange in her behaviour, was simply the effect of inexperience, timidity, and a retired education, for I find her informed, sensible, and intelligent. She is not, indeed, like most modern young ladies, to be known in half an hour; her modest worth, and fearful excellence, require both time and encouragement to shew themselves. She does not, beautiful as she is, seize the soul by surprise, but, with more dangerous fascination, she steals it almost imperceptibly."

"Enough, my Lord," cried Sir Clement, "your solicitude for her welfare is now sufficiently explained."

"My friendship and esteem," returned Lord Orville, "I do not wish to disguise; but assure yourself, Sir Clement, I should not have troubled *you* upon this subject, had Miss Anville and I ever conversed but as friends. However, since you do not chuse to avow your intentions, we must drop the subject."

"My intentions," cried he, "I will frankly own, are hardly known to myself. I think Miss Anville the loveliest of her sex, and, were I a *marrying man,* she, of all the women I have seen, I would fix upon for a wife: but I believe that not even the philosophy of your Lordship would recommend to me a connection of that sort, with a girl of obscure birth, whose only dowry is her beauty, and who is evidently in a state of dependency."

"Sir Clement," cried Lord Orville, with some heat, "we will discuss this point no further; we are both free agents, and must act for ourselves."

Here Mrs. Selwyn, fearing a surprise, and finding my apprehensions of danger were groundless, retired hastily into another walk, and soon after came to give me this account.

Good Heaven, what a man is this Sir Clement! so designing, though so easy; so deliberately artful, though so flighty! Greatly, however, is he mistaken, all confident as he seems, for the girl, obscure, poor, dependent as she is, far from wishing the honour of his alliance, would not only *now,* but *always* have rejected it.

As to Lord Orville, — but I will not trust my pen to mention him, — tell me, my dear Sir, what *you* think of him? — tell me if he is not the noblest of men? — and if you can either wonder at, or blame my admiration?

The idea of being seen by either party, immediately after so singular a conversation, was both awkward and distressing to me; but I was obliged to appear at dinner. Sir Clement, I saw, was absent and uneasy; he watched me, he watched Lord Orville, and was evidently disturbed in his mind. Whenever he spoke to me, I turned from him with undisguised disdain, for I am too much irritated against him, to bear with his ill-meant assiduities any longer.

But, not once, — not a moment did I dare meet the eyes of Lord Orville! All consciousness myself, I dreaded his penetration, and directed mine every way — but towards his. The rest of the day, I never quitted Mrs. Selwyn.

Adieu, my dear Sir: to-morrow I expect your directions whether I am to return to Berry Hill, or once more visit London.

## LETTER XV

### Evelina in Continuation

Oct. 6th.

And now, my dearest Sir, if the perturbation of my spirits will allow me, I will finish my last letter from Clifton Hill.

This morning, though I did not go down stairs early, I was the only person in the parlour when Lord Orville entered it. I felt no small confusion at seeing him alone, after having so long and success-fully avoided such a meeting. As soon as the usual compliments were over, I would have left the room, but he stopped me by saying, "If I disturb you, Miss Anville, I am gone."

"My Lord," said I, rather embarrassed, "I was just going."

"I flattered myself," cried he, "I should have had a moment's con-versation with you."

I then turned back; and he seemed himself in some perplexity: but after a short pause, "You are very good," said he, "to indulge my re-quest; I have, indeed, for some time past, most ardently desired an opportunity of speaking to you."

Again he paused; but I said nothing, so he went on.

"You allowed me, Madam, a few days since, you allowed me to lay claim to your friendship, — to interest myself in your concerns, — to call you by the affectionate title of sister, — and the honour you did me, no man could have been more sensible of; I am ignorant, therefore, how I have been so unfortunate as to forfeit it: — but, at present, all is changed! you fly me, — your averted eye shuns to meet mine, and you sedulously avoid my conversation."

I was extremely disconcerted at this grave, and but too just accusa-tion, and I am sure I must look very simple;[1] but I made no answer.

"You will not, I hope," continued he, "condemn me unheard; if there is any thing I have done, — or any thing I have neglected, tell me, I beseech you, *what,* and it shall be the whole study of my thoughts how to deserve your pardon."

"Oh, my Lord," cried I, penetrated at once with shame and grati-tude, "your too, too great politeness oppresses me! — you have done nothing, — I have never dreamt of offence; — if there is any pardon to be asked, it is rather for *me,* than for *you,* to ask it."

"You are all sweetness and condescension!" cried he, "and I flatter myself you will again allow me to claim those titles which I find

---

[1]*simple:* Silly or stupid.

myself so unable to forego. Yet, occupied as I am with an idea that gives me the severest uneasiness, I hope you will not think me impertinent, if I still solicit, still entreat, nay implore you to tell me, to what cause your late sudden, and to me most painful, reserve was owing?"

"Indeed, my Lord," said I, stammering, "I don't, — I can't, — indeed, my Lord, — "

"I am sorry to distress you," said he, "and ashamed to be so urgent, — yet I know not how to be satisfied while in ignorance, — and the *time* when the change happened, makes me apprehend — may I, Miss Anville, tell you *what* it makes me apprehend?"

"Certainly, my Lord."

"Tell me, then, — and pardon a question most essentially important to me; — Had, or had not, Sir Clement Willoughby, any share in causing your inquietude?"

"No, my Lord," answered I, with firmness, "none in the world."

"A thousand, thousand thanks!" cried he: "you have relieved me from a weight of conjecture which I supported very painfully. But one thing more; is it, in any measure, to Sir Clement that I may attribute the alteration in your behaviour to myself, which, I could not but observe, began the very day of his arrival at the Hotwells?"

"To Sir Clement, my Lord," said I, "attribute nothing. He is the last man in the world who would have any influence over my conduct."

"And will you, then, restore to me that share of confidence and favour with which you honoured me before he came?"

Just then, to my great relief, — for I knew not what to say, — Mrs. Beaumont opened the door, and, in a few minutes, we went to breakfast.

Lord Orville was all gaiety; never did I see him more lively or more agreeable. Very soon after, Sir Clement Willoughby called, to pay his respects, he said, to Mrs. Beaumont. I then came to my own room, where, indulging my reflections, which now soothed, and now alarmed me, I remained very quietly till I received your most kind letter.

Oh Sir, how sweet are the prayers you offer for your Evelina! how grateful to her are the blessings you pour upon her head! — You *commit me to my real parent,* — Ah, Guardian, Friend, Protector of my youth! — by whom my helpless infancy was cherished, my mind formed, my very life preserved, — *you* are the Parent my heart acknowledges, and to you do I vow eternal duty, gratitude, and affection.

I look forward to the approaching interview with more fear than hope; but important as is this subject, I am, just now, wholly engrossed with another, which I must hasten to communicate.

I immediately acquainted Mrs. Selwyn with the purport of your letter. She was charmed to find your opinion agreed with her own, and settled that we should go to town to-morrow morning. And a chaise is actually ordered to be here by one o'clock.

She then desired me to pack up my cloaths; and said she must go, herself, to *make speeches,* and *tell lies* to Mrs. Beaumont.

When I went down stairs to dinner, Lord Orville, who was still in excellent spirits, reproached me for secluding myself so much from the company. He sat next me, — he *would* sit next me, — at table; and he might, I am sure, repeat what he once said of me before, *that he almost exhausted himself in fruitless endeavours to entertain me;* — for, indeed, I was not to be entertained: I was totally spiritless and dejected; the idea of the approaching meeting, — and oh Sir, the idea of the approaching parting, — gave a heaviness to my heart, that I could neither conquer nor repress. I even regretted the half explanation that had passed, and wished Lord Orville had supported his own reserve, and suffered me to support mine.

However, when, during dinner, Mrs. Beaumont spoke of our journey, my gravity was no longer singular; a cloud instantly overspread the countenance of Lord Orville, and he became nearly as thoughtful and as silent as myself.

We all went together to the drawing-room. After a short and unentertaining conversation, Mrs. Selwyn said she must prepare for her journey, and begged me to see for some books she had left in the parlour.

And here, while I was looking for them, I was followed by Lord Orville. He shut the door after he came in, and approaching me with a look of great anxiety, said, "Is this true, Miss Anville, are you going?"

"I believe so, my Lord," said I, still looking for the books.

"So suddenly, so unexpectedly must I lose you?"

"No great loss, my Lord," cried I, endeavouring to speak chearfully.

"Is it possible," said he, gravely, "Miss Anville can doubt my sincerity?"

"I can't imagine," cried I, "what Mrs. Selwyn has done with these books."

"Would to Heaven," continued he, "I might flatter myself you would allow me to prove it!"

"I must run up stairs," cried I, greatly confused, "and ask what she has done with them."

"You are going, then," cried he, taking my hand, "and you give me not the smallest hope of your return! — will you not, then, my too lovely friend! — will you not, at least, teach me, with fortitude like your own, to support your absence?"

"My Lord," cried I, endeavouring to disengage my hand, "pray let me go!"

"I will," cried he, to my inexpressible confusion, dropping on one knee, "if you wish to leave me!"

"Oh, my Lord," exclaimed I, "rise, I beseech you, rise! — such a posture to me! — surely your Lordship is not so cruel as to mock me!"

"Mock you!" repeated he earnestly, "no, I revere you! I esteem and I admire you above all human beings! — you are the friend to whom my soul is attached as to its better half! you are the most amiable, the most perfect of women! and you are dearer to me than language has the power of telling!"

I attempt not to describe my sensations at that moment; I scarce breathed; I doubted if I existed, — the blood forsook my cheeks, and my feet refused to sustain me: Lord Orville, hastily rising, supported me to a chair, upon which I sunk, almost lifeless.

For a few minutes, we neither of us spoke; and then, seeing me recover, Lord Orville, though in terms hardly articulate, entreated my pardon for his abruptness. The moment my strength returned, I attempted to rise, but he would not permit me.

I cannot write the scene that followed, though every word is engraven on my heart: but his protestations, his expressions, were too flattering for repetition: nor would he, in spite of my repeated efforts to leave him, suffer me to escape; — in short, my dear Sir, I was not proof against his solicitations — and he drew from me the most sacred secret of my heart!

I know not how long we were together, but Lord Orville was upon his knees, when the door was opened by Mrs. Selwyn! To tell you, Sir, the shame with which I was overwhelmed, would be impossible; — I snatched my hand from Lord Orville, — he, too, started and rose, and Mrs. Selwyn, for some instants, stood facing us both in silence.

At last, "My Lord," said she, sarcastically, "have you been so good as to help Miss Anville to look for my books?"

"Yes, Madam," said he, attempting to rally, "and I hope we shall soon be able to find them."

"Your Lordship is extremely kind," said she, drily, "but I can by no means consent to take up any more of your time." Then, looking on the window-seat, she presently found the books, and added,

"Come, here are just three, and so, like the servants in the Drummer,[2] this important affair may give employment to us all." She then presented one to Lord Orville, another to me, and taking a third herself, with a most provoking look, she left the room.

I would instantly have followed her; but Lord Orville, who could not help laughing, begged me to stay a minute, as he had many important matters to discuss.

"No, indeed, my Lord, I cannot, — perhaps I have already stayed too long."

"Does Miss Anville so soon repent her goodness?"

"I scarce know what I do, my Lord, — I am quite bewildered!"

"One hour's conversation," cried he, "will I hope compose your spirits, and confirm my happiness. When, then, may I hope to see you alone? — shall you walk in the garden to-morrow before breakfast?"

"No, no, my Lord; you must not, a second time, reproach me with making an *appointment.*"

"Do you, then," said he, laughing, "reserve that honour only for Mr. Macartney?"

"Mr. Macartney," said I, "is poor, and thinks himself obliged to me; otherwise — "

"Poverty," cried he, "I will not plead; but if being *obliged* to you has any weight, who shall dispute *my* title to an appointment?"

"My Lord, I can stay no longer, — Mrs. Selwyn will lose all patience."

"Deprive her not of the pleasure of her *conjectures; —* but, tell me, are you under Mrs. Selwyn's care?"

"Only for the present, my Lord."

"Not a few are the questions I have to ask Miss Anville: among them, the most important is, whether she depends wholly on herself, or whether there is any other person for whose interest I must solicit?"

"I hardly know, my Lord, I hardly know myself to whom I most belong!"

"Suffer, suffer me then," cried he, with warmth, "to hasten the time when that shall no longer admit a doubt! — when your grateful Orville may call you all his own!"

At length, but with difficulty, I broke from him. I went, however, to my own room, for I was too much agitated to follow Mrs. Selwyn.

---

[2] *the Drummer:* Joseph Addison's comedy *The Drummer* (1716) went through a revival in the 1770s. The reference is to the fifth act, in which three servants — the butler, coachman, and gardener — bring paper, ink, and pen to the conjurer.

Good God, my dear Sir, what a scene! surely the meeting for which I shall prepare to-morrow, cannot so greatly affect me! To be loved by Lord Orville, — to be the honoured choice of his noble heart, — my happiness seemed too infinite to be borne, and I wept, even bitterly I wept, from the excess of joy which overpowered me.

In this state of almost painful felicity, I continued, till I was summoned to tea. When I re-entered the drawing-room, I rejoiced much to find it full of company, as the confusion with which I met Lord Orville was rendered the less observable.

Immediately after tea, most of the company played at cards, and then, — and till supper-time, Lord Orville devoted himself wholly to me.

He saw that my eyes were red, and would not let me rest till he had made me confess the cause; and when, though most reluctantly, I had acknowledged my weakness, I could with difficulty refrain from weeping again at the gratitude he expressed.

He earnestly desired to know if my journey could not be postponed; and when I said no, entreated permission to attend me to town.

"Oh, my Lord," cried I, "what a request!"

"The sooner," answered he, "I make my devotion to you public, the sooner I may expect, from your delicacy, you will convince the world you encourage no mere *danglers*."

"You teach me, then, my Lord, the inference I might expect, if I complied."

"And can you wonder I should seek to hasten the happy time, when no scruples, no discretion, will demand our separation? and when the most punctilious delicacy will rather promote, than oppose, my happiness in attending you?"

To this I was silent, and he re-urged his request.

"My Lord," said I, "you ask what I have no power to grant. This journey will deprive me of all right to act for myself."

"What does Miss Anville mean?"

"I cannot now explain myself; indeed, if I could, the task would be both painful and tedious."

"O Miss Anville," cried he, "when may I hope to date the period[3] of this mystery? when flatter myself that my promised friend will indeed honour me with her confidence?"

[3] *the period:* The end.

"My Lord," cried I, "I mean not to affect any mystery, — but my affairs are so circumstanced, that a long and most unhappy story, can alone explain them. However, if a short suspence will give your Lordship any uneasiness, — "

"My beloved Miss Anville," cried he, eagerly, "pardon my impatience! — You shall tell me nothing you would wish to conceal, — I will wait your own time for information, and trust to your goodness for its speed."

"There is *nothing*, my Lord, I wish to conceal; — to *postpone* an explanation is all I desire."

He then requested, that, since I would not allow him to accompany me to town, I would permit him to write to me, and promise to answer his letters.

A sudden recollection of the two letters which had already passed between us, occurring to me, I hastily answered, "No, indeed, my Lord! — "

"I am extremely sorry," said he, gravely, "that you think me too presumptuous. I must own I had flattered myself that to soften the inquietude of an absence which seems attended by so many inexplicable circumstances, would not have been to incur your displeasure."

This seriousness hurt me; and I could not forbear saying, "Can you indeed desire, my Lord, that I should, a second time, expose myself, by an unguarded readiness to write to you?"

"A *second time! unguarded readiness!*" repeated he; "you amaze me!"

"Has your Lordship then quite forgot the foolish letter I was so imprudent as to send you when in town?"

"I have not the least idea," cried he, "of what you mean."

"Why then, my Lord," said I, "we had better let the subject drop."

"Impossible!" cried he, "I cannot rest without an explanation!"

And then, he obliged me to speak very openly of both the letters; but, my dear Sir, imagine my surprise, when he assured me, in the most solemn manner, that far from having ever written me a single line, he had never received, seen, or heard of my letter!

This subject, which caused mutual astonishment and perplexity to us both, entirely engrossed us for the rest of the evening; and he made me promise to shew him the letter I had received in his name to-morrow morning, that he might endeavour to discover the author.

After supper, the conversation became general.

And now, my dearest Sir, may I not call for your congratulations upon the events of this day? a day never to be recollected by me but with the most grateful joy! I know how much you are inclined to think well of Lord Orville, I cannot, therefore, apprehend that my frankness to him will displease you. Perhaps the time is not very distant when your Evelina's choice may receive the sanction of her best friend's judgment and approbation, — which seems now all she has to wish!

In regard to the change in my situation which must first take place, surely I cannot be blamed for what has passed! the partiality of Lord Orville must not only reflect honour upon me, but upon all to whom I do, or may belong.

Adieu, most dear Sir. I will write again when I arrive at London.

## LETTER XVI

### Evelina in Continuation

Clifton, Oct. 7th.

You will see, my dear Sir, that I was mistaken in supposing I should write no more from this place, where my residence, now, seems more uncertain than ever.

This morning, during breakfast, Lord Orville took an opportunity to beg me, in a low voice, to allow him a moment's conversation before I left Clifton; "May I hope," added he, "that you will strole into the garden after breakfast?"

I made no answer, but I believe my looks gave no denial; for, indeed, I much wished to be satisfied concerning the letter. The moment, therefore, that I could quit the parlour I ran up stairs for my calash,[1] but before I reached my room, Mrs. Selwyn called after me, "If you are going to walk, Miss Anville, be so good as to bid Jenny bring down my hat, and I'll accompany you."

Very much disconcerted, I turned into the drawing-room, without making any answer, and there I hoped to wait unseen, till she had otherwise disposed of herself. But, in a few minutes, the door opened, and Sir Clement Willoughby entered.

Starting at the sight of him, in rising hastily, I let drop the letter which I had brought for Lord Orville's inspection, and, before I could recover it, Sir Clement, springing forward, had it in his hand. He was

---

[1] *calash:* A woman's hood, made of silk and supported by whalebone or cane ribbings that held the fabric away from the face.

just presenting it to me, and, at the same time, enquiring after my health, when the signature caught his eye, and he read aloud "Orville."

I endeavoured, eagerly, to snatch it from him, but he would not permit me, and, holding it fast, in a passionate manner exclaimed, "Good God, Miss Anville, is it possible you can value such a letter as this?"

The question surprised and confounded me, and I was too much ashamed to answer him; but finding he made an attempt to secure it, I prevented him, and vehemently demanded him to return it.

"Tell me first," said he, holding it above my reach, "tell me if you have, since, received any more letters from the same person?"

"No, indeed," cried I, "never!"

"And will you, also, sweetest of women, promise that you never will receive any more? Say that, and you will make me the happiest of men."

"Sir Clement," cried I, greatly confused, "pray give me the letter."

"And will you not first satisfy my doubts? — will you not relieve me from the torture of the most distracting suspence? — tell me but that the detested Orville has written to you no more!"

"Sir Clement," cried I, angrily, "you have no right to make any conditions, — so pray give me the letter directly."

"Why such solicitude about this hateful letter? can it possibly deserve your eagerness? tell me, with truth, with sincerity tell me; Does it really merit the least anxiety?"

"No matter, Sir," cried I, in great perplexity, "the letter is mine, and therefore — "

"I must conclude, then," said he, "that the letter deserves your utmost contempt, — but that the name of Orville is sufficient to make you prize it."

"Sir Clement," cried I, colouring, "you are quite — you are very much — the letter is not — "

"O Miss Anville," cried he, "you blush! — you stammer! — Great Heaven! it is then all as I feared!"

"I know not," cried I, half frightened, "what you mean; but I beseech you to give me the letter, and to compose yourself."

"The letter," cried he, gnashing his teeth, "you shall never see more. You ought to have burnt it the moment you had read it!" And, in an instant, he tore it into a thousand pieces.

Alarmed at a fury so indecently outrageous, I would have run out of the room; but he caught hold of my gown, and cried, "Not yet, not yet must you go! I am but half-mad yet, and you must stay to finish your work. Tell me, therefore, does Orville know your fatal partiality? — Say *yes,*" added he, trembling with passion, "and I will fly you for ever!"

"For Heaven's sake, Sir Clement," cried I, "release me! — if you do not, you will force me to call for help."

"Call then," cried he, "inexorable and most unfeeling girl; call, if you please, and bid all the world witness your triumph! — but could ten worlds obey your call, I would not part from you till you had answered me. Tell me, then, does Orville know you love him?"

At any other time, an enquiry so gross would have given me inexpressible confusion; but now, the wildness of his manner terrified me, and I only said, "Whatever you wish to know, Sir Clement, I will tell you another time; but for the present, I entreat you to let me go!"

"Enough," cried he, "I understand you! — the art òf Orville has prevailed; — cold, inanimate, phlegmatic as he is, you have rendered him the most envied of men! — One thing more, and I have done; — Will he marry you?"

What a question! my cheeks glowed with indignation, and I felt too proud to make any answer.

"I see, I see how it is," cried he, after a short pause, "and I find I am undone for ever!" Then, letting loose my gown, he put his hand to his forehead, and walked up and down the room in a hasty and agitated manner.

Though now at liberty to go, I had not the courage to leave him: for his evident distress excited all my compassion. And this was our situation, when Lady Louisa, Mr. Coverley, and Mrs. Beaumont, entered the room.

"Sir Clement Willoughby," said the latter, "I beg pardon for making you wait so long, but — "

She had not time for another word; Sir Clement, too much disordered to know or care what he did, snatched up his hat, and, brushing hastily past her, flew down stairs, and out of the house.

And with him went my sincerest pity, though I earnestly hope I shall see him no more. But what, my dear Sir, am I to conclude from his strange speeches concerning the letter? does it not seem as if he was himself the author of it? How else should he be so well acquainted with the contempt it merits? Neither do I know another human being who could serve any interest by such a deception. I remember, too, that just as I had given my own letter to the maid, Sir Clement came into the shop; probably he prevailed upon her, by some bribery, to give it to him, and afterwards, by the same means, to deliver to me an answer of his own writing. Indeed I can in no other manner account for this affair. Oh, Sir Clement, were you not yourself unhappy, I know not how I could pardon an artifice that has caused me so much uneasiness!

His abrupt departure occasioned a kind of general consternation.

"Very extraordinary behaviour this!" cried Mrs. Beaumont.

"Egad," said Mr. Coverley, "the Baronet has a mind to tip us a touch of the heroicks this morning!"

"I declare," cried Lady Louisa, "I never saw any thing so monstrous in my life! it's quite abominable, — I fancy the man's mad; — I'm sure he has given me a shocking fright!"

Soon after, Mrs. Selwyn came up stairs, with Lord Merton. The former, advancing hastily to me, said, "Miss Anville, have you an almanack?"

"Me! — no, Ma'am."

"Who has one, then?"

"Egad," cried Mr. Coverley, "I never bought one in my life; it would make me quite melancholy to have such a time-keeper in my pocket. I would as soon walk all day before an hour-glass."

"You are in the right," said Mrs. Selwyn, "not to *watch time,* lest you should be betrayed, unawares, into reflecting how you employ it."

"Egad, Ma'am," cried he, "if Time thought no more of me, than I do of Time, I believe I should bid defiance, for one while, to old-age and wrinkles; — for deuce take me if ever I think about it at all."

"Pray, Mr. Coverley," said Mrs. Selwyn, "why do you think it necessary to tell me this so often?"

"Often!" repeated he, "Egad, Madam, I don't know why I said it now, — but I'm sure I can't recollect that ever I owned as much before."

"Owned it before!" cried she, "why, my dear Sir, you own it all day long; for every word, every look, every action proclaims it."

I know not if he understood the full severity of her satire, but he only turned off with a laugh: and she then applied to Mr. Lovel, and asked if *he* had an almanack?

Mr. Lovel, who always looks alarmed when she addresses him, with some hesitation, answered, "I assure you, Ma'am, I have no manner of antipathy to an almanack, — none in the least, I assure you; — I dare say I have four or five."

"Four or five! — pray may I ask what use you make of so many?"

"Use! — really, Ma'am, as to that, — I don't make any particular use of them, — but one must have them, to tell one the day of the month; — I'm sure, else, I should never keep it in my head."

"And does your time pass so smoothly umarked, that, without an almanack, you could not distinguish one day from another?"

"Really, Ma'am," cried he, colouring, "I don't see any thing so very particular in having a few almanacks; other people have them, I believe, as well as me."

"Don't be offended," cried she, "I have but made a little digression. All I want to know, is the state of the moon, — for if it is at the *full* I shall be saved a world of conjectures, and know at once to what cause to attribute the inconsistencies I have witnessed this morning. In the first place, I heard Lord Orville excuse himself from going out, because he had business of importance to transact at home, — yet have I seen him sauntering alone in the garden this half-hour. Miss Anville, on the other hand, I invited to walk out with me; and, after seeking her every where round the house, I find her quietly seated in the drawing-room. And, but a few minutes since, Sir Clement Willoughby, with even more than his usual politeness, told me he was come to spend the morning here, — when, just now, I met him flying down stairs, as if pursued by the Furies; and, far from repeating his compliments, or making any excuse, he did not even answer a question I asked him, but rushed past me, with the rapidity of a thief from a bailiff!"

"I protest," said Mrs. Beaumont, "I can't think what he meant; such rudeness from a man of any family is quite incomprehensible."

"My Lord," cried Lady Louisa to Lord Merton, "do you know he did the same by *me?* — I was just going to ask him what was the matter, but he ran past me so quick, that I declare he quite dazzled my eyes. You can't think, my Lord, how he frighted me; I dare say I look as pale — don't I look very pale, my Lord?"

"Your Ladyship," said Mr. Lovel, "so well becomes the lilies, that the roses might blush to see themselves so excelled."

"Pray, Mr. Lovel," said Mrs. Selwyn, "if the roses should blush, how would you find it out?"

"Egad," cried Mr. Coverley, "I suppose they must blush, as the saying is, like a blue dog,[2] — for they are *red* already."

"Prithee, Jack," said Lord Merton, "don't you pretend to talk about blushes, that never knew what they were in your life."

[2] *like a blue dog:* i.e., not blush.

"My Lord," said Mrs. Selwyn, "if experience alone can justify mentioning them, what an admirable treatise upon the subject may we not expect from your Lordship!"

"O, pray, Ma'am," answered he, "stick to Jack Coverley, — he's your only man; for my part, I confess I have a mortal aversion to arguments."

"O fie, my Lord," cried Mrs. Selwyn, "a senator of the nation! a member of the noblest parliament in the world! — and yet neglect the art of oratory?"

"Why, faith, my Lord," said Mr. Lovel, "I think, in general, your House is not much addicted to study; we of the lower House[3] have indubitably most application; and, if I did not speak before a superior power," (bowing low to Lord Merton) "I should presume to add, we have likewise the most able speakers."

"Mr. Lovel," said Mrs. Selwyn, "you deserve immortality for that discovery! But for this observation, and the confession of Lord Merton, I protest I should have supposed that a peer of the realm, and an able logician, were synonymous terms."

Lord Merton, turning upon his heel, asked Lady Louisa, if she should *take the air* before dinner?

"Really," answered she, "I don't know; — I'm afraid it's monstrous hot; besides," (putting her hand to her forehead) "I a'n't half well; it's quite horrid to have such weak nerves! — the least thing in the world discomposes me: I declare, that man's oddness has given me such a shock, — I don't know when I shall recover from it. But I'm a sad weak creature — don't you think I am, my Lord?"

"O, by no means," answered he, "your Ladyship is merely delicate, — and devil take me if ever I had the least passion for an Amazon."

"I have the honour to be quite of your Lordship's opinion," said Mr. Lovel, looking maliciously at Mrs. Selwyn, "for I have an insuperable aversion to strength, either of body or mind, in a female."

"Faith, and so have I," said Mr. Coverley; "for egad I'd as soon see a woman chop wood, as hear her chop logic."

"So would every man in his senses," said Lord Merton; "for a woman wants nothing to recommend her but beauty and good-nature; in every thing else she is either impertinent or unnatural. For

---

[3] *your House . . . we of the lower House:* Lord Merton's house of Parliament is the House of Lords; Lovel's is the House of Commons.

my part, deuce take me if ever I wish to hear a word of sense from a woman as long as I live!"

"It has always been agreed," said Mrs. Selwyn, looking round her with the utmost contempt, "that no man ought to be connected with a woman whose understanding is superior to his own. Now I very much fear, that to accommodate all this good company, according to such a rule, would be utterly impracticable unless we should chuse subjects from Swift's hospital of idiots."[4]

How many enemies, my dear Sir, does this unbounded severity excite! Lord Merton, however, only whistled; Mr. Coverley sang; and Mr. Lovel, after biting his lips some time, said, "'Pon honour, that lady — if she was *not* a lady, — I should be half tempted to observe, — that there is something, — in such severity, — that is rather, I must say, — rather — *oddish.*"

Just then, a servant brought Lady Louisa a note, upon a *waiter,*[5] which is a ceremony always used to her Ladyship; and I took the opportunity of this interruption to the conversation, to steal out of the room.

I went immediately to the parlour, which I found quite empty; for I did not dare walk in the garden after what Mrs. Selwyn had said.

In a few minutes, a servant announced Mr. Macartney, saying, as he entered the room, that he would acquaint Lord Orville he was there.

Mr. Macartney rejoiced much at finding me alone. He told me he had taken the liberty to enquire for Lord Orville, by way of pretext for coming to the house.

I then very eagerly enquired if he had seen his father.

"I have, Madam," said he; "and the generous compassion you have shewn made me hasten to acquaint you, that upon reading my unhappy mother's letter, he did not hesitate to acknowledge me."

"Good God," cried I, with no little emotion, "how similar are our circumstances! And did he receive you kindly?"

"I could not, Madam, expect that he would: the cruel transaction that obliged me to fly Paris, was too recent in his memory."

"And, — have you seen the young lady?"

"No, Madam," said he mournfully, "I was forbid her sight."

"Forbid her sight! — and why?"

---

[4] *Swift's hospital of idiots:* Jonathan Swift, satiric and political writer and dean of the Church of England, founded St. Patrick's hospital for "idiots" in Dublin in 1757.
[5] *waiter:* A serving tray.

"Partly, perhaps, from prudence, — and partly from the remains of a resentment which will not easily subside. I only requested leave to acquaint her with my relationship, and be allowed to call her sister; — but it was denied me! — *You have no sister,* said Sir John, *you must forget her existence.* Hard, and vain command!"

"You have, you have a sister!" cried I, from an impulse of pity which I could not repress, "a sister who is most warmly interested in all your concerns, and who only wants opportunity to manifest her friendship and regard."

"Gracious Heaven!" cried he, "what does Miss Anville mean?"

"Anville," said I, "is not my real name; Sir John Belmont is my father, — he is your's, — and I am your sister! — You see, therefore, the claim we mutually have to each other's regard; we are not merely bound by the ties of friendship, but by those of blood. I feel for you, already, all the affection of a sister, — I felt it, indeed, before I knew I was one. — Why, my dear brother, do you not speak? — do you hesitate to acknowledge me?"

"I am so lost in astonishment," cried he, "that I know not if I hear right!" —

"I have then found a brother," cried I, holding out my hand, "and he will not own me!"

"Own you! — Oh, Madam," cried he, accepting my offered hand, "is it, indeed, possible *you* can own *me?* — a poor, wretched adventurer! who so lately had no support but from your generosity? — whom your benevolence snatched from utter destruction? — Can *you,* — Oh Madam, can you indeed, and without a blush, condescend to own such an outcast for a brother?"

"Oh, forbear, forbear," cried I, "is this language proper for a sister? are we not reciprocally bound to each other? — Will you not suffer me to expect from *you* all the good offices in your power? — But tell me, where is our father at present?"

"At the Hotwell, Madam; he arrived there yesterday morning."

I would have proceeded with further questions, but the entrance of Lord Orville prevented me. The moment he saw us, he started, and would have retreated; but, drawing my hand from Mr. Macartney's, I begged him to come in.

For a few moments we were all silent, and, I believe, all in equal confusion. Mr. Macartney, however, recollecting himself, said, "I hope your Lordship will forgive the liberty I have taken in making use of your name?"

Lord Orville, rather coldly, bowed, but said nothing.

Again we were all silent, and then Mr. Macartney took leave.

"I fancy," said Lord Orville, when he was gone, "I have shortened Mr. Macartney's visit?"

"No, my Lord, not at all."

"I had presumed," said he, with some hesitation, "I should have seen Miss Anville in the garden; — but I knew not she was so much better engaged."

Before I could answer, a servant came to tell me the chaise was ready, and that Mrs. Selwyn was enquiring for me.

"I will wait on her immediately," cried I, and away I was running; but Lord Orville, stopping me, said, with great emotion, "Is it thus, Miss Anville, you leave me?"

"My Lord," cried I, "how can I help it? — perhaps, soon, some better opportunity may offer — "

"Good Heaven!" cried he, "do you indeed take me for a Stoic? What better opportunity may I hope for? — is not the chaise come? — are you not going? have you even deigned to tell me whither?"

"My journey, my Lord, will now be deferred. Mr. Macartney has brought me intelligence which renders it, at present, unnecessary."

"Mr. Macartney," said he, gravely, "seems to have great influence, — yet he is a very young counsellor."

"Is it possible, my Lord, Mr. Macartney can give you the least uneasiness?"

"My dearest Miss Anville," said he, taking my hand, "I see, and I adore the purity of your mind, superior as it is to all little arts, and all apprehensions of suspicion; and I should do myself, as well as you, injustice, if I were capable of harbouring the smallest doubts of that goodness which makes you mine for ever: nevertheless, pardon me, if I own myself surprised, — nay, alarmed, at these frequent meetings with so young a man as Mr. Macartney."

"My Lord," cried I, eager to clear myself, "Mr. Macartney is my brother!"

"Your brother! you amaze me! — What strange mystery, then, makes his relationship a secret?"

Just then, Mrs. Selwyn opened the door. "O, you are here!" cried she; "Pray is my Lord so kind as to assist you in *preparing* for your journey, — or in *retarding* it?"

"I should be most happy," said Lord Orville, smiling, "if it were in my power to do the *latter*."

I then acquainted her with Mr. Macartney's communication.

She immediately ordered the chaise away, and then took me into her own room, to consider what should be done.

A few minutes sufficed to determine her, and she wrote the following note.

### "To Sir John Belmont, Bart.

"Mrs. Selwyn presents her compliments to Sir John Belmont, and, if he is at leisure, will be glad to wait on him this morning, upon business of importance."

She then ordered her man to enquire at the pump-room for a direction, and went herself to Mrs. Beaumont to apologise for deferring her journey.

An answer was presently returned, that he would be glad to see her.

She would have had me immediately accompany her to the Hotwells; but I entreated her to spare me the distress of so abrupt an introduction, and to pave the way for my reception. She consented rather reluctantly, and, attended only by her servant, walked to the Wells.

She was not absent two hours, yet so miserably did time seem to linger, that I thought a thousand accidents had happened, and feared she would never return. I passed the whole time in my own room, for I was too much agitated even to converse with Lord Orville.

The instant that, from my window, I saw her returning, I flew down stairs, and met her in the garden.

We both walked to the arbour.

Her looks, in which disappointment and anger were expressed, presently announced to me the failure of her embassy. Finding that she did not speak, I asked her, in a faultering voice, Whether or not I had a father?

"You have *not*, my dear!" said she, abruptly.

"Very well, Madam," said I, with tolerable calmness, "let the chaise, then, be ordered again, — I will go to Berry Hill, — and there, I trust, I shall still find one!"

It was some time ere she could give, or I could hear, the account of her visit; and then she related it in a hasty manner; yet I believe I can recollect every word.

"I found Sir John alone. He received me with the utmost politeness. I did not keep him a moment in suspence as to the purport of my visit. But I had no sooner made it known, than, with a supercilious smile, he said, 'And have you, Madam, been prevailed upon to revive that ridiculous old story?' Ridiculous, I told him, was a term

which he would find no one else do him the favour to make use of, in
speaking of the horrible actions belonging to the *old story* he made so
light of; 'actions,' continued I, 'which would dye still deeper the black
annals of Nero or Caligula.'[6] He attempted in vain to rally, for I pursued him with all the severity in my power, and ceased not painting
the enormity of his crime, till I stung him to the quick, and, in a voice
of passion and impatience, he said, 'No more, Madam, — this is not
a subject upon which I need a monitor.' 'Make, then,' cried I, 'the
only reparation in your power. — Your daughter is now at Clifton;
send for her hither, and, in the face of the world, proclaim the legiti-
macy of her birth, and clear the reputation of your injured wife.'
'Madam,' said he, 'you are much mistaken, if you suppose I waited
for the honour of this visit, before I did what little justice now depends upon me, to the memory of that unfortunate woman: her
daughter has been my care from her infancy; I have taken her into my
house; she bears my name, and she will be my sole heiress.' For some
time this assertion appeared so absurd, that I only laughed at it; but
at last, he assured me, I had myself been imposed upon, for that the
very woman who attended Lady Belmont in her last illness conveyed
the child to him while he was in London, before she was a year old.
'Unwilling,' he added, 'at that time to confirm the rumour of my
being married, I sent the woman with the child to France; as soon as
she was old enough, I put her into a convent, where she has been
properly educated; and now I have taken her home, I have acknowledged her for my lawful child, and paid, at length, to the memory of
her unhappy mother, a tribute of fame which has made me wish to
hide myself hereafter from all the world.' This whole story sounded
so improbable, that I did not scruple to tell him I discredited every
word. He then rung his bell, and enquiring if his hair-dresser was
come, said he was sorry to leave me, but that, if I would favour him
with my company to-morrow, he would do himself the honour of introducing Miss Belmont to *me,* instead of troubling me to introduce
her to *him.* I rose in great indignation, and, assuring him I would
make his conduct as public as it was infamous, I left the house."

Good Heaven, how strange a recital! how incomprehensible an affair! The Miss Belmont, then, who is actually at Bristol, passes for the
daughter of my unhappy mother! — passes, in short, for your Evelina!
Who she can be, or what this tale can mean, I have not any idea.

---

[6] *Nero or Caligula:* Roman emperors noted for the cruelty of their crimes against
the weaker.

Mrs. Selwyn soon after left me to my own reflections. Indeed they were not very pleasant. Quietly as I had borne her relation, the moment I was alone I felt most bitterly both the disgrace and the sorrow of a rejection so cruelly inexplicable.

I know not how long I might have continued in this situation, had I not been awakened from my melancholy reverie by the voice of Lord Orville. "May I come in," cried he, "or shall I interrupt you?"

I was silent, and he seated himself next me.

"I fear," he continued, "Miss Anville will think I persecute her; yet so much as I have to say, and so much as I wish to hear, with so few opportunities for either, she cannot wonder, — and I hope she will not be offended, — that I seize with such avidity every moment in my power to converse with her. You are grave," added he, taking my hand; "I hope you do not regret the delay of your journey? — I hope the pleasure it gives to *me* will not be a subject of pain to *you?* — You are silent? — Something, I am sure, has afflicted you: — Would to Heaven I were able to console you! — Would to Heaven I were worthy to participate in your sorrows!"

My heart was too full to bear this kindness, and I could only answer by my tears. "Good Heaven," cried he, "how you alarm me! — My love, my sweet Miss Anville, deny me no longer to be the sharer of your griefs! — tell me, at least, that you have not withdrawn your esteem! — that you do not repent the goodness you have shewn me! — that you still think me the same grateful Orville whose heart you have deigned to accept!"

"Oh, my Lord," cried I, "your generosity overpowers me!" And I wept like an infant. For now that all my hopes of being acknowledged seemed finally crushed, I felt the nobleness of his disinterested attachment so forcibly, that I could scarce breathe under the weight of gratitude that oppressed me.

He seemed greatly shocked, and in terms the most flattering, the most respectfully tender, he at once soothed my distress, and urged me to tell him its cause.

"My Lord," said I, when I was able to speak, "you little know what an outcast you have honoured with your choice! — a child of bounty, — an orphan from infancy, — dependent, even for subsistence dependent, upon the kindness of compassion! — Rejected by my natural friends, — disowned for ever by my nearest relation, — Oh, my Lord, so circumstanced, can I deserve the distinction with which you honour me? No, no, I feel the inequality too painfully; — you must leave me, my Lord, you must suffer me to return to obscurity, —

and there, in the bosom of my first, best, — my only friend, — I will pour forth all the grief of my heart! — while you, my Lord, must seek elsewhere — "

I could not proceed; my whole soul recoiled against the charge I would have given, and my voice refused to utter it.

"Never!" cried he, warmly; "my heart is yours, and I swear to you an attachment eternal! — You prepare me, indeed, for a tale of horror, and I am almost breathless with expectation, — but so firm is my conviction, that, whatever are your misfortunes, to have merited them is not of the number, that I feel myself more strongly, more invincibly attached to you than ever! — Tell me but where I may find this noble friend, whose virtues you have already taught me to reverence, — and I will fly to obtain his consent and intercession, that henceforward our fates may be indissolubly united, — and then shall it be the sole study of my life to endeavour to soften your past, — and guard you from future misfortunes!"

I had just raised my eyes, to answer this most generous of men, when the first object they met was Mrs. Selwyn!

"So, my dear," cried she, "what, still courting the rural shades! — I thought ere now you would have been satiated with this retired seat, and I have been seeking you all over the house. But I now see the only way to meet with *you*, — is to enquire for *Lord Orville*. However, don't let me disturb your meditations; you are possibly planning some pastoral dialogue."

And, with this provoking speech, she walked on.

In the greatest confusion, I was quitting the arbour, when Lord Orville said, "Permit *me* to follow Mrs. Selwyn, — it is time to put an end to all impertinent conjectures; will you allow me to speak to her openly?"

I assented in silence, and he left me.

I then went to my own room, where I continued till I was summoned to dinner; after which, Mrs. Selwyn invited me to her's.

The moment she had shut the door, "Your Ladyship," said she, "will, I hope, be seated."

"Ma'am!" cried I, staring.

"O the sweet innocent! So you don't know what I mean? — but, my dear, my sole view is to accustom you a little to your dignity elect, lest, when you are addressed by your title, you should look another way, from an apprehension of listening to a discourse not meant for you to hear."

Having, in this manner, diverted herself with my confusion, till her raillery was almost exhausted, she congratulated me very seriously upon the attachment of Lord Orville, and painted to me, in the strongest terms, his disinterested desire of being married to me immediately. She had told him, she said, my whole story; and yet he was willing, nay eager, that our union should take place of any further application to my family. "Now, my dear," continued she, "I advise you by all means to marry him directly; nothing can be more precarious than our success with Sir John; and the young men of this age are not to be trusted with too much time for deliberation, where their interests are concerned."

"Good God, Madam," cried I, "do you think I would *hurry* Lord Orville?"

"Well, do as you will," said she; "luckily you have an excellent subject for Quixotism;[7] — otherwise, this delay might prove your ruin: but Lord Orville is almost as romantic as if he had been born and bred at Berry Hill."

She then proposed, as no better expedient seemed likely to be suggested, that I should accompany her at once in her visit to the Hotwells to-morrow morning.

The very idea made me tremble; yet she represented so strongly the necessity of pursuing this unhappy affair with spirit, or giving it totally up, that, wanting her force of argument, I was almost obliged to yield to her proposal.

In the evening, we all walked in the garden: and Lord Orville, who never quitted my side, told me he had been listening to a tale, which, though it had removed the perplexities that had so long tormented him, had penetrated him with sorrow and compassion. I acquainted him with Mrs. Selwyn's plan for to-morrow, and confessed the extreme terror it gave me. He then, in a manner almost unanswerable, besought me to leave to him the conduct of the affair, by consenting to be his before an interview took place.

I could not but acknowledge my sense of his generosity; but I told him I was wholly dependent upon you, and that I was certain your opinion would be the same as mine, which was, that it would be highly improper I should dispose of myself for ever, so very near the time which must finally decide by whose authority I ought to be

[7] *Quixotism:* The allusion is to Cervantes's *Don Quixote* (1605, 1615); Quixotism had, by the eighteenth century, become a byword for an innocent, even blind idealism.

guided. The subject of this dreaded meeting, with the thousand conjectures and apprehensions to which it gives birth, employed all our conversation then, as it has all my thoughts since.

Heaven only knows how I shall support myself, when the long-expected, — the wished, — yet terrible moment arrives, that will prostrate me at the feet of the nearest, the most reverenced of all relations, whom my heart yearns to know, and longs to love!


## LETTER XVII

### Evelina in Continuation

Oct. 9.

I could not write yesterday, so violent was the agitation of my mind, — but I will not, now, lose a moment till I have hastened to my best friend an account of the transactions of a day I can never recollect without emotion.

Mrs. Selwyn determined upon sending no message, "Lest," said she, "Sir John, fatigued with the very idea of my reproaches, should endeavour to avoid a meeting: all we have to do, is to take him by surprise. He cannot but see who you are, whether he will do you justice or not."

We went early, and in Mrs. Beaumont's chariot; into which, Lord Orville, uttering words of the kindest encouragement, handed us both.

My uneasiness, during the ride, was excessive, but, when we stopped at the door, I was almost senseless with terror! the meeting at last, was not so dreadful as that moment! I believe I was carried into the house; but I scarce recollect what was done with me: however, I know we remained some time in the parlour, ere Mrs. Selwyn could send any message up stairs.

When I was somewhat recovered, I entreated her to let me return home, assuring her I felt myself quite unequal to supporting the interview.

"No," said she, "you must stay now; your fears will but gain strength by delay, and we must not have such a shock as this repeated." Then, turning to the servant, she sent up her name.

An answer was brought, that he was going out in great haste, but would attend her immediately. I turned so sick, that Mrs. Selwyn was apprehensive I should have fainted; and opening a door which led to an inner apartment, she begged me to wait there till I was somewhat composed, and till she had prepared for my reception.

Glad of every moment's reprieve, I willingly agreed to the proposal, and Mrs. Selwyn had but just time to shut me in, ere her presence was necessary.

The voice of a *father* — Oh dear and revered name! — which then, for the first time, struck my ears, affected me in a manner I cannot describe, though it was only employed to give orders to a servant as he came down stairs.

Then, entering the parlour, I heard him say, "I am sorry, Madam, I made you wait, but I have an engagement which now calls me away: however, if you have any commands for me, I shall be glad of the honour of your company some other time."

"I am come, Sir," answered Mrs. Selwyn, "to introduce to you your daughter."

"I am infinitely obliged to you," answered he, "but I have just had the satisfaction of breakfasting with her. Ma'am, your most obedient."

"You refuse, then, to see her?"

"I am much indebted to you, Madam, for this desire of encreasing my family, but you must excuse me if I decline taking advantage of it. I have already a daughter, to whom I owe every thing; and it is not three days since, that I had the pleasure of discovering a son; how many more sons and daughters may be brought to me, I am yet to learn, but I am, already, perfectly satisfied with the size of my family."

"Had you a thousand children, Sir John," said Mrs. Selwyn, warmly, "this only one, of which Lady Belmont was the mother, ought to be most distinguished; and, far from avoiding her sight, you should thank your stars, in humble gratitude, that there yet remains in your power the smallest opportunity of doing the injured wife you have destroyed, the poor justice of acknowledging her child!"

"I am very unwilling, Madam," answered he, "to enter into any discussion of this point; but you are determined to compel me to speak. There lives not, at this time, the human being who should talk to *me* of the regret due to the memory of that ill-fated woman; no one can feel it so severely as myself: but let me, nevertheless, assure you I have already done all that remained in my power to prove the respect she merited from me; her child I have educated, and owned for my lawful heiress; if, Madam, you can suggest to me any other means by which I may more fully do her justice, and more clearly manifest her innocence, name them to me, and though they should wound my character still deeper, I will perform them readily."

"All this sounds vastly well," returned Mrs. Selwyn, "but I must own it is rather too enigmatical for *my* faculties of comprehension. You can, however, have no objection to seeing this young lady?"

"None in the world."

"Come forth, then, my dear," cried she, opening the door, "come forth, and see your father!" Then, taking my trembling hand, she led me forward. I would have withdrawn it, and retreated, but as he advanced instantly towards me, I found myself already before him.

What a moment for your Evelina! — an involuntary scream escaped me, and covering my face with my hands, I sunk on the floor.

He had, however, seen me first; for in a voice scarce articulate he exclaimed, "My God! does Caroline Evelyn still live!"

Mrs. Selwyn said something, but I could not listen to her; and, in a few minutes, he added, "Lift up thy head, — if my sight has not blasted thee, — lift up thy head, thou image of my long-lost Caroline!"

Affected beyond measure, I half arose, and embraced his knees, while yet on my own.

"Yes, yes," cried he, looking earnestly in my face, "I see, I see thou art her child! she lives — she breathes — she is present to my view! — Oh God, that she indeed lived! — Go, child, go," added he, wildly starting, and pushing me from him, "take her away, Madam, — I cannot bear to look at her!" And then, breaking hastily from me, he rushed out of the room.

Speechless, motionless myself, I attempted not to stop him: but Mrs. Selwyn, hastening after him, caught hold of his arm. "Leave me, Madam," cried he, with quickness, "and take care of the poor child; — bid her not think me unkind, — tell her I would at this moment plunge a dagger in my heart to serve her, — but she has set my brain on fire, and I can see her no more!" Then, with violence almost frantic, he ran up stairs.

Oh Sir, had I not indeed cause to dread this interview? — an interview so unspeakably painful and afflicting to us both! Mrs. Selwyn would have immediately returned to Clifton; but I entreated her to wait some time, in the hope that my unhappy father, when his first emotion was over, would again bear me in his sight. However, he soon after sent his servant to enquire how I did, and to tell Mrs. Selwyn he was much indisposed, but would hope for the honour of seeing her to-morrow, at any time she would please to appoint.

She fixed upon ten o'clock in the morning, and then, with a heavy heart, I got into the chariot. Those afflicting words, *I can see her no more* were never a moment absent from my mind.

Yet the sight of Lord Orville, who handed us from the carriage, gave some relief to the sadness of my thoughts. I could not, however, enter upon the painful subject, but begging Mrs. Selwyn to satisfy him, I went to my own room.

As soon as I communicated to the good Mrs. Clinton the present situation of my affairs, an idea occurred to her, which seemed to clear up all the mystery of my having been so long disowned.

The woman, she says, who attended my ever-to-be-regretted mother in her last illness, and who nursed me the first four months of my life, soon after being discharged from your house, left Berry Hill entirely, with her baby, who was but six weeks older than myself. Mrs. Clinton remembers, that her quitting the place appeared, at the time, very extraordinary to the neighbours, but, as she was never heard of afterwards, she was, by degrees, quite forgotten.

The moment this was mentioned, it struck Mrs. Selwyn, as well as Mrs. Clinton herself, that my father had been imposed upon, and that the nurse who said she had brought his child to him, had, in fact, carried her own.

The name by which I was known, the secrecy observed in regard to my family, and the retirement in which I lived, all conspired to render this scheme, however daring and fraudulent, by no means impracticable, and, in short, the idea was no sooner started, than conviction seemed to follow it.

Mrs. Selwyn determined immediately to discover the truth or mistake of this conjecture; therefore, the moment she had dined, she walked to the Hotwells, attended by Mrs. Clinton.

I waited in my room till her return, and then heard the following account of her visit.

She found my poor father in great agitation. She immediately informed him of the occasion of her so speedy return, and of her suspicions of the woman who had pretended to convey to him his child. Interrupting her with quickness, he said he had just sent her from his presence: that the certainty I carried in my countenance, of my real birth, made him, the moment he had recovered from a surprise which had almost deprived him of reason, suspect, himself, the imposition she mentioned. He had, therefore, sent for the woman, and questioned her with the utmost austerity: she turned pale, and was extremely embarrassed, but still she persisted in affirming, that she had really brought him the daughter of Lady Belmont. His perplexity, he said, almost distracted him; he had *always* observed that his daughter bore no resemblance of either of her parents, but, as he had never doubted the veracity of the nurse, this circumstance did not give birth to any suspicion.

At Mrs. Selwyn's desire, the woman was again called, and interrogated with equal art and severity; her confusion was evident, and her answers often contradictory, yet she still declared she was no impostor. "We will see that in a minute," said Mrs. Selwyn, and then desired Mrs. Clinton might be called up stairs. The poor wretch, changing colour, would have escaped out of the room, but, being prevented, dropt on her knees, and implored forgiveness. A confession of the whole affair was then extorted from her.

Doubtless, my dear Sir, you must remember *Dame Green*, who was my first nurse? The deceit she has practised, was suggested, she says, by a conversation she overheard, in which my unhappy mother besought you, that, if her child survived her, you would take the sole care of its education; and, in particular, if it should be a female, you would by no means part with her early in life. You not only consented, she says, but assured her you would even retire abroad with me yourself, if my father should importunately demand me. Her own child, she said, was then in her arms, and she could not forbear wishing it were possible to give *her* the fortune which seemed so little valued for me. This wish once raised, was not easily suppressed; on the contrary, what at first appeared a mere idle desire, in a short time seemed a feasible scheme. Her husband was dead, and she had little regard for any body but her child; and, in short, having saved money for the journey, she contrived to enquire a direction to my father, and, telling her neighbours she was going to settle in Devonshire, she set out on her expedition.

When Mrs. Selwyn asked her, how she dared perpetrate such a fraud, she protested she had no ill designs, but that, as *Miss* would be never the worse for it, she thought it pity *nobody* should be the better.

Her success we are already acquainted with. Indeed every thing seemed to contribute towards it: my father had no correspondent at Berry Hill, the child was instantly sent to France, where being brought up in as much retirement as myself, nothing but accident could discover the fraud.

And here, let me indulge myself in observing, and rejoicing to observe, that the total neglect I thought I met with, was not the effect of insensibility or unkindness, but of imposition and error; and that, at the very time we concluded I was unnaturally rejected, my deluded father meant to shew me most favour and protection.

He acknowledges that Lady Howard's letter flung him into some perplexity; he immediately communicated it to Dame Green, who confessed it was the greatest shock she had ever received in her life; yet she had the art and boldness to assert, that Lady Howard must herself have been deceived: and as she had, from the beginning of her enterprize, declared she had stolen away the child without your knowledge, he concluded that some deceit was *then* intended him; and this thought occasioned his abrupt answer.

Dame Green owned, that from the moment the journey to England was settled, she gave herself up for lost. All her hope was to have had her daughter married before it took place, for which reason she had so much promoted Mr. Macartney's addresses: for though such a match was inadequate to the pretensions of *Miss Belmont,* she well knew it was far superior to those *her daughter* could form, after the discovery of her birth.

My first enquiry was, if this innocent daughter was yet acquainted with the affair? No, Mrs. Selwyn said, nor was any plan settled how to divulge it to her. Poor unfortunate girl! how hard is her fate! She is entitled to my kindest offices, and I shall always consider her as my sister.

I then asked whether my father would again allow me to see him?

"Why no, my dear, not yet," answered she; "he declares the sight of you is too much for him: however, we are to settle every thing concerning you to-morrow, for this woman took up all our time to-day."

This morning, therefore, she is again gone to the Hotwell. I am waiting in all impatience for her return; but as I know you will be anxious for the account this letter contains, I will not delay sending it.

## LETTER XVIII

### Evelina in Continuation

Oct. 9.

How agitated, my dear Sir, is the present life of your Evelina! every day seems important, and one event only a prelude to another.

Mrs. Selwyn, upon her return this morning from the Hotwell, entering my room very abruptly, said, "Oh my dear, I have terrible news for you!"

"For me, Ma'am! — Good God! what now?"

"Arm yourself," cried she, "with all your Berry Hill philosophy; — con over every lesson of fortitude or resignation you ever learnt in your life — for know, — you are next week to be married to Lord Orville!"

Doubt, astonishment, and a kind of perturbation I cannot describe, made this abrupt communication alarm me extremely, and, almost breathless, I could only exclaim, "Good God, Madam, what do you tell me?"

"You may well be frightened, my dear," said she, ironically, "for really there is something mighty terrific, in becoming, at once, the wife of the man you adore, — and a Countess!"

I entreated her to spare her raillery, and tell me her real meaning. She could not prevail with herself to grant the *first* request, though she readily complied with the second.

My poor father, she said, was still in the utmost uneasiness. He entered upon his affairs with great openness, and told her he was equally disturbed how to dispose either of the daughter he had discovered, or the daughter he was now to give up: the former he dreaded to trust himself with again beholding, and the latter he knew not how to shock with the intelligence of her disgrace. Mrs. Selwyn then acquainted him with my situation in regard to Lord Orville; this delighted him extremely, and, when he heard of his Lordship's eagerness, he said he was himself of opinion, the sooner the union took place the better: and, in return, he informed her of the affair of Mr. Macartney. "And, after a very long conversation," continued Mrs. Selwyn, "we agreed, that the most eligible scheme for all parties, would be to have both the real and the fictitious daughter married without delay. Therefore, if either of you have any inclination to pull caps for the title of Miss Belmont, you must do it with all speed, as next week will take from both of you all pretensions to it."

"Next week! — dear Madam, what a strange plan! — without my being consulted — without applying to Mr. Villars, — without even the concurrence of Lord Orville!"

"As to consulting *you*, my dear, it was out of all question, because, you know, young ladies hearts and hands are always to be given with reluctance; — as to Mr. Villars, it is sufficient we know him for your friend; — and as for Lord Orville, he is a party concerned."

"A party concerned! — you amaze me!"

"Why, yes; for as I found our consultation likely to redound to his advantage, I persuaded Sir John to send for him."

"Send for him! — Good God!"

"Yes, and Sir John agreed. I told the servant, that if he could not hear of his Lordship in the house, he might be pretty certain of encountering him in the arbour. — Why do you colour, my dear? — Well, he was with us in a moment; I introduced him to Sir John, and we proceeded to business."

"I am very, very sorry for it! — Lord Orville must, himself, think this conduct strangely precipitate."

"No, my dear, you are mistaken, Lord Orville has too much good sense. Every thing was then discussed in a rational manner. You are to be married privately, tho' not secretly, and then go to one of his Lordship's country seats: and poor little Miss Green and your brother, who have no house of their own, must go to one of Sir John's."

"But why, my dear Madam, why all this haste? why may we not be allowed a little longer time?"

"I could give you a thousand reasons," answered she, "but that I am tolerably certain *two* or *three* will be more than you can controvert, even with all the logic of genuine coquetry. In the first place, you doubtless wish to quit the house of Mrs. Beaumont, — to whose, then, can you with such propriety remove, as to Lord Orville's?"

"Surely, Madam," cried I, "I am not more destitute now, than when I thought myself an orphan?"

"Your father, my dear," answered she, "is willing to save the little impostor as much of the mortification of her disgrace as is in his power: now if you immediately take her place, according to your right, as Miss Belmont, why not all that either of you can do for her, will prevent her being eternally stigmatized, as the bantling[1] of Dame Green, wash-woman and wet nurse of Berry Hill, Dorsetshire. Now such a genealogy will not be very flattering, even to Mr. Macartney, who, all-dismal as he is, you will find by no means wanting in pride and self-consequence."

"For the universe," interrupted I, "I would not be accessary to the degradation you mention; but, surely, Madam, I may return to Berry Hill."

"By no means," said she; "for though compassion may make us wish to save the poor girl the confusion of an immediate and public fall, yet justice demands you should appear, henceforward, in no other light than that of Sir John Belmont's daughter. Besides, between

---

[1] *bantling*: An infant, although the word also carried connotations of illegitimate birth.

friends, I, who know the world, can see that half this prodigious delicacy for the little usurper, is the mere result of self-interest; for while
*her* affairs are husht up, Sir John's, you know, are kept from being
brought further to light. Now the double marriage we have projected,
obviates all rational objections. Sir John will give you, immediately,
£30,000; all settlements, and so forth, will be made for you in the
name of Evelina Belmont; — Mr. Macartney will, at the same time,
take poor Polly Green, — and yet, at first, it will only be generally
known, that *a daughter of Sir John Belmont's* is married."

In this manner, though she did not convince me, yet the quickness
of her arguments silenced and perplexed me. I enquired, however, if I
might not be permitted to again see my father, or whether I must regard myself as banished his presence for ever?

"My dear," said she, "he does not know you; he concludes that
you have been brought up to detest him, and therefore he is rather
prepared to dread, than to love you."

This answer made me very unhappy; I wished, most impatiently,
to remove his prejudice, and endeavour, by dutiful assiduity, to engage his kindness, yet knew not how to propose seeing him, while
conscious he wished to avoid me.

This evening, as soon as the company was engaged with cards,
Lord Orville exerted his utmost eloquence to reconcile me to this
hasty plan: but how was I startled, when he told me that next *Tuesday* was the day appointed by my father to be the most important of
my life!

"Next Tuesday!" repeated I, quite out of breath, "Oh my Lord! — "

"My sweet Evelina," said he, "the day which will make me the happiest of mortals, would probably appear awful to you, were it to be deferred a twelvemonth: Mrs. Selwyn has, doubtless, acquainted you
with the many motives which, independent of my eagerness, require it
to be speedy; suffer, therefore, its acceleration, and generously complete my felicity, by endeavouring to suffer it without repugnance."

"Indeed, my Lord, I would not wilfully raise objections, nor do I
desire to appear insensible of the honour of your good opinion; —
but there is something in this plan, so very hasty, — so unreasonably
precipitate, — besides, I shall have no time to hear from Berry Hill, —
and believe me, my Lord, I should be for ever miserable, were I, in
an affair so important, to act without the sanction of Mr. Villars'
advice."

He offered to wait on you himself; but I told him I had rather
write to you. And then he proposed, that, instead of my immediately

accompanying him to Lincolnshire, we should, first, pass a month at *my native Berry Hill.*

This was, indeed, a grateful proposal to me, and I listened to it with undisguised pleasure. And, — in short, I was obliged to consent to a compromise, in merely deferring the day till Thursday! He readily undertook to engage my father's concurrence in this little delay, and I besought him, at the same time, to make use of his influence to obtain me a second interview, and to represent the deep concern I felt in being thus banished his sight.

He would then have spoken of *settlements,*[2] but I assured him, I was almost ignorant even of the word.

And now, my dearest Sir, what is your opinion of these hasty proceedings? believe me, I half regret the simple facility with which I have suffered myself to be hurried into compliance, and, should you start but the smallest objection, I will yet insist upon being allowed more time.

I must now write a concise account of the state of my affairs to Howard Grove, and to Madame Duval.

Adieu, dearest and most honoured Sir! every thing, at present, depends upon your single decision, to which, though I yield in trembling, I yield implicitly.

[2] *settlements:* It was common among monied families to draw up premarriage legal agreements stipulating the wife's independent income, or pin money, and what portion of the estate should be hers upon her husband's death. These agreements were all the more desirable from the wife's point of view since under English law the husband automatically owned whatever income or capital his wife brought into the marriage.


## LETTER XIX

### Evelina in Continuation

October 11.

Yesterday morning, as soon as breakfast was over, Lord Orville went to the Hotwells, to wait upon my father with my double petition.

Mrs. Beaumont then, in general terms, proposed a walk in the garden. Mrs. Selwyn said she had letters to write, but Lady Louisa arose to accompany her.

I had had some reason to imagine, from the notice with which her Ladyship had honoured me during breakfast, that her brother had acquainted her with my present situation: and her behaviour now confirmed my conjecture; for, when I would have gone up stairs, instead of suffering me, as usual, to pass disregarded, she called after me, with an affected surprise, "Miss Anville, don't you walk with us?"

There seemed something so little-minded in this sudden change of conduct, that, from an involuntary emotion of contempt, I thanked her, with a coldness like her own, and declined her offer. Yet, observing that she blushed extremely at my refusal, and recollecting she was sister to Lord Orville, my indignation subsided, and upon Mrs. Beaumont's repeating the invitation, I accepted it.

Our walk proved extremely dull; Mrs. Beaumont, who never says much, was more silent than usual; Lady Louisa strove in vain to lay aside the restraint and distance she has hitherto preserved; and as to me, I was too conscious of the circumstances to which I owed their attention, to feel either pride or pleasure from receiving it.

Lord Orville was not long absent; he joined us in the garden, with a look of gaiety and good-humour that revived us all. "You are just the party," said he, "I wished to see together. Will you, Madam," taking my hand, "allow me the honour of introducing you, by your real name, to two of my nearest relations? Mrs. Beaumont, give me leave to present to you the daughter of Sir John Belmont; a young lady who, I am sure, must long since have engaged your esteem and admiration, tho' you were a stranger to her birth."

"My Lord," said Mrs. Beaumont, graciously saluting me,[1] "the young lady's rank in life, — your Lordship's recommendation, — or her own merit, would any one of them have been sufficient to have entitled her to my regard; and I hope she has always met with that respect in my house which is so much her due; though, had I been sooner made acquainted with her family, I should, doubtless, have better known how to have secured it."

"Miss Belmont," said Lord Orville, "can receive no lustre from family, whatever she may give to it. Louisa, you will, I am sure, be happy to make yourself an interest in the friendship of Miss Belmont, whom I hope shortly," kissing my hand, and joining it with her Ladyship's, "to have the happiness of presenting to you by yet another name, and by the most endearing of all titles."

I believe it would be difficult to say whose cheeks were, at that moment, of the deepest dye, Lady Louisa's or my own; for the conscious pride with which she has hitherto slighted me, gave to her an

---

[1] *saluting me:* A formal kiss of greeting.

embarrassment which equalled the confusion that an introduction so unexpected gave to me. She saluted me, however, and, with a faint smile, said, "I shall esteem myself very happy to profit by the honour of Miss Belmont's acquaintance."

I only courtsied, and we walked on; but it was evident, from the little surprise they expressed, that they had been already informed of the state of the affair.

We were, soon after, joined by more company: and Lord Orville then, in a low voice, took an opportunity to tell me the success of his visit. In the first place, Thursday was agreed to; and, in the second, my father, he said, was much concerned to hear of my uneasiness, sent me his blessing, and complied with my request of seeing him, with the same readiness he should agree to any other I could make. Lord Orville, therefore, settled that I should wait upon him in the evening, and, at his particular request, unaccompanied by Mrs. Selwyn.

This kind message, and the prospect of so soon seeing him, gave me sensations of mixed pleasure and pain, which wholly occupied my mind till the time of my going to the Hotwells.

Mrs. Beaumont lent me her chariot, and Lord Orville absolutely insisted upon attending me. "If you go alone," said he, "Mrs. Selwyn will certainly be offended; but, if you allow me to conduct you, tho' she may give the freer scope to her raillery, she cannot possibly be affronted; and we had much better suffer her laughter, than provoke her satire."

Indeed, I must own I had no reason to regret being so accompanied; for his conversation supported my spirits from drooping, and made the ride seem so short, that we actually stopt at my father's door, ere I knew we had proceeded ten yards.

He handed me from the carriage, and conducted me to the parlour, at the door of which I was met by Mr. Macartney. "Ah, my dear brother," cried I, "how happy am I to see you here!"

He bowed and thanked me. Lord Orville, then, holding out his hand, said, "Mr. Macartney, I hope we shall be better acquainted; I promise myself much pleasure from cultivating your friendship."

"Your Lordship does me but too much honour," answered Mr. Macartney.

"But where," cried I, "is my sister? for so I must already call, and always consider her: — I am afraid she avoids me; — you must endeavour, my dear brother, to prepossess her in my favour, and reconcile her to owning me."

"Oh, Madam," cried he, "you are all goodness and benevolence! but at present, I hope you will excuse her, for I fear she has hardly fortitude sufficient to see you: in a short time, perhaps — "

"In a *very* short time, then," said Lord Orville, "I hope you will yourself introduce her, and that we shall have the pleasure of wishing you both joy: allow me, my Evelina, to say *we,* and permit me, in your name as well as my own, to entreat that the first guests we shall have the happiness of receiving, may be Mr. and Mrs. Macartney."

A servant then came to beg I would walk up stairs.

I besought Lord Orville to accompany me; but he feared the displeasure of Sir John, who had desired to see me alone. He led me, however, to the head of the stairs, and made the kindest efforts to give me courage; but indeed he did not succeed, for the interview appeared to me in all its terrors, and left me no feeling but apprehension.

The moment I reached the landing-place, the drawing-room door was opened, and my father, with a voice of kindness, called out, "My child, is it you?"

"Yes, Sir," cried I, springing forward, and kneeling at his feet, "it is your child, if you will own her!"

He knelt by my side, and folding me in his arms, "Own thee!" repeated he, "yes, my poor girl, and Heaven knows with what bitter contrition!" Then, raising both himself and me, he brought me into the drawing-room, shut the door, and took me to the window, where, looking at me with great earnestness, "Poor unhappy Caroline!" cried he, and, to my inexpressible concern, he burst into tears. Need I tell you, my dear Sir, how mine flowed at the sight?

I would again have embraced his knees; but, hurrying from me, he flung himself upon a sopha, and leaning his face on his arms, seemed, for some time, absorbed in bitterness of grief.

I ventured not to interrupt a sorrow I so much respected, but waited in silence, and at a distance, till he recovered from its violence. But then it seemed, in a moment, to give way to a kind of frantic fury; for, starting suddenly, with a sternness which at once surprised and frightened me, "Child," cried he, "hast thou yet sufficiently humbled thy father? — if thou hast, be contented with this proof of my weakness, and no longer force thyself into my presence!"

Thunderstruck by a command so unexpected, I stood still and speechless, and doubted whether my own ears did not deceive me.

"Oh, go, go!" cried he, passionately, "in pity — in compassion, — if thou valuest my senses, leave me, — and for ever!"

"I will, I will!" cried I, greatly terrified; and I moved hastily towards the door: yet stopping when I reached it, and, almost involuntarily, dropping on my knees, "Vouchsafe," cried I, "oh, Sir, vouchsafe but once to bless your daughter, and her sight shall never more offend you!"

"Alas," cried he, in a softened voice, "I am not worthy to bless thee! — I am not worthy to call thee daughter! — I am not worthy that the fair light of heaven should visit my eyes! — Oh God! that I could but call back the time ere thou wast born, — or else bury its remembrance in eternal oblivion!"

"Would to Heaven," cried I, "that the sight of me were less terrible to you! that, instead of irritating, I could soothe your sorrows! — Oh Sir, how thankfully would I then prove my duty, even at the hazard of my life!"

"Are you so kind?" cried he, gently; "come hither, child, — rise, Evelina; — alas, it is for *me* to kneel, not you! — and I *would* kneel, — I would crawl upon the earth, — I would kiss the dust, — could I, by such submission, obtain the forgiveness of the representative of the most injured of women!"

"Oh, Sir," exclaimed I, "that you could but read my heart! — that you could but see the filial tenderness and concern with which it overflows! — you would not then talk thus, — you would not then banish me your presence, and exclude me from your affection!"

"Good God," cried he, "is it then possible that you do not hate me? — Can the child of the wronged Caroline look at, — and not execrate me? Wast thou not born to abhor, and bred to curse me? did not thy mother bequeath thee her blessing, on condition that thou shouldst detest and avoid me?"

"Oh no, no, no!" cried I, "think not so unkindly of her, nor so hardly of me." I then took from my pocket-book her last letter, and, pressing it to my lips, with a trembling hand, and still upon my knees, I held it out to him.

Hastily snatching it from me, "Great Heaven!" cried he, " 'tis her writing! — Whence comes this? — who gave it you? — why had I it not sooner?"

I made no answer; his vehemence intimidated me, and I ventured not to move from the suppliant posture in which I had put myself.

He went from me to the window, where his eyes were for some time rivetted upon the direction of the letter, though his hand shook so violently he could hardly hold it. Then, bringing it to me, "Open it," — cried he, — "for I cannot!"

I had, myself, hardly strength to obey him; but, when I had, he took it back, and walked hastily up and down the room, as if dreading to read it. At length, turning to me, "Do you know," cried he, "its contents?"

"No, Sir," answered I; "it has never been unsealed."

He then again went to the window, and began reading. Having hastily run it over, he cast up his eyes with a look of desperation; the letter fell from his hand, and he exclaimed, "Yes! thou art sainted! — thou art blessed! — and I am cursed for ever!" He continued some time fixed in this melancholy position; after which, casting himself with violence upon the ground, "Oh wretch," cried he, "unworthy of life and light, in what dungeon canst thou hide thy head?"

I could restrain myself no longer; I rose and went to him; I did not dare speak, but with pity and concern unutterable, I wept and hung over him.

Soon after, starting up, he again seized the letter, exclaiming, "Acknowledge thee, Caroline! — yes, with my heart's best blood would I acknowledge thee! — Oh that thou couldst witness the agony of my soul! — Ten thousand daggers could not have wounded me like this letter!"

Then, after again reading it, "Evelina," he cried, "she charges me to receive thee; — wilt thou, in obedience to her will, own for thy father the destroyer of thy mother?"

What a dreadful question! I shuddered, but could not speak.

"To clear her fame, and receive her child," continued he, looking stedfastly at the letter, "are the conditions upon which she leaves me her forgiveness: her fame, I have already cleared; — and oh how willingly would I take her child to my bosom, — fold her to my heart, — call upon her to mitigate my anguish, and pour the balm of comfort on my wounds, were I not conscious I deserve not to receive it, and that all my affliction is the result of my own guilt!"

It was in vain I attempted to speak; horror and grief took from me all power of utterance.

He then read aloud from the letter, "*Look not like thy unfortunate mother!* — Sweet soul, with what bitterness of spirit hast thou written! — Come hither, Evelina: Gracious Heaven!" looking earnestly at me, "never was likeness more striking! — the eye, — the face, — the form, — Oh my child, my child!" Imagine, Sir, — for I can never describe my feelings, when I saw him sink upon his knees before me! "Oh dear resemblance of thy murdered mother! — Oh all that remains of the most-injured of women! behold thy father at thy feet! —

bending thus lowly to implore you would not hate him; — Oh then, thou representative of my departed wife, speak to me in her name, and say that the remorse which tears my soul, tortures me not in vain!"

"Oh rise, rise, my beloved father," cried I, attempting to assist him, "I cannot bear to see you thus; — reverse not the law of nature, rise yourself, and bless your kneeling daughter!"

"May Heaven bless thee, my child! — " cried he, "for *I* dare not." He then rose, and embracing me most affectionately, added, "I see, I see that thou art all kindness, softness, and tenderness; I need not have feared thee, thou art all the fondest father could wish, and I will try to frame my mind to less painful sensations at thy sight. Perhaps the time may come when I may know the comfort of such a daughter, — at present, I am only fit to be alone: dreadful as are my reflections, they ought merely to torment myself. — Adieu, my child; — be not angry, — I cannot stay with thee, — oh Evelina! thy countenance is a dagger to my heart! — just so, thy mother looked, — just so — "

Tears and sighs seemed to choak him! — and waving his hand, he would have left me, — but, clinging to him, "Oh, Sir," cried I, "will you so soon abandon me? — am I again an orphan? — oh my dear, my long-lost father, leave me not, I beseech you! take pity on your child, and rob her not of the parent she so fondly hoped would cherish her!"

"You know not what you ask," cried he; "the emotions which now rend my soul are more than my reason can endure: suffer me, then, to leave you, — impute it not to unkindness, but think of me as well as thou canst. — Lord Orville has behaved nobly; — I believe he will make thee happy." Then, again embracing me, "God bless thee, my dear child," cried he, "God bless thee, my Evelina! — endeavour to love, — at least not to hate me — and to make me an interest in thy filial bosom by thinking of me as thy father."

I could not speak; I kissed his hands on my knees; and then, with yet more emotion, he again blessed me, and hurried out of the room, — leaving me almost drowned in tears.

Oh Sir, all goodness as you are, how much will you feel for your Evelina, during a scene of such agitation! I pray Heaven to accept the tribute of his remorse, and restore him to tranquillity!

When I was sufficiently composed to return to the parlour, I found Lord Orville waiting for me with the utmost anxiety; — and then, a new scene of emotion, though of a far different nature, awaited me;

for I learnt, by Mr. Macartney, that this noblest of men had insisted the so-long-supposed Miss Belmont should be considered *indeed* as my sister, and as the co-heiress of my father! though not in *law,* in *justice,* he says, she ought ever to be treated as the daughter of Sir John Belmont.

Oh Lord Orville! — it shall be the sole study of my happy life, to express, better than by words, the sense I have of your exalted benevolence, and greatness of mind!

## LETTER XX

### Evelina in Continuation

Clifton, Oct. 12

This morning, early, I received the following letter from Sir Clement Willoughby.

### "To Miss Anville

"I have this moment received intelligence that preparations are actually making for your marriage with Lord Orville.

"Imagine not that I write with the imbecile idea of rendering those preparations abortive. No, I am not so mad. My sole view is to explain the motive of my conduct in a particular instance, and to obviate the accusation of treachery which may be laid to my charge.

"My unguarded behaviour when I last saw you, has, probably, already acquainted you, that the letter I then saw you reading was written by myself. For your further satisfaction, let me have the honour of informing you, that the one you had designed for Lord Orville, had fallen into my hands.

"However I may have been urged on by a passion the most violent that ever warmed the heart of man, I can by no means calmly submit to be stigmatised for an action seemingly so dishonourable; and it is for this reason that I trouble you with my justification.

"Lord Orville, — the happy Orville, whom you are so ready to bless, — had made me believe he loved you not, — nay, that he held you in contempt.

"Such were my thoughts of his sentiments of you, when I got possession of the letter you meant to send him; I pretend not to vindicate either the means I used to obtain it, or the action of breaking the seal; — but I was impelled by an impetuous curiosity to discover the terms upon which you wrote to him.

"The letter, however, was wholly unintelligible to me, and the perusal of it only added to my perplexity.

"A tame suspence I was not born to endure, and I determined to clear my doubts at all hazards and events.

"I answered it, therefore, in Orville's name.

"The views which I am now going to acknowledge, must, infallibly, incur your displeasure, — yet I scorn all palliation.

"Briefly, then, — I concealed your letter to prevent a discovery of your capacity, — and I wrote you an answer which I hoped would prevent your wishing for any other.

"I am well aware of every thing which can be said upon this subject. Lord Orville will, possibly, think himself ill used; — but I am extremely indifferent as to his opinion, nor do I now write by way of offering any apology to him, but merely to make known to yourself the reasons by which I have been governed.

"I intend to set off next week for the Continent. Should his Lordship have any commands for me in the mean time, I shall be glad to receive them. I say not this by way of defiance, — I should blush to be suspected of so doing through an indirect channel, — but simply that, if you shew him this letter, he may know I dare defend, as well as excuse my conduct.

"CLEMENT WILLOUGHBY."

What a strange letter! how proud and how piqued does its writer appear! To what alternate *meanness* and *rashness* do the passions lead, when reason and self-denial do not oppose them! Sir Clement is conscious he has acted dishonourably, yet the same unbridled vehemence which urged him to gratify a blameable curiosity, will sooner prompt him to risk his life, than confess his misconduct. The rudeness of his manner of writing to me springs from the same cause: the proof he has received of my indifference to him, has stung him to the soul, and he has neither the delicacy nor forbearance to disguise his displeasure.

I determined not to shew this letter to Lord Orville, and thought it most prudent to let Sir Clement know I should not. I therefore wrote the following note.

### "To Sir Clement Willoughby

"Sir,

"The letter you have been pleased to address to me, is so little calculated to afford Lord Orville any satisfaction, that you may depend
upon my carefully keeping it from his sight. I will bear you no resentment for what is past; but I most earnestly entreat, nay implore, that
you will not write again, while in your present frame of mind, by *any*
channel, direct or indirect.

"I hope you will have much pleasure in your purposed expedition,
and I beg leave to assure you of my good wishes."

Not knowing by what name to sign, I was obliged to send it without any.

The *preparations* which Sir Clement mentions, go on just as if
your consent were arrived: it is in vain that I expostulate; Lord
Orville says, should any objections be raised, all shall be given up,
but that, as his hopes forbid him to expect any, he must proceed as if
already assured of your concurrence.

We have had, this afternoon, a most interesting conversation, in
which we have traced our sentiments of each other from our first acquaintance. I have made him confess how ill he thought of me, upon
my foolish giddiness at Mrs. Stanley's ball; but he flatters me with assurances, that every succeeding time he saw me, I appeared to something less and less disadvantage.

When I expressed my amazement that he could honour with his
choice a girl who seemed so infinitely, in *every* respect, beneath his alliance, he frankly owned, that he had fully intended making more
minute enquiries into my family and connections, and particularly
concerning *those people* he saw with me at Marybone, before he acknowledged his prepossession in my favour: but the suddenness of
my intended journey, and the uncertainty of seeing me again, put him
quite off his guard, and "divesting him of prudence, left him nothing
but love." These were his words; and yet, he has repeatedly assured
me, that his partiality has known no bounds from the time of my residing at Clifton.

\*    \*    \*    \*    \*

Mr. Macartney has just been with me, on an embassy from my father. He has sent me his kindest love, and assurances of favour, and
desired to know if I am happy in the prospect of changing my situa-

tion, and if there is any thing I can name which he can do for me. And, at the same time, Mr. Macartney delivered to me a draught on my father's banker for a thousand pounds, which he insisted that I should receive entirely for my own use, and expend in equipping myself properly for the new rank of life to which I seem destined.

I am sure I need not say how much I was penetrated by this goodness; I wrote my thanks, and acknowledged, frankly, that if I could see *him* restored to tranquillity, my heart would be without a wish.


## LETTER XXI

### Evelina in Continuation

Clifton, October 13.

The time approaches now, when I hope we shall meet, — yet I cannot sleep, — great joy is as restless as sorrow, — and therefore I will continue my journal.

As I had never had any opportunity of seeing Bath,[1] a party was formed last night for shewing me that celebrated city; and this morning, after breakfast, we set out in three phaetons. Lady Louisa and Mrs. Beaumont with Lord Merton; Mr. Coverley with Mr. Lovel; and Mrs. Selwyn and myself with Lord Orville.

We had hardly proceeded half a mile, when a gentleman from a post-chaise, which came galloping after us, called out to the servants, "Holla, my Lads, — pray is one Miss Anville in any of them *thing-em-bobs?*"

I immediately recollected the voice of Captain Mirvan, and Lord Orville stopt the phaeton. He was out of the chaise, and with us in a moment. "So, Miss Anville," cried he, "how do you do? so I hear you're Miss Belmont now; — pray how does old Madame French do?"

"Madame Duval," said I, "is, I believe, very well."

"I hope she's in *good case,*"[2] said he, winking significantly, "and won't flinch at seeing service: she has laid by long enough to refit and be made tight. And pray how does poor Monsieur Doleful do? is he as lank-jawed[3] as ever?"

"They are neither of them," said I, "at Bristol."

---

[1] *Bath:* See the headnote to Christopher Anstey, "From *The New Bath Guide*" in Part Two, Chapter 2.

[2] *good case:* Good physical condition.

[3] *lank-jawed:* Having slack jaws, as with a mouth that hangs open.

"No!" [cried he, with a look of disappointment,] "but surely the old dowager intends coming to the wedding! 'twill be a most excellent opportunity to shew off her best Lyons' silk. Besides, I purpose to dance a new-fashioned jig with her. Don't you know when she'll come?"

"I have no reason to expect her at all."

"No! — 'Fore George, this here's the worst news I'd wish to hear! — why I've thought of nothing all the way but what trick I should serve her!"

"You have been very obliging!" said I, laughing.

"O, I promise you," cried he, "our Moll would never have wheedled me into this jaunt, if I'd known she was not here; for, to let you into the secret, I fully intended to have treated the old buck with another frolic."

"Did Miss Mirvan, then, persuade you to this journey?"

"Yes, and we've been travelling all night."

"*We!*" cried I: "Is Miss Mirvan, then, with you?"

"What, Molly? — yes, she's in that there chaise."

"Good God, Sir, why did not you tell me sooner?" cried I; and immediately, with Lord Orville's assistance, I jumpt out of the phaeton, and ran to the dear girl. Lord Orville opened the chaise-door, and I am sure I need not tell you what unfeigned joy accompanied our meeting.

We both begged we might not be parted during the ride, and Lord Orville was so good as to invite Captain Mirvan into his phaeton.

I think I was hardly ever more rejoiced than at this so seasonable visit from my dear Maria; who had no sooner heard the situation of my affairs, than, with the assistance of Lady Howard and her kind mother, she besought her father with such earnestness to consent to the journey, that he had not been able to withstand their united entreaties; though she owned that, had he not expected to have met with Madame Duval, she believes he would not so readily have yielded. They arrived at Mrs. Beaumont's but a few minutes after we were out of sight, and overtook us without much difficulty.

I say nothing of our conversation, because you may so well suppose both the subjects we chose, and our manner of discussing them.

We all stopped at a great hotel, where we were obliged to enquire for a room, as Lady Louisa, *fatigued to death,* desired to *take something* before we began our rambles.

As soon as the party was assembled, the Captain, abruptly saluting me, said, "So, Miss Belmont, I wish you joy; so I hear you've quarrelled with your new name already?"

"Me! — no, indeed, Sir."

"Then please for to tell me the reason you're in such a hurry to change it."

"Miss Belmont!" cried Mr. Lovel, looking round him with the utmost astonishment, "I beg pardon, — but, if it is not impertinent, — I must beg leave to say, I always understood that Lady's name was Anville."

" 'Fore George," cried the Captain, "it runs in my head, I've seen you somewhere before! and now I think on't, pray a'n't you the person I saw at the play one night, and who did n't know, all the time, whether it was a tragedy or a comedy, or a concert of fidlers?"

"I believe, Sir," said Mr. Lovel, stammering, "I had once, — I think — the pleasure of seeing you last spring."

"Ay, and if I live an hundred springs," answered he, "I shall never forget it; by Jingo, it has served me for a most excellent good joke ever since. Well, however, I'm glad to see you still in the land of the living," shaking him roughly by the hand, "pray, if a body may be so bold, how much a night may you give at present to keep the undertakers aloof?"

"Me, Sir!" said Mr. Lovel, very much discomposed; "I protest I never thought myself in such imminent danger as to — really, Sir, I don't understand you."

"O, you don't! — why then I'll make free for to explain myself. Gentlemen and Ladies, I'll tell you what; do you know this here gentleman, simple as he sits there, pays five shillings a night to let his friends know he's alive!"

"And very cheap too," said Mrs. Selwyn, "if we consider the value of the intelligence."

Lady Louisa, being now refreshed, we proceeded upon our expedition.

The charming city of Bath answered all my expectations. The Crescent, the prospect from it, and the elegant symmetry of the Circus, delighted me. The Parades, I own, rather disappointed me; one of them is scarce preferable to some of the best paved streets in London, and the other, though it affords a beautiful prospect, a charming view of Prior Park and of the Avon, yet wanted something in *itself* of more striking elegance than a mere broad pavement, to satisfy the ideas I had formed of it.[4]

---

[4] *The Crescent . . . formed of it:* The Crescent, the Circus, and the Parades in Bath were known for their views and were fashionable in the mid-eighteenth century for their newly built, elegant houses. A fine mansion close to Bath, Prior Park was one of the more attractive views in the area.

At the pump-room, I was amazed at the public exhibition of the ladies in the bath: it is true, their heads are covered with bonnets, but the very idea of being seen, in such a situation, by whoever pleases to look, is indelicate.

"'Fore George," said the Captain, looking into the bath, "this would be a most excellent place for old Madame French to dance a fandango in! By Jingo, I would n't wish for better sport than to swing her round this here pond!"

"She would be very much obliged to you," said Lord Orville, "for so extraordinary a mark of your favour."

"Why, to let you know," answered the Captain, "she hit my fancy mightily; I never took so much to an old tabby[5] before."

"Really, now," cried Mr. Lovel, looking also into the bath, "I must confess it is, to me, very incomprehensible why the ladies chuse that frightful unbecoming dress to bathe in![6] I have often pondered very seriously upon the subject, but could never hit upon the reason."

"Well, I declare," said Lady Louisa, "I should like of all things to set something new a going; I always hated bathing, because one can get no pretty dress for it; now do, there's a good creature, try to help me to something."

"Who? me! — O dear Ma'am," said he, simpering, "I can't pretend to assist a person of your Ladyship's taste; besides, I have not the least head for fashions, — I really don't think I ever invented [above] three in my life! — but I never had the least turn for dress, — never any notion of fancy or elegance."

"O fie, Mr. Lovel! how can you talk so? — don't we all know that you lead the *ton* in the *beau monde?* I declare, I think you dress better than any body."

"O dear Ma'am, you confuse me to the last degree! *I* dress well! — I protest I don't think I'm ever fit to be seen! — I'm often shocked to death to think what a figure I go. If your Ladyship will believe me, I was full half an hour this morning thinking what I should put on!"

"Odds my life," cried the Captain, "I wish I'd been near you! I warrant I'd have quickened your motions a little! Half an hour thinking what you'd put on? and who the deuce, do you think, cares the snuff of a candle whether you've any thing on or not?"

---

[5] *tabby:* An elderly, usually unmarried woman; also a name for a cat.
[6] *unbecoming dress to bathe in:* See Tobias Smollett, "On a Visit to Bath" in Part Two, Chapter 2.

"O pray, Captain," cried Mrs. Selwyn, "don't be angry with the gentleman for *thinking*, whatever be the cause, for I assure you he makes no common practice of offending in that way."

"Really, Ma'am, you're prodigiously kind!" said Mr. Lovel, angrily.

"Pray, now," said the Captain, "did you ever get a ducking in that there place yourself?"

"A ducking, Sir!" repeated Mr. Lovel; "I protest I think that's rather an odd term! — but if you mean a *bathing*, it is an honour I have had many times."

"And pray, if a body may be so bold, what do you do with that frizle-frize top of your own?[7] Why I'll lay you what you will, there is fat and grease enough on your crown, to buoy you up, if you were to go in head downwards."

"And I don't know," cried Mrs. Selwyn, "but that might be the easiest way, for I'm sure it would be the lightest."

"For the matter of that there," said the Captain, "you must make him a soldier, before you can tell which is lightest, head or heels. Howsomever, I'd lay ten pounds to a shilling, I could whisk him so dexterously over into the pool, that he should light plump upon his foretop, and turn round like a tetotum."[8]

"Done!" cried Lord Merton; "I take your odds!"

"Will you?" returned he; "why then, 'fore George, I'd do it as soon as say Jack Robinson."

"He, he!" faintly laughed Mr. Lovel, as he moved abruptly from the window, " 'pon honour, this is pleasant enough; but I don't see what right any body has to lay wagers about one, without one's consent."

"There, Lovel, you are out;" cried Mr. Coverley; "any man may lay what wager about you he pleases; your consent is nothing to the purpose: he may lay that your nose is a sky-blue, if he pleases."

"Ay," said Mrs. Selwyn, "or that your mind is more adorned than your person; — or any absurdity whatsoever."

"I protest," said Mr. Lovel, "I think it's a very disagreeable privilege, and I must beg that nobody may take such a liberty with *me*."

"Like enough you may," cried the Captain; "but what's that to the purpose? suppose I've a mind to lay that you've never a tooth in your head? — pray, how will you hinder me?"

---

[7] *frizle-frize top of your own:* By mid-century it had become unfashionable for men to wear wigs. Lovel has his own hair dressed in a slightly more restrained version of the manner which Evelina describes on page 73. See footnote 9 to Volume I, Letter X.

[8] *tetotum:* A small disk, with an initial letter on each side and a spindle that enabled it to be twirled like a top to decide the outcome of a game or bet. The tetotum would fall to leave one letter uppermost.

"You'll allow me, at least, Sir, to take the liberty of asking how you'll *prove* it?"

"How! — why, by knocking them all down your throat."

"Knocking them all down my throat, Sir!" repeated Mr. Lovel, with a look of horror, "I protest I never heard any thing so shocking in my life; and I must beg leave to observe, that no wager, in my opinion, could justify such a barbarous action."

Here Lord Orville interfered, and hurried us to our carriages.

We returned in the same order we came. Mrs. Beaumont invited all the party to dinner, and has been so obliging as to beg Miss Mirvan may continue at her house during her stay. The Captain will lodge at the Wells.

The first half-hour after our return, was devoted to hearing Mr. Lovel's apologies for dining in his riding-dress.

Mrs. Beaumont then, addressing herself to Miss Mirvan and me, enquired how we liked Bath?

"I hope," said Mr. Lovel, "the Ladies do not call this seeing Bath."

"No! — what should ail 'em?" cried the Captain; "do you suppose they put their eyes in their pockets?"

"No, Sir; but I fancy you will find no person, — that is, no person of any condition, — call going about a few places in a morning *seeing Bath.*"

"Mayhap, then," said the literal Captain, "you think we should see it better by going about at midnight?"

"No, Sir, no," said Mr. Lovel, with a supercilious smile, "I perceive you don't understand me, — *we* should never call it *seeing Bath,* without going at the right season."[9]

"Why, what a plague, then," demanded he, "can you only see at one season of the year?"

Mr. Lovel again smiled; but seemed superior to making any answer.

"The Bath amusements," said Lord Orville, "have a sameness in them, which, after a short time, renders them rather insipid: but the greatest objection that can be made to the place, is the encouragement it gives to gamesters."

"Why I hope, my Lord, you would not think of abolishing *gaming,*" cried Lord Merton; " 'tis the very *zest* of life! Devil take me if I could live without it!"

---

[9] *right season:* Spring and fall were considered the fashionable seasons to visit Bath, but Lovel seems to suggest that one must see Bath in the spring.

"I am sorry for it," said Lord Orville, gravely, and looking at Lady Louisa.

"Your Lordship is no judge of this subject," continued the other; — "but if once we could get you to a gaming-table, you'd never be happy away from it."

"I hope, my Lord," cried Lady Louisa, "that nobody *here* ever occasions *your* quitting it."

"Your Ladyship," said Lord Merton, recollecting himself, "has power to make me quit any thing."

"Except *herself*," said Mr. Coverley. "Egad, my Lord, I think I've helpt you out there."

"You men of wit, Jack," answered his Lordship, "are always ready; — for my part, I don't pretend to any talents that way."

"Really, my Lord?" asked the sarcastic Mrs. Selwyn; "well, that is wonderful, considering success would be so much in your power."

"Pray, Ma'am," said Mr. Lovel to Lady Louisa, "has your Ladyship heard the news?"

"News! — what news?"

"Why, the report circulating at the Wells concerning a certain person?"

"O Lord, no; pray tell me what it is!"

"O no, Ma'am, I beg your La'ship will excuse me; 'tis a profound secret, and I would not have mentioned it, if I had not thought you knew it."

"Lord, now, how can you be so monstrous? — I declare, now, you're a provoking creature! But come, I know you'll tell me; — won't you, now?"

"Your La'ship knows I am but too happy to obey you; but, 'pon honour, I can't speak a word, if you wont all promise me the most inviolable secrecy."

"I wish you'd wait for that from me," said the Captain, "and I'll give you my word you'd be dumb for one while. Secrecy, quoth a! — 'Fore George, I wonder you a'n't ashamed to mention such a word, when you talk of telling it to a woman. Though, for the matter of that, I'd as lieve blab it to the whole sex at once, as to go for to tell it to such a thing as you."

"Such a thing as me, Sir!" said Mr. Lovel, letting fall his knife and fork, and looking very important: "I really have not the honour to understand your expression."

"It's all one for that," said the Captain; "you may have it explained whenever you like it."

" 'Pon honour, Sir," returned Mr. Lovel, "I must take the liberty to tell you, that I should be extremely offended, but that I suppose it to be some sea-phrase, and therefore I'll let it pass without notice."

Lord Orville then, to change the discourse, asked Miss Mirvan if she should spend the ensuing winter in London?

"No, to be sure," said the Captain, "what should she for? she saw all that was to be seen before."

"Is London, then," said Mr. Lovel, smiling at Lady Louisa, "only to be regarded as a *sight?*"

"Why pray, Mr. Wiseacre, how are you pleased for to regard it yourself? — Answer me to that?"

"O Sir, *my* opinion I fancy you would hardly find intelligible. I don't understand *sea-phrases* enough to define it to your comprehension. Does n't your La'ship think the task would be rather difficult?"

"Oh Lard, yes," cried Lady Louisa, "I declare I'd as soon teach my parrot to talk Welch."

"Ha! ha! ha! admirable! — 'Pon honour your La'ship's quite in luck to day; — but that, indeed, your La'ship is every day. Though, to be sure, it is but candid to acknowledge, that the gentlemen of the ocean have a set of ideas, as well as a dialect, so opposite to *ours,* that it is by no means surprising *they* should regard London as a mere *shew* that may be seen by being *looked at.* Ha! ha! ha!"

"Ha! ha!" echoed Lady Louisa: "Well, I declare you are the drollest creature!"

"He! he! 'pon honour I can't help laughing at the conceit of *seeing London* in a few weeks!"

"And what a plague should hinder you?" cried the Captain; "do you want to spend a day in every street?"

Here again Lady Louisa and Mr. Lovel interchanged smiles.

"Why, I warrant you, if I had the shewing it, I'd haul you from St. James's to Wapping the very first morning."

The smiles were now, with added contempt, repeated; which the Captain observing, looked very fiercely at Mr. Lovel, and said, "Hark'ee, my spark, none of your grinning! — 'tis a lingo I don't understand; and if you give me any more of it, I shall go near to lend you a box o' the ear."

"I protest, Sir," said Mr. Lovel, turning extremely pale, "I think it's taking a very particular liberty with a person, to talk to one in such a style as this!"

"It's like you may," returned the Captain; "but give a good gulp and I warrant you'll swallow it." Then, calling for a glass of ale, with a very provoking and significant nod, he drank to his easy digestion.

Mr. Lovel made no answer, but looked extremely sullen: and soon after, we left the gentlemen to themselves.

I had then two letters delivered to me; one from Lady Howard and Mrs. Mirvan, which contained the kindest congratulations; and the other from Madame Duval, — but not a word from *you*, — to my no small surprise and concern.

Madame Duval seems greatly rejoiced at my late intelligence: a violent cold, she says, prevents her coming to Bristol. The Branghtons, she tells me, are all well; Miss Polly is soon to be married to Mr. Brown, but Mr. Smith has changed his lodgings, "which," she adds, "has made the house extremely dull. However, that's not the worst news; *pardie*, I wish it was! but I've been used like nobody, — for Monsieur Du Bois has had the baseness to go back to France without me." In conclusion, she assures me, as you prognosticated she would, that I shall be sole heiress of all she is worth, when Lady Orville.

At tea-time, we were joined by all the gentlemen but Captain Mirvan, who went to the hotel where he was to sleep, and made his daughter accompany him, to separate her *trumpery*, as he called it, from his cloaths.

As soon as they were gone, Mr. Lovel, who still appeared extremely sulky, said, "I protest, I never saw such a vulgar, abusive fellow in my life, as that Captain: 'pon honour, I believe he came here for no purpose in the world but to pick a quarrel; however, for my part, I vow I won't humour him."

"I declare," cried Lady Louisa, "he put me in a monstrous fright, — I never heard any body talk so shocking in my life!"

"I think," said Mrs. Selwyn, with great solemnity, "he threatened to box your ears, Mr. Lovel, — did not he?"

"Really, Ma'am," said Mr. Lovel, colouring, "if one was to mind every thing those low kind of people say, — one should never be at rest for one impertinence or other, — so I think the best way is to be above taking any notice of them."

"What," said Mrs. Selwyn, with the same gravity, "and so receive the blow in silence!"

During this discourse, I saw the Captain's chaise drive up to the gate, and ran down stairs to meet Maria. She was alone, and told me that her father, who, she was sure, had some scheme in agitation against Mr. Lovel, had sent her on before him. We continued in the garden till his return, and were joined by Lord Orville, who begged me not to insist on a patience so unnatural, as submitting to be excluded our society. And let me, my dear Sir, with a grateful heart let me own, I never before passed half an hour in such perfect felicity.

I believe we were all sorry when we saw the Captain return; yet his inward satisfaction, from however different a cause, did not seem inferior to what ours had been. He chucked Maria under the chin, rubbed his hands, and was scarce able to contain the fullness of his glee. We all attended him to the drawing-room, where, having composed his countenance, without any previous attention to Mrs. Beaumont, he marched up to Mr. Lovel, and abruptly said, "Pray have you e'er a brother in these here parts?"

"Me, Sir? — no, thank Heaven, I'm free from all incumbrances of that sort."

"Well," cried the Captain, "I met a person just now, so like you, I could have sworn he had been your twin-brother."

"It would have been a most singular pleasure to me," said Mr. Lovel, "if I also could have seen him; for, really, I have not the least notion what sort of a person I am, and I have a prodigious curiosity to know."

Just then, the Captain's servant opening the door, said, "A little gentleman below desires to see one Mr. Lovel."

"Beg him to walk up stairs," said Mrs. Beaumont. "But pray what is the reason William is out of the way?"

The man shut the door without any answer.

"I can't imagine who it is," said Mr. Lovel; "I recollect no little gentleman of my acquaintance now at Bristol, — except, indeed, the Marquis of Carlton, — but I don't much fancy it can be him. Let me see, who else is there so very little?" —

A confused noise among the servants now drew all eyes towards the door; the impatient Captain hastened to open it, and then, clapping his hands, called out, " 'Fore George, 'tis the same person I took for your relation!"

And then, to the utter astonishment of every body but himself, he hauled into the room a monkey! full dressed, and extravagantly *á-la-mode!*

The dismay of the company was almost general. Poor Mr. Lovel seemed thunderstruck with indignation and surprise; Lady Louisa began a scream, which for some time was incessant; Miss Mirvan and I jumped involuntarily upon the seats of our chairs; Mrs. Beaumont herself followed our example; Lord Orville placed himself before me as a guard; and Mrs. Selwyn, Lord Merton, and Mr. Coverley, burst into a loud, immoderate, ungovernable fit of laughter, in which they were joined by the Captain, till, unable to support himself, he rolled on the floor.

The first voice which made its way thro' this general noise, was that of Lady Louisa, which her fright and screaming rendered extremely shrill. "Take it away!" cried she, "take the monster away, — I shall faint, I shall faint if you don't!"

Mr. Lovel, irritated beyond endurance, angrily demanded of the Captain "what he meant?"

"Mean?" cried the Captain, as soon as he was able to speak, "why only to shew you in your proper colours." Then rising, and pointing to the monkey, "Why now, Ladies and Gentlemen, I'll be judged by you [all]! — Did you ever see any thing more like? Odds my life, if it was n't for this here tail, you would n't know one from t'other."

"Sir," cried Mr. Lovel, stamping, "I shall take a time to make you feel my wrath."

"Come, now," continued the regardless Captain, "just for the fun's sake, doff your coat and waistcoat, and swop with Monsieur *Grinagain* here, and I'll warrant you'll not know yourself which is which."

"Not know myself from a monkey? — I assure you, Sir, I'm not to be used in this manner, and I won't bear it, — curse me if I will!"

"Why heyday," cried the Captain, "what, is Master in a passion? well, don't be angry, — come, he sha'n't hurt you; — here, shake a paw with him, — why he'll do you no harm, man! — come, kiss and friends!" —

"Who I?" cried Mr. Lovel, almost mad with vexation, "as I'm a living creature, I would not touch him for a thousand worlds!"

"Send him a challenge," cried Mr. Coverley, "and I'll be your second."

"Ay, do," said the Captain, "and I'll be second to my friend Monsieur Clapperclaw here. Come, to it at once! — tooth and nail!"

"God forbid!" cried Mr. Lovel, retreating, "I would sooner trust my person with a mad bull!"

"I don't like the looks of him myself," said Lord Merton, "for he grins most horribly."

"Oh I'm frightened out of my senses!" cried Lady Louisa, "take him away, or I shall die!"

"Captain," said Lord Orville, "the ladies are alarmed, and I must beg you would send the monkey away."

"Why, where can be the mighty harm of one monkey more than another?" answered the Captain; "howsomever, if it's agreeable to the ladies, suppose we turn them out together?"

"What do you mean by that, Sir?" cried Mr. Lovel, lifting up his cane.

"What do *you* mean?" cried the Captain, fiercely: "be so good as to down with your cane."

Poor Mr. Lovel, too much intimidated to stand his ground, yet too much enraged to submit, turned hastily round, and, forgetful of consequences, vented his passion by giving a furious blow to the monkey.

The creature, darting forwards, sprung instantly upon him, and clinging round his neck, fastened his teeth to one of his ears.

I was really sorry for the poor man, who, though an egregious fop, had committed no offence that merited such chastisement.

It was impossible, now, to distinguish whose screams were loudest, those of Mr. Lovel, or the terrified Lady Louisa, who, I believe, thought her own turn was approaching: but the unrelenting Captain roared with joy.

Not so Lord Orville: ever humane, generous, and benevolent, he quitted his charge, whom he saw was wholly out of danger, and seizing the monkey by the collar, made him loosen the ear, and then, with a sudden swing, flung him out of the room, and shut the door.

Mr. Lovel was now a dreadful object; his face was besmeared with tears, the blood from his ear ran trickling down his cloaths, and he sunk upon the floor, crying out, "Oh I shall die, I shall die! — Oh I'm bit to death!"

"Captain Mirvan," said Mrs. Beaumont, with no little indignation, "I must own I don't perceive the wit of this action; and I am sorry to have such cruelty practised in my house."

"Why, Lord, Ma'am," said the Captain, when his rapture abated sufficiently for speech, "how could I tell they'd fall out so? — by Jingo, I brought him to be a messmate for t'other."

"Egad," said Mr. Coverley, "I would not have been served so for a thousand pounds!"

"Why then there's the odds on't," said the Captain, "for you see he is served so for nothing. But come," (turning to Mr. Lovel,) "be of good heart, all may end well yet, and you and Monsieur Longtail be as good friends as ever."

"I'm surprised, Mrs. Beaumont," cried Mr. Lovel, starting up, "that you can suffer a person under your roof to be treated so inhumanly."

"What argufies so many words?" said the unfeeling Captain, "it is but a slit of the ear; it only looks as if you had been in the pillory."[10]

"Very true," added Mrs. Selwyn, "and who knows but it may acquire you the credit of being an anti-ministerial writer?"[11]

"I protest," cried Mr. Lovel, looking ruefully at his dress, "my new riding-suit's all over blood!"

"Ha, ha, ha!" cried the Captain; "see what comes of studying for an hour what you shall put on."

Mr. Lovel then walked to the glass, and looking at the place, exclaimed, "Oh Heaven, what a monstrous wound! my ear will never be fit to be seen again!"

"Why then," said the Captain, "you must hide it; — 'tis but wearing a wig."

"A wig!" repeated the affrighted Mr. Lovel, "*I* wear a wig? — no, not if you would give me a thousand pounds an hour!"

"I declare," said Lady Louisa, "I never heard such a shocking proposal in my life!"

Lord Orville then, seeing no prospect that the altercation would cease, proposed to the Captain to walk. He assented; and having given Mr. Lovel a nod of exultation, accompanied his Lordship down stairs.

" 'Pon honour," said Mr. Lovel, the moment the door was shut, "that fellow is the greatest brute in nature! he ought not to be admitted into a civilized society."

"Lovel," said Mr. Coverley, affecting to whisper, "you must certainly pink him:[12] you must not put up with such an affront."

"Sir," said Mr. Lovel, "with any common person, I should not deliberate an instant; but, really, with a fellow who had done nothing but fight all his life, 'pon honour, Sir, I can't think of it!"

"Lovel," said Lord Merton, in the same voice, "you *must* call him to account."

---

[10] *slit of the ear . . . pillory:* Cutting off all or part of the outer ear was sometimes a punishment for criminal behavior. The pillory was a common punishment for a number of crimes in the eighteenth century. The convicted criminal was locked into a heavy wooden frame, usually on a platform in a public place, so that he or she was unable to move head, arms, or legs. If the convict was unpopular for the onerousness of his or her crime, or some other reason, this punishment could be quite severe, as the mob was allowed to inflict both physical and verbal abuse on the helpless criminal. Occasionally this abuse would be severe enough to result in death.

[11] *anti-ministerial writer:* One who published a book that libeled the government. Ear-slitting and the pillory were both used to punish such a crime.

[12] *pink him:* Stab him; in other words, challenge him to a duel.

"Every man," said he, pettishly, "is the best judge of his own affairs, and I don't ask the honour of any person's advice."

"Egad, Lovel," said Mr. Coverley, "you're in for it! — you can't possibly be off!"

"Sir," cried he, very impatiently, "upon any proper occasion, I should be as ready to shew my courage as any body; — but as to fighting for such a trifle as this, — I protest I should blush to think of it!"

"A trifle!" cried Mrs. Selwyn; "good Heaven! and have you made this astonishing riot about a *trifle?*"

"Ma'am," answered the poor wretch, in great confusion, "I did not know at first but that my cheek might have been bit: — but as 'tis no worse, why it does not a great deal signify. Mrs. Beaumont, I have the honour to wish you good evening; I'm sure my carriage must be waiting." And then, very abruptly, he left the room.

What a commotion has this mischief-loving Captain raised! Were I to remain here long, even the society of my dear Maria could scarce compensate for the disturbances he excites.

When he returned, and heard of his quiet exit, his triumph was intolerable. "I think, I think," cried he, "I have peppered him well![13] I'll warrant he won't give an hour to-morrow morning to settling what he shall put on; why his coat," turning to me, "would be a most excellent match for old Madame Furbelow's[14] best Lyons' silk. 'Fore George, I'd desire no better sport, than to have that there old cat here, to go her snacks!"[15]

All the company then, Lord Orville, Miss Mirvan, and myself excepted, played at cards, and *we* — oh how much better did we pass our time!

While we were engaged in a most delightful conversation, a servant brought me a letter, which he told me had, by some accident, been mislaid. Judge my feelings, when I saw, my dearest Sir, your revered hand-writing! My emotions soon betrayed to Lord Orville whom the letter was from: the importance of the contents he well knew, and, assuring me I should not be seen by the card-players, he besought me to open it without delay.

Open it, indeed, I did; — but read it I could not, — the willing, yet aweful consent you have granted, — the tenderness of your expressions, — the certainty that no obstacle remained to my eternal union with the loved owner of my heart, gave me sensations too various,

[13] *I have peppered him well*: Made him hurt, punished him.
[14] *Furbelow*: Literally, the flounce of a skirt or petticoat; the term also carried connotations of ostentatious showiness.
[15] *to go her snacks*: To give her her share.

and though joyful, too little placid for observation. Finding myself unable to proceed, and blinded by the tears of gratitude and delight which started into my eyes, I gave over the attempt of reading, till I retired to my own room: and, having no voice to answer the enquiries of Lord Orville, I put the letter into his hands, and left it to speak both for me and itself.

Lord Orville was himself affected by your kindness; he kissed the letter as he returned it, and, pressing my hand affectionately to his heart, "You are now," (said he, in a low voice) "all my own! Oh my Evelina, how will my soul find room for its happiness? — it seems already bursting!" I could make no reply; indeed I hardly spoke another word the rest of the evening; so little talkative is the fullness of contentment.

O my dearest Sir, the thankfulness of my heart I must pour forth at our meeting, when, at your feet, my happiness receives its confirmation from your blessing, and when my noble-minded, my beloved Lord Orville, presents to you the highly-honoured and thrice-happy Evelina.

A few lines I will endeavour to write on Thursday, which shall be sent off express, to give you, should nothing intervene, yet more certain assurance of our meeting.

Now then, therefore, for the first — and probably the last time I shall ever own the name, permit me to sign myself,

Most dear Sir,
Your gratefully affectionate,
EVELINA BELMONT

Lady Louisa, at her own particular desire, will be present at the ceremony, as well as Miss Mirvan and Mrs. Selwyn: Mr. Macartney will, the same morning, unite himself with my foster-sister, and my father himself will give us both away.

## LETTER XXII

### Mr. Villars to Evelina

Every wish of my soul is now fulfilled — for the felicity of my Evelina is equal to her worthiness!

Yes, my child, thy happiness is engraved, in golden characters, upon the tablets of my heart! and their impression is indelible; for, should the rude and deep-searching hand of Misfortune attempt to pluck them from their repository, the fleeting fabric of life would give way, and in tearing from my vitals the nourishment by which they are supported, she would but grasp at a shadow insensible to her touch.

Give thee my consent? — Oh thou joy, comfort, and pride of my life, how cold is that word to express the fervency of my approbation! yes, I do indeed give thee my consent, and so thankfully, that, with the humblest gratitude to Providence, I would seal it with the remnant of my days.

Hasten, then, my love, to bless me with thy presence, and to receive the blessings with which my fond heart overflows! — And, oh my Evelina, hear and assist in one only, humble, but ardent prayer which yet animates my devotions: that the height of bliss to which thou art rising may not render thee giddy, but that the purity of thy mind may form the brightest splendor of thy prosperity! — and that the weak and aged frame of thy almost idolizing parent, nearly worn out by time, past afflictions, and infirmities, may yet be able to sustain a meeting with all its better part holds dear; and then, that all the wounds which the former severity of fortune inflicted, may be healed and purified by the ultimate consolation of pouring forth my dying words in blessings on my child! — closing these joy-streaming eyes in her presence, and breathing my last faint sighs in her loved arms!

Grieve not, oh child of my care, grieve not at the inevitable moment; but may thy own end be equally propitious! Oh may'st thou, when full of days, and full of honour, sink down as gently to rest, — be loved as kindly, watched as tenderly as thy happy father! And may'st thou, when thy glass is run, be sweetly but not bitterly mourned, by some remaining darling of thy affections, — some yet surviving Evelina!

ARTHUR VILLARS

## LETTER XXIII

### Evelina to the Rev. Mr. Villars

All is over, my dearest Sir, and the fate of your Evelina is decided! This morning, with fearful joy, and trembling gratitude, she united herself for ever with the object of her dearest, her eternal affection!

I have time for no more; the chaise now waits which is to conduct me to dear Berry Hill, and to the arms of the best of men.

EVELINA

FINIS

# Part Two

*Evelina*
## Cultural Contexts

Portrait of Frances Burney by her cousin Edward Francesco Burney, 1782. Courtesy Henry W. and Albert A. Berg Collection, The New York Public Library, Astor, Lenox, and Tilden Foundations.

# 1

# The Young Lady

The materials gathered in this section offer two different contexts for understanding Evelina's entrance into the world. First, two prominent English clergymen, James Fordyce and Thomas Gisborne, place women in general and young ladies in particular at the moral center of their society. Fordyce's thoughts on these subjects take the form of collected sermons that were highly popular in the late eighteenth century and went through many printings, while Gisborne's equally popular treatise takes the form of "advice to young ladies" — a sort of how-to book on the proper roles and behaviors for young women. This mixture of religious and secular writings about the proper character and conduct of women might seem a bit odd to readers in the modern world for whom these two realms of thought usually have far more separation than they did in the eighteenth century. Popular clergymen such as Fordyce wrote at length about "secular" matters like how young women should spend their time, and they were widely published and read. Gisborne's text might be thought of as a precursor to articles in twentieth-century magazines that give young women advice on how to manage their love life or what to do with their summer vacations. Both Fordyce and Gisborne emphasize the moral importance of women to society at large. The good woman is at the heart of the social order. Implicit in woman's role as moral model and influence is the normative standard of marriage as her life goal and work, and both authors assume that the young lady's "entrance" — the courtship period that should lead to that marriage — is a highly critical, even dangerous period in her life. Will the young lady fulfill her idealized role as her culture's moral conscience? Will she succeed in realizing the goal of becoming a wife and mother?

The excerpts from Burney's personal diaries and letters in the second part of this chapter give us some insight into how a particular woman came to her own terms with the burden of "being good" and the normative standard of marriage as woman's vocation in life. Burney's record of her experiences as a young woman facing marriage through economic necessity makes it clear that feeling and thought did not always conform unproblematically to the imperative of marriage as woman's destiny. It is hard, Burney tells us, to be the object of the idealizations thrust on her by a well-intentioned young man. Her experience of the crucial period of courtship accords with the perilousness attributed to it by Gisborne and Fordyce; Burney, too, sees the entrance into married life as critical to her happiness and fraught with danger, but she differs from these religious educators on where the threat lies. Unlike Gisborne, who worries about young ladies' failures of judgment, Burney is concerned that others will force her into a course of life that she knows is antithetical to her well-being. Danger lies in society's rules, not the young lady's intellectual and moral capacity. Burney's middle-aged reflections on her experiences as the Second Keeper of the Robes to Charlotte, queen to George III of England, similarly suggest that the female mind often resisted the rules of conduct even as the female body suffered under them.

Fordyce's primary concern is with shifting women's attention away from the cultivation of external, bodily attractions toward a concern for moral and intellectual values. His emphasis on inner beauty is expressed in terms of Christian doctrine, but his views on the importance of "feminine" inner value were dominant across both sacred and secular writing in the eighteenth century. As the hero of Samuel Richardson's *Pamela,* a highly popular novel of the 1740s, admits, the physical perfection of his beloved first attracted him, but it was the beauties of her mind and soul that caused him to love her. Similarly, Lord Orville does not fall in love with Evelina's silent loveliness when he first meets her but comes to value her as a result of her conversation and actions. Fordyce's emphasis on inner "ornamentation" takes its imperative from the role he gives women as moral and emotional centers of social life. Women soften the harsh edges of culture, and they act as moral checks on men too prone to self-indulgence.

As symbols of moral purity before and after marriage, and as mothers and wives who give the sanction of family to men's labor in the world of business, women are represented as bringing moral order to the late-eighteenth-century world. Hence, it is understandable that both Fordyce and Gisborne fear that young women might fail as moral models. If women err, the logic follows, civilization as Fordyce knows it will fail. In Fordyce and Gisborne we can see a form of what is referred to today as a pernicious "double standard" of conduct for men and women, which holds women to stricter rules for behavior than men. These eighteenth-century instructional and religious texts demonstrate that such double standards are historically rooted in a system of morality based on representations of the female character's "progress" from pure young woman to virtuous wife and mother.

Both Fordyce and Gisborne are invested in the process of female education — in the shaping of model wives and mothers. What, it should be asked, did "female education" consist of in the mid- to late eighteenth century? Some upper- and middle-class young women attended newly flourishing boarding schools, but most received their learning at home. Educational institutions for all but the poor were strictly segregated by sex, and young men received a very different sort of education from that of young women. At home or at school, young English women of the upper classes were taught to read and write, to do arithmetic, and often to speak French or Italian. It was not unheard of for history and geography to be taught, and a taste for English literature, especially, was often encouraged. Much of women's education, however, was invested in marriageability — the talents (such as music and conversation) that would make them good companions to the men they were expected to marry. Implicit in the texts collected here is an assumption that the young lady is made rather than born. While Fordyce and Gisborne may refer to "natural" feminine delicacy, modesty, and beauty as parts of divine creation, these writers point out very clearly that education makes or breaks the young lady's value to her culture as prospective wife and mother.

Fordyce's and Gisborne's belief in the importance of education is in line with theories of human psychology that were becoming increasingly important in the eighteenth century. The idea that human character is formed by its experiences — secular as well as spiritual — was central to the highly influential theories of John Locke and the very different but equally influential ideas of Jean-Jacques Rousseau.

Both writers gave the educational process pride of place in the forma-
tion of human character — an emphasis that we have inherited and
that is still important to theories of human development and psychology. Locke tended to minimize differences between men and women
in his theories of education, while Rousseau emphasized the differences between the educations appropriate to men and women, respectively. There was, to make a long story short, no consensus about
what sort of education best contributed to the making of young
ladies. However, the fact that women's education was discussed in a
variety of cultural forums reflects a widespread concern that if
women are to fulfill the idealized, civilizing role depicted by such
writers as Fordyce, they must have the proper education.

The question of what is the proper education for young ladies is
complicated by the degree to which innocence is represented as contributing to women's moral value. As Gisborne points out, too limited knowledge of the world can lead a young lady into serious errors, jeopardizing her idealized moral status. On the other hand, too
much knowledge is seen by Gisborne as poisonous to female moral
character. If education is a process by which one grows more knowledgeable, and knowledge may contaminate feminine innocence, how
is the young lady to be educated? What can she be taught without
jeopardizing the innocence that makes her valuable? The young lady
must, for example, read in order to be knowledgeable, but she must
not read anything that might destroy her innocence — such as the
"wrong" kind of novel. Novels are, indeed, generally discussed by
eighteenth-century theorists of women's education as parts of the
wrong sort of education given to young ladies. As critics since Joyce
Hemlow (*The History of Fanny Burney,* 1958) have noted, *Evelina* is
both a contribution to the genre of texts designed for the education of
young, middle-class women and a not-uncritical commentary on how
that education was often conceived in Burney's culture. *Evelina* both
models the process by which the young lady should enter into the
world and is critical of how the young lady is generally educated in
order to negotiate this risky period in her life. Burney draws attention
to the fact that the innocence so valued by Fordyce, Gisborne, and
Villars is precisely what makes Evelina vulnerable to fops such as
Lovel and sexual opportunists like Sir Clement.

The materials in this section represent the period of life just before
the young lady's marriage as being critical to her own happiness and
her ability to live out those feminine ideals that contribute indirectly

to the good of the social order. Gisborne and Fordyce portray the shaping of moral character as central to the young lady's safe passage into maturity. The right female education entails a complete disciplining of the female mind and body. In particular, the young lady's time must be carefully regulated and her energies employed in the right reading, the correct implementation of domestic chores, prescribed exercise, and so on. Under proper regulation, she will constitute the moral center of her world. Without such regulation, Gisborne darkly implies that she will bring moral havoc to society. Burney's diaries and letters offer us a different understanding of the young lady's crucial entrance. They suggest that strict regulation of female life poses as great a threat to the young woman's well-being and sanity in this critical period as does the transgression of prescribed boundaries.

Burney's biography has traditionally been written as the story of a highly conventional, even straightlaced lady who was uncritically committed to the social conventions governing life for women of her class. Recent feminist rethinkings of the novelist and her works, including my own *Divided Fictions* (1987), Julia Epstein's *The Iron Pen* (1989), and Margaret Doody's *Frances Burney: The Life in the Works* (1988), argue that this image is misconceived and that Burney offered considerable resistance to "the rules" of conventional femininity that are reflected in the excerpts from Gisborne and Fordyce. In fact, Burney led a highly unconventional life for a woman of her time and class. She was unusually assertive in the matter of marriage, fending off an early, "appropriate" offer in her twenties and marrying the penniless French immigrant Alexandre d'Arblay, whom she loved, in her forties. The biographical materials gathered in this section reflect both Burney's awareness of the conventional expectations for "young ladies" and her own critical distance from them. The excerpts included here from Burney's *Early Diary* concern a proposal of marriage made to her as a woman in her early twenties. Burney successfully resisted this offer, despite the relief it would have afforded her from economic dependence on her father's limited resources. The second, much shorter excerpt is from a letter written at a period of Burney's life when she unhappily lived with the negative consequences of her earlier choice not to marry a man she did not love.

Even though she was a popular novelist and something of a literary celebrity, Burney was without the economic support that women of her class achieved almost exclusively through marriage. At this juncture in her life, she felt unable to refuse her father's request that she accept a prestigious but personally disastrous appointment to the court of Queen Charlotte and George III. A single woman was, after all, her father's economic and moral responsibility, no matter what her age. While Burney had successfully avoided the tedium and pain of an unloving marriage, she was unable to resist her father's ambition to see his daughter honored as Second Keeper to the Robes. In her letter to her sister Esther, the critical distance with which the young Frances Burney approached marriage is applied to the court conventions under which she suffered every day. Although Burney could not entirely prevent her victimization as a dependent woman, her diaries and letters, like her fiction, demonstrate more than a passive acceptance of the rules and regulations of feminine discipline. They reveal a social satirist who maintained devastatingly tight control over the representation of her own painful experiences.

# For the Young Lady

## JAMES FORDYCE

### "On the Importance of the Female Sex"

James Fordyce (1720–1796) was a highly popular Presbyterian clergyman and sometimes poet. He was born in Aberdeen, Scotland, the third son to a merchant and one of twenty children. The popularity of his printed sermons probably grew out of his charismatic performances as a preacher in London during the 1760s. His eloquence and his imaginative presentation of the problems of everyday middle-class life won him a large congregation and the friendship of Samuel Johnson, the great English writer and lexicographer. The famous actor David Garrick is said to have gone to hear him preach on more than one occasion. The following selection is from *Sermons to Young Women,* one of the most popular of several collections of sermons Fordyce published. It went through several reprintings after its initial appearance in 1765 and became one of Britain's most frequently mentioned texts on female conduct and education in the late eighteenth century.

I will — that women adorn themselves in modest apparel, with shame-facedness and sobriety; not with broidered hair, or gold, or pearls, or costly array, but (which becometh women professing godliness) with good works.

— I. TIM. ii. 8, 9, 10.

"Can a maid forget her ornaments or a bride her atire?" is the Almighty's question by the mouth of a prophet.[1] Splendid attire and rich ornaments are in many places of scripture spoken of without censure, and in some with approbation. "The king's daughter," says the psalmist, "is all glorious within:" he adds, "her clothing is of wrought gold; she shall be brought unto the king in raiment of needle-work."[2] The Virtuous Woman is in the Proverbs applauded for "clothing her houshold with scarlet, and herself with silk and purple."[3] The Creator has poured unbounded beauty over his works. Witness the flowers of the field, celebrated by our Saviour himself;[4] witness the gems of the mine, mentioned in the Revelation of St. John, as employed to give additional lustre even to the New Jerusalem;[5] witness, in general, all that wonderful colouring, and those fair proportions, that please the eye, and amuse the imagination, with endless variety. Who can resist, who indeed ought to resist, the agreeable effect? Surely the Author of Nature does nothing in vain. He surely meant, that by beholding her with delight we might be led to copy her with care, and from contemplating the inferior orders of beauty rise to the admiration of that which is supreme.

As he has furnished infinite materials for the exercise and entertainment, no less than for the provision and accommodation of man; so has he inspired that genius, and supplied those powers, by which they are moulded into form, and heightened into splendor. In saying this we are warranted by revelation itself, where we are expressly told, that "the spirit of the Lord filled Bezaleel, Aholiab," and others, "with wisdom, and understanding, and knowledge, to devise and

[1] *mouth of a prophet:* Jeremiah 2:32.
[2] *her clothing . . . needle-work:* Psalms 45:13–15.
[3] *The Virtuous Woman . . . silk and purple:* "A good wife" is described in Proverbs 31:10–31.
[4] *the flowers of the field, celebrated by our Saviour himself:* Matthew 2:28–29: "Consider the lilies of the field, how they grow; they toil not, neither do they spin. Even Solomon in all his glory was not arrayed like one of these."
[5] *gems of the mine . . . New Jerusalem:* Revelation 21:18–23 describes the vision of the New Jerusalem, the holy city to come at the Apocalypse.

work all manner of curious and cunning works of the carver of wood, the cutter of stones, the jeweller, the engraver, the weaver, the embroiderer in blue and in purple, in scarlet and in fine linen."[6] What multitudes are daily employed and comfortably supported by these and such like ornamental arts; hardly any one is ignorant.

That works of ingenuity and elegance are particularly becoming in your sex, and that the study of them ought to enter into female education as much as possible, all, I think, are agreed. In fine, none but the most contracted, or the most prejudiced, will deny that women may avail themselves of every decent attraction, that can lead to a state for which they were manifestly formed; and that, should they by any neglect of their persons render themselves less amiable than God has made them, they would so far disappoint the design of their creation. . . .

Princes, it has been said, and young women, seldom hear truth. It is a melancholy consideration. Flattery you have often heard, and sometimes, I doubt not, listened to. May He hope for your attention, whose character forbids him to flatter, and whose principles are equally averse to it? Nothing, I am convinced, can be more pernicious to your best interests, than the adulation with which you are so early and so generally entertained. You will not look for it here. But be not afraid, on the other hand, of the bitterness of reproach, the bluntness of incivility. If any thing should appear harsh, be assured it proceeds from real regard. We would not willingly offend, we are naturally solicitous to please you; but we dare not promote your pleasure at the expence of your improvement. To tenderness and respect you are entitled: but certainly faithful and candid admonition is not incompatible with the latter; and of the former, if I be not mistaken, it is the truest proof.

The Almighty has thrown you upon the protection of our sex. To yours we are indebted on many accounts. He that abuses you dishonours his mother. Virtuous women are the sweetners, the charm of human life. "A Virtuous Woman — her price is far above rubies."[7] This is not flattery; it is just praise: and that every one of you may deserve such commendation, is my earnest prayer. Much, I am sure depends on you. And this shall be my First Point; to which I will devote the present discourse, as a proper foundation for what is to follow.

---

[6] *with wisdom, . . . and in fine linen:* This alludes to the building of the Tabernacle in Exodus 36.
[7] *A Virtuous Woman . . . rubies:* Proverbs 31:10–31.

That I thus address you in particular, is principally owing to the idea I have formed of your consequence.

He that depreciates your sex is as unkind to society, as he is unjust to you. Yet to do so in your absence is, I am sorry to say, too common with many men; with those very men that soothe you to your faces, and are dupes to your smiles. Is this either manly or fair? Because there are foolish and vicious women, does it follow that there are hardly any other? Were such an opinion to prevail generally, what would become of human kind? Were so ungracious a system once established, is there not reason to fear, it would soon grow to be too well founded? The world, we know, is mightily influenced by reputation. Applause incites and animates; contempt has the contrary effect. A concern for character is, from their constitution, education, and circumstances, particularly strong in women; in all but those who, having lost their native honours, have with them lost their sense of shame; an infamy to which they would have hardly descended, had they not first sunk in their own estimation.

That admired maxim of heathen antiquity,[8] "Reverence thyself," seems to me peculiarly proper for a woman. She that does not reverence herself must not hope to be respected by others. I would therefore remind you of your own value. By encouraging you to entertain a just esteem for yourselves, I would on one hand guard you against every thing degrading, and on the other awaken your ambition to act up to the best standard of your sex; to aspire at every amiable, every noble quality that is adapted to your state, or that can insure the affection and preserve the importance to which you were born. Now this importance is very great, whether we consider you in your present single condition, or as afterwards connected in wedlock.

Considering you in your present Single condition, I would begin where your duty in society begins, by putting you in mind how deeply your Parents are interested in your behaviour. For the sake of the argument, I suppose your parents to be alive. Those that have had the misfortune to be early deprived of theirs, are commonly left to the care of some friend or guardian, who is understood to supply their place; and to such my remarks on this head will not be altogether inapplicable. But I must likewise suppose that your parents deserve the name, that they are really concerned for your virtue and welfare. — Great God! are there then any of thy creatures so unnatural, as to

---

[8] *heathen antiquity:* The classical authors of Greece and Rome were pre-Christian, hence "heathen."

neglect the culture and happiness of the children thou hast given them? Yes, and worse than to neglect it. "Be astonished, O ye heavens, at this!" There are beings called Parents, and Christian parents, who are at pains to introduce their unexperienced offspring to folly, to vice, to every practice that can plunge them in misery! — What, Mothers too, and mothers "professing godliness!" Is it possible that They can train up the fruit of their womb, their own daughters, to dishonour and destruction? Alas! it is done every day, and passes unregarded. There is not perhaps in the whole science of female vanity, female luxury, or female falsehood, a single article that is not taught, and also exemplified, by those Christian Mothers, to the poor young creatures whom every dictate of nature, as well as every principle of the gospel, should engage their parents to bring up in modesty, sobriety, and simplicity of manners. What words can paint the guilt of such a conduct?

Are you who now hear me blest with parents that even in these times, and in this metropolis, where all the corruption and futility of these times are concentrated, discover a zeal for your improvement and salvation? How thankful should you be for the mighty blessing! Would you show that you are thankful? Do nothing to make them unhappy; do all in your power to give them delight. Ah, did you but know how much it is in your power to give them! —— But who can describe the transports of a breast truly parental, on beholding a daughter shoot up like some fair but modest flower, and acquire, day after day, fresh beauty and growing sweetness, so as to fill every eye with pleasure, and every heart with admiration; while, like that same flower, she appears unconscious of her opening charms, and only rejoices in the sun that chears, and the hand that shelters her? In this manner shall you, my lovely friend, repay most acceptably a part (you never can repay the whole) of that immense debt you owe for all the pains and fears formerly suffered; and for all the unutterable anxieties daily experienced, on your account.

Perhaps you are the only daughter, perhaps the only child of your mother, and her a widow. All her cares, all her sensations point to you. Of the tenderness of a much loved and much lamented husband you are the sole remaining pledge. On you she often fixes her earnest melting eye; with watchful attention she marks the progress of your rising virtues; in every softened feature she fondly traces your father's sense, your father's probity. Something within her whispers, you shall live to be the prop of comfort of her age, as you are now her companion and friend. Blessed Lord, what big emotions swell her labouring soul! But lest, by venting them in your company, she should affect you too much, she silently withdraws to pour them forth in tears of rapture; a rapture only augmented by the sweetly sad remembrance that mingles with it, while at the same time it is exalted and consecrated doubly by ardent vows to heaven for your preservation and prosperity. Is there a young woman that can think of this with indifference? Is there a young woman that can reverse the description, suppose herself the impious creature that could break a widowed mother's heart, and support the thought?

When a daughter, it may be a favourite daughter, turns out unruly, foolish, wanton; when she disobeys her parents, disgraces her education, dishonours her sex, disappoints the hopes she had raised; when she throws herself away on a man unworthy of her, or if disposed, yet by his or her situation unqualified, to make her happy; what her parents in any of these cases must necessarily suffer, we may conjecture, they alone can feel.

The world, I know not how, overlooks in our sex a thousand irregularities, which it never forgives in yours; so that the honour and peace of a family are, in this view, much more dependant on the conduct of daughters than of sons; and one young lady going astray shall subject her relations to such discredit and distress, as the united good conduct of all her brothers and sisters, supposing them numerous, shall scarce ever be able to repair. But I press not any farther an argument so exceedingly plain. We can prognosticate nothing virtuous, nothing happy, concerning those wretched creatures of either sex, that do not feel for the satisfaction, ease, or honour of their parents.

Another and a principal source of your importance is the very great and extensive influence which you, in general, have with Our sex. There is in female youth an attraction, which every man of the least sensibility must perceive. If assisted by beauty, it becomes in the first impression irresistible. Your power so far we do not affect to conceal. That He who made us meant it thus, is manifest from his having attempered our hearts to such emotions. Would to God you knew how to improve this power to its noblest ends! We should then rejoice to see it increased: then indeed it would be increased of course. Youth and beauty set off with sweetness and virtue, capacity and discretion — what have not they accomplished?

Far be it from me, my fair hearers, to damp your spirits, or to wish in the least to abridge your triumphs: on the contrary, by assisting you to direct, we would contribute to exalt and extend them. We are always sorry when we see them misplaced or abused; and — I was

going to add, there is nothing more common. To give them their just
direction, is truly a nice point. Power, from whatever source derived,
is always in danger of turning the head. It has turned many an old
one. What then shall become of a young woman, placed on such a
precipice? What can balance or preserve her, but sobriety and caution, a good providence, and good advice?

There are few young women who do not appear agreeable in the
eyes of some men. And what might not be done by the greater part of
you to secure solid esteem, and to promote general reformation,
among our sex? Are such objects unworthy of your pursuit? or will
ye say, that those which frequently engage it are of superior or equal
importance?

If men discover that you study to captivate them by an outside
only, or by little frivolous arts, there are, it must be confessed, many
of them who will rejoice at the discovery; and while they themselves
seem taken by the lure, they will endeavour in reality to make you
their prey. Some more sentimental spirits, who might be dazzled in
the beginning, will be soon disabused; and a few more honourable
characters will scorn to take advantage of your folly. Folly most undoubtedly it is, by a wrong application of your force, to lose the substance for the shadow.

Now and then a giddy youth may be caught. But what is the shal-
low admiration of an hundred such, or the smooth address of artful
destroyers, to the heartfelt respect of men of worth and discernment,
or the well-earned praise of reclaiming were it but one offender? I
verily believe you might reclaim a multitude. I can hardly conceive
that any man would be able to withstand the soft persuasion of your
words, but chiefly of your looks and actions, habitually exerted on
the side of goodness. . . .

The influence of the sexes is, no doubt, reciprocal; but I must ever
be of opinion, that yours is the greatest. How often have I seen a
company of men who were disposed to be riotous, checked all at
once into decency by the accidental entrance of an amiable woman;
while her good sense and obliging deportment charmed them into at
least a temporary conviction, that there is nothing so beautiful as female excellence, nothing so delightful as female conversation in its
best form! Were such conviction frequently repeated, (and it would
be frequently repeated, if such excellence and such conversation were
more general) what might we not expect from it at last? In the mean
time, it were easy to point out instances of the most evident reformation wrought on particular men, by their having happily conceived a

passion for virtuous women: but among the least valuable of your sex, when have you known any that were amended by the society or example of the better part of ours?

To form the manners of men various causes contribute; but nothing, I apprehend, so much as the turn of the women with whom they converse. Those who are most conversant with women of virtue and understanding will be always found the most amiable characters, other circumstances being supposed alike. Such society, beyond every thing else, rubs off the corners that give many of our sex an ungracious roughness. It produces a polish more perfect, and more pleasing, than that which is received from a general commerce with the world. This last is often specious, but commonly superficial. The other is the result of gentler feelings, and a more elegant humanity: the heart itself is moulded; habits of undissembled courtesy are formed; a certain flowing urbanity is acquired; violent passions, rash oaths, coarse jests, indelicate language of every kind, are precluded and disrelished. Understanding and virtue, by being often contemplated in the most engaging lights, have a sort of assimilating power. I do not mean, that the men I speak of will become feminine; but their sentiments and deportment will contract a grace. Their principles will have nothing ferocious or forbidding; their affections will be chaste and soothing at the same instant. In their case the Gentleman, the Man of worth, the Christian, will all melt insensibly and sweetly into one another. How agreeable the composition! In the same way too, honourable love is inspired and cherished. — Honourable love! that great preservative of purity, that powerful softener of the fiercest spirit, that mighty improver of the rudest carriage, that all-subduing, yet all-exalting principle of the human breast, which humbles the proud, and bends the stubborn, yet fills with lofty conceptions, and animates with a fortitude that nothing can conquer — what shall I say more? — which converts the savage into a man, and lifts the man into a hero! What a happy change should we behold in the minds, the morals, and the demeanour of our youth, were this charming passion to take place of that false and vicious gallantry which gains ground amongst us every day, to the disgrace of our country, to the discouragement of holy wedlock, to the destruction of health, fortune, decency, refinement, rectitude of mind, and dignity of manners! For my part, I despair of feeling the effeminate, trifling, and dissolute character of the age reformed, so long as this kind of gallantry is the mode. But it will be the mode, so long as the present fashionable system of Female Education continues.

Parents now a days almost universally, down to the lowest tradesman, or mechanic, who to ape his superiors strains himself beyond
his circumstances, send their duaghters to Boarding-schools. And
what do they mostly learn there? I say, Mostly; for there are exceptions, and such as do the Mistresses real honour. Need I mention
that, making allowance for those exceptions, they learn, chiefly to
dress, to dance, to speak bad French, to prattle much nonsense, to
practise I know not how many pert conceited airs, and in consequence of all to conclude themselves Accomplished Women? I say
nothing here of the alarming suggestions I have heard as to the corruption of their morals. Thus prepared they come forth into the
world. Their parents, naturally partial, fancy them to be every thing
that is fine, and are impatient to show them, or, according to the
fashionable phrase, to let them see Company; by which is chiefly
meant exhibiting them in public places. Thither at least many of them
are conducted. They have youth, and perhaps beauty. The effect of
both is heightened by all possible means, at an expence frequently felt
for a long time after. They are intoxicated by so many things concur-
ring to deprive them of their little senses. Gazers and flatterers they
meet with every where. All is romance and distraction, the extravagance of vanity, and the rage of conquest. They think of nothing that
is domestic or rational. Alas! they were never taught it. How to appear abroad with the greatest advantage, is the main concern. In sub-
serviency to that, as well as from the general love of amusement, Parties of Pleasure, as they are called, become the prevailing demand.
The same dispositions on the side of the men, sometimes stimulated
by the worst designs, often seconded by good nature, and not seldom
perhaps pushed on by the fear of appearing less generous or less gallant, prompt them to keep pace with all this folly. They are soon fired
in the chace; every thing is gay and glittering; prudence appears too
cold a monitor; gravity is deemed severe; the Ladies must be pleased;
mirth and diversion are all in all. The phantoms pass: the female adventurers must return home; it is needless to say, with what impressions. The young gentlemen are not always under equal restraint;
their blood boils; the tavern, the streets, the stews,[9] eke out the
evening; riot and madness conclude the scene: or if this should be prevented, it is not difficult to imagine the dissipation that must naturally grow out of those idle gallantries often repeated. Nor shall we
be surprised to find the majority of our youth so insignificant, and so

[9] *stews:* Brothels.

profligate; when to these we join the influence of bad or giddy women grown up, the infection of the most pestilent books, and the pattern of veterans in sin, who are ever zealous to display the superiority of their talents by the number of their disciples, and secretly solicitous by the strength of their party to make amends for the weakness of their cause.

That men are sometimes dreadfully successful in corrupting the women, cannot be denied. But do women on the other side never corrupt the men? I speak not at present of those abandoned creatures that are the visible ruin of so many of our unhappy youth; but I must take the liberty to say that, amongst a number of your sex who are not sunk so low, there is a forwardness, a levity of look conversation and demeanour, unspeakably hurtful to young men. Their reverence for female virtue it in a great measure destroys; it even tempts them to suspect that the whole is a pretence, that the sex are all of a piece. The consequences of this, with regard to their behaviour while they remain single, the prejudices it must necessarily produce against marriage, and the wild work it is likely to make if they ever enter into that state, I leave you to imagine.

Hitherto I have spoken only of the interest young women have with our sex. Let me now say something of that which they have with their Own. It is not perhaps so extensive as the other; but for obvious reasons it cannot be inconsiderable. Do they always use it to good purposes? Do they never corrupt one another? Do none of them assist the common enemy; those wicked and designing men that are combined against the sex, especially against the innocent and unwary? Do the old never initiate the young in those low arts of dissimulation and cunning, which a wise woman cannot want, and which a worthy woman will not practise? Do the young — But I hasten from so painful a topic, to consider the Importance of your sex in another light. As you have certainly great influence at present, so, in the next place, it may be probably in your power to communicate much happiness, or to occasion much misery hereafter. I think now of the chances you have to be connected in Wedlock. These it is impossible to calculate: but there are not, I suppose, many young women who, at one time or another, unless they themselves be in fault, may not form that connexion with the usual prospects; and I say, that the men you marry, the children you bring, and the community at large, will be all deeply interested in your conduct.

As to the first, I am not ignorant that there are some men so grossly insensible, as to be for the most part little or nothing affected by the temper or behaviour of their wives; provided only they do not ruin their affairs. And in truth, if those wives be ill tempered or ill behaved, such want of feeling is so far well for the husbands. If otherwise, how much are they themselves objects of compassion, thus condemned to drag a wretched life with beings, on whom all their endeavours to delight are lost! How sensibly must such a situation pain a delicate and ingenuous mind! What can reconcile her to it, but the strongest principles of religion?

Some sordid or saturnine spirits of either sex there may be, who can support a connexion of this kind with a stupid indifference; plodding along through a tasteless existence, without attachment or gratitude, desire or hope. Whether the case be very common, I leave others to decide. Of both sexes there are certainly many who are not made of such dull materials. With respect to them —— But surely it cannot be necessary to display the felicity, or the wo, which must unavoidably arise to them from their partners. Here indeed, as in most instances where the modes of life happen to influence, it must be allowed the men have the advantage. If they find themselves unequally yoked, they are generally furnished with various means of beguiling their wretchedness at a distance from home; whereas, if such be the fate of the poor women, they are commonly left to pine away in solitary misery. For them scarce any allowance is made; to them little or no pity is shown: while the former make themselves judges in their own cause, and the partial world is ready to side with them. But yet, if the usages of that leave them often more room to elude the ideas of domestic distress, the feelings of nature will never suffer them fairly to escape it. A woman, it is certain, if she be so minded, has still the power of plaguing her partner out of every real enjoyment; — a power however, of which nothing can justify the exercise, and which when exercised is, like every other act of tyranny, sure to recoil upon the tyrant.

It is natural for me to wish well to my own sex; and therefore you will not wonder, if I be solicitous for your possessing every quality that can render you agreeable companions in a relation which of all others is the most intimate, should be the most endearing, and must be the happiest or the worst. But to this solicitude my friendship for you is at least an equal motive. Were the lower springs of self-love to have no effect on your conduct, I must yet think, that the more refined principles of generosity and goodness ought to prompt it. Ah! my young friends, what pleasure can be compared to that of conferring felicity? What honour can be enjoyed by your sex, equal to that of showing yourselves every way worthy of a virtuous tenderness from ours? What can be conceived so properly female as inspiring, improving, and continuing such a tenderness, in all its charming extent? Contrasted with this, how unamiable, and how miserable, must we pronounce the passion for ungentle command, for petulant dominion, so shamefully indulged by some women as soon as they find a man in their power!

But lastly, let us suppose you Mothers; a character which, in due time, many of you will sustain. How does your importance rise! A few years elapsed, and I please myself with the prospect of seeing you, my honoured auditress,[10] surrounded with a family of your own, dividing with the partner of your heart the anxious, yet delightful labour, of training your common offspring to virtue and society, to religion and immortality; while, by thus dividing it, you leave him more at leisure to plan and provide for you all; a task, which he prosecutes with tenfold alacrity, when he reflects on the beloved objects of it, and finds all his toils both soothed and rewarded by the wisdom and sweetness of your deportment to him and his children.

I think I behold you, while he is otherwise necessarily engaged, casting your fond maternal regards round and round through the pretty smiling circle; not barely to supply their bodily wants, but chiefly to watch the gradual openings of their minds, and to study the turns of their various tempers, that you may "teach the young idea how to shoot," and lead their passions by taking hold of their hearts. I admire the happy mixture of affection and skill which you display in assisting Nature, not forcing her; in directing the understanding, not hurrying it; in exercising without wearying the memory, and in moulding the behaviour without constraint. I observe you prudently overlooking a thousand childish follies. You forgive any thing but falsehood or obstinacy: you commend as often as you can: you reprove only when you must; and then you do it to purpose, with moderation and temper, but with solemnity and firmness, till you have carried your point. You are at pains to excite honest emulation: you take care to avoid every appearance of partiality; to convince your dear charge, that they are all dear to you, that superior merit alone can entitle to superior favour, that you will deny to none of them what is proper, but that the kindest and most submissive will be

[10] *auditress:* The reader herself.

always preferred. At times, you even partake in their innocent amusements, as if one of them; that they may love you as their friend, while
they revere you as their parent. In graver hours, you insinuate knowledge and piety by your conversation and example, rather than by formal lectures and awful admonitions. And finally, to secure as far as
possible the success of all, you dedicate them daily to God, with the
most fervent supplications for his blessing —— Thus you show yourself a conscientious and a judicious mother at the same moment; and
in that light I view you with veneration. I honour you as sustaining a
truly glorious character on the great theatre of humanity. Of the part
you have acted I look forward to the consequences, direct and collat-
eral, future and remote. Those lovely plants which you have reared I
see spreading, and still spreading, from house to house, from family
to family, with a rich increase of fruit. I see you diffusing virtue and
happiness through the human race; I see generations yet unborn rising up to call you Blessed! I worship that Providence which has destined you for such usefulness, for such felicity. I pity the man that is
not charmed with the image of so much excellence; an image which,
in one degree or another, has been realized by many women of worth
and understanding in every age: I will add, an image which, when realized, cannot fail of being contemplated with peculiar delight by all
the benevolent spirits of heaven, with the Father and Saviour of the
world at their head! And are there, amongst the sons of men, any that
will presume to depreciate such women, to speak of them with an air
of superiority, or to suggest that your sex are not capable of filling
the more important spheres of life?

    . . . Why, ye daughters of Britain, are so many of you insensible to
those brightest glories of your sex? Where is your love for your native
country, which, by thus excelling, you might so nobly serve? where
your emulation of those Heroic Women, that have in ancient days
graced this happy land? How long will you be ambitious of flaunting
in French attire, of fluttering about with the levity of that fantastic
people? When will you be satisfied with the simplicity of elegance,
and the gracefulness of modesty, so becoming in a nation like this,
supported by trade, polished by taste, and enlightened by true religion? Say, when will you relinquish delusive pursuits, and dangerous
pleasures, the gaze of fools, and the flattery of libertines, for the
peaceful and solid study of whatever can adorn your nature, do honour to your country, reflect credit on your profession of christianity,
give joy to all your connexions, and confer dignity on Womankind?

# THOMAS GISBORNE

## "On the Mode of Introducing Young Women into General Society"

## "On the Employment of Time"

Like James Fordyce, Thomas Gisborne (1758–1846) was a clergyman noted for preaching highly popular sermons. Unlike Fordyce, who
was a Presbyterian, Gisborne held a curacy under his country's primary
organized religion, the Church of England. He was of an old and respectable family who had played an active role in Staffordshire politics
for two centuries. Educated at Cambridge, Gisborne could have followed his forefathers and gone into politics, but he chose instead to settle into the relatively quiet life of a country squire and clergyman. His
writings fall mainly within the genre of moral philosophy, ranging from
*Principles of Moral Philosophy* (1789) to the frequently reprinted (and
even translated into German) *An Enquiry into the Duties of the Female
Sex* (1797). Gisborne was closely associated with the evangelical movement within the Anglican Church — a movement that sought religious
and social reforms — and he was friends with William Wilberforce, the
famous English abolitionist. He also wrote and published poetry. Although his *Enquiry* was written nearly twenty years after *Evelina*'s publication, it reflects much of the popular thinking about middle-class female life that was contemporary to Burney's novel. Indeed, many of Mr.
Villars's concerns over Evelina's entrance into public life are echoed in
Gisborne's portrait of the young lady's entrance into the world.

## "On the Mode of Introducing Young Women into General Society"

When the business of education, whether conducted at home or at
a public seminary, draws towards a conclusion, the next object that
occupies the attention of the parent is what she terms the introduction of her daughter into the world. Emancipated from the shackles
of instruction, the young woman is now to be brought forward to act
her part on the public stage of life. And as though liberty were a gift
unattended with temptations to unexperienced youth; as though

vivacity, openness of heart, the consciousness of personal accomplishments and of personal beauty, would serve rather to counteract than to aggravate those temptations; the change of situation is not unfrequently heightened by every possible aid of contrast. Pains are taken, as it were, to contrive, that when the dazzled stranger shall step from the nursery and the lecture-room, she shall plunge at once into a flood of vanity and dissipation. Mewed up from every prying gaze, taught to believe that her first appearance is the subject of universal expectation, tutored to beware above all things of tarnishing the lustre of her attractions by *mauvaise honte,*[1] stimulated with desire to outshine her equals in age and rank, she burns with impatience for the hour of displaying her perfections; till at length, intoxicated beforehand with anticipated flatteries, she is launched, in the pride of ornament, on some occasion of festivity; and from that time forward thinks by day and dreams by night of amusements, and of dress, and of compliments, and of admirers.

I believe this picture to convey no exaggerated representation of the state of things which is often witnessed in the higher ranks of society. I fear, too, that it is a picture to which the practice of the middle ranks, though at present not fully corresponding, bears a continually increasing resemblance. The extreme, however, which has been described, has, like every other extreme, its opposite. There are mothers who profess to initiate their daughters, almost from the cradle, into what they call the knowledge of life; and pollute the years of childhood with an instilled attachment to the card-table; with habits of flippancy and pertness, denominated wit; with an "easiness" of manners, which ought to be named effrontery; and with a knowledge of tales of scandal unfit to be mentioned by any one but in a court of justice. Both these extremes are most dangerous to every thing that is valuable in the female character; to every thing on which happiness in the present world and in a future world depends. But of the two the latter is the more pernicious. In that system war is carried on almost from infancy, and carried on in the most detestable manner, against female delicacy and innocence. In the former, that delicacy and that innocence are exposed under the greatest disadvantages to the sudden influence of highly fascinating allurements. It may be hoped, however, that, coming to the encounter as yet little impaired, they may have some chance of escaping without severe injury. At any rate, be this chance ever so small, it is greater than the probability, that when

---

[1] *mauvaise honte:* A painful and awkward bashfulness.

assailed from their earliest dawn, by slow poison incessantly administered, they should ultimately survive.

To accustom the mind by degrees to the trials which it must learn to withstand, yet to shelter it from insidious temptations, while it is unable to discern and to shun the snare, is the first rule which wisdom suggests with regard to all trials and temptations whatever. To this rule too much attention cannot be paid in the mode of introducing a young woman into the common habits of social intercourse. Let her not be distracted in the years by nature particularly designed for the cultivation of the understanding and the acquisition of knowledge, by the turbulence and glare of polite amusements: nor be suffered to taste the draught which the world offers to her, till she has learnt, that if there is sweetness on the surface there is venom deeper in the cup; and is fortified with those principles of temperance and rectitude which may guard her against unsafe indulgence. Let vanity, and other unwarrantable springs of action, prompt, at all times, to exert their influence on the female character, and at no time likely to exert an influence more dangerous than when a young woman first steps into public life, be curtailed, as far as may be safely practicable, of the powerful assistance of novelty. Altogether to preclude that assistance is impossible. But it may be disarmed of much of its force by gradual familiarity. Let that gradual familiarity take place under the superintendence of parents and near relations, and of friends of approved sobriety and discretion. Let not the young woman be consigned to some fashionable instructress, who, professing at once to add the last polish to education, and to introduce the pupil into the best company, will probably dismiss her thirsting for admiration; inflamed with ambition; devoted to dress and amusements; initiated in the science and the habit of gaming; and prepared to deem every thing right and indispensable, which is or shall be recommended by modish example. Let her not be abandoned in her outset in life to the giddiness and mistaken kindness of fashionable acquaintance in the metropolis, or forwarded under their convoy to public places, there to be whirled, far from maternal care and admonition, in the circle of levity and folly. Let parental vigilance and love gently point out to the daughter, on every convenient occasion, what is proper or improper in the conduct of the persons of her own age, with whom she is in any degree conversant, and also the grounds of the approbation or disapprobation expressed. Let parental counsel and authority be prudently exercised in regulating the choice of her associates. And at the same time that she is habituated to regard distinctions of wealth and rank, as circumstances wholly unconnected with personal worth; let her companions be in general neither much above her own level, nor much below it: lest she should be led to ape the opinions, the follies, and the expensiveness of persons in a station higher than her own; or, in her intercourse with those of humbler condition, to assume airs of contemptuous and domineering superiority. Solicitude on the part of parents, to consult the welfare of their child in these points, will probably be attended with a further consequence of no small benefit to themselves; when it persuades them to an encreased degree of circumspection as to the visitors whom they encourage at home, and the society which they frequent abroad.

## "On the Employment of Time"

To occupy the mind with useful employments is among the best methods of guarding it from surrendering itself to dissipation. To occupy it with such employments regularly, is among the best methods of leading it to love them. Young women sometimes complain, and more frequently the complaint is made for them, that they have nothing to do. Yet few complaints are urged with less foundation. To prescribe to a young person of the female sex the precise occupations to which she should devote her time, is impossible. It would be to attempt to limit, by inapplicable rules, what must vary according to circumstances which cannot previously be ascertained. Differences in point of health, of intellect, of taste, and a thousand nameless particularities of family occurrences and local situation, claim, in each individual case, to be taken into the account. Some general reflections, however, may be offered.

I advert not yet to the occupations which flow from the duties of matrimonial life. When, to the rational employments open to all women, the entire superintendence of domestic economy is added; when parental cares and duties press forward to assume the high rank in a mother's breast to which they are entitled; to complain of the difficulty of finding proper methods of occupying time, would be a lamentation which nothing but politeness could preserve from being received by the auditor with a smile. But in what manner, I hear it replied, are they, who are not wives and mothers, to busy themselves? Even at present young women in general, notwithstanding all their efforts to quicken and enliven the slow-paced hours, appear, if we may judge from their countenances and their language, not unfrequently to feel themselves unsuccessful. If dress then, and what is called dissipation, are not to be allowed to fill so large a space in the course of female life as they now overspread; and your desire to curtail them in the exercise of this branch of their established prerogative is, by no means, equivocal; how are well-bred women to support themselves in the single state through the dismal vacuity that seems to await them? This question it may be sufficient to answer by another. If young and well-bred women are not accustomed, in their single state, regularly to assign a large proportion of their hours to serious and instructive occupations; what prospect, what hope is there that, when married, they will assume habits to which they have ever been strangers, and exchange idleness and volatility for steadiness and exertion?

To every woman, whether single or married, the habit of regularly allotting to improving books a portion of each day, and, as far as may be practicable, at stated hours, cannot be too strongly recommended. I use the term *improving* in a large sense; as comprehending whatever writings may contribute to her virtue, her usefulness, and her innocent satisfaction, to her happiness in this world and in the next. She who believes that she is to survive in another state of being through eternity, and is duly impressed by the awful conviction, will not be seduced from an habitual study of the Holy Scriptures, and of other works calculated to imprint on her heart the comparatively small importance of the pains and pleasures of this period of existence; and to fill her with that knowledge, and inspire her with those views and dispositions, which may enable her to rejoice in the contemplation of futurity. With the time allotted to the regular perusal of the word of God, and of performances which enforce and illustrate the rules of Christian duty, no other kind of reading ought to be permitted to interfere. At other parts of the day let history, biography, poetry, or some of the various branches of elegant and profitable knowledge, pay their tribute of instruction and amusement. But let her studies be confined within the strictest limits of purity. Let whatever she peruses in her most private hours be such as she needs not to be ashamed of reading aloud to those whose good opinion she is most anxious to deserve. Let her remember that there is an all-seeing eye, which is ever fixed upon her, even in her closest retirement.

There is one species of writings which obtains from a considerable proportion of the female sex a reception much more favourable than is accorded to other kinds of composition more worthy of encouragement. It is scarcely necessary to add the name of romances.[2] Works of this nature not unfrequently deserve the praise of ingenuity of plan and contrivance, of accurate and well-supported discrimination of character, and of force and elegance of language. Some have professedly been composed with a design to favour the interests of morality. And among those which are deemed to have on the whole a moral tendency, a very few perhaps might be selected which are not liable to the disgraceful charge of being contaminated occasionally by incidents and passages unfit to be presented to the reader; a charge so very generally to be alleged with justice, that even of the novels which possess great and established reputation, some are totally improper, in consequence of such admixture, to be perused by the eye of delicacy. Poor, indeed, are the services rendered to virtue by a writer, however he may boast that the object of his performance is to exhibit the vicious as infamous and unhappy, who, in tracing the progress of vice to infamy and unhappiness, introduces the reader to scenes and language adapted to wear away the quick feelings of modesty, which form at once the ornament and the safeguard of innocence; and like the bloom upon a plum, if once effaced, commonly disappear for ever. To indulge in a practice of reading romances is, in several other particulars, liable to produce mischievous effects. Such compositions are, to most persons, extremely engaging. That story must be uncommonly barren, or wretchedly told, of which, after having heard the beginning, we desire not to know the end. To the pleasure of learning the ultimate fortunes of the heroes and heroines of the tale, the novel commonly adds, in a greater or in a less degree, that which arises from animated description, from lively dialogue, or from interesting sentiment. Hence the perusal of one romance leads, with much more frequency than is the case with respect to works of other kinds, to the speedy perusal of another. Thus a habit is formed, a habit at first, perhaps, of limited indulgence, but a habit that is continually found more formidable and more encroaching. The appetite becomes too keen to be denied; and in proportion as it is more urgent, grows less nice and select in its fare. What would formerly have given offence, now gives none. The palate is vitiated or made dull. The produce of the book-club, and the contents of the circulating library[3] are de-

---

[2] *romances:* In the late eighteenth century, the term *romance* often referred to novels.
[3] *book-club . . . circulating library:* Books were expensive commodities in the eighteenth century. As literacy rates in England improved over the course of the century, a growing reading public developed institutions for making books more cheaply available. Book clubs were organized to buy volumes that could be passed around and shared by their members. The circulating library was established as a flourishing institution by the turn of the century.

voured with indiscriminate and insatiable avidity. Hence the mind is secretly corrupted. Let it be observed too, that in exact correspondence with the increase of a passion for reading novels, an aversion to reading of a more improving nature will gather strength. There is yet another consequence too important to be overlooked. The catastrophe and the incidents of romances commonly turn on the vicissitudes and effects of a passion the most powerful of all those which agitate the human heart.[4] Hence the study of them frequently creates a susceptibility of impression and a premature warmth of tender emotions, which, not to speak of other possible effects, have been known to betray young women into a sudden attachment to persons unworthy of their affection, and thus to hurry them into marriages terminating in unhappiness. . . .

But it is not from books alone that a considerate young woman is to seek her gratifications. The discharge of relative duties, and the exercise of benevolence form additional sources of activity and enjoyment. To give delight in the affectionate intercourse of domestic society; to relieve a parent in the superintendence of family affairs; to smooth the bed of sickness, and cheer the decline of age; to examine into the wants and distresses of the female inhabitants of the neighbourhood; to promote useful institutions for the comfort of mothers, and for the instruction of children; and to give to those institutions that degree of attention, which, without requiring either much time or much personal trouble, will facilitate their establishment and extend their usefulness: these are employments congenial to female sympathy; employments in the precise line of female duty; employments which diffuse genuine and lasting consolation among those whom they are designed to benefit, and never fail to improve the heart of her who is engaged in them.

In pointing out what ought to be done, let justice be rendered to what has been done. In the discharge of the domestic offices of kindness, and in the exercise of charitable and friendly regard to the neighbouring poor, women in general are exemplary. In the latter branch of Christian virtue, an accession of energy has been witnessed within a few years. Many ladies have shewn, and still continue to shew, their earnest solicitude for the welfare of the wretched and the

---

[4] *a passion the most powerful . . . the human heart:* Gisborne probably had in mind the sorts of novels written by, among many others, Eliza Haywood in the 1720s. We might call them "bodice-rippers," and compare them to the highly popular Harlequin romances of the twentieth century. These novels tended to focus on a heroine's adventures and misadventures in love, and though they were by no means pornographic, they favored a more frank consideration of sexuality than Gisborne condones for young ladies.

ignorant, by spontaneously establishing schools of industry and of religious instruction; and with a still more beneficial warmth of benevolence, have taken the regular inspection of them upon themselves. May they stedfastly persevere, and be imitated by numbers!

Among the employments of time, which, though regarded with due attention by many young women, are more or less neglected by a considerable number, moderate exercise in the open air claims to be noticed. Sedentary confinement in hot apartments on the one hand, and public diversions frequented, on the other, in buildings still more crowded and stifling, are often permitted so to occupy the time as by degrees even to wear away the relish for the freshness of a pure atmosphere, for the beauties and amusements of the garden, and for those "rural sights and rural sounds," which delight the mind uncorrupted by idleness, folly, or vice. Enfeebled health, a capricious temper, low and irritable spirits, and the loss of many pure and continually recurring enjoyments, are among the consequences of such misconduct.

But though books obtain their reasonable portion of the day, though health has been consulted, the demands of duty fulfilled, and the dictates of benevolence obeyed, there will yet be hours remaining unoccupied; hours for which no specific employment has yet been provided. For such hours it is not the intention of these pages to prescribe any specific employment. What if some space be assigned to the useful and elegant arts of female industry? But is industry to possess them all? Let the innocent amusements which home furnishes claim their share. It is a claim which shall cheerfully be allowed. Do amusements abroad offer their pretensions? Neither shall they, on proper occasions, be unheard. A well-regulated life will never know a vacuum sufficient to require an immoderate share of public amusements to fill it.

# By the Young Lady

## FRANCES BURNEY

## *An Unwanted Proposal of Marriage*

These excerpts from Burney's correspondence and diaries are taken from *The Early Journals and Letters of Fanny Burney*, compiled and edited by Lars E. Troide (Montreal and Kingston: McGill-Queen's UP, 1990). Burney (1752–1840) was an inveterate writer all her life and, at her death, left huge quantities of letters to and from friends and family, as well as personal diaries and journals written both for herself and for family members. It is clear from her own editorial work on these manuscripts that Burney was at least thinking of the possibility of publication after her death. Indeed, her niece Charlotte Barrett edited her personal papers, and the first edition of Burney's diaries and letters was published in 1842. Nineteenth-century England saw a lively interest in and a strong market for the lives and letters of the famous or almost famous. Burney, a well-known novelist and a public figure of some note, drew significant numbers of readers as a diarist and letter writer, and throughout the late nineteenth and twentieth centuries she has been as known for her personal writings as for her fiction and plays.

At the time of the events related in these excerpts from Frances Burney's diaries and letters, the Burney family was a large and rather complicated clan. Burney's mother, Esther Sleepe Burney, had died in 1762 when Frances was ten, leaving six children in the care of her husband, Charles Burney. Burney's older brother, James, was at sea from the age of eleven and went on to become an admiral in the British navy. Her sister Esther carried on her father's talents in a musical career, while her younger brother, Charles, became a noted classical scholar. Burney was closest to her younger sister Susanna, who was herself a lively writer of journals and letters. Her youngest sister, Charlotte, was the baby of the family, and it was her daughter, Charlotte Barrett, who went on to publish the first edition of Frances Burney's diaries and letters. In 1767 the elder Charles Burney married Elizabeth Allen, with whom he had three children who were all young at the time that Burney kept this diary. The youngest, Sarah Harriet, eventually became a novelist herself. Allen also brought two children from a previous marriage into the family, and Burney was later to become a sympathetic if reluctant confidante to her unhappily married stepsister Maria.

Charles Burney was a well-liked and hard-working musician who became the foremost musicologist of his day. He was the author of *History
of Music,* published in four volumes between 1776 and 1789. Burney
served as his amanuensis and, as should be apparent from the following
excerpts, adored her gregarious, charming, if all-too-busy father. She and
her stepmother were never close and were sometimes mutually antag-
onistic, which may explain Burney's extreme emotional dependence on
her father's approval and support.

Another important figure in Burney's letters and diaries is Samuel
Crisp, who became a friend of the Burney household around 1763 and
died in 1783. He provided surrogate parenting to the Burney children,
especially Frances, in the frequent absence of their father. Burney often
referred to Crisp as "Daddy," as she does in some of the letters that follow. Crisp was a retired man of letters who was somewhat sensitive
about an unsuccessful play that he had written earlier in his life. His
home at times offered Frances a haven from the rather hectic life of the
Burney household — particularly after her father's remarriage — and he
served as one of Frances's favorite correspondents until his death. After
Burney's success with *Evelina,* Crisp joined her father in providing not
always welcome advice concerning her literary career. Crisp and Charles
Burney thwarted her attempts to write for the stage after her initial success with *Evelina,* a bit of career interference about which she remained
bitter, despite the fact that she was always lovingly dutiful to her paternal mentors.

While Burney's father managed to build a fine reputation for his
musical skill and knowledge, he was forced to do so through long
hours of teaching, performing, and writing. He was subsidized by well-
to-do patrons of the arts, as much for his company as for his music,
and this marketing of his social as well as professional skills kept him
from home for many hours of the day and night. The urgency with
which Samuel Crisp argues for Frances Burney's marriage to Thomas
Barlow, the suitor whose proposal distresses her in the following letters
and journals, derives in large part from the economic realities of the
Burney family. While not wanting for the means to live comfortably,
Charles Burney could not give his daughters the dowers that would
have made them attractive on the highly competitive marriage market
of the late eighteenth century. If his sometimes precarious health had
failed through overwork, Frances Burney would indeed have been in a
difficult economic position.

## Journal Entry for May 8, 1775

This month is Called a *tender* one — It has proved so *to* me — but not *in* me — I have not breathed one sigh, — felt one sensation, — or uttered one folly the more for the softness of the season. — However — I have met with a youth whose Heart, if he is to be Credited, has been less guarded — indeed it has yielded itself so suddenly, that had it been in any other month — I should not have known how to have accounted for so easy a Conquest.

The First Day of this month I Drank Tea & spent the Evening at M^r Burney's, at the request of my sister,[1] to meet a very stupid Family, which she told me it would be Charity to herself to give my Time to.

This Family consisted of M^rs O'Connor, & her Daughter, by a first marriage, Miss Dickenson, who, poor Creature, has the misfortune to be both Deaf & Dumb. They are very old acquaintances of my Grandmother Burney, to oblige whom my sister Invited them. My Grandmother & 2 aunts therefore were of the Party: — as was also, M^r Barlow, a young man who has Boarded with M^rs O'Connor for about 2 years.

M^r Barlow is rather short but handsome, he is a very well behaved, civil, good tempered & sensible young man. He bears an excellent character, both for Disposition & morals. He has Read more than he has Conversed, & seems to know but little of the World; his Language is stiff & uncommon, he has a great desire to please, but no elegance of manners; niether, though he may be very worthy, is he at all agreeable.

Unfortunately, however, he happened to be prodigiously Civil to me, & though I have met with much more gallantry occasionally, yet I could not but observe a *seriousness* of attention much more expressive than Complimenting.

As my sister knew not well how to *wile away the Time,* I proposed, after supper, a round of Cross Questions.[2] This was agreed to. M^r Barlow, who sat next to me, took near half an Hour to settle upon what he should ask me, — & at last his question was — "what I thought most necessary in Love?" I answered. *Constancy.* I hope, for

---

[1] *Mr. Burney's . . . my sister:* Burney's sister Esther married her cousin, a musician also named Charles Burney.

[2] *Cross Questions:* "A game of questions and answers in which a ludicrous effect is produced by connecting questions and answers which have nothing to do with one another; as *e.g.* the question of one's neighbour on the right with the answer given to another question by one's neighbour on the left" (*Oxford English Dictionary*).

his own sake, he will not remember this answer long, though he readily subscribed to it at the Time.

The Coach came for me about Eleven. I rose to go. He earnestly entreated me to stay only 2 minutes. I did not, however, think such compliance at all requisite, & therefore only offered to set my Grandmother down in my way. The Party then broke up. M$^{rs}$ O'Connor began an urgent Invitation to all present to return the visit the next Week. M$^r$ Barlow, who followed me, repeated it very pressingly, to *me,* hoping I would make one. I promised that I would.

When we had all taken leave of our Host & Hostess, — my Grandmother, according to custom, gave me a kiss & her blessing. I would fain have eluded my aunts, as Nothing can be so disagreeable as kissing before young men; however, they chose it should go round; & after them, M$^{rs}$ O'Connor also saluted me,[3] as did her Daughter, desiring to be better Acquainted with me. This disagreeable Ceremony over, M$^r$ Barlow, came up to me, & making an apology which, not suspecting his intention, I did not understand, — he gave me a most ardent salute! I have seldom been more surprised. I had no idea of his taking such a freedom. However, I have told my friends that for the future I will not chuse to lead, or have led, so contagious an Example.

He came down stairs with us, & waited at the Door, I believe, till the Coach was out of sight.

Four Days after this meeting [5 May], my mother & M$^{rs}$ Young happened to be in the Parlour, when I received a Letter which from the strong resemblance of the Hand writing to that of M$^r$ Crisp, I immediately opened & thought came from Chesington. But what was my surprise, to see Madam, at the beginning, & at the Conclusion

your sincere Admirer &

very humble serv$^t$ Tho$^s$ Barlow

I Read it 3 or 4 Times before I could credit my Eyes. An Acquaintance so short, & a procedure so hasty astonished me. It is a most tender Epistle & contains a passionate Declaration of Attachment, hinting at hopes of a *return,* & so forth.

Mad$^m$

Uninterrupted happiness we are told is of a short duration, & is quickly succeeded by Anxiety, which moral Axiom I really experienc'd on the Conclusion of May day at M$^r$ Charles Burney's, as the

---

[3] *saluted me:* A kiss on the cheek was a polite but affectionate mark of greeting or parting.

singular Pleasure of your Company was so soon Eclips'd by the rapidity of ever-flying Time; but the felicity, tho' short, was too great to keep within the limits of one Breast, I must therefore intreat your Pardon for the Liberty I take, in attempting to reiterate the satisfaction I then felt, & paying a Tythe of Justice to the amiable Lady from whom it proceeded, permit me then Mad^m, with the greatest sincerity, to assure you, that the feelings of that Evening were the most refined I ever enjoy'd, & discovered such a latent Spring of Happiness from the Company of the Fair, which I had positively before then been a Stranger to; I had 'til then thought, all Ladys might be flattered, but I now experience the contrary, & am assur'd, Language cannot possibly depict the soft Emotions of a mind captivated by so much merit; & have now a Contest between my ardorous Pen, stimulated by so pleasing & so just a subject on the one side, & a dread of being accused of Adulation on the other; however, endeavouring at Justice, & taking Truth (in her plainest Attire) for my Guide, I will venture to declare, that the Affability, Sweetness, & Sensibility, which shone in your every Action, lead me irresistably to Love & Admire the mistress of them & I should account it the road to the highest Felicity, if my *sincerity* might in any degree meet your Approbation; as I am persu[a]ded *that is the first Principle* which can be offer'd as a foundation for the least hope of a Ladys regard; & I must beg leave to observe, I greatly admire that Quality which yourself so justly declar'd, was most necessary in Love, I mean CONSTANCY, from which I would presume to infer, that we are naturally led from Admiration, to Imitation & Practice: All which in being permitted to declare to you — woud constitute my particular happiness, as far as Expression coud be prevail'd on to figure the Ideas of the mind; mean while I woud particularly Request, you woud condescend to favour me with a Line, in which I hope to hear you are well, & that you will honour us with your Company with good M^rs Burney & Family some day next week, which that Lady is to fix; in which request I trust we shall not be deny'd, as 'twill not be possible to admit separating so particularly desirable a part of the Company and as I am persuaded we are honoured with your Assent to the Engagement: I am D^r Miss Fanny's

> most sincere Admirer & very hble Serv^t
> Tho^s Barlow.

I took not a moment to deliberate. — I felt that my Heart was totally insensible — & felt that I could never Consent to unite myself to a man who I did not *very* highly value.

However, as I do not consider myself as an independant member of society, & as I knew I could depend upon my Father's kindness, I thought it incumbent upon me to act with his Concurrence. I therefore, at Night, before I sent an answer, shewed him the Letter. He asked me a great many Questions — I assured him that forming a Connection without attachment — (& that I was totally indifferent to the Youth in Question) was what I could never think of. My Father was all indulgence & goodness; he at first proposed that I should write him Word that our acquaintance had been too short to authorise so high an opinion as he expressed for me; but I objected to that, as seeming to infer that a *longer* acquaintance might be Acceptable. He therefore concluded upon the whole, that I should send no answer at all.

I was not very easy at this determination, as it seemed to treat M^r Barlow with a degree of Contempt, which his partiality to me by no means merited from myself; & as I apprehended it to be possible for him to put, perhaps, *another* & more favourable interpretation upon my silence. I shewed Hetty[4] the Letter next Day. She most vehemently took the young man's part: urged me to think differently, & above all advised me to certainly Write an answer, & to be of their party, according to my promise, when they went to M^rs O'Connor's.

I told her I would speak to my Father again in regard to writing an Answer, which I wished much to do, but could not now without his consent: but as to the Party, I could not make one, as it would be a kind of tacit approbation & assent of his further attentions.

I went afterwards to call on my Grandmother; my sister followed me, & directly told her & my aunts of the affair. They all of them became most zealous Advocates for M^r Barlow; they spoke most highly of the Character they had heard of him, & my aunt Anne humourously bid me beware of her & Beckey's fate!

I assured them I was not intimidated, & that I had rather a thousand Times Die an old maid than be married, except from affection.

When I came Home, I wrote the following Answer which I proposed sending, with my Father's leave.

Miss Burney presents her Compliments to M^r Barlow; she is much obliged for, though greatly surprised at the good opinion with which on so short an Acquaintance he is pleased to Honour her; she wishes M^r Barlow all happiness, but must beg leave to recommend to him to Transfer to some person better known to him a partiality which she so little merits.

---

[4] *Hetty:* Burney's sister Esther.

My Father, however, did not approve of my Writing. I could not imagine why, but have since heard from my sister that he was unwilling I should give a No without some further knowledge of the young man.

Further knowledge will little avail. In Connections of this sort, the *Heart* ought to be heard.

My sister was not contented with giving her own advice; she Wrote about the affair to M$^r$ Crisp, representing in the strongest light the utility of my listening to M$^r$ Barlow. He has written me such a Letter! God knows how I shall have Courage to answer it. Every body is against me but my beloved Father. My mother, indeed, knows nothing of the matter & yet has had a downright Quarrel with me upon the subject & though Hetty was at first very kind, she has at last also Quarrelled with me. My 2 aunts will hardly speak to me — Mr. Crisp is in a *rage*.

They all of them are kindly interested in my welfare; but they know not so well as myself what may make me happy or miserable. To unite myself for Life to a man who is not *infinitely* dear to me, is what I can never, never Consent to. Unless, indeed, I was strongly urged by my Father. I thank God most gratefully he has not interfered.

They tell me they do not desire me to *marry*, but not to give up the *power* of it, without seeing more of the proposer: but this reasoning I cannot give into. — it is foreign to all my Notions: how can I see more of M$^r$ Barlow without encourageing him to believe I am willing to think of him?

### Samuel Crisp to Frances Burney

Chesington May 8.

So much of the future Good or Ill of your Life seems now depending, Fanny, that I cannot dispense with myself from giving You (without being call'd upon) my whole sentiments on a subject which I dare say you already guess at — Hetty, (as she told You she would) has disclos'd the affair to me — the Character she gives of the Young man is in these Words.

" — a Young man, whose Circumstances, I have heard are Easy, but am not throughly inform'd of them — but he bears an extraordinary Character for a Young man now a Days — I have it from some who have known him long, that he is remarkably even-temper'd, sedate & sensible he is 24 Years of Age, is greatly esteem'd for Qualities rarely found at his Age — Temperance & Industry — well Educated, understands Books & Words, better than the World. Which gives him something of a stiffness & formality, which discovers him unus'd to Company, but which might wear off" —

Is all this true, Fanny? — if it is, is such a man so very determinately to be rejected, because from the overflowings of an innocent, honest mind (I wont call it *ignorant* but) *untainted with* the World, (instead of a thousand pitiful Airs & disguises, mixt perhaps with treachery & design) he with trembling & diffidence ventures to write, what he is unable to declare in person, & forsooth, to raise your indignation to the highest pitch, is so indelicate as to hint, that his intentions aim at *matrimony* — god damn my blood but You make me mad! — if you dont put me in mind of Moliere's Precieuses Ridicules![5] — Read it; [*two to three words missing*] You Young Devil, & blush! — tis scene the 4th & instead of Gorgibus & Madelon, read Crispin & Fanchon & the Dialogues will run thus.

*Fanchon.*

La belle galanterie que la sienne! Quoi, débuter d'abord par la mariàge!

*Crispin.*

Et par où veux-tu donc qu'il débute? par la concubinage? n'est-ce pas un procedé, dont vous avez sujet de vous loüer, aussi-bien que moi? est il rien de plus obligeant que cela? et ce lien sacré, où il aspire, n'est-il pas un témoignage de l'honnêteté de ses intentiòns?

*Fanchon.*

Ah mon Pere! ce que vous dites là est du dernier Bourgeois. Cela me fait honte de vous oüir parler de la sorte, & vous devriez un peu vous faire apprendre le bel air des choses.[6]

---

[5] *Moliere's Precieuses Ridicules:* Molière was the name taken by Jean Baptiste Poquelin (1622–1673), a French actor who became one of the most well-known comic dramatists of the seventeenth century. *Les précieuses ridicules* (*The Precious Damsels*) was first acted in Paris in 1659 and was the first of Molière's comedies to gain him reputation as the great satirist of French society. He was often copied by English dramatists and even more often cited for the acuteness of his wit and observations on human life and manners.

[6] *Fanchon . . . le bel air des choses:* "Fanchon: Such beautiful chivalry on his part! What, starting off with marriage! Crispin: And where would you have him begin? With co-habitation? Isn't this a solution of which you and I can both be equally proud? Is there anything more obliging than that? And this holy union to which he aspires, isn't it a testimony to the honesty of his intentions? Fanchon: Ah, Father! What you're saying is hopelessly middle class. I'm ashamed to hear you talk like that, you really ought to learn to see things as they are."

How does this happen? Were there Fanchons in Moliere's days, or
are there Madelons now? — But seriously, Fanny, all the ill-founded
Objections You make, to me appear strong & invincible marks of a
violent & sincere Passion — what You take it into your head to be
displeas'd with, as too great a Liberty, I mean, his presuming to write
to You, & in so tender & respectful & submissive a strain, if You
knew the World, & that villanous Yahoo, call'd man,[7] as well as I
do, You would see in a very different Light — in its true light — fear-
fulness, a high opinion of You, a consciousness (an unjust one I will
call it) of his own inferiority; & at last, as he thinks the happiness of
his Life is at stake, summoning up a trembling resolution of disclos-
ing in writing the situation of his mind, which he has not the courage
to do to Your Face — & do You call, or think this — can You judge
so ill, as to look on this as an undue, or impertinent Liberty? — Ah
Fany [*sic*], such a disposition promises a thousand fold more happiness,
more solid, lasting, home-felt happiness, than all the seducing, exterior
Airs, Graces, Accomplishments, & Address of an Artful rake — such
a man, as this Young Barlow, if ever You are so lucky, & so well-
advis'd, as to be united to him, will improve upon You every hour;
You will discover in him Graces, & Charms, which kindness will
bring to light, that at present You have no Idea, of — I mean if his
Character is truly given by Hetty — that is the grand Object of Inquiry — as likewise his Circumstances. This last, as the great sheet
Anchor,[8] on which we are to depend in our Voyage thro' life, ought
most minutely to be scrutiniz'd. Is he of any profession, or only of an
independent Fortune? — if either, or both, sufficient to promise a
really comfortable [Income,] You may live to the Age of your Grandmother, & not meet with so Valuable an offer — Shakespear says,

> There is a Tide in the affairs of men,
> Which taken at the heighth, leads on to Fortune;
> But being neglected, &c[9]

I forget how it goes on, but the sense is, (what You may guess,) that
the Opportunity is never to be recover'd — the Tide is lost, & You

[7] *Yahoo, call'd man:* Yahoos are fictional creatures created by the author Jonathan
Swift (1667–1745) in his famous satire *Gulliver's Travels*. Filthy, violent, and morally
corrupt, they embody what is worst in Swift's view of humanity.

[8] *sheet Anchor:* The sheet anchor was the largest of a ship's anchors, usually used
only in emergencies.

[9] *There is a tide . . . neglected, &c:* See Shakespeare's *Julius Caesar,* 4.3.217:
"There is a tide in the affairs of men, / Which, taken at the flood, leads on to fortune; /
Omitted, all the voyage of their life / Is bound in shallows and in miseries."

are left in shallows, fast aground, & struggling in Vain for the remainder of your life to get on — doom'd to pass it in Obscurity & regret — look around You Fany — look at y$^r$ Aunts — *Fanny Burney* wont always be what she is now! — M$^{rs}$ Hamilton once had an Offer of £3000 a Year or near it — a parcel of young giggling Girls laugh'd her out of it — the man forsooth was not quite smart enough, tho' otherwise estimable — Oh Fanny this is not a marrying Age, without a handsome Fortune! — how happy does Hetty feel herself to have married [*five words missing*] — Suppose You to lose y$^r$ Father — take in all Chances. Consider the situation of an unprotected, unprovided Woman —

Excuse my being so Earnest with You — Assure Yourself it proceeds from my regard, & from (let me say it, tho' it savours of Vanity) a deep knowledge of the World — Observe, how far I go — I dont urge You, hand over head, to have this man at all Events; but for Gods sake, & your own sake, give him & yourself fair Play — dont decide so positively against it — if You do, You are ridiculous to a high degree — if You dont answer his letter, dont avoid seeing him — at all Events, I charge You on my blessing to attend Hetty in her Visit to the O'Connors, according to y$^r$ Promise, & which You cant get off without positive rudeness — this binds You to Nothing; it leaves an opening for future Consideration & Inquiry, & is barely decent — I have wrote so much on this subject, (which is now next my heart) that I cannot frame myself to any thing else for this bout — so Adieu, You have the best wishes of y$^r$ Affectionate Daddy SC

## Journal Entry for Sunday, May 15, 1775

The Visit to M$^{rs}$ O Connor was made yesterday. I Commissioned my Aunts — — though they would hardly hear me — to say that I was prevented from Waiting on her by a bad Cold. How the message was taken, & what passed, I know not; but this morning, while we were all at Breakfast, except my Father, who was in the study; John[10] came into the Parlour, & said that a Gentleman wanted me.

I guessed who it was — & was inexpressibly Confused. Mama stared, but desired he might walk in — the Door opened — & he appeared. — He had Dressed himself elegantly — but could hardly

---

[10] *John:* John is a servant of the household, part of whose duties would include announcing visitors.

speak. — He Bowed two or three Times — I coloured like scarlet, & I believe he was the only person in the Room who did not see it.

"M^rs O Connor — he called — my Cold — he understood — he was very sorry — "

He could not get on. — My voice too, failed me terribly — for his silence at his first Entrance made me fear he was going to reproach me for not answering his Letter. — I told him my Cold had been too bad to allow me to go out — but I was so terribly frightened lest my mother should say *what Cold — I did not know you had one*! — that I had great difficulty to get out the Words: & he himself after wards took Notice that my *Voice* spoke how bad my Cold was! — though in fact I have no Cold at all: my mother then asked him to sit down — & Sukey,[11] very good naturedly, entered into Conversation with him, to our mutual relief, — particularly to his, as he seemed so confounded he scarse knew where he was. I sat upon Thorns from the fear he would desire to speak to me alone — I looked another way, & hardly opened my mouth, & when, in about ½ an Hour, he rose to go, I kept my Eyes from him — & Sukey went to the Parlour Door with him.

I don't know what my mother thought, but she has not said a Word. Whether he was induced to make this visit from expecting he might speak to me, or whether in order to see if I had any Cold or not, I cannot tell: but it proved cruelly distressing to him, & confusing to me.

Had I sent an answer, this would not have happened: but it is now too late. I am very sorry to find this young man seems so serious; — however, an attachment so precipitately formed, so totally discouraged, & *so* placed — cannot be difficult to Cure.

### Frances Burney to Samuel Crisp

[St Martin's Street, May 15, 1775]

And so it is all over with me!

& I am to be given up — to forfeit your blessing — to lose your good opinion — to be doomed to regret & the Horrors — *because* — I have not a mind to be married.

Forgive me — my dearest M^r Crisp — forgive me — but indeed I cannot act from *Worldly motives* — you know, & have long known

---

[11] *Sukey:* Nickname for Burney's sister Susanna, her closest confidante and friend until the latter's death in 1800.

& laughed at my Notions & Character. Continue still to *Laugh* at me — but pray don't make *me* Cry — for your last Letter really made me unhappy — I am grieved that you can so earnestly espouse the Cause of a person you never saw — I heartily wish him well — he is, I believe, a worthy young man — but I have long accustomed myself to the idea of being an old maid — & the Title has lost all its terrors in my Ears. I feel no repugnance to the expectation of being ranked among the Number.

As to the Visit to Hoxton — my dear Daddy, *how* could I make it, without leaving M^r Barlow to infer — the Lord knows what? — by what he says in his Letter, it is evident he would have taken it to himself: — he is hasty — & I dreaded being some how or other entangled — I have no dislike to him — the whole party were strongly his friends — & upon the whole, I though it necessary to keep away. I would not for the World be thought to *trifle* with any man. [I could not] now have made that Visit without giving him reason to draw conclusions very disagreeable to me.

Don't imagine by what I say that I have made a *Vow* for a single Life — no. But on the other Hand I have no *Objection* to it, & have all my life determined never to marry without having the highest value & esteem for the man who should be my Lord.

Were I ever so well disposed to follow your advice & see more of this Youth — I am convinced he would not let me; — he is so extremely precipitate — I *must* either determine for or against him — or at least enter into such conditions as I should think myself in honour bound to abide by.

If you ask my Objections — I must frankly own they are such as perhaps will only satisfy myself — for I have none to make to his Character — Disposition or person — they are all good; *but* — he is not used to Company or the World — his Language is stiff, studied, & even affected — in short — he does not *hit my fancy* —

> I do not like you, Dr. Fell —
> The Reason why I cannot tell —
> But I don't *like* you, Dr. Fell![12]

Hetty, & the Party, went on Saturday [13 May] to Hoxton. I desired them to say I was not well — how the Day passed I know not — they have all Quarrelled with me about this affair, & I don't care to

---

[12] *I do not like . . . Dr. Fell:* While a student at Christ Church, Oxford, the popular wit and writer Thomas Brown (1663–1704) wrote of John Fell, dean of Christ Church, "I do not love thee, Doctor Fell. / The reason why I cannot tell; / But this alone I know full well, / I do not love thee, Doctor Fell."

go either to Queen Street or York Street. But while we were at Breakfast yesterday morning — John came in & said a Gentleman desired to speak to me. — M^r Barlow came in — to enquire after my Health — *You* would have Laughed had you been present — for I was so much frightened lest my mother should blab my being well, & lest he should desire to speak to me — that I quite lost my Voice — in so much, that he himself afterwards took notice how bad my Cold was — though in fact I have none at all! — while on the other Hand, he was so terribly confused that he made 3 several Bows before he could get out a word. My mother, Bessy & Charlotte all stared with amazement, wondering who he was, & what his visit meant — as to Sukey, she could not keep her Countenance at first — though soon after, she very good naturedly entered into Conversation with M^r Barlow, to our mutual relief.

I am very uneasy at not having answered his Letter — I should be equally grieved to have him take my silence either for *Contempt* or for *Compliance*; but my Father to whom I shewed it, desired me not to answer it. — *why* I cannot imagine. If *he* sided against me — I could not resist the stream — for Sukey is firmly his friend — but I thank Heaven he does not interfere — he is all indulgence — & to quit *his* Roof requires inducements which I am sure I shall never have. I never — never can love any human being as I love him!

Once more I entreat your forgiveness — & that you will write me word you forgive me —

Don't be uneasy about my welfare, my dear Daddy, I dare say I shall do very well. — I cannot persuade myself to *snap* at a settlement — & I do assure you this young man would not suffer me to deliberate long. —

Had marriage from prudence & Convenience been my desire — I believe I had it quite as much in my power if I designed it as now — there was a certain youth, not *quite* so hasty to be sure, as M^r Barlow, but not far otherwise, who took much pains for increasing our Acquaintance — I happened to Dance with him at a private masquerade[13] at M^r. Lalauze's — & he called two or 3 Times afterward, & wrote 2 notes, with most pressing requests that Hetty & I would

[13] *private masquerade:* Masquerade balls, in which the participants wore costumes, masks, and even disguised their voices so that they would not be recognized, were highly popular, if much criticized, amusements in eighteenth-century London. The most heavily censured masquerades were large public affairs for which one paid an admission price. People from different walks of life could mix indiscriminately at a public masquerade, and it was often said that the general atmosphere of disguise and the anonymity of the crowd led to licentious behavior. A private masquerade was a far more respectable, if still very exciting, experience for a young person, as it retained the element of disguise within the relative safety of a controlled and limited guest list.

accept Tickets for Balls & that *he might exist again* — however,
after the answer he received to the 2ᵈ Note, I heard of him no more.
In short, I long since settled to either attach myself with my whole
Heart — or to have the Courage to lead Apes.[14]

I have now — & I shall ever have the most grateful sense of your
kindness, & of the interest you take in my concerns. — I heartily wish
I *could* act by your advice, & that I could return an attachment,
which, strange as it seems to me, I so little deserve.

After all — so long as I live to be of some comfort (as I flatter myself I am) to my Father, — I can have no motive to wish to sign myself other than his & your

> ever obliged & ever affectionate & devoted
> Frances Burney to
> the End of the Chapter.
> Amen!

As to his circumstances, I have made no Enquiries — for I honestly
[c]onfess they wᵈ have but little Influence with me one way or other.


### Frances Burney to Samuel Crisp

[St Martin's Street, c. May 22–25, 1775]

My dear Daddy,

I was extremely happy at the Receipt of your last Letter, because
you assure me you are not angry with me, though, believe me, I cannot with unconcern Read your cautions & prognostics. I am *not tri-
umphant* — but I am not *desponding*: & I must again repeat what I
have so often had the hardiesse to say, that I have no idea why a
single Life may not be happy. Liberty is not without its value — with
women as well as with men, though it has not *equal* recommenda-
tions for both, — & I hope never without a prospect brighter to myself to lose mine: & I have no such prospect in view.

Had I ever *Hesitated* about Mʳ Barlow, your advice, my dear sir,
would have turned the Balance on his side; but I never did or could.
So now to other matters. . . .


Thursday May 25

And now, my dear Mʳ Crisp, I am going to ask you advice, for I
am in some perplexity. — all concerning this Mʳ Barlow.

My Grandmother, 2 aunts & sister spent the Day with us last
Wednesday [17 May]. They told me that my *Cold* was very well

---

[14] *lead Apes:* An old saying: old maids lead apes in hell.

swallowed at Hoxton & that M^r Barlow was *immensely shocked,* & all that. — My Aunt Beckey teized me to Drink Tea with her the next Day [18 May] — I was engaged, & could not, but said I would on Saturday [20 May]. Accordingly I went. I ran up stairs, as usual — but when I opened the Door, the first object I saw was M^r Barlow. I was much surprised, & rather provoked, fearing that my aunt Beckey, whose Temper is much superior to her Understanding, had purposely led me to this meeting. You will believe I was tolerably shy & forbidding, at first, but afterwards I tried to behave as if I had never received his Letter, & it was not difficult to me to appear quite unconcerned, & as usual.

I made my visit [*two to three words missing*] very short, & was hurrying away as soon as Tea was over when I found that I should not be allowed to go [*one and a half lines missing*] had I slipt out, he would have followed me. I therefore sat down again, determined to wait till he went, or till I was sent for by the Mama.

I have since wished that I had let him have his way — speak to me — & answered him, — to End the affair for ever. But at the Time, I really had not sufficient presence of mind: — he appeared so humbly at my service, that I dreaded lest, in the fear of being impertinent, I should be involved in some scrape from being *civil*; — in short, I much wished to avoid a private Conversation in which I could hear nothing that would be agreeable to me, & could say nothing that would not be highly *disagreeable* to him. — I am heartily sorry his Letter was not answered at once. It is now too late to take any Notice of it. He was excessively urgent with my Grandmother to fix a Day for another visit to Hoxton *with me*; & he *entreated* me not to have a Cold then! I laughed the Cold off as well as I could, but would by no means promise to be of the Party — niether, indeed, would I do any single thing that he requested, lest he should construe even common complaisance into a wish of obliging him.

I should be quite sorry for the apparent *seriousness* of this young man's attachment, but that I am p[r]etty persuaded what so easily came, will without difficulty depart.

I hope — as I endeavoured — that my *general manner* has convinced him of his having chosen ill. Nevertheless, — I beg you to advise me what to do whether to go to Hoxton & force myself to say (as Lord Ogleby expresses it) *shocking* things to Him[15] — I

---

[15] *shocking things to Him:* An allusion to David Garrick's and George Colman's *The Clandestine Marriage,* act 4, scene 3.

don't care to say any thing more to my Father about it. — I could not resist *him*.

I certainly ought not to keep him [Barlow] in *suspence,* if it is *possible* he can think himself so. Pray Instruct me — only remember that I am *fixed*.

Adieu my dear sir, I am now and ever

most faithfully & truly yours,
Frances


### Frances Burney to Samuel Crisp

[St Martin's Street, June 2, 1775]
Friday Night

My dear Sir,

My Father can not see you before Sunday, when he proposes to be with you as s[oo]n as he can. Whether *alone* — or with any body else — or whether your anecdote-monger will accompany him, as yet none but the *great gods can tell*!

If I do *not* see you — I must take this opportunity of entreating & convincing you not to use your Influence with my Father for M^r B. in case he should mention that personage to you. I have not Time at present to tell you *all about it* — but a great deal has passed since I wrote last, & I have suffered the most cruel & terrifying uneasiness — I am *now* again at peace & hope to continue so. Should my Father happen to speak to you of what *I* have said, — (as it is well known that I write very openly to you) I entreat you to assure him that I have expressed the greatest aversion to forming a connection with M^r B. I have not dared to speak so much to the purpose myself, — for I have been — & I am, determined at all Events not to oppose *his* will & advice — but I know he wishes only for my happiness, & I am sensible that I should be wretched for ever if induced to marry where I have no manner of affection or regard. — O M^r Crisp — it is dreadful to me to think of Uniting my Destiny — Spending my Time — Devoting my Life — to one whose Face I never desire to see Again!

Had I with equal bluntness expressed myself to my Father, I am certain he would not ever think of M^r B. more — but — his interference was so unexpected — it silenced, confounded, & frightened me.

I see you did not care to send me your advice — which, however would be too late — as M^r B. is no *Dreaming Lover.* — I hope all is over.

I don't think my mother will be able to be with you, as Miss Lidderdale of Lynn is expected here — but all this is unsettled.
Adieu, my dear Daddy,

> I am ever most truly yours
> F. Burney

## Journal Entry for June 6, 1775

A Week passed after this, without my hearing or seeing any more of M^r Barlow & I hoped that he had resigned his pretensions. But on Saturday morning [27 May], while we were at Breakfast, I had a Letter brought me in a Hand which I immediately knew to be Barlow's. As it by no means is so *high flown* as his first, I will Copy it.

Madam,

I have somewhere seen that powerful Deity Cupid, & the invincible Mars habited in a similar manner, & each have in their Train several of the same dispositioned Attendants: the propriety of which Thought I own pleased me, for when drawn from the Allegory, it is acknowledged both Love & War are comparative in several particulars; they each require Constancy, & the hope of success stimulate each to perseverance, & as the one is warmed & encouraged by the Desire of Glory, so the other is much more powerfully fired & transported by the Charms of the Fair sex: I have been told that Artifice & Deception are connected to both; but those Qualities I should determine to discard, & substitute in their place an open Frankness, & undisguised Truth & Honour, & for Diligence, Attention, Assiduity & Care, which are essential to both, & which some place in the Catalogue of the Labours of Love, I should have them happily converted to pleasures, in the honour of devoting them to Miss Fanny Burney, if the Destinys auspiciously avert a disagreeable sequel, for as the bravest General may miscarry, so the most sincere Lover may lose the wished for Prize; to prevent which, I should continue to invoke my Guardian Genius,[16] that she may ever inspire me with such Principles & Actions as may enable me to reach the summit of my Ambition, in Approveing [*sic*] myself not unworthy the Esteem of your amiable self, & not unworthy — but stop, Oh *arduous Pen, & presume not* — 'till in the front you can place Permission to hope — ascending such sublime heights.

---

[16] *my Guardian Genius:* According to classical mythology, the spirit delegated to people at birth, who will guide their personal fortune and shape their character.

It has given me great uneasiness that the excessive hurry of Business has so long prevented me the honour of Waiting on You, & enquiring after your Welfare, which I earnestly wish to hear; but I determine, with your leave, ere long to do myself that pleasure, as methinks Time moves very slowly in granting me an opportunity to declare, in some small degree, (for I could never reach what I should call otherwise) how much I am, with the greatest Respect immaginable, dear Miss Fanny,

Your most Devoted & most Obedient servant<br>Tho<sup>s</sup> Barlow.

Notwithstanding I was at once sorry & provoked at perceiving how sanguine this youth chose to be, I was not absolutely concerned at receving this 2<sup>d</sup> Letter, because I regarded it as a fortunate opportunity of putting an unalterable Conclusion to the whole Affair. However, as I had begun by asking my Father's advice, I thought it my duty to speak to Father before I sent an Answer, never doubting his immediate concurrence.

My mother, Sukey & I went to the opera that Evening; it was therefore too late when I returned to send a Letter to Hoxton — but I went up stairs into the study, & told my Father I had received another Epistle from M<sup>r</sup> Barlow which I could only attribute to my not answering, as I had wished, his first; I added that I proposed, with his leave, to Write to M<sup>r</sup> Barlow the next morning.

My Father looked grave, asked me for the Letter, put it in his Pocket unread, & wished me good Night.

I was siezed with a kind of pannic — I trembled at the idea of his Espousing, however mildly, the Cause of this young man: — I passed a restless Night, & in the morning dared not Write without his permission, which I was now half afraid to ask.

About 2 O'clock, while I was dawdling in the study, & Waiting for an opportunity to speak, we heard a Rap at the Door — & soon after, John came up, & said "A Gentleman is below, who asks for Miss Burney, — M<sup>r</sup> Barlow."

I think I was never more mad in my life — to have taken pains to avoid a private Conversation so highly disagreeable to me, & at last to be forced into it at so unfavourable a Juncture, — for I had now 2 Letters from him, both Unanswered & consequently open to his Conjectures. I exclaimed "Lord! — how provoking! what shall I do?"

My Father looked uneasy & perplexed: — he said something

about not being hasty, which I did not desire him to explain, but only said as I left the Room —

"Well, I must soon tell him I *have* answered his letter, & so send one tomorrow, & let him think it kept at the Post office." In this determination, I went down stairs. — I saw my mother pass into the Back Parlour; which did not add to the *Graciousness* of my Reception of poor M^r Barlow, who I found alone in the Parlour. I was not sorry that none of the Family were there, as I now began to seriously dread any protraction of this affair.

He came up to me, & with an Air of *tenderness* & satisfaction, began some anxious Enquiries about my Health, but I interrupted him with saying "I fancy, Sir, You have not received a Letter I have written to you — I — "

"A Letter? — no, Ma'am!"

"You will have it, then, to-morrow, Sir."

We were both silent for a minute or two, when he said "In consequence, I presume, Ma'am, of the one I — "

"Yes Sir!" Cried I.

"And pray — Ma'am — Miss Burney! — may I — beg to ask the contents? that is — the — the — " he could not go on.

"Sir — I — it was only — it was merely — in short, you will see it to-morrow."

"But if you would favour me with the Contents now, I could perhaps Answer it at once?"

"Sir, it requires no Answer!"

A second silence ensued. I was really distressed myself to see *his* distress, which was very apparent. After some time, he stammered out something of *hoping* — & *beseeching,* — which, gathering more firmness, I announced — "I am much obliged to You, Sir, for the great opinion You are pleased to have of me — but I should be sorry you should lose any more Time upon my account — as I have no thoughts at all of changing my situation."

He seemed to be quite overset: having, therefore so freely explained myself, I then asked him to sit down, & began to talk of the Weather. When he had a little recovered himself, he drew a Chair close to me, & began making most ardent professions of respect & regard, & so forth. I interrupted him, as soon as I could, & begged him to rest satisfied with my Answer.

"*Satisfied?*" repeated he — "my dear Ma'am — is that possible?"

"Perhaps, Sir," said, I, "I ought to make some apologies for not answering your first Letter — but really, I was so much surprised — upon so short an Acquaintance."

He then began making Excuses for having written but as to *short acquaintance,* he owned it was a reason for *me* — but for *him* — fifty Years could not have more convinced him of my &c &c.

"You have taken a sudden, & far too partial idea of my character," answered I. "If you look round among your older Acquaintance, I doubt not but you will very soon be able to make a better choice."

He shook his Head: "I have seen, Madam, a great many Ladies, it is true — but never — "

"You do me much honour;" cried I, "but I must desire you would take no further trouble about me — for I have not, at present, the slightest thoughts of ever leaving this House."

"*At present?*" repeated he, eagerly, — "no, I would not expect it — I would not *wish* to precipitate — but in future — "

"Niether now or ever, Sir," returned I, "have I any view of changing my situation."

"But surely — surely this can never be! so severe a resolution — you cannot mean it — it would be wronging all the world!"

"I am extremely sorry, Sir, that you did not receive my Letter — because it might have saved you this trouble."

He looked very much mortified, & said, in [a] dejected voice — "If there is any thing in me — in my connections — or in my situation in Life — which you wholly think unworthy of You — & beneath you — — or if my Character or Disposition meet with your disapprobation — I will immediately forgo all — I will not — I would not — "

"No, indeed, Sir," cried I, "I have niether seen or heard any thing of your character that was to your disadvantage — & I have no doubts of your worthiness — "

He thanked me, & seemed reassured; but renewed his solicitations in the most urgent manner. He repeatedly begged my permission to acquaint my Family of the state of his affairs, & to abide by their decision — but I would not let him say two words following upon that subject. I told him that the Answer I had written was a final one, & begged him to take it as such.

He remonstrated very earnestly. "This is the severest decision! — I am persuaded, Madam, you cannot be so cruel? — Surely you must allow that the *social state* is what we were all meant for? — that we were created for one another? — that to form such a resolution is contrary to the design of our Being? — "

"All this may be true, — " said I; — "I have nothing to say in contradiction to it — but you know there are many odd Characters in the World — & I am one of them."

"O no, no, no, — that can never be! — but is it possible you can have so bad an opinion of the married state? It seems to me the *only* state for happiness! — "

"Well, Sir, *You* are attached to the married Life — *I* am to the single — therefore, *every man in his humour* — [17] do *you* follow *your* opinion, — & let *me* follow *mine.*"

"But surely — is not this — *singular?* — "

"I give you leave, Sir," cried I, laughing, "to think me singular — odd — Queer — nay, even whimsical, if you please."

"But, my *dear* Miss Burney, only — "

"I entreat you, Sir, to take my Answer — You really pain me by being so urgent. — "

"That would not I do for the World! — I only beg You to suffer me — perhaps in future — "

"No, indeed; I shall never change — I do assure you you will find me very obstinate!"

He began to lament his own Destiny. I grew extremely tired of saying so often the same thing; — but I could not absolutely turn him out of the House, & indeed he seemed so dejected & unhappy, that I made it my study to soften my refusal as much as I could without leaving room for future expectation.

About this Time, my mother came in. We both rose. — I was horridly provoked at my situation —

"I am only come in for a Letter," cried she, — "pray don't let me disturb you. — " & away she went.

Very obliging indeed!

She was no sooner gone, than Mr. Barlow began again the same story, & seemed determined not to give up his Cause. He hoped, at least, that I would allow him to enquire after my Health? —

"I must beg you, Sir, to send me no more Letters."

He seemed much hurt.

---

[17] *every man in his humour:* An allusion to a play by the English dramatist Ben Jonson (1572–1637). *Every Man in his Humour,* first performed with Shakespeare in the cast in 1598, drew on English humors theory, which held that every human being was composed of different combinations of heat, cold, moisture, and dryness. The combination determined a person's "humour" — what we might call his or her disposition or personality.

"You had better, Sir, think of me no more — if you study your own happiness — "

"I *do* study my own happiness — more than I have ever had Any probability of doing before — !"

"You have made an unfortunate Choice, Sir; but you will find it easier to forget it than you imagine. You have only to suppose I was not at M^r Burney's on May Day — & it was a mere chance my being there — & then you will be —

"But if I *could* — could I also forget seeing you at [old] M^rs Burney's? — and if I did — can I forget that I see you now? — "

"O yes! — in 3 months Time you may forget you ever knew me. You will not find it so difficult a Task as you suppose."

"You have heard, Ma'am, of an Old man being Growed young? — perhaps you believe *that*? — But you will not deny me leave to sometimes see you? — "

"My Father, Sir, is seldom, — hardly ever, indeed, at Home — "[18]

"I have never seen the Doctor — but I hope he would not refuse me permission to enquire after your Health? I have no wish without his Consent."

"Though I acknowledge myself to be *singular* I would not have you think me either *affected* or *trifling*, — & therefore I must assure you that I am *fixed* in the Answer I have given You; *Unalterably* fixed."

His entreaties grew extremely urgent & very distressing to me: — he besought me to take more Time, said it should be the study of his life to make me happy. "Allow me — my *dear* Miss Burney — only to hope that my future Conduct — "

"I shall always think myself obliged, nay honoured by your good opinion — & you are entitled to my best wishes for your Health & Happiness — but indeed, the less we meet the better."

"What — what can I do?" cried he, very sorrowfully.

"Why — go & ponder upon this affair for about half an Hour — then say, what an odd, queer, strange Creature she is! & then — think of something else."

"O no; no! — you cannot suppose all that? — I shall think of nothing else; *your* refusal is more pleasing than any other Lady's acceptance — "

---

[18] *My Father . . . at Home:* This claim might be literally true. Charles Burney's professional obligations often kept him away from home, and when there, he was often engaged in writing and therefore was not "at home" to company.

He said this very simply, but too seriously for me to Laugh at it. Just then, Sukey came in — but did not stay two minutes. It would have been shocking to be thus left purposely as if with a declared Lover, & yet I was not sorry to have an opportunity of preventing future doubts or expectations.

I rose & Walked to the Window, thinking it high Time to End a Conversation already much too long; & when he again began to entreat me not to be so *very severe,* I told him that I was *sure* I should never alter the Answer I made at first; that I was very happy at Home, & not at all inclined to try my fate elsewhere; I then desired my Compliments to M^rs O'Connor, & Miss Dickenson, & made a *reverence*[19] by way of leave taking.

"I am extremely sorry to detain you so long, Ma'am, — " said he, in a melancholy Voice. I made no answer. He Walked about the Room; & then again besought my leave to ask me how I did some other Time — I absolutely, though Civilly, refused it; & told him frankly that, fixed as I was, it was better for himself that we should not meet.

He then took his leave: — returned back — took leave — returned again: — he had then a new Petition, for then I took a more formal leave of him, expressing my good wishes for his Welfare, in a sort of way that implied I expected never to see him again — he would fain have taken a more *tender* leave of me, — but I repulsed him with great surprise & displeasure. I did not, however, as he was so terribly sorrowful, refuse him my Hand, which he had made sundry vain attempts to take in the course of our Conversation; when I withdrew it, as I did presently, I rang the Bell,[20] to prevent him again returning from the Door.

Though I was really sorry for the unfortunate & misplaced attachment which this Young man professes for me, yet I could almost have *Jumped* for Joy when he was gone, to think that the affair was thus finally over.

Indeed I think it hardly possible for a Woman to be in a more irksome situation, than when rejecting an honest man who is all humility, Respect & submission, & who throws himself & his Fortune at her Feet.

I had no opportunity of speaking to my Father all that Day. In the Evening M^r Burney & Hetty came. Hetty told me, that the Day

[19]*reverence:* A formal nod, a modified bow.
[20]*I rang the Bell:* To call the servant to see him out.

before, M$^{rs}$ O Connor had Called on her, & told her of Mr. Barlow's having owned to her his Attachment to me, & requested of her to let him know, first, whether I had any pre-engagement, & secondly, whether I had ever expressed any *Antipathy* to him. She answered both these in the Negative, & then M$^{rs}$ O'Connor, in M$^{r}$ Barlow's Name, entreated her to be his Advocate; which she readily promised.

After his Conversation with me, he Called on her himself. She says he was all dejection & sadness. He expressed the greated *Respect* for me, feared I thought him wanting in it; — apologised for his early Declaration, which, he said, resulted from his sincerity, & his having no Experience either in the arts, or the ways of men.

My Father sent for Hetty up stairs, & made a thousand Enquiries concerning M$^{r}$ Barlow.

The next Day [29 May] — a Day the remembrance of which will be never erased from my memory — my Father first spoke to me *in favour* of M$^{r}$ Barlow! & desired me not to be *peremtory* in the Answer I was going to Write.

I scarce made any answer — I was terrified to Death — I felt the utter impossibility of resisting not merely my Father's *persuasion,* but even his *Advice.* — I felt, too, that I had no *argumentative* objections to make to M$^{r}$ Barlow, his Character — Disposition — situation — I knew nothing against — but O! — I felt he was no Companion for my Heart! — I wept like an Infant — Eat nothing — seemed as if already married — & passed the whole Day in more misery than, merely on my own account, I ever did before in my life, — except upon the loss of my own beloved mother — & ever revered & most dear Grandmother![21]

After supper, I went into the study, while my dear Father was alone, to wish him Good Night, which I did as chearfully as I could, though pretty evidently in dreadful uneasiness. When I had got to the Door, he called me back, & asked me concerning a new mourning Gown I had bought for the mourning of Queen Caroline — [22] he de-

---

[21]*most dear Grandmother:* Burney refers here to her maternal grandmother. Her paternal grandmother was still living, although she died shortly after this was written. For a discussion of the death of Burney's mother, Esther Sleepe Burney, see the headnote to this selection.

[22]*new mourning Gown . . . Queen Caroline:* Court mourning was a formal period of mourning ordered by the royal court. Public appearances during such a period required special dark clothing, usually of silk or some rich fabric. George III's sister, Caroline Matilda, married to the king of Denmark, had died on May 10 of this year, and a general mourning was ordered between May 24 and July 5.

sired to know what it would come to, & as our allowance for Cloaths is not *sumptuous,* said he would assist Sukey & me which he accordingly did, & affectionately embraced me, saying "I wish I could do more for Thee, Fanny!" "O Sir! — " cried I — "*I* wish for Nothing! — only let me Live with you! — " — "My life!" cried he, kissing me kindly, "Thee shalt live with me for ever, if Thee wilt! Thou canst not think I meant to get rid of thee?"

"I could not, Sir! I could not!" cried I, [I could not outlive] such a thought — " I saw his dear Eyes full of Tears! a mark of his tenderness which I shall never forget!

"God knows" — continued he — "I wish not to part with my Girls! — they are my greatest Comfort! — only — do not be too hasty! — "

Thus relieved, restored to future hopes, I went to Bed as light, happy & thankful as if Escaped from Destruction.

I had, however, written my Letter before my Father spoke, & as I had expressly told M[r] Barlow it contained a Refusal, I thought it would be even ridiculous to alter it, & I rather determined, if my Father had persisted in desiring it, to *unsay* a rejection, than not to write it after having declared I already had. This is the Copy:

St Martin's Street<br>Leicester Fields.

Sir,

I am much concerned to find that my silence to the first Letter with which you honoured me, has not had the Effect it was meant to produce, of preventing your giving yourself any further trouble upon my Account.

The good opinion you are pleased to express of me, however extraordinary upon so short an Acquaintance, certainly claims my Acknowledgements; but as I have no intention of changing my present situation, I can only assure You of my good wishes for Your Health & Happiness, & request & desire that you will bestow no further Thoughts, Time, or Trouble upon,

Sir,<br>Your most humble servant,<br>F. Burney.

From that Day to this, my Father, I thank [H]eaven, has never again mentioned M[r] Barlow.

## Journal Entry for June 8, 1775

I called at my sister's lately, & was very sorry to hear that M^r Barlow, who has been again to visit her, expressed himself to be as strongly as ever Attached to me, & requested of her to suffer him to meet me some Day at her House, by letting him know when I was with her. She told him I should be very angry with her — he promised to appear so much surprised, that I should never know the meeting was not accidental, — & she was at length prevailed with to promise him her assistance.

However, reflecting upon it afterwards, she repented, & therefore told me of what had passed. I Assured her I was extremely glad she had saved me so disagreeable [a] Task as a second refusal should have been — for as *his* motives are obvious, so *my* resolution is unalterable. — but by my Father, who, I am sure is too indulgent to require me to give my Hand without my Heart.

I Commissioned her, when she saw him, to tell him that she found by my Conversation I was so *determined,* that she thought it was only exposing both of us to uneasiness to promote a meeting.

I wish this young man Well — I believe him to be worthy — but am sorry he will not be Answered. . . .

On Wednesday morning, while my mother & I were with her, [*one-half line missing*] the maid came up stairs, & said a *Gentleman* was in the parlour, waiting for me — "Did not he send up his Name?" cried Mama. "No, Ma'am," answered she. "Do you know who he is?" "No, Ma'am."

I supposed it was M^r Barlow, & heartily wished I had been out. I went down stairs, nevertheless, perforce, & found him Alone. He Bowed. I curtsied. He seemed at a loss what to say — & as I determined not to ask him to sit down, or to say any thing that might encourage him either to stay, or to repeat his Visit, I was silent also. At length, he stammered out "I hope — ma'am — you — are well? — "

"Very well, I thank You, Sir," was my laconic reply.

Another silence; & then — "Your Cold? — I hope, Ma'am, I hope you have quite — "

"O it is quite gone," cried I; "I am perfectly well."

"I am very happy to hear it — I could not, — Ma'am — I could not deny myself — the satisfaction of enquiring after your Health. — "

"I am sorry, Sir," answered I very gravely, "that You should have taken the trouble to Call."

"Does it give you — I hope, Ma'am — it does not give you — any *uneasiness?* — "

I made no answer, but went towards the Window, where I saw Dick & Miss Fydell, a lady who was coming to see Miss Lidderdale, in the street; I was rejoiced at so speedy an opportunity of Ending our Tete à Tete, & flew myself to the Door to let them in. I then began to talk with Miss Fydell, all the Time standing myself, that I might not be obliged to ask M^r Barlow to sit.

He seemed a good deal agitated. I was truly quite sorry to be so rude to him — but what can a Woman do when a man will not take an answer? I would with all my Heart, have been civil & sociable with him in a friendly manner, from gratitude for the real regard he seems to have for me — but I have heard too much of mankind to believe he would not draw *Inferences,* & entertain *Expectations* from such *friendliness,* that might greatly distress & embarrass me: besides, ever since the Day that my *Father* spoke for him, I have quite dreaded the continuation of his addresses.

His situation was too uneasy to be long supported, &, after enquiring about the Family, he took his leave, with a look so mortified & unhappy, that I felt shocked at myself for what, in fact, I could not help. — how ever, when I heard the street Door opened, I just shewed my self in the Passage, & called out that I wished him a good Walk. He started back & seemed going to return — but I immediately came into the Parlour, yet not before I could see by his change of Countenance that he was pleased at this little mark of Civility.

I hope, however, that this Visit will be his last. I think he will never have the courage to make Another. I have not mentioned it to my Father. Indeed I dare not renew a subject which has caused me so much uneasiness & fright. Sorry as I am for M^r Barlow, who is a worthy young man, I cannot involve myself in a Life of discomfort for his satisfaction.

I have had the great pleasure of a Letter from my dear M^r Crisp, in answer to my pleas against marrying *Heart-whole,* in which he most kindly gives up the Cause, & allows of my reasoning & Opinion.

What my mother thinks of the Affair I know not, but the other Day, when Hetty & M^t Burney were here, she suddenly, in a *laughing way,* turned to me, & said "O but — Fanny! — was you cruel? — or kind, the other morning? — upon my Word — it is Time to enquire! — a Gentleman *whose Visits are admitted!*"[23]

---

[23]*whose Visits are admitted:* Burney's stepmother is teasingly referring to Mr. Barlow as Frances's acknowledged suitor.

I only laughed, not caring to be serious so publicly, but really it was a very provoking *turn* to give to M^r Barlow's Calls; — & will make me doubly desirous that they should not be renewed.

I forgot to mention that one Evening, about a fortnight since, as we Were all Walking in the Park, we met M^rs Pringle again. I introduced to her her *young old* friend, Charlotte,[24] & they were mutually glad to see each other. She was extremely cordial in her Invitation to all of us, & I much wish it was in my power to accept them.

We also saw poor Miss Laluze, whose Face immediately shewed that she recollected my Eldest sister & me; however, we Walked on, wishing to avoid speaking to her: but when we were at Spring Garden Gate, she just touched my shoulder, as she came suddenly behind us, & said "Miss Burney! — how do you do, Ma'am?" —

I answered her rather coldly — & Hetty turned from her abruptly. I was afterwards very sorry that I did not speak with more kindness to her, for Sukey says that she looked greatly disappointed. It is, however, impossible & improper to keep up acquaintance with a Female who has lost her character, however sincerely they may be objects of Pity. What way this unfortunate Girl is in, at present, I know not; but Miss Strange believes her to be as culpable as ever. She was with [a] very decent looking Party, & was very genteely Dressed, without shew or frippery, & looked very handsome.

Much is to be said in Excuse of a poor credulous young Creature, whose Person is Attractive, while her mind is unformed. Should she quit her way of life before she grows more abandonned, I shall have great pleasure in shewing her any Civility in my circumscribed power, from the remembrance of her Innocence when I first knew her. Miss Strange has heard the story of her *marriage* all contradicted. . . .[25]

I called lately upon my Grandmother, & found her at Cards with my Aunts & M^rs O Connor, who I saw looked rather gravely upon me. I enquired after Miss Dickenson, & sat & chatted about a Quarter of an Hour, & then I said I must be gone, for Miss Cooke from Chesington, & M^rs & Miss Simmons were to Drink Tea with us. Just as I rose, & was taking leave, M^rs O Connor called out "No! stop a moment! — " I stood, suspended, — & in a solemn kind of manner, she addressed herself to my Grandmother & said "Would you think this lady to be one of the greatest Cheats that ever was Born?"

---

[24] *Charlotte:* Frances Burney's sister.

[25] *marriage all contradicted:* Miss Laluze appears to be living with a man to whom she is not married. Hence, she is not a proper acquaintance for the respectable Burney women.

They all stared, & she went on.

"Who — to look in her Face, & see so much good Nature would believe her to have *none?* — to be actually *cruel?* — here has she sat this half Hour — & never once had the common Civility to ask how my poor Mʳ Barlow does, whose Heart she has been breaking! — Fie! — Fie!"

I was much surprised at this Attack, — & made no immediate answer, hardly knowing whether she meant it seriously, or as badinage²⁶ — my aunts looked rather displeased, & my Grandmother said — "I'll assure you, I began to wonder what you *meant,* by Calling *my* Grand Daughter a Cheat!"

"O yes!" cried Mʳˢ O Connor, "I expected to make you all angry! — I thought as much! but I could not contain — poor Mʳ Barlow! how will he wish *he* had happened to have been here, when I tell him — but you need not, I shall say, for she never once asked how you did!"

"If Mʳ Barlow would have been *the better* for any Enquiry, said I, I should certainly — "

"O — if you meant *nothing else,*" cried she, "it may be as well as it is! but you *will* — you *will* say *yes* yet? — "

"Let us hope, said my Aunt Anne, very judiciously, that they may *both* do better."

"Ay — well — I don't know — I can't say — all I know is that poor Mʳ Barlow is almost dying with grief — you — you — *naughty* thing! you have broke his Heart!"

"O, cried I (endeavouring to laugh it off) I dare say he will *survive* — "

"O! — very well, Ma'am — very well — pray *exult* — it is always the way with you young ladies — "

I determined to make no more answer, as I was quite affronted at this speech; — *Exult* — ! I would not for the World! — but how affected would it sound in *me* to *pity* a man for my own *cruelty,* as she Calls it!

"He is a good & most Worthy Young man," continued she; "& I have the greatest regard for him — however — perhaps — before twice 7 years Time — you may *repent* — "

How excessively impertinent! I was quite silent, & so were my Grand mother & Aunt Anne; — but my poor Aunt Becky simply

---

²⁶ *badinage:* A sort of joke, taunting the person to whom it is directed but without real seriousness.

added to M^rs O'Connor's prediction, by saying — "Ay — when you are *like us!*"

Perhaps she [M^rs O'Connor] thought she had gone too far, for she afterwards seemed to endeavour to *soften* her Attack by saying a great deal of the good *nature* of my *looks;* — & wishing — though with an air of doubt — that I might be *happier.*

As to my enquiring after M^r Barlow, I own I felt too *conscious* to mention his Name, & had I *looked* so, & spoke of him at the same Time, I am certain she would have put a wrong construction upon it; — besides, M^r Barlow, I believe, would *catch at a shadow,* & if he heard I meerly asked after his Health, he would be anxious, I doubt not, to answer me himself, & I should be extremely uneasy to have, or to give, any further trouble about this affair.

### Frances Burney to Samuel Crisp

[St Martin's Street, October 30, 1775]

My dear Daddy.

It is so long since I wrote to you that I suppose you conclude we are all gone a fortune Hunting in some other planet; — however though I cannot totally exculpate myself from the charge of Negligence, yet a great part of the Time during which I have been silent, has been employed in a manner that would have given you no pleasure to have heard of, — for my poor grandmother Burney, after a long painful, lingering Illness, in the course of which we all contributed our mites towards assisting as Nurses, — has Breathed her last. I shall not dwell upon this melancholy subject, as I know your peculiar aversion to the *Horrors,* — but shall proceed to write upon those topics which you have yourself made choice of. . . .

In regard to M^r Barlow — I have not seen him for many months — but I *hear* of him very often, from a certain M^rs O'Connor, who was an old friend & favourite of my poor Grandmother, & continues to be so of my Aunts. It was by her means that he became acquainted with our Family, as he said he was [*one-half line missing*] This Gentle woman & I never meet, without her most officiously telling me Tales of his goodness, worth & so forth, — & expatiating upon my *cruelty,* & my *own loss,* & his *broken Heart,* & such sort of stuff. I have, however, sent her a message by my Aunt Anne, desiring her to forbear these attacks, & letting her know, in as civil words as possible, that I was too much determined for them to answer any possible purpose. She has thought fit to make an Apology, & I hope she will desist in future. My Father, thank Heaven, has not once mentioned his Name, since the *Tragical tragedy*[27] which I gave you a hint of.

As to any *other* person — my dear M^r Crisp your wishes for me are very kind, — but I am a queer sort of charcter, & without *particular inducements,* cannot bear ever the thought of uniting myself for life with one who must have full power to make me miserable, & perhaps none to make me happy — for it is such a Chance! — & as the constable says,[28] there are Gifts which God gives — & do not fall to the lot of every one.

But though I am difficult & saucy, as you call me, in regard to giving *another* the sole power of settling my fate, yet I am by no means difficult to be pleased & happy *as I am,* — on the contrary, I niether want spirits nor *pliability* of Temper, to enjoy all the *Good* that I can meet with: & as to the *Bad,* — though I am sometimes tempted to think I can never have *more,* yet, *upon the whole,* perhaps I shall never have *less!* & the more sensible I am of the Comforts I actually possess, the more careful it makes me of foregoing them.

[27] *Tragical tragedy:* Probably an allusion to Henry Fielding's farcical play *Tragedy of Tragedies; or, The Life and Death of Tom Thumb the Great* (1731).
[28] *as the constable says:* A reference to a speech made by Dogberry in Shakespeare's *Much Ado about Nothing,* 3.5.43.

FRANCES BURNEY

## Directions for Coughing and Sneezing
## before the King and Queen

This letter, taken from the first edition of *The Diary and Letters of Madame d'Arblay* (London: H. Colburn, 1842–46), which was edited by Charlotte Barrett, Burney's niece, has been widely reprinted and discussed, perhaps most interestingly in Julia Epstein's *The Iron Pen* (1989). It was written to Burney's sister Esther just before Burney's presentation at the court of George III in preparation for her new position as Second Keeper to the Robes.

Burney published *Evelina* anonymously, but within months it was known in London literary circles that Charles Burney's hitherto unnoticed daughter Frances had written this highly acclaimed novel. *Evelina*'s huge success, combined with its author's relationship to the already well-known Charles Burney, made Frances Burney a celebrity overnight. She was then befriended by many London artists, musicians, writers, and intellectuals on her own account — not just as her father's daughter. Among the most famous of her new friends was the author Samuel Johnson and his patrons, Henry and Hester Thrale, who subsequently became Burney's patrons. After an abortive attempt to produce a play on the London Stage (see the Introduction to this volume), Burney published her second novel, *Cecilia*, in 1782. While not the sensation that *Evelina* had been, this novel was well received. Despite her growing reputation as an author, however, Burney did not make enough money from her first two novels to establish economic independence. When Henry Thrale died and Hester Thrale married her children's music teacher, Gabriel Piozzi in 1784 — a match that precipitated a breach between Burney and her patron — Burney faced a future of economic dependency on her father's uncertain resources.

In 1786 Burney's friends succeeded in gaining Queen Charlotte's interest in patronizing her through an invitation to become Second Keeper to the Robes. Burney had been received at court before: her friend Mary Delany benefited from a royal pension and was instrumental in introducing Burney to court life and court patronage. It is certain, from reading Burney's journals and letters, that she would never have accepted this position if her father had not urged her to do so. Court life, with its formality and lack of privacy, was antithetical to the close, domestic relations and quiet habits of life that suited her best. The Second Keeper kept long hours at the service of the queen and of her immediate superior, the Keeper of the Robes, Elizabeth Juliana Schwellenberg. She had little time for her private life, kept killing hours, and endured the tedium and physical hardship of "waiting" — often quite literally standing for long hours without relief — on the queen. The experience of court life was even worse than Burney had feared. Schwellenberg proved to be a tyrant, jealous of the attentions of her royal mistress and shrewish and cruel to Burney. Burney's court service nearly destroyed her health and devastated her peace of mind. She finally convinced her father of the seriousness of her situation and left the service of Queen Charlotte, with a pension of one hundred pounds, in 1791.

Burney reveals her feelings about the queen's invitation in the following letter to her sister Esther, written in December of 1785. On the one hand, she is aware of the financial incentive to accept; on the other, she knows the mental and physical anguish that conformity to court rules and "etiquette" will entail. The violent, dark satire of this piece might be usefully compared to Burney's description of the old women's race in *Evelina*. In both cases, women are portrayed as damaging their own bodies in the course of being manipulated by social conventions.

Windsor, Dec. 17th, 1785.

My dearest Hetty,

I am sorry I could not more immediately write; but I really have not had a moment since your last.

Now I know what you next want is, to hear accounts of kings, queens, and such royal personages. O ho! do you so? Well.

Shall I tell you a few matters of fact? — or, had you rather a few matters of etiquette?[1] Oh, matters of etiquette, you cry! for matters of fact are short and stupid, and anybody can tell, and everybody is tired with them.

Very well, take your own choice.

To begin, then, with the beginning.

You know I told you, in my last, my various difficulties, what sort of preferment to turn my thoughts to, and concluded with just starting a young budding notion of decision, by suggesting that a handsome pension for nothing at all would be as well as working night and day for a salary.

This blossom of an idea, the more I dwelt upon, the more I liked. Thinking served it for a hot-house, and it came out into full blow as I ruminated upon my pillow. Delighted that thus all my contradictory and wayward fancies were overcome, and my mind was peaceably settled what to wish and to demand, I gave over all further meditation upon choice of elevation, and had nothing more to do but to make my election known.

My next business, therefore, was to be presented.[2] This could be no difficulty; my coming hither had been their own desire, and they

---

[1] *matters of etiquette:* By referencing Esther's alleged interest in etiquette, Burney makes an ironic comment on the proliferation of "conduct" books for young ladies in the eighteenth century. These were widely produced and read, and no doubt they had much to do with how Burney's culture defined middle-class femininity.

[2] *to be presented:* That is, formally introduced at court to the king and queen in order to voice her petition for a pension.

had earnestly pressed its execution. I had only to prepare myself for the rencounter.

You would never believe — you, who, distant from courts and courtiers, know nothing of their ways, — the many things to be studied, for appearing with a proper propriety before crowned heads. Heads without crowns are quite other sort of rotundas.

Now, then, to the etiquette. I inquired into every particular, that no error might be committed. And as there is no saying what may happen in this mortal life, I shall give you those instructions I have received myself, that, should you find yourself in the royal presence, you may know how to comport yourself.

### Directions for Coughing, Sneezing, or Moving, before the King and Queen

In the first place, you must not cough. If you find a cough tickling in your throat, you must arrest it from making any sound; if you find yourself choking with the forbearance, you must choke — but not cough.

In the second place, you must not sneeze. If you have a vehement cold, you must take no notice of it; if your nose-membranes feel a great irritation, you must hold your breath; if a sneeze still insists upon making its way, you must oppose it, by keeping your teeth grinding together; if the violence of the repulse breaks some blood-vessel, you must break the blood-vessel — but not sneeze.

In the third place, you must not, upon any account, stir either hand or foot. If, by chance, a black pin[3] runs into your head, you must not take it out. If the pain is very great, you must be sure to bear it without wincing; if it brings the tears into your eyes, you must not wipe them off; if they give you a tingling by running down your cheeks, you must look as if nothing was the matter. If the blood should gush from your head by means of the black pin, you must let it gush; if you are uneasy to think of making such a blurred appearance, you must be uneasy, but you must say nothing about it. If, however, the agony is very great, you may, privately, bite the inside of your cheek, or of your lips, for a little relief; taking care, meanwhile, to do it so cautiously as to make no apparent dent outwardly. And, with that precaution, if you even gnaw a piece out, it will not be

---

[3] *black pin:* Black pins, similar to what we might call hat pins, were used to secure women's elaborate hairstyles. See the description of Evelina having her hair dressed for the first time on page 73 of this volume.

minded, only be sure either to swallow it, or commit it to a corner of the inside of your mouth till they are gone — for you must not spit.

I have many other directions, but no more paper; I will endeavor, however, to have them ready for you in time. Perhaps, meanwhile, you would be glad to know if I have myself had opportunity to put in practice these receipts?

How can I answer in this little space? My love to Mr. B. and the little ones, and remember me kindly to cousin Edward, and believe me, my dearest Esther,

Most affectionately yours,<br>F. B.

"Hints to the Ladies to Take Care of Their Heads." Published by R. Sayer &
Bennett, Fleet Street, London, 1776. In this caricature, which is set in the
large assembly room at the Pantheon, a lady's headdress has caught fire from
the lights in the chandelier.

# 2

# The Fashionable World

The materials gathered in this section give insight into the social and economic relations that make up the world of fashion and leisure entered by Evelina once she leaves the rural isolation of Berry Hill. The novel's fictional representations of London amusements and fashionable resort life at Bristol Hotwells may, on first reading, leave the impression of a rather rarified atmosphere in which fashionable aristocrats and gentry do the "right" things at the "right" places, interrupted only by those loutish outsiders to fashion such as Evelina's grandmother and cousins. But Evelina's experience at public pleasure grounds such as the Spring Gardens at Vauxhall and even at private balls and ridottos also points toward larger cultural patterns that connect the glamour of fashion with the more matter-of-fact realities of economic and social relations. The social relations between men and women, different classes, and even different nationalities of people are inextricable parts of the world of leisure and fashion that the young lady enters.

The first five selections illustrate some of the economic, social, and national relations that produced the fashionable world that Evelina enters. The excerpts from *The London Tradesman* of 1747 give some details of the trades and professions that went into making the amusements and fashions enjoyed by Evelina. The language used to explain the labor, status, and responsibilities of tradesmen and tradeswomen is scarcely neutral. Rather, it draws on specific

eighteenth-century cultural attitudes toward gender and national
identity in describing both the labor done by the tradesman or
tradeswoman and his or her social status. Even music, the most seemingly abstract of arts and the one most unequivocally enjoyed by
Evelina (and her author, who came from a family of fine musicians),
is seen to be a trade that carries certain highly concrete social and
economic implications for its practitioners. The musician is characterized as too feminine and thus suspiciously linked to "effeminate" foreign cultures such as those of France and Italy. Not surprisingly,
those trade positions characterized as "effeminate" and those most
frequently assumed by women are the most economically vulnerable.

But those whose labor makes the world of fashion and leisure possible
live and work within the frameworks of nationalism, class hierarchy,
gender systems, and economic relations. Joseph Addison's view of the
Royal Exchange, the center of international trade in London, gives a
sort of bird's-eye view of trade in the context of global economic
power and an emerging English nationalism. The commodities of
English trade are celebrated as unproblematic signs of economic
growth and "progress"; what must be read between the lines is the
oppression of peoples indigenous to those countries subjugated by
British economic and military dominance, particularly in the Caribbean, the Americas, and North Africa. More obvious in these texts
is the implied competition between England and other European
countries for economic and military supremacy. Addison's satiric letter from *The Spectator* on French fashions demonstrates, as do *The
London Tradesman* articles, a sense of English national superiority in
relation to competitor nations such as France.

But not all of the following materials on trade are celebratory of
England's new era of economic expansion. Oliver Goldsmith's hap-
less Chinese visitor to London finds himself trapped in a commerce
of luxury that perverts the fulfillment of needs into the creation of
false desires. And Henry Fielding's cynical account of how the definition and location of fashion changes in defense of the economically
and socially privileged reveals a social system that may work against
traditional values and ideals. In any case, whether fashion and
leisure pursuits are celebrated as part of economic development and
social growth or portrayed as signs of moral decadence, they become
vehicles for implicitly or explicitly expressing different views on the
economic and social relations between England and its European
competitors, England and its colonial conquests, and different groups
within England's own highly class-conscious society.

The last five selections on fashion give several accounts of the fashionable places that Evelina visits in London and Bath. Some, such as the anonymous *A Sketch of the Spring-Gardens, Vaux-hall*, are uncritical celebrations of a relatively new social phenomenon: public places that allowed for the mixing on a large scale of middle-class and aristocratic consumers of leisured pastimes and fashion. In Goldsmith's "On a Visit to Vauxhall Gardens," class distinctions, far from being erased in a place such as Vauxhall, are represented as shaping the very nature of the pleasure taken from such public places. *The Spectator*'s critical look at British theater audiences suggests the rowdy, even violent potential of this particular public space, and Tobias Smollett's and Christopher Anstey's satires on the fashionable resort of Bath point to a world that could be darkly absurd in its very fashionableness.

*Evelina* itself takes part in this social commentary on places of fashion and leisure. Evelina's enjoyment of *The New Bath Guide* (see Volume III, Letter IV) points toward her growing attachment to Orville, her co-reader, but it also suggests that for all her innocence, the heroine at least partakes of the sometimes satirical, sometimes amused, sometimes downright cynical views of fashion and leisure that we can find in writings about resort and London life in the mid-eighteenth century. The places Burney describes in her novel are not fairy-tale locations — castle ballrooms or magic gardens — but very real parts of London and such fashionable resorts as Bath. As we can see from the following selections, these places of pleasure and fashion had, by the mid-eighteenth century, become objects of social debate over the nature of the economic and social changes that had led to their creation.

# Making Fashion

## RICHARD CAMPBELL

### *From* The London Tradesman

Richard Campbell was one of many publishers at mid-century who themselves wrote and compiled books that they hoped would turn a profit. *The London Tradesman*, published in 1747, offers advice to parents about a wide range of trades to which the latter might apprentice their children. It can be seen as a sort of "how-to" book, in roughly the same genre as Thomas Gisborne's *Enquiry* (see the headnote to the Gisborne selections in Part Two, Chapter 1), but for a different audience and with some differences in purpose. Whereas Gisborne addresses young middle-class women with the intent of preparing them for their domestic and maternal roles, Campbell gives parents a sometimes unsettling view of the lines of work their sons and daughters might enter through the apprentice system. While Gisborne assumes that women have a domestic vocation, Campbell discusses work for women outside of their roles as mothers and wives.

It is helpful, in reading this text, to know something about how training in the crafts or trades took place in eighteenth-century England. Craftsmen specialized in the production of particular items. A staymaker, for instance, made the whalebone or metal supports that went into women's corsets, while a milliner specialized in making women's gowns and petticoats. Trades were organized into a tiered system that included masters, journeymen, and apprentices. A master, in addition to practicing his craft, owned his (and in some cases her) own shop, bought his or her own materials, and negotiated the sale of wares. In order to learn a trade, young men and women were apprenticed to a master. This meant that they worked and often boarded on the master's premises. Theoretically, they were supposed to learn their craft within a specified time period, at the end of which their apprenticeship would end. In return for teaching a craft, the master would gain a cheaply maintainable work force. Often the apprentice's friends or family would even pay the master a fee. At the end of the apprenticeship, the successful apprentice became a journeyman who could sell his or her labor to any master for wages. A journeyman who managed to amass some capital might eventually become a master.

In actuality, the apprenticeship system was badly abused in the eighteenth century. Many masters exploited apprentices as a cheap labor force without ever bothering to teach them a trade. The abuse and physical ill treatment of apprentices was common. An apprentice who did make it to the journeyman level rarely earned enough to enable him or her to become a master.

The social class of the young people about whose future line of work Campbell writes would have been highly variable, both in terms of the family from which they came and the class standing that they could, eventually, attain. This variability was symptomatic of a new fluidity in class relations. Although there were still very real constraints on social mobility, such as the difficulty of finding a good apprenticeship and of making enough money to advance socially and economically once it was completed, it is worth noting that a rigidly hierarchical society in which children automatically took up their parents' line of work would not have created the market for a book such as *The London Tradesman*. The following excerpts are taken from the 1747 edition published in London by T. Gardner.

## Of Music

I Begin with music, as Harmony is the first and chief Beauty in all Arts. Music is reckoned among the Liberal arts, only as it is studied as a genteel and pleasant Accomplishment, calculated to sooth the Mind, and unbend its most racking Cares and Anxiety; but in this Country especially, those who practice it for Bread are in but small Repute. The Grave and Rigid of all Ages have looked upon Music as of no public Utility: They imagine it effeminates the Mind, enervates the more Manly Faculties, and erases from the Soul all manner of Martial Ardour. Soft Music lulls asleep all the active Passions, fills the Imagination with delicate Languishment, and moulds the whole Frame into a thoughtless Delirium. There is nothing in Nature has so great an Effect upon the Soul of Man as Music: He must be less than Man, he must be merely half-animated Clay who cannot be moved by Harmony; in it there is such boundless Variety, that every Temper and Disposition meet with something agreeable to his Genius; the Dull, the Stupid, and the Thoughtless may be raised out of their lethargic Trance, and divested of their Inanity by its brisk Airs; the martial firy Genius of the Soldier may be raised yet higher, and every Thought of Danger banished from his Breast by the Harmony of Warlike Instruments of Music; and the same Person, whose Soul is fired by the Sound of Trumpets and transported to Acts of Madness by Drum and Clarion, may be melted down to the Softness of a Woman by the soft bewitching Melody of the Harp and Violin. It was this wonderful Effect of Music that made the Ancients fable, that the Damned were charmed with the Pipe of *Orpheus,* and that Trees, Stones, and Things inanimate danced to the Music of *Apollo.*[1]

---

[1] *Damned . . . Apollo:* Orpheus was a poet of Greek legend who was said to be such a skilled player on the lyre that when his wife Eurydice died, his music charmed Pluto, the ruler of hell, into allowing her to return to the world of the living with Orpheus. He was, however, unable to adhere to Pluto's condition that he not look at his beloved on their journey from hell, and the lovers were lost to each other. Apollo, also a figure out of Greek myth, was the god of the sun, as well as of music and poetry.

Brisk Martial Music communicates a Vivacity to the Soul of Man, that makes him despite all Danger, and meet Death cloathed in all his Terrors with Intrepidity and Resolution; whereas soft Airs, and elaborate Melody has the contrary Effect: From whence it is observed, that the Spirit of most Nations may be learned by the Nature of the Music with which they are delighted: Florid sprightly Airs denote a fierce, hardy, and valiant People; but soft, delicate, and harmonious Notes bespeak the effeminate, lazy, and voluptuous Coward. While the Music of *Italy* was full of Discord, and consisted more in Noise than Harmony, then was she the Mistress of the World: Her hardy Sons fought to the Tune of their rude artless Instruments, with Courage and Intrepidity, and courted Death in the most distant Climes; but since she refined in her Taste of Music, and has been polished out of her rustic Melody, by degrees she has degenerated into what she is, a Nation of Priests, something less than Women; into a Race of mere effeminate Cowards.

What may be observed of the *Italians* will be found true of Nations nearer home: As *Italian* Music, and the Love of it, has prevailed in these Islands, Luxury, Cowardice, and Venality has advanced upon us in exact Proportion. In the Southern Parts, where this bewitching *Demon* is best known, we find less of Martial Ardor than in the more remote and Northern Parts, where they have not been squeaked out of their old Music, or Antient Courage: One may discern in the Music of the *Scotch Highlanders* something of the hot firy ungovernable Temper of that unhappy warlike People: Observe but with Attention one of their Marches, and you may mark in the sonorous Noise, the haughty proud Step of the Highland Chieftain; in the Shortness of the Stops and Quickness of the Measure, their firy hot and hasty Disposition; and when you come to the Chorus, you may fancy you see him, with his mad Followers, rushing into Battle like the Wind, and dealing Death and Destruction about him every where. Even in their Dead Marches, and Funeral *Dirges,* their Martial Disposition may be traced; their Complaints are not in soft Murmurs, or melodious Wailings, they seem in a Passion, and rather scold than complain, and the Sound seems to express more of Anger than of Grief.

Cross but the Narrow Seas, over into *Ireland,* where the Manners and Customs of the People are much the same; yet we find a wonderful Difference in their Music, and in the Disposition of the Inhabitants.

The *Irish* were once a warlike hardy People, and still have retained some Part of their old Disposition: They are hardy at this Day; their

Poverty makes them so; and they prove, when once out of *Ireland* very good Soldiers; but at home, their Spirit is broke, they groan under the Yoke of their new Governors; they but remember they were once free. This affects their Music sensibly: Their Instruments are rude, and have as little Harmony in them as those of the *Highlanders*, but they want that Life and Spirit; there is a dead Langour in all their Tunes; they have a mourning complaining Sound, and you must fancy you hear the Rattling of Chains in their most sprightly Compositions.

From all this I would only infer, that a Refinement of our Taste into a Love of the soft *Italian* Music, is debasing the Martial Genius of the Nation; and may one Day be a Means to fiddle us out of our Liberties. I would chuse, if we are to be improved in Music, that the Composers would keep to the old *British* Key, and let us sing *English* as well as speak it.[2]

A Genius for Music is discerned early; a good Ear is absolutely necessary, and without it all the Art on Earth cannot make either a Composer or Performer. There are some who have a good Ear, and become excellent Judges and Composers of Music, who cannot play well upon any Instrument, or turn a Tune with their Voice; but a Performer must have an Ear. Those who discover any liking to Music ought to be early set to learn: The Ear may be improved, the Taste refined, much easier than in advanced Years, and the Joints and Fingers are then most pliable, and acquire a natural Facility in Performance.

But if a Youth is not resolved to turn Musician entirely, or has not an independent Fortune, I would have him avoid any Improvements in Singing. If he is obliged to follow any Business that requires Application, this Amusement certainly takes him off his Business, exposes him to Company and Temptations to which he would otherwise have been a Stranger. I believe it will agree with every Body's Observation what I have always remarked, that a Tradesman who could sing a good Song, or play upon any Instrument, seldom or never prospered in his Business: I declare it, I never found one, but in the end became Beggars. While they had any thing to spend, their facetious Turn gave them Access to, and made them coveted in all tippling Companies:[3] The Praise, the Respect and little Flattery of these Bottle Companions, pleased so much, that they could never deny to make one in a

---

[2] *old British Key . . . speak it:* This passage speaks against the influence of Italian opera on English music, particularly within the British theater.
[3] *tippling Companies:* Drinking parties.

Party of Pleasure; the Love of Company and the Bottle naturally grow upon them; Neglect of Business, late Hours, and unnecessary Expence, beget Poverty and Diseases, and the poor Man has been so happy as to sing himself into Misery, and to purchase Poverty to his Family with a Tune of the Fiddle.

If a Parent cannot make his Son a Gentleman, and finds, that he has got an Itch of Music, it is much the best Way to allot him entirely to that Study. The present general Taste of Music in the Gentry may find him better Bread than what perhaps this Art deserves. The Gardens[4] in the Summer Time employ a great Number of Hands; where they are allowed a Guinea[5] a Week and upwards, according to their Merit. The Opera, the Play-Houses, Masquerades, Ridottoes, and the several Music-Clubs,[6] employ them in the Winter. But I cannot help thinking, that any other Mechanic Trade is much more useful to the Society than the whole Tribe of Singers and Scrapers;[7] and should think it much more reputable to bring my Son up a Blacksmith (who was said to be the Father of Music) than bind him Apprentice to the best Master of Music in *England*. This I know must be reckoned an unfashionable Declaration in this Musical Age; but I love my Country so well, that I hate every thing that administers to Luxury and Effeminacy: I would rather *Britons* were rude, unpolished, and free, than to see them Slaves, with all the polite Delicacies and Improvements of the Eastern and Western World.

### Of the Barber and Peruke-Maker

. . . We next employ the Peruke[8]-Maker. This is a Branch of Trade but of short Date: Our Forefathers were contented with their own

---

[4] *Gardens:* Probably Vauxhall Gardens, a public resort in London in the summertime, which offered various concerts and musical entertainments. See the headnote to the excerpt from *A Sketch of the Spring-Gardens, Vaux-hall*, in this chapter.

[5] *Guinea:* A gold coin, minted between 1663 and 1813, with the nominal value of 20 shillings, although after 1717 it generally circulated at the value of 21 shillings.

[6] *Opera . . . Music-Clubs:* Italian opera was very popular in London, however decried, as it is here, for its "effeminacy," and the London stage included various musical entertainments along with plays as part of an evening's theater entertainment. Librettists such as Isaac Bickerstaffe wrote what we might call musicals for the London theaters at mid-century. Masquerades and ridottoes were popular gatherings at which music and dancing played some part of the entertainment. They might be held privately or publicly, with an admission charge. Along with Music Clubs, they offered smaller, more private vehicles for a musician's talent than the stage or the opera.

[7] *Scrapers:* Slang for fiddler or violinist.

[8] *Peruke:* Wig.

Hair, and never dreamed of thatching their Sculls with false Curls.[9] It is a foreign Invention, but of what Country I cannot learn, and appeared among us at the Restoration.[10] Like all other Inventions, it has received great Improvements. It was originally but rude and simple, but kept a nearer Resemblance to Nature than it does at present; the Fashion was to wear Wigs nearly resembling the natural Colour of our Hair, and shaped in such manner as to make the artificial Locks appear like a natural Production; but in Process of Time full-bottomed Wiggs became the Mode; and the Heads of our Beaus and Men of Fashion were loaded with Hair: To these the Tie-Wigg succeeded, and the Natural Colour was laid aside for Silver Locks. The Bobb, the Pig-tail, Tupee, Ramilie, and a Number of Shapes, that bear no Relation to the Human Head, are now become the Mode. Sometimes the Beaus appear plaistered all over with Powder and Pomatum, and their Curls frizzled out with laborious Nicety; at other Times the Powder Puff is laid aside, and they affect to dress in Wanton Ringlets. Originally Wiggs were confined to the Male Part of the Species, but of late, that usurping Sex the Ladies, are grown ashamed of the Natural Production of their own Heads, and lay Snares for our Hearts in artificial Buckles and *Têtes de Mouton*:[11] The Black, the Brown, the Fair and Carroty, appear now all in one Livery; and you can no more judge of your Mistress's natural Complexion by the Colour of her Hair, than by that of her Ribbons. The whole Species of our Modern Beaus and Belles appear in a perpetual Masquerade, and seem contending with one another who shall deviate most from Nature, and the antient Simplicity of their Forefathers.

The Peruke-Maker has his Fashions from *Paris,* like all other Tradesmen, and the nearer he can approach to the Patterns of that fickle Tribe, the better Chance he has to succeed with his *English* Customers. His Business is governed but by a few Rules, and it

[9] *false Curls:* In the late seventeenth and early eighteenth centuries, it was fashionable for men to shave their heads and wear long, flowing, curly wigs called full-bottomed perriwigs. Men's wigs went through numerous style changes over the eighteenth century, with several different options being possible at any given time. One popular style involved teasing the hair to give it fullness and covering it with a hair dressing (pomatum) and powder (usually white or silver).

[10] *Restoration:* After a brief period of mid-seventeenth-century rule by parliament and the "Lord Protector," Oliver Cromwell, the British monarchy was "restored" to England in the person of Charles II, whose long, flowing perriwig set men's hair fashions for many years.

[11] *artificial Buckles . . . Mouton:* Women's elaborate hairdos often called for hair supplements. The *Tête de Mouton* was a popular style resembling its literal translation: head of a lamb.

requires Experience to be Master of them; the continual Flux and Re-
flux of Fashions, obliges him to learn something new almost every
Day. There is a good deal of Ingeniuty in his Business as a Wig-
Maker, and a considerable Profit attends it; but he is not only a
Wigg-Maker but a Barber. They generally all Shave and Dress,
though some keep the Branches distinct. As a Barber, he reckons himself of an old Profession, though I cannot justly settle his Chronology:
With this Branch of his Trade was formerly connected that of a Surgeon; and Numbers of them in *London* and *Westminster,* let Blood
and draw Teeth, which I think is the only Part of Surgery they ever
pretended to practise.[12]

I own I cannot understand the Connection there is between a Barber and a Surgeon, nor can I too much condemn the Folly of trusting
those Bunglers to perform one of the nicest, tho' common Operations
in Surgery. I never saw a good Surgeon, but was under some Apprehension when he was about to let Blood; yet these Fellows for Three-
pence, break a Vien at random, without the least Hesitation, or the
smallest Notion of the Danger of a Miscarriage. They used Lancets,
which ought more properly to be termed Horse Flimes,[13] and if they
miss to prick an Artery every Time they let Blood, it is more owing to
Chance than any Precaution of theirs. When we consider that such an
Accident may happen to the most skillful Surgeon, and consequently,
that the ignorant Barber is much more liable, and is utterly incapable
to remedy the Mischief when done, I apprehend it a Degree of Madness to trust them upon any Consideration.

I observed in the Chapter upon Surgery, that the Barbers and Surgeons were one Corporation. While they remained in that Situation
they had some small Pretence to the Practice of Surgery, but now they
are separated, and become plain Barbers, I believe that ridiculous and
dangerous Part of their Trade will be laid aside.

The Trade of a Barber and Peruke-Maker is sufficiently profitable,
and their Journeymen pretty constantly employed. They are generally

---

[12] *let Blood . . . practise:* The eighteenth-century medical therapy of letting blood
was supposed to give relief to fevers or other maladies caused, according to eighteenth-
century medical pathology, by a superfluence of heat in the body. Often this bleeding,
along with tooth extraction, was practiced by the barbers who also shaved and cut
hair. Over the course of the eighteenth century, the medical functions of the barber
generally became the professional responsibility of surgeons, a newly consolidated professional group. At mid-century, however, there was still considerable blurring between the groups in question. A barber who claimed his traditional surgical function
might well go into wig-making as a lucrative way to add to his receipts.

[13] *Horse Flimes:* A large lancet used to bleed horses.

hired by the Year or the Quarter, and are allowed Twelve or Fifteen Pounds a Year, besides Bed and Board. It requires no great Strength, and a Boy may be bound about Twelve or Thirteen Years of Age, without any Education but that of reading and writing.

The Hair-Merchant is the principal Tradesman the Wig-Maker deals with; he is furnished by him with Hair, ready picked, dressed, and curled, fit for weaving. The Hair-Merchant buys Hair of those who go up and down the Country of *England* to procure it, and imports some from abroad; he then sorts it into Parcels, according to its Colour and Fineness; employs Pickers, to pick the Black from the White, and the Dead from the Live Hair, and Hands to mix it into proper Shades of Colour, and curl it, which is done by rolling it up on Pipes and baking it in the Oven. They have a Method of dying Hair black, and bleaching other Hair white, of putting off Horse and Goat Hair for Human Hair, and many other Tricks peculiar to their Trade. There are Hair-Merchants who only deal in wholesale, and sell their Commodity in the Rough; but the greatest Part of them prepare their Hair in the Manner I have mentioned. Country Wig-Makers, and some few in Town, curl and prepare their own Hair likewise; but most of them find it more their Advantage to buy it from the Hair-Merchant.

The Wig-Maker employs the Net-Worker for Cauls[14] to his Wigs: They are generally made in the Country by Women, and bought up by the Haberdasher,[15] who furnishes the Wig-Maker with them, and Silk for weaving his Hair on, and Ribbons for mounting his Wigs. He buys his Blocks from the Turner;[16] but I shall defer mentioning that Trade, till I can range it under a more proper Head.

## Of the Milliner

The Milliner, though no Male Trade, has a just Claim to a Place on this Occasion, as the Fair Sex, who are generally bound to this Business, may have as much Curiosity to know the Nature of their Employment before they engage in it, and stand as much in need of

---

[14] *Cauls:* Caps.

[15] *Haberdasher:* In the eighteenth century, the haberdasher sold small miscellaneous articles pertaining to dress, such as ribbons, thread, and tape. Before the sixteenth century, the haberdasher was also the primary carrier of caps and hats, although by the eighteenth century this part of his trade had gone to the hatter. Perhaps his role in providing cauls to the wig-maker is residual from this former practice.

[16] *Turner:* A craftsman who worked objects of wood, metal, and bone on a lathe. These blocks were probably wood.

sound Advice in the Choice of an Occupation, as the Youth of our own Sex.

The Milliner is concerned in making and providing the Ladies with Linen[17] of all sorts, fit for Wearing Apparel, from the Holland Smock to the Tippet and Commode; but as we are got into the Lady's Articles, which are so very numerous, the Reader is not to expect that we are to give an exact List of every thing belonging to them; let it suffice in general, that the Milliner furnishes them with Holland, Cambrick, Lawn, and Lace of all sorts, and makes these Materials into Smocks, Aprons, Tippits, Handerchiefs, Neckaties, Ruffles, Mobs, Caps, Dressed-Heads,[18] with as many *Etceteras* as would reach from *Charing-Cross* to the *Royal Exchange.*

They make up Cloaks, Manteels, Mantelets, Cheens and Capucheens, of Silk, Velvet, plain or brocaded, and trim them with Silver and Gold Lace, or Black Lace: They make up and sell Hats, Hoods, and Caps of all Sorts and Materials; they find them in Gloves, Muffs, and Ribbons; they sell quilted Petticoats, and Hoops of all Sizes, *&c.* and lastly, some of them deal in Habits for Riding, and Dresses for the Masquerade:[19] In a word, they furnish every thing to the Ladies, that can contribute to set off their Beauty, increase their Vanity, or render them ridiculous.

The Milliner must be a neat Needle-Woman in all its Branches, and a perfect Connoisieur in Dress and Fashion: She imports new

[17] *Linen:* Originally referring to cloth made of flax, the term "linen" came to refer by extension to the personal apparel that was often made of that material, such as men's shirts and a woman's undergarments.

[18] *Holland . . . Dressed-Heads: Holland* refers to a type of linen produced in the province of the same name in the Netherlands; a smock is a woman's undergarment, like a chemise or a shift. *Tippits* were usually of fur or wool and were worn over the shoulders like a loose cape. A *commode* is a type of headdress popular in the late seventeenth and early eighteenth centuries. It was a tall wire frame that could be decorated with lace, silk, or ribbons. *Cambrick* originally referred to a very fine white linen produced in France, but it could also mean a coarser imitation made of cotton. *Lawn* was also a fine linen, closely resembling cambrick. *Handerchiefs* were scarves worn over a woman's shoulders and tucked tightly into the bosom of her gown, while *neckaties* were worn around women's necks. *Ruffles* were ornamental frills made of strips of gathered cloth. *Mobs, caps,* and *dressed-heads* are women's head coverings, primarily for inside wear.

[19] *Cloaks . . . Dresses for the Masquerade:* A *manteel* is a kind of cape; a *mantelet,* a cape that just covers the shoulders. *Cheens* and *Capucheens* are hooded cloaks. *Quilted petticoats* worn under the outer petticoat gave breadth to a woman's long, wide skirts, as did the *hoop,* which was usually made of either whalebone or iron and could hold the skirts out and away from her body. *Masquerade* balls sometimes required elaborate character costumes, such as a fanciful version of a milkmaid's costume, a nun's habit, or the robes of some goddess from classical mythology.

Whims from *Paris* every Post, and puts the Ladies Heads[20] in as many different Shapes in one Month as there are different Appearances of the Moon in that Space. The most noted of them keep an Agent at *Paris*, who have nothing else to do but to watch the Motions of the Fashions, and procure Intelligence of their Changes, which she signifies to her Principals, with as much Zeal and Secrecy as an Ambassador or Plenipo[21] would the important Discovery of some political Intrigue. They have vast Profits on every Article they deal in; yet give but poor, mean Wages to every Person they employ under them: Though a young Woman can work neatly in all manner of Needle Work, yet she cannot earn more than Five or Six Shillings a Week, out of which she is to find herself in Board and Lodging. Therefore, out of Regard to the Fair Sex, I must caution Parents, not to bind their Daughters to this Business: The vast Resort of young Beaus and Rakes[22] to Milliner's Shops, exposes young Creatures to many Temptations, and insensibly debauches their Morals before they are capable of Vice. A young Coxcomb[23] no sooner is Master of an Estate, and a small Share of Brains, but he affects to deal with the most noted Milliner: If he chances to meet in her Shop any thing that has the Appearance of Youth, and the simple Behaviour of undesigning Innocence, he immediately accosts the young Sempstress[24] with all the little Raillery he is Master of, talks loosely, and thinks himself most witty, when he has cracked some obscene Jest upon the young Creature. The Mistress, tho' honest, is obliged to bear the Wretch's Ribaldry, out of Regard to his Custom, and Respect to some undeserved Title of Quality he wears, and is forced to lay her Commands upon the Apprentice to answer all his Rudeness with Civility and Complaisance. Thus the young Creature is obliged every Day to hear a Language, that by degrees undermines her Virtue, deprives her of that modest Delicacy of Thought, which is the constant Companion of uncorrupted Innocence, and makes Vice become familiar to the Ear, from whence there is but a small Transition to the grosser Gratification of the Appetite.

I am far from charging all Milliners with the Crime of Connivance at the Ruin of their Apprentices; but fatal Experience must convince

---

[20] *Heads:* Headdresses.

[21] *Plenipo:* A colloquial shortening of plenipotentiary, meaning an agent with full power to act for his or her sovereign.

[22] *Beaus and Rakes:* A *beau* is a fashionably dressed young man, while a *rake* is a man with a reputation for seducing or raping women.

[23] *Coxcomb:* A silly young man who is overly vain of his appearance.

[24] *Sempstress:* Seamstress.

the Public, that nine out of ten of the young Creatures that are obliged to serve in these Shops, are ruined and undone: Take a Survey of all the common Women of the Town, who take their Walks between *Charing-Cross* and *Fleet-Ditch*,[25] and, I am persuaded, more than one Half of them have been bred Milliners, have been debauched in their Houses, and are obliged to throw themselves upon the Town[26] for Want of Bread, after they have left them. Whether then it is owing to the Milliners, or to the Nature of the Business, or to whatever Cause it is owing, the Facts are so clear, and the Misfortunes attending their Apprentices so manifest, that it ought to be the last Shift a young Creature is driven to. But if Parents will needs give their Daughters this kind of Education, let them avoid your private Hedge Milliners; those who pretend to deal only with a few select Customers, who scorn to keep open Shop, but live in some remote Corner: These are Decoys for the Unwary; they are but Places for Assignations, and take the Title of Milliner, a more polite Name for a Bawd, a Procuress, a Wretch who lives upon the Spoils of Virtue, and supports her Pride by robbing the Innocent of Health, Fame, and Reputation: They are the Ruin of private Families, Enemies of conjugal Affection, and promote nothing but Vice, and live by Lust.

## Of the Stay-Maker

The Stay-Maker is employed in making Stays, Jumps, and Bodice[27] for the Ladies: He ought to be a very polite Tradesman, as he approaches the Ladies so nearly; and possessed of a tolerable Share of Assurance and Command of Temper to approach their delicate Persons in fitting on their Stays, without being moved or put out of Countenance. He is obliged to inviolable Secrecy in many Instances, where he is obliged by Art to mend a crooked Shape, to bolster up a fallen Hip, or distorted Shoulder: The delicate easy Shape we so much admire in *Miranda*[28] is entirely the Workmanship of the Stay-Maker; to him she reveals all her natural Deformity, which she industriously conceals from the fond Lord, who was caught by her slender

[25] *between Charing-Cross and Fleet-Ditch:* A common area for prostitutes to work the streets.

[26] *throw themselves upon the Town:* Become a prostitute.

[27] *Stays . . . Bodice: Jumps* were underbodices, fitted tightly to the body and often taking the place of stays. *Stays* were sets of connected metal or whalebone strips worn tightly laced around the waist and mid-torso. *Bodices* were tightly fitting garments that supported the breasts with whalebone and were placed on the upper body rather than the waist.

[28] *Miranda:* A beautiful woman.

Waist: Her Shape she owes to Steel and Whalebone, her black Locks to the Tire-Woman,[29] and her florid Complexion to Paint and Pomatum: She is like the Jack-Daw in the Fable,[30] dressed out in borrowed Plumes, and her natural Self, when deposited in the Bridal-Bed, is a mere Lump of animated Deformity, fitter far for the Undertaker than to be initiated in the Mysteries of Connubial Joy. How necessary a Qualification is it in that kind of Tradesmen to keep the Deformed secret? and how dangerous to the Repose of the Fair Sex would it be to blab the misshapen Truth? I am surprised that Ladies have not found out a Way to employ Women Stay-Makers rather than trust our Sex with what should be kept as inviolably as Free-Masonry;[31] But the Work is too hard for Women, it requires more Strength than they are capable of, to raise Walls of Defence about a Lady's Shape, which is liable to be spoiled by so many Accidents.

The Materials in Stays are Tabby, Canvass, and Whale-Fin, commonly called Whale-Bone:[32] The Stay-Maker takes the Lady's Shape as nicely as he can; if it is natural, and where it is not, he supplies the Deficiency, then he cuts out the Tabby and Canvass by the Shape in Quarters, which are given out to Women to be stitched, at so much the Pair of Stays: This Part of the Stay-making Trade is but poor Bread; a Woman cannot earn above a Crown or Six Shillings a Week, let her fit as close as she pleases.

The Whale-Fin we have mostly from *Holland*, and the preparing it for Use was till of late a Secret, in a few Hands; though, like *Columbus's* Egg,[33] there appears little in it, now it is discovered. Those who cut it and prepare it for the Shops have a long, square Copper, about the Length of a Fin; in these the Fins are boiled till they grow soft: They are taken out while hot, and placed in a Vice to support them, while the Workman cuts them, or rather splits them into long square

[29] *Tire-Woman:* A woman who assisted at the elaborate toilet of middle- and upper-class women by fixing hair, adjusting clothes, applying makeup, and so forth.

[30] *Jack-Daw in the Fable:* Aesop tells the tale of a jackdaw — normally a drab, dark bird — who borrowed the feathers of more brightly colored birds in order to appear more spectacular than he was. The borrowed feathers fall out, and the jackdaw is revealed as foolish for his pretensions.

[31] *Free-Masonry:* The free masons originally consisted of organized groups of masons formed to pass on the "secrets" of their trade. By the eighteenth century, membership extended beyond the practitioners of this particular trade, and its purposes had more to do with sociability aend conviviality than with craftsmanship.

[32] *Tabby . . . Whale-Bone: Tabby* was padding or quilting combined with stays to reshape the figure; *whale-fin* or *whale-bone* was actually baleen, a flexible, platelike material extracted from the jaws of some kinds of whales.

[33] *Columbus's Egg:* Christopher Columbus is said to have impressed the king and queen of Spain by making an egg balance on its end; he accomplished this feat by slightly flattening one end of the egg.

Pieces, such as they are sold in the Shops; it requires no other Dexterity but to follow the Grain of the Fin with the Knife, in the same manner as a Cooper splits a Hoop for a Cask.[34]

The Stay-Maker buys it from the Haberdashers in their Branch in Lengths, and cuts it in thin Slices fit for their own Use. After the Stays are stitched, and the Bone cut into thin Slices of equal Breadths and the proper Lengths, it is thrust in between the Rows of Stitching: This requires a good deal of Strength, and is by much the nicest Part of Stay Work; there is not above one Man in a Shop who can execute this Work, and he is either Master or Foreman, and has the best Wages. When the Stays are boned, they are loosly sewed together, and carried Home to the Lady to be fitted; if they answer according to Expectation they are bound, the Braiding laid along the Seam and the Lacing down the Stomacher,[35] and are then fit for the Lady's Use.

This is a Species of the Taylor's Business, and rather the most ingenious Art belonging to the Mechanism of the Needle. The Masters have large Profits when they are paid, and the Journeymen's Wages are the same with the Taylors, and regulated by Act of Parliament: They are, like them, much overstocked; though the Press[36] for the War about a Year ago has thinned them. They are three or four Months of the Year out of Business, and are not over-and-above good Oeconomists of the Time they may expect to be employed. Their Education has no Connexion with their Business, and a Boy may be bound about fourteen Years of Age.

There are a Species of Tradesmen who make nothing else but Bodice, which every Woman knows differ from Stays; but Women are chiefly employ'd. They are made, if I mistake not, of Pack-Thread[37] instead of Whale-Bone; and those employed, either as Masters or Journey People, earn a tolerable Substance: Women that can apply themselves, and refrain from Gin,[38] may get from Five to Eight Shillings a Week.

Child's-Coat-making is another Branch of the Taylor and Stay making Business, chiefly engrossed by Women, who make a good Living of it: It requires a tolerable Genius, but not much Strength.

[34] *Cooper . . . Cask:* A cooper made the hoops that held together casks, or barrels.
[35] *Stomacher:* A decorative garment worn over the chest, under a woman's bodice.
[36] *the Press:* The English navy recruited sailors through a process of legalized kidnapping by what were called press-gangs. These gangs usually preyed upon working-class men whom they could isolate and take aboard ship before anyone else could protest.
[37] *Pack-Thread:* A type of strong twine.
[38] *Gin:* Cheap, strong gin, made available from new uses for byproducts in the brewing of beer at mid-century, was consumed at alarming rates by the London laboring class. Alcoholism reached near epidemic proportions during the 1740s and brought with it death, disease, and crime.

## Of the Mantua-Maker

The Mantua-Maker,[39] as she is a Servant of the Ladies, may take it amiss if she is not allowed a Place among the many Arts and Mysteries we are treating of. Her Business is to make Night-Gowns, Mantuas, and Petticoats, *Rob de Chambres*,[40] &c. for the Ladies. She is Sister to the Taylor, and, like him, must be a perfect Connoisieur in Dress and Fashions; and, like the Stay-Maker, she must keep the Secrets she is entrusted with, as much as a Woman can: For, though the Stay-Maker does his Business as nicely as possible, and conceals all Deformities with the greatest Art, yet the Mantua-Maker must discover them at some times; she must see them, and pretend to be blind, and at all times she must swear herself to an inviolable Secrecy: She must learn to flatter all Complexions, praise all Shapes, and, in a word, ought to be compleat Mistress of the Art of Dissimulation. It requires a vast Stock of Patience to bear the Tempers of most of their Customers, and no small Share of Ingenuity to execute their innumerable Whims. Their Profits are but inconsiderable, and the Wages they give their Journeywomen small in proportion; they may make a Shift with great Sobriety and Oeconomy to live upon their Allowance; but their Want of Prudence, and general Poverty, has brought the Business into small Reputation: If a young Creature, when out of her Time, has no Friend to advise with, or be a Check upon her Conduct, it is more than ten to one but she takes some idle, if not vicious Course, by the many Temptations to which her Sex and narrow Circumstances subject her. It is a Misfortune to the Fair Sex, when they are left young to their own Management, that they can scarce avoid falling into the many Snares laid for them by designing Men: Even their Virtues contribute to their Undoing; Men pride themselves in debauching such as betray any Marks of modest Virtue; their natural Innocence and Good-nature make them credulous, and too soon yields them a Prey to the affected Sighs and perjured Oaths of those who have no other View but their Ruin. In short, nothing can properly save them from falling but their Pride, which the servile Condition of a Journeywoman too often humbles: I would conclude from this, that Parents, who bind their Daughters to this Business, must

---

[39] *Mantua-Maker:* A dressmaker, distinguished from the milliner, who produced what we might call accessories to the main article.

[40] *Night-Gowns . . . Rob de Chambres: Night-Gowns* were not bedwear, as we might expect, but rather dressy gowns for evening wear. The *mantua* was a loose-fitting gown for daywear. *Petticoats*, in this sense, were the overskirts, worn over the underpetticoats. A *rob de chambre* was a dressing gown.

not think they have done their Duty, when, according to the Phrase, they have put a Trade into their Hands; they must instil into them early Principles of Piety, and inspire them with a virtuous Pride, and a delicate Concern for their Reputation: They ought to watch their Motions, and assist their unexperienced Years with good Advice; and never think themselves discharged of their Parental Duty, till they have settled them in the World under the Protection of some Man of Sagacity, Industry, and Good-nature: A Woman is always under Age till she comes (in the Law Phrase) to be under Cover.[41] A Youth may be set a-float in the World as soon as he has got a Trade in his Head, without much Danger of spoiling; but a Girl is such a tender, ticklish Plant to rear, that there is no permitting her out of Leading-strings[42] till she is bound to a Husband.

[41] *under Cover:* Under English law, a woman was literally "covered" by her father before marriage and her husband after. Her property and her debts were legally those of her father or husband; she had no independent legal standing as an economic agent, whatever her age.

[42] *Leading-strings:* Cords or a leash used to restrain small children.

## JOSEPH ADDISON

### On the Royal Exchange
### (The Spectator, No. 69)

Joseph Addison (1672–1719) was educated at the Charterhouse, where he met his future collaborator on the popular periodical *The Spectator,* Richard Steele (1672–1729). A published author by 1704, he was also an active politician in the Whig administration from 1706 (as undersecretary of state) until 1711, when the Whig government fell from power. He returned to his political career in 1715, after the Whigs regained control. During this hiatus from active political service, Addison began his famous collaboration with Steele on *The Spectator* (published from 1711 to 1712), a project that followed naturally enough from Addison's contribution to the latter's earlier *Tatler.* He also wrote a successful tragic play, *Cato,* produced in 1713, and continued to write for his *Freeholder* political newspaper from 1715 to 1716, when he became lord commissioner of trade. He retired with a pension of £1,500 in 1718 (as compared to Burney's pension of £100).

The dominant political parties of eighteenth-century England, Whig and Tory, are characterized more by changes in policy over the first half of the century than by fixed political positions. In general, the Whigs during the first half of the century favored a "progressive" model for social order based on a centralized bureaucratic government administration, the growth of regulatory laws legitimating the authority of that administration, and a monetary and trade system that nurtured the accumulation of capital. The Tories tended to stress more traditional models of government anchored by the monarchy, and often criticized Whig economic policy as greedy and short-sighted and Whig governance as corrupt and nepotistic. In the following excerpt from *The Spectator*, Addison's Whig political position is evident if not explicit. The Whig government of which Addison was part favored the global expansion of British trade while downplaying the military dominance that was needed to support successful economic competition with other European nations, particularly France, Spain, and Holland. Addison's glorification of mercantile trade and the figure of the merchant offers a peaceful, almost utopic vision of English mercantile dominance.

The persona that Addison assumes here is that of "Mr. Spectator," through whose eyes many of *The Spectator*'s observations on contemporary life are made. In creating a fictionalized, detached observer through which to voice their views on culture, Addison and Steele tapped into a newly important investment in empirical observation as the means to achieving knowledge. *The Spectator* was only one of many London periodicals that took their name from the activity of observation; others included *The London Spy*, *The Mirror*, and *The Invisible Spy*. In introducing Mr. Spectator to his readers, Addison emphasized his detachment from partisan politics and his theoretical, rather than practical, interest in the practices and institutions of human life. Ironically, Addison the politician claimed, through Mr. Spectator, the authorial pose of distance on England's political and economic life.

The Royal Exchange that Addison describes was built in 1669 to replace a market that had burned down in the Great Fire that demolished much of London in 1666. It was a large, two-story structure with a paved court within. Around this court were the "walks" of various merchants, divided by nationality and ethnicity: Spanish, French, Portuguese, Italian, Jewish, Scotch, Irish, German, and the English-American plantations. Londoners were located in the court's middle, open space. The Royal Exchange housed around two hundred different shops selling various items, but especially men's and women's clothes and dress accessories. Excerpted here is Number 69 from *The Spectator*, ed. Donald F. Bond, vol. I (Oxford: Clarendon Press, 1965), 292–96.

## No. 69
### Saturday, May 19, 1711

*Hic segetes, illic veniunt felicius uvæ:*
*Arborei fœtus alibi, atque injussa virescunt*
*Gramina. Nonne vides, croceos ut Tmolus odores,*
*India mittit ebur, molles sua thura Sabæi?*
*At Chalybes nudi ferrum, virosaque Pontus*
*Castorea, Eliadum palmas Epirus equarum?*
*Continuo has leges æternaque fœdera certis*
*Imposuit Natura locis . . .*

— Vir.[1]

There is no Place in the Town which I so much love to frequent as the *Royal-Exchange*. It gives me a secret Satisfaction, and, in some measure, gratifies my Vanity, as I am an *Englishman*, to see so rich an Assembly of Country-men and Foreigners consulting together upon the private Business of Mankind, and making this Metropolis a kind of *Emporium* for the whole Earth. I must confess I look upon High-Change[2] to be a great Council, in which all considerable Nations have their Representatives. Factors[3] in the Trading World are what Ambassadors are in the Politick World; they negotiate Affairs, conclude Treaties, and maintain a good Correspondence between those wealthy Societies of Men that are divided from one another by Seas and Oceans, or live on the different Extremities of a Continent. I have often been pleased to hear Disputes adjusted between an Inhabitant of *Japan* and

---

[1] *Hic segetes . . . locis:* The motto is taken from Virgil's *Georgics*. Dryden translates "This Ground with *Bacchus*, that with *Ceres* suits: / That other loads the Trees with happy Fruits. / A fourth with Grass, unbidden, decks the Ground: / Thus *Tmolus* is with yellow Saffron crown'd: / *India*, black Ebon and white Ivory bears: / And soft *Idume* weeps her od'rous Tears. / Thus *Pontus* sends her Beaver Stones from far; / And naked *Spanyards* temper Steel for War. / *Epirus* for th' *Elean* Chariot breeds. / (In hopes of Palms,) a Race of running Steeds. / This is the Orig'nal contract; these the Laws / Impos'd by Nature, and by Nature's Cause, / O sundry Places."

[2] *High-Change:* The busiest trading time in the Exchange.

[3] *Factors:* Agents for different business concerns.

Courtyard of the Royal Exchange. From an engraving by Bartolozzi, 1788. Copyright Museum of London.

an Alderman[4] of *London,* or to see a Subject of the *Great Mogul*[5] entering into a League with one of the *Czar* of *Muscovy.* I am infinitely delighted in mixing with these several Ministers of Commerce, as they are distinguished by their different Walks and different Languages: Sometimes I am justled among a Body of *Armenians:* Sometimes I am lost in a Crowd of *Jews,* and sometimes make one in a Groupe of *Dutch-men.* I am a *Dane, Swede,* or *French-Man* at different times, or rather fancy my self like the old Philosopher, who upon being asked what Countryman he was, replied, That he was a Citizen of the World.[6]

---

[4] *Alderman:* In London, the chief officer of a ward (an administrative division within a municipality).

[5] *Great Mogul:* Common European term for the emperor of Delhi, a domain that at one time included most of Hindustan.

[6] *old Philosopher . . . Citizen of the World:* Probably Diogenes the Cynic, although Cicero also puts these words in the mouth of Socrates.

Though I very frequently visit this busie Multitude of People, I am known to no Body there but my Friend, Sir ANDREW,[7] who often smiles upon me as he sees me bustling in the Croud, but at the same time connives at my Presence without taking any further notice of me. There is indeed a Merchant of *Egypt,* who just knows me by sight, having formerly remitted me some Mony to *Grand Cairo;*[8] but as I am not versed in the Modern *Coptik,*[9] our Conferences go no further than a Bow and a Grimace.[10]

This grand Scene of Business gives me an infinite Variety of solid and substantial Entertainments. As I am a great Lover of Mankind, my Heart naturally overflows with Pleasure at the sight of a prosperous and happy Multitude, insomuch that at many publick Solemnities I cannot forbear expressing my Joy with Tears that have stolen down my Cheeks. For this reason I am wonderfully delighted to see such a Body of Men thriving in their own private Fortunes, and at the same time promoting the Publick Stock; or in other Words, raising Estates for their own Families, by bringing into their Country whatever is wanting, and carrying out of it whatever is superfluous.

Nature seems to have taken a particular Care to disseminate her Blessings among the different Regions of the World, with an Eye to this mutual Intercourse and Traffick among Mankind, that the Natives of the several Parts of the Globe might have a kind of Dependance upon one another, and be united together by their common Interest. Almost every *Degree* produces something peculiar to it. The Food often grows in one Country, and the Sauce in another. The Fruits of *Portugal* are corrected by the Products of *Barbadoes:* The Infusion of a *China* Plant sweetned with the Pith of an *Indian* Cane: The *Philippick* Islands give a Flavour to our *European* Bowls. The single Dress of a Woman of Quality is often the Product of an hundred Climates. The Muff and the Fan come together from the different Ends of the Earth. The Scarf is sent from the Torrid Zone, and the Tippet[11] from beneath the Pole. The Brocade Petticoat rises out of

---

[7] *Sir ANDREW:* Sir Andrew Freeport, a recurring character in *The Spectator,* represents the interests of commerce.

[8] *Merchant of Egypt . . . Grand Cairo:* In his first number of *The Spectator,* Addison's Mr. Spectator talks of his travels to Egypt.

[9] *Modern Coptik:* The language spoken by Christian Egyptians.

[10] *Grimace:* In Addison's day, this term meant a facial expression that expressed recognition — something like a nod in our culture.

[11] *Tippet:* A long, narrow piece of cloth, usually forming part of the hood, headdress, or sleeve of a woman's dress.

the Mines of *Peru*, and the Diamond Necklace out of the Bowels of *Indostan.*

If we consider our own Country in its natural Prospect, without any of the Benefits and Advantages of Commerce, what a barren uncomfortable Spot of Earth falls to our Share! Natural Historians tell us, that no Fruit grows originally among us, besides Hips and Haws, Acorns and Pig-Nutts, with other Delicacies of the like Nature; That our Climate of it self, and without the Assistances of Art, can make no further Advances towards a Plumb than to a Sloe, and carries an Apple to no greater a Perfection than a Crab:[12] That our Melons, our Peaches, our Figs, our Apricots, and Cherries, are Strangers among us, imported in different Ages, and naturalized in our *English* Gardens; and that they would all degenerate and fall away into the Trash of our own Country, if they were wholly neglected by the Planter, and left to the Mercy of our Sun and Soil. Nor has Traffick more enriched our Vegetable World, than it has improved the whole Face of Nature among us. Our Ships are laden with the Harvest of every Climate: Our Tables are stored with Spices, and Oils, and Wines: Our Rooms are filled with Pyramids of *China,* and adorned with the Workmanship of *Japan:* Our Morning's-Draught comes to us from the remotest Corners of the Earth: We repair our Bodies by the Drugs of *America,* and repose our selves under *Indian* Canopies. My Friend Sir ANDREW calls the Vineyards of *France* our Gardens; the Spice-Islands our Hot-Beds; the *Persians* our Silk-Weavers, and the *Chinese* our Potters. Nature indeed furnishes us with the bare Necessaries of Life, but Traffick gives us a great Variety of what is Useful, and at the same time supplies us with every thing that is Convenient and Ornamental. Nor is it the least part of this our Happiness, that whilst we enjoy the remotest Products of the North and South, we are free from those Extremities of Weather which give them Birth; That our Eyes are refreshed with the green Fields of *Britain,* at the same time that our Palates are feasted with Fruits that rise between the Tropicks.

For these Reasons there are not more useful Members in a Commonwealth than Merchants. They knit Mankind together in a mutual Intercourse of good Offices, distribute the Gifts of Nature, find Work for the poor, add Wealth to the Rich, and Magnificence to the Great. Our *English* Merchant converts the Tin of his own Country into Gold, and exchanges his Wooll for Rubies. The *Mahometans* are

[12]*Sloe . . . Crab:* A *sloe* is the fruit of the English blackthorn, *crab* refers to a crab apple.

cloathed in our *British* Manufacture, and the Inhabitants of the Frozen Zone warmed with the Fleeces of our Sheep.

When I have been upon the *'Change,* I have often fancied one of our old Kings[13] standing in Person, where he is represented in Effigy, and looking down upon the wealthy Concourse of People with which that Place is every Day filled. In this Case, how would he be surprized to hear all the Languages of *Europe* spoken in this little Spot of his former Dominions, and to see so many private Men, who in his Time would have been the Vassals of some powerful Baron, Negotiating like Princes for greater Sums of Mony than were formerly to be met with in the Royal Treasury! Trade, without enlarging the *British* Territories, has given us a kind of additional Empire: It has multiplied the Number of the Rich, made our Landed Estates infinitely more Valuable than they were formerly, and added to them an Accession of other Estates as Valuable as the Lands themselves.

[13] *our old Kings:* There were statues of the British monarchs since the Norman Conquest in niches in the walls of the Exchange.

JOSEPH ADDISON

## The Influence of French Fashions
## (The Spectator, No. 45)

At the time when Addison wrote this satire on the English vogue for French fashions in clothing and manners, English diplomats were negotiating the shaky Peace of Utrecht (1713), which brought a temporary truce to the French/English military conflict that dominated much of the late seventeenth and eighteenth centuries. The issue of clothing and goods imported from France was especially loaded because of the economic rivalry that underpinned the military conflict between the two countries. Addison's preference for English manners and customs over the French can be best understood in the light of England's rising dominance as a global military and economic power — a dominance most nearly rivaled by France.

Addison's distaste for "French Fopperies" bears some resemblance to Goldsmith's critique of English "luxury" in *The Citizen of the World* (see the excerpt reprinted in this chapter), and Burney's satiric portrait of Madame Duval. Addison critiques the mindless consumption of goods, along with the assumption of "foreign" manners. However, it is helpful to compare his disparaging view of imported French fashions in the following *Spectator* essay with his glowing view of global economic exchange in the preceding excerpt on the Royal Exchange. It is clearly not consumption itself that troubles Addison. Rather, his dislike of "French fopperies" derives more specifically from the economic rivalry among European nations competing for conquest of newly discovered nations and their resources. Reprinted here is Number 45 from *The Spectator*, ed. Donald F. Bond, vol. 1 (Oxford: Clarendon Press, 1965), 191–95.

## No. 45
## Saturday, April 21, 1711

*Natio Comœda est . . .*
— Jux.[1]

There is nothing which I more desire than a safe and honourable Peace, tho' at the same time I am very apprehensive of many ill Consequences that may attend it. I do not mean in regard to our Politicks, but to our Manners. What an Inundation of Ribbons and Brocades will break in upon us? What Peals of Laughter and Impertinence shall we be exposed to? For the Prevention of these great Evils, I could heartily wish that there was an Act of Parliament for Prohibiting the Importation of *French* Fopperies.

The Female Inhabitants of our Island have already received very strong Impressions from this ludicrous Nation, tho' by the Length of the War[2] (as there is no Evil which has not some Good attending it) they are pretty well worn out and forgotten. I remember the time when some of our well-bred Country Women kept their *Valet de Chambre*,[3] because forsooth, a Man was much more handy about them than one of their own Sex. I my self have seen one of these Male *Abigails*[4] tripping about the Room with a Looking-Glass in his hand, and combing his Lady's Hair a whole Morning together. Whether or no there was any Truth in the Story of a Lady's being got with Child

---

[1] *Natio Comœda est:* From Juvenal's *Satires:* "They are a nation of play-actors."
[2] *War:* The War of Spanish Succession ended, in 1701, a short and tenuous period of peace between England and France.
[3] *Valet de Chambre:* Manservant, usually in the employ of fashionable, aristocratic men.
[4] *Male Abigails:* Abigail was a type name for personal maidservants.

by one of these her Hand-maids I cannot tell, but I think at present the whole Race of them is extinct in our own Country.

About the Time that several of our Sex were taken into this kind of Service, the Ladies likewise brought up the Fashion of receiving Visits in their Beds.[5] It was then looked upon as a piece of Ill Breeding, for a Woman to refuse to see a Man, because she was not stirring; and a Porter would have been thought unfit for his Place, that could have made so awkward an Excuse. As I love to see every thing that is new, I once prevail'd upon my Friend WILL HONEYCOMB to carry me along with him to one of these Travell'd Ladies, desiring him, at the same time, to present me as a Foreigner who could not speak *English*, that so I might not be obliged to bear a Part in the Discourse. The Lady, tho' willing to appear undrest, had put on her best Looks, and painted her self for our Reception. Her Hair appeared in a very nice Disorder, as the Night-Gown which was thrown upon her Shoulders was ruffled with great Care. For my part, I am so shocked with every thing which looks immodest in the Fair Sex, that I could not forbear taking off my Eye from her when she moved in her Bed, and was in the greatest Confusion imaginable every time she stirred a Leg or an Arm. As the Coquets, who introduced this Custom, grew old, they left it off by degrees, well knowing that a Woman of Threescore may kick and tumble her Heart out, without making any Impressions.

*Sempronia*[6] is at present the most profest Admirer of the *French* Nation, but is so modest as to admit her Visitants no farther than her Toilet. It is a very odd Sight that beautiful Creature makes, when she is talking Politicks with her Tresses flowing about her Shoulders, and examining that Face in the Glass, which does such Execution upon all the Male Standers-by. How prettily does she divide her Discourse between her Woman and her Visitants? What sprightly Transitions does she make from an Opera or a Sermon, to an Ivory Comb or a Pin-Cushion? How have I been pleased to see her interrupted in an Account of her Travels, by a Message to her Foot man? and holding her Tongue, in the midst of a Moral Reflection, by applying the tip of it to a Patch.[7]

---

[5] *Visits in their Beds:* Addison's target here is the fashionable custom of the *ruelle*, or morning visit, which was paid in the bedroom or *boudoir* before the host or hostess had completed the elaborate toilet that was part of fashionable grooming.

[6] *Sempronia:* One of Addison's fictional "type" characters. Sempronia in classical literature was known for exceeding the bounds of "proper" feminine behavior.

[7] *Patch:* Small, decorative marks worn by men and women of fashion.

There is nothing which exposes a Woman to greater Dangers, than that Gaiety and Airiness of Temper, which are Natural to most of the Sex. It should be therefore the Concern of every Wise and Virtuous Woman, to keep this Sprightliness from degenerating into Levity. On the contrary, the whole Discourse and Behaviour of the *French* is to make the Sex more Fantastical, or (as they are pleased to term it,) *more awaken'd,*[8] than is consistent either with Virtue or Discretion. To speak Loud in Publick Assemblies, to let every one hear you Talk of Things that should only be mentioned in Private, or in Whispers, are looked upon as Parts of a refined Education. At the same time, a Blush is unfashionable, and Silence more ill-bred than any thing that can be spoken. In short, Discretion and Modesty, which in all other Ages and Countries have been regarded as the greatest Ornaments of the Fair Sex, are considered as the Ingredients of narrow Conversation, and Family Behaviour.

Some Years ago, I was at the Tragedy of *Macbeth*, and unfortunately placed my self under a Woman of Quality that is since Dead; who, as I found by the Noise she made, was newly returned from *France.* A little before the rising of the Curtain, she broke out into a loud Soliloquy, *When will the dear Witches enter;* and immediately upon their first Appearance, asked a Lady that sat three Boxes from her, on her Right Hand, if those Witches were not charming Creatures. A little after, as *Betterton*[9] was in one of the first Speeches of the Play, she shook her Fan at another Lady, who sat as far on the left Hand, and told her with a Whisper, that might be heard all over the Pit, We must not expect to see *Balloon*[10] to Night. Not long after, calling out to a young Baronet by his Name, who sat three Seats before me, she asked him whether *Macbeth's* Wife was still alive; and (before he could give an Answer) fell a talking of the Ghost of *Banquo.* She had by this time formed a little Audience to her self, and fixed the Attention of all about her. But as I had a mind to hear the Play, I got out of the Sphere of her Impertinence, and planted my self in one of the remotest Corners of the Pit.

---

[8] *more awaken'd:* From the French *eveillé,* meaning something like knowing although not necessarily in a positive sense.

[9] *Betterton:* Thomas Betterton was one of the most acclaimed actors of the late seventeenth and early eighteenth centuries. He was known for the grandeur and dignity of his elocution.

[10] *Balloon:* Balon, a popular French dancer in the London theaters. Compare this description with Evelina's account of trying to hear the actors over the conversation of the theater audience.

This pretty Childishness of Behaviour is one of the most refined Parts of Coquetry, and is not to be attained in Perfection, by Ladies that do not Travel for their Improvement. A natural and unconstrained Behaviour has something in it so agreeable, that it is no wonder to see People endeavouring after it. But at the same time, it is so very hard to hit, when it is not Born with us, that People often make themselves Ridiculous in attempting it.

A very Ingenious *French* Author[11] tells us, that the Ladies of the Court of *France,* in his Time, thought it ill Breeding, and a kind of Female Pedantry, to pronounce an hard Word right; for which Reason they took frequent occasion to use hard Words, that they might shew a Politeness in murdering them. He further adds, that a Lady of some Quality at Court, having accidentally made use of an hard Word in a proper Place, and Pronounced it right, the whole Assembly was out of Countenance for her.

I must however be so just to own, that there are many Ladies who have Travell'd several thousands of Miles without being the worse for it, and have brought Home with them all the Modesty, Discretion and good Sense, that they went abroad with. As on the contrary, there are great Numbers of *Travell'd* Ladies, who have lived all their Days within the Smoak of *London.* I have known a Woman that never was out of the Parish of St. *James*'s, betray as many Foreign Fopperies in her Carriage, as she could have Gleaned up in half the Countries of *Europe.*

[11] *French Author:* La Bruyère, "De la Société et de la Conversation," *Les Caractères,* vol. 5.

## OLIVER GOLDSMITH

### On London Shops
### (From The Citizen of the World)

Oliver Goldsmith (1730?–1774) is perhaps best known for his novel, *The Vicar of Wakefield* (1766), and a highly successful comic play, *She Stoops to Conquer,* first performed in 1773. His fellow author, friend, and biographer, Samuel Johnson, wrote in an epitaph for Goldsmith that "there was hardly any kind of writing that he did not touch upon, and he touched none that he did not adorn." Works well received in his day include a long poem, *The Deserted Village* (1770), and *The Citizen of the World* (1762), from which the following excerpts are taken. Perhaps some of Goldsmith's versatility was forced upon him by economic necessity: he needed to write in popular genres to please as large a paying audience as possible. Johnson wryly commented, when Goldsmith died with debts of more than £2,000, "Was ever poet so trusted before?"

Goldsmith's use of his fictional "citizen," Lien Chi Altangi, a visitor from China to London, follows in the tradition of Montesquieu's *Lettres Persanes* (1721), in which the fictional viewpoint of a visitor from Asia is used as a means to critique European customs and social institutions. It is interesting to compare the citizen's experience in visiting London shops with that of Evelina on her trip to the city. The fact that Lien Chi Altangi is shopping for silk is significant in both the context of London labor politics and of contemporary discussions of England as corrupted by "foreign" luxuries. Silk was increasingly the fabric of choice among the upper classes in England, and the market for this fabric created competition between the domestic silk produced by laborers in London's textiles industry and goods imported from England's Asian economic and political conquests. Goldsmith puts less emphasis on the struggles of laborers in the silk industry for fair wages and working conditions than on the English upper-class consumption of "foreign" goods — a consumption that he sees as having nothing to do with the fulfillment of real needs. The citizen's pointless purchases reflect what Goldsmith saw as the growing selfishness and thoughtlessness of a rapidly expanding English consumer economy.

The text of the following excerpt is taken from *The Collected Works of Oliver Goldsmith*, ed. Arthur Friedman (Oxford: Clarendon Press, 1966), 318–20.

Letter LXXVII.
From Lien Chi Altangi, to Fum Hoam,
First President of the Ceremonial Academy
at Pekin, in China.

The Shops of London are as well furnished as those of Pekin.[1] Those of London have a picture hung at their door, informing the passengers what they have to sell, as those at Pekin have a board to assure the buyer, that they have no intentions to cheat him.

[1] *Pekin:* Peking, the capital of China.

I was this morning to buy silk for a night-cap; immediately upon entering the mercer's[2] shop, the master and his two men, with wigs plaistered with powder, appeared to ask my commands. They were certainly the civilest people alive; if I but looked, they flew to the place, where I cast my eye; every motion of mine sent them running round the whole shop for my satisfaction. I informed them that I wanted what was good, and they shewed me not less than forty pieces, and each was better than the former; the prettiest pattern in nature, and the fittest in the world for night-caps. My very good friend, said I to the mercer, you must not pretend to instruct me in silks, I know these in particular to be no better than your mere flimsy *Bungees*.[3] *That may be,* cried the mercer, who I afterwards found had never contradicted a man in his life, *I can't pretend to say but they may; but I can assure you, my Lady Trail has had a sacque[4] from this piece this very morning.* But friend, said I, though my Lady has chosen a sacque from it, I see no necessity that I should wear it for a night-cap. *That may be,* returned he again, *yet what becomes a pretty Lady, will at any time look well on a handsome Gentleman.* This short compliment was thrown in so very seasonably upon my ugly face, that even tho' I disliked the silk, I desired him to cut me off the pattern of a night-cap.

While this business was consigned to his journeyman,[5] the master himself took down some pieces of silk still finer than any I had yet seen, and spreading them before me, *There, cries he, there's beauty, my Lord Snakeskin has bespoke the fellow to this for the birth-night[6] this very morning; it would look charmingly in waistcoats.* But I don't want a waistcoat, replied I: *Not want a waistcoat,* returned the mercer; *then I would advise you to buy one; when waistcoats are wanted, you may depend upon it they will come dear. Always buy before you want, and you are sure to be well used, as they say in*

---

[2] *mercer's:* A dealer in textile fabrics. It was customary to pick a fabric and then have it made into clothing; "ready-to-wear" clothes are a relatively modern phenomenon.

[3] *Bungees:* A kind of fabric.

[4] *sacque:* A fashionable, loose gown.

[5] *journeyman:* A craftsman who has completed his apprenticeship, but does not run his own shop. See the headnote to the selection from *The London Tradesman* in this chapter.

[6] *birth-night:* Those of noble birth customarily purchased a special, splendid suit of clothes to wear to court in celebration of the king's birthday.

*Cheapside.*[7] There was so much justice in his advice, that I could not refuse taking it; besides, the silk, which was really a good one, encreased the temptation, so I gave orders for that too.

As I was waiting to have my bargains measured and cut, which I know not how, they executed but slowly; during the interval, the mercer entertained me with the modern manner of some of the nobility receiving company in their morning gowns;[8] *Perhaps, Sir,* adds he, *you have a mind to see what kind of silk is universally worn.* Without waiting for my reply, he spreads a piece before me, which might be reckoned beautiful, even in China. *If the nobility, continues he, were to know I sold this to any, under a Right Honourable,*[9] *I should certainly lose their custom; you see, my Lord, it is at once rich, tastey, and quite the thing.* I am no Lord, interrupted I——*I beg pardon,* cried he, *but be pleased to remember, when you intend buying a morning-gown, that you had an offer from me of something worth money. Conscience, Sir, conscience, is my way of dealing; you may buy a morning-gown now, or you may stay till they become dearer and less fashionable, but it is not my business to advise.* In short, most reverend *Fum,* he persuaded me to buy a morning-gown also, and would probably have persuaded me to have bought half the goods in his shop, if I had stayed long enough, or was furnished with sufficient money.

Upon returning home, I could not help reflecting with some astonishment, how this very man with such a confined education and capacity, was yet capable of turning me as he thought proper, and molding me to his inclinations! I knew he was only answering his own purposes, even while he attempted to appear solicitous about mine; yet by a voluntary infatuation, a sort of passion compounded of vanity and good nature, I walked into the snare with my eyes open, and put myself to future pain in order to give him immediate pleasure. The wisdom of the ignorant, somewhat resembles the instinct of animals; it is diffused in but a very narrow sphere, but within that circle it acts with vigour, uniformity, and success.    Adieu.

---

[7]*Cheapside:* The site of a market in medieval times, this street in London took its name from the Anglo-Saxon *ceap,* meaning barter or purchase. It was famous from Tudor times for its goldsmith shops and was generally associated with craftsmen and trade. At mid-century, it was a fashionable and rather expensive place to shop.

[8]*morning gowns:* A loose gown, generally worn at home for informal occasions, often with a night cap.

[9]*Right Honourable:* A form of address applied to peers (those with inherited titles) below the rank of marquess.

HENRY FIELDING

# People of Fashion
## *(From* The Covent-Garden Journal*)*

Henry Fielding (1707–1754) is established in modern studies of the novel as one of the "fathers" of English prose fiction, and he is currently best known as a novelist. His career was in fact rather more complicated than this representation suggests. Fielding contributed to the popular periodical *The Champion,* a periodical oppositional to the Whig government of Robert Walpole, which lasted from 1721 to 1742. Unlike the Whigs Addison and Steele, who tended to veil their political positions in "common sense," allegedly nonpartisan rhetoric, Fielding was specific and pointed in his political satire. Most notably, he wrote comic plays for and managed London's Haymarket Theatre during the most troubled and contentious years of Walpole's administration. Farcical plays such as *The Tragedy of Tragedies* invited audiences to laugh while making devastating critiques of corrupt government practices. In 1737 Parliament passed a Licensing Act that required all plays proposed for the government-sanctioned London theaters to receive government approval before they could be performed. Fielding was unable to survive in the theater under these censorious conditions. After 1737 he turned his energies to his duties as a London justice of the peace and to writing the novels for which he is famous today: *Joseph Andrews* (1742), *Tom Jones* (1749), and *Amelia* (1751).

As a justice of the peace, Fielding also continued his activities as an author of pamphlets and other topical and occasional forms of literature. *The Covent-Garden Journal* ran between January and November of 1752. The following excerpt is taken from *The Covent-Garden Journal and A Plan of the Universal Register-Office,* ed. Bertrand A. Goldgar (Middletown, Conn.: Wesleyan UP, 1988), 217–21.

Saturday, May 9, 1752

*Scilicet in Vulgus manent Exempla Regentum.*
— CLAUDIAN.
THE CREATURES *will endeavour to ape their Betters.*

There are many Phrases that Custom renders familiar to our Ears, which, when looked into, and closely examined, will appear extremely strange, and of which it must greatly puzzle a very learned Etymologist to account for the Original.

Of this Sort is the Term, PEOPLE OF FASHION. An Expression of such very common Use, and so universally understood, that it is entirely needless to set down here what is meant by it: But how it first acquired its present Meaning, and became a Title of Honour and Distinction, is a Point, I apprehend, of no small Difficulty to determine.

I have on this Occasion consulted several of my Friends, who are well skilled in Etymology. One of these traces the Word Fashion through the French Language up to the Latin. He brings it from the Verb FACIO, which, among other Things, signifies TO DO. Hence he supposes *People of Fashion*, according to the old Derivation of *Lucus a non lucendo*,[1] to be spoken of those who do Nothing. But this is too general, and would include all the Beggars in the Nation.

Another carries the Original no farther than the French Word FACON, which is often used to signify *Affectation*. This likewise will extend too far, and will comprehend Attorney's Clerks, Apprentices, Milliners, Mantua-makers, and an infinite Number of the lower People.

A third will bring Fashion from φάσις.[2] This in the genitive Plural makes φασέων, which in English is the very Word. According to him, by People of Fashion are meant People whose Essence consisteth in Appearances, and who, while they seem to be something, are really nothing.

But tho' I am well apprized that much may be said to support this Derivation, there is a fourth Opinion, which to speak in the proper Language, hath yet a *more smiling* Aspect. This supposes the Word Fashion to be a Corruption from Fascination,[3] and that these people were formerly believed by the Vulgar to be a Kind of Conjurers, and to possess a Species of the Black Art.

In Support of this Opinion, my Friend urges the Use which these People have always made of the Word Circle, and the Pretence to be enclosed in a certain Circle, like so many Conjurers, and by such Means to keep the Vulgar at a Distance from them.

---

[1] *Lucus a non lucendo:* A phrase from Quintilian — "A grove is so called because it excludes the light" — that suggests how words are derived from their opposites. Fielding exhibits pseudo classical learning here to increase the mock-solemnity of his ridiculous etymology.

[2] φάσις: This Greek word means "appearance."

[3] *Fascination:* A casting of a spell, as in magic.

"Pantheon Macaroni," 1782. The term *macaroni* was used to refer to effeminate young men of fashion in the second half of the eighteenth century. The Pantheon was just the sort of fashionable public place where a macaroni would go to show off himself and his clothes.

To this Purpose likewise he quotes the Phrases, a polite Circle, the Circle of one's Acquaintance, People that live within a certain Circle, and many others. From all which he infers, that in those dark and ignorant Ages, when Conjurers were held in more Estimation than they are at present, the credulous Vulgar believed these People to be of the Number, and consequently called them *People of Fascination*, which hath been since corrupted into *People of Fashion.*

However whimsical this Opinion may seem, or however far fetched the Derivation may sound to those who have not much considered the barbarous Corruption of Language, I must observe in its Favour how difficult it is by any other Method, to account not only for that odd Phrase, People of Fashion; but likewise for that Circle within which those People have always affected to live.

Even now, when Conjurers have been long laughed out of the World, the Pretence to the Circle is nevertheless maintained, and within this Circle the People of Fascination do actually insist upon living at this Day.

It is moreover extremely pleasant to observe what wonderful Care these People take to preserve their Circle safe and inviolate, and with how jealous an Eye they guard against any Intrusion of those whom they are pleased to call the Vulgar; who are on the other Hand as vigilant to watch, and as active to improve every Opportunity of invading this Circle, and breaking into it.

Within the Memory of many now living, the Circle of the People of Fascination included the whole Parish of Covent-Garden, and great Part of St. Giles's in the Fields; but here the Enemy broke in, and the Circle was presently contracted to Leicester-Fields, and Golden-Square. Hence the People of Fashion again retreated before the Foe to Hanover-Square; whence they were once more driven to Grosvenor-Square, and even beyond it, and that with such Precipitation, that had they not been stopped by the Walls of Hyde-Park, it is more than probable they would by this Time have arrived at Kensington.[4]

In many other Instances we may remark the same Flight of these People, and the same Pursuit of their Enemies. They first contrived a certain Vehicle called a Hackney-Coach[5] to avoid the Approach of

[4] *the Circle . . . Kensington:* The movement of the boundaries of "Fashion's" magic circle reflects the westward growth of London beyond the perimeters of the original city. The "City" increasingly came to mean the unfashionable business district, while the wealthy gravitated toward the newly developed "suburb" of Westminster.

[5] *Hackney-Coach:* Visitors to London commented on Londoners' ability to hire a coach for trips in town, much as we would hire a taxi today.

the Foe in the open Streets. Hence they were soon routed, and obliged to take Shelter in Coaches of their own. Nor did this protect them long. The Enemy likewise in great Numbers mounted into the same *armed* Vehicles.[6] The People of Fascination then betook themselves to Chairs;[7] in which their exempt Privileges being again invaded, I am informed that several Ladies of Quality have bespoke a Kind of Couch somewhat like the *Lectica*[8] of the Romans; in which they are next Winter to be carried through the Streets upon Men's Shoulders.

The Reader will be pleased to observe, that beside the local Circle which I have described above, there is an imaginary or figurative one, which is invaded by every Imitation of the Vulgar.

Thus those People of Fascination, or if they like it better, of Fashion, who found it convenient to remain still in Coaches, observing that several of the Enemy had lately exhibited Arms[9] on their Vehicles, by which Means, those Ornaments became vulgar and common, immediately ordered their own Arms to be blotted out, and a Cypher substituted in their Room; perhaps cunningly contriving to represent themselves instead of their Ancestors.[10]

Numberless are the Devices made use of by the People of Fashion of both Sexes, to avoid the Pursuit of the Vulgar, and to preserve the Purity of the Circle. Sometimes the Perriwig covers the whole Beau, and he peeps forth from the midst like an Owl in an Ivy-Bush; at other Times his Ears stand up behind half a dozen Hairs, and give you the Idea of a different Animal. Sometimes a large black Bag, with Wings spread as broad as a Raven's adorns his Back, at other Times, a little lank Silk appears like a dead Blackbird in his Neck. To Day he borrows the Tail of a Rat, and Tomorrow that of a Monkey; for he will transform himself into the Likeness of the vilest Animal, to avoid the Resemblance of his own Species.[11]

Nor are the Ladies less watchful of the Enemy's Motions, or less anxious to avoid them. What Hoods and Hats and Caps and Coifs

---

[6] *armed Vehicles:* Coaches carrying the owners' coat of arms.

[7] *Chairs:* Sedan chairs, carried by men who made their living as bearers.

[8] *Lectica:* A litter.

[9] *Arms:* Coats of arms, the family sign or signature design.

[10] *Cypher . . . themselves instead of their Ancestors:* A pun: "cypher" means both symbol and nothing.

[11] *the Perriwig . . . his own Species:* This passage reflects a variety of fashions in men's hairstyles and wigs popular in the first half of the century, from the long, loosely flowing perriwig to the tie-wig, which ended in a tail down the back. (The "tails" of various animals in this passage may refer to the practice of using animals' fur to supplement wigs and hairpieces.)

have fallen a Sacrifice in this Pursuit! Within my Memory the Ladies of the Circle covered their lovely Necks with a Cloak; this being routed by the Enemy, was exchanged for the Manteel; this again was succeeded by the Pelorine, the Pelorine by the Neckatee, the Neckatee by the Capuchine;[12] which hath now stood its Ground a long Time, but not without various Changes of Colour, Shape, Ornaments, &c.

And here I must not pass by the many admirable Arts made use of by these Ladies, to deceive and dodge their Imitators; when they are hunted out in any favourite Mode, the Method is to lay it by for a Time, and then to resume it again all at once, when the Enemy least expect it. Thus Patches[13] appear and disappear several Times in a Season. I have myself seen the Enemy in the Pit, with Faces all over spotted like the Leopard, when the Circle in the Boxes have with a conscious Triumph displayed their native Alabaster, without a simple Blemish, tho' they had a few Evenings before worn a thousand: within a Month afterwards the Leopards have appeared in the Boxes to the great Mortification of the Fair Faces in the Pit.[14]

In the same Manner the Ruff after a long Discontinuance some Time since began to revive in the Circle, and advanced downwards, till it almost met the Tucker.[15] But no sooner did the Enemy pursue, than it vanished all at once, and the Boxes became a Collection of little Hills of Snow, extremely delightful to the Eyes of every Beholder.[16]

Of all the Articles of Distinction the Hoop hath stood the longest, and with the most obstinate Resistance. Instead of giving Way, this the more it hath been pushed, hath encreased the more; till the Enemy hath been compelled to give over the Pursuit from mere

[12] *Cloak . . . Capuchine:* Different styles of women's shoulder and neck coverings.

[13] *Patches:* Small, dark beauty marks or moles were considered attractive, and false beauty marks, or patches were worn variably, as Fielding suggests, by the fashionable or unfashionable of both genders. They sometimes took decorative shapes and colors other than the "natural" black or dark-brown round dot. While often fashionable for affluent and aristocratic women, patches were also popular with prostitutes who used them to hide the skin sores of venereal disease.

[14] *Boxes . . . Pit:* The box seats at the theater were more expensive than a place on the main floor, or pit, and hence, usually kept by those of higher class standing. Fashionable women in the boxes often came as much to display their finery and beauty as to watch the play. In any case, they certainly were part of the theater's spectacle.

[15] *Ruff . . . Tucker:* A ruff was usually worn high on the neck, while the tucker was a ruffle that rode low on the bosom.

[16] *Collection . . . Beholder:* Bare chests, with prominently displayed cleavage became fashionable.

Necessity; it being found impossible to convey seven Yards of Hoop into a Hackney-Coach, or to slide with it behind a Counter.[17]

But as I have mentioned some of the Arts of the Circle, it would not be fair to be silent as to those of the Enemy, among whom a certain Citizen's Wife distinguished herself very remarkably, and appeared long in the very Top of the Mode. It was at last however discovered that she used a very unfair Practice, and kept a private Correspondence with one of those Milliners[18] who were intrusted with all the Secrets of the Circle.

[17] *Hoop . . . Counter:* Complaints about the wide hoops, made of whalebone or metal and worn under women's outer petticoat, were common in the eighteenth century. The would-be-fashionable middle-class "Enemy" gives up trying to emulate the wide skirts of aristocratic women because of the relative physical constraints of their world. Unlike her upper-class counterparts, she must take the narrower hackney coach or even work "behind a Counter" in the shop of a tradesman husband or father.

[18] *Milliners:* Milliners dealt in the design and marketing of a variety of women's clothing, primarily accessory apparel such as ribbons, bonnets, scarves, and so forth.

# Placing Fashion

## JOSEPH ADDISON AND RICHARD STEELE

### On the London Theatre
### (From The Spectator, Nos. 235, 240, and 502)

Addison and his partner in writing *The Spectator,* Sir Richard Steele, maintained an ongoing interest in English drama and the London theater. Both wrote successful plays. Addison's tragedy *Cato,* first performed in 1713 and performed 226 times prior to 1776, was well received as a serious attempt to adhere to Aristotole's rules for dramatic decorum, and Steele's sentimental comedy *The Conscious Lovers* (1722) was also popular, as a refined and "sentimental" comedy, throughout the century. Working in tragedy and comedy, respectively, Addison and Steele engaged in the ongoing cultural project of "reforming" English drama and the English theater: that is, they wished to bring what they considered more refined standards to an art form that often depended as much on the broad strokes of spectacular display as on "tasteful" writing and elocution.

Along with reforming English drama, Addison and Steele wished to reform the theater itself. Even the supposedly more sophisticated urban audiences of London were more than a little demonstrative in their reception of plays and the actors that performed them. It was not uncommon for performances to be brought to a halt by the displeasure of a rowdy audience; the crowd's approbation, on the other hand, could result in a favorite actor repeating a favorite scene over and over again, at the expense of any coherent performance of a play. It was common practice to interrupt performances with noisy demonstrations of approval or disapprobation. And this rowdy responsiveness was, perhaps, preferable to the total disregard some parts of an audience might have for a performance. As we can see from Evelina's experience at the theater and Fielding's complaints in *The Covent-Garden Journal,* many "fashionable" people came to socialize and display their new finery rather than to see the play. The following excerpts from *The Spectator* speak to forms of playhouse behavior that had not altogether died out by the date of *Evelina*'s publication, although the practice of allowing smart young men or beaux to sit on the stage during a performance to show off their clothing and figures had been discontinued.

Excerpted here are Numbers 235, 240, and 502 from *The Spectator,* ed. Donald F. Bond, 5 vols. (Oxford: Clarendon Press, 1965).

## No. 235
## Thursday, November 29, 1711

*. . . Populares*
*Vincentem strepitus . . .*[1]
— Hor.

There is nothing which lies more within the Province of a Spectator than Publick Shows and Diversions; and as among these there are none which can pretend to Vie with those Elegant Entertainments that are exhibited in our Theatres, I think it particularly Incumbent on me to take Notice of every thing that is remarkable in such numerous and refined Assemblies.

---

[1] *. . . Populares Vincentem strepitus . . .* : From Horace, *Ars poetica:* ". . . stilling the tumultuous noises of the pit . . ."

It is observed, that of late Years, there has been a certain Person in the Upper Gallery of the Play-house, who when he is pleased with any thing that is acted upon the Stage, expresses his Approbation by a loud Knock upon the Benches, or the Wainscot, which may be heard over the whole Theatre. This Person is commonly known by the Name of the *Trunk-maker in the Upper-Gallery*. Whether it be, that the Blow he gives on these Occasions resembles that which is often heard in the Shops of such Artizans, or that he was supposed to have been a real Trunk-maker, who after the finishing of his Day's Work, used to unbend his Mind at these Publick Diversions with his Hammer in his Hand, I cannot certainly tell. There are some, I know, who have been foolish enough to imagine it is a Spirit which haunts the Upper-Gallery, and from time to time makes those strange Noises; and the rather, because he is observed to be louder than ordinary every time the Ghost of *Hamlet* appears. Others have reported, that it is a Dumb Man, who has chosen this way of uttering himself, when he is transported with any thing he sees or hears. Others will have it to be the Play-house Thunderer, that exerts himself after this manner in the Upper Gallery, when he has nothing to do upon the Roof.[2]

But having made it my business to get the best Information I cou'd in a matter of this Moment, I find that the Trunk-maker, as he is commonly called, is a large black[3] Man, whom no body knows. He generally leans forward on a huge Oaken Plant[4] with great Attention to every thing that passes upon the Stage. He is never seen to Smile; but upon hearing any thing that pleases him, he takes up his Staff with both Hands, and lays it upon the next piece of Timber that stands in his way with exceeding Vehemence: After which he composes himself in his former Posture, 'till such time as something new sets him again at Work.

It has been observed his Blow is so well timed, that the most judicious Critick could never except against it. As soon as any shining Thought is expressed in the Poet, or any uncommon Grace appears in the Actor, he smites the Bench or Wainscot. If the Audience does not concur with him, he smites a second time; and if the Audience is not yet awaked, looks round him with great Wrath, and repeats the Blow

---

[2] *Play-house Thunderer . . . Roof:* New methods for producing thunder during a performance had been introduced early in the century and were much commented on in the popular press.

[3] *black:* "Black" in this context probably refers to a dark-complected European, not an African or Indian.

[4] *Oaken Plant:* Staff.

a third time, which never fails to produce the Clap. He sometimes lets the Audience begin the Clap of themselves, and at the Conclusion of their Applause ratifies it with a single Thwack.

He is of so great use to the Play-house, that it is said a former Director of it, upon his not being able to pay his Attendance by reason of Sickness, kept one in Pay to officiate for him 'till such time as he recovered; but the Person so employed, tho' he laid about him with incredible Violence, did it in such wrong Places, that the Audience soon found out it was not their old Friend the Trunk-maker.

It has been remarked, that he has not yet exerted himself with Vigour this Season. He sometimes plies at the Opera; and upon *Nicolini's* first Appearance,[5] was said to have demolished three Benches in the Fury of his Applause. He has broken half a dozen Oaken Plants upon *Dogget*,[6] and seldom goes away from a Tragedy of *Shakespear*, without leaving the Wainscot extreamly shattered.

The Players do not only connive at this his obstreperous Approbation, but very chearfully repair at their own Cost whatever Damages he makes. They had once a Thought of erecting a kind of Wooden Anvil for his use, that should be made of a very sounding Plank, in order to render his Stroaks more deep and mellow; but as this might not have been distinguished from the Musick of a Kettle Drum, the Project was laid aside.

In the mean while I cannot but take notice of the great use it is to an Audience, that a Person should thus preside over their Heads, like the Director of a Consort, in order to awaken their Attention, and beat Time to their Applauses. Or to raise my Simile, I have sometimes fancied the Trunk-maker in the Upper Gallery to be like *Virgil's* Ruler of the Winds,[7] seated upon the Top of a Mountain, who, when he struck his Sceptre upon the side of it, roused an Hurricane, and set the whole Cavern in an Uproar.

It is certain the Trunk-maker has saved many a good Play, and brought many a graceful Actor into Reputation, who would not otherwise have been taken notice of. It is very visible, as the Audience is not a little abashed, if they find themselves betrayed into a Clap, when their Friend in the Upper Gallery does not come into it; so the

---

[5] *Nicolini's first Appearance:* Nicolino Grimaldi came to London in 1708. Richard Steele praises both his voice and acting in *The Tatler*, January 3, 1710. The actor, playwright, and theater manager Colley Cibber says of him that "no singer, since his time had so justly, and gracefully acquitted himself, in whatever character he appear'd, as Nicolini" (*Apology*, 1740 edition, 225).

[6] *Dogget:* Thomas Dogget, an Irish actor extremely popular for his "low" comic performances.

[7] *Ruler of the Winds:* Aeolus, from the *Aeneid*, line 52 and following.

Actors do not value themselves upon the Clap, but regard it as a meer *Brutum fulmen,* or empty Noise, when it has not the Sound of the Oaken Plant in it. I know it has been given out by those, who are Enemies to the Trunk-maker, that he has sometimes been bribed to be in the Interest of a bad Poet, or a vicious Player; but this is a Surmise, which has no Foundation; his Stroaks are always just, and his Admonitions seasonable; he does not deal about his Blows at Random, but always hits the right Nail upon the Head. The inexpressible Force wherewith he lays them on, sufficiently shews the Evidence and Strength of his Conviction. His Zeal for a good Author is indeed outrageous, and breaks down every Fence and Partition, every Board and Plank, that stands within the Expression of his Applause.

As I do not care for terminating my Thoughts in Barren Speculations, or in Reports of pure Matter of Fact, without drawing something from them for the Advantage of my Countrymen, I shall take the Liberty to make an humble Proposal, that whenever the Trunk-maker shall depart this Life, or whenever he shall have lost the Spring of his Arm by Sickness, Old Age, Infirmity, or the like, some able-bodied Critick should be advanced to this Post, and have a competent Salary setled on him for Life, to be furnished with Bamboos for Operas, Crabtree-Cudgels for Comedies, and Oaken Plants for Tragedy, at the publick Expence. And to the End that this Place should always be disposed of, according to Merit, I would have none preferred to it, who has not given convincing Proofs, both of a sound Judgment and a strong Arm, and who could not, upon Occasion, either knock down an Ox or write a Comment upon *Horace*'s Art of Poetry. In short, I would have him a due Composition of *Hercules* and *Apollo,* and so rightly qualifyed for this important Office, that the *Trunk-maker* may not be missed by our Posterity.

### From No. 240
### Wednesday, December 5, 1711

*Mr.* SPECTATOR,[8]  *December* 3d, 1711.

"I was the other Night at *Philaster*,[9] where I expected to hear your famous Trunk-maker, but was unhappily disappointed of his Company, and saw another Person who had the like Ambition to distin-

---

[8] It was common for Addison and Steele to print letters from readers. Sometimes these were written by friends of the authors; often they were the work of Addison or Steele themselves.

[9] *Philaster:* A popular play by the seventeenth-century playwrights Francis Beaumont and John Fletcher.

guish himself in a noisy Manner, partly by Vociferation or talking loud, and partly by his bodily Agility. This was a very lusty Fellow, but withal a sort of Beau, who getting into one of the Side-Boxes on the Stage before the Curtain drew, was disposed to shew the whole Audience his Activity by leaping over the Spikes;[10] he pass'd from thence to one of the ent'ring Doors, where he took Snuff with a tolerable good Grace, display'd his fine Cloaths, made two or three feint Passes at the Curtain with his Cane, then faced about and appear'd at t'other Door: Here he affected to survey the whole House, bow'd and smil'd at Random, and then shew'd his Teeth (which were some of them indeed very white): After this he retir'd behind the Curtain, and obliged us with several Views of his Person from every Opening.

"During the Time of acting he appear'd frequently in the Prince's Apartment, made one at the Hunting-Match, and was very forward in the Rebellion. If there were no Injunctions to the contrary, yet this Practice must be confess'd to diminish the Pleasure of the Audience, and for that Reason presumptuous and unwarrantable: But since her Majesty's late Command has made it criminal,[11] you have Authority to take Notice of it.

*SIR,*

*Your humble Servant,*

Charles Easy."

**From No. 502**
**Monday, October 6, 1712**

According to what you may observe there on our Stage, you see them [the audience] often moved so directly against all common Sense and Humanity, that you would be apt to pronounce us a Nation of Savages. It cannot be called a Mistake of what is pleasant, but the very Contrary to it is what most assuredly takes with them. The other Night an old Woman carried off with a Pain in her Side, with all the Distortions and Anguish of Countenance which is natural to one in that Condition, was laughed and clapped off the Stage . . .

The intolerable Folly and Confidence of Players putting in Words of their own, does in a great measure feed the absurd Taste of the Audience. But, however that is, it is ordinary for a Cluster of Coxcombs to take up the House to themselves, and equally insult both

---

[10] *Spikes:* Spikes separated the stage from the audience.
[11] *her Majesty's late . . . criminal:* Queen Anne barred the audience from going behind the scenes, a fact that was frequently advertised on playbills. The royal decree was usually ignored, however, in Addison and Steele's day.

the Actors and the Company. These Savages, who want all manner of Regard and Deference to the rest of Mankind, come only to shew themselves to us, without any other Purpose than to let us know they despise us.

The Gross of an Audience is compos'd of two Sorts of People, those who know no Pleasure but of the Body, and those who improve or command corporeal Pleasures by the Addition of fine Sentiments of the Mind. At present the intelligent Part of the Company are wholly subdued by the Insurrections of those who know no Satisfactions but what they have in common with all other Animals.

This is the Reason that when a Scene tending to Procreation is acted, you see the whole Pit in such a Chuckle, and old Letchers, with Mouths open, stare at the loose Gesticulations on the Stage with shameful Earnestness, when the justest Pictures of Humane Life in its calm Dignity, and the properest Sentiments for the Conduct of it, pass by like meer Narration, as conducing only to somewhat much better which is to come after. I have seen the whole House at some Times in so proper a Disposition, that indeed I have trembled for the Boxes, and feared the Entertainment would end in the Representation of the Rape of the *Sabines*.

I would not be understood in this Talk to argue, that nothing is tolerable on the Stage but what has an immediate Tendency to the Promotion of Virtue. On the contrary, I can allow, provided there is nothing against the Interests of Virtue, and is not offensive to good Manners, that Things of an indifferent Nature may be represented. For this Reason I have no Exception to the well-drawn Rusticities in the *Country-Wake;*[12] and there is something so miraculously pleasant in *Dogget's* acting the awkard Triumph and comick Sorrow of *Hob* in different Circumstances, that I shall not be able to stay away whenever it is acted. All that vexes me is, that the Gallantry of taking the Cudgels for *Gloucestershire,* with the Pride of Heart in tucking himself up, and taking Aim at his Adversary, as well as the other's Protestation in the Humanity of low Romance, That he could not promise the Squire to break *Hob's* Head, but he would, if he could, do it in Love; then flourish and begin: I say, what vexes me is, that such excellent Touches as these, as well as the Squire's being out of all Patience at *Hob's* Success, and venturing himself into the Crowd, are Circumstances hardly taken Notice of, and the Height of the Jest

---

[12] *Country-Wake:* A popular farce, authored by and acted in by Thomas Dogget. (An instance of "low" comedy.)

is only in the very Point that Heads are broken. I am confident, were there a Scene written, wherein *Penkethman* should break his Leg by wrestling with *Bullock*, and *Dicky*[13] come in to set it, without one Word said but what should be according to the exact Rules of Surgery in making this Extention, and binding up the Leg, the whole House should be in a Roar of Applause at the dissembled Anguish of the Patient, the Help given by him who threw him down, and the handy Address and arch Looks of the Surgeon. To enumerate the Entrance of Ghosts, the Embattling of Armies, the Noise of Heroes in Love, with a thousand other Enormities, would be to transgress the Bounds of this Paper, for which Reason it is possible they may have hereafter distinct Discourses; not forgetting any of the Audience who shall set up for Actors, and interrupt the Play on the Stage; and Players who shall prefer the Applause of Fools to that of the reasonable Part of the Company.

[13] *Penkethman . . . Dicky:* All popular comic actors on the London stage.

ANONYMOUS

## *From* A Sketch of the Spring-Gardens, Vaux-hall

Vauxhall Gardens opened in the early summer of 1661. The gardens were brought to the height of their popularity by Jonathan Tyers, who purchased them in 1728 for £250 and developed them into the fashionable pleasure grounds they became after about 1752. The Tyers family sold the gardens in 1821 for £28,000. By then, the popularity of the gardens had waned, and they were no longer the favored resort of "the quality"; nor did they draw the number of visitors, from different walks of life, that they had in Evelina's day.

W. S. Scott, a historian of the gardens, explains their lengthy popularity in his *Green Retreats: The Story of Vauxhall Gardens, 1661–1859* (1955), by referring to the "inherent love of the English people for out-of-doors amusements." During the Restoration years, the gardens drew crowds reacting against the Puritan suppression of public amusements during the Interregnum period. Later in the eighteenth century, the popularity of "picturesque" landscapes in gardening dovetailed with a literary fashion for scenic descriptions to make the gardens all the more popular. In addition, Vauxhall, located about two miles from the city of London,

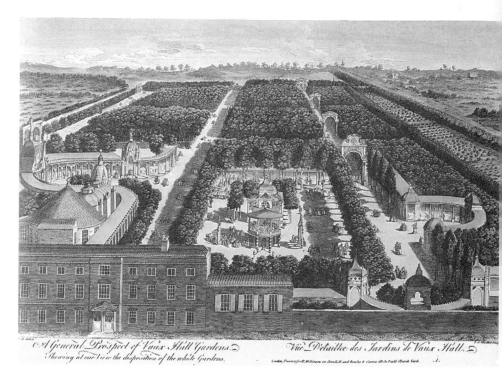

A General Prospect of Vaux Hall Gardens.
Shewing at one View the disposition of the whole Gardens.

Vüe Detaillée des Jardins de Vaux Hall.

London, Printed for R. Wilkinson in Cornhill, and Bowles & Carver, 69 St Paul's Church Yard.

was "over the water," on the Surrey side of the Thames, and therefore going to the gardens gave the pleasant impression of leaving the city for a rural setting. Aside from the gardens themselves, music contributed to much of Vauxhall's attraction. During the summer months, one could hear a variety of outdoor concerts, and visitors commented on the charm of hearing the music as one approached the gardens over the Thames. Dining was also available for those who tired of strolling, enjoying the lighted gardens, crowd-watching, and being watched.

Scott also notes that Vauxhall's popularity grew in part because it afforded a socially acceptable form of amusement for women, as well as men, in a society in which public entertainment was frequently gender-segregated. Besides being mixed in gender, the crowds that frequented Vauxhall also tended to be mixed in class. The price of admission (one shilling until 1792, when it was raised to two shillings) allowed a wide range of people to enjoy the gardens. At the same time, "most of the nobility and gentry, then in and near London" frequented the gardens, as well as "some of the royal family" (*Royal Gazetter*, 1751). In some accounts, such as the following, Vauxhall Gardens is portrayed as an ideal public space, in which order prevails, despite the mixing of genders and classes. In others, including Burney's and Goldsmith's, class and gender conflicts occasionally detract from the enjoyment of the music and spectacle of the gardens.

The pamphlet from which the following excerpt is taken was published anonymously in London, probably around mid-century.

*Opposite, top:* "A General Prospect of Vauxhall Gardens." From a drawing by Samuel Wale, 1751. Courtesy of the Board of Trustees of the Victoria & Albert Museum.

*Opposite, bottom:* "Vauxhall Gardens," by Thomas Rowlandson. Exhibited at the Royal Academy, 1784. The Prince of Wales is shown talking to his mistress, the poet and actress Mary Perdita Robinson on the right; seated in the box on the left are James Boswell, Burney's mentor Dr. Johnson, her patron Mrs. Thrale, and Oliver Goldsmith. Courtesy of the Board of Trustees of the Victoria & Albert Museum.

'Twould be endless to attempt a Description of every Beauty in these Gardens; many Parts of which being illuminated, shine forth in all their Glory, in a dark Night; and seem a strong Representation of the fam'd *Elizium,*[1] (as was observed) on which antient Poets have lavished the most lovely Colours. Was it possible for *Homer* and *Virgil* to return to Earth, and visit this *Spot,* with Extasy would they seize their Lyres, and sing the various Charms of this Garden.

> What different Pleasures here are found! —
> Now wand'ring lonely, up and down,
> The lofty Trees, which Shade us round,
> Waft us in Fancy Far from Town

> Lo! the Magician waves his Wand,
> And in some Monarch's Court we seem,
> Such Crouds move round, so bright each Band: —
> The whole is a delicious Dream!

After the Music is ended for the Night, 'tis vastly agreeable to wind round the Ranges of *Pavillions,* and gaze at the numberless *Parties,* (some of whom are frequently attended by *French* Horns) supping in their several Bowers. The Multitude of Groops surveyed on this Occasion, varying in Figure, Age and Dress; the different Attitudes in which the *Parties* appear, and the Disparity of their Humours, form methinks, (altogether) an exquisite School of Painting. And so many of our lovely Countrywomen visit these blissful Bowers, that was *Zeuxis*[2] again to attempt the Picture of *Venus,* 'tis from hence, and not from *Greece,* that he would compose his Image of perfect Beauty.

After the Sketch thus attempted of these *Gardens,* it may not be improper just to hint at one Circumstance, that contributes very much to the Convenience, as well as to the Beauty, of this *Entertainment,* and for want whereof, indeed, it could not well subsist: I mean the Readiness with which the numberless *Tables* are serv'd, with whatever may be call'd for; a Decorum that could not take Place, nor the Master of the Gardens[3] keep a just Account of the various Articles deliver'd out to his Waiters, was it not for *Order.* This, indeed, is so exact, that Many have wonder'd, how it could be possible for three or four thousand Persons to be regularly entertain'd, at differ-

---

[1] *Elizium:* The heaven of the gods in classical mythology.
[2] *Zeuxis:* A Greek painter from the south of Italy in the late fifth century B.C. His most famous painting was actually of the legendary Helen of Troy, who was Venus's competitor in a famous contest over who was the most beautiful woman in the world.
[3] *Master of the Gardens:* Jonathan Tyers, the owner of Vauxhall.

ent Tables, at one and the same Time. The *Bands* thus feasting, form (altogether) as grand a Picture as the Imagination can frame. — . . .

As these *Gardens* abound with so many Beauties, both natural and artificial (the Latter of which are increasing every Year,) 'tis no Wonder, that they should have been the darling Resort of all Persons of Taste, ever since their being opened in this Form. The extraordinary and very just Success, which the several *Entertainments* of them always met with, gave rise to many *Copies* in the Neighbourhood of our Metropolis, as well as in different Parts of our Island; but then, like *Copies*, they sink far below the admired ORIGINAL; *Vaux-hall* Garden being more immediately the *Thing* for which it was intended. Farther, this Imitation has not been confined merely to *Great Britian;* there having been one, to which the Manager gave the Name of *Vaux-hall*, at the *Hague*.[4] This *Entertainment* met with Success, it having been frequented by Persons of the first Figure in *Holland;* and honoured with the Presence of the STATHOLDER and his illustrious CONSORT.[5] There is an *Entertainment* of the same Kind in *Ireland*.

To return to *Vaux-hall Garden*. — The Charm and Innocence of the *Entertainments* exhibited there, have made them the Delight (as was declared) of all Persons of Reputation and Taste; so that even Bishops have been seen in this Recess, without injuring their Character. Its Fame is spread to such a Degree, in every Quarter of the World, that one of the first Enquiries made, by a polite Foreigner, who visits us in the Summer, is, when he may share in the Diversions of these Gardens. The Master, in return for the Favours with which he is perpetually honour'd by the Public, is adding Improvements to them every Year, as was hinted. — Whilst he is greatly indebted to the Public for their Countenance; They, (if I mistake not) may almost be said to owe some Obligations to him, upon a double Account. — First, for his having suppress'd a much-frequented rural Brothel, (as it once was;) which gave rise to the following Lines on seeing leud Women refused Admittance into *Vaux-hall* Garden, after that an Orchestra had been introduced into it:

> This SPOT in all the Pride of Spring array'd,
> Improv'd by Music warbling thro' the Shade,
> But, for the Serpent, did fam'd Eden seem,
> (Sweet Fancy aiding the delicious Dream.)
> The Serpent banish'd, justly 'tis design'd,
> To charm an elegant and virtuous Mind.

[4] *Hague:* The capital of Holland.
[5] *STATHOLDER . . . CONSORT:* The chief magistrate of the Dutch republic. The title was hereditary to the rulers of Holland, the House of Orange.

'Twas in Allusion to the Sobriety and Chastity of this mirthful *Entertainment*, that the following Verses were hit off:

> The Maid to whom Honour is dear,
> Uncensur'd may take off her Glass:
> And stray among Beaux without Fear,
> No Snake lurking here in the Grass.

> In blissful Arcadia[6] of Old,
> Where Mirth, Wit, and Innocence join'd;
> The Swains thus discreetly were bold,
> The Nymphs[7] were thus prudently kind.

To return to my Argument. — The Public are (I presume,) obliged in some little measure, to the Master, on a second Account, *viz.* for his, having chang'd the leud Scene above-mentioned, to another of the most rational, elegant, and innocent Kind. Those serious Persons who look upon it as One of the great Instruments of Luxury, (the Extremes whereof are very fatal to a Nation, and which makes too rapid a Progress among us) may please to reflect, that Multitudes, who inhabit this vast City, will take a Bottle, somewhere or other, every Evening; whatever grave Divines[8] and Moralists might preach or write to the contrary: And that it is far more healthy, for such Persons to rove about, and take a Glass in these *Gardens,* than to be coop'd up every Night, in a Tavern in *London*, as was the Practice, before the *Entertainment* in question took place. Let me add, that many might not scruple to intoxicate themselves with Wine, when conceal'd by a Room; who yet would not hazard their being seen in Liquor, in a Place free and open to Thousands. 'Tis confess'd, that Inconveniences and Abuses, (from the Texture of all mortal things) will creep into the wisest human Institutions; and that even *Religion* (fair Daughter of the Sky!) is not exempt from them: But it must be granted, on the other hand, that *Diversions,* of one sort or another, are absolutely necessary to Mankind; and therefore, the great Wisdom of Legislators seems to be, to make choice of such Diversions as may polish; without corrupting the Minds, or enervating the Bodies, of the People whom they govern. The wise, rich Men among the Antients us'd to recreate their Spirits, after the Fatigues and Toils of the Day, with a Concert of *Music;* but never in a Morning, as is the

---

[6] *Arcadia:* A district in the Peloponnese mountains. In Greek legend, it was the home of Pan, god of shepherds, and an ideal image of rural peace and contentment.

[7] *Swains . . . Nymphs:* Traditional names for shepherds and shepherdesses in a pastoral, or a story of idealized love in an idealized rural setting.

[8] *Divines:* Christian ministers, clergymen.

Custom crept in lately among us; a Custom extremely illaudable, since it may (especially) prevent many of our Superiors, from discharging the Duties they owe to their native Country; and transform them to so many *Sybarites*.[9] Farther, it seems not proper, that even these Summer-Evening *Entertainments* should be permitted to multiply, (especially the pedling ones;) because such lessen the Industry, promote the Expence, and consequently impoverish the common People, who are well known to be the Basis of a State. Let all Ranks among us be more or less industrious, but let us not be *Goths*.[10] The Industry of the *Dutch* is very much to be commended; but then their Indelicacy deserves proportionable Contempt. The *useful* and the *polite* ARTS should go Hand in Hand, and be consider'd as Sisters; and none, except the Tasteless, will think their Union impracticable. To possess, like the *Dutch*, a mighty Magazine[11] of all things useful and curious, for which every part of the Globe had been ransack'd, and not enjoy them; could convey (one would think) no other Satisfaction than that groveling one which a Miser feels, in counting over perpetually his Treasure, without daring to employ a single Farthing of it. Methinks one of the great Arts of Life is, to pass thro' it with elegant Innocence, if that Epithet may be allow'd. — 'Tis evident, that what is said above, relates only to People of Education, and a polite Turn of Mind. — But to wave all Reflections of this Cast: Providence seems to have indulg'd these *Gardens*, one special Mark of its Favour, in not permitting a single Person to be drown'd, tho' so many Thousands have return'd from them by the Thames, in very boisterous Weather. And now all Fears of perishing in the Water, in the Passage to, or from *Vaux-hall*, are happily remov'd, by the very fine Bridge lately built cross our River at *Westminster*; a structure, which is justly the Admiration of Foreigners; and forms one of the noblest Pieces of Art in this Island; and indeed, in the World, of the kind: The View of which Bridge, especially when illuminated, adds to the Delight of the Curious, in their Return from *Vaux-hall*. Another Pleasure found (occasionally,) in going to, or coming from thence by Water, is to hear the Trumpets or *French* Horns, which frequently attend on the Boats of Persons of Distinction. A Concert of this kind, in a fine Moon-light Night, is a great Addition to our Joy. —

[9] *Sybarites:* Residents of an ancient Greek town in southern Italy, known for their voluptuousness and overindulgence in pleasure.

[10] *Goths:* Originally a Germanic tribe that invaded Rome's eastern and western empires in the third, fourth, and fifth centuries. The term had come to mean anyone who behaves like a barbarian, particularly in regard to neglecting the fine arts.

[11] *Magazine:* A storehouse or repository. The Dutch were highly successful competitors with England in global trade.

# OLIVER GOLDSMITH

## On a Visit to Vauxhall Gardens
## (*From* The Citizen of the World)

Oliver Goldsmith's "citizen," Lien Chi Altangi, gives us a very differ-
ent view of Vauxhall Gardens than that of the author of the preceding
*Sketch*. He is struck by the beauties of the place, but his account focuses
more on the people who enjoy — or affect not to enjoy — those beauties.
The citizen's party is closer in class and manners to Evelina's cousins the
Branghtons than to the aristocratic circle of Orville. The eccentric but
good-hearted Man in Black, a recurring character in Goldsmith's *The
Citizen of the World,* is genuinely worthy of Lien Chi Altangi's affection
and respect, but he is not a man of high birth and social standing to
whom fashion would come easily. Despite their aristocratic pretensions
to superior tastes and manners, the tradesmen friends of the Man in
Black illustrate the very real tensions of class differences that were as
much a part of Vauxhall as the more purely aesthetic enjoyments of art,
nature, and music. A place such as Vauxhall held out the promise that all
could share in "refinement," but one's class status had much to do with
how one experienced the entertainments that were offered.

For more background on Goldsmith and his *Citizen of the* World, see
the headnote to "On London Shops" in this chapter. The following excerpt is taken from *The Collected Works of Oliver Goldsmith,* ed.
Arthur Friedman (Oxford: Clarendon Press, 1966), 293–98.

## Letter LXXI.
### From Lien Chi Altangi, to Fum Hoam,
### First President of the Ceremonial Academy
### at Pekin, in China.

The People of *London* are as fond of walking as our friends at
*Pekin* of riding; one of the principal entertainments of the citizens
here in summer is to repair about nightfall to a garden not far from
town, where they walk about, shew their best cloaths and best faces,
and listen to a concert provided for the occasion.

I accepted an invitation a few evenings ago from my old friend, the
man in black, to be one of a party that was to sup there, and at
the appointed hour waited upon him at his lodgings. There I found
the company assembled and expecting my arrival. Our party consisted of my friend in superlative finery, his stockings rolled, a black

velvet waistcoat which was formerly new, and his grey wig combed down in imitation of hair.[1] A pawn-broker's widow, of whom, by the bye, my friend was a professed admirer, dressed out in green damask with three gold rings on every finger. Mr. *Tibbs* the second rate beau, I have formerly described, together with his lady, in flimsy silk, dirty gauze instead of linen, and an hat as big as an umbrello.

Our first difficulty was in settling how we should set out. Mrs. *Tibbs* had a natural aversion to the water, and the widow being a little in flesh, as warmly protested against walking,[2] a coach was therefore agreed upon; which being too small to carry five, Mr. *Tibbs* consented to sit in his wife's lap.

In this manner therefore we set forward, being entertained by the way with the bodings of Mr. *Tibbs,* who assured us, he did not expect to see a single creature for the evening above the degree of a cheesemonger; that this was the last night of the gardens, and that consequently we should be pestered with the nobility and gentry from *Thames-street* and *Crooked-lane,* with several other prophetic ejaculations, probably inspired by the uneasiness of his situation.[3]

The illuminations began before we arrived, and I must confess, that upon entering the gardens, I found every sense overpaid with more than expected pleasure; the lights every where glimmering through the scarcely moving trees; the full-bodied consort bursting on the stillness of the night; the natural consort of the birds, in the more retired part of the grove, vying with that which was formed by art; the company gayly dressed looking satisfaction; and the tables spread with various delicacies, all conspired to fill my imagination with the visionary happiness of the *Arabian* lawgiver, and lifted me into an extasy of admiration. Head of *Confucius,* cried I to my friend, this is fine! this unites rural beauty with courtly magnificence, if we except

---

[1] *his grey wig . . . of hair:* At times during the century it became fashionable for men to wear their own hair, in a natural style, as opposed to a wig. The Man in Black is attempting this fashionable look, probably without his own hair to comb down. (Many men who habitually wore wigs simply shaved their heads.)

[2] *natural aversion to the water . . . walking:* Earlier in the century, the gardens were accessible only by taking a boat across the Thames; by Evelina's and the widow's day, a bridge had been built, making it possible to walk, drive, or take a boat. As we can see in *Evelina,* many opted for the boat ride for reasons of enjoyment.

[3] *the last night of the gardens . . . situation:* Vauxhall was open for approximately three months of the year, usually beginning in May. The last night of the season was notorious for the rowdy behavior of the crowds. Historical accounts of last-night riots suggest that young men of the upper classes may have been as much to blame for the damage and confusion as the ironically named lower-class "nobility and gentry from Thames-street and Crooked-lane" (*not* high-class addresses) that Mr. Tibbs names.

the virgins of immortality that hang on every tree, and may be
plucked at every desire, I don't see how this falls short of *Mahomet's
Paradise!* [4] As for virgins, cries my friend, it is true, they are a fruit
that don't much abound in our gardens here; but if ladies as plenty as
apples in autumn, and as complying as any *houry* [5] of them all can
content you, I fancy we have no need to go to heaven for Paradise.

I was going to second his remarks when we were called to a consultation by Mr. Tibbs and the rest of our company, to know in what
manner we were to lay out the evening to the greatest advantage.
Mrs. Tibbs was for keeping the genteel walk of the garden, where she
observed there was always the very best company; the widow, on the
contrary, (who came but once a season) was for securing a good
standing place to see the water-works, [6] which she assured us would
begin in less than an hour at farthest; a dispute therefore began, and
as it was managed between two of very opposite characters, it threatened to grow more bitter at every reply. Mrs. Tibbs wondered how
people could pretend to know the polite world who had received all
their rudiments of breeding behind a compter; [7] to which the other
replied, that tho' some people sat behind compters, yet they could sit
at the head of their own tables too, and carve three good dishes of
hot meat whenever they thought proper, which was more than some
people could say for themselves, that hardly knew a rabbet and
onions from a green goose and gooseberries. It is hard to say where
this might have ended, had not the husband, who probably knew the
impetuosity of his wife's disposition, proposed to end the dispute by
adjourning to a box, [8] and try if there was any thing to be had for
supper that was supportable. To this we all consented, but here a new
distress arose, Mr. and Mrs. Tibbs would sit in none but a genteel
box, a box where they might see and be seen, one, as they expressed
it, in the very focus of public view; but such a box was not easy to be
obtained, for tho' we were perfectly convinced of our own gentility,
and the gentility of our appearance, yet we found it a difficult matter
to persuade the keepers of the boxes to be of our opinion; they chose
to reserve genteel boxes for what they judged more genteel company.

---

[4] *Arabian lawgiver . . . Mahomet's Paradise!*: Lien Chi evokes, in his enthusiasm, a
rather confused mix of "oriental" images, in which Arabic and Chinese images of sublimity and beauty indiscriminately jostle each other.

[5] *houry:* Female slaves in a harem.

[6] *water-works:* The cascade was a relatively new attraction at the time of Goldsmith's writing. It was an artificial waterfall built so as to turn a mill in a simulated
landscape.

[7] *compter:* A counter, as in a shop.

[8] *box:* An enclosed table, rather like a booth, in which one could dine.

At last however we were fixed, tho' somewhat obscurely, and supplied with the usual entertainment of the place. The widow found the
supper excellent, but Mrs. Tibbs thought every thing detestable:
come, come, my dear, cries the husband, by way of consolation, to be
sure we can't find such dressing here as we have at lord Crumps or
lady Crimps; but for Vauxhall dressing it is pretty good, it is not their
victuals indeed I find fault with, but their wine; their wine, cries he,
drinking off a glass, indeed, is most abdominable.

By this last contradiction the widow was fairly conquered in point
of politeness. She perceived now that she had no pretensions in the
world to taste, her very senses were vulgar, since she had praised detestable custard, and smacked at wretched wine; she was therefore
content to yield the victory, and for the rest of the night to listen and
improve. It is true she would now and then forget herself and confess
she was pleased, but they soon brought her back again to miserable
refinement. She once praised the painting of the box in which we
were sitting, but was soon convinced that such paltry pieces ought
rather to excite horror than satisfaction; she ventured again to commend one of the singers, but Mrs. Tibbs soon let her know, in the
style of a connoisseur, that the singer in question had neither ear,
voice, nor judgment.

Mr. Tibbs now willing to prove that his wife's pretensions to music
were just, entreated her to favour the company with a song; but to this
she gave a positive denial, for you know very well, my dear, says she,
that I am not in voice to day, and when ones voice is not equal to ones
judgment, what signifies singing; besides as there is no accompany-
ment, it would be but spoiling music. All these excuses however were
overruled by the rest of the company who, though one would think they
already had music enough, joined in the entreaty. But particularly the
widow, now willing to convince the company of her breeding, pressed
so warmly that she seem'd determined to take no refusal. At last then
the lady complied, and after humming for some minutes, began with
such a voice and such affectation, as I could perceive gave but little satisfaction to any except her husband. He sate with rapture in his eye, and
beat time with his hand on the table.

You must observe, my friend, that it is the custom of this country,
when a lady or gentleman happens to sing, for the company to sit as
mute and motionless as statues. Every feature, every limb must seem to
correspond in fixed attention, and while the song continues, they are to
remain in a state of universal petrifaction. In this mortifying situation
we had continued for some time, listening to the song, and looking with
tranquility, when the master of the box came to inform us that the

water-works were going to begin. At this information I could instantly perceive the widow bounce from her seat; but correcting herself, she saw down again, repressed by motives of good breeding. Mrs. Tibbs, who had seen the water-works an hundred times, resolving not to be interrupted, continued her song without any share of mercy, nor had the smallest pity on our impatience. The widow's face, I own, gave me high entertainment; in it I could plainly read the struggle she felt between good breeding and curiosity; she had talked of the water-works the whole evening before, and seemed to have come merely in order to see them, but then she could not bounce out in the very middle of a song, for that would be forfeiting all pretensions to high life, or high-lived company ever after: Mrs. *Tibbs* therefore kept on singing, and we continued to listen, till at last, when the song was just concluded, the waiter came to inform us that the water-works were over.

The water-works over, cried the widow! the water-works over already, that's impossible, they can't be over so soon! It is not my business, replied the fellow, to contradict your ladyship, I'll run again and see; he went, and soon returned with a confirmation of the dismal tidings. No ceremony could now bind my friend's disappointed mistress, she testified her displeasure in the openest manner; in short, she now began to find fault in turn, and at last insisted upon going home, just at the time that Mr. and Mrs. Tibbs assured the company, that the polite hours were going to begin, and that the ladies would instantaneously be entertained with the horns.[9]

Adieu.

[9] *horns:* The author of A *Sketch of the Spring-Gardens, Vaux-hall,* writes that elegant parties often brought french horns to accompany their dining (see p. 551). Evelina also mentions a concert in the open air.

## TOBIAS SMOLLETT

## On a Visit to Bath
### (From Humphry Clinker)

The town of Bath became a popular health and pleasure resort in the eighteenth century, especially during the reigns of George II and George III (1751–1820). The waters of its natural, hotwater springs were supposed to have curative powers, but by the mid-eighteenth century Bath drew more than the sick, and its waters were only part of its attraction. It became a highly fashionable social center where people gathered to attend concerts and the theater, dance in balls and assemblies, shop, and generally see and be seen in such places as the Pump Room, where one could also, incidentally, drink the famous water. Bath was the largest and most famous of English resorts in the eighteenth century; it was also noted for its social diversity. It was the resort of royalty, the aristocracy, and many of the lower classes who were affluent enough to afford a holiday where the rich and powerful took their pleasure.

Tobias Smollett (1721–1771) would, perhaps, have been interested in Bath both as a health resort and as a fashionable social center. Smollett was a physician as well as a popular novelist and writer of travel literature. *Humphry Clinker,* published in 1771, is, like *Evelina,* an epistolary novel, or story made up of letters. More than *Evelina,* which relies heavily on its title character's observations and reports, *Humphry Clinker* tells its story through the development of multiple points of view. As we can see, the two characters whose letters are represented here have very different takes on the town and its amusements. Matthew Bramble, the writer of the first letter in this excerpt, is the guardian of Lydia Melford, his young niece, whose letter to a female friend follows. The former is prone to gout, depression, and a jaundiced view of life, while the latter, though sensible enough to qualify her pleasure in some of Bath's less attractive aspects, is charmed by the bustle and modishness of resort life. Bramble tends to see the growth of Bath in terms of the cultural narrative of luxury and English decadence. Melford takes an innocent enjoyment in the consumption of "modern" pleasures. The following letters serve to underscore the cultural changes brought about by the mixing of classes and genders in such fashionable places as Bath, where money, as opposed to traditional class divisions, now enabled participation in "diversions."

This excerpt is from *The Expedition of Humphry Clinker,* ed. Thomas R. Preston and O M Brack, Jr. (Athens: U of Georgia P, 1990), 33–41.


### To Dr. Lewis.

Bath, April 23.

DEAR DOCTOR,

If I did not know that the exercise of your profession has habituated you to the hearing of complaints, I should make a conscience of troubling you with my correspondence, which may be truly called *the lamentations of Matthew Bramble.* Yet I cannot help thinking, I have some right to discharge the overflowings of my spleen upon you, whose province it is to remove those disorders that occasioned it; and let me tell you, it is no small alleviation of my grievances, that I have a sensible friend, to whom I can communicate my crusty humours, which, by retention, would grow intolerably acriminious.[1]

You must know, I find nothing but disappointment at Bath; which is so altered, that I can scarce believe it is the same place that I frequented about thirty years ago. Methinks I hear you say, "Altered it is, without all doubt; but then it is altered for the better; a truth which, perhaps, you would own without hesitation, if you yourself were not altered for the worse." The reflection may, for aught I know, be just. The inconveniences which I overlooked in the high-day of health, will naturally strike with exaggerated impression on the irritable nerves of an invalid, surprised by premature old age, and shattered with long-suffering — But, I believe, you will not deny, that this place, which Nature and Providence seem to have intended as a resource from distemper and disquiet, is become the very center of racket and dissipation. Instead of that peace, tranquility and ease, so necessary to those who labour under bad health, weak nerves, and irregular spirits; here we have nothing but noise, tumult, and hurry; with the fatigue and slavery of maintaining a ceremonial, more stiff, formal, and oppressive, than the etiquette of a German elector.[2] A national hospital it may be; but one would imagine, that none but lunatics are admitted; and, truly, I will give you leave to call me so, if I stay much longer at Bath. — But I shall take another opportunity to explain my sentiments at greater length on this subject — I was impatient to see the boasted improvements in architecture, for which the upper parts of the town have been so much celebrated, and t'other day I made a circuit of all the new buildings. The Square,[3] though irregular, is, on the whole, pretty well laid out, spacious, open, and airy; and, in my opinion, by far the most wholsome and agreeable sit-

---

[1] *discharge the overflowings . . . acrimonious:* Bramble is talking about his ill health in terms of English humors theory, which held that mental and physical health relied on a proper balance between certain body fluids and elements. Too much spleen resulted in an angry, pessimistic disposition.

[2] *German elector:* One of the princes of Germany allowed to take part in the election of the emperor.

[3] *The Square:* Queen Square, built by John Wood in 1729–36, consisted of about twenty-five houses.

uation in Bath, especially the upper side of it; but the avenues to it are mean, dirty, dangerous, and indirect. Its communication with the Baths, is through the yard of an inn, where the poor trembling valetudinarian is carried in a chair, betwixt the heels of a double row of horses, wincing under the curry-combs of grooms and postilions, over and above the hazard of being obstructed, or overturned by the carriages which are continually making their exit or their entrance — I suppose after some chairmen[4] shall have been maimed, and a few lives lost by those accidents, the corporation will think, in earnest, about providing a more safe and commodious passage.The Circus[5] is a pretty bauble; contrived for shew, and looks like Vespasian's amphitheatre[6] turned outside in. If we consider it in point of magnificence, the great number of small doors belonging to the separate houses, the inconsiderable height of the different orders, the affected ornaments of the architrave,[7] which are both childish and misplaced, and the areas projecting into the street, surrounded with iron rails, destroy a good part of its effect upon the eye; and, perhaps, we shall find it still more defective, if we view it in the light of convenience. The figure of each separate dwelling house, being the segment of a circle, must spoil the symmetry of the rooms, by contracting them towards the street windows, and leaving a larger sweep in the space behind. If, instead of the areas and iron rails, which seem to be of very little use, there had been a corridore with arcades all round, as in Covent-Garden,[8] the appearance of the whole would have been more magnificent and striking; those arcades would have afforded an agreeable covered walk, and sheltered the poor chairmen and their carriages from the rain, which is here almost perpetual. At present, the chairs stand soaking in the open street, from morning to night, till they become so many boxes of wet leather, for the benefit of the gouty and rheumatic, who are transported in them from place to place. Indeed this is a shocking inconvenience that extends over the

[4]*chairmen:* The men who made their living by carrying passengers in sedan chairs.

[5] *Circus.* The King's Circus was planned by John Wood and completed in 1765. It is notable for its combination of Doric, Ionic, and Corinthian styles and includes 324 columns.

[6] *Vespasian's amphitheatre:* The Colosseum in Rome.

[7] *architrave:* In this context, *architrave* seems to refer to the ornamental molding around a door frame.

[8] *Covent-Garden:* This London district was known for its churches, coffeehouses, elegant residences, and, most notably, its marketplace.

whole city; and, I am persuaded, it produces infinite mischief to the delicate and infirm; even the close chairs,[9] contrived for the sick, by standing in the open air, have their frize[10] linings impregnated, like so many spunges, with the moisture of the atmosphere, and those cases of cold vapour must give a charming check to the perspiration of a patient, piping hot from the Bath, with all his pores wide open.

But, to return to the Circus: it is inconvenient from its situation, at so great a distance from all the markets, baths, and places of public entertainment. The only entrance to it, through Gay-street, is so difficult, steep, and slippery, that, in wet weather, it must be exceedingly dangerous, both for those that ride in carriages, and those that walk a-foot, and when the street is covered with snow, as it was for fifteen days successively this very winter, I don't see how any individual could go either up or down, without the most imminent hazard of broken bones. In blowing weather, I am told, most of the houses in this hill are smothered with smoke, forced down the chimneys, by the gusts of wind reverberated from the hill behind, which (I apprehend likewise) must render the atmosphere here more humid and unwholesome than it is in the square below; for the clouds, formed by the constant evaporation from the baths and rivers in the bottom, will, in their ascent this way, be first attracted and detained by the hill that rises close behind the Circus, and load the air with a perpetual succession of vapours: this point, however, may be easily ascertained by means of an hygrometer,[11] or a paper of salt of tartar exposed to the action of the atmosphere. The same artist, who planned the Circus, has likewise projected a Crescent;[12] when that is finished, we shall probably have a Star; and those who are living thirty years hence, may, perhaps, see all the signs of the Zodiac exhibited in architecture at Bath. These, however fantastical, are still designs that denote some ingenuity and knowledge in the architect; but the rage of building has laid hold on such a number of adventurers, that one sees new houses starting up in every out-let and every corner of Bath; contrived without judgment, executed without solidity, and stuck together, with so little regard to plan and propriety, that the different lines of the new rows and buildings interfere with,

---

[9] close chairs: Enclosed sedan chairs.
[10] frize: A kind of woolen cloth, with a nap.
[11] hygrometer: An instrument for measuring the humidity in the air.
[12] Crescent: The Royal Crescent was begun in 1767 and completed in 1775.

and intersect one another in every different angle of conjunction. They look like the wreck of streets and squares disjointed by an earthquake, which hath broken the ground into a variety of holes and hillocks; or, as if some Gothic devil[13] had stuffed them altogether in a bag, and left them to stand higgledy piggledy, just as chance directed. What sort of a monster Bath will become in a few years, with those growing excrescences, may be easily conceived: but the want of beauty and proportion is not the worst effect of these new mansions; they are built so slight, with the soft crumbling stone found in this neighbourhood, that I should never sleep quietly in one of them, when it blowed (as the sailors say) a cap-full of wind; and, I am persuaded, that my hind,[14] Roger Williams, or any man of equal strength, would be able to push his foot through the strongest part of their walls, without any great exertion of his muscles. All these absurdities arise from the general tide of luxury, which hath overspread the nation, and swept away all, even the very dregs of the people. Every upstart of fortune, harnessed in the trappings of the mode, presents himself at Bath, as in the very focus of observation — Clerks and factors[15] from the East Indies, loaded with the spoil of plundered provinces; planters, negro-drivers, and hucksters, from our American plantations, enriched they know not how; agents, commissaries, and contractors, who have fattened, in two successive wars,[16] on the blood of the nation; usurers, brokers, and jobbers[17] of every kind; men of low birth, and no breeding, have found themselves suddenly translated into a state of affluence, unknown to former ages; and no wonder that their brains should be intoxicated with pride, vanity, and presumption. Knowing no other criterion of greatness, but the ostentation of wealth, they discharge their affluence without taste or conduct, through every channel of the most absurd extravagance; and all of them hurry to Bath, because here, without any further qualification, they can mingle with the princes and nobles of the land. Even the wives and daughters of low tradesmen, who, like

---

[13] *Gothic devil:* A demon used in medieval architecture and art.

[14] *hind:* Manservant.

[15] *factors:* A factor was a mercantile agent, probably buying and selling for the powerful East India Company.

[16] *two successive wars:* The War of Austrian Succession (1739–48) and the Seven Years War (1756–63).

[17] *jobbers:* Usually small traders or brokers who sold to other merchants as well as consumers; middle men.

shovel-nosed sharks, prey upon the blubber of those uncouth whales of fortune, are infected with the same rage of displaying their importance; and the slightest indisposition serves them for a pretext to insist upon being conveyed to Bath, where they may hobble country-dances and cotillons among lordlings, 'squires, counsellors, and clergy. These delicate creatures from Bedfordbury, Butcher-row, Crutched-Friers, and Botolph-lane,[18] cannot breathe in the gross air of the Lower Town, or conform to the vulgar rules of a common lodging-house; the husband, therefore, must provide an entire house, or elegant apartments in the new buildings. Such is the composition of what is called the fashonable company at Bath; where a very inconsiderable proportion of genteel people are lost in a mob of impudent plebeians, who have neither understanding nor judgment, nor the least idea of propriety and decorum; and seem to enjoy nothing so much as an opportunity of insulting their betters.

Thus the number of people, and the number of houses continue to increase; and this will ever be the case, till the streams that swell this irresistible torrent of folly and extravagance, shall either be exhausted, or turned into other channels, by incidents and events which I do not pretend to foresee. This, I own, is a subject on which I cannot write with any degree of patience; for the mob is a monster I never could abide, either in its head, tail, midriff, or members: I detest the whole of it, as a mass of ignorance, presumption, malice, and brutality; and, in this term of reprobation, I include, without respect of rank, station, or quality, all those of both sexes, who affect its manners, and court its society.

But I have written till my fingers are crampt, and my nausea begins to return — By your advice, I sent to London a few days ago for half a pound of Gengzeng;[19] though I doubt much, whether that which comes from America is equally efficacious with what is brought from the East Indies. Some years ago, a friend of mine paid sixteen guineas for two ounces of it; and, in six months after, it was sold in the same shop for five shillings the pound. In short, we live in a vile world of fraud and sophistication; so that I know nothing of equal value with

---

[18] *Bedfordbury* . . . *Botolph-lane:* Poor and unfashionable areas of London. Butcher Row was named for the butchers whose shops were located there.

[19] *Gengzeng:* Also spelled ginseng, this term refers to a plant found in China, Nepal, Canada, and the eastern United States. It is alleged to have certain curative powers, especially that of restoring virility to the old and impotent.

the genuine friendship of a sensible man; a rare jewel! which I cannot help thinking myself in possession of, while I repeat the old declaration, that I am, as usual,

Dear Lewis,
Your affectionate
M. BRAMBLE.

After having been agitated in a short hurricane, on my first arrival, I have taken a small house in Milsham-street, where I am tolerably well lodged, for five guineas a week. I was yesterday at the Pump-room, and drank about a pint of water, which seems to agree with my stomach; and to-morrow morning I shall bathe, for the first time; so that in a few posts you may expect farther trouble; mean while, I am glad to find that the inoculation[20] has succeeded so well with poor Joyce, and that her face will be but little marked —— If my friend Sir Thomas was a single man, I would not trust such a hand-some wench in his family; but as I have recommended her, in a particular manner, to the protection of Lady G —— , who is one of the best women in the world, she may go thither without hesitation, as soon as she is quite recovered, and fit for service — Let her mother have money to provide her with necessaries, and she may ride behind her brother on Bucks; but you must lay strong injunctions on Jack, to take particular care of the trusty old veteran, who has faithfully earned his present ease, by his past services.

### To Miss Willis, at Gloucester.

Bath, April 26.

MY DEAREST COMPANION,

The pleasure I received from yours, which came to hand yester-day, is not to be expressed. Love and friendship are, without doubt, charming passions; which absence serves only to heighten and

---

[20] *inoculation:* The reference here is to the inoculation for smallpox, a disease that ravaged England up to and through the eighteenth century. In 1718, Lady Mary Wort-ley Montagu brought from Turkey to England the practice of inoculation with a live form of the virus taken from the scabs of the disease's victims. The inoculated devel-oped a mild case of the disease (hence, Joyce is "little marked") that would leave the patient immune to the mortal or seriously disfiguring or disabling effects of a more se-vere bout of the illness.

improve. Your kind present of the garnet bracelets, I shall keep as carefully as I preserve my own life; and I beg you will accept, in return, of my heart-housewife,[21] with the tortoise-shell memorandum-book, as a trifling pledge of my unalterable affection.

Bath is to me a new world —— All is gayety, good-humour, and diversion. The eye is continually entertained with the splendour of dress and equipage;[22] and the ear with the sound of coaches, chaises, chairs, and other carriages. *The merry bells ring round*,[23] from morn till night. Then we are welcomed by the city-waits[24] in our own lodgings: we have musick in the Pump-room every morning, cotillons every fore-noon in the rooms, balls twice a week, and concerts every other night, besides private assemblies and parties without number — As soon as we were settled in lodgings, we were visited by the Master of the Ceremonies;[25] a pretty little gentleman, so sweet, so fine, so civil, and polite, that in our country he might pass for the prince of Wales; then he talks so charmingly, both in verse and prose, that you would be delighted to hear him discourse; for you must know he is a great writer, and has got five tragedies ready for the stage. He did us the favour to dine with us, by my uncle's invitation; and next day 'squired my aunt and me to every part of Bath; which, to be sure, is an earthly paradise. The Square, the Circus, and the Parades, put you in mind of the sumptuous palaces represented in prints and pictures; and the new buildings, such as Princes-row, Harlequin's-row, Bladud's-row,[26] and twenty other rows, look like so many enchanted castles, raised on hanging terraces.

---

[21] *heart-housewife:* A housewife was a small, pocket-sized case used for holding needles, thread, scissors, and other implements needed for mending and sewing.

[22] *equipage:* Carriages and their trappings.

[23] *The merry bells . . . round:* Quoted from Milton, *L'Allegro*, 1. 93.

[24] *city-waits:* A small group of wind instrumentalists maintained at municipal expense.

[25] *Master of the Ceremonies:* Richard "Beau" Nash, whose deft and diplomatic (if sometimes despotic) regulation of the routines and pleasures at Bath was responsible for much of the resort's popularity, was succeeded by Samuel Derrick, an actor and writer, in 1761.

[26] *Princes-row . . . Bladud's-row:* Residential streets, called "rows," as in rows of houses. Harlequin's Row took its name from its mixture of brick and stone, while Bladud's row was named for the legendary British king who was cured of leprosy by bathing in Bath's springs.

At eight in the morning, we go in dishabille[27] to the Pump-room; which is crowded like a Welsh fair; and there you see the highest quality, and the lowest trades folks, jostling each other, without ceremony, hail-fellow well-met. The noise of the musick playing in the gallery, the heat and flavour of such a crowd, and the hum and buz of their conversation, gave me the headache and vertigo the first day; but, afterwards, all these things became familiar, and even agreeable. — Right under the Pump-room windows is the King's Bath;[28] a huge cistern, where you see the patients up to their necks in hot water. The ladies wear jackets and petticoats of brown linen, with chip hats,[29] in which they fix their handkerchiefs to wipe the sweat from their faces; but, truly, whether it is owing to the steam that surrounds them, or the heat of the water, or the nature of the dress, or to all these causes together, they look so flushed, and so frightful, that I always turn my eyes another way — My aunt, who says every person of fashion should make her appearance in the bath, as well as in the abbey church, contrived a cap with cherry-coloured ribbons to suit her complexion, and obliged Win to attend her yesterday morning in the water. But, really, her eyes were so red, that they made mine water as I viewed her from the Pump-room; and as for poor Win, who wore a hat trimmed with blue, what betwixt her wan complexion and her fear, she looked like the ghost of some pale maiden, who had drowned herself for love. When she came out of the bath, she took assafœtida drops,[30] and was fluttered all day; so that we could hardly keep her from going into hysterics:[31] but her mistress says it will do her good; and poor Win curtsies, with the tears in her eyes. For my part, I content myself with drinking about half a pint of the water every morning.

The pumper, with his wife and servant, attend within a bar; and the glasses, of different sizes, stand ranged in order before them, so

[27] *dishabille:* Literally "undress," but dishabille usually simply meant day wear, as opposed to more formal evening wear.

[28] *King's Bath:* The largest and most popular of the public baths, it was overlooked by the pump room.

[29] *chip hats:* Hats made of strips of wood.

[30] *assafœtida drops:* A strong-smelling, resinous gum, produced by a plant in India and used as an antispasmodic.

[31] *hysterics:* In eighteenth-century medical theory, a systemic disorder that could manifest itself in convulsions or even madness. It was supposed to be a disorder of the womb.

you have nothing to do but to point at that which you chuse, and it is filled immediately, hot and sparkling from the pump. It is the only hot water I could ever drink, without being sick — Far from having that effect, it is rather agreeable to the taste, grateful to the stomach, and reviving to the spirits. You cannot imagine what wonderful cures it performs — My uncle began with it the other day; but he made wry faces in drinking, and I'm afraid he will leave it off — The first day we came to Bath, he fell into a violent passion; beat two black-a-moors, and I was afraid he would have fought with their master; but the stranger proved a peaceable man. To be sure, the gout had got into his head, as my aunt observed: but, I believe, his passion drove it away; for he has been remarkably well ever since. It is a thousand pities he should ever be troubled with that ugly distemper; for, when he is free from pain, he is the best-tempered man upon earth; so gentle, so generous, so charitable, that every body loves him; and so good to me, in particular, that I shall never be able to shew the deep sense I have of his tenderness and affection.

Hard by the Pump-room, is a coffee-house for the ladies; but my aunt says, young girls are not admitted, inasmuch as the conversation turns upon politics, scandal, philosophy, and other subjects above our capacity; but we are allowed to accompany them to the book-sellers shops, which are charming places of resort; where we read novels, plays, pamphlets, and news-papers, for so small a subscription as a crown a quarter; and in these offices of intelligence, (as my brother calls them) all the reports of the day, and all the private transactions of the Bath, are first entered and discussed. From the bookseller's shop, we make a tour through the milliners and toy-men;[32] and commonly stop at Mr. Gill's, the pastry-cook, to take a jelly, a tart, or a small bason of vermicelli.[33] There is, moreover, an-other place of entertainment on the other side of the water, opposite to the Grove;[34] to which the company cross over in a boat — It is called Spring Gardens;[35] a sweet retreat, laid out in walks and ponds,

---

[32] *toy-men:* Sellers of trinkets, knickknacks, and other small ornamental objects.

[33] *Mr. Gill's . . . vermicelli:* Mr. Gill was a famous Bath cook. A "jelly" would be more like a bowl of gelatin than what our modern usage suggests. "Vermicelli" refers generally to the flour-and-egg-based food that we call pasta.

[34] *Grove:* A residential area near Bath Abbey, it was known as "Orange Grove" for the obelisk erected by Beau Nash in 1734 in honor of the Prince of Orange.

[35] *Spring Gardens:* A pleasure garden located across the Avon River and accessed from Bath by ferry.

and parterres of flowers; and there is a long-room for breakfasting and dancing. As the situation is low and damp, and the season has been remarkably wet, my uncle won't suffer me to go thither, lest I should catch cold: but my aunt says it is all a vulgar prejudice; and, to be sure, a great many gentlemen and ladies of Ireland frequent the place, without seeming to be the worse for it. They say, dancing at Spring Gardens, when the air is moist, is recommended to them as an excellent cure for the rheumatism. I have been twice at the play; where, notwithstanding the excellence of the performers, the gayety of the company, and the decorations of the theatre, which are very fine, I could not help reflecting, with a sigh, upon our poor homely representations at Gloucester — But this, in confidence to my dear Willis — You know my heart, and will excuse its weakness. ——

After all, the great scenes of entertainment at Bath, are the two public rooms;[36] where the company meet alternately every evening — They are spacious, lofty, and, when lighted up, appear very striking. They are generally crowded with well-dressed people, who drink tea in separate parties, play at cards, walk, or sit and chat together, just as they are disposed. Twice a-week there is a ball; the expence of which is defrayed by a voluntary subscription among the gentlemen; and every subscriber has three tickets. I was there Friday last with my aunt, under the care of my brother, who is a subscriber; and Sir Ulic Mackilligut recommended his nephew, captain O Donaghan, to me as a partner; but Jerry excused himself, by saying I had got the headach; and, indeed, it was really so, though I can't imagine how he knew it. The place was so hot, and the smell so different from what we are used to in the country, that I was quite feverish when we came away. Aunt says it is the effect of a vulgar constitution, reared among woods and mountains; and, that as I become accustomed to genteel company, it will wear off. — Sir Ulic was very complaisant, made her a great many high-flown compliments; and, when we retired, handed her with great ceremony to her chair. The captain, I believe, would have done me the same favour; but my brother, seeing him advance, took me under his arm, and wished him good night. The Captain is a pretty man, to be sure; tall and strait, and well made; with light-grey eyes, and a Roman nose; but there is a certain boldness in his look and manner, that puts one out of

---

[36] *two public rooms:* Thomas Harrison's spacious Assembly Rooms, erected in 1708, were often used for balls. In 1728 a second set of assembly rooms was opened.

countenance — But I am afraid I have put you out of all patience with this long unconnected scrawl; which I shall therefore conclude, with assuring you, that neither Bath nor London, nor all the diversions of life, shall ever be able to efface the idea of my dear Letty, from the heart of her ever affectionate

LYDIA MELFORD.

## CHRISTOPHER ANSTEY

### *From* The New Bath Guide

Christopher Anstey (1724–1805) was a country gentleman and sometimes poet whose *New Bath Guide* was one of the most popular satires of the 1760s. The *Guide*'s popularity probably had much to do with the fascination of the resort it satirized. The socially naive, probably nouveau riche Blunderhead family, including the romantic young lady whose letter begins this excerpt, was Anstey's fictional vehicle for poking fun at the many who came to Bath hoping to absorb the fashionable airs of the great.

The following is from *The New Bath Guide; or, Memoirs of the B---R----D Family. In a Series of Poetical Epistles* (London: J. Dodsley, 1766).

Miss Jenny W — D — R, to Lady Eliz. M — D — SS,
at ——Castle, North.
Letter IX.
A Journal.

To humbler Strains, ye Nine,[1] descend,
And greet my poor sequester'd Friend.
Not Odes with rapid Eagle flight,
That soar above all human Sight;
Not Fancy's fair and fertile Field,

---

[1] *ye Nine:* The nine muses of classical antiquity.

To all the fame Delight can yield.
But come CALLIOPE[2] and say
How Pleasure wastes the various Day:
   Whether thou art wont to rove
   By Parade, or Orange Grove,
   Or to breathe a purer Air
   In the Circus or the Square;[3]
Wheresoever be thy Path,
Tell, O tell the Joys of *Bath*.

   Ev'ry Morning, ev'ry Night,
Gayest Scenes of fresh Delight:
When AURORA[4] sheds her Beams,
Wak'd from soft Elysian Dreams,
Music calls me to the Spring
Which can Health and Spirits bring;
There HYGEIA,[5] Goddess, pours
Blessings from her various Stores,
Let me to her Altars haste,
Tho' I ne'er the Waters taste,
Near the Pump to take my Stand,
With a Nosegay in my Hand,
And to hear the Captain say,
"How d'ye do dear Miss to-day?"
The Captain! — Now you'll say my Dear,
Methinks I long his Name to hear, —
Why then — but don't you tell my Aunt
The Captain's Name is — CORMORANT:[6]
But hereafter, you must know,
I shall call him ROMEO,
And your Friend, dear Lady BET,
JENNY no more but JULIET.

---

[2] *CALLIOPE:* The muse of poetry.
[3] *Parade . . . Square:* These were all well-known places in Bath. See footnotes 3 and 5 to "On a Visit to Bath" in this chapter.
[4] *AURORA:* Goddess of the dawn.
[5] *HYGEIA:* The Greek goddess of health.
[6] *CORMORANT:* A large and voracious sea bird; this term also referred to a greedy and insatiable person.

O ye Guardian Spirits fair,
All who make true Love your Care,
May I oft my ROMEO meet,
Oft enjoy his Converse sweet;
I alone his Thoughts employ
Thro' each various Scene of Joy.
Lo! where all the jocund Throng
From the Pump-Room hastes along,
To the Breakfast all invited
By Sir TOBY, lately knighted.
See with Joy my ROMEO comes,
He conducts me to the Rooms;
There he whispers, not unseen,
Tender Tales behind the Screen;
While his Eyes are fix'd on mine,
See each Nymph with Envy pine,
And with Looks of forc'd Disdain
Smile Contempt, but sigh in vain.

O the charming Parties made !
Some to walk the South Parade,
Some to LINCOMB's shady Groves,
Or to SIMPSON's proud Alcoves;
Some for Chapel trip away,
Then take Places for the Play:
Or we walk about in Pattins,[7]
Buying Gauzes, cheap'ning Sattins,
Or to PAINTER's we repair,
Meet Sir PEREGRINE HATCHET there,
Pleas'd the Artist's Skill to trace
In his dear Miss GORGON's Face:
Happy Pair! who fix'd as Fate
For the sweet connubial State,
Smile in Canvass *Tete a Tete*.
If the Weather, cold and chill,
Calls us all to Mr. GILL,

---

[7] *Pattins:* Also spelled pattens, these were shoes raised on metal or wooden plat-
forms that allowed women to walk muddy streets without soiling their feet or the bottoms of their skirts.

ROMEO hands to me the Jelly,
Or the Soup of Vermicelli;[8]
If at TOYSHOP[9] I step in,
He presents a Diamond Pin,
Sweetest Token I can wear,
Which at once may grace my Hair;
And in Witness of my Flame,
Teach the Glass to bear his Name:[10]
See him turn each Trinket over,
If for me he can discover
Ought his Passion to reveal,
Emblematic Ring or Seal;
CUPID whetting pointed Darts,
For a Pair of tender Hearts;
HYMEN[11] lighting sacred Fires,
Types of chaste and fond Desires:
Thus enjoy we ev'ry Blessing,
Till the Toilet[12] calls to Dressing;
Where's my Garnet, Cap and Sprig?[13]
Send for SINGE[14] to dress my Wig:
Bring my silver'd Mazarine,[15]
Sweetest Gown that e'er was seen:
TABITHA, put on my Ruff;
Where's my dear delightful Muff?
Muff, my faithful ROMEO's Present;
Tippet[16] too from Tail of Pheasant!
Muff from downy Breast of Swan,
O the dear enchanting Man!

[8] *Jelly . . . Vermicelli:* See footnote 3 to "On a Visit to Bath" in this chapter.

[9] *TOYSHOP:* A shop that sold jewelry, trinkets, small decorative objects.

[10] *Teach the Glass . . . Name:* It was fashionable for ladies to write on glass window panes the names of the admirers who had given them the diamonds used as writing implements.

[11] *HYMEN:* The god of marriage.

[12] *Toilet:* The procedure of dressing, coifing the hair, and so forth.

[13] *Sprig:* An ornament in the shape of a spray or sprig, sometimes in diamonds.

[14] *SINGE:* A type name for a hairdresser, probably commenting on the tendency to singe the hair when curling it with hot irons.

[15] *Mazarine:* A fabric of a deep, rich blue.

[16] *Tippet:* A long, narrow piece of cloth, usually part of a headdress or hood.

Muff, that makes me think how JOVE
Flew to LEDA[17] from above. —
Muff that —— TABBY, see who rapt then?
"Madam, Madam, 'tis the Captain!
Sure his Voice I hear below,
'Tis, it is my ROMEO;
Shape and Gate, and careless Air,
Diamond Ring, and Solitair,[18]
Birth and Fashion all declare.
How his Eyes that gently roll
Speak the Language of his Soul;
See the Dimple on his Cheek,
See him smile and sweetly speak,
"Lovely Nymph, at your Command
I have something in my Hand,
Which I hope you'll not refuse,
'Twill us both at Night amuse:
What tho' Lady WHISKER crave it,
And Miss BADGER longs to have it,
'Tis, by Jupiter I swear,
'Tis for you alone, my Dear:
See this Ticket, gentle Maid,
At your Feet an Off'ring laid,
Thee the Loves and Graces call
To a little private Ball:
And to Play I bid adieu,
Hazard, Lansquenet and Loo,[19]
Fairest Nymph to dance with you. —
— I with Joy accept his Ticket,
And upon my Bosom stick it:
Well I know how ROMEO dances,
With what Air he first advances,
With what Grace his Gloves he draws on,

[17] JOVE . . . LEDA: In classical mythology, the god Jove in the form of a swan made love to the mortal Leda.
[18] Solitair: A loose necktie of black silk, sometimes a broad ribbon, worn by fashionable men in the eighteenth century.
[19] Hazard . . . Loo: Fashionable card games.

Claps, and calls up *Nancy Dawson;*[20]
Me thro' ev'ry Dance conducting,
And the Music oft instructing;
See him tap the Time to shew,
With his light fantastic Toe;
Skill'd in ev'ry Art to please,
From the Fan to waft the Breeze,
Or his Bottle to produce
Fill'd with pungent *Eau de Luce.* — [21]
Wonder not, my Friend, I go
To the Ball with ROMEO.

Such Delights if thou canst give
*Bath,* at thee I choose to live.

BATH, 1766.                    *J——W---D---R.*

Mr. S—— B — N — R----D, to Lady B — N---R----D,
at——Hall, North.

### Letter XII.
### A Modern Head-Dress,
### with a Little Polite Conversation.

What base and unjust Accusations we find
Arise from the Malice and Spleen of Mankind!
One would hope, my dear Mother, that Scandal would spare
The tender, the helpless, and delicate Fair;
But alas! the sweet Creatures all find it the Case,
That *Bath* is a very censorious Place.
Would you think that a Person I met since I came,
(I hope you'll excuse my concealing his Name)
A splenetic ill-natur'd Fellow, before
A Room full of very good Company, swore,
That, in spight of Appearance, 'twas very well known,
Their Hair and their Faces were none of their own;

---

[20] *Nancy Dawson:* A popular country dance.
[21] *Eau de Luce:* Smelling salts, used to revive people (especially women) from spells of faintness or dizziness.

And thus without Wit, or the least Provocation,
Began an impertinent formal Oration:
"Shall Nature thus lavish her Beauties in vain
For Art and nonsensical Fashion to stain?
The fair JEZEBELLA what Art can adorn,
Whose Cheeks are like Roses that blush in the Morn?
As bright were her Locks as in Heaven are seen,
Presented for Stars by th'*Egyptian* Queen;[22]
But alas! the sweet Nymph they no longer must deck,
No more shall they flow o'er her Ivory Neck;
Some Runaway Valet, some outlandish Shaver[23]
Has spoil'd all the Honours that Nature has gave her;
Her Head has he robb'd with as little Remorse
As a Fox-Hunter crops both his Dogs and his Horse:
A Wretch that, so far from repenting his Theft,
Makes a Boast of tormenting the little that's left:
And first at her Porcupine Head he begins
To fumble and poke with his Irons and Pins,
Then fires all his Crackers with horrid Grimace,
And puffs his vile *Rocambol* Breath[24] in her Face,
Discharging a Steam, that the Devil would choak,
From Paper, Pomatum,[25] from Powder, and Smoke:
The Patient submits, and with due Resignation
Prepares for her Fate in the next Operation.
When lo! on a sudden, a Monster appears,
A horrible Monster, to cover her Ears;
What Sign of the Zodiac is it he bears?
Is it *Taurus's Tail,* or the *Tete de Mouton,*
Or the *Beard of the Goat,* that he dares to put on?[26]
'Tis a Wig *en Vergette,* that from *Paris* was brought
Un *Tete comme il faut,* that the Varlet has bought
Of a Beggar, whose Head he has shav'd for a Groat:
Now fix'd to her Head does he frizzle and dab it;

---

[22] *th'Egyptian Queen:* Cleopatra.
[23] *Valet . . . Shaver:* A hairdresser, in other words.
[24] *Rocambol Breath:* Smelling of onion and garlic.
[25] *Pomatum:* Hair-dressing cream.
[26] *Taurus's Tail . . . to put on:* Names of fashionable hairstyles into which wigs were shaped.

Her Foretop's no more.—'Tis the Skin of a Rabbit.—
'Tis a Muff.—'tis a Thing that by all is confest
Is in Colour and Shape like a Chalfinch's Nest.[27]

O cease, ye fair Virgins, such Pains to employ,
The Beauties of Nature with Paint to destroy;
See VENUS lament, see the Loves and the Graces,
How they pine at the Injury done to your Faces!
Ye have Eyes, Lips, and Nose, but your Heads are no more
Than a Doll's that is plac'd at a Milliner's Door.——"[28]

I'm asham'd to repeat what he said in the Sequel,
Aspersions so cruel as nothing can equal!
I declare I am shock'd such a Fellow should vex,
And spread all these Lyes of the innocent Sex,
For whom, while I live, I will make Protestation
I've the highest Esteem and profound Veneration;
I never so strange an Opinion will harbour,
That they buy all the Hair they have got of a Barber:
Nor ever believe that such beautiful Creatures
Can have any Delight in abusing their Features.
One Thing tho' I wonder at much, I confess, is
Th'Appearance they make in their different Dresses,
For indeed they look very much like Apparitions
When they come in the Morning to hear the Musicians,
And some I am apt to mistake, at first Sight,
For the Mothers of those I have seen over Night;
It shocks me to see them look paler than Ashes,
And as dead in the Eye as the Busto of NASH is,[29]
Who the Ev'ning before were so blooming and plump:
— I'm griev'd to the Heart when I go to the Pump;

[27] *'Tis a Wig . . . Nest:* The elaborate, often towering hairstyles of the day some-times required supplementing native hair with hair pieces. This passage implies that some of these came from rather dubious or unsavory sources.

[28] *Doll's . . . Door:* The milliner sold dress accessories, and probably used a doll, or mannequin, to show off her wares.

[29] *It shocks . . . NASH is:* See also Lydia Melford's description of the women bathing at Bath in Smollett, "On a Visit to Bath," in this chapter. The Nash whose bust, or sculpted portrait, is referred to is Beau Nash, who came to Bath in 1704 and became its self-appointed authority on manners and politeness. Nash later became the official Master of Ceremonies presiding over public assemblies, a position he kept until 1758.

For I take ev'ry Morning a Sup at the Water,
Just to hear what is passing, and see what they're a'ter:
For I'm told, the Discourses of Persons refin'd
Are better than Books for improving the Mind:
But a great deal of Judgment's requir'd in the skimming
The polite Conversation of sensible Women,
For they come to the Pump, as before I was saying,
And talk all at once, while the Music is playing:
"Your Servant, Miss FITCHET," "good Morning, Miss STOTE,
My dear Lady RIGGLEDUM, how is your Throat?
Your Ladyship knows that I sent you a Scrawl,
Last Night to attend at your Ladyship's Call,
But I hear that your Ladyship went to the Ball."
" — Oh FITCHET — don't ask me — good Heavens preserve,
I wish there was no such a Thing as a Nerve;
Half dead all the Night I protest and declare —
My dear little FITCHET, who dresses your Hair?—
You'll come to the Rooms, all the World will be there.
Sir TOBY MAC'NEGUS is going to settle
His Tea-drinking Night with Sir PHILIP O'KETTLE."
"I hear that they both have appointed the same;[30]
The Majority think that Sir PHILIP's to blame;
I hope they won't quarrel, they're both in a Flame:
Sir TOBY MAC'NEGUS much Spirit has got,
And Sir PHILIP O'KETTLE is apt to be hot. — "
"Have you read the *Bath Guide*,[31] that ridiculous Poem?
What a scurrilous Author! does nobody know him?"
Young BILLY PENWAGGLE, and SIMIUS CHATTER,
Declare 'tis an ill-natur'd half-witted Satire."
"You know I'm engag'd, my dear Creature, with you,
And Mrs. PAMTICKLE, this Morning at Loo;
Poor Thing! though she hobbled last Night to the Ball,
To-Day she's so lame that she hardly can crawl;

[30] *have appointed the same:* Two noblemen, Sir Toby Mac'Negus and Sir Philip O'Kettle, are quarrelling over which of them can claim a certain night as his "Tea-drinking Night." The joke names make reference to the alleged hot-headedness of the Scottish and Irish nobility.
[31] *Bath Guide:* A satire of fashionable Bath, published prior to *The New Bath Guide,* after which Anstey modeled the title for his book.

Major LIGNUM has trod on the first Joint of her Toe —
— That Thing they play'd last was a charming Concerto;
I don't recollect I have heard it before;
The Minuet's good, but the Jig I adore;
Pray speak to Sir TOBY to cry out, *Encore.*"

Dear Mother I think this is excellent Fun,
But, if all I must write, I should never have done:
So myself I subscribe your most dutiful Son,

Bath, 1766.                                              S—— B—N—R—D.

*An English* JACK-TAR *giving* MONSIEUR *a* Drubbing.

Publish'd May 1st 1779.

"An English Jack-Tar Giving Monsieur a Drubbing." Mezzotint published by Robert Sayer, London, 1779. In this print, a sailor and ship's boy attack a fashionable French gentleman. Reproduced by permission of the Library of Congress, Prints and Photographs Division.

# 3

# Beyond the Fashionable World

As we can see from the materials collected in the previous section, fashion and the public uses of leisure time were inextricably part of larger patterns of social and economic change in eighteenth-century English culture. The fashionable elegance of the elite circle of Orville and Sir Clement Willoughby may offer Evelina different experiences from the more obviously economics-driven life of the shopkeeping Branghtons, but the relationship between the two is more permeable than the glamorous image of "fashion" would lead one to expect. Similarly, the image of the ideal "young lady" is inextricably bound up with cultural narratives of English nationalism and imperialist expansion, as we can see from Addison's image of Woman dressed in the commodities of colonialism (see pp. 522–23).

The materials in this section help place the concepts of "the young lady" and "fashion" within the larger framework of English economic and military expansion. The selections under "Visitors to London" convey some of the day-to-day experiences of urban life in London around mid-century, as seen from European perspectives outside the frame of the native Londoner. The points of view of visitors to the city give us more detailed descriptions of practices and institutions than we might get from a native. We can learn, for instance, about the systems of transportation available to Evelina and her friends. What was it like to be carried in a sedan chair (or knocked

down by one, in the manner of one of our unfortunate "visitors")?
How did hackney coaches operate, and why was it so advantageous
to keep one's own coach? It is possible to use these descriptions of the
London streets, transportation, and populace to fill out the brief
sketches that *Evelina* gives us.

Our "visitors" — Saussure, Archenholtz, Moritz, and Campbell —
also write about the darker, grittier aspects of London life, introducing us to the illicit world hiding beneath the surface of fashion.
Archenholtz's description of London prostitution, for instance, helps
make Evelina's unpleasant encounter with two "ladies" of the wrong
sort socially explicable rather than anomalous. Similarly, the visitors'
reflections on urban crime, particularly highwaymen, give us a cultural context in which to read both Macartney's desperate intentions
and Captain Mirvan's most vicious practical joke on Madame Duval.

We also gain a sense, from these accounts, of how violently English national pride and a sense of national superiority could affect
foreign visitors. London was not a gentle environment for those who
did not know the "rules" of everyday life, and an ignorant visitor
could find himself thrown against a wall or to the ground by passing
traffic if he could not read the code for "get out of the way." He
could find himself the recipient of even rougher treatment if he wore
the wrong, "Frenchified" clothes among the wrong kind of people.

In general, however, the visitors to London whose writings are
represented here show us a city that was exciting to its visitors. They
offer us useful descriptions of London topography and other concrete, material features. London was growing beyond its seventeenth-
century boundaries to swallow up surrounding farmlands and villages, some of which were themselves becoming new, fashionable
residential areas. The parish of Westminster was rapidly becoming
the site of fashionable homes for the landed gentry, while the old,
walled city of London increasingly belonged to the "cits" — tradesmen, merchants, and artisans — who worked for their money. Patterns of poverty and wealth were discernible, with a rich north and
west opposed to the poorer areas of east and south. As Archenholtz
writes in *A Picture of England* (1785), "the east end, especially along
the shores of the Thames, consists of old houses, the streets there are
narrow, dark and ill-paved; inhabited by sailors and other workmen
who are employed in the construction of ships and by a great part
of the Jews. The contrast between this and the West end is astonishing: the houses here are mostly new and elegant; the squares are superb, the streets straight and open. . . . If all London were as well

built, there would be nothing in the world to compare to it." While the economic divisions of London were clear enough, it is important to note that poverty could be even more virulent within "wealthier" areas, where laborers were isolated from the trade work that was available in the city's "poorer" regions. Architectural elegance was often cheek by jowl with crumbling, derelict buildings in which the homeless population of London found a sleeping place after dark. If one looks at maps from the first half of the century, one can see a steady growth to the west and south from the old walled city and its environs, following the direction of existent roads. The third quarter of the century brought a new type of development: in addition to new buildings, new roads appear across fields and other areas previously untraversed.

In addition to the growth of public pleasure sites that is a focus of the previous section, transportation and roads were becoming more complicated and sophisticated, a penny post was developed, and street lighting and indoor water supplies were becoming more and more common. The English, in London at least, were, as we can see from some of our visitors' reactions, gaining a reputation for cleanliness and an orderly public life. One should not overinflate this reputation; that the English poor had shoes in winter is more a reflection on the misery of the poor in France and Germany than unequivocal proof of an advanced English conscience. And the numbers of London prostitutes and various kinds of thieves observed by nearly all the visitors to London suggest that poverty had driven many Londoners to live outside the bounds of dominant morality and the law.

We can see from the following accounts that the growing sophistication of urban amenities in London coexists with certain rough, even violent social practices directed against foreigners and other "outsiders." In *Evelina*, Burney contrasts the politeness and restraint exemplified by Orville with a rudeness and violence that is not confined to the lower-class characters in the novel, as a tradition of class snobbery would teach us to expect. If anything, the young aristocrats who abuse poor, elderly women for sport are more violent than the loutish Tom Branghton. Rather, the juxtaposition of gentleness with violence cuts across class and gender lines to suggest the more complex and various tensions in English culture also discernible in the visitors' accounts.

The final group of materials in this section offers still another context in which to read the novel's pervasive contrasts of order and refinement against confusion and violence. This section contains the letters, journals, and memoirs of English sea captains and sailors who made their livings as Captain Mirvan might have done. The dangerous, sometimes brutal life of English seamen is perhaps most obvious in the rough and ready yarns of James Anthony Gardner with his sea jargon and blunt expression, but one can see that the higher-class Thomas Pasley and Edward Boscawen, although gentler in expression, lived far from gentle lives at sea. Pasley eventually lost his leg in a sea battle, and both men were professional warriors in a world where it was often difficult to distinguish between piracy and "legitimate" warfare. While Pasley and Boscawen were often recipients of others' violence, it is important to remember that they were not innocent victims. Pasley's work was primarily convoyance — that is, the protection of English merchant ships from both actual pirates and the "legal" piracy of hostile ships at war with England. Boscawen was himself an aggressor whose job was to assault and hopefully capture any vessels, military or otherwise, belonging to a nation with which England was at war. It is fascinating, and a little disconcerting, to read his accounts of capturing French ships alongside his musing on the peaceful, domestic life at home on his estate, especially when one reflects that Boscawen's estate could well have been purchased by ransom money and sale proceeds from his entirely "legal" acts of piracy. Also disconcerting is the fact that the particular capture recorded here began, with relative casualness, the Seven Years War.

Olaudah Equiano's autobiographical narrative provides yet another perspective from which to view the world of London fashion and the central role that the young lady takes within it. Kidnapped from his Ibo village in Africa at an early age and eventually sold to English traders as a slave, Equiano speaks from the position of an African who found himself forced into complex and often contradictory relations with English culture. Equiano was, for part of his life, a sailor aboard English ships. He was also a slave. As a sailor, he shares in the "Englishness" of the other sea-faring men whose words we read here. The experience of slavery distanced him, at the same time, from English investments in chattel slavery. While slavery was controversial in England throughout the eighteenth century, English commercial wealth depended in large part directly or indirectly on the violent seizure and transportation to the Caribbean and North America of West Africans. In addition to the capital gained from the trade itself, the growth of English colonies, particularly in the Caribbean, was fed by the English slave trade. The fashionable world that Evelina enters was in part supported by a traffic in human bodies that was rationalized by an English racism that refused the full humanity of those bodies. Equiano's words are an important reminder of this racial and global dimension to the violence that Burney critiques in English culture.

Despite *Evelina*'s focus on the world of fashion — a world seemingly distant from the military exploits of sea captains — the contrasts between violence and peace within the novel's apparently isolated and rarified world are as much a part of English global strategies for military and economic dominance as they are part of the young lady's experience. Or perhaps a better way to put it is that the young lady's experience is only apparently separate from the larger world beyond the ballroom, the fashionable walks, and the ridottos.

# Visitors to London

## CÉSAR DE SAUSSURE

### From A Foreign View of England in the Reigns of George I and George II

César de Saussure was born in Lorraine, France, in 1702. His family fled Lorraine for Lausanne to avoid anti-Protestant persecutions during the reign of Louis XIV. In 1725 Saussure left home and traveled for eleven years, all the while writing observant, descriptive letters to his family at home. Over a twenty-year period, his letters were copied and read by so large a group of people in Berne and Geneva, as well as Lausanne, that Saussure edited them into bound volumes which have been translated and republished in more than one edition. The great French philosopher and writer Voltaire is said to have sought out Saussure's letters and read them with pleasure.

The popular appeal of these letters both in England and France is due in part to the more general popularity of travel writing. Europeans in the eighteenth century bought goods from countries whose material and cultural resources were only recently known to them. The exploration of the Caribbean and the Americas and the growing European economic and political interests in Africa and Asia form a context that fostered much interest in "new" people and places. There was also a growth in published accounts of European cities and other places of natural or civilized interest. Saussure's letters would have had obvious interest for the French student of English culture, but they also appealed to the English as an "outsider's" view of their country, not unlike that of the fictionalized "outsider," Goldsmith's Citizen of the World.

At the same time that Saussure is "outside" English culture, he is, by virtue of his class position and education, "inside." He speaks with the authority of the relatively privileged — those "in the know." In 1729, for example, he traveled to Turkey with Lord Kinnoull, the English ambassador to Constantinople, and was appointed the first secretary to the British Embassy there. In 1740 he nearly traveled with Lord Cathcart, who commanded a portion of the British fleet sent against Spanish settlements in America, but his mother evidently convinced him to stay closer to home. He apparently wished to marry an Englishwoman at one point, but was prevented by his family's wishes that he marry one of his own countrywomen.

These excerpts are from *A Foreign View of England in the Reigns of George I and George II: The Letters of Monsieur César de Saussure to His Family*, trans. Madame van Muyden (London: John Murray, 1902).

London, Sept. 17, 1725

You are kind enough to tell me the interest you took in my long letter to you, and that you will be pleased to hear from me again and to know more about England. It is a difficult task for such an inexperienced pen as mine, and I feel as if I ought to refuse your request rather than disappoint you by my style; but a young man of my age cannot refuse the request of an old friend and I will do the best I can, according to your desire.

The reason why I have not sent off my second letter sooner is that I thought I had better see more of London before attempting to describe it to you.

I have often heard travellers and scholars declare that London is undoubtedly the largest and most populous city in the whole of Europe. The city is ten miles long from Millbank to Blackwall, and its width is about three miles from Southwark to Moorfields;[1] it contains more than one million inhabitants. The streets are long, wide, and straight, some of them being more than a mile in length. On either side of the street the ground is raised and paved with flat stones, so that you can walk in the streets without danger of being knocked down by coaches and horses. The City of London itself is not very large, being only three miles in circumference. It is inclosed by stone walls and has gates; but so many houses have been built around, especially on the western side, that London has been joined to Westminster, which latter place was formerly two miles distant. The space between consisted of fields and pastures, but now is part of the town. That which is surrounded by walls is called the City,[2] and is almost entirely inhabited by merchants; the other part of London is called the Liberty of Westminster,[3] and here you will find the Court, and the residences of the peers and noblemen and of other persons of distinction.

A few days after my arrival in London I had an unpleasant experience. Wishing one evening to walk in the park, and having already visited it twice, I thought I could easily find my way there and back alone. The evening was very fine, and I stayed in the park till ten o'clock, enjoying my stroll and the amusing sights around me, the park being very crowded that evening. When I wished to go home again and cross the Mews, a large square occupied by the King's stables, by which way I had come, I found the gates already closed. I immediately set about trying to find out my whereabouts and a new way home. Unfortunately I could not speak a word of English, and wandered aimlessly about, trying to find my way, unable to ask anyone's help or to hire a hackney-coach,[4] as I could not make a driver

---

[1] *Millbank . . . Moorfields:* Millbank to Blackwall would define the length of the city as it stretched along the Thames, while Moorfields and Southwark marked its development back from river banks to what was largely undeveloped land. Moorfields, for instance, was relatively open country at mid-century but developed rapidly during the third quarter of the century.

[2] *City:* By mid-century, urban buildings had outgrown the old, walled city of London, which was referred to as "the City." As Saussure notes, it was primarily the residence of the tradesmen who also worked and had their shops there. The Branghtons live and work in the City.

[3] *Liberty of Westminster:* Westminster was originally a village proximate to the City of London, but by the time of this writing, the growth of the latter had made it virtually contiguous with it and therefore a "liberty" or district of it. It was both the newer and more fashionable end of what was coming to be known, collectively, as "the Town" — that is, London and its environs.

[4] *hackney-coach:* A coach for hire.

understand me or give him my address. The only thing I could do was to walk from street to street, in the hopes of recognising some landmark or other; but after hoping this for about an hour I found myself in an entirely unknown part. It was now past midnight; the streets were empty, and I did not know what to do. I sat down on a seat in front of a shop and longed for day. After I had been seated there for half an hour or so, to my intense relief two gentlemen happened to go by, and you can imagine my delight when I heard them conversing in French. I almost thought they were angels sent to my help! I hastened to stop them, to explain to them my unpleasant situation. They inquired where I lived, which I could not tell them, the name of the street having completely escaped my memory. After questioning me for some minutes as to what country I came from, how long I had been in London, whether I had any acquaintances, it turned out most fortunately for me that these gentlemen were acquainted with a friend of mine, and that they lived at no great distance from him. They were kind enough to show me the way themselves, and we walked two miles together before I got back to my rooms. Since then I have taken good care not to lose myself again. I am too much afraid of spending such another weary night. . . .

After the Royal Family had left the circle, we went to walk in St. James's Park. At one end of the park is a space called the Parade, for every morning a battalion of the foot-guards parade in this place, and from thence proceed to mount guard before St. James's Palace, before the Prince of Wales's mansion, and at the Tower. Along one side of the Palace is a magnificent place for the game of pall-mall,[5] which extends the entire length of the park, and is bordered on either side by a long avenue of trees. This place is no longer used for the game, but is a promenade, and every spring it is bestrewn with tiny sea-shells, which are then crushed by means of a heavy roller. St. James's Park contains several avenues of elm and lime trees, two large ponds, and a pretty little island; in a word, this is an enchanting spot in summer time. Society comes to walk here on fine, warm days, from seven to ten in the evening, and in winter from one to three o'clock. English men and women are fond of walking, and the park is so crowded at times that you cannot help touching your neighbour. Some people come to see, some to be seen, and others to seek their

---

[5] *pall-mall:* A game, introduced into England in the seventeenth century, in which players used wooden mallets to knock a ball down a certain course of ground into a metal ring. The least number of strokes used to place the ball successfully won.

fortunes; for many priestesses of Venus[6] are abroad, some of them magnificently attired, and all on the look-out for adventures, and many young men are not long in repenting that they have become acquainted with such beautiful and amiable nymphs:[7] The ponds are covered with wild ducks and geese, deer and roe-deer are so tame that they eat out of your hand, and there is little danger of being attacked in the park or in the neighbourhood of the Palace, for should the offender be taken up in any of these privileged parts, the laws would condemn him to lose his hand. No one can be taken up and imprisoned for debt so long as he does not leave the vicinity of the Palace. . . .

London, Dec. 16, 1725

. . . Do not expect me to describe to you all the streets of London. I should have too much to do, and we should get tired of one another. A number of them are dirty, narrow, and badly built; others again are wide and straight, bordered with fine houses. Most of the streets are wonderfully well lighted, for in front of each house hangs a lantern or a large globe of glass, inside of which is placed a lamp which burns all night. Large houses have two of these lamps suspended outside their doors by iron supports, and some have even four. The streets of London are unpleasantly full either of dust or of mud. This arises from the quality of houses that are continually being built, and also from the large number of coaches and chariots rolling in the streets day and night. Carts are used for removing mud, and in the summer time the streets are watered by carts carrying barrels or casks, pierced with holes, through which the water flows.

Another of the unpleasantnesses of the streets is that the pavement is so bad and rough that when you drive in a coach you are most cruelly shaken, whereas if you go on foot you have a nice smooth path paved with wide flat stones, and elevated above the road; but I believe I have mentioned this before.

London does not possess any watchmen, either on foot or on horseback as in Paris, to prevent murder and robbery; the only watchman you see is a man in every street carrying a stick and a lantern, who, every time the clock strikes, calls out the hour and state of the weather. The first time this man goes on his rounds he

---

[6]*priestesses of Venus:* Prostitutes.
[7]*repenting . . . nymphs:* The repentance of young men is due to their infection with venereal disease.

pushes the doors of the shops and houses with his stick to ascertain whether they are properly fastened, and if they are not he warns the proprietors.

I must own that Englishmen build their houses with taste; it is not possible to make a better use of ground, or to have more comfortable houses. It is surprising to see in what a small space they will build, and in what an incredibly short time. The houses are of bricks; the walls are thin, most of them having only one foot and a half thickness. The finest houses sometimes have cornices and borders to divide the floors, and round the doors and windows you occasionally see a sort of polished marble. In all the newly-built quarters the houses have one floor made in the earth, containing the kitchens, offices, and servants' rooms. This floor is well lighted, and has as much air as the others have. In order to accomplish this a sort of moat, five or six feet in width and eight or nine deep, is dug in front of all the houses, and is called the "area." This moat is edged on the side next the street with an iron railing. The cellars and vaults where coal is stored are very strongly built beneath the streets, and to reach them you cross the area. Hangings are little used in London houses on account of the coal smoke, which would ruin them, besides which woodwork is considered to be cleaner and prevents damp on the walls. Almost all the houses have little gardens or courtyards at the back. . . .

London, Feb., 1726

. . . You cannot imagine the quantity of people there are at the windows, balconies, and in the streets to see the pageant pass. The Lord Mayor's Day[8] is a great holiday in the City. The populace on that day is particularly insolent and rowdy, turning into lawless freedom the great liberty it enjoys. At these times it is almost dangerous for an honest man, and more particularly for a foreigner, if at all well dressed, to walk in the streets, for he runs a great risk of being insulted by the vulgar populace, which is the most cursed brood in exis-

---

[8] *Lord Mayor's Day:* On his inauguration day, the lord mayor of London would make a ceremonial journey from the old city of London to Westminster. The lord mayor was London's highest civil authority, and this event was an occasion for pageantry and show. The city poet would compose poems addressed to the mayor and write an account of the floats and fancy dress of those who took part in the procession. The latter started at Guildhall and went down King Street to the Three Crane Wharf. Then the lord mayor and his party traveled by barge, accompanied by other decorated boats, to Westminster Hall to take the oath of office. From there he traveled back by water to Blackfriars Landing.

tence. He is sure of not only being jeered at and being bespattered with mud, but as likely as not dead dogs and cats will be thrown at him, for the mob makes a provision beforehand of these playthings so that they may amuse themselves with them on the great day. If the stranger were to get angry his treatment would be all the worse. The best thing to be done on these occasions is not to run the risk of mixing with the crowd; but, should you desire to do so from curiosity, you had better dress yourself as simply as possible in the English fashion, and trust to pass unnoticed. I daresay it would interest you to hear of the style and the way Englishmen usually dress. They do not trouble themselves about dress, but leave that to their womenfolk. When the people see a well-dressed person in the streets, especially if he is wearing a braided coat, a plume in his hat, or his hair tied in a bow, he will, without doubt, be called "French dog" twenty times perhaps before he reaches his destination. This name is the most common, and evidently, according to popular idea, the greatest and most forcible insult that can be given to any man, and it is applied indifferently to all foreigners, French or otherwise. Englishmen are usually very plainly dressed, they scarcely ever wear gold on their clothes; they wear little coats called "frocks," without facings and without pleats, with a short cape above. Almost all wear small, round wigs, plain hats, and carry canes in their hands, but no swords. Their cloth and linen are of the best and finest. You will see rich merchants and gentlemen thus dressed, and sometimes even noblemen of high rank, especially in the morning, walking through the filthy and muddy streets. Englishmen are, however, very lavish in other ways. They have splendid equipages[9] and costly apparel when required. Peers and other persons of rank are richly dressed when they go to Court, especially on gala days, when their grand coaches, with their magnificent accoutrements, are used. The lower classes are usually well dressed, wearing good cloth and linen. You never see wooden shoes in England, and the poorest individuals never go with naked feet. . . .

Highwaymen are generally well mounted; one of them will stop a coach containing six or seven travellers. With one hand he will present a pistol, with the other his hat, asking the unfortunate passengers most politely for their purses or their lives. No one caring to run the risk of being killed or maimed, a share of every traveller's money is thrown into the hat, for were one to make the slightest attempt at

---

[9] *equipages:* Privately maintained carriages or coaches.

self-defence the ruffian would turn bridle and fly, but not before attempting to revenge himself by killing you. If, on the contrary, he receives a reasonable contribution, he retires without doing you any injury. When there are several highwaymen together, they will search you thoroughly and leave nothing. Again, others take only a part of what they find; but all these robbers ill-treat only those who try to defend themselves. I have been told that some highwaymen are quite polite and generous, begging to be excused for being forced to rob, and leaving passengers the wherewithal to continue their journey. All highwaymen that are caught are hanged without mercy.

East Sheen, Near Richmond, June 14, 1726

. . . Fifty paces from London Spa[10] you see another big house, Sadler's Wells.[11] An entertainment is given here all the summer through, which lasts from four o'clock in the afternoon till ten o'clock at night. You first see rope-dancers, tumblers, and acrobats; after that tricks of skill and daring are performed, amongst others that of men going up ladders which lean against nothing, their heads downwards and their feet in the air, and all kinds of tricks of equilibrium and diversions of that sort. The entertainment ends with a pantomime, acted on a very pretty little theatre with good scenery. Besides this there is quite a good orchestra; but the best of it is you pay nothing for this entertainment — you need only throw the actors a few coins. Each party of spectators sits in a kind of box, which contains a little table on which to place plates and glasses, for everyone must have something to eat or to drink, as none are allowed into this house for the diversion of the eyes and ears only, enjoyment must also be given to the palate. You may order any sort of wine, cold meats, and sweetmeats, which are not dearer than elsewhere, the only difference being that the bottles here contain about one glass less than at other places. Notwithstanding the cheapness, the proprietor is quite satisfied with the profits, for many persons come daily, and much wine is drunk. . . .

[10] *London Spa:* There were seventeen spas in London. This is most probably a reference to the spa in Clerkenwell, the Fountain Inn, owned by John Holland, who claimed medicinal and tonic qualities in his water.

[11] *Sadler's Wells:* A place for refreshments and musical, among other, entertainments, Sadler's Wells can be seen as a lower-class Vauxhall. During the eighteenth century, it carried a somewhat disreputable image for the rowdy behavior of its clientele.

East Sheen, Near Richmond, October 29, 1726

In my preceding letter I gave you what you may perhaps have thought an insipid description of London and its surroundings. I think that I will do well to tell you of a few of the advantages of this city, for they are many, and are not to be found in other towns. Foremost amongst the number I must place the penny post, which is a most useful institution. It would be very inconvenient in such a large town as London to have to run from one end of it to the other every time you had anything special to communicate. In order to provide for this difficulty, a large number of small offices have been established in every quarter of the town and in the principal streets. You may, if you wish it, write twice a day to anyone living in the town or suburbs, and once in the day to about one hundred and fifty small towns and villages in the vicinity of London. Should the letter be addressed to any place further than London and its suburbs, the person who sends it, in giving it to be posted, will have to pay one penny, and the receiver will also have to pay the same sum; but if the letter is addressed to the town or suburbs the sender alone pays the penny. You can send parcels in the same way; a parcel weighing a pound will not cost more than a simple letter. Whatever is sent by the penny post is well cared for, provided you have taken the trouble of registering it at the office, because should the parcel get lost, the clerk is in that case answerable for it. . . .

The common people and low populace have their taverns, or rather spirit shops; for nothing but strong liquor is sold in this class of tavern. Spirits are made from grains or from juniper. These taverns are almost always full of men and women, and even sometimes of children, who drink with so much enjoyment that they find it difficult to walk on going away. Though these liquors are a sort of poison, and many people die from making too free a use of them, it would be most difficult to abolish these pothouses. On the whole the people of this country are very fond of liquors, which are said to be necessary because of the thickness and dampness of the atmosphere. You can easily imagine that London possesses many inns and hostelries and shops where you can purchase cooked food. Men and more especially foreigners live in furnished apartments, and take their meals in eating-houses. You can have rooms from sixpence to half a guinea a head.

The hackney coaches in London are a great convenience. About one thousand of these vehicles are to be found day and night in the public places and principal streets of the city and town. Most of them, to tell the truth, are ugly and dirty. The driver is perched high up on a wooden seat, as elevated as the imperial of a coach. The body of the carriage is very badly balanced, so that when inside you are most cruelly shaken, the pavement being very uneven, and most of the horses excellent and fast trotters. A drive costs one shilling, provided you do not go further than a certain distance; other drives will cost two or sometimes three shillings, according to distance. The drivers often ask more than is their due, and this is the case especially when they have to do with foreigners. To avoid being cheated, you must take the number of the coach marked on the door, and offer the driver a handful of coins, telling him to take his fare out of it. In this fashion of dealing he will not take more than his due, for should he do so you have a right to go and complain at the coach office, and the driver will be punished by being made to pay a fine, half of which would go to the plaintiff, and the other half to the officers of the office.

Besides these conveyances there are a great number of chariots and coaches belonging to noblemen and gentlemen. Some are magnificent, and most are drawn by fine and excellent horses. The chariots belonging to noblemen are recognisable by the small gilt coronets placed at each of the four corners of the imperial; those belonging to dukes have ducal coronets, and so on. These fine chariots, behind which stand two or three footmen attired in rich liveries, are certainly a great ornament to a town, and a convenience to rich people, but they are a great hindrance to those who are not wealthy and go on foot, for the streets being generally very muddy, the passers-by get terribly bespattered and dirty. Pedestrians, it is true, would be far worse off were there not on either side of the street a sort of elevated footpath for their convenience, but I think I have already told you of this.

Near the palace and in its vicinity there are more than three hundred Sedan chairs for hire; like the cabs, they are found in the principal streets and thoroughfares. Chairs are very convenient and pleasant for use, the bearers going so fast that you have some difficulty in keeping up with them on foot. I do not believe that in the whole of Europe better or more dexterous bearers are to be found; all foreigners are surprised at their strength and skill. Like coaches, Sedan chairs are most convenient for the wealthy, but often very embarrassing for those of another class, for these chairs are allowed to be carried on the footpaths, and when a person does not take heed, or a stranger does not understand the "Have care," or "By your leave, sir," of the bearers, and does not make room to let them pass, he will run a great risk of being knocked down, for the bearers go very fast and cannot turn aside with their burden.

I went through this experience on first coming to London. Not understanding the "By your leave" addressed to me, I did not draw aside, and repented quickly, for I received a tremendous push which hurled me four feet further on, and I should undoubtedly have fallen on my back had it not been for the wall of a house which broke my fall, but much to the injury of my arm. To my cost I thus learnt what the cry of the bearer means. Sedan chairs are also numbered, and there is an office where you can go and make your complaint if cheated by your bearers.

Besides hackney coaches and Sedan chairs, London possesses another means of public conveyance in its boats. I believe there are about fifteen thousand of these on the Thames, in London and its vicinity. All these boats are numbered, and the boatmen likewise possess an office where you can apply should you have a complaint to lodge against one of their number. These boats are very attractive and cleanly kept, and are light in weight, painted generally in red or in green, and can hold six persons comfortably. On rainy days these boats are covered with coarse, strong tents, so that the rain cannot pass, and in summer, when the sun is burning hot, with an awning made of thin green or red woollen stuff. . . .

London, February 7, 1727

. . . I do not think there is a people more prejudiced in its own favour than the British people, and they allow this to appear in their talk and manners. They look on foreigners in general with contempt, and think nothing is as well done elsewhere as in their own country, and certainly many things contribute to keep up this good opinion of themselves, their love for their nation, its wealth, plenty, and liberty, and the comforts that are enjoyed. They see, on the other hand, what a number of foreigners come to England to seek their fortunes, and comparatively few out of mere curiosity, whilst Englishmen, on the contrary, do not leave their country, but if they do it is only for a few years, and generally only for pleasure.

# W. DE ARCHENHOLTZ

## *From* A Picture of England

Johann Wilhem de Archenholtz (1743–1812) was a German historian and man of letters. Before turning to writing as a career, he was an officer who served and was wounded in the Seven Years War. He retired as a captain from the military in 1763 and traveled extensively in Europe. Settling in Magdeburgh in 1780, Archenholtz founded and ran the periodical *Litterature und Volkerkunde* between 1782 and 1791. His travel narrative *England und Italien* was published in 1785 and went through many German editions. Excerpts from this work were reprinted separately and translated into English. The following selections are from *A Picture of England: Containing a Description of the Laws, Customs, and Manners of England. Interspersed with Curious and Interesting Anecdotes of Many Eminent Persons*, published in London in 1797. Archenholtz's reputation as a historian was founded on his twenty-volume work, *Annalen der britischen Geschichte* (1789–98), and he was well known in Germany toward the end of his life for editing the scholarly journal *Minerva*.

Every shop and warehouse is open by eight o'clock in the morning in the city; all is in motion and every body at work; whereas at the west end of this immense place,[1] the streets are still empty and the houses shut; all, without excepting the servants, are still locked in the arms of sleep. The noise of carriages is not heard, and one seems to wander in a desart place. This difference, which holds even in the hours of eating and drinking, in the kinds of amusements, the dress and manner of speaking, &c. has given rise to a degree of mutual contempt by the inhabitants of each of these quarters for the other. Those of the city reproach them of the other end for their idleness, luxury, manner of living, and desire to imitate every thing that is French: these in their turn never mention an inhabitant of the city but as an animal gross and barbarous, whose only merit is his strong-box.[2] It is chiefly when the deputies of these last come to ask an audi-

---

[1] *city . . . place:* The "city" here means the old, walled city where most of London's commerce took place and most of its tradespeople lived. The "west end" refers to the newer and more fashionable area of Westminster.
[2] *strong-box:* The place where he keeps his money.

ence of the king, to compliment him on some great event, or to present some petition, that the courtiers take a malicious pleasure in ridiculing them. The deputation is generally very numerous, and the king receives, them seated on his throne. It may be easily imagined that a simple citizen, to whom the manners and customs of a court are totally strangers, will not acquit himself in this solemn act with the ease of a courtier who makes etiquette his chief and only study, and who even considers it as the most interesting and only useful occupation. This mutual dislike is sung in the streets, it is introduced upon the stage, and even in parliament it is not forgotten. In Italy, in similar circumstances, daggers would be drawn and blood spilt; but far from having these fatal effects in England, the matter seems only to divert, at times, the spleen[3] of the nation. When the young citizens however happen to be in company with their antagonists, they carefully conceal the place of their abode, that an unfavourable idea of their manners may not be entertained by the persons present.

The English nobility have at all times passed three-fourths of the year on their estates. This antient custom is the cause that there are so few great houses in the capital. It must be observed, however, that the residence in this place having now many more attractions than formerly, the nobility stay for a longer time than they used to do, but they still regard their estates as their home, and their houses in London merely as lodgings. Many individuals, worth twenty thousand a year or more, have small houses in London in comparison, and consequently with a small number of domestics are indifferently lodged. But this inconvenience will soon cease, as many of the nobility are now beginning to build superb houses in town. Let it not be supposed that these establishments are encouraged by the government; for although the first wish of courts is to draw around them a numerous nobility, who while adding to their splendour, relieve them from the fear of any commotion which might be raised by powerful lords in the heart of the country, I can affirm that nothing of this is the case, but that the pleasures of London alone are the source of attraction. The passion for the chace[4] is already beginning to abate, and that for the fine arts, and for whatever tends to add to the luxuries of life to increase. It is even probable that the English nobility will fix at last like those of France, in the capital. When it is considered that since this custom has been generally adopted in Europe, troubles in the

---

[3] *spleen:* Melancholy, ill-humor.
[4] *chace:* Fox-hunting, more commonly spelled chase.

interior parts of the kingdom, which were either raised or fomented by the nobles, have ceased, and that it is only in Poland and in England, that they have been known in our times, because it is only in these two countries that the nobility still live on their estates, we shall be forced to allow that luxury, against which we so much cry out, has often been good for something.

This new disposition in the rich among the English to make London their principal abode, has suggested to speculators the idea of forming whole streets and large squares, decorated with houses built at their expence. Such speculations had never before been attempted in London. These houses, which may be considered as so many palaces, are very large, exceedingly commodious, and have all two floors under ground, which are lighted by a sort of court before. These two floors contain some very good apartments in which the servants and domestics live. Here is also the kitchen, the larder, the wine cellar, &c. so that the ground floor and others above, are entirely at the disposal of the master and family. . . .

I come now to a subject which I am sorry to say is inexhaustible, I mean the women of the town in London. It is well known how much nature has done for the English women, but I maintain that the greatest part of the pretty girls in that metropolis, shamefully abuse the charms she has bestowed on them. It is computed that there are fifty thousand common prostitutes in London. Their customs and conduct divide them into different classes. The lowest sort live under the direction of an old bawd who furnishes them with cloaths. Others live in houses of their own or in furnished lodgings. The uncertainty of the payment, makes the proprietors of those houses, demand double the ordinary rent. Without such lodgers, there would be thousands of empty houses in the west end of the town. In the parish of Marylebone alone, which is indeed the largest and most populous of any in England, there were thirteen thousand of these inhabitants a few years ago, of whom seventeen hundred occupied entire houses. These last live decently, and without being disturbed. They are mistresses in their own house, and if any of the magistrates should think of troubling them, they might shew him the door; for paying the same taxes with other householders they are entitled to the same privileges.

Their houses are neatly and sometimes magnificently furnished, they have waiting maids, house maids, livery[5] servants, and some of

---

[5] *livery:* The uniform for a domestic servant. Those who could afford to often chose to put their servants in a distinctive uniform that was recognizable as theirs.

them even keep a carriage. Many of them have annuities, which they have obtained from their seducers, or which they have coaxed out of their lovers in the moment of intoxication. These annuities, it is true, secure them from want, but are not always sufficient to enable them to live as they please in a capital where every pleasure is so dear; accordingly they receive visits from particular people, but their door is always shut against the crowd. The testimony of these nymphs, even of the lowest among them, is received in courts of justice, and this gives them in general a certain pride and principles which it is difficult to reconcile with their course of life.

Among those of the higher class, a person is secure of not being robbed; he may even give them his purse to keep. They think it dishonourable likewise to grant favours to the lovers of their friends. A countryman of mine solicited a poor girl of this profession, and offered her a considerable reward but in vain. Surprized at her refusal, he made an English gentleman ask her the reason; "Sir, said she, I am a poor girl and forced to live by this trade, and Heaven knows how much need I have of money; but it would be dishonourable to consent to this gentleman's proposal. If he were an Englishman I might perhaps be prevailed upon, but as he is a foreigner what would he think of us?" At elections for members of parliament these girls have been known to refuse large sums, and to reserve their favours for those who could procure votes to the patriots whom they esteemed. Such virtues take off the stigma attached to their profession. I have seen well known persons give them their arm on a public walk. I have even seen more than one minister plenipotentiary[6] conversing publicly in Vauxhall gardens with celebrated courtezans. Although their rank requires a certain dignity, which an English Lord never affects, yet they easily conform to the manners of a country, in matters when something is gained on the side of liberty. . . .

The descriptions of the multiplied pleasures of the town, give the country girls the most ardent desire to partake of them. Imagination inflames their little brains and presents every object in an exaggerated shape. Young persons of both sexes, who live at a distance, regard the Metropolis as the Mahometans consider the Paradise promised them by their prophet. It is not astonishing then that so many young people are daily forming innumerable projects to get at that centre of pleasure. How easily is a young girl without experience tempted by a proposal of this sort, made to her by her lover! If there is no other ray

---

[6] *minister plenipotentiary:* A high-ranking state official.

of hope left that her parents will consent to her marriage with him, the inconsiderate creature imagines that she will force them to it by eloping. Thus she arrives in London. This proceeding irritates her parents, they remain deaf to her prayers; her lover grows every day more indifferent, abandons her, leaves her without resource, alone, unknown in an immense city, where art and intrigue every day, exhibit the most atrocious scenes. Many a severe censor will perhaps exact that in this deplorable situation, and while repentance is yet strong in her mind, she should beg her way back to her father's house, or if she had received a proper education, she should go to service.[7] These two resources are totally wanting in England. The respectable professor Moritz,[8] has shewn by his own example that journeys on foot, are absolutely inpracticable in that island. How could a beautiful girl hazard herself alone on the highway! Besides, a person without character or recommendation can never procure service in London. Had she even such an intention, would her creditors allow her the time? Bawds and false officers of justice are ever on the watch, the most infernal stratagems are practised, and the most abominable snares are laid for her, till yielding to necessity, the poor abandoned creature consents to her irretrievable undoing.

It will not therefore be surprising that there should be so many women of the town in London, who possess those virtues we admire in the sex, youth, beauty, the graces, gentleness, education, principles, and even that delightful modesty which is the most powerful attraction to pleasure. They give us an idea of those celebrated Greek courtezans, who charmed the Athenian heroes, and whom Socrates himself honoured with his visits.

It is to be observed that I am here talking only of the higher class, for it is rare if not impossible to find these qualities among the vile prostitutes whose manner of life chokes every seed of virtue, if any had ever been sown in their heart. In every season of the year at the approach of night, they sally from their homes well dressed, and every street and square is crowded with them.

If such abuses, which are the natural consequences of luxury and a superabundance of wealth, were to be reformed, the effects would be very pernicious to the trade and commerce of a country like England.

---

[7] *go to service:* Become a domestic servant.
[8] *Moritz:* For a discussion of Moritz's wanderings on foot, see the headnote to the selection from his *Travels* in this chapter.

If it was resolved to establish at London, as there was at Vienna, a tribunal of chastity,[9] that great city would soon be depopulated; the natural melancholy of the English[10] would exceed all bounds; the fine arts in terror, would fly from the country; numberless methods of subsisting, which give bread to one half of the inhabitants would be annihilated, and that superb metropolis be changed into a wild and dreary desert. What is said above sufficiently justifies this conclusion. If more convincing proofs are demanded, let us enter into all the shops in the city, and ask who are their best customers, and those from whom they receive most punctual payments? They will answer, that these unhappy creatures, who deny themselves every necessary of life in order to furnish their wardrobe, will often expend with them in an instant the whole gain of a week. Without them, the public entertainments would be abandoned; not only are they there in crowds themselves, but multitudes of young persons go thither only to see and to speak to them. All who are acquainted with London will be of my opinion. . . .

England surpasses all the other nations of Europe in the luxury of dress and apparel, and this luxury is increasing daily. Twenty years ago, neither gold nor silver were to be seen on a coat, except at court or the theatre. Persons in dress went in carriages; on foot they never wore swords, and the petit maitres[11] put on their hats. This last custom remains, but all the rest are changed. Even the common people have embroidered vests. Every body in summer as well as in winter wears a plain coat but of the finest cloth; no tradesman will wear any thing else. No furs are used, but great surtouts[12] which protect from the rain in summer, and the cold in winter. In this simple dress, do the first ministers of state walk the streets of London, without being followed by a single servant. Many people do not allow their shoes to

---

[9] *Vienna . . . tribunal of chastity:* In 1747 the Empress of Austria, Maria Theresa, established a "Chastity Commission" designed to discourage licentious behavior in both men and women. The commissioners could search houses, arrest men caught "entertaining" opera singers or other women of "loose character," and could lock up any offending women in a convent or banish them from the kingdom. At least two acting companies and a soprano were expelled by this commission. Maria Theresa's commission was not popular in many quarters and was widely ridiculed. It was abolished after about six months.

[10] *melancholy of the English:* The English were reputed to be of a melancholic, or splenatic character, a characteristic often attributed to the dampness of the island. Melancholy was, in some medical theories, caused by an excess of fluid. See footnote 1 to Smollett, "On a Visit to Bath," in Part Two, Chapter 2.

[11] *petit maitres:* "Little masters," or vain and rather petty young men.

[12] *surtouts:* Overcoats.

be cleaned in the house but in the open street. The shoe blacks of London earn a deal of money. They are seen at the corners of every street amidst a heap of shoes brought to them from the houses in the neighbourhood. Nobody, even among the common people, wears a turned coat, or a soled shoe.[13] Shirts of the finest linen are generally worn, and even the lower sort have a clean one every day. The cleanliness of the English in every thing is admirable. Fine linen, clean stockings, a neat hat and good shoes distinguish the men of easy circumstances. The coat is not so much observed. This is generally the dress of the rich citizens, who go to 'Change[14] sometimes in threadbare coats. The custom of wearing fanciful buttons, has increased very much within these few years, so that a plain frock will sometimes cost as much as a laced coat. Young people of quality get them by dozens. Linen warehouses of every kind, are dispersed over every other quarter of the town; but those of shoes and furniture are fixed in particular districts. The quantity of ready made goods alone is astonishing; you would think there was sufficient to furnish a whole city, and yet no great house goes thither to purchase, but applies to some fashionable broker who charges an advanced price. I have already taken notice of the extravagance in the dress of the women.

The English have adopted the custom of dressing their hair almost against their will; and accordingly their friseurs[15] are the most unskillful of any in Europe. They perform as in France, the office of barber and hairdresser, and they are equally awkward at both.

I have had more than one opportunity to remark, that the great characteristic differences between the people of England and the other nations of Europe, arise from that freedom, which the former enjoy, and which gives occasion to many singular and extraordinary customs. It is not therefore by our measures that we are to calculate the distance that separates the different classes of that republican monarchy. This observation extends even to menial servants. The first citizen dare not strike his domestics, for they can sue him for ill usage, or defend themselves against him. In the first case, a pecuniary

---

[13] *turned coat . . . soled shoe:* A turned coat was an old, worn coat that had been unstitched and resewn with the fabric reversed to give it a newer appearance and a longer-wearing life. Shoe soles were a sign of class status and affluence. The lower classes who had to face the muddy streets wore clogs or, when they went out of fashion after mid-century, "patten" shoes with high, wooden platform soles. "Soled shoe" would seem to refer to pattens here.

[14] *'Change:* That is, to the sites of trade and business, such as the Royal Exchange.

[15] *friseurs:* Hairdressers.

fine, and many other disagreeable circumstances, are always the consequence. The English justly think that, as poverty and dependance are none of the comforts of life, it would be cruel to aggravate the hard fate of those who are born in such circumstances, by a submission which the laws do not authorise. If a domestic is in fault, the master can only dismiss him, except the fault is punishable by law. To give harsh names would only expose him to a return of the same kind, which are the less tolerable as they are not actionable; except when they affect his honour or reputation. All other injurious expressions, however provoking or humiliating, cannot be redressed by any court. . . .

It is customary in all the great houses to give their servants board wages; but in other houses their victuals[16] are provided for them. The rule observed in this case is very singular. They receive the dishes immediately on their being removed from the table of their masters; and none are ever put aside, till the servants have dined. If every ones meal was portioned out to them, they would not touch it, however ample it might be, and they would immediately demand their dismission. They must have the absolute choice of all the dishes that were served up to their master, without exception of number or quality. This of all English customs is the most disagreeable to the families of foreigners who come to settle among them, being too opposite to their own principles of economy, and diminishing too much the distance between them and their servants. This approach of the different classes of citizens to one another, which arises from the sentiment of natural equality, and is encouraged by the laws, is even observable among the lowest of the people, who might sometimes be supposed to exalt themselves over those who do not live so well as they do. The proof of this I shall take from the class of the grossest and most savage of men who are more accustomed to live with horses than with reasonable beings. It never comes into the head of the splendid and well fed coachman of a Duke, to think himself above the driver of a miserable hackeny coach that plies night and day on the streets of London. He treats him as his equal, and without knowing him, he will descend from his seat to do him a service, he will turn his carriage aside to let him pass.

[16] *victuals:* Food.

## CARL PHILLIP MORITZ

## *From* Travels, Chiefly on Foot,
## Through Several Parts of England, in 1782

Carl Phillip Moritz (1756–1793) was a professor in Berlin who wrote philosophical prose on language and psychology. He grew up in a poor family and suffered many economic hardships as a young scholar, but eventually he became an educator and writer known and respected by Goethe, one of the greatest authors of his day. Moritz's travels in England were highly unusual for being undertaken on foot. Travel on foot, or hiking as we might call it today, was very rare and even quite dangerous in the late eighteenth century. Moritz often suffered rejection and, at best, serious snubbing when he stopped to find a bed or refreshment on his travels; for people assumed that only the very poorest would find themselves traveling on foot. Actually, Moritz found his first experience with traveling in an English coach so uncomfortable that he chose walking as a preferable manner of seeing the country. His travel writings are notable for their particularly well-informed, sympathetic approach to English life and customs. Although an "outsider" by nationality, Moritz was familiar with the language and politics of England. One might say he was something of an enthusiast for the English way of life.

Moritz's *Travels* were first published in 1783 and translated into English in 1795. The following excerpts are from the second translation into English, done by an anonymous "lady": *Travels, Chiefly on Foot, Through Several Parts of England, in 1782. Described in Letters to a Friend*, trans. "a lady" (London: G. G. and J. Robinson, 1795).

It might be about ten or eleven o'clock when we arrived here. After the two Englishmen had first given me some breakfast, at their lodgings, which consisted of tea and bread and butter, they went about with me themselves, in their own neighbourhood, in search of an apartment, which they at length procured for me, for sixteen shillings a week, at the house of a taylor's widow, who lived opposite to them. It was very fortunate, on other accounts, that they went with me, for, equipped as I was, having neither brought clean linen, nor change of cloaths from my trunk, I might, perhaps have found it difficult to obtain good lodgings.

It was a very uncommon, but pleasing sensation I experienced, on being now, for the first time in my life, entirely among Englishmen;

among people whose language was foreign, their manners foreign, and in a foreign climate, with whom, notwithstanding, I could converse as familiarly as though we had been educated together from our infancy. It is certainly an inestimable advantage to understand the language of the country through which you travel. I did not at first give the people I was with any reason to suspect I could speak English; but I soon found that the more I spoke, the more attention and regard I met with. I now occupy a large room in front on the ground floor, which has a carpet and matts, and is very neatly furnished; the chairs are covered with leather, and the tables are of mahogany. Adjoining to this I have another large room. I may do just as I please, and keep my own tea, coffee, bread and butter; for which purpose my landlady has given me a cupboard in my room, which locks up.

The family consists of the mistress of the house, her maid and her two sons, *Jacky* and *Jerry;* singular abbreviations for *John* and *Jeremiah.* The eldest, Jacky, about twelve years old, is a very lively boy, and often entertains me in the most pleasing manner, by relating to me his different employments at school; and afterwards desiring me, in my turn, to relate to him all manner of things about Germany. He repeats his *amo, amas, amavi,*[1] in the same singing tone as our common school-boys. As I happened once, when he was by, to hum a lively tune, he stared at me with surprize, and then reminded me it was Sunday; and so, that I might not forfeit his good opinion, by any appearance of levity, I gave him to understand, that in my hurry of my journey, I had forgotten the day. He has already shewn me St. James's Park, which is not far from hence; and now let me give you some description of the renowned.

### St. James's Park

This Park is nothing more than a semicircle, formed of an alley of trees, which enclose a large green area, in the middle of which is a marshy pond.

The cows feed on this green turf, and their milk is sold here on the spot, quite new.

In all the alleys, or walks, there are benches, where you may rest yourself. When you come through the Horse-Guards (which is provided with several passages) into the Park, on the right hand is St. James's Palace, or the King's place of residence, one of the meanest publick buildings in London. At the lower end, quite at the

---

[1] *amo . . . amavi:* Jacky is memorizing the conjugation of Latin verbs.

extremity, is the Queen's Palace, an handsome and modern building, but very much resembling a private house. As for the rest, there are generally every where about St. James's Park very good houses, which is a great addition to it. There is also before the semicircle of the trees just mentioned, a large vacant space, where the soldiers are exercised.

How little this famous park is to be compared with our park at Berlin I need not mention. And yet one cannot but form an high idea of St. James's Park, and other public places in London; this arises, perhaps, from their having been oftener mentioned in romances and other books than ours have. Even the squares and streets of London are more noted, and better known, than many of our principal towns.

But what again greatly compensates for the mediocrity of this park, is the astonishing number of people who, towards evening, in fine weather, resort here; our finest walks are never so full even in the midst of summer. The exquisite pleasure of mixing freely with such a concourse of people, who are for the most part well dressed and handsome, I have experienced this evening for the first time.

Before I went to the park I took another walk with my little *Jacky,* which did not cost me much fatigue, and yet was most uncommonly interesting. I went down the little street in which I live to the Thames; nearly at the end of it, towards the left, a few steps led me to a singularly pretty terrace, planted with trees, on the very brink of the river.

Here I had the most delightful prospect you can possibly imagine. Before me was the Thames with all its windings, and the stately arches of its bridges; Westminster with its venerable Abbey[2] to the right, to the left again London, with St. Paul's,[3] seemed to wind all along the windings of the Thames; and on the other side of the water lay Southwark[4]; which is now also considered as part of London.

---

[2] *Westminster . . . Abbey:* Originally a monastery founded in the seventh or eighth century, this abbey is famous for its "Poet's Corner," which contains monuments to Chaucer, Spenser, Shakespeare, Ben Jonson, and Milton. English sovereigns are crowned here.

[3] *St. Paul's:* The famous cathedral designed by Christopher Wren (1631–1723), completed in 1710.

[4] *Southwark:* The south bank of the Thames had been the site of much of London's entertainment in the sixteenth and seventeenth centuries, with the Thames watermen rowing revelers across to the Old Bear Gardens, Pye Gardens, and the theaters farther east. In the eighteenth century it was not entirely respectable, the site of Southwark Fair and the location of Mint Street, a criminal quarter alluded to in John Gay's *Beggar's Opera* (1728).

Thus, from this single spot, I could nearly, at one view, see the whole City, at least that side of it towards the Thames. Not far from hence, in this charming quarter of the town, lived the renowned *Garrick*.[5] Depend upon it I shall often visit this delightful walk, during my stay in London.

To day my two Englishmen carried me to a neighbouring tavern, or rather an eating-house, where we paid a shilling each for some roast-meat, and a sallad, giving, at the same time, nearly half as much to the waiter; and yet this is reckoned a cheap house, and a cheap stile of living. — But, I believe, for the future, I shall pretty often dine at home; I have already begun this evening with my supper. I am now sitting by the fire, in my own room in London; the day is nearly at an end, the first I have spent in England, and I hardly know, whether I ought to call it only one day, when I reflect what a quick and varied succession of new and striking ideas have, in so short a time, passed in my mind. . . .

## Vauxhall

I yesterday visited Vauxhall for the first time. I had not far to go from my lodgings, in the Adelphi-buildings,[6] to Westminster-Bridge,[7] where you always find a great number of boats on the Thames, which are ready on the least signal to serve those who will pay them a shilling or sixpence, according to the distance.

---

[5] *Garrick:* David Garrick was the most highly acclaimed and respected actor of his generation — perhaps, indeed, of a whole century of English actors. He brought to English acting style a new "naturalness" of gesture and elocution; he also brought respectability to what was often seen as a rather disreputable profession. A playwright as well as an actor, he managed Drury Lane Theatre during the height of his career. He was also a friend of Charles Burney and a frequent visitor to the Burney house when Frances was a young woman.

[6] *Adelphi-buildings:* "Adelphi" is the latinized Greek term for brothers, and these buildings were so called in honor of their architects, Robert Adam and his brothers. Robert was architect to George III, but the Adelphi buildings were a private venture that nearly bankrupted the brothers. In 1772 Burney visited her friend David Garrick, who was residing in the buildings, and the actor was impressed with the size and elegance of the house, as well as its "sweet situation." The ground on which the buildings rested sloped sharply from the Strand to the river, and the Adams had to build on the level of the Strand a riverside terrace that was supported by huge dramatic arches.

[7] *Westminster-Bridge:* Westminster was an island encircled by two branches of the Tyburn. A bridge was built across the Thames in 1736, making it possible to travel from the old City of London without aid from the watermen who successfully resisted its building until that date.

From hence I went up the Thames to Vauxhall, and as I passed along, I saw Lambeth;[8] and the venerable old palace belonging to the archbishops of Canterbury, lying on my left.

Vauxhall is, properly speaking, the name of a little village in which the garden, now almost exclusively bearing the same name, is situated. You pay a shilling on entrance.

On entering it, I really found, or fancied I found, some resemblance to our Berlin Vauxhall; if, according to Virgil, I may be permitted to compare small things with great ones. The walks at least, with the paintings at the end, and the high trees, which, here and there, form a beautiful grove, or wood, on either side, were so similar to those of Berlin, that often, as I walked along them, I seemed to transport myself, in imagination, once more to Berlin, and forgot for a moment, that immense seas and mountains, and kingdoms now lie between us. I was the more tempted to indulge in this reverie, as I actually met with several gentlemen, inhabitants of Berlin; in particular Mr. S***r, and some others, with whom I spent the evening in the most agreeable manner. Here and there (particularly in one of the charming woods which art has formed in this garden) you are pleasingly surprized by the sudden appearance of the statues of the most renowned English poets and philosophers; such as Milton, Thomson, and others. But, what gave me most pleasure, was the statue of the German composer, Handel, which, on entering the garden, is not far distant from the orchestra.

This orchestra is among a number of trees situated as in a little wood, and is an exceedingly handsome one. As you enter the garden, you immediately hear the sound of vocal and instrumental music. There are several female singers constantly hired here to sing in public.

On each side of the orchestra are small boxes, with tables and benches, in which you sup. The walks before these, as well as in every other part of the garden, are crowded with people of all ranks. I supped here with Mr. S***r, and the secretary of the Prussian ambassador; besides a few other gentlemen from Berlin; but what most astonished me, was the boldness of the women of the town; who, along with their pimps, often rushed in upon us by half dozens; and in the most shameless manner importuned us for wine, for themselves and their followers. Our gentlemen thought it either unwise, unkind, or unsafe, to refuse them so small a boon altogether.

[8] *Lambeth:* The parish in which Vauxhall was located.

An Englishman passed our box with hasty steps, and on our acquaintance's asking him, where he was going in such a hurry, he answered with an air of ridiculous importance, which set us all a laughing, "I have lost my girl!" He seemed to make his search, just as if he had been looking for a glove or a stick, which he had accidently dropt, or forgotten somewhere.

Lateish in the evening, we were entertained with a sight, that is indeed singularly curious and interesting. In a particular part of the garden, a curtain was drawn up, and by means of some mechanism, of extraordinary ingenuity, the eye and the ear are so completely deceived, that it is not easy to persuade one's-self it is a deception; and that one does not actually see and hear a natural waterfall from an high rock. As every one was flocking to this scene in crowds, there arose all at once, a loud cry of, "Take care of your pockets." This informed us, but too clearly, that there were some pick-pockets among the crowd; who had already made some fortunate strokes.

The rotunda, a magnificent circular building, in the garden, particularly engaged my attention. By means of beautiful chandeliers, and large mirrors, it was illuminated in the most superb manner; and every where decorated with delightful paintings, and statues, in the contemplation of which you may spend several hours very agreeably, when you are tired of the crowd and the bustle, in the walks of the garden.

Among the paintings one represents this surrender of a besieged city. If you look at this painting with attention, for any length of time, it affects you so much, that you even shed tears. The expression of the greatest distress, even bordering on despair, on the part of the besieged, the fearful expectation of the uncertain issue, and what the victor will determine concerning those unfortunate people, may all be read so plainly, and so naturally in the countenances of the inhabitants who are imploring for mercy, from the hoary head to the suckling whom his mother holds up, that you quite forget yourself, and in the end scarcely believe it to be a painting before you.

You also here find the busts of the best English authors, placed all round on the sides. Thus a Briton again meets with his Shakespear, Locke, Milton, and Dryden, in the public places of his amusements; and there also reveres their memory. Even the common people thus become familiar with the names of those who have done honour to their nation; and are taught to mention them with veneration. For this rotunda is also an orchestra, in which the music is performed, in rainy weather. But enough of Vauxhall!

Certain it is, that the English classical authors are read more generally, beyond all comparison than the German; which in general are read only by the learned; or, at most, by the middle class of people. The English national authors are in all hands, and read by all people, of which the innumerable editions they have gone through, are a sufficient proof.

My landlady, who is only a taylor's widow, reads her Milton; and tells me, that her late husband first fell in love with her, on this very account; because she read Milton with such proper emphasis. This single instance perhaps would prove but little; but I have conversed with several people of the lower class, who all knew their national authors, and who all have read many, if not all of them. This elevates the lower ranks, and brings them nearer to the higher. There is hardly any argument, or dispute in conversation, in the higher ranks, about which the lower cannot also converse or give their opinion. Now in Germany, since Gellert,[9] there has as yet been no poet's name familiar to the people. But the quick sale of the classical authors, is here promoted also, by cheap and convenient editions. They have them all bound in pocket volumes; as well as in a more pompous stile. I myself bought Milton in duodecimo[10] for two shillings, neatly bound; it is such an one as I can, with great convenience, carry in my pocket. It also appears to me to be a good fashion, which prevails here, and here only, that the books which are most read, are always to be had, already well and neatly bound. At stalls, and in the streets, you every now and then meet with a sort of antiquarians, who sell single or odd volumes; sometimes perhaps of Shakespear, &c. so low as a penny; nay even sometimes for an halfpenny a piece. Of one of these itinerant antiquarians I bought the two volumes of the Vicar of Wakefield,[11] for sixpence, i.e. for the half of an English shilling. In what estimation our German literature is held in England, I was en-

---

[9] *Gellert:* Christian Furchtegott Gellert (1715–1769) was the author of *Leben der schwedischen Grafin von G\*\*\** (1746–48), a novel translated into English four times between 1752 and 1776 as *History of the Swedish Countess of Guildenstern*. He began his writing career as a playwright and poet of some moderate success, but his only novel made him an international European celebrity and one of the few German writers well known in England at mid-century.

[10] *duodecimo:* A book made by dividing a sheet of paper into twelve leaves (or twenty-four pages). Although the size of these volumes varied according to the dimensions of the sheet of paper that was used, they were generally small enough to fit into a pocket and were often thought of as "ladies' editions."

[11] *Vicar of Wakefield:* Oliver Goldsmith's popular novel. See the headnote to "On London Shops" in Part Two, Chapter 2.

abled to judge, in some degree, by the printed proposals of a book, which I saw. The title was "The Entertaining Museum, or Complete Circulating Library;" which is to contain a list of all the English classical authors, as well as translations of the best French, Spanish, Italian, and *even German novels.*

The moderate price of this book deserves also to be noticed; as by such means books in England come more within the reach of the people; and of course are more generally distributed among them. The advertisement mentions, that in order that every one may have it in his power to buy this work and at once to furnish himself with a very valuable library, without perceiving the expense, a number will be sent out weekly, which, stitched, costs sixpence, and bound with the title on the back, nine-pence. The twenty-fifth and twenty-sixth number, contain the first and second volume of the vicar of Wakefield, which I had just bought of the antiquarian above mentioned. . . .

Often as I had heard Ranelagh spoken of, I had yet formed only an imperfect idea of it. I supposed it to be a garden some-what different from that of Vauxhall; but, in fact, I hardly knew what I thought of it. Yesterday evening I took a walk, in order to visit this famous place of amusement; but I missed my way and got to Chelsea;[12] where I met a man with a wheelbarrow, who not only very civilly shewed me the right road, but also conversed with me the whole of the distance, which we walked together. And finding, on enquiry, that I was a subject of the King of Prussia, he desired me, with much eagerness, to relate to him some anecdotes concerning that mighty monarch.

At length I arrived at Ranelagh; and having paid my half-crown, on entrance, I soon enquired for the garden door, and it was readily shewn to me; when, to my infinite astonishment, I found myself in a poor, mean-looking, and ill-lighted garden, where I met but few people. I had not been here long before I was accosted by a young lady, who also was walking there, and who, without ceremony, offered me her arm, asking me why I walked thus solitarily? I now concluded, this could not possibly be the splendid, much-boasted Ranelagh; and so, seeing not far from me a number of people entering a door, I followed them, in hopes either to get out again, or to vary the scene.

But it is impossible to describe, or indeed to conceive, the effect it had on me, when, coming out of the gloom of the garden, I suddenly entered a round building, illuminated by many hundred lamps; the

---

[12] *Chelsea:* Chelsea, an attractive, rural village only a few miles from both the City and the newly fashionable Westminster, was the site of Ranelagh Gardens.

A view of the Rotunda, House & Gardens, at Ranelagh, with an exact representation of the Jubilee. Vüe de la Maison & Rotonde, des Jardins, & de Ranelagh, et du Bal, public donné le 24 May 1759, pour la Naissance de sa altesse Royale George, Prince de Galle.

Representing the Celebrating the Birth-Day of his Royal Highness George, Prince of Wales.

Printed for Robert Sayer, Fleet Street, London.

73

splendor and beauty of which surpassed every thing of the kind I had ever seen before. Every thing seemed here, to be round: above, there was a gallery, divided into boxes; and in one part of it an organ with a beautiful choir, from which issued both instrumental and vocal music. All around, under this gallery, are handsome painted boxes for those who wish to take refreshments: the floor was covered with mats; in the middle of which are four high black pillars; within which there are neat fire places for preparing tea, coffee, and punch: and all around also there are placed tables, set out with all kinds of refreshments. Within these four pillars, in a kind of magic rotundo, all the beau-monde of London move perpetually round and round.

I at first mixed with this immense concourse of people, of all sexes, ages, countries, and characters: and I must confess, that the incessant change of faces, the far greater number of which were strikingly beautiful, together with the illumination, the extent and majestic splendor of the place, with the continued sound of the music, makes an inconceivably delightful impression on the imagination; and I take the liberty to add, that, on seeing it now for the first time, I felt pretty nearly the same sensations, that I remember to have felt, when, in early youth, I first read the Fairy Tales.

Being however at length tired of the crowd, and being tired also, with always moving round and round in a circle, I sat myself down in one of the boxes, in order to take some refreshment, and was now contemplating at my ease, this prodigious collection and crowd of an happy, chearful world, who were here enjoying themselves devoid of care, when a waiter very civilly asked me what refreshment I wished to have, and in a few moments returned with what I asked for. To my astonishment, he would accept no money for these refreshments; which I could not comprehend, till he told me that everything was included in the half-crown I had paid at the door; and that I had only to command, if I wished for any thing more; but that, if I pleased, I might give him as a present a trifling douceur.[13] This I gave him with pleasure, as I could not help fancying, I was hardly entitled to so much civility and good attendance for one single half-crown.

[13] *douceur:* Tip.

*Opposite:* **The Rotunda House and Gardens at Ranelagh on the occasion of the Jubilee Ball, May 24, 1759, celebrating the birthday of the Prince of Wales. From a drawing by Canaletto. Copyright British Museum.**

I now went up into the gallery, and seated myself in one of the boxes there: and from thence becoming, all at once, a grave and moralizing spectator, I looked down on the concourse of people, who were still moving round and round in the fairy circle; and then I could easily distinguish several stars, and other orders, of knighthood; French queues and bags[14] contrasted with plain English heads of hair, or professional wigs; old age and youth, nobility and commonalty, all passing each other in the motley swarm. An Englishman who joined me, during this my reverie, pointed out to me on my enquiring, princes, and lords with their dazzling stars; with which they eclipsed the less brilliant part of the company.

Here some moved round in an eternal circle to see and be seen; there a groupe of eager connoisseurs had placed themselves before the orchestra and were feasting their ears, while others, at the well supplied tables, were regaling the parched roofs of their mouths, in a more substantial manner, and again others like myself were sitting alone, in the corner of a box in the gallery, making their remarks and reflexions on so interesting a scene.

I now and then indulged myself in the pleasure of exchanging, for some minutes, all this magnificence and splendor, for the gloom of the garden, in order to renew the pleasing surprize I experienced on my first entering the building. Thus I spent here some hours in the night, in a continual variation of entertainment; when the crowd now all at once began to lessen, and I also took a coach and drove home.

At Ranelagh, the company appeared to me much better, and more select than at Vauxhall; for those of the lower class, who go there, always dress themselves in their best; and thus endeavour to copy the great. Here I saw no one who had not silk stockings on. Even the poorest families are at the expence of a coach, to go to Ranelagh, as my landlady assured me. She always fixed on some one day in the year, on which, without fail, she drove to Ranelagh. On the whole the expense at Ranelagh is nothing near so great as it is at Vauxhall, if you consider the refreshments; for anyone who sups at Vauxhall, which most people do, is likely for a very moderate supper, to pay at least half-a-guinea.

---

[14] *bags:* Referring to a cloth bag enclosing a man's pigtail at the nape of his neck.

# THOMAS CAMPBELL

## From Dr. Campbell's Diary
## of a Visit to England in 1775

Thomas Campbell (1733–1795) was an Irish clergyman who visited England shortly before the publication of *Evelina*. He was an important dignitary in the Irish Protestant church, an author and antiquarian interested in Irish history, and a well-known and respected pulpit orator. James Boswell, in his biography of the famous man of letters Samuel Johnson, records that Campbell had come to England to meet Johnson. Whether this is true or not, Campbell did become acquainted with Johnson at the home of the literary patrons Hester and Henry Thrale, who were also close friends of Burney's. Hester Thrale wrote of Campbell, "He was a fine showy talking man. Johnson liked him of all things in a year or two" (*Autobiography, Letters, and Literary Remains of Mrs. Piozzi*, 1861).

Campbell's diaries were first published in Sydney, Australia, in 1854 through the agency of a nephew. The excerpts reprinted here give us Campbell's view of a theater audience in London and some general opinions on the national character of the English in relation to the French. Campbell's description of a disrupted theater performance testifies to the rudeness, even brutality, of the London audiences. At the same time, he records reactions that suggest that the "civilizing" influence represented by Addison and Steele (see pp. 538–45) had at least registered in the consciousness of some London playgoers. Indeed, we see it in Evelina's desire that she be allowed to sit and watch a play without interruptions. Campbell clearly admires many aspects of what he sees as an English national character, but his admiration is always that of an outsider, an Irishman whose most serious investment is in the promotion of knowledge about his homeland. One of the aspects of the English that struck Campbell most forcefully on his trip was their ignorance of Ireland — its history, geography, and culture. His *Philosophical Survey of the South of Ireland* (1778) was intended to educate the English through a series of fictional letters. These views of Ireland were written as if by an Englishman, a ruse Campbell believed was the best strategy for winning over English readers.

The following selection is from *Dr. Campbell's Diary of a Visit to England in 1775*, ed. James L. Clifford (Cambridge: Cambridge UP, 1947), 44–45, 103–06.

February 4, 1775

Braganza[1] went off well — the poetry is happy enough & the Catastrophe is striking. After the representation of this play a scene ensued which strongly marked the English character — It was the tenth night of the play & it seems that custom hath decided that after the nineth night the prologue & epilogue[2] should be discontinued. Neither was announced in the bills — However when the players came on the prologue was called for, & Mr. Palmer — a very handsome mouthing blockhead — answered the call. — When the overture for the farce[3] began to be played the Epilogue was called for — the musick ceased for it could not be heared — a long interval ensued — the players came on — they stood their ground for a long time — but were hissed at length off — Mr. Vernon attempted to speak, but he would not be heared — still the cry was off, off, the epilogue, &c — after a long pause the bell rang for the musick[4] — this set the house in an uproar — the women however who were singers came on in hopes of charming these savage beasts — but they were a second time pelted off — then Weston — a mighty favourite of the town came on — he was pelted with oranges[5] — however he stuck to the stage as if he had vegetated on the spot, & only looked at the gallery & pointed up at it when the orange fell, as if to say I know you that threw that — Once he took up an orange as if in thankfulness & put it in his pocket — this & a thousand other humorous tricks he played yet all to no purpose — John Bull[6] roared on — & poor Weston could not prevail. The Players came again & again & Vernon after a third effort was allowed to tell the pit that Mrs. Yates[7] was sent for & begged leave that the farce might go on till she came — But this was denied — the

---

[1] *Braganza: Braganza,* a tragedy by Robert Jephson (1736–1803), was performed at the Theatre Royal in Drury Lane and published in London in 1775.

[2] *prologue & epilogue:* It was customary for especially popular actors to speak the epilogue and prologue to plays; often these occasions were the scene of playful (or not so playful) exchanges between audience and actor.

[3] *farce:* A farce was a short theatrical piece, humorous in nature, that followed the performance of the regular play.

[4] *musick:* Musical performances and dancing often accompanied plays.

[5] *pelted with oranges:* Oranges were among the refreshments sold in the theater. They sometimes served additionally as ammunition.

[6] *John Bull:* Term denoting the typically English, usually of a lower-class nature and often applied to a crowd acting in concert.

[7] *Mrs. Yates:* A popular actress who apparently spoke the epilogue in prior performances.

house grew more & more clamourous calling for Garrick[8] or Mrs. Yates — at length Mr. Yates comes on & tho' he declared in the most solemn manner that his wife[9] was gone sick to bed, yet this would not tame the savages of the gallery — The players were twice hissed off after this till a promise of Mrs. Yates's appearance on Monday &c somewhat abated their madness. — But what to me seemed most expressive of Angloism was the conduct of some in the pit beside me — some were more moderate & asked others why they made such a noise — one before asked another behind, how he dared make such a noise & told him — after some altercation — that he deserved to be turned out of the pit — This produced no other effect but to make my friend behind me more vociferous. — The smallest fraction of such language would have produced a duel in the Dublin Theatres — And the millioneth part of the submissions made by these poor players would have appeased an Irish audience — yea if they have murdered their fathers. . . .

August 1, 1787

The general appearance of the English was to my eye, fresh from Paris, what it never before had been, strangely awkward & clownish,[10] at this ball — The French deserve most richly that character of preeminent politeness which they have universally obtained — I never saw a awkward person in France even in the lowest department — They are, upon the whole, a strange but agreeable mixture of pomp & beggary — the latter is visible in every avenue of Versailles, even in the Palace — I listened in the street to a woman who sung ballads, with the assistance of her husbands tambour, with more pleasure than I ever did at Ranelagh, Vauxhall or the Rotunda[11] — The French language & Musick seem adapted to engage the heart in small matters &c. . . .

---

[8] *Garrick:* David Garrick, the manager of the Drury Lane Theatre and one of the most popular and influential actors of the British stage. See Footnote 5 to the excerpt from Carl Phillip Moritz's *Travels* in this chapter.

[9] *Mr. Yates . . . his wife:* Mr. Yates was also an actor for the company. Acting couples were fairly common to the theater.

[10] *clownish:* Having a loutish appearance usually associated with lower-class, rural people.

[11] *Ranelagh, Vauxhall . . . Rotunda:* For a description of Ranelagh, see Moritz, pages 609–12. For Vauxhall, see Moritz, pages 605–07, *Sketch of the Spring-Gardens,* pages 545–51, and Goldsmith, pages 552–56.

On Monday July the 30th between 11 & 12 I left Paris & on Wednesday the first of Augt about one oclock I found myself at Brighthelmstone, so that after spending two hours at Rouen & more at Dieppe I passed from Paris to Brighton in about 49 hours — This is scarce worthy notice — but upon the whole I must observe that according to the impressions made upon me in this short excursion the two countries bear an exact image of the governments in each — In England the laws are made by the people & therefore they are there for the people & their interests — In France the people are only considered as if made for the use of the court of Versailles & city of Paris — & therefore the people of France do not reflect that image of happiness which the English nation does in every quarter — & yet it is said that the English are less happy than the French — now, though I dont believe this, yet it possibly may be the case — for the English are so pampered by a redundance of meat & money, that they may be said at all times to be under a plethora of both, & therefore may not enjoy that happiness which is within their reach — The laws too being made by & for them (as I have observed) gives them frequent advantages, on trials by jury, over their superiors in rank, which renders them rough & savage in their manners & like children *wilful* peevish & discontented, repining at their own inferiority of condition, & of course unhappy in their stations; not considering that an equality of ranks is incompatible with any form of society ever yet established — Which verifies the French Maxim "Tout chose a le bon & le mal." — [12]

I have thought that if the persons & things of both countries be supposed to be divided into ten classes, there will be found in France one class of these to be so superior to any thing of the kind in England as to have no parallel there — another class may be found in both countries perfectly on *par,* — but that the remaining eight classes in the lower walks of life will be found every way superior in England — That is to say, among the mass of the people, which I count as *eight,* the whole advantage as to the means of the comforts & conveniencies of life lie on the side of the English — And to explain myself as to that highest rank in France for which, I say, England can produce no parallel, I instance in the pomp of a court, the elegance of mind & manners prevalent among the highest orders in France, the general refinement among the more numerous orders of

[12] *Tout . . . mal:* Roughly, "one takes the good with the bad."

clergy & lawyers, the unrivaled accomplishments of the female sex which more than compensates for that beauty of person which distinguishes English ladies, but which is rarely embellished by that expressive eye & those acquired accomplishments which characterize the French Ladies & place them not only above competition in the present age, but challenge antiquity to produce any thing equal to them — NB. I speak of classes of persons & things not of individuals — England may & I doubt not does produce individuals equal to any in any other country — but elegance (I dont mean cleanliness, on which the English pride themselves) of ranks is not as yet to be found in England — The Gentry are cold, lifeless & reserved — the *mauvais honte*[13] is still prevalent among them — They may perhaps in general see what is decorous in behaviour, but they have not acquired the habits of it — of this they are conscious, & therefore they are generally stiff, if not awkward, in their carriage; & always afraid of being incorrect they seldom arrive at excellence, in the exhibition of those good qualities, which they frequently possess. — The French most richly deserve that character of superlative politeness which they have obtained — the despotism of their government has contributed to it — they are compelled to restrain those ebulitions of passion, which sometimes disfigure the behaviour of a free people & this general awe, with which they are impressed, smooths the perturbations of the mind & disposes the people to suavity of demeanour & to those resources from the anguish of thought upon public affairs which is only to be found in the mutual endearments of private society.

---

[13] *mauvais honte:* An awkward shame or bashfulness.

# Seafaring Men

## JAMES ANTHONY GARDNER

### Voyages of a Seaman

James Anthony Gardner (1770?–1846) was born into a naval family at Waterford. He entered the navy at a very young age but apparently had some career disappointments, as he retired from active sea duty as a lieutenant on half-pay at the age of thirty-two. Gardner's memoirs seem to have been written up from journals and logs that he kept at sea when a young man. The following excerpts give a vivid picture of the rough, colorful, and dangerous life of a seaman in the latter half of the eighteenth century. I have tried to keep the burden of footnotes light, but additional information is often needed to follow Gardner's meaning. As some of Captain Mirvan's dialogue in *Evelina* suggests, sailors were notorious for speaking a language so specialized as to be incomprehensible to "landlubbers."

The naval battles recounted by Gardner took place in the last year of the War of American Independence, which ended in 1783. Gardner first went to sea in May 1782 on the *Panther* and was present at battles between the English and the combined French and Spanish fleet off Gibraltar and Cape Spartel in 1782. The fighting in which he took part involved the European allies of the Americans, particularly the French. As Gardner's memoirs indicate, the capture of trading ships belonging to the enemy was as much a part of maritime combat as the direct confrontation between military ships equipped specifically for war.

The following excerpts are from *Recollections of James Anthony Gardner,* ed. Sir R. Vesey Hamilton and John Knox Laughton, in Publications of the Navy Records Society, vol. 31 (London: Navy Records Society, 1946), 19–26, 30–36, 64–68, 74–78, 83–85, 88–90.

> When I remember all
>     The friends so link'd together,
> I've seen around me fall,
>     Like leaves in windy weather;
>     I feel like one

Who treads alone
Some banquet-hall deserted,
Whose lights are fled,
Whose garlands dead,
And all but me departed.
Thus in the stilly night,
Ere slumber's chain has bound me,
Sad memory brings the light
Of other days around me.
— MOORE.[1]

When I was on board the Boreas and Conqueror with my father I had nothing to do with the midshipmen,[2] as I lived in the gunroom[3] of the former and wardroom[4] of the latter. But in this ship I took my degrees (not as a doctor of Oxford, thank God!) but as a midshipman in the cockpit of H.M. ship Panther, with some of the best fellows that ever graced the British navy. I joined her early in 1782 fitting in Portsmouth Harbour, commanded by Captain Thomas Piercy of glorious memory. I had eleven shillings given me by some friends in Gosport, and I thought my fortune was made.

On my introduction to my new shipmates I was shown down to the starboard wing berth.[5] I had not been long seated before a rugged-muzzled midshipman came in, and having eyed me for a short time, he sang out with a voice of thunder: "Blister my tripes[6] — where the hell did you come from? I suppose you want to stick your grinders (for it was near dinner-time) into some of our a la mode beef;" and without waiting for a reply, he sat down and sang a song that I shall remember as long as I live. The first verse, being the most moral, I shall give:

A Duchess from Germany
Has lately made her will;
Her body she's left to be buried,
Her soul to the devil in hell.

---

[1] MOORE: Edward Moore (1712–1757), author of the comedy *Gil Blas* (1751).
[2] *midshipmen:* In the navy, the rank between that of cadet and the lowest of commissioned officers.
[3] *gunroom:* A compartment for the accommodation of junior officers.
[4] *wardroom:* The mess cabin (or dining room) of the navy's commissioned officers.
[5] *starboard wing berth:* The starboard is the right-hand side of a ship; Gardner's berth is his personal sleeping and storage accommodation.
[6] *tripes:* Innards, bowels.

"Jack in the Bilboes," by William Ward, from a painting by George Mor-
land, ca. 1790. This engraving shows a waterman — one of the seamen who
operated the light boats generally used in river traffic — being "pressed" into
service on a ship. Courtesy of the National Maritime Museum, London.

This gentleman's name was Watson; and notwithstanding the song
and his blunt manner of speaking, he proved to be a very good fellow, and was the life and soul of the mess.

I must now describe our starboard wing berth and compare it with
the manners and customs of the present day. In this ship our mess-
place had canvas screens scrubbed white, wainscot tables, well polished, Windsor chairs, and a pantry fitted in the wing to stow our
crockery and dinner traps[7] with safety. The holystones and hand or-

---

[7] *traps:* Equipment for dining.

gans,[8] in requisition twice a week, made our orlop[9] deck as white as the boards of any crack drawing-room, the strictest attention being paid to cleanliness; and everything had the appearance of Spartan simplicity. We used to sit down to a piece of salt beef, with sour krout, and dine gloriously with our pint of black-strap[10] after, ready at all calls, and as fit for battle as for muster.[11] Here mark the difference. The cockpit[12] abandoned, and my lords and gentlemen ushered into the gunroom fitted up in luxurious style, with window curtains, blinds, buffets, wine coolers, silver forks, and many other appendages of that delicate nature, unknown in the good old times; and, if I am correctly informed, a brass knocker fixed at the gunroom door, which ever and anon announces the approach of the mighty members with as much pomp as a Roman consul with his lictors[13] thundering at the door for admittance. But enough of this. When war comes we shall see.

When I joined the Panther, Mr. Price, the purser,[14] who I knew nothing of, furnished me with everything I stood in need of, as the ship was hurried off to join Lord Howe and I had not time to get fitted out. When the ship was paid,[15] he refused to take any remuneration when I called to repay the obligation, but said he would do the same again with pleasure. I stand indebted to his kindness, which I shall remember for ever with heartfelt gratitude and respect for his memory, and grieved I am that the service should have lost so good an officer, lamented by every person who had the pleasure of his acquaintance.

We sailed (I think) in May with the grand fleet under Lord Howe, to cruise in the North Sea after the Dutch.[16] On our arrival in the Downs, Captain Piercy, from ill health, left the ship, to the great

---

[8] *holystones and hand organs:* The holystone was a soft sandstone used to scrub the decks of ships. "Hand organ" probably refers here to a cleaning implement used with the holystone.

[9] *orlop:* The floor or deck covering the hold of the ship.

[10] *black-strap:* Red wine.

[11] *muster:* An assembly of men for inspection in the military.

[12] *cockpit:* The after part of the orlop deck in a man-of-war; sometimes used for housing junior officers, and in combat used for tending to the wounded.

[13] *lictors:* Attendant officers.

[14] *purser:* An officer aboard ship who has control over provisions, as well as accounts.

[15] *ship was paid:* At the end of a voyage, the crew received its pay, in many cases, the proceeds from cargos captured in battle.

[16] *North Sea after the Dutch:* The Dutch entered the war in 1780.

regret of every officer and man on board, and was succeeded in the command by Captain Robert Simonton.

> Nor he unworthy to conduct the host,
> Yet still they mourned their ancient leader lost.
>                 — *Iliad.*

. . . About the middle of July, in the Bay of Biscay[17] we took, after a long chase, three prizes,[18] the Pigmy cutter,[19] Hermione victualler,[20] with ninety bullocks[21] for the combined fleet, and a brig[22] laden with salt. A day or two after, when blowing very hard and under a close-reefed main topsail and foresail,[23] on the starboard tack,[24] a fleet was seen to leeward[25] on the beam and lee bow.[26] The commodore made the private signal which was not answered, and then the signal for an enemy and to wear and make sail on the other tack. Wore accordingly, and set close-reefed topsails, with fore and main tacks[27] on board, which worked the old ship most charmingly. In loosing the mizen[28] topsail, and before letting it fall, I slipped my foot from the horse[29] and fell off the yard[30] into the top, and saved my life by catching hold of the clewline,[31] having fallen from the bunt[32] of the sail. The captain saw this and gave me a terrible rub down for not taking more care of myself. One of the prizes (the brig with salt) was

---

[17] *Bay of Biscay:* A bay on the Mediterranean off the west coast of France, also bordering Spain.

[18] *prizes:* Enemy ships, often merchant ships with cargo, taken during wartime.

[19] *cutter:* A small oared boat used for conveying stores or passengers to a ship.

[20] *victualler:* A ship that carries provisions for a fleet.

[21] *bullocks:* Cattle. Given the lack of refrigeration, it was common to carry livestock on board.

[22] *brig:* A ship with two masts.

[23] *close-reefed . . . foresail:* To reef a sail was to bind it close, so as to offer the least amount of wind resistance. The topsail was the upper-most, and the foresail was the main sail of the foremast.

[24] *starboard tack:* The wind is coming from the starboard side of the ship.

[25] *leeward:* The side of the ship away from the wind.

[26] *beam and lee bow:* Beams were the horizontal timbers that held the ship together, hence "beam" designated the side of the ship. A fleet is sighted off the side and bow of the ship that is away from the wind.

[27] *fore and main tacks:* Tacks were the ropes used to attach the corners of the ship's lower sails to its sides; the fore tack belonged to the foresail; the main belonged to the mainsail, or the principal sail of the ship.

[28] *mizen:* The aftermost mast on the ship.

[29] *horse:* Foot rope.

[30] *yard:* A long, slender rod that crosses the mast to support a sail.

[31] *clewline:* The line attaching the clew, or lower corner of a sail, to the yard or mast.

[32] *bunt:* Middle part.

retaken. The next morning, the weather being moderate, saw the enemy about three leagues to leeward. Sent down one of our frigates, the Monsieur who sailed remarkably well, to reconnoitre; in the evening they were out of sight. Soon after, we fell in with the Sandwich, 90, Vice-Admiral Sir Peter Parker (white at the fore), with the Count de Grasse[33] on board a prisoner, and a large convoy[34] from the West Indies bound to England. Parted company from Sir Peter. Several ships of the line joined our squadron, which proceeded to cruise off the coast of Ireland for a short time, and then returned to Spithead,[35] where we found the grand fleet fitting for the relief of Gibraltar.[36] Caught fire in the marine storeroom near the after magazine,[37] which damaged several knapsacks before it could be got under. We had only one boat alongside, the others being absent getting off the stores from the dockyard. A quartermaster's wife and three others jumped out of one of the lower-deck ports into this boat, and casting off the painter[38] pulled away for the hospital beach as well as any bargemen, leaving their husbands to take care of themselves.

August the 29th, one of our fleet, the Royal George, 100, Rear-Admiral Kempenfelt (blue[39] at the mizen), being on a careen,[40] to the astonishment of every person upset at Spithead, and more than two thirds of her crew drowned, and among the number that brave and meritorious officer Admiral Kempenfelt, a man that has never been surpassed as an able tactician. We saved twenty-seven of her hands. One of them told a curious story. He said he was boat-keeper of the pinnace,[41] whose painter was fast to the stern-ladder; and just as the ship was going over, the hairdresser took a flying leap out of the stern gallery with a powder bag in his hand and had nearly jumped into his boat. He was so much alarmed that he could not cast off the painter,

---

[33] *Count de Grasse:* The captured commander in chief of the French fleet.

[34] *convoy:* Ships would travel in convoys, escorted by man-of-wars, for protection in wartime.

[35] *Spithead:* A well-traveled sea passage between Portsmouth, on the southern coast of England, and the Isle of Wight.

[36] *Gibraltar:* An important fortress and sea port still held by the British.

[37] *magazine:* Storage area.

[38] *painter:* The rope attached to the bow of a shop or boat, used to make it fast.

[39] *blue:* For more than two hundred years, the British Fleet had three divisions, each with its own flag or ensign. Merchant marines carried a red ensign, the Royal Navy a white ensign, and the Naval Reserves a blue.

[40] *careen:* The position of a ship laid over or tipping to one side.

[41] *pinnace:* A small, light-weight boat, usually eight-oared, belonging to a man-of-war.

nor could he find his knife to cut it, and was obliged to jump and swim for his life, when our boat picked him up. His own boat went down with the ship. It was a sad sight to see the dead bodies floating about Spithead by scores until we sailed. The poor admiral and several officers were never found. Captain Waghorn (the admiral's captain) was saved and tried by a court martial and acquitted. God knows who the blame ought to light on, for blame there must have been somewhere, for never was a ship lost in such a strange and unaccountable manner. The ship might have been weighed[42] had proper steps been taken. A stupid attempt was made, but failed, as well it might; for neither officers nor men exerted themselves. The Royal William and Diligente were placed one on each side, and would have raised her, but energy was wanting, and there she remains, a disgrace to this day.

Lord Howe having hoisted his flag (blue at the main) on board the Victory, 110, and the fleet being ready, the signal was made on the 11th of September to get under way, and that we were to take charge of the convoy as commodore[43] with a broad blue pennant, and the Buffalo, 60, to bring up the rear. The convoy consisted of fifty sail of victuallers for the relief, with which we went through the Needles[44] and joined the grand fleet at the back of the Isle of Wight, the Bristol, 50, and East India fleet under her charge, in company. In forming the line of battle the Goliath was to lead on the starboard tack and the Vengeance on the larboard. The fleet consisted of thirty-four sail of the line, besides frigates,[45] and their names I shall give when I come to the action with the combined fleets. We had moderate weather down Channel, and the number of convoys collected, and under the protection of the grand fleet to a certain distance, made up several hundred sail, which cut a fine appearance.

But, when the fleet got well into the Bay of Biscay, things began to alter, the wind shifting to the SW, with heavy squalls, which increased from a gale to a furious hurricane. I remember being at dinner in the wardroom when the height of the gale came on, the ship being under a close-reefed main topsail, and a very heavy sea running, which made her labour prodigiously. Our third lieutenant

---

[42] *weighed:* Raised up.

[43] *commodore:* Commanding officer. In the British navy this was usually a temporary title given to the officer in charge of a detached squadron.

[44] *the Needles:* A cluster of rocks, eighteen miles off Newport on the Isle of Wight.

[45] *frigates:* A small, lightweight vessel, quick but not big enough to carry many guns or a large cargo.

(Montagu) came down and said: "Gentlemen, prepare for bad weather; the admiral has handed[46] his main topsail and hove to under storm staysails."[47] Our main topsail was not handed ten minutes before she gave a roll that beggared all description; "chaos seemed to have come again," and it appeared doubtful whether she would right. The quarter-deck guns were out of sight from this lee lurch, and the weather roll was equally terrible. The scuttle butts[48] broke adrift and were stove;[49] a lower-deck gun started and with great difficulty was secured; one of our poor fellows was lost overboard, and serious apprehensions were entertained for the safety of the ship, who cut such dreadful capers that we expected she would founder. I must here mention that when the Panther came from abroad, the devil tempted the navy board to order her proper masts to be taken out, and [a] fifty-gun ship's placed in their room, and this occasioned her to roll so dreadfully. It was in this gale that the Ville de Paris, Glorieux, Hector, Centaur, and others were lost on their passage to England from the West Indies. It lasted a considerable time, and it was near the middle of October before the fleet entered the Gut of Gibraltar. . . .

I had a very narrow escape while standing on the quarter deck with Captain Forrester of the marines. The first lieutenant (the late Admiral Alexander Fraser) came up to us, and while speaking a shot passed between us and stuck on the larboard[50] side of the quarter deck. We were very close at the time, so that it could only have been a few inches from us. It knocked the speaking-trumpet out of Fraser's hand, and seemed to have electrified Captain Forrester and myself. The shot was cut out and weighed either 12 or 18 pounds — I forget which. Our rigging fore and aft was cut to pieces; the booms[51] and boats also, and every timber-head on the forecastle,[52] with the sheet and spare anchor stocks,[53] were shot away, and the fluke[54] of the latter. Our side, from the foremost gun to the after, was like a riddle, and it was astonishing that we had not more killed and wounded. Several shot-holes were under water, and our worthy old carpenter

---

[46] *handed:* Furled.
[47] *staysails:* Triangular sails.
[48] *scuttle butts:* Large casks for holding water.
[49] *stove:* Broken.
[50] *larboard:* The left-hand side of the ship.
[51] *boom:* A spar or rod extending out from the base of a sail.
[52] *forecastle:* A small, raised deck at the fore of the ship.
[53] *anchor stocks:* The metal cross-bar perpendicular to and intersecting with the main shaft of the anchor.
[54] *fluke:* The broad, triangular pieces of metal at the ends of the anchor stock.

(Mr. Cock) had very near been killed in the wing, and was knocked down by a splinter, but not materially hurt. The enemy set off in the night and could only be seen from the masthead in the morning. It was supposed they went for Cadiz.

A curious circumstance took place during the action. Two of the boys who had gone down for powder fell out in consequence of one attempting to take the box from the other, when a regular fight took place. It was laughable to see them boxing on the larboard side, and the ship in hot action on the starboard. One of our poor fellows was cut in two by a double-headed shot on the main deck, and the lining of his stomach (about the size of a pancake) stuck on the side of the launch, which was stowed amidships on the main deck with the sheep inside.[55] The butcher who had the care of them, observing what was on the side of the boat, began to scrape it off with his nails, saying, "Who the devil would have thought the fellow's paunch would have stuck so? I'm damned if I don't think it's glued on!"

We had a fellow by the name of Mulligan who ran from his quarters and positively hid in the coppers![56] and had put on the drummer's jacket. When the firing had ceased he was seen coming out, and was taken for the poor drummer, and ran forward taking off the jacket, which he hid in the round house; but one of the boatswain's mates observed the transaction and Mr. Mulligan got well flogged just as the action was over. The poor drummer had greatly distinguished himself, and had taken off his jacket in the heat of the action, which this fellow stole to hide his rascality. . . .

A court martial was held on board the Dunkirk on one of our midshipmen (Mr. Foularton) on some trifling charge brought against him by Lieutenant Hanwell of the Dublin, on which he was fully acquitted. One of our main-top men (Martin Anguin), in sending down the topgallant mast, fell from the fore part of the main topmast crosstrees and pitched on the collar of the main stay, from which he went down, astern of the barge upon the booms, into the hold, the gratings being off. He was sent to the hospital without a fractured limb, but much bruised about the breast. He recovered and came on board to receive his pay on the day the ship was paid off. Such a fall and to escape with life, I believe is not to be found in the annals of naval his-

---

[55] *sheep inside:* The sheep would have been part of the ship's live provisions.
[56] *coppers:* Large vessels made of copper or iron and used for cooking and doing laundry aboard ship.

tory. Hoisted the flag (blue at the fore) of Vice-Admiral Milbanke as port admiral, second in command.

The peace soon after taking place, a mutiny broke out in the men of war, and some of the ships began to unrig without orders, and were in a high state of insubordination, particularly the Blenheim, Crown, Standard, Medway, and Artois. I do not remember that any examples were made, but this I am sure of, that the ringleaders richly deserved hanging. Having received orders we dismantled the ship and struck Admiral Milbanke's flag, and in a few days after the old Panther was paid off to the great regret of every officer on board. It was like the parting of a family who had lived long together in the strictest friendship; and while writing this, it brings to mind many circumstances that make me bitterly lament the inroads death has made among those worthy fellows. . . .

Before closing my account of the Panther, I must relate a few anecdotes that happened during the time I belonged to her. I was placed with another youngster, by the name of Owen, under the tuition of the captains of the fore and main top. We were both in the same watch, which we kept first in one top and then in the other, to learn to knot and splice and to reef a sail; and for their attention we remunerated them with our grog. I remember the captain of the fore top (Joe Moulding), a very droll fellow, teaching us what he called a catechism, which we were obliged to repeat to him at two bells in every middle watch. It was as follows:

> So fine the Conflustions!! of old Mother Damnable, who jumped off the fore topsail yard and filled the main topgallant sail; run down the lee leach of the mizen and hauled the main tack on board, that all the devils in hell could not raise it; clapped a sheep-shank on the main mast, a bowline knot on the foremast, and an overhand knot on the mizen mast; run the keel athwart ships, coiled the cables in the binnacle, tossed the quarter deck overboard, and made a snug ship for that night; when up jumped the little boy Fraser with a handspike stuck in his jaws to fend the seas off, with which he beat them into peas porridge, and happy was the man who had the longest spoon. AMEN!![57]

After repeating this rigmarole we were obliged to start up to the mast head, if topgallant yards were across to blow the dust out of the

---

[57] *So fine . . . AMEN!!:* This piece echoes a comic speech attributed to the English actor and playwright Samuel Foote.

topgallant clueline[58] blocks.[59] One night, blowing and raining like the devil, I proposed to Owen about five bells in the middle watch to steal down out of the top and take the raisins that were intended for the pudding next day. When we got down to our berth we found the raisins were mixed with the flour and we had the devil's own job to pick them out. After filling our pockets, one of the watch came down for grog and found us out. We ran off as fast as we could and got in the weather main rigging, where poor Owen was caught, seized up and made a spread eagle of[60] for the remainder of the watch and part of the next. I made my escape and remained some time on the collar of the main stay, until all was quiet. One of the watch came up, but not finding me in the top gave over chase; but I got cobbed[61] in the morning, and no pudding for dinner.

While in Hamoaze[62] we had a draught of Irish Volunteers, about sixty in number. One of them was seven feet high, and when the hands were turned up to muster on the quarter deck, he stood like Saul the King of Israel, with head and shoulders above the host. This man used to head his countrymen when on shore upon leave, and was the terror of the people about Dock,[63] particularly North Corner Street, flourishing an Irish shillelah[64] of enormous size, [so] that the constables when called out would fly like chaff at the very sight of him. He was, like the rest of his countrymen, honest and brave, and very inoffensive, but woe betide those that insulted him. Being in the dockyard returning stores, some of the shipwrights called him a walking flagstaff; for which compliment he gave two or three of them a terrible beating, and then challenged to fight twelve of the best men among them, taking two a day, but the challenge was not accepted from so queer a customer.

The night before we were paid off our ship's company gave a grand supper and the lower deck was illuminated. Several female visitors were of the party from Castlerag[65] and other fashionable places, who danced jigs and reels the whole of the night, with plenty of grog

---

[58] *topgallant clueline: Topgallant* refers to a sail; for *clueline*, see footnote 31.

[59] *blocks:* Pulleys.

[60] *made a spread eagle of:* Tied up with arms and legs stretched out.

[61] *cobbed:* "Cobbing" involved being struck on the posterior a specific number of times with a heavy instrument made for that purpose.

[62] *Hamoaze:* A western division of Plymouth Sound, at the mouth of the Tamar River, Hamoaze formed an important passage for the British navy at Devonport.

[63] *Dock:* The town of Devonport.

[64] *shillelah:* Club.

[65] *Castlerag:* A port town in Ireland.

and flip;[66] and what was remarkable, not a soul was drunk in the morning. . . .

## Edgar

Early in 1787 I joined the Edgar, a guard-ship in Portsmouth Harbour — Charles Thompson, Esq., captain, formerly of the Boreas. . . .

Coming out of his cabin early one morning in a great hurry, he fell over a signal lantern, and was going to play hell with the lieutenant of the watch for having lanterns upon deck at that time of day — about half-past two in the morning. The Crown being out of her station, he was going to make the signal for an officer from that ship, and going to the office to write the order he could not get in, the clerk having the key; which put him into such a rage that he swore he would flog the clerk and those that wrote under him. However, his rage abated and he did not make the signal, it blowing very hard; but he would not suffer the clerk or his under-scribes to show themselves in the office while his flag was flying. . . .

He was a mortal foe to puppyism,[67] and one of our midshipmen going aloft with gloves on, attracted his eye; for which he got such a rub down that I am certain he remembers to the present day, although he is a post captain, and as proud as the devil, without any reason. Another of his freaks was threatening to have a bowl put upon our heads and our hair cut round in the newest fashion by that measure. He told one of our midshipmen (Pringle) who was a very stout man and who happened to be in his way when looking at the compass, "That he was too big for a midshipman but would do very well as a scuttle butt," and, Pringle having his hands in his pockets, he was going to send for the tailor to sew them up. When he first came on board to muster, a little before we sailed, everyone was dressed in full uniform to receive him. He took notice of this, and with a smile (a lurking devil in it), complimented us on our good looks, at the same time observing, "You knew who was coming; but notwithstanding your looking so well, I think I can see a little rust on you yet which I shall endeavour to rub off."

Our captain was as gruff as the devil, and had a voice like a mastiff whose growling would be heard superior to the storm. He was very particular respecting dress as the following order will shew: —

[66] *flip:* A mixture of beer and spirits, sweetened with sugar and heated with a hot iron.

[67] *puppyism:* Affectation of fashionable apparel or manners.

*Memo:* —
> If any officer shall so far forget himself as to appear when on shore without his uniform, I shall regard it as a mark of his being ashamed of his profession and discharge him from the ship accordingly.
>
> (Signed) CHARLES THOMPSON,
> Captain.

He had very near caught some of us in Middle Street, Gosport, but fortunately an alley was at no great distance through which we made a hasty but safe retreat, and by that means prevented a few vacancies for midshipmen taking place in the Edgar. . . .

Like all ships we had some droll hands, and with the exception of about half a dozen, all good and worthy fellows. One or two of the half dozen I shall mention, and begin with Geo. Wangford, who had been in the Boreas, and was a follower of the captain. He was an immoderate drinker, and from his fiery countenance had the nickname of Bardolph.[68] While in the Edgar his mother died and left him one thousand pounds. He lived about six months after receiving the money in one scene of debauchery; and with the assistance of a noted prostitute, named Poll Palmer, in that short time made away with nearly five hundred pounds. I remember his being taken ill after a hard drinking match, and then he got religious and requested one of the midshipmen (Patrick Flood), another strange fish, to read the Bible to him. This Patrick readily agreed to; but before he got through a chapter pretended to have a violent pain in his stomach, upon which Wangford requested him to take capillaire[69] and brandy, and that he would join him, and desired that, in mixing, two thirds should be brandy. Flood was immediately cured, and began to read a chapter in Job; and when he came to that part, "Then Job answered and said," Wangford started up and roared out — "that I am going to hell before the wind." I lay close by them and heard every word. He soon after turned to upon Hollands,[70] his favourite beverage, and thought no more of Job or the Bible. Soon after he was sent to the hospital, where he remained some time and died mad. A little before his death Pringle (one of the midshipmen) went to see him, and while sitting on the foot of his bed he started up and seized hold of Pringle by the hair singing out, "—— —— ——, catch that bird"; the other calling out for the nurse to assist him, which was of little use for he

---

[68] *Bardolph:* A comic character in Shakespeare's *Henry IV* and *Henry V*, known for his red face and heavy drinking.
[69] *capillaire:* An herb-based medicinal syrup.
[70] *Hollands:* A grain spirit manufactured in Holland.

nearly broke her arm before others came up to secure him. Several of us attended his funeral.

Our time passed cheerfully in the harbour; plenty of fun and going on shore. One night several of us supped in the main hatchway berth on the orlop deck, when old Andrew Macbride, the schoolmaster[71] (a man of splendid abilities but unfortunately given to drinking, though the goodness of his heart made him much respected and did away in a great measure with that infirmity) on this occasion got so drunk that Ned Moore (my worthy messmate) handed him a couple of tumblers of the juice of red pickled cabbage and told him it was brandy and water, which he drank without taking the least notice. I believe it did him good as an aperient,[72] for he was cruising about all night and next day, and could not imagine what it was that affected him so.

One of our midshipmen (Millar), as worthy a fellow as ever lived, told me the following anecdote of himself and Macbride. On his joining the Hector, 74, a guard-ship in Portsmouth Harbour, Morgan, the first lieutenant, came up to him and said, "Millar, my boy, how glad I am to see you. You must dine with me to-day." Millar, who had never seen him before, thought it rather queer that he should be so friendly at first sight; however, he accepted the invitation. When dinner was over, Morgan declared that he was under a great obligation to him and that he should at all times be happy to acknowledge it. Poor Millar said he was really at a loss to understand him. "Well then," says Morgan, "I'll tell you. It is this. I was considered the ugliest son of a bitch in the fleet before you came on board, but you beat me dead hollow, and surely you cannot wonder at my being sensible of the obligation." Millar laughed heartily, and they were ever after on the best terms. It happened in about three months after this, Macbride also joined the Hector. The moment he came on board, down came the quartermaster to Millar saying that Lieutenant Morgan wanted to see him immediately. As soon as Millar came on the quarter-deck, Morgan went up to him and wished him joy; and pointing to Macbride observed, "You, Millar, are a happy dog for being relieved so soon. I was considered the ugliest son of a bitch in the fleet for more than a year; you then came on board and outdid me; but there stands one that beggars all description, and if they were to rake hell they could not find his fellow." Then going and shaking

---

[71] *schoolmaster:* Because many boys were apprenticed to work at sea (as was Frances Burney's older brother, James), it was customary to provide a schoolmaster for their education.

[72] *aperient:* A laxative.

Macbride by the hand, asked him and Millar to dine with him that day to celebrate the happy relief.

Poor Andrew once made a vow that he would not get drunk, and said that not only the taste but the smell of the liquor was so disagreeable that he could not bear to stay where it was. He also gave Watson, the boatswain, leave to thrash him with his cane if ever he found him drunk. Poor fellow, he kept his promise for about three months, and then turned to as bad as ever, and Watson did not forget to give him a lacing with his cane, which occasioned the following song written by John Macredie: —

> Of all the delights that a mortal can taste,
> A bottle of liquor is surely the best;
> Possessed of that treasure my hours sweetly glide,
> Oh! there's nothing like grog, says sweet Andrew Macbride.
>
> When I sit in my school I think my time lost
> Where with dry sines[73] and tangents my temper is crossed;
> But how sweetly I smile with the glass by my side:
> Grog helps mathematics, says Andrew Macbride.
>
> The boatswain, God damn him, would fain me control
> With a promise when sober I made like a fool;
> With his cursed rattan he so curried my hide,
> That I'll drink his damnation, says Andrew Macbride.
>
> When the sweet powers of grog have my reason betrayed,
> And free from sad care on the deck I am laid,
> Then the boys black my face, and my actions deride;
> The whelps may be damned, says Andrew Macbride.
>
> From the raptures of grog shall a sage be controlled,
> And a man like myself submit to be schooled?
> If I'm drunk, the lieutenant and captain may chide;
> But I'll drink till I die, says sweet Andrew Macbride.
>
> When I said the smell hurt me, the fools did believe;
> Och hone! my dear friends, I did you deceive;
> When the taste or smell hurts me, may hell open wide,
> And I, damned there with water to drink, says Macbride.

Nothing disrespectful was intended by this song. Every officer in the ship was a friend to poor Andrew, and Macredie would have been one of the first to resent an insult offered to him. . . .

[73] *sines:* A term from trigonometry.

We had a custom when the officers were at dinner in the ward-room, of dividing into parties; one division was to storm the other on the poop. In one of those attacks I succeeded in getting on the poop, when Kiel (who I have mentioned before) attacked me with a fixed bayonet and marked me in the thigh (all in good part). I then got hold of a musket, put in a small amount of powder, and as he advanced, I fired. To my horror and amazement he fell flat on the deck, and when picked up his face was as black as a tinker's,[74] with the blood running down occasioned by some of the grains of powder sticking in. I shall never forget the terror I was in, but thank God he soon got well; only a few blue spots remained in his phiz, which never left him. This was the only time I ever fired a musket and probably will be the last. They used to say in the cockpit that he was troubled with St. Anthony's fire[75] (alluding to my name).

Another time when attacking the poop, I was standing on one of the quarter-deck guns, when I received a violent blow on the face from a broomstick, which made my nose bleed off and on for several days. It was thrown at me by J. S. Carden (now Captain Carden) and a hand swab[76] was thrown at him, which falling short, entered one of the office windows, which put an end to the attack. It was laughable to see John Macredie take the part of Ajax Telamon,[77] with a half-port[78] for a shield and a boarding-pike[79] for a lance. Culverhouse used to take the part of Diomede,[80] but instead of a lance would use the single-stick,[81] with which he was superior to anyone in the fleet. He was a very clever fellow, full of fun and drollery, and sung humorous songs in the most comic style. I remember a verse or two of one:

[74] *tinker's:* A term applied to gypsies, who often plied the trade of tinker, or a mender of small household utensils, such as pots and kettles. "Black" was often used to refer to any skin darker than the fair, English standard.

[75] *St. Anthony's fire:* A common name for the contagious disease called, in modern terminology, erysipelas, which causes fever and widespread inflammation of the skin.

[76] *hand swab:* A mop used for scrubbing the decks.

[77] *Ajax Telamon:* Along with Achilles, one of the bravest of Greek heroes at the battle of Troy in Homer's *Iliad*.

[78] *half-port:* A particular kind of shutter for a porthole, out of which the muzzle of a gun could extend.

[79] *boarding-pike:* A spiked instrument used to board enemy ships.

[80] *Diomede:* One of the Greek princes who fought alongside Ajax and Achilles.

[81] *single-stick:* A wooden stick used onboard ships for teaching crew members how to use the cutlass.

When first they impressed[82] me and sent me to sea,
'Twas in the winter time in the making of hay,
They sent me on board of a ship called Torbay,
Oh! her white muzzle guns they did sore frighten me,
    Musha tudey, etc.

Says the boatswain to Paddy, And what brought you here?
For the making of hay 'tis the wrong time of year.
By Jasus, says Paddy, I wish I was gone,
For your small wooden kingdom I don't understand.
    Musha tudey, etc.

Oh! the first thing they gave me it was a long sack,
Which they tould me to get in and lay on my back;
I lay on my back till the clock struck one bell,
And the man overhead he sung out, All is well.
    Musha tudey, etc.

We had a very droll midshipman who lately died an old post captain, and was one of the best officers in the service. This gentleman was a kind of ventriloquist, and when we sat in the officers' seat in Gosport chapel, and opposite to old Paul the clerk, of beer-drinking memory, whenever this man would begin to sing, the other would go Quack, Quack, Quack; sometimes high and sometimes low, according as the clerk would sing the psalm. I have seen the old fellow look round with amazement, the people whispering to one another, while others could not keep their countenance but would hold their heads down and laugh. I remember him coming on board late one night in a wherry[83] from Gosport,[84] and it being calm we could hear him quacking a long way off. We then lay at the Hardway moorings. When the wherry got alongside the waterman swore he would be damned sooner than have that chap in his boat again. Had he known as much, he would not have taken him off for any money; he certainly was the devil or his near relation, for some hell-hound or other had been following him on the water all the way from Burrow Castle (near the Magazine and reported to be haunted) until he got alongside. He said he knew that Burrow Castle was haunted and he'd take

---

[82] *impressed:* The British navy replenished its forces through the practice of pressing, a kind of legalized kidnapping. Press gangs working for the navy would seize upon able-bodied men who could not prove their status as a "house-holder" — that is, one who had a permanent address — and "press" them into service on ships.

[83] *wherry:* A light boat, usually used in river traffic.

[84] *Gosport:* A market town on the west side of Portsmouth Harbor.

good care to return on the other side of the harbour, and blast him if he'd ever come that way at night. I had the watch upon deck at the time and remember every word, and I thought I should have died a-laughing. . . .

Our first lieutenant was a devil for scrubbing decks, and in the dead of winter we frequently had to shovel the snow from the quarter-deck, and take a spell, about half-past four in the morning, with the holystone and hand organs, while the water would freeze as soon as it was thrown on the deck. The general order, made into rhyme by Flood [was] as follows:

> The decks, as usual, to be washed and scrubbed;
> And with the holystone severely rubbed.

To show the superstition of sailors I must mention the following anecdote. Not a hundred miles from Portsmouth lived a great nabob,[85] who formerly possessed a large fortune, but from gambling and other bad management had greatly fallen off, and the neighbours used to say he had dealings with the devil, and at night would converse with him in his cellar. We have a raven on board that came from this neighbourhood; and from the number of strange pranks it was in the habit of playing, was supposed by the ship's company not to have been one of this world; and what strengthened this opinion was Macredie giving it out that he had heard the raven speak, and say that he had been the nabob's coachman, and should resume his office as soon as the ship was paid off, and he had got some recruits for his master. This made him be looked at with an evil eye by the ship's company; and one evening when the provisions were serving out and several of the people were in the cockpit about the steward's room, the raven caught hold of the gunner's mate by the trowsers, croaking and snapping at his legs. He then flew on the shoulder of the corporal of marines, took off his hat and hid it in the tier.[86] "I'm damned," says old Phillips, the quartermaster, "if he has not marked you for his master." He had hardly said this when the raven came hopping back and seized upon the cheese belonging to the quartermaster, and walked off with a large piece of it, the other being afraid to follow.

Another of his tricks I was an eye-witness to. Our sergeant of marines had leave to go on shore, and was on the poop showing a

---

[85] *nabob:* Usually someone who had returned from India with a fortune.
[86] *tier:* A row of guns on a man-of-war.

half-guinea to the corporal, saying "With this bit of gold I shall take a cruise, it will last as long as I like to stay." He was holding the half-guinea between his finger and thumb, and asked the raven, who was on the poop, if he would take a trip with him. Ralph, ever on the watch, in an instant snapped the half-guinea out of his hand, and flew up to the main topmast head and remained more than an hour aloft, the sergeant all the time in the greatest anxiety, and some of the fellows saying to him, "Now, don't you believe he's the devil?" At last the raven flew down upon the booms and went into the stern sheets of the barge lying there and hid the half-guinea, which the sergeant found, but swore it was not the same that was taken from him, while several called out "Sold! Sold!"

I shall now conclude the Edgar after saying a word for Davy Reed, the master. He was what we call a hard officer, as well as a very strange sort of fish, and had the misfortune, like many others, to lose his teeth. I was at dinner in the wardroom when a small parcel was handed in directed for Mr. Reed. "What the hell can this be?" says Davy (who did not like to have sixpence to pay the waterman[87]), "and who gave it to you?" continued he. "Sir," says the waterman, "it was a young lady who sent it off from Common Hard." As several tricks had been played with Davy before, he was afraid to open the parcel, and begged of one of the officers at the table to do so for him, but when opened, what was his amazement to find a set of sheep's teeth for David Reed, Esq., with directions for fixing, and a box of tooth powder that, by the smell, appeared to be a mixture of everything abominable. Poor Davy was in a dreadful rage, and never heard the last of it. The Edgar was paid off in January 1790, and we had a parting dinner at the India Arms, Gosport, and kept it up until twelve that night. With the exception of the half dozen, they were some of the best fellows I ever met with. The Edgar was commissioned immediately after by Captain Anthony James Pye Molloy, and some of the midshipmen rejoined her.

---

[87] *waterman:* This term could refer to a seaman or, more specifically, to one who operated a wherry. Because the teeth came from shore, the latter is the more likely meaning.

# EDWARD BOSCAWEN

## Waging War against France

Edward Boscawen (1711–1761) was the third son of Hugh, first viscount of Falmouth. His mother was related to the duke of Marlborough. He took part in a victorious battle with the French in 1746, in which he was severely wounded by a musket ball in the shoulder, and was shortly thereafter appointed commander in chief by sea and land of the king's forces in the East Indies. In 1755 he was appointed to command a squadron ordered to North America to stop French reinforcements from reaching their colonies in Canada. At the time when Admiral Boscawen was writing the letters reprinted here, the French and Engish were technically at peace. In 1748 the tenuous Peace of Aix-la-Chapelle ended war between the two countries, but continuing clashes in North America made this truce shakey at best. Boscawen was given orders to provoke renewed conflict with the French; the naval maneuvers described in the following letters led to the Seven Years War, declared in 1756, with England and Prussia allied against France. Boscawen took two French vessels — the *Lys* and the *Alcide* — but missed the main fleet. What constituted an act of war was, in fact, a debatable point in the eighteenth century, but when the French minister in London was told of the admiral's orders, he replied that the French would take Boscawen's acting on his orders as a declaration of war. Boscawen's military aggression prior to an official declaration of war caused some embarrassment for George II in the international community — and the British did not even achieve the benefit of preventing reinforcements from reaching Canada. In the final analysis, it was not so much Boscawen's intervention that led to the eventual British victory as the British navy's disruption of French commercial shipping in 1755, which had seriously damaged French power at sea. After his crucial attack on the *Lys* and *Alcide*, Boscawen was forced to seek harbor for the health of his men, among whom a violent "fever" raged. Before his squadron reached England again, about two thousand men had died of this illness.

Boscawen had a clear economic interest in the war. The financial rewards of commanding a man-of-war depended on the "prizes" he took; that is, he kept a percentage of the profits made from capturing enemy vessels, both military and merchant. His epitaph refers to Hatchlands Park, his estate in Surrey, as "just finished at the expense of the enemies of his country." Boscawen was popularly known for his courage in battle and his concern for and efforts to improve the health of his men.

Portrait of Edward Boscawen ca. 1754, engraved after Allan Ramsay. Courtesy of the National Maritime Museum, London.

He married France Glanville in 1742 and had three sons and two daughters; the third son, George Evelyn, succeeded his uncle as Viscount Falmouth. The following letters are from *Boscawen's Letters to His Wife*, ed. Christopher Lloyd, in *The Naval Miscellany*, vol. 4 (London: Navy Records Society, 1952), 177–84, 187–89, 193–94, 205, 216, 220–21.

*Torbay* at sea at least 300 miles from England,
Saturday, May 3, 1755.

Dearest Fanny, — If you can tell where I am a-going it is more than anybody with me can, for I have told no one, and I believe they don't judge by the course we steer. But as the post goes out but seldom from hence, I will not miss an opportunity when it does go, and I hear tomorrow is the day, and wish you may have this in ten days, which is the ordinary from hence. Could you but send to me as easily, I should then hear from you how my dear little Billyboy is.[1] By this time you have almost certain hopes of his doing well, or your fears are great, but as the odds are so much in his favour, I will conclude all is well with him, and I hope the rest of your family. . . .

We have very fine weather and a jolly company. I don't dislike my ship, she sails well, at this time the best of any of the fleet, and generally better than most of them. Mostyn[2] sometimes flatters himself he can outgo us, but in many situations, we are the best sailors.

Pray don't be angry with me for leaving off the custom of writing something to you every day, it was your own self that was the occasion. You seemed to dislike the trite account of wind and weather which was almost the whole my journal afforded, and the daily occurrences of a sea life are scarce intelligible to you, so little variety that they do not entertain even us who have no other amusements. I am told we have a mortal sight of dancers on board, and a good scraper[3] to play to them. They divert themselves every evening in fine weather and I believe have shaken all their clothes off their backs, for

---

[1] *how my dear little Billyboy is:* Boscawen's son has been inoculated for smallpox. This process made the patient ill for a time, although usually less so than if the virus was contracted through contagion. There was some anxiety about the severity of the illness associated with inoculation as well as fears that the patient might be permanently marked by the pox. See footnote 20 to Smollett, "On a Visit to Bath" in Part Two, Chapter 2.

[2] *Mostyn:* Savage Mostyn, rear admiral or second-in-command of the fleet.

[3] *scraper:* Fiddler.

they are a ragged set of rogues. As yet we are tolerably healthy, and I hope shall continue so. We are 709 on board, a jovial crew locked up in the same wooden case.

Don't conceive I live one day without thinking of you. Many things occur that I wish to have your opinion of, and many others that I wish you to see. I want to know how the farm goes on under your care, but you have scarce given any direction yet, though your own walk should be rolled and mowed. I hope that is not forgot, though if you have any distress at home you will scarce think of that. If Black Tom was now on board he would be coming aft with the tea kettle (if as heretofore) but I have left off that custom, and have not seen the tea kettle in an evening since I have been on board.

The irregular life of London, the attendance on the Mitchell affair,[4] etc., has made that custom not necessary, so that I save at least one shilling per diem in this article. Could I but do as the Rear Admiral does, and go to bed without supper, I should save something more, but I must have my bit of something at night and a little punch to drink Fanny's health with (that of) her dear son Ned and the rest of the charming babes. Rest assured, by dearest love, that I am well, that I love you, and think of you constantly, that I wish you and our children as good health as I enjoy myself and I am your faithful and affectionate

ED. BOSCAWEN.

I go to sleep before ten and rise before six.

*Torbay*, at sea, May 7, 1755.

My dearest wife, — We are now many leagues at sea, and I don't doubt but by this time you know where we are gone. We have very pleasant weather, it is lucky for us it is so or we should be very sickly. The hurry we came out in, the dread of going to the West Indies, as well as the regret of being pressed,[5] hangs heavy on many, so that we have at present a long sick list, which Ramsay[6] flatters himself will not be long so, but as it increases daily, I cannot agree with him, and

---

[4] *Mitchell affair:* Cornelius Mitchell was a captain in the navy in command of a squadron in the Windward Passage off Cape Nicolas in 1746. Meeting a French convoy of inferior force, Mitchell inexplicably failed to attack and was pursued by the French. He was court-martialed in 1747–48 and dismissed from service. There was considerable belief that Mitchell had got off too light, and in 1749 Parliament revised the code of naval discipline.

[5] *regret of being pressed:* The men are understandably depressed after being forced to join Boscawen's crew. See footnote 1 to Gardner, "Voyages of a Seaman" in this chapter.

[6] *Ramsay:* The ship's surgeon.

am afraid of worse consequences than he thinks of at present. Mr. Mostyn dined with me the day before yesterday but is not yet quite well. I am perfectly so. He has not yet left off a fire in his cabin, I never have had one in mine and I assure you it is quite sultry weather, what you would call hot, though we are not got much to the southward of England. . . .

I have little else to tell you but how we live, and how we chat. First then for living. We rise before six, breakfast at eight, dine at one, and sup at eight again, and all very regularly. My mess at dinner consists of six, at breakfast and supper only Colby and Macpherson. I have cards but have not yet played, nor do I hear that the officers play below, your favourite backgammon they are always at. Exercising the squadron, our own men, and looking out which ship sails best, employs all our time. I have read some of the French books you gave me without much entertainment; the History of Gustavus Vasa[7] is entertaining; you will like to read it. I have gone through Mr. Hume's[8] *History of James the First and Charles the First,* I can't say he is very fond of that same James, but speaks of Charles as the honestest and best man that ever lived, and most certainly the whole system of Government and the Constitution was altered at that time. As to the conversation I mentioned, we have little of it, but the repetition of old voyages etc. Capt. Colby, who is a sportsman, now and then gives us a fox chase, but I don't think much of that, as Ramsay would say.

But I now think of Hatchlands,[9] and suppose you do so too sometimes, and desire you will direct now about weeding the park or the docks, thistles, etc., will rejoice in my absence. And I desire you will direct Messrs. Miel & Wright for their amusement to level the three roads in the park, the horse walk, the road to (the) brewhouse gate, and that from the barn to the hurdles.[10] . . . Adieu my dearest love for tonight, I find I have left a blank side on the other sheet.

[7] *History of Gustavus Vasa:* Apparently a history of Gustavus Vasa, who liberated the Swedes from the domination of the Danes and ascended the Swedish throne in 1523. Perhaps Boscawen refers to a tragedy written on this subject by Henry Brooke. Olaudah Equiano, another of our sea-faring men, was ironically named after this Gustavus Vasa. Equiano served under Boscawen at sea (see the headnote to Equiano, "Serving with the English Navy" in this chapter).

[8] *Mr. Hume's:* David Hume (1711–1776) was a Scottish philosopher, political economist, and historian. His *History of Great Britain* was published in four volumes between 1754 and 1761. The first two volumes, dealing with the Stuart kings of the seventeenth century and apparently the ones read by Boscawen, were often criticized for their errors and Tory prejudice but became very popular in the eighteenth century.

[9] *Hatchlands:* The name of Boscawen's country estate.

[10] *hurdles:* Fencing, made from the native hawthorne found in English hedgerows.

I have entertained myself with reading my dear's letters, that I have received since we parted, fourteen in number, and have ranged them in order. God knows when you will have this, for I know not from whence I shall send it, I am now beyond the Post. The last I wrote will be long going to you, as the *Hazard* that carried it has had a contrary wind ever since she left us.

*Sunday, May 11th,* My dear, I have nothing to say to my dearest but that I constantly think of her and the dear children. This day three weeks poor Billy was inoculated, how fares it with him, how fares it with Mamma, and if Doctor Barnard[11] has not altered the holidays, you have got your friend and companion Neddyboy with you, and both you and him longing to go to Hatchlands, which I hope your Billy is well enough for you to accomplish this week. I figure to myself a charming summer. You know the leaves in your walk were bursting when we were there together.

This afternoon I sent a how d'ye do to the Rear Admiral.[12] He sends word his rheumatism is well and he in good spiritis. Whilst my boat went on board of him, Master Geary called on board the *Torbay,* but we talked of no other ploughing but the ocean, not one word of farming. Our men are very merry, we have most excellent dancers, but, alas, the fiddler was in a scrape and was whipped. But he has since played; they sometimes dance to the fife and drum and fiddle altogether, so well that you and I could dance country dances. I am sorry to tell you Ramsay has been ill with a fever for some days, and thinks of being blooded[13] again this evening; he is very careful and solicitous about the health of the people, and he has had pretty good success with them hitherto. But I am afraid of the scurvy, which man cannot prevent. All my other officers are perfectly well and behave very well.

I have read some pages of Doctor Hill's book and am sure you will like it. It is very serious, the subject is so, and I believe very learned, but of that I am no judge. I hope Lord Granville has seen it and should be glad to know his opinion of it, or that of your friend, Mr. West. To be sure he will read it. Our weather continues fine and we have a fair wind. But let me go as pleasant as possible, I shall be impatient to return to the arms of my dear Fanny.

[11] *Doctor Barnard:* The headmaster at Eton from 1754 until 1765. "Neddyboy," Boscawen's son, is apparently in school there.

[12] *Rear Admiral:* Mostyn.

[13] *blooded:* Eighteenth-century English medical practice included the deliberate letting of blood, supposedly to relieve a fever.

*Wednesday, May 14th,* My dearest love cannot think what a lazy life I live. I almost wish for bad weather for exercise. At present we have a westerly wind and hot sunshine with very smooth water, but for aught I see we are got into an unfrequented part of the globe, for we see nobody but ourselves, not even a fish to be caught, though many have put out their lines. I often think of dear *Beeboy* and his smallpox, and hope by this time you have done thinking of it, indeed that is the only reason I have now taken up my pen for I have nothing more to say to my dear wife, but to hope she and the dear babes are all well.

I must tell you the best sort of table-cloths that you bought of Mr. Faux are good, but the others too small and very coarse, we have no room to wipe. I fancy soon we shall want a laundry maid, but none can we have for want of water. . . .

Few of the officers think we shall fight if we do meet the French,[14] that I can scarce persuade them to prepare properly. But I believe the officers are in general good, and will do their duty on occasion. Besides Mostyn and Colby, here is only Spry and Geary that you know. Harvey has, as I am writing, been with me to desire me to kill a hog. You'll say it is the wrong time of year, but when we go to sea, we leave all dates and seasons on shore and eat what we can get, so that I shall hear of liver and bacon tomorrow though near Midsummer. I wish I had the recipe for boiling rice. Mr Fash has no idea of a *Pulloo,* which is a very usual sea dish, but we have got a black Jack[15] cook to the lieutenants, an acquaintance of Tom's, they say does it well. We will try his hand tomorrow.

Dearest, may God bless you and Mr. Edward — Fanny, Bessy, and Mr. William. My love to them. If I meet a West Indiaman you may have this before they return to school. How does Billy become his breeches? I long to see you all. I hope he was not very *tross*[16] and will

---

[14] *Few of the officers . . . French:* One can sympathize with these reluctant officers. The uncertain nature of the peace between France and England and the difficulties of communication with ships long at sea might well have left some officers puzzled about whether French ships should be treated as hostile or not. Boscawen himself later expresses some doubts about attacking the French prior to the official declaration of war.

[15] *black Jack:* "Jack" was used to refer to a knave or rascal; the adjective "black" might mean African, East Indian, or dark-skinned European.

[16] *tross:* Also spelled *truss,* this term was applied to a tight-fitting pair of pants, which Billy has just assumed. Up to a certain age, boys and girls alike wore a dresslike garment; graduating to pants marked an important point in a boy's maturing process. There's probably a pun here, as truss was also used to refer to a smart, firm, young man.

not want whipping to set him to rights again after the indulgence he has lately had when in the smallpox.

*June 9th, 1755.* If I mistake not, my dearest Fanny's birthday,[17] and this day, *pour la troisième fois,*[18] Monsieur Hoquart is my prisoner. He was in the *Alcide,* of 64 guns, which was taken this day and is now on board the *Torbay.* We have likewise taken the *Lys,* of 74, with 680 men, but she had not her lower battery mounted. Capt. Howe, in the *Dunkirk,* was the only ship that engaged. I came up second but on my firing one single gun he struck. Howe has about seven men killed, and 28 wounded, the *Alcide* 50 killed and as many wounded, five of the French slain are officers, among which are a Colonel and a nephew of Hoquart's, who is so used to be taken that he does not seem in the least concerned about it. I had two private men killed and two wounded. The *Defiance* came up with the *Lys* and took her with no loss at all and firing very few guns. In this ship there is near a whole battalion of soldiers, so that if we go no farther, we shall in part disappointment their schemes and answer the purpose for which we were sent. Not but what I expect to take more, having seen one, the *Dauphin Royal,* that escaped yesterday, and four with two admirals two days ago.

We live in continual fogs, and seldom see half our own friends. They came out 20 sail and are dispersed, and we by our superior seamanship have all kept company. We heard of a single one a few days ago, but I am afraid he got into Louisbourg, *alias* Cape Breton,[19] near which place we now are. I assure you it is a country not worth fighting for, and I believe those that are in it would be glad to lose it. . . .

*13th at 4 p.m.* I know not what I was going to say when I finished the other page. Since the evening we took the two ships, I have seen nothing of them, nor three of our own ships. Both yesterday and till noon today we have had fine weather, eight of us in company, not but this ship and any two of the others are strong enough to defend us

---

[17] *If I mistake not . . . Fanny's birthday:* The "New Style" (or Gregorian) calendar was adopted in England in 1752. This change made it quite possible to confuse dates such as birthdays.

[18] *pour la troisième fois:* For the third time.

[19] *Louisbourg, alias Cape Breton:* In the 1740s American militia had joined with British troops to capture this French fort in Canada. The French regained possession, however, in exchange for Madras. As the result of fighting in the Seven Years War, the British gained all of New France along the St. Lawrence and the Great Lakes, as well as the east side of the Mississippi.

from any attack the French can make on us here. And I yet hope to pick up some more of them. It will give me much trouble if my dearest Fanny should be alarmed about me, as our great folks had their fears for me and have sent a reinforcement after me. I had yesterday a letter from the Admiralty, and one from Lord Anson. What could be the meaning Mr. Cleveland did not write me three words, or give you five minutes warning he was sending me orders?[20] But not a syllable. What am I to think, what to conclude about poor Billy who I left inoculated? You may conclude I am uneasy about the dear rogue. Every hour that we have clear weather I expect to see Rear-Admiral Holburne with a squadron from England in which are both Norris and Brett; by them to be sure I shall have letters and hear from you, my dearest. And indeed this reinforcement will be welcome to me as it will enable me to return directly and bring you this letter myself. . . .

Would you think it, the French are so sunk in their discipline that many of their land officers have quitted the service rather than come to this country and indeed it is the very worst I every yet saw, and still the severest weather I ever experienced. The whole ship's company have chilblains on their hands and feet; my feet have not escaped, my great coat is never off my back, and a thick handkerchief round my neck. What is still worse, we have an ugly fever in the ship which has gone through the common men. Ramsay and all his mates have had it, but I think it begins to leave us and we grow better, though we have lost 20 men by it. William has had a severe fit of it, but is now about his business again. My cook is still on board the *Alcide,* and my dinner dressed by a soldier. We sit down ten every day to the table, and soon shall have another French officer, who now stays below being much wounded. A pretty quantity of victuals I consume. Unless we do make prizes of these ships I shall be ruined, and if we do at the old rate, I shall get £5,000 and something more. Adieu, dearest, for this evening.

*Monday, 16th at 6 p.m.* — We have now lost company with our prizes eight days, and with them three of our men-of-war, and have not seen one ship of the enemy. But I have still hopes the French are not all of them got in. A few days will give me the satisfaction of a letter from my dearest, as we have had a strong easterly wind

---

[20] *he was sending me orders:* Boscawen is annoyed that the British naval command has sent him orders without notifying his wife, which would have allowed her to send recent news.

which will bring Mr. Holbum (Holburne) near to us. Perhaps we may see him tomorrow, and I flatter myself I shall be with you in August at farthest. I suppose this attack on the French will make a great noise, but if I was not sent here to do this, I was sent for nothing. I have not much fear of (not) being supported in it. I hope I may find you and yours well, I long to see you all. Hoquart and all his officers seem well contented, they are well behaved men. We grow very sickly; it is lucky there is a relief coming, (for) we could not stay here long.

June 26, 1755.

*At 8 a.m.* My dearest Fanny cannot think how easy I have found myself since I dispatched the *Gibraltar* for England. The account I have given of myself, good or bad, being gone from me, has taken a great burden from my spirits. To begin a war between two great and powerful nations without an absolute order or declaration for it, now and then gives me some serious thoughts. Some will abuse me but as it is on the fighting side, more will commend me. Had I been lucky enough to have fallen in with more of them, I should have been more commended. Not but that I have the secret satisfaction to know I have done all that man could do in this part of the world, which no man that has not seen can be any judge of; the sudden and continual fogs, the cold in this southern latitude at midsummer and, on our first coming on the coast, the dismal prospect of floating islands of ice, sufficient to terrify the most daring seaman. I know what I have done is acting up to the spirit of my order. I know it is agreeable to the King, the Ministry and the majority of the people, but I am afraid they will expect I should have done more. The whole scheme is the demolishing the naval power of France, and indeed the falling in with those that have escaped me and demolishing them would have been a decisive stroke and prevented a war. But what I have done will add fuel to the fire only and make them complain at all the Courts in Europe. If our great men dare begin first in Europe they will yet take some (of the French ships) on their return; they have not provisions to stay here all the winter. If they attempt to stay, all their men will perish. My friend Hoquart is surprised to see so many of us here, and yet will not believe we can have more in England fitted. How great will his surprise be when he gets to Spithead and finds at least 30 sail of large ships there! Breakfast appears.

*12th at 6 a.m.* My dear love, I am in great spirits and have persuaded myself all night that the captive *Warwick* will yet go to England, as I am sure we are between the land and them, and have now a fresh breeze, which is against them and will carry us in their road that they must come.

If these French gentry do not escape me this time, they will pay for the house and furniture too, besides something to save hereafter for all our dear children. I am obliged to send two ships away. We have this chase in view, but I can't keep them any longer. Don't be under any uneasiness about me; there are but two fighting ships and we don't sail so as to be either the first or second, and if we did they would not stand us five minutes cannonading.

I have intelligence from that lucky soul Harland that he has taken four more sugar ships, so that my love sees that these little hits keep up my spirits. And to show you we live well, our venison is not yet gone, and we have now one of the best turtle I ever saw to dress and a whole pipe of Madeira, with a cask of rum sent with it for to wash it down. I have also the best baker I ever had, he makes the best French bread hot every morning, which I cut with orange marmalade, the best anti-scorbutic[21] we know of, for my breakfast. Observe four "best" in this page, with all these I must do well. But I must add another "best," that is that I shall hereafter think it the best cruise I ever went in my life hitherto, as it produces the best profit, which I hope will make the best of wives easy at so long an absence. I am, dearest love, your faithful and affectionate husband

ED. BOSCAWEN.

*June 1st 1756 at 7 p.m.* My spirits are in a great hurry. I have today received the Proclamation of War and have been proclaiming it, and ordering of it to be proclaimed, on board all the ships, and have seen all the captains, and had at least ten of them to dine with me. So that I have little leisure at present in my mind (for I am now alone) from the very interesting event, to reply or in any shape thank my dearest partner for her many kind letters. I have also much business to do, but cannot dispatch it all till tomorrow. But I must tell you, we have taken at least five or six sugar ships since the 17th May, all which will be good prizes, and by my address we have, in a manner

---

[21] *anti-scorbutic:* A substance that prevents scurvy, a common disease for eighteenth-century sailors. The ascorbic acid found in citrus was a preventative.

unanimously, appointed the Bretts, Mason, and Stephens our agents. This will encourage us to go on with our scheme of building.

What may be the calamities of the Mother country upon this occasion, I know not, but we must make the best we can of a melancholy event. Thank God we continue in health and spoils and I think on any occasion shall do our duty well. I have as yet twelve good ships with me and I assure (you) the event of today has done us in general much good. I have a very civil letter from Lord Anson, which I must answer tomorrow when I shall seal this. I must add I am obliged to you, for the Masons', Mrs. Montague's, and dear Ned's letter. I shall peruse yours again very early in the morning. I expect Mostyn every hour. Adieu for tonight. . . .

*6th at 4 p.m.* My dearest Fanny may know by the use of the letters, and the distance of the lines, that it was late when I wrote last night. . . .

I was the first that cruised here last French war,[22] I think I shall make more of it this war than the last. Mr. McPherson in this first instance will get £500 by it. The spirits I am in and the money I shall get will make me worry Mr. Ledbeater till he goes about our building and when can it be better undertaken than when I can't live in the old one, that I may have a comfortable, warm, new house to hide my diminished head in when war is no more and military men, as well as us seamen, are looked on as monsters, or at least as very burthensome useless subjects. I am sure in our tattered old house we shall find no comfort when we grow old which, if we live to do, the prospect is not far distant. But that we may ever live to be the same comfort to each other we now are, is the sincere and hearty prayer of your faithful and affectionate

E. B.

---

[22] *last French War:* In 1748 the Peace of Aix-la-Chapelle ended war between England and France, but by 1751 the two nations were involved in continuing skirmishes, which culminated in the declaration of the Seven Years War in 1756.

# THOMAS PASLEY

## A Voyage to the Cape of Good Hope

Thomas Pasley (1734–1808) was the fifth son of what the *Naval Chronicle* (1799–1818) refers to as "an ancient and honourable family in North Britain." He gained his first independent command of a ship during the last years of the Seven Years War with France. His sea journals excerpted here were written during the years of his command of the H M S *Sybil* during the War of American Independence. His military assignment was to convoy British trading ships — that is, to protect them from attack by American ships and their European allies. This task could be thankless and unprofitable. Merchant ships in the eighteenth century were themselves often armed and independent and were not necessarily cooperative with the captain of the ship convoying them. In addition, any money to be made as a navy officer came from the taking of prizes — that is, the capture of enemy trading vessels. While convoyers might well stumble upon an opportunity to take a prize, their primary mission was otherwise defined. They could not make money at the expense of leaving their own merchant ships unprotected. If the convoyers' opportunities to take prizes were limited, their danger was not, as escort work could easily turn into battle. After these journals were written, Pasley was made a rear admiral and lost a leg in battle in 1794. He was granted an annual pension of £1,000 and was created a baronet and shortly thereafter a vice admiral.

Pasley's journals convey the prejudices of an English sea captain of his class and upbringing. While not an unjust or unkind man, Pasley clearly believes that his Englishness makes him superior to his Irish subordinates and the dark-skinned Islanders with whom he trades for water and food. The following excerpts are from *Private Sea Journals 1778–1782*, ed. Rodney M. S. Pasley (London: J. M. Dent & Sons Ltd., 1931), 59–72.

*Thursday, February 10th, 1780.* After an infinity of hurry and consequent confusion, being pushed by daily Expresses from the Board and hourly letters from Admiral Gambier to combate impossibilities, I was at last in some sort of situation to slip the moorings between the Island and main, which I did this morning at daylight.

The first Express was to countermand my Newfoundland Orders, and command me to join the *Intrepid* when she appeared off the

Sound, to assist in convoying the Troops to the West Indies.[1] The next Express was to set at nought those orders and put in force my original ones, with the indulgence of a Cruize till the end of March, then to call at Lisbon for the Salt Vessels and convoy them to Newfoundland[2] — these were favorable to my wish. But alas! On the Eve of my sailing arrived another Express with Orders for me to proceed instantly to Sea with an enclosed Sealed Pacquet, which I was directed to open off the Lizard[3] — how very unsteady are those great Lords and Masters of ours! So triffling a Ship to occation no less than five different Expresses from London to Plymouth in the space of Eight days — Poor Old England!

Before the Day dawned, I repaired on board after having bid aideu to Mrs. Pasley, *the Wife, the friend of my heart;* and slip'd the moorings as soon as possible afterwards, as I have said above, and towed into the Sound. A light Air springing up, by two O'clock P.M. we got as far out as the Ram Head, where we remained Becalmed till after dark. At 8 P.M. a Breeze from the S.E. freshened favorably, which we made the best use of in pushing down Channel with all our Canvas.

What those Sealed Orders are, or where I am destined to by them, I cannot divine. The Admiral's Idea is that they convey an Express to Sir George Rodney;[4] that I am to continue my Cruize, and Call at Lisbon agreable to Orders for the Salt Vessels. I confess it my Idea likewise, and I heartily wish it may be so. Patience! Tomorrow I shall break the Seal.

*Friday, February 11th.* Patience! — Well might I say so. Abreast of the Lizard at two in the morning and acquainted of it by the Master, yet did not choose to break the Secret Seal, lest if disagreable or contrary to my wishes and expectations, I should be rob'd of my rest for the remaining part of the night. I only judged too right — at Seven I got up, sent for the 1st Lieutenant and Master, and in their presence broke the Enchantment. Great God! Thou knowest the wonder and amazement I was seized with, on perusing such unexpected Orders: — "To proceed with all possible dispatch to the Cape of Good Hope, to

---

[1] *to assist . . . West Indies:* Pasley had previously commanded the *Glasgow* in convoying British merchant ships to and from ports in the British colonies of the West Indies.

[2] *then to call . . . to Newfoundland:* These orders would have kept Pasley in northerly waters, not too far from British and European shores, convoying vessels to and from British colonies in Newfoundland.

[3] *Lizard:* The Lizard peninsula, off Cornwall.

[4] *Sir George Rodney:* Naval commander, then with a fleet near Gibraltar.

Convoy the India Ships to England."[5] A Frigate of 28 Guns[6] — a noble convoy for such valuable Ships! But at present I cannot help saying that this is the least of my consideration. I hold it an act of unthinking and unprecedented cruelty in the Admiralty — Ships of the *Sybil's* class are well known to Seamen neither to have capacity to stow water, nor provisions, for such a Voyage out and Home. I was indeed under orders to take on board Eight months', but with difficulty stowed Six of all stores except Bread, of that four; and even to accomplish this I was under the disagreable necessity of taking 50 Casks between Decks, and reducing my water to a proportion of Eight weeks. What steps am I to take with only two Months' water on board, when three Months is esteemed a quick passage from Europe to the place I am ordered to go? Even time admits of my calling nowhere; if it did, St. Iago, one of the Cape de Verds, is the only place; and if I may believe Forster who writes Cook's Voyages,[7] little is to be procured, and that little brackish. Once more I say — Patience! I am under orders and must proceed, or lose what is dearer, far dearer to me than Life — my Character. . . . In thy Almighty and Providential protection, Most Merciful God, I place all my hopes — and proceed without fear or dread in execution of my Orders.

*Saturday, February 12th.* The first day is past — and, I thank God, wind still favorable. The Officers and Ship's Company look a little gloomy, but say little; and whatever my private and secret sentiments may be, I hold in public the Language of an Officer, laugh at and obviate every arising difficulty started. If I had been thought worthy by their Lordships of the smallest hint, my Ship should have been very differently prepared for the Voyage. I would have added to my water; carried no Beer; and floored my Ship between decks with Casks, however fatal to my Ship's company. At the Yard they refused to fix my Coppers[8] for the distillation of Salt water, so that resource is denied me. Vinegar to wash my Ship, an article so essentially necessary to the very Life and well-being of the Ship's Company in Hot Climates — to sum up the account —, was likewise denied me. Poor

---

[5] *Cape of Good Hope . . . to England:* Instead of a relatively short voyage to Newfoundland, Pasley discovers he is to sail to the southern tip of Africa to convoy British ships coming home from Indian ports.

[6] *Frigate of 28 Guns:* A frigate was a small, lightweight vessel, quick but not big enough to carry many guns or a large cargo.

[7] *Cook's Voyages:* James Cook (1728–1779) was famous for his exploratory sea voyages, which took him around the globe.

[8] *Coppers:* Large copper or iron containers used for laundry and cooking aboard ship.

Sailors — you are the only class of Beings in our famed Country of Liberty really *Slaves*, devoted and hardly used, tho' the very Being of the Country depends on you. . . .

*Wednesday, February 16th.* As I suspected, the Wind is at S.W. Patience: my firm reliance on this and on all other occations is Above. In the middle of the Night I was seized with a violent Flux, which kept me dancing till morning when the Surgeon gave me a little Rhubarb. I hope it will have the desired effect, as I intend keeping my Cabin all day. Wednesdays and Saturdays I constantly Scrape, Wash, and Fumigate between decks; yet this cursed lurking Fever still hangs about the Ship. There is not, I am convinced, more if so much attention paid in any other Ship in the Service to keeping her Clean: I constantly Fumigate and Wash with Vinegar twice a week, and Muster every Man shaved and clean once.

*Thursday, February 17th.* Calm till midnight, when a Breeze sprung up from the Northward and encreased sufficiently to push my *Sybil* on at the rate of Eleven miles an hour before daylight; if it continues, it will do — that is, serve to ease our aching hearts. . . .

*Monday, February 21st.* Found great fault this morning with cleaning the Ship. Written orders every Watching Officer has to move every Arm Chest, Hencoop &Ca abaft[9] daily; yet this morning I had only too incontestable a proof that my orders were not complied with. Above ten days since we sailed; yet I discovered lodged between the Coops the whole dirt made by the Stock since the day of taking them on board, Bushells of it — Horrid. I am sorry to say (but I cannot help thinking) that Mr. Newton does not improve upon me as a first officer. Whether he is in Love or what is the matter, I know not; but he seems neither to have memory nor recollection for the Ship's duty. Fitting out the Ship in the Harbour this last time was a disgrace to every Officer in her, and more particularly the first — but 'tis past, and I heartily wish to forget it. . . .

*Thursday, February 24th.* Weather moderate, Sea smooth, and Wind right aft, judged it a favorable opportunity to new seize in the Fore Shrouds properly (which was never done in the Harbour), and to endeavour to get a bend out of the Foremast, which it had acquired to Starboard by inattention in first setting the rigging up. Accomplished this last nearly, and finished the whole a little after noon. After having taken the exact Measure of the Mast from the Head of the Topsail Sheet Bitts I was returning to the Quarter Deck, when

---

[9] *abaft:* To the rear, behind.

on stepping off the Forecastle I unfortunately missed my foot, and tumbled headlong down on the main Deck where I lay some time insensible. The Gun which I struck in falling, together with my taking off some part of the force by supporting myself on my left Hand, certainly prevented a fracture, and in all probability the fall proving fatal — as I had too great reason to apprehend from my Corpulent and unwieldy habit. It pleased God, however, to preserve my Life, at the expense of a Violent contusion on my left Hip and loss of my left Thumb, which by my weight was broke short off by a dislocation at the first joint. I am all gratitude and praise for this instance of His Particular Providential Protection — Blissed, for ever Blissed, be His Holy Name!

*Friday, February 25th.* Passed the Night, my heart overflowing with gratitude and thanks to him whose mercies are over all his works, tho' by no means on a bed of Down, the pain being extreme from my Hip and Thumb, the consequence of my fall. Exercised Great Guns and small arms: N.B.: — The Marines are under Arms every morning at Six, those of the Watch I mean, yet they fire infamously — Worthless Rascals! But I impute the fault solely to the Officer, whose abilities in that line might be stuff'd in a Nutshell. . . .

*Monday, February 28th.* Stood off and on all night; by Seven in the morning were close in with the Land — still so very thick and foggy that the Breakers and white beach were the only discernible marks of Land at two miles distant. Kept running along shore to the West and S.W. in soundings, taking care to keep without 6 fathoms, till we opened a little Bay on the East point of which we saw a number of Hutts and many heaps of Salt, which convinced us that it was assuredly the Isle of May[10] — before this we had our doubts. A little schooner was riding in this bay; sent an Officer on board her for intelligence, who on his return acquainted us that this was Englishman's Bay, the accustomed place for the Vessells of that Nation to load Salt for America; and that we might get plenty of Water and every other Refreshment, which we could not depend on at St. Iago, as there were at that time two large Ships watering at that Island — one a Sweedish East India Ship, the other a French Ship of 64 Guns last from Senegal. This particular piece of information determined me in a moment to remain where I was; the Portugueze Fort at St. Iago I knew not to be of sufficient Force to protect me from the Insults of a

---

[10] *Isle of May:* The Isle of Maio, a flat, barren island near Santiago, in the Cape Verde islands off the coast of what was then known as Guinea, West Africa.

Saucy Frenchman, with power in his hands.[11] Came therefore to an Anchor, and moor'd Ship; sent imedeately on shore, sunk a number of Butts, and found the water very tolerable.

*Tuesday, February 29th.* This day employed watering; got off by night Twenty Butts, the Black Rascals of inhabitants having stole the water out of our sunk casks in the night. Found that there were to be purchased plenty of Fowls, Goats, Pigs, Eggs, all very reasonable. Had the honor of a Visit today from His Sutty Excellency[12] and his Father Confessor, the High Priest and the only one in the Island.

*Wednesday, March 1st.* Completed our Water before night, in all 23 Ton. Allowed a free and general market, both on board and at the watering place, of which the Sailors made most excellent use: very few messes had less Sea stock than three or four Pigs, as many fat Goats, and half a Dozen of Fowls.

The Convalescents recovered during our stay past belief, by broths and Vegetables — I thank God! In the Ship there is not one Man really sick — Six in the Doctor's list, who expects to turn them out (being greatly advanced in their recovery) in a day or two. In the morning I shall bid this Island adieu as soon as the Breeze sets in.

*Thursday, March 2nd.* At 8 A.M. Weighed our Anchor, having first sent as a present to His Sutty Excellency my Plaid shooting-dress, partly intended as a Bribe to induce him to forward a letter for my Brother at Lisbon, a Vessel at St. Iago being to sail for Lisbon some time this month. Enclosed was one for my Beloved Mary, my Wife, friend, and Companion; if it does arrive safe I know that it will afford her infinite pleasure; if it does not, 'tis only my trouble and a sheet of paper lost. The Black chief, on my hoisting my Colours when we weighed, spread on a Pole at the end of his House a white handker-

---

[11] *Portugueze Fort . . . in his hands:* Portugal was neutral in the War of American Independence, and any hostilities between enemy ships within its waters would have breached that neutrality. Pasley does not seem to depend on the French adhering to this prohibition, however.

[12] *His Sutty Excellency:* The uninhabited Cape Verde islands were colonized in the 1400s by the Portuguese, who almost immediately began to bring African slaves to the islands. The population was composed, through subsequent centuries, of white Europeans, dark-skinned Africans, and an increasingly numerous mixed-race progeny. By 1700 the islanders were thought of as a people in their own right, though Creole in the mixture of African languages and Portuguese that they spoke. At the time of Pasley's writing, the dominant social order was still that of a slavocracy, in which skin color was tied to social and economic status, but many "maroon" settlements had developed on Santiago and adjacent islands. "His Sutty Excellency" might have been quite light-skinned, from our perspective, but his "blackness" was defined, in Pasley's eyes, by the sheer fact of his difference from the light-skinned English and Europeans.

chief as a Flag; 'twas the only way he had to express his good wishes and respect on parting.

The Inhabitants are all black. Their principal Town is called Penhouse, about 8 miles from where the Ship lay; it consists of about 1,000 Houses, tho' the Island contains not 400 Inhabitants. In the years 1773 and '74, a dreadful Famine happened in these Islands, which sweep'd off about one half the Inhabitants in this Island and nearly the same proportion in all the rest; in this chief Town 30 or 40 died of a day for want of sustenance. Representations to the Bigoted Court of Portugal on this melancholy occation had little effect; scanty triffles they were supplied with, but not in quantity to preserve Life. A Black Man named Silvester is at present stiled Governor, tho' more Properly Collector of the Customs as he receives all the King's dues; above him there is a chief stiled Captain Moor[13] — the Etymology of the Title we could not learn. He is Commander-in-chief of the Forts, Troops, and Militia. Between those two great men there is no small jealousy, which my little partial presents gave me early notice of.

The better sort, that is those in authority (for the whole are Blacks), wear old ragged European Cloaths obtained by barter from Ships that have touched here. The rest content themselves with one or more articles of finery as they can procure them; with either a shirt, Waistcoat, pair of Breeches, or Hatt, they hold themselves in full dress and strut proudly, not a little pleased with consequential self.

The women arc in general exceeding ugly, if I may be allowed to judge from the sample we saw; they wear a striped cotton covering over their shoulders, which reaches down below their knees before and behind. The children of both sexes remain Naked till the Years of Puberty. The Cloths are of their own manufactory, similar to the Guinea Cloths.[14] The proportion exceeds two Women to one Man in this Island at present; about 20 to 30 came down, the rest remained at their City Penhouse. Those few kept close at the Landing place night and day while we stayed, and gave incontestable proofs of their *wants* by the earnestness with which they pressed to be admitted on

---

[13] *Silvester . . . Governor . . . Captain Moor:* The Cape Verde islands operated on a system of royal charter from the Portuguese crown between the fifteenth and nineteenth centuries. From 1755–1778 the Majestic Company held the lease for the slave trade that prospered in and through the Cape Verde islands. This company appointed the governor of the islands who was essentially the company's tool, the Collector of the Customs (that is, the King's dues).

[14] *Guinea Cloths:* Textiles from what Europeans called Guinea, a portion of the West African coast extending from Sierra Leone to Benin.

board to have those wants supplied; but, in faith, even the Johns[15] thought them too ugly; they were therefore, poor creatures, only partially supplied. They stand in great Awe of their Priest, who is a monster above Six foot and more than Corpulent in proportion; Captain Moore exceeds him in height, but is a Skeleton figure. The Poor Wretches' situation is most lamentable from their despotic Governor and Bigoted Priest (whose black faces are characteristic of the harsh cruelty of their Souls), unattended to by the indolence of the Court of Portugal.

A very little inland from the shore, the soil seems equal to cultivation; but the indolent inhabitants raise little, and that little depends intirely on the Early and later Rains — deprived of which one Year, an inevitable Famine succeeds. Experience of such fatal periods so very often must deter them from indulging in the sweets of conjugal connections: we saw no young children. At this Bay are only a few temporary Huts, intended for a covering for those who come to ship off Salt.

*Friday, March 3rd.* Half an hour after we sailed Yesterday, took my departure from the Island; still so very thick that in little more than that we were out of sight of it. Breeze continues Brisk and pleasant; a few degrees to the Southward and adieu to Fogs, I hope. Ship absolutely full of Hogs and Goats: the first I must order to be killed — Goats make little dirt. Not one Fever in the Ship, nor has been for these some days past, thank God; it is the first time I could make this boast since I commanded the *Sybil.*

*Saturday, March 4th.* Light winds inclinable to Calms most of the Night — I cannot think our Trade will yet leave us; at this season we have reason to expect its company to 4° North. From thence to 4° South we must take our chance; then for the S.E. Trade to dance away with all our Canvass.

*Sunday, March 5th.* Nearly calm, one and two knots — when shall we cross the Line with this tedious movement? My Stewart, John, never was in a Man-of-War before — too milky — ; he has many good qualities, but as the old adage says, has not Divil enough in him; had he more I should be more at my ease. He acquainted me this morning that my Coops under the Forecastle were in the night Rob'd of Seven Fowls; turned all Hands up, talked to them, and pictured in the strongest possible terms the infamy and disgrace of such a conduct. There are many good and honest on board, but intermixed with

---

[15] *Johns:* Slang term for Marines.

a set of Damned Irish Villains, espetially amongst the Marines; many Sailor men have I turned out but I cannot so easily Marines, tho' I have a few by stratagem.

*Monday, March 6th.* Light winds still — an effort it made in the night for a couple of hours, but failed again. Began to Paint the Ship, the sides being done at the Isle of May; at the Cape she shall look smart. Natural Beauties she has many — well decorated and set off she must look Elegantly Handsome.

*Tuesday, March 7th.* Light winds and Variable this 24 hours, expected a severe Tornado, and prepared accordingly; it ended in a hard spate of Rain — filled Water. The Marines to day fired as usual — infamously. Took a view of the Ship in the boat; gave directions to alter the manner of painting the Stern and Head; when done, I am convinced she will look uncommonly handsome. The most Elegant Frigate I ever saw on the water is — my *SYBIL*.

*Wednesday, March 8th.* Squalls of rain, with wind from the S.W. — make the best use of every spurt that offers to push to the Southward, my point at present. Very tedious, yet we must have Patience — that's disagreable, so is every force hard of digestion. The Line — when shall we step over this said Line? The Rains have cooled the Air a little, and rendered the Intense Heat more bearable.

*Thursday, March 9th.* Calm all night, and still so — hard fate. We live in hopes — all men does so. Tired of calms and teizing whifs from all points of the Compass, I sat down to a party at my favorite game of Chess with Mr. Virgin, a Sweedish Gentleman on board. In the midst of our Game I heard an uncommon bustle on Deck; I instantly run up; a man overboard was the general cry — too true. Most affirmed that he jumped intentionally off the Gangway, but no one knew the person. A capstan Bar[16] was thrown within three foot of him under the Stern, and the Jolly Boat launched over the Gunwale in an instant of time, into which the 2nd Lieutenant and three Men jumped and went in quest of him; the Ship brought to, very little wind, the little boat could not be 40 yards from him; but after Rowing and calling for some time, they returned without success.

On enquiry I found it was one Lloyd, a quarter Gunner, who had for some days past been feverish but by no means supposed in danger. He had actually in a raving insane fitt jumped overboard, supposing the Sea a green field — at least this was our conjecture, as

---

[16] *capstan Bar:* The capstan is a mechanism used for raising heavy sails; the bar was used as a lever to make the mechanism work.

such fancies are not uncommon in Fevers. Such a Fever raged on board the *St. Albans* when in North America; in spite of Centinels and every possible precaution, above a hundred jumped overboard from that ship. Most of them drowned, but some were saved, and when recovered they gave that as a reason for leaping into the Sea.

This unfortunate fellow's Fate affects me much — a very fine young fellow he was. Can this be imputed to a man as self-murder? Surely not; a Just and unerring God cannot punish involuntary crimes.

The heat begins to be intolerable; when calm 'tis allmost impossible to breathe. . . .

*Sunday, March 12th.* Five Days complete since we were to the Southward of Six Degrees, and not yet to the Southward of five — Constant Calms. All last night not a breath of wind, and the Calm still continues. My God! When will we see an end of this more than disagreable Weather? The Sun allmost Vertical and not one breath of Air to cool his scorching rays, the Heat allmost unbearable.

To day entertained Mr. Farghar the Surgeon, and treated him with a Bottle of Claret, as a small sense of my gratitude for his particular attention to the preservation of my Broken Thumb, this day unswaddled and cleared of his attendance. The cure from his attention and my particular good habit of body has been completed in very little more than a fortnight. In some degree I have the use of that joint; whether time will restore it in perfection to me again or not, Time alone can discover. Another Bottle too I gave to my friend Mr. Scot, for his trouble in taking the head of my Table during the time of my inability to Carve or do the honors.

I am all gratitude on this occation to God for his Merciful protection — Grant, Almighty God, that my heart may ever be unfeignedly thankfull for this as well as every other instance of thy Divine Mercy, repeatedly shewn by innumerable proofs of thy particular Providential protection at all times.

How truly unhappy would my Mary have been, had she known how very nearly she was losing her friend, her Pasley! But I rejoice her extreme sensibility has not been put to the proof. May God of his infinite Mercy preserve, protect, her and the Dear Lovely little ones[17] to a once more joyful and happy Meeting in Manchester Buildings. "Hope travels on, nor quits us when we Die" — we indeed Live *In* and *By* hopes.

[17] *Dear Lovely little ones:* Pasley's daughters, Maria, then four, and Magdalene, three.

# OLAUDAH EQUIANO

## Serving with the English Navy

Olaudah Equiano (1745–1797) was born in the village of Issekein in what is now Eastern Nigeria. His native language was Ibo. He was kidnapped and enslaved at the age of eleven by another African nation and, after a short time, sold to the English. He survived the harrowing middle passage from West Africa to North America — an experience that probably has much to do with his youthful expectations of English barbarity and cruelty. After a brief interval at a Virginia plantation, he was sold again to a British naval officer, a Captain Pascal. He served with Pascal during General Wolfe's campaigns in Canada, spent some time in England, and served with Admiral Boscawen (see preceding selection) in the Seven Years War. He was finally released from slavery at the age of twenty-one and continued to work as a seaman for much of his free life.

Equiano was well-known in England for his political work against slaveholding in the British colonies. He was initially part of the disastrous Sierra Leone project, which was undertaken to resettle indigent former slaves in Africa. He was dismissed from the project in 1787, perhaps for being critical of the undertaking. In fact, the expedition proved to be fatally underfunded and underprovided, and many of the freed slaves who returned to Africa died in the attempt to settle there. After his dismissal, Equiano wrote his book and became famous for his speeches against the slave trade.

*The Interesting Narrative of the Life of Olaudah Equiano*, first published in 1789, was extremely popular, having gone into eight editions by 1794. The following excerpt, which is based on the first American edition (New York, 1791), is reprinted from *The Interesting Narrative of the Life of Olaudah Equiano: Written by Himself*, ed. Robert J. Allison (Boston: Bedford Books, 1995), 59–78, 80–86.

## Chapter III

I now totally lost the small remains of comfort I had enjoyed in conversing with my countrymen;[1] the women too, who used to wash and take care of me were all gone different ways, and I never saw one of them afterwards.

---

[1] *conversing with my countrymen:* Although Equiano had become fluent in several different African languages during his slavery in Africa, his fellow slaves in Virginia are from nations whose languages are unfamiliar to him.

I stayed in this island for a few days, I believe it could not be above a fortnight, when I, and some few more slaves that were not saleable amongst the rest, from very much fretting, were shipped off in a sloop for North America. On the passage we were better treated than when we were coming from Africa, and we had plenty of rice and fat pork. We were landed up a river a good way from the sea, about Virginia county, where we saw few or none of our native Africans, and not one soul who could talk to me. I was a few weeks weeding grass and gathering stones in a plantation; and at last all my companions were distributed different ways, and only myself was left. I was now exceedingly miserable, and thought myself worse off than any of the rest of my companions, for they could talk to each other, but I had no person to speak to that I could understand. In this state, I was constantly grieving and pining, and wishing for death rather than anything else.

While I was in this plantation, the gentleman, to whom I suppose the estate belonged, being unwell, I was one day sent for to his dwelling-house to fan him; when I came into the room where he was I was very much affrighted at some things I saw, and the more so as I had seen a black woman slave as I came through the house, who was cooking the dinner, and the poor creature was cruelly loaded with various kinds of iron machines; she had one particularly on her head, which locked her mouth so fast that she could scarcely speak; and could not eat nor drink. I was much astonished and shocked at this contrivance, which I afterwards learned was called the iron muzzle. Soon after I had a fan put in my hand, to fan the gentleman while he slept; and so I did indeed with great fear. While he was fast asleep I indulged myself a great deal in looking about the room, which to me appeared very fine and curious.

The first object that engaged my attention was a watch which hung on the chimney, and was going. I was quite surprised at the noise it made, and was afraid it would tell the gentleman anything I might do amiss; and when I immediately after observed a picture hanging in the room, which appeared constantly to look at me, I was still more affrighted, having never seen such things as these before. At one time I thought it was something relative to magic; and not seeing it move, I thought it might be some way the whites had to keep their great men when they died, and offer them libations as we used to do our friendly spirits. In this state of anxiety I remained till my master awoke, when I was dismissed out of the room, to my no small satisfaction and relief; for I thought that these people were all made up of wonders.

In this place I was called Jacob; but on board the *African Snow,* I was called Michael. I had been some time in this miserable, forlorn, and much dejected state, without having anyone to talk to, which made my life a burden, when the kind and unknown hand of the Creator (who in every deed leads the blind in a way they know not) now began to appear, to my comfort; for one day the captain of a merchant ship, called the *Industrious Bee,* came on some business to my master's house. This gentleman, whose name was Michael Henry Pascal, was a lieutenant in the Royal Navy, but now commanded this trading ship, which was somewhere in the confines of the county many miles off. While he was at my master's house, it happened that he saw me, and liked me so well that he made a purchase of me. I think I have often heard him say he gave thirty or forty pounds sterling for me; but I do not remember which. However, he meant me for a present to some of his friends in England: and as I was sent accordingly from the house of my then master (one Mr. Campbell) to the place where the ship lay; I was conducted on horseback by an elderly black man (a mode of travelling which appeared very odd to me). When I arrived I was carried on board a fine large ship, loaded with tobacco, &c., and just ready to sail for England.

I now thought my condition much mended; I had sails to lie on, and plenty of good victuals to eat; and everybody on board used me very kindly, quite contrary to what I had seen of any white people before; I therefore began to think that they were not all of the same disposition. A few days after I was on board we sailed for England. I was still at a loss to conjecture my destiny. By this time, however, I could smatter a little imperfect English; and I wanted to know as well as I could where we were going. Some of the people of the ship used to tell me they were going to carry me back to my own country, and this made me very happy. I was quite rejoiced at the idea of going back, and thought if I could get home what wonders I should have to tell. But I was reserved for another fate, and was soon undeceived when we came within sight of the English coast.

While I was on board this ship, my captain and master named me *Gustavus Vassa.*[2] I at that time began to understand him a little, and refused to be called so, and told him as well as I could that I would be

---

[2] *Gustavus Vassa:* The name of an early seventeenth-century king of Sweden. It was common to give slaves the names of the powerful, perhaps to underscore their powerlessness. See also footnote 7 to Boscawen, "Waging War against France" in this chapter.

called Jacob; but he said I should not, and still called me Gustavus: and when I refused to answer to my new name, which I at first did, it gained me many a cuff; so at length I submitted, and by which I have been known ever since.

The ship had a very long passage; and on that account we had very short allowance of provisions. Toward the last, we had only one pound and a half of bread per week, and about the same quantity of meat, and one quart of water a day. We spoke with only one vessel the whole time we were at sea, and but once we caught a few fishes. In our extremities the captain and people told me in jest they would kill and eat me; but I thought them in earnest, and was depressed beyond measure, expecting every moment to be my last. While I was in this situation, one evening they caught, with a good deal of trouble, a large shark, and got it on board. This gladdened my poor heart exceedingly, as I thought it would serve the people to eat instead of their eating me; but very soon, to my astonishment, they cut off a small part of the tail, and tossed the rest over the side. This renewed my consternation; and I did not know what to think of these white people, though I very much feared they would kill and eat me.

There was on board the ship a young lad who had never been at sea before, about four or five years older than myself: his name was Richard Baker. He was a native of America, had received an excellent education, and was of a most amiable temper. Soon after I went on board, he showed me a great deal of partiality and attention, and in return I grew extremely fond of him. We at length became inseparable; and, for the space of two years, he was of very great use to me, and was my constant companion and instructor. Although this dear youth had many slaves of his own, yet he and I have gone through many sufferings together on shipboard; and we have many nights lain in each other's bosoms when we were in great distress. Thus such a friendship was cemented between us as we cherished till his death, which, to my very great sorrow, happened in the year 1759, when he was up the Archipelago,[3] on board his Majesty's ship the *Preston:* an event which I have never ceased to regret, as I lost at once a kind interpreter, an agreeable companion, and a faithful friend; who, at the age of fifteen, discovered a mind superior to prejudice; and who was not ashamed to notice, to associate with, and to be the friend and instructor of one who was ignorant, a stranger, of a different complexion, and a slave!

---

[3] *Archipelago:* The Greek islands.

My master had lodged in his mother's house in America; he respected him very much, and made him always eat with him in the cabin. He used often to tell him jocularly that he would kill and eat me. Sometimes he would say to me — the black people were not good to eat, and would ask me if we did not eat people in my country. I said, No; then he said he would kill Dick (as we always called him) first, and afterwards me. Though this hearing relieved my mind a little as to myself, I was alarmed for Dick, and whenever he was called I used to be very much afraid he was to be killed; and I would peep and watch to see if they were going to kill him; nor was I free from this consternation till we made the land.

One night we lost a man overboard; and the cries and noise were so great and confused, in stopping the ship, that I, who did not know what was the matter, began, as usual, to be very much afraid, and to think they were going to make an offering with me, and perform some magic; which I still believed they dealt in. As the waves were very high, I thought the Ruler of the seas was angry, and I expected to be offered up to appease him. This filled my mind with agony, and I could not any more, that night, close my eyes again to rest. However, when daylight appeared, I was a little eased in my mind; but still, every time I was called, I used to think it was to be killed. Some time after this, we saw some very large fish, which I afterwards found were called grampusses.[4] They looked to me exceedingly terrible, and made their appearance just at dusk, and were so near as to blow the water on the ship's deck. I believed them to be the rulers of the sea; and as the white people did not make any offerings at any time, I thought they were angry with them; and, at last, what confirmed my belief was, the wind just then died away, and a calm ensued, and in consequence of it the ship stopped going. I supposed that the fish had performed this, and I hid myself in the fore part of the ship, through fear of being offered up to appease them, every minute peeping and quaking; but my good friend Dick came shortly towards me, and I took an opportunity to ask him, as well as I could, what these fish were. Not being able to talk much English, I could but just make him understand my question; and not at all, when I asked him if any offerings were to be made to them; however, he told me these fish would swallow anybody which sufficiently alarmed me. Here he was called away by the captain, who was leaning over the quarter-deck railing, and looking at the fish; and most of the people were busied in

---

[4] *grampusses:* Whales.

getting a barrel of pitch to light for them to play with. The captain now called me to him, having learned some of my apprehensions from Dick; and having diverted himself and others for some time with my fears, which appeared ludicrous enough in my crying and trembling, he dismissed me. The barrel of pitch was now lighted and put over the side into the water. By this time it was just dark, and the fish went after it; and, to my great joy, I saw them no more.

However, all my alarms began to subside when we got sight of land; and at last the ship arrived at Falmouth,[5] after a passage of thirteen weeks. Every heart on board seemed gladdened on our reaching the shore, and none more than mine. The captain immediately went on shore, and sent on board some fresh provisions, which we wanted very much. We made good use of them, and our famine was soon turned into feasting, almost without ending. It was about the beginning of the spring 1757, when I arrived in England, and I was near twelve years of age at that time. I was very much struck with the buildings and the pavement of the streets in Falmouth; and, indeed, every object I saw, filled me with new surprise.

One morning, when I got upon deck, I saw it covered all over with the snow that fell over night. As I had never seen anything of the kind before, I thought it was salt: so I immediately ran down to the mate, and desired him, as well as I could, to come and see how somebody in the night had thrown salt all over the deck. He, knowing what it was, desired me to bring some of it down to him. Accordingly I took up a handful of it, which I found very cold indeed; and when I brought it to him he desired me to taste it. I did so, and I was surprised beyond measure. I then asked him what it was; he told me it was snow, but I could not in anywise understand him. He asked me, if we had no such thing in my country; I told him, No. I then asked him the use of it, and who made it; he told me a great man in the heavens, called God. But here again I was to all intents and purposes at a loss to understand him; and the more so, when a little after I saw the air filled with it, in a heavy shower, which fell down on the same day.

After this I went to church; and having never been at such a place before, I was again amazed at seeing and hearing the service. I asked all I could about it, and they gave me to understand it was worshipping God, who made us and all things. I was still at a great loss, and soon got into an endless field of inquiries, as well as I was able to speak and ask about things. However, my little friend Dick used to be

---

[5] *Falmouth:* A seaport and market town in Cornwall at the mouth of the River Fal.

my best interpreter; for I could make free with him, and he always instructed me with pleasure. And from what I could understand by him of this God, and in seeing these white people did not sell one another as we did, I was much pleased; and in this I thought they were much happier than we Africans. I was astonished at the wisdom of the white people in all things I saw; but was amazed at their not sacrificing, or making any offerings, and eating with unwashed hands, and touching the dead. I likewise could not help remarking the particular slenderness of their women, which I did not at first like; and I thought they were not so modest and shame-faced as the African women.

I had often seen my master and Dick employed in reading; and I had a great curiosity to talk to the books as I thought they did, and so to learn how all things had a beginning. For that purpose I have often taken up a book, and have talked to it, and then put my ears to it, when alone, in hopes it would answer me; and I have been very much concerned when I found it remained silent.

My master lodged at the house of a gentleman in Falmouth, who had a fine little daughter about six or seven years of age, and she grew prodigiously fond of me, insomuch that we used to eat together, and had servants to wait on us. I was so much caressed by this family that it often reminded me of the treatment I had received from my little noble African master.[6] After I had been here a few days, I was sent on board of the ship; but the child cried so much after me that nothing could pacify her till I was sent for again. It is ludicrous enough, that I began to fear I should be betrothed to this young lady; and when my master asked me if I would stay there with her behind him, as he was going away with the ship, which had taken in the tobacco again, I cried immediately, and said I would not leave him. At last, by stealth, one night I was sent on board the ship again; and in a little time we sailed for Guernsey,[7] where she was in part owned by a merchant, one Nicholas Doberry.

As I was now amongst a people who had not their faces scarred, like some of the African nation where I had been, I was very glad I did not let them ornament me in that manner when I was with them.

---

[6] *little noble African master:* Equiano's earlier African enslavement did not carry with it the physical constraints and cruelties of his enslavement by Europeans. In the family referenced here, he was treated much like a brother to the little boy who was his master.

[7] *Guernsey:* An island in the English channel near the coast of Brittany and Normandy that provided safe harbor to British ships and their allies.

When we arrived at Guernsey, my master placed me to board and lodge with one of his mates, who had a wife and family there; and some months afterwards he went to England, and left me in care of this mate, together with my friend Dick. This mate had a little daughter, aged about five or six years, with whom I used to be much delighted. I had often observed that when her mother washed her face it looked very rosy, but when she washed mine it did not look so. I therefore tried oftentimes myself if I could not by washing make my face of the same color as my little play-mate, Mary, but it was all in vain; and I now began to be mortified at the difference in our complexions. This woman behaved to me with great kindness and attention, and taught me everything in the same manner as she did her own child, and, indeed, in every respect, treated me as such. I remained here till the summer of the year 1757, when my master, being appointed first lieutenant of his Majesty's ship the *Roebuck,* sent for Dick and me, and his old mate. On this we all left Guernsey, and set out for England in a sloop, bound for London.

As we were coming up towards the Nore,[8] where the *Roebuck* lay, a man-of-war's boat came along side to press[9] our people, on which each man run to hide himself. I was very much frightened at this, though I did not know what it meant, or what to think or do. However I went and hid myself also under a hencoop. Immediately afterwards, the press-gang came on board with their swords drawn, and searched all about, pulled the people out by force, and put them into the boat. At last I was found out also; the man that found me held me up by the heels while they all made their sport of me, I roaring and crying out all the time most lustily; but at last the mate, who was my conductor, seeing this, came to my assistance, and did all he could to pacify me; but all to very little purpose, till I had seen the boat go off. Soon afterwards we came to the Nore, where the *Roebuck* lay; and, to our great joy, my master came on board to us, and brought us to the ship.

When I went on board this large ship, I was amazed indeed to see the quantity of men and the guns. However, my surprise began to diminish as my knowledge increased; and I ceased to feel those apprehensions and alarms which had taken such strong possession of me when I first came among the Europeans, and for some time after. I began now to pass to an opposite extreme; I was so far from being

---

[8] *Nore:* A district near the mouth of the Thames, often used as anchorage by the navy.
[9] *press:* See footnote 1 to Gardner, "Voyages of a Seaman" in this chapter.

afraid of anything new which I saw, that after I had been some time in this ship, I even began to long for an engagement. My griefs, too, which in young minds are not perpetual, were now wearing away; and I soon enjoyed myself pretty well, and felt tolerably easy in my present situation. There was a number of boys on board, which still made it more agreeable; for we were always together, and a great part of our time was spent in play.

I remained in this shop a considerable time, during which we made several cruises, and visited a variety of places; among others we were twice in Holland, and brought over several persons of distinction from it, whose names I do not now remember. On the passage, one day, for the diversion of those gentlemen, all the boys were called on the quarter-deck, and were paired proportionably, and then made to fight; after which the gentlemen gave the combatants from five to nine shillings each. This was the first time I ever fought with a white boy; and I never knew what it was to have a bloody nose before. This made me fight most desperately, I suppose considerably more than an hour; and at last, both of us being weary, we were parted. I had a great deal of this kind of sport afterwards, in which the captain and the ship's company used very much to encourage me.

Sometime afterwards, the ship went to Leith in Scotland, and from thence to the Orkneys,[10] where I was surprised in seeing scarcely any night; and from thence we sailed with a great fleet, full of soldiers, for England. All this time we had never come to an engagement, though we were frequently cruising off the coast of France; during which we chased many vessels, and took in all seventeen prizes.[11] I had been learning many of the maneuvres of the ship during our cruise; and I was several times made to fire the guns. One evening, off Havre de Grace, just as it was growing dark, we were standing off shore, and met with a fine large French built frigate. We got all things immediately ready for fighting; and I now expected I should be gratified in seeing an engagement, which I had so long wished for in vain. But the very moment the word of command was given to fire, we heard those on board the other ship cry, "Haul down the jib"; and in that instant she hoisted English colors. There was instantly with us an amazing cry of — "Avast!" or stop firing; and I think one or two guns had been let off, but happily they did no mischief. We had hailed them several times, but they not hearing, we received no answer, which

---

[10] *Orkneys:* The Orkney Islands, off the coast of Scotland.
[11] *prizes:* See footnote 8 to Gardner, "Voyages of a Seaman."

was the cause of our firing. The boat was then sent on board of her, and she proved to be the *Ambuscade,* man-of-war, to my no small disappointment.

We returned to Portsmouth,[12] without having been in any action, just at the trial of Admiral Byng[13] (whom I saw several times during it); and my master having left the ship, and gone to London for promotion, Dick and I were put on board the *Savage,* sloop-of-war,[14] and we went in her to assist in bringing off the *St. George,* man-of-war, that had run ashore somewhere on the coast. After staying a few weeks on board the *Savage,* Dick and I were sent on shore at Deal,[15] where we remained for some short time, till my master sent for us to London, the place I had long desired exceedingly to see. We therefore both with great pleasure got into a wagon, and came to London, where we were received by a Mr. Guerin, a relation of my master. This gentleman had two sisters, very amiable ladies, who took much notice and great care of me.

Though I had desired so much to see London, when I arrived in it I was unfortunately unable to gratify my curiosity; for I had at this time the chilblains[16] to such a degree that I could not stand for several months, and I was obliged to be sent to St. George's hospital. There I grew so ill that the doctors wanted to cut my leg off, at different times, apprehending a mortification; but I always said I would rather die than suffer it, and happily (I thank God) I recovered without the operation. After being there several weeks, and just as I had recovered, the smallpox broke out on me, so that I was again confined; and I thought myself now particularly unfortunate. However, I soon recovered again; and by this time, my master having been pro-

---

[12] *Portsmouth:* Also spelled Portsmith. Portsmouth boasted a fine harbor that could offer safe protection for a large fleet.

[13] *Admiral Byng:* John Byng (1704–1757) was made commander in chief of the British navy in the Mediterranean in 1747. In 1755 he relieved Edward Hawkes in the Bay of Biscay and was ordered to defend Minorca from a threatened French invasion. Possibly, the British ministry did not fully believe that the French threat was real, as Byng's squadron was woefully small for such an assignment. Byng requested troops from the governor of Gibraltar but was refused; when the French did indeed attack, Byng fled back to Gibraltar. The loss of Minorca and Byng's flight caused a public uproar in England, and the commander was tried by court-martial in 1757. Convicted of neglect of duty, he was sentenced to death and shot on the quarterdeck of the *Monarque* in Portsmouth Harbor on March 14, 1757.

[14] *sloop-of-war:* The sloop, as opposed to a man-of-war, was a relatively small, light-weight vessel carrying guns only on the upper deck.

[15] *Deal:* A market town and seaport in Kent, seventy-two miles southeast of London; supposedly the spot where Julius Caesar landed in Britain.

[16] *chilblains:* The inflamed, swollen areas of flesh left by frostbite.

moted to be first lieutenant of the *Preston,* man-of-war, of fifty guns, then new at Deptford, Dick and I were sent on board her, and soon after, we went to Holland to bring over the late Duke of Cumberland to England.

While I was in the ship an incident happened, which, though trifling, I beg leave to relate, as I could not help taking particular notice of it, and considered it then as a judgment of God. One morning a young man was looking up to the foretop, and in a wicked tone, common on shipboard, d —— d his eyes about something. Just at the moment some small particles of dirt fell into his left eye, and by the evening it was very much inflamed. The next day it grew worse, and within six or seven days he lost it.

From this ship my master was appointed a lieutenant on board the *Royal George.* When he was going he wished me to stay on board the *Preston,* to learn the French horn; but the ship being ordered for Turkey, I could not think of leaving my master, to whom I was very warmly attached; and I told him if he left me behind, it would break my heart. This prevailed on him to take me with him; but he left Dick on board the *Preston,* whom I embraced at parting for the last time. The *Royal George* was the largest ship I had ever seen, so that when I came on board of her I was surprised at the number of people, men, women, and children, of every denomination; and the largeness of the guns, many of them also of brass, which I had never seen before. Here were also shops or stalls of every kind of goods, and people crying their different commodities about the ship as in a town.

To me it appeared a little world, into which I was again cast without a friend, for I had no longer my dear companion Dick. We did not stay long here. My master was not many weeks on board before he got an appointment to the sixth lieutenant of the *Namur,* which was then at Spithead,[17] fitting up for Vice-admiral Boscawen,[18] who was going with a large fleet on an expedition against Louisburg.[19]

The crew of the *Royal George* were turned over to her, and the flag of that gallant admiral was hoisted on board, the blue at the maintop gallant mast head. There was a very great fleet of men-of-war of every description assembled together for this expedition, and I was in hopes soon to have an opportunity of being gratified with a

[17]*Spithead:* A wide passage for ships between Portsmouth, on the southern coast of England, and the Isle of Wight.

[18]*Vice-admiral Boscawen:* See the headnote to Boscawen, "Waging War against France," in this chapter.

[19]*Louisburg:* See footnote 19 to Boscawen, "Waging War against France."

sea-fight. All things being now in readiness, this mighty fleet (for there was also Admiral Cornish's fleet in company, destined for the East Indies) at last weighed anchor, and sailed. The two fleets continued in company for several days, and then parted; Admiral Cornish, in the *Lenox,* having first saluted our Admiral in the *Namur,* which he returned. We then steered for America; but, by contrary winds, we were driven to Tenerife,[20] where I was struck with its noted peak. Its prodigious height, and its form, resembling a sugar loaf, filled me with wonder. We remained in sight of this island some days, and then proceeded for America, which we soon made, and got into a very commodious harbor called St. George, in Halifax,[21] where we had fish in great plenty, and all other fresh provisions. We were here joined by different men-of-war and transport ships with soldiers; after which, our fleet being increased to a prodigious number of ships of all kinds, we sailed for Cape Breton in Nova Scotia. We had the good and gallant General Wolfe on board our ship, whose affability made him highly esteemed and beloved by all the men. He often honored me, as well as other boys, with marks of his notice, and saved me once a flogging for fighting with a young gentleman.

We arrived at Cape Breton in the summer of 1758; and here the soldiers were to be landed, in order to make an attack upon Louisburg. My master had some part in superintending the landing; and here I was in a small measure gratified in seeing an encounter between our men and the enemy. The French were posted on the shore to receive us, and disputed our landing for a long time; but at last they were driven from their trenches, and a complete landing was effected. Our troops pursued them as far as the town of Louisburg. In this action many were killed on both sides.

One thing remarkable I saw this day. A lieutenant of the *Princess Amelia,* who, as well as my master, superintended the landing, was giving the word of command, and while his mouth was open, a musket ball went through it, and passed out at his cheek. I had that day, in my hand, the scalp of an Indian king, who was killed in the engagement; the scalp had been taken off by an Highlander. I saw the king's ornaments too, which were very curious, and made of feathers.

Our land forces laid siege to the town of Louisburg, while the French men-of-war were blocked up in the harbor by the fleet, the batteries at the same time playing upon them from the land. This they

[20] *Tenerife:* One of the Canary Islands off the west coast of Africa.
[21] *Halifax:* This southeastern Canadian seaport served as a naval base for the expedition against Louisburg.

did with such effect, that one day I saw some of the ships set on fire by the shells from the batteries, and I believe two or three of them were quite burnt. . . .

At last, Louisburg was taken, and the English men-of-war came into the harbor before it, to my very great joy; for I had now more liberty of indulging myself, and I went often on shore. When the ships were in the harbor, we had the most beautiful procession on the water I ever saw. All the Admirals and Captains of the men-of-war, full dressed, and in their barges, well ornamented with pendants, came alongside of the *Namur.* The Vice-admiral then went on shore in his barge, followed by the other officers in order of seniority, to take possession, as I suppose, of the town and fort. Some time after this, the French Governor and his lady, and other persons of note, came on board our ship to dine. On this occasion our ships were dressed with colors of all kinds, from the top-gallant mast head to the deck; and this, with the firing of guns, formed a most grand and magnificent spectacle.

As soon as everything here was settled, Admiral Boscawen sailed with part of the fleet for England, leaving some ships behind with Rear-admirals Sir Charles Hardy and Durell. It was now winter; and one evening, during our passage home, about dusk, when we were in the channel, or near soundings,[22] and were beginning to look for land, we descried seven sail of large men-of-war, which stood off shore. Several people on board of our ship said, as the two fleets were (in forty minutes from the first sight) within hail of each other, that they were English men-of-war; and some of our people even began to name some of the ships. By this time both fleets began to mingle, and our Admiral ordered his flag to be hoisted. At that instant, the other fleet, which were French, hoisted their ensigns,[23] and gave us a broadside[24] as they passed by. Nothing could create greater surprise and confusion among us than this. The wind was high, the sea rough, and we had our lower and middle deck guns housed in, so that not a single gun on board was ready to be fired at any of the French ships. However, the *Royal William* and the *Somerset,* being our sternmost ships, became a little prepared, and each gave the French ships a broadside as they passed by.

---

[22] *near soundings:* Close enough to shore to begin to locate the deeper channels through which one could safely approach. A line with a lead weight on the end was used to test how deep the waters were.

[23] *ensigns:* Flags.

[24] *broadside:* Shots fired at the broadside of the ship.

I afterwards heard this was a French squadron, commanded by Monsieur Corflans; and certainly, had the Frenchmen known our condition, and had a mind to fight us, they might have done us great mischief. But we were not long before we were prepared for an engagement. Immediately many things were tossed overboard, the ships were made ready for fighting as soon as possible, and about ten at night we had bent a new main-sail, the old one being split. Being now in readiness for fighting, we wore ship, and stood after the French fleet, who were one or two ships in number more than we. However we gave them chase, and continued pursuing them all night; and at day-light we saw six of them, all large ships of the line, and an English East Indiaman, a prize they had taken. We chased them all day till between three and four o'clock in the evening, when we came up with, and passed within a musket shot of one seventy-four gun, and the Indiaman also, who now hoisted her colors, but immediately hauled them down again. On this we made a signal for the other ships to take possession of her; and, supposing the man-of-war would likewise strike, we cheered, but she did not; though if we had fired into her, from being so near we must have taken her. To my utter surprise, the *Somerset,* who was the next ship astern of the *Namur,* made way likewise; and, thinking they were sure of this French ship, they cheered in the same manner, but still continued to follow us.

The French Commodore was about a gun-shot ahead of all, running from us with all speed; and about four o'clock he carried his foretopmast overboard. This caused another loud cheer with us; and a little after the topmast came close by us; but, to our great surprise, instead of coming up with her, we found she went as fast as ever, if not faster. The sea grew now much smoother; and the wind lulling, the seventy-four-gun ship we had passed, came again by us in the very same direction, and so near that we heard her people talk as she went by, yet not a shot was fired on either side; and about five or six o'clock, just as it grew dark, she joined her Commodore. We chased all night; but the next day we were out of sight, so that we saw no more of them; and we had only the old Indiaman (called *Carnarvon,* I think) for our trouble.

After this we stood in for the channel, and soon made the land; and, about the close of the year 1758–9, we got safe to St. Helen's.[25] Here the *Namur* ran aground, and also another large ship astern of

---

[25] *St. Helen's:* Probably St. Helena, midway between the southwest coast of Africa and the east coast of South America.

us; but, by starting our water, and tossing many things overboard to lighten her, we got the ships off without any damage. We stayed for a short time at Spithead, and then went into Portsmouth harbor to refit. From whence the Admiral went to London; and my master and I soon followed, with a press-gang, as we wanted some hands to complete our complement.

## Chapter IV

It was now between two and three years since I first came to England, a great part of which I had spent at sea;[26] so that I became inured to that service, and began to consider myself as happily situated, for my master treated me always extremely well; and my attachment and gratitude to him were very great. From the various scenes I had beheld on shipboard, I soon grew a stranger to terror of every kind, and was, in that respect at least, almost an Englishman. I have often reflected with surprise that I never felt half the alarm at any of the numerous dangers I have been in, that I was filled with at the first sight of the Europeans, and at every act of theirs, even the most trifling, when I first came among them, and for some time afterwards. That fear, however, which was the effect of my ignorance, wore away as I began to know them. I could now speak English tolerably well, and I perfectly understood everything that was said. I not only felt myself quite easy with these new countrymen, but relished their society and manners. I no longer looked upon them as spirits, but as men superior to us; and therefore I had the stronger desire to resemble them, to imbibe their spirit, and imitate their manners. I therefore embraced every occasion of improvement, and every new thing that I observed I treasured up in my memory. I had long wished to be able to read and write; and for this purpose I took every opportunity to gain instruction, but had made as yet very little progress. However, when I went to London with my master, I had soon an opportunity of improving myself, which I gladly embraced. Shortly after my arrival, he sent me to wait upon the Miss Guerins, who had treated me with much kind ness when I was there before; and they sent me to school.

While I was attending these ladies, their servants told me I could not go to Heaven unless I was baptized. This made me very uneasy,

---

[26] *a great part of which I had spent at sea:* Equiano had sailed with Pascal, under General Wolfe and Admiral Boscawen, on the expedition against the French in Canada in February of 1758. Boscawen had since become commander in chief in the Mediterranean, and it is joining his fleet that takes Equiano on this second expedition.

for I had now some faint idea of a future state: accordingly I communicated my anxiety to the eldest Miss Guerin, with whom I was become a favorite, and pressed her to have me baptized; when to my great joy, she told me I should. She had formerly asked my master to let me be baptized, but he had refused. However she now insisted on it; and he being under some obligation to her brother, complied with her request. So I was baptized in St. Margaret's church, Westminster, in February 1759, by my present name. The clergyman at the same time, gave me a book, called *A Guide to the Indians,* written by the Bishop of Sodor and Man.[27] On this occasion, Miss Guerin did me the honor to stand as god-mother, and afterwards gave me a treat.

I used to attend these ladies about the town, in which service I was extremely happy; as I had thus many opportunities of seeing London, which I desired of all things. I was sometimes, however, with my master at his rendezvous house,[28] which was at the foot of Westminster bridge. Here I used to enjoy myself in playing about the bridge stairs, and often in the waterman's wherries,[29] with other boys. On one of these occasions there was another boy with me in a wherry, and we went out into the current of the river; while we were there, two more stout boys came to us in another wherry, and abusing us for taking the boat, desired me to get into the other wherry-boat. Accordingly, I went to get out of the wherry I was in, but just as I had got one of my feet into the other boat, the boys shoved it off, so that I fell into the Thames; and, not being able to swim, I should unavoidably have been drowned, but for the assistance of some watermen who providentially came to my relief.

The *Namur* being again got ready for sea, my master, with his gang, was ordered on board; and, to my no small grief, I was obliged to leave my school-master, whom I liked very much, and always attended while I stayed in London, to repair on board with my master. Nor did I leave my kind patronesses, the Miss Guerins, without uneasiness and regret. They often used to teach me to read, and took great pains to instruct me in the principles of religion and the knowledge of God. I therefore parted from those amiable ladies with reluc-

---

[27] *Guide to the Indians . . . Sodor and Man: The Knowledge and Practice of Christianity made Easy for the Meanest Mental Capacities; or, An Essay towards an Instruction for the Indians* (1740) was written by Thomas Wilson, bishop of Sodor and Man from 1697 to 1755.

[28] *rendezvous house:* A place designated for officers to gather to receive orders while on shore.

[29] *wherries:* Small boats used to transport passengers and light cargo, usually used in rivers.

tance, after receiving from them many friendly cautions how to conduct myself, and some valuable presents.

When I came to Spithead, I found we were destined for the Mediterranean, with a large fleet, which was now ready to put to sea. We only waited for the arrival of the Admiral, who soon came on board. And about the beginning of the spring of 1759, having weighed anchor, and got under way, sailed for the Mediterranean; and in eleven days, from the Land's End, we got to Gibraltar. While we were here I used to be often on shore, and got various fruits in great plenty, and very cheap.

I had frequently told several people, in my excursions on shore, the story of my being kidnapped with my sister, and of our being separated, as I have related before; and I had as often expressed my anxiety for her fate, and my sorrow at having never met her again. One day, when I was on shore, and mentioning these circumstances to some persons, one of them told me he knew where my sister was, and, if I would accompany him, he would bring me to her. Improbable as this story was, I believed it immediately, and agreed to go with him, while my heart leaped for joy; and, indeed, he conducted me to a black young woman, who was so like my sister, that at first sight, I really thought it was her; but I was quickly undeceived. And, on talking to her, I found her to be of another nation.

While we lay here the *Preston* came in from the Levant.[30] As soon as she arrived, my master told me I should now see my old companion, Dick, who was gone in her when she sailed for Turkey. I was much rejoiced at this news, and expected every minute to embrace him; and when the captain came on board of our ship, which he did immediately after, I ran to inquire after my friend; but, with inexpressible sorrow, I learned from the boat's crew that the dear youth was dead! and that they had brought his chest, and all his other things, to my master. These he afterwards gave to me, and I regarded them as a memorial of my friend, whom I loved, and grieved for, as a brother.

While we were at Gibraltar, I saw a soldier hanging by the heels, at one of the moles.[31] I thought this a strange sight, as I had seen a man hanged in London by his neck. At another time I saw the master of a frigate towed to shore on a grating, by several of the men-of-war's boats, and discharged the fleet, which I understood was a mark

[30] *Levant:* The eastern Mediterranean.
[31] *moles:* He had drowned himself in endeavoring to desert [Equiano's note]. A mole is a stone pier or breakwater.

of disgrace for cowardice. On board the same ship there was also a sailor hung up at the yardarm.

After laying at Gibraltar for some time, we sailed up the Mediterranean, a considerable way above the Gulf of Lyons;[32] where we were one night overtaken with a terrible gale of wind, much greater than any I had ever yet experienced. The sea ran so high, that, though all the guns were well housed, there was great reason to fear their getting loose, the ship rolled so much; and if they had, it must have proved our destruction. After we had cruised here for a short time, we came to Barcelona, a Spanish sea-port, remarkable for its silk manufactures. Here the ships were all to be watered; and my master, who spoke different languages, and used often to interpret for the Admiral, superintended the watering of ours. For that purpose, he and the other officers of the ship, who were on the same service, had tents pitched in the bay; and the Spanish soldiers were stationed along the shore, I suppose to see that no depredations were committed by our men.

I used constantly to attend my master; and I was charmed with this place. All the time we stayed it was like a fair with the natives, who brought us fruits of all kinds, and sold them to us much cheaper than I got them in England. They used also to bring wine down to us in hog and sheep skins, which diverted me very much. The Spanish officers here treated our officers with great politeness and attention; and some of them, in particular, used to come often to my master's tent to visit him; where they would sometimes divert themselves by mounting me on the horses or mules, so that I could not fall, and setting them off at full gallop; my imperfect skill in horsemanship all the while affording them no small entertainment.

After the ships were watered, we returned to our old station of cruising off Toulon,[33] for the purpose of intercepting a fleet of French men-of-war that lay there. One Sunday, in our cruise, we came off a place where there were two small French frigates laying in shore; and our Admiral, thinking to take or destroy them, sent two ships in after them — the *Culloden* and the *Conqueror*. They soon came up to the Frenchmen, and I saw a smart fight here, both by sea and land; for the frigates were covered by batteries, and they played upon our ships most furiously, which they as furiously returned; and for a long time a constant firing was kept up on all sides at an amazing rate. At last,

---

[32] *Gulf of Lyons:* Gulf off the Mediterranean on the southeast coast of France.
[33] *Toulon:* Port city on the Mediterranean, on the southeast coast of France.

one frigate sunk; but the people escaped, though not without much difficulty. And soon after, some of the people left the other frigate also, which was a mere wreck. However, our ships did not venture to bring her away, they were so much annoyed from the batteries, which raked them both in going and coming. Their topmasts were shot away, and they were otherwise so much shattered, that the Admiral was obliged to send in many boats to tow them back to the fleet. I afterwards sailed with a man who fought in one of the French batteries during the engagement, and he told me our ships had done considerable mischief that day, on shore and in the batteries.

After this we sailed for Gibraltar, and arrived there about August 1759. Here we remained with all our sails unbent, while the fleet was watering and doing other necessary things. While we were in this situation, one day the Admiral, with most of the principal officers and many people of all stations, being on shore, about seven o'clock in the evening we were alarmed by signals from the frigates stationed for that purpose; and in an instant there was a general cry that the French fleet was out, and just passing through the straits. The Admiral immediately came on board with some other officers; and it is impossible to describe the noise, hurry, and confusion throughout the whole fleet, in bending their sails and slipping their cables;[34] many people and ship's boats were left on shore in the bustle. We had two captains on board of our ship who came away in the hurry and left their ships to follow. We showed lights from the gun-wales to the main topmast head; and all our lieutenants were employed amongst the fleet to tell the ships not to wait for their captains, but to put the sails to the yards, slip their cables, and follow us; and in this confusion of making ready for fighting, we set out for sea in the dark after the French fleet. Here I could have exclaimed with Ajax,[35]

> O Jove! O father! if it be thy will
> That we must perish, we thy will obey,
> But let us perish by the light of day.

They had got the start of us so far that we were not able to come up with them during the night; but at day light we saw seven sail of the line of battle some miles ahead. We immediately chased them till

---

[34] *bending . . . cables:* Raising their sails and pulling their ropes aboard.

[35] *Ajax:* A brave warrior and hero from Homer's *Iliad*, which Equiano misquotes. In Alexander Pope's translation, the lines read: "Oh king! oh father! hear my humble prayer . . . / If Greece must perish, we thy will obey / But let us perish in the face of day" (17.728–32).

about four o'clock in the evening, when our ships came up with them; and, though we were about fifteen large ships, our gallant Admiral only fought them with his own division, which consisted of seven; so that we were just ship for ship. We passed by the whole of the enemy's fleet in order to come at their commander, Monsieur Le Clue,[36] who was in the *Ocean,* an eighty-four gun ship. As we passed they all fired on us, and at one time three of them fired together, continuing to do so for some time. Notwithstanding which our Admiral would not suffer a gun to be fired at any of them, to my astonishment; but made us lie on our bellies on the deck until we came quite close to the *Ocean,* who was ahead of them all; when we had orders to pour the whole three tiers[37] into her at once.

The engagement now commenced with great fury on both sides. The *Ocean* immediately returned our fire, and we continued engaged with each other for some time; during which I was frequently stunned with the thundering of the great guns, whose dreadful contents hurried many of my companions into awful eternity. At last the French line was entirely broken, and we obtained the victory, which was immediately proclaimed by loud huzzas and acclamations. We took three prizes, *La Modeste,* of sixty-four guns, and *Le Temeraire* and *Centaur,* of seventy-four guns each. The rest of the French ships took to flight with all the sail they could crowd. Our ship being very much damaged, and quite disabled from pursuing the enemy, the Admiral immediately quitted her and went in the broken and only boat we had left on board the *Newark,* with which, and some other ships, he went after the French. The *Ocean,* and another large French ship, called the *Redoubtable,* endeavoring to escape, ran ashore at Cape Logas, on the coast of Portugal, and the French Admiral and some of the crew got ashore; but we, finding it impossible to get the ships off, set fire to them both. About midnight I saw the *Ocean* blow up, with a most dreadful explosion. I never beheld a more awful scene. In less than a minute, the midnight for a certain space seemed turned into day by the blaze, which was attended with a noise louder and more terrible than thunder, that seemed to rend every element around us.

My station during the engagement was on the middle deck, where I was quartered with another boy, to bring powder to the aftermost gun; and here I was a witness of the dreadful fate of many of my companions, who, in the twinkling of an eye, were dashed in pieces,

---

[36] *Monsieur Le Clue:* Admiral de la Clue Sabran, commander of the French fleet.
[37] *whole three tiers:* To fire all the ship's guns (on three levels) at one time.

and launched into eternity. Happily I escaped unhurt, though the shot and splinters flew thick about me during the whole fight. Towards the latter part of it, my master was wounded, and I saw him carried down to the surgeon; but though I was much alarmed for him, and wished to assist him, I dared not leave my post. At this station, my gun-mate (a partner in bringing powder for the same gun) and I ran a very great risk, for more than half an hour, of blowing up the ship. For, when we had taken the cartridges out of the boxes, the bottoms of many of them proving rotten, the powder ran all about the deck, near the match tub; we scarcely had water enough at the last to throw on it. We were also, from our employment, very much exposed to the enemy's shots; for we had to go through nearly the whole length of the ship to bring the powder. I expected, therefore, every minute to be my last, especially when I saw our men fall so thick about me; but, wishing to guard as much against the dangers as possible, at first I thought it would be safest not to go for the powder till the Frenchmen had fired their broadside; and then, while they were charging, I could go and come with my powder. But immediately afterwards I thought this caution was fruitless; and, cheering myself with the reflection that there was a time allotted for me to die as well as to be born, I instantly cast off all fear or thought whatever of death, and went through the whole of my duty with alacrity; pleasing myself with the hope, if I survived the battle, of relating it and the dangers I had escaped to the Miss Guerins, and others, when I should return to London.

Our ship suffered very much in this engagement; for, besides the number of our killed and wounded, she was almost torn to pieces, and our rigging so much shattered, that our mizen-mast, main-yard,[38] &c., hung over the side of the ship; so that we were obliged to get many carpenters, and others from some of the ships of the fleet, to assist in setting us in some tolerable order. And, notwithstanding which, it took us some time before we were completely refitted; after which we left Admiral Broderick to command, and we, with the prizes, steered for England. On the passage, and as soon as my master was something recovered of his wounds, the Admiral appointed him Captain of the *Etna*, fire ship,[39] on which he and I left the *Namur*,

---

[38] *mizen-mast, main-yard:* The mizen mast was the rear mast of a three-masted ship. The yards are the cross beams that support the sail on the mast. The main yard supports the main sail on the main mast.
[39] *fire ship:* A ship filled with flammable material that would be ignited and set to sail among enemy ships at sea.

and went on board of her at sea. I liked this little ship very much. I now became the captain's steward, in which situation I was very happy; for I was extremely well treated by all on board, and I had leisure to improve myself in reading and writing. The latter I had learned a little of before I left the *Namur,* as there was a school on board. When we arrived at Spithead, the *Etna* went into Portsmouth harbor to refit, which being done, we returned to Spithead and joined a large fleet that was thought to be intended against the Havannah;[40] but about that time the king died.[41] Whether that prevented the expedition, I know not, but it caused our ship to be stationed at Cowes, in the isle of Wight, till the beginning of the year sixty-one. Here I spent my time very pleasantly; I was much on shore, all about this delightful island, and found the inhabitants very civil.

While I was here, I met with a trifling incident, which surprised me agreeably. I was one day in a field belonging to a gentleman who had a black boy about my own size; this boy having observed me from his master's house, was transported at the sight of one of his own countrymen, and ran to meet me with the utmost haste. I not knowing what he was about, turned a little out of his way at first, but to no purpose; he soon came close to me, and caught hold of me in his arms, as if I had been his brother, though we had never seen each other before. After we had talked together for some time he took me to his master's house, where I was treated very kindly. This benevolent boy and I were very happy in frequently seeing each other, till about the month of March 1761, when our ship had orders to fit out again for another expedition. When we got ready, we joined a very large fleet at Spithead, commanded by Commodore Keppel, which was destined against Belle Isle;[42] and, with a number of transport ships, with troops on board, to make a descent on the place, we sailed once more in quest of fame. I longed to engage in new adventures, and see fresh wonders. . . .

When we had refitted our ship, and all things were in readiness for attacking the place, the troops on board the transports were ordered to disembark; and my master, as a junior captain, had a share in the command of the landing. This was on the 12th of April. The French were drawn up on the shore, and had made every disposition to oppose the landing of our men, only a small part of them this day being able to effect it; most of them, after fighting with great bravery, were

---

[40] *the Havannah:* England captured Havana, Cuba, in 1762.
[41] *the king died:* George II died in 1760.
[42] *Belle Isle:* Island off the French coast, in the Bay of Biscay.

cut off; and General Crawford, with a number of others, were taken prisoners. In this day's engagement we had also our lieutenant killed.

On the 21st of April we renewed our efforts to land the men, while all the men-of-war were stationed along the shore to cover it, and fired at the French batteries and breast-works from early in the morning till about four o'clock in the evening, when our soldiers effected a safe landing. They immediately attacked the French; and, after a sharp encounter, forced them from the batteries. Before the enemy retreated, they blew up several of them, lest they should fall into our hands. Our men now proceeded to besiege the citadel, and my master was ordered on board to superintend the landing of all the materials necessary for carrying on the siege; in which service I mostly attended him.

While I was there I went about to different parts of the island; and one day, particularly, my curiosity almost cost me my life. I wanted very much to see the mode of charging the mortars, and letting off the shells, and for that purpose I went to an English battery that was but a very few yards from the walls of the citadel. There, indeed, I had an opportunity of completely gratifying myself in seeing the whole operation, and that not without running a very great risk, both from the English shells that burst while I was there, but likewise from those of the French. One of the largest of their shells bursted within nine or ten yards of me. There was a single rock close by, about the size of a butt;[43] and I got instant shelter under it in time to avoid the fury of the shell. Where it burst, the earth was torn in such a manner that two or three butts might easily have gone into the hole it made, and it threw great quantities of stones and dirt to a considerable distance. Three shots were also fired at me and another boy, who was along with me, one of them in particular seemed

Wing'd with red lightning and impetuous rage;[44]

for, with a most dreadful sound it hissed close by me, and struck a rock at a little distance, which it shattered to pieces. When I saw what perilous circumstances I was in, I attempted to return the nearest way I could find, and thereby I got between the English and the French sentinels. An English sergeant, who commanded the out-posts, seeing me, and surprised how I came there (which was by stealth along the seashore), reprimanded me severely for it, and

---

[43] *butt:* Large cask.
[44] *Wing'd . . . rage:* Quotation from Milton, *Paradise Lost,* 1.175.

instantly took the sentinel off his post into custody, for his negligence in suffering me to pass the lines.

While I was in this situation, I observed at a little distance a French horse, belonging to some islanders, which I thought I would now mount, for the greater expedition of getting off. Accordingly I took some cord, which I had about me, and making a kind of bridle of it, I put it round the horse's head, and the tame beast very quietly suffered me to tie him thus, and mount him. As soon as I was on the horse's back, I began to kick and beat him, and try every means to make him go quick, but all to very little purpose: I could not drive him out of a slow pace. While I was creeping along, still within reach of the enemy's shot, I met with a servant well mounted on an English horse; I immediately stopped, and crying, told him my case, and begged of him to help me, and this he effectually did. For, having a fine large whip, he began to lash my horse with it so severely that he set off full speed with me towards the sea, while I was quite unable to hold or manage him. In this manner I went along till I came to a craggy precipice. I now could not stop my horse, and my mind was filled with apprehensions of my deplorable fate, should he go down the precipice, which he appeared fully disposed to do. I therefore thought I had better throw myself off him at once, which I did immediately, with a great deal of dexterity, and fortunately escaped unhurt. As soon as I found myself at liberty I made the best of my way for the ship, determined I would not be so foolhardy again in a hurry.

We continued to besiege the citadel till June, when it surrendered. During the siege, I have counted above sixty shells and carcases[45] in the air at once. When this place was taken I went through the citadel, and in the bomb-proofs under it, which were cut in the solid rock; and I thought it a surprising place, both for strength and building: notwithstanding which our shots and shells had made amazing devastation, and ruinous heaps all around it. . . .

After our ship was fitted out again for service, in September she went to Guernsey, where I was very glad to see my old hostess, who was now a widow, and my former little charming companion, her daughter. I spent some time here very happily with them, till October, when we had orders to repair to Portsmouth. We parted from each other with a great deal of affection; and I promised to return soon, and see them again, not knowing what all powerful fate had

---

[45] *carcases:* Iron-shelled missiles filled with burning materials.

determined for me. Our ship having arrived at Portsmouth, we went into the harbor, and remained there till the latter end of November, when we heard great talk about a peace; and, to our very great joy, in the beginning of December we had orders to go up to London with our ship, to be paid off.[46] We received this news with loud huzzas, and every other demonstration of gladness; and nothing but mirth was to be seen throughout every part of the ship. I too was not without my share of the general joy on this occasion.

I thought now of nothing but being freed, and working for myself, and thereby getting money to enable me to get a good education; for I always had a great desire to be able at least to read and write; and while I was on ship-board, I had endeavored to improve myself in both. While I was in the *Etna*, particularly, the captain's clerk taught me to write, and gave me a smattering of arithmetic, as far as the rule of three. There was also one Daniel Queen, about forty years of age, a man very well educated, who messed with me on board this ship, and he likewise dressed and attended the captain. Fortunately this man soon became very much attached to me, and took very great pains to instruct me in many things. He taught me to shave and dress hair a little, and also to read in the Bible, explaining many passages to me, which I did not comprehend. I was wonderfully surprised to see the laws and rules of my own country written almost exactly here; a circumstance which I believe tended to impress our manners and customs more deeply on my memory. I used to tell him of this resemblance, and many a time we have sat up the whole night together at this employment. In short, he was like a father to me, and some even used to call me after his name; they also styled me the black Christian. Indeed, I almost loved him with the affection of a son. Many things I have denied myself that he might have them; and when I used to play at marbles, or any other game, and won a few half-pence, or got any little money, which I sometimes did, for shaving anyone, I used to buy him a little sugar or tobacco, as far as my stock of money would go. He used to say, that he and I never should part; and that when our ship was paid off, as I was as free as himself, or any other man on board, he would instruct me in his business, by which I might gain a good livelihood.

This gave me new life and spirits; and my heart burned within me, while I thought the time long till I obtained my freedom. For though

---

[46] *to be paid off:* See footnote 15 to Gardner, "Voyages of a Seaman" in this chapter.

my master had not promised it to me, yet, besides the assurances I had received, that he had no right to detain me,[47] he always treated me with the greatest kindness, and reposed in me an unbounded confidence; he even paid attention to my morals, and would never suffer me to deceive him, or tell lies, of which he used to tell me the consequences; and that if I did so, God would not love me. So that, from all this tenderness, I had never once supposed, in all my dreams of freedom, that he would think of detaining me any longer than I wished.

In pursuance of our orders, we sailed from Portsmouth for the Thames, and arrived at Deptford[48] the 10th of December, where we cast anchor just as it was high water. The ship was up about half an hour, when my master ordered the barge to be manned; and all in an instant, without having before given me the least reason to suspect anything of the matter, he forced me into the barge, saying, I was going to leave him, but he would take care I should not. I was so struck with the unexpectedness of this proceeding, that for some time I did not make a reply, only I made an offer to go for my books and chest of clothes, but he swore I should not move out of his sight, and if I did, he would cut my throat, at the same time taking his hanger. I began, however, to collect myself, and plucking up courage, I told him I was free, and he could not by law serve me so. But this only enraged him the more: and he continued to swear, and said he would soon let me know whether he would or not, and at that instant sprung himself into the barge from the ship, to the astonishment and sorrow of all on board.

The tide, rather unluckily for me, had just turned downward, so that we quickly fell down the river along with it, till we came among some outward-bound West Indiamen; for he was resolved to put me on board the first vessel he could get to receive me. The boat's crew, who pulled against their will, became quite faint, different times, and would have gone ashore, but he would not let them. Some of them strove then to cheer me, and told me he could not sell me, and that

---

[47] *he had no right to detain me:* The legal right of slave owners in England was not compromised until 1772, when Lord Mansfield ruled that owners could not force their slaves to leave England and return to the Caribbean. Mansfield's ruling was often misinterpreted to mean that slaves were free on English soil. The slave trade was not abolished until 1807, and slaves in the British Caribbean were not emancipated until 1838. Slaves who came to England with their owners might, however, gather support for their moral right to freedom through the growing English movement to abolish slavery in the last half of the eighteenth century.

[48] *Deptford:* A town in Kent, on the Thames, about four miles east of London.

they would stand by me, which revived me a little, and I still entertained hopes; for, as they pulled along, he asked some vessels to receive me, but they would not. But, just as we had got a little below Gravesend,[49] we came alongside of a ship which was going away the next tide for the West Indies. Her name was the *Charming Sally,* Captain James Doran, and my master went on board, and agreed with him for me; and in a little time I was sent for into the cabin.

When I came there, Captain Doran asked me if I knew him. I answered that I did not. "Then," said he, "you are now my slave." I told him my master could not sell me to him, nor to anyone else. "Why," said he, "did not your master buy you?" I confessed he did. "But I have served him," said I, "many years, and he has taken all my wages and prize-money, for I had only got one six pence during the war; besides this I have been baptized, and by the laws of the land no man has a right to sell me." And I added that I had heard a lawyer and others at different times tell my master so. They both then said that those people who told me so, were not my friends; but I replied, "It was very extraordinary that other people did not know the law as well as they."

Upon this Captain Doran said I talked too much English; and if I did not behave myself well, and be quiet, he had a method on board to make me. I was too well convinced of his power over me to doubt what he said; and my former sufferings in the slave-ship presenting themselves to my mind, the recollection of them made me shudder. However, before I retired I told them that, as I could not get any right among men here, I hoped I should hereafter in Heaven; and I immediately left the cabin, filled with resentment and sorrow. The only coat I had with me my master took away with him, and said, "If your prize money had been £10,000, I had a right to it all, and would have taken it."

I had about nine guineas, which, during my long sea-faring life, I had scraped together from trifling perquisites and little ventures; and I hid it at that instant, lest my master should take that from me likewise, still hoping that by some means or other I should make my escape to the shore; and indeed some of my old shipmates told me not to despair, for they would get me back again; and that, as soon as they could get their pay, they would immediately come to Portsmouth to me, where the ship was going. But, alas! all my hopes were

[49] *Gravesend:* A market town in Kent, the first port on the Thames within London's jurisdiction.

baffled, and the hour of my deliverance was yet far off. My master, having soon concluded his bargain with the captain, came out of the cabin, and he and his people got into the boat and put off. I followed them with aching eyes as long as I could, and when they were out of sight I threw myself on the deck, with a heart ready to burst with sorrow and anguish.

# Selected Bibliography

### Burney's Autobiographical Writings

*Diary and Letters of Madame d'Arblay.* 4 vols. Ed. Charlotte Barrett. London: George Bell & Sons, 1891.

*The Early Diary of Frances Burney, 1768–1778.* Ed. Annie Raine Ellis. London: George Bell & Sons, 1889.

*The Early Journals and Letters of Fanny Burney.* 3 vols. Ed. Lars E. Troide. Montreal and Kingston, London and Buffalo: Oxford UP and McGill-Queen's UP, 1990.

*The Journals and Letters of Fanny Burney* (Madame d'Arblay). 12 vols. Ed. Joyce Hemlow et al. Oxford: Clarendon, 1972–1984.

*Memoirs of Dr. Burney,* 3 vols. London: Edward Moxon, 1832.

### Critical and Biographical Works on Burney

Adelstein, Michael E. *Fanny Burney.* New York: Twayne, 1968.

Bloom, Edward A., and Lillian D. Bloom. "Fanny Burney's Novels: the Retreat from Wonder." *Novel* 12 (1979): 367–93.

Bloom, Harold, ed. *Fanny Burney's "Evelina."* Modern Critical Interpretations. New York: Chelsea, 1988.

Brown, Martha G. "Fanny Burney's 'Feminism': Gender or Genre." *Fetter'd or Free: British Women Novelists, 1770–1815.* Ed. Mary Anne Schofield and Cecilia Macheski. Athens: Ohio UP, 1986. 29–39.

Campbell, D. Grant. "Fashionable Suicide: Conspicuous Consumption and the Collapse of Credit in Frances Burney's *Cecilia*." *Studies in Eighteenth-Century Culture* 20 (1990): 131–45.

Campbell, Gina. "Bringing Belmont to Justice: Burney's Quest for Paternal Recognition in *Evelina*." *Eighteenth-Century Fiction* 3:4 (1991): 321–40.

———. "How to Read like a Gentleman: Burney's Instructions to Her Critics in *Evelina*." *ELH* 57:3 (1990): 557–84.

Cutting, Rose Marie. "A Wreath for Fanny Burney's Last Novel — the *Wanderer*'s Contribution to Women's Studies." *Illinois Quarterly* 37 (1975): 45–64.

Cutting-Gray, Joanne. *Woman as "Nobody" and the Novels of Fanny Burney*. Gainesville: UP of Florida, 1992.

Doody, Margaret Anne. "Beyond *Evelina*: The Individual Novel and the Community of Literature." *Eighteenth-Century Fiction* 3:4 (1991): 358–71.

———. *Frances Burney: The Life in the Works*. New Brunswick: Rutgers UP; Cambridge: Cambridge UP, 1988.

Dowling, William C. "*Evelina* and the Genealogy of Literary Shame." *Eighteenth-Century Life* 16:3 (1992): 208–20.

Epstein, Julia. *The Iron Pen: Frances Burney and the Politics of Women's Writing*. Madison: U of Wisconsin P, 1989.

Fizer, Irene. "The Name of the Daughter: Identity and Incest in *Evelina*." In *Refiguring the Father: New Feminist Readings of Patriarchy*, ed. Patricia Yaeger and Beth Kowaleski-Wallace. Carbondale: U of Illinois P, 1989.

Greenfield, Susan. "'Oh Dear Resemblance of Thy Murdered Mother': Female Authorship in *Evelina*." *Eighteenth-Century Fiction* 3:4 (1991): 301–20.

Hemlow, Joyce. *The History of Fanny Burney*. Oxford: Clarendon, 1958.

Oakleaf, David. "The Name of the Father: Social Identity and the Ambition of Evelina." *Eighteenth-Century Fiction* 3:4 (1991): 341–58.

Pawl, Amy J. "'And What Other Name May I Claim?': Names and Their Owners in Frances Burney's *Evelina*." *Eighteenth-Century Fiction* 3 (1991): 283–300.

Rogers, Catharine M. *Frances Burney: The World of "Female Difficulties."* New York: Harvester, 1990.

Shaffer, Julie. "Not Subordinate: Empowering Women in the Marriage Plot — the Novels of Frances Burney, Maria Edgeworth, and Jane Austen." *Criticism: A Quarterly for Literature and the Arts* 34:1 (1992): 51–73.

Simons, Judy. *Fanny Burney*. Totowa, N.J.: Barnes & Noble, 1987.

Staves, Susan. "*Evelina*; or Female Difficulties." *Modern Philology* 73 (1976): 368–81.

Straub, Kristina. *Divided Fictions: Fanny Burney and Feminine Strategy.* Lexington: UP of Kentucky, 1987.

Thaddeus, Janice. "Hoards of Sorrow: Hester Lynch Piozzi, Frances Burney d'Arblay, and Intimate Death." *Eighteenth-Century Life* 14:3 (1990): 108–29.

Tucker, Irene. "Writing Home: *Evelina*, the Epistolary Novel and the Paradox of Propriety." *ELH* 60 (1993): 419–39.

Wiltshire, John. "Love unto Death: Fanny Burney's 'Narrative of the Last Illness and Death of General d'Arblay' (1820)." *Literature and Medicine* 12:2 (1993): 215–34.


## General Literary Studies

Armstrong, Nancy. *Desire and Domestic Fiction: A Political History of the Novel.* New York: Oxford UP, 1987.

Brown, Laura. *The Ends of Empire: Women and Ideology in Early Eighteenth-Century English Literature.* Ithaca, N.Y.: Cornell UP, 1993.

Butler, Marilyn. *Romantics, Rebels and Reactionaries: English Literature and Its Background, 1760–1830.* Oxford: Oxford UP, 1981.

DeRitter, Jones. *The Embodiment of Characters: The Representation of Physical Experience on Stage and in Print, 1728–1749.* Philadelphia: U of Pennsylvania P, 1994.

Doody, Margaret Anne. "Deserts, Ruins, and Troubled Waters: Female Dreams in Fiction and the Development of the Gothic Novel." *Genre* 10 (1977): 529–72.

Fraiman, Susan. *Unbecoming Women: British Women Writers and the Novel of Development.* New York: Columbia UP, 1993.

Gallagher, Catherine. *Nobody's Story: The Vanishing Acts of Women Writers in the Marketplace, 1670–1820.* Berkeley: U of California P, 1994.

Greene, Katherine. *The Courtship Novel, 1740–1830: A Feminized Genre.* Lexington: UP of Kentucky, 1991.

Hunter, J. Paul. *Before Novels: The Cultural Contexts of Eighteenth-Century English Fiction.* New York: Norton, 1990.

Jones, Vivien, ed. *Women in the Eighteenth Century: Constructions of Femininity.* New York: Routledge, 1990.

Langbauer, Laurie. *Women and Romance: The Consolations of Gender in the English Novel.* Ithaca, N.Y.: Cornell UP, 1990.

McKeon, Michael. "Historicizing Patriarchy: The Emergence of Gender Difference in England, 1660–1760." *Eighteenth-Century Studies* 28 (1995): 295–322.

———. *The Origins of the English Novel, 1600–1740.* Baltimore: Johns Hopkins UP, 1987.

Newton, Judith Lowder. *Women, Power, and Subversion: Social Strategies in British Fiction, 1778–1860.* Athens: U of Georgia P, 1981.

Nussbaum, Felicity A. *The Autobiographical Subject: Gender and Ideology in Eighteenth-Century England.* Baltimore: Johns Hopkins UP, 1989.

Parke, Catherine. "Vision and Revision: A Model for Reading the Eighteenth-Century Novel of Education." *Eighteenth-Century Studies* 16 (1982–83): 162–74.

Perry, Ruth. *Women, Letters, and the Novel.* New York: AMS, 1980.

Rogers, Katharine. *Feminism in Eighteenth-Century England.* Urbana: U of Illinois P, 1985.

Scheuermann, Mona. *Her Bread to Earn: Women, Money, and Society from Defoe to Austen.* Lexington: UP of Kentucky, 1993.

———. *Social Protest in the Eighteenth-Century Novel.* Columbus: Ohio State UP, 1985.

Spacks, Patricia Meyer. *Desire and Truth: The Function of Plot in Eighteenth-Century English Novels.* Chicago: U of Chicago P, 1990.

———. *Imagining a Self: Autobiography and the Novel in Eighteenth-Century England.* Cambridge: Harvard UP, 1976.

Spencer, Jane. *The Rise of the Woman Novelist: From Aphra Behn to Jane Austen.* Oxford: Basil Blackwell, 1986.

Spender, Dale. *Mothers of the Novel: One Hundred Good Women Writers before Jane Austen.* London: Pandora, 1986.

Stallybrass, Peter, and Allon White. *The Politics and Poetics of Transgression.* Ithaca, N.Y.: Cornell UP, 1986.

Staves, Susan. *Married Women's Separate Property in England, 1660–1833.* Cambridge: Harvard UP, 1990.

Thompson, James. *Models of Value: Eighteenth-Century Political Economy and the Novel.* Durham and London: Duke UP, 1996.

Van Sant, Ann. *Eighteenth-Century Sensibility and the Novel: The Senses in Social Context.* Cambridge: Cambridge UP, 1992.

Watt, Ian. *The Rise of the Novel: Studies in Defoe, Richardson, and Fielding.* Berkeley: U of California P, 1957.

Williams, Raymond. *The Country and the City.* New York: Oxford UP, 1973.

———. *Keywords: A Vocabulary of Culture and Society*. New York: Oxford UP, 1976.

Yeazell, Ruth. *Fictions of Modesty: Women and Courtship in the English Novel*. Chicago: U of Chicago P, 1991.

Zomchick, John. *Family and the Law in Eighteenth-Century Fiction: The Public Conscience in the Private Sphere*. Cambridge: Cambridge UP, 1993.


## Social History

Brewer, John. *The Sinews of Power: War, Money, and the English State, 1688–1783*. London: Unwin Myman, 1989.

Clay, Christopher. "Marriage, Inheritance, and the Rise of Large Estates in England, 1660–1815." *Economic History Review* 2d ser. 21 (1968): 503–18.

Davidoff, Leonore, and Catherine Hall. *Family Fortunes: Men and Women of the English Middle Class, 1780–1850*. Chicago: U of Chicago P, 1987.

Hobsbawm, E. J. *Industry and Empire: From 1750 to the Present Day*. Volume 3 of *The Pelican Economic History of England*. Harmondsworth: Penguin, 1968.

Macfarlane, Alan. *Marriage and Love in England: Modes of Reproduction, 1300–1840*. Oxford: Basil Blackwell, 1986.

Macpherson, C. B. *The Political Theory of Possessive Individualism*. Oxford: Clarendon, 1962.

Mathias, Peter. *The First Industrial Nation: An Economic History of Britain, 1700–1914*. London: Methuen, 1983.

McKendrick, Neil; John Brewer; and J. H. Plumb. *The Birth of a Consumer Society: The Commercialization of Eighteenth-Century England*. Bloomington: Indiana UP, 1983.

Newman, Gerald. *The Rise of English Nationalism: A Cultural History, 1720–1830*. New York: St. Martin's, 1987.

Rediker, Marcus. *Between the Devil and the Deep Blue Sea: Merchant Seamen, Pirates, and the Anglo-American Maritime World*. Cambridge and New York: Cambridge UP, 1987.

Rendall, Jane. *Women in an Industrializing Society: England, 1750–1880*. Oxford: Basil Blackwell, 1990.

Rodger, N. A. M. *The Wooden World: An Anatomy of the Georgian Navy*. London: Collins, 1986.

Stock, Phyllis. *Better than Rubies: A History of Women's Education*. New York: E. P. Putnam's Sons, 1978.

Stone, Lawrence. *The Family, Sex, and Marriage in England, 1500–1800*. New York: Harper & Row, 1977.

———. *Uncertain Unions: Marriage in England, 1660–1753.* Oxford: Oxford UP, 1992.

Thompson, E. P. *The Making of the English Working Class.* New York: Vintage, 1966.

Trumbach, Randolph. *The Rise of the Egalitarian Family: Aristocratic Kinship and Domestic Relations in Eighteenth-Century England.* New York: Academic, 1978.

The text of *Evelina* by Frances Burney is reprinted from the Oxford English Novels edition of *Evelina* by Frances Burney, edited by Edward A. Bloom (1968; World's Classics Paperback 1982) by permission of Oxford University Press.

Excerpts from *Spectator* #45 and #69 by Joseph Addison; and *Spectator* #240, #245, and #502 by Joseph Addison and Richard Steele, reprinted from *The Spectator*, edited by Donald F. Bond (1965), by permission of Oxford University Press.

Edward Boscawen, excerpts from *Boscawen's Letters to His Wife*, edited by Christopher Lloyd, in *The Naval Miscellany*, vol. 4 (1952), reprinted courtesy of the Navy Records Society.

Excerpts from *The Early Journals and Letters of Frances Burney*, vol. 2, edited by Lars E. Troide (1990), reprinted by permission of McGill-Queen's University Press.

Thomas Campbell, excerpts from *Dr. Campbell's Diary of a Visit to England in 1775*, edited by James L. Clifford (1947), reprinted with the permission of Cambridge University Press.

Number 37 from Henry Fielding's *The Covent-Garden Journal and a Plan of the Universal Register-Office* © 1988 by Wesleyan University Press. Reprinted by permission of University Press of New England.

Excerpts from *Recollections of James Anthony Gardner*, edited by Sir R. Vesey Hamilton and John Know Laughton, in *Publications of the Navy Records Society*, vol. 21 (1946), reprinted courtesy of the Navy Records Society.

Oliver Goldsmith, excerpts from *The Citizen of the World* in *The Collected Works of Oliver Goldsmith*, edited by Arthur Friedman (1966), reprinted by permission of Oxford University Press.

Admiral Sir Thomas Pasley, excerpts from *Private Sea Journals, 1778–1782*, edited and introduced by Rodney M. S. Pasley (1931), reprinted by permission of J. M. Dent and Sons, Ltd.

Tobias Smollett, selection from *The Expedition of Humphry Clinker: Tobias Smollett*, Thomas R. Preston and O. M. Brack, Jr., editor. Copyright © 1990 by the University of Georgia Press, Athens, Georgia.